A CHILD OF THE WILDERNESS,
SHE TURNED TO THE MOTHER
SHE HAD NEVER KNOWN . . .

Hammerwater Kate walked on. She passed the Russian Orthodox church, now being used as a storage building by the ACCo traders, and then turned back. Wandering around to the small cemetery behind the log building with its strange, cross-topped onion dome, she found the mound of white stones and the bleached wooden cross upon which could still faintly be traced the carved letters spelling out the legend *Grushenka Karloff, d. 1855*.

Hammerwater Kate stood before the weathered Russian cross that marked her blood mother's grave. She knelt at last and laid her lips on the faintly decipherable letter *G*.

"I have come again, Mother I never knew," she whispered. "It is Katrina. Do you remember me, Mother? Do the dead remember the living at all?"

As Kate knelt, a raven drifted over the old church, came low to the ground, circled and then flapped away toward the river. Faintly from the distance came sounds of laughter. It was Koyukon children batting a moose bladder filled with dried grass, shouting, yelling at one another.

"I am well," Kate continued, "but I am not happy. I am twenty-five years old and I have found only one man with whom I wish to spend my life. But he is married to another and she is my friend. She came from the land to the west, your land, my mother. She was a princess there as she is here. Princess Ludmila was a child when you married the man called Karloff. . . ."

THE RUSSIANS

JUDITH SHEARS

Miles Standish Press

Published by
Miles Standish Press, Inc.
353 West Lancaster Avenue
Wayne, Pennsylvania 19087

Dell ® TM 681510, Dell Publishing Co., Inc.

ISBN: 0-440-07553-X

Printed in the United States of America

First printing—September 1984

For my husband, Bill Hotchkiss, co-author of
The Russians.

Book One:
GRUSHENKA

Chapter 1
The Marriage of Grushenka

Perhaps you have heard of Maryushka? Though she was an orphan with no mother to teach her, the beautiful maiden grew famous for her embroidery, her skill with colored silks and glass beads. Merchants heard of her art and came to her, promising great wealth, but she refused them all, insisting that she had no need for riches. She had chosen never to leave the small village where she had been born and to whose citizens she owed her life, inasmuch as they had been very kind to her after the deaths of her father and mother.

"I wish only to sell my work to those around me, for they find it beautiful, and I know that they care for me."

And so the merchants went away disappointed, but they continued to marvel at the lovely things they had beheld in Maryushka's cottage, and the stories they continued to tell spread across Mother Russia from east to west, from north to south.

The evil sorcerer Kaschei the Immortal heard these tales, and he determined to possess both the woman and her art. With this purpose in mind he transformed himself into a handsome youth and flew across mountain and river and ocean until he reached Maryushka's village.

Kaschei presented himself at Maryushka's doorway and said he wished to purchase some of her work. She invited him within and showed him all she had, telling him he could pay her later if he wished. If he did not care for what he saw, she would attempt to do something at his direction.

Kaschei grew furious, for even with his powers of magic he could not match the beauty Maryushka's skilled hands created. He smiled and begged her to come with him; he would make her a queen and provide her with a palace built of jewels. Her utensils would be of gold and her bed of eiderdown. In the orchard would grow birds of paradise and golden apples.

"I cannot leave this village," she said, "for here is where my parents lie buried, nor could I ever embroider for you alone."

Kaschei's anger burst forth and he transformed Maryushka into a firebird. Then he became a dark-plumaged hawk. He grasped her in his talons and flew away with her.

She was dying; the claws pierced her. She shed her brilliant feathers and they fell over Russia like a crimson snowstorm. And to this day they lie hidden among the grasses and weeds, visible only to those who love beauty or who seek to create it.

November 1853

It was easy to get lost in the taiga, as indeed Grushenka Kosnova was. The sky threatened snow and early winter darkness in a couple of hours. The pine and fir trees stretched for thousands of miles east and west, several hundred at least north and south, from the mixed woods and black land of the steppes all the way to the beginning of the tundra, the northern timberline near the Arctic Circle.

Not that Grushenka minded being lost. She rather enjoyed the adventure and would frequently wander in the forest for the express purpose of losing herself. Then she could spin out one of her stories, making it up as she went along, acting out all the parts.

Perhaps she would live for days alone, gathering pine nuts and berries, sleeping huddled beneath pine needles until she was discovered by a kindly prince with hair like the sun and eyes like the clear sky of summer. Or perhaps it would be a gentle bear who would carry her off to his den among the fallen logs and tend to her. He would bring her fish every day from the nearby stream, yes, and delectable berries and tender wild onions. He would warm her with his great shaggy body at night until at last she consented to kiss him, upon which he would turn into a prince with hair like the sun and eyes like the clear sky of summer. . . .

"Well, this is foolishness and I know it," she sighed aloud to one of the tiny black-headed birds who hopped and scratched among the duff at the edge of a patch of frozen snow.

Foolishness; that would be her father's word. When she went out into the woods now, she would take an axe with her, telling her father she was going to gather wood. "Wood gathering," he would snort. "Wool-gathering, I should say." But he seldom ordered her to remain at home, confined to the little cabin and occupied with sewing or weaving.

Her mother, Irena, fretted about wolves. When Grushenka explained that she had seen the big grey canines several times and that they always ran away, Irena was not comforted.

It was always Aunt Sofia who interceded. "Let the child go, Andrei, Irena. Heaven knows there is little enough for her to do around here."

Aunt Sofia had been to Moscow, had lived there for years when her husband, in service to the czar, was alive. She used to go to balls and concerts, had even met His

Holiness the Emperor. Grushenka would happily listen for hours to tales of this magical world; Aunt Sofia talked on and on about a life that seemed as distant from the village of Seeneestaken as if it existed on the moon.

Sofia loved to weave this fairy dust, but her brother Andrei would soon lose patience and growl, "Hush, Sofia. The child's head is already so full of moonbeams that I can hardly get her to pull a weed in the garden."

That accusation was of course untrue, as Grushenka knew quite well. In the short summer months she worked as hard as anyone else, plowing and tilling and planting, weeding and turning water and harvesting alongside the Michaelovich family. These latter, mother and father and two adolescent sons, belonged nominally to the Kosnovovich estate as bonded serfs, along with Dietrik and Marya Borsoy, a childless couple too old to be of any use in the fields.

Grushenka's family was of the *dvoriane*, the landed gentry. Their eighty-acre farm was a gift to Andrei's great-grandfather for services rendered to the Czarina Catherine.

"Dvoriane," her father would snort. "We eat cabbage soup and live in a log shack and grub in the dirt until our fingernails are as black as anyone else's. I fail to see the distinction." Then he would go across to drink kvass with old Dietrik if there was no work to be done.

To Irena the distinction was very important. She herself did not socialize with the peasant women, but in her gentle, indomitable way discouraged Grushenka from associating with them.

And so Grushenka grew up essentially alone, feeding on Sofia's stories and her few books from Moscow. From these the aunt taught Grushenka to read, making the two of them the only literate individuals for miles around.

Grushenka sighed and glanced up at the threatening sky. When she looked at things squarely, which she avoided as much as possible, she had to admit that although at sixteen she was acknowledged to be the most beautiful girl in Seeneestaken as well as the daughter of landowners, her prospects were severely limited.

In summertime everyone worked frantically through the short growing season, battling the elements to plant, grow and harvest their crops of rye and hard wheat, turnips, cabbages, onions and beets. In the winter, when there was little to do, the walls of the small house would begin to close in on Grushenka, and at times she felt she would go mad if she could not escape.

These were the times when she would venture away from the cabin, from the village with its single road of frozen mud and its two rows of houses, away from the dormant fields and into the dark mystery of the evergreen woods. In that imponderably vast and shadowed kingdom, at least in the mind of a sixteen-year-old daydreamer, wonderful and unexpected things could happen.

One of the tiny birds ventured very close, even darting forward to peck tentatively at Grushenka's heavy boot. It cocked its head, fixing her with a shiny stare. She smiled and knelt down, at which movement the creature darted away, emitting a shrill peep as it fluttered to where its companions scratched among the damp pine needles some yards distant.

"Well, little bird," she said, no longer certain which had been the bold member of the small flock, "I don't suppose I really thought you had a message for me."

She pondered briefly, as she often did, the notion of venturing farther and farther into the woods to find what was out there instead of returning home. But it would be dark before long and the biting cold penetrated even her heavy sheepskin coat. Besides, at home there would be hot cabbage soup and black bread, perhaps even a little mutton.

Grushenka turned her attention to the trees around her. She selected one that looked taller than the others, tucked her woolen skirt between her legs and began to shinny up to the lower branches. From the top of the tree she would be able to spot the clearing where Seeneestakan and the fields lay.

She was still within two or three yards of the ground when a branch splintered in front of her face and a blunderbuss roared almost in her ears. The heavy explosion rebounded oddly among the trees. Blinded by splinters and considerably shocked, Grushenka lost her grip and slid to the ground. A moment later a deer crashed past her in panic. Dogs bayed in hot pursuit.

Furious, tears pouring to cleanse her eyes, she stepped out into the path of the dogs and shouted. As the pair of spotted hounds tried to flank her she kicked one of them and sent it sprawling and yelping. It scrambled to its feet and took off after its quarry with no more than a glance at Grushenka.

"You come back," she shouted. "Where's your blasted master? I'll tell him a thing or two about looking before he shoots!" She shook her fist and ran after the dogs, intent on taking out her anger on the hunting party if not the trigger man.

Eventually she came out of the trees into a clearing beside a small stream, frozen solid. Heedless, she thrust through a tangle of leafless willow brush along the stream. Brittle branches caught her kerchief and pulled it from her head, then tangled in her red-gold hair and loosed a halo-cloud.

It was only when her foot skidded on the ice and she sprawled headlong against the low bank of the creek that she noticed the other sounds: hoofbeats, an equine snort and clatter, hoofbeats stopping, a wordless exclamation followed by deep-throated male laughter.

Alex Karloff, thirty-nine years old, schooled in Moscow and a veteran of seventeen years in service to His Majesty, was veteran as well of half a dozen dalliances with the bored ladies of that city's society. Despite those and countless arrangements with Indian women in the wilds of Russian America Alex Karloff, long thought to be beyond schoolboy infatuations, was enchanted.

Sprawled on the ice with her skirts momentarily up around her ears, she displayed legs that even in their heavy winter stockings were extraordinarily shapely, long and lithe. Her hair in disarray looked like a fine cloud of flame in the dead black and white November landscape; her face, flushed from exertion and emotion, glowed like another small fire. The eyes were such a vivid blue that they also seemed to blaze as she glared at him and scrambled to her feet.

Karloff quickly dismounted, still laughing, not taking his eyes off Grushenka. "I can hardly credit my senses. Are you a wood nymph, or perhaps a fury? Diana herself?"

"You fool," Grushenka raged, "can't you shoot at all? You nearly shot me out of a tree back there."

Karloff shook his head regretfully. "To you, little goddess of the woods, I must certainly make my profoundest apologies, but you must see that in this humdrum modern world I could never expect to get near such a magical creature, let alone shoot her."

Grushenka stared at the man. "You speak nonsense," she snapped. She glanced at the lowering sky and turned to climb another tree.

Karloff caught her arm, pulled her back. "Wait," he urged. "I am sorry for my marksmanship, but perhaps I can make it up to you, eh?"

Grushenka Kosnova stared up at the tall man in his handsome furs, tears of frustration and anger beginning to well up in her eyes despite her best efforts to keep them back. She recognized him now, although she had not seen him for over six years. It was Baron Karloff, of course, the landlord of the vast estate that bordered her parents' small holding. He did not live on his land but rather pursued his career in government, the only way anyone got ahead these days.

The management of his property was left to Danin, a serf, remarkably competent and in fact a good deal wealthier than Grushenka's father. So far as Grushenka knew Karloff himself had last come to inspect his properties the winter when she was ten. She remembered seeing him dressed in an officer's uniform and astride a magnificent black gelding. At the time he seemed like a figure from one of her fairy tales, very handsome and dashing, and she was torn between hopeless infatuation and intense hostility.

Even in her fury now she was not oblivious to the fact that he was a very handsome man. Close as she was, she had to admit that it was not all fine clothing and military bearing. His face looked carved from rough stone, the skin dark and weathered, the chin hard and jutting, the nose also prominent and slightly humped. He was saved from harshness by rich, dark wavy hair. His lips were half hidden below a heavy black mustache and were wide and thicker than usual for a man, but there was a hint of humor in the stern lines of the cheeks and around the deep brown eyes.

There was something else about him—*danger*. He had the look of a man quite at home with the inflicting of pain.

Just now, however, Alex Karloff was smiling, almost tender. He touched a finger to a last tear on Grushenka's eyelashes, ran the finger gently over her cheekbone down to the corner of her mouth.

"You are a lovely creature," he murmured. "If you are not a wood sprite, then you must be—let me think. Perhaps you are Gossof's daughter? He had a red-haired girl, I seem to remember. . . ."

Grushenka had been almost mesmerized by Karloff's bemused caresses on her face. Now she jerked away. "I am not one of your girls," she snapped, drawing her back very straight and standing as tall as she could. "My parents are dvoriane also, Baron Karloff. If you will excuse me, I must be getting home. It will be dark soon and I am sure my parents wonder what has become of me."

"Forgive me for everything, including the potshot," Karloff returned, pulling off his tall shako and bowing grandly from the waist. The gesture and the apology were, Grushenka suspected, not entirely sincere; a faint mocking smile remained on the baron's full lips. "I should have known you at once. I would be honored, Kosnova, if you would permit me to escort you home. You shall, of course, ride Thunder, and I shall lead him."

"*Merci, monsieur le baron,*" Grushenka simpered, displaying the words from her small store of French like banners that proclaimed her equality. "But I am sure you have other matters to attend to, and I am perfectly capable of finding my way back to the village." She looked once more for a tall tree.

"No, please wait," Karloff said. His demeanor changed suddenly, the mockery leaving his face. "You are insulted because you think I have been laughing at you. I would never forgive myself if you walked off into the forest alone. I will follow you even if you don't want my company."

Grushenka paused, searching his face carefully. "You were making fun of me. I'm not sure you aren't still. I don't much care, but I really must be getting home, and you need to wait for your dogs to come back."

"Devil take the ungovernable brutes. They'll find their way. No more argument, now. You make me feel ungallant." Without further ado he grasped her elbow, swung her around and lifted her bodily onto the back of the great black horse. In the next instant, before she could so much as murmur her surprised protest, he swung himself up behind her. Circling her waist with one arm and taking the reins in the other, he murmured in her ear,

"I've changed my mind. I hope you don't mind if I ride too, mademoiselle. Thunder is a powerful beast, and it's a long walk back to Seeneestakan.

"I know your last name because I know who your father is," he said without pausing, "but you must have a Christian name as well. Mine is Alex, and I'd be pleased if you'd call me by it."

"Grushenka," she replied automatically, "but—"

"Grushenka," he interrupted. "I'm in love with you, Grushenka."

"Don't speak that way, Baron Karloff," she cried, aware that she was blushing bright scarlet. "I've told you I'm not one of your peasants. You may not toy with me."

"I'll prove to you that I'm quite serious, my beautiful Grushenka," he whispered, putting his lips closer to her ear and tightening his hold around her waist. "You will see."

Just before they reached the fields Karloff drew his gelding to a halt and helped Grushenka down from the big black.

"So your neighbors will not have anything to wag their tongues about," he said. "You see, I do care about your reputation."

"My thanks to you, Baron Karloff," Grushenka muttered as she turned to dash away.

He caught her quite suddenly by the wrist, drew her around and close to him and kissed her full on the lips, holding her firmly for several seconds despite her struggles. When he released her, she slapped him as hard as she could and ran off across the frozen fields, her face once again flaming and the sound of his laughter ringing in her ears.

She didn't speak of her encounter with Karloff when she got home, but that night she slept very little. She shared her wide goose-feather mattress with Aunt Sofia and so had to restrain herself as much as possible from turning and sighing, but as the hours of the night crept past and Grushenka lay staring into the thick dark and listening to her aunt's delicate, monotonous snores, remaining still became more and more difficult.

She did not wish to think about Alex Karloff. She was certain she did not trust the great landowner in the slightest, and yet her rebellious mind rehearsed over and over the feelings of his hard body pressed against her back, his arm about her waist. Yes, especially the kiss, the strong hand at the back of her head, holding her motionless, the insistent pressure of his mouth—these were the sensations that despite her outrage had thrilled her to her toes.

Never before had she imagined such a complete separation of the will governed by mind, her ideas of what was right from the independent will of the body and the senses. The conflict confused her, even frightened her.

Nonetheless, if Karloff had been a different person instead of an absentee landlord, one whom she deeply mistrusted and believed culpable of capricious disregard for his dependents, if he had been gentle and perhaps younger, then the day's encounter would have come very near to fulfilling her daydreams.

The situation would not resolve itself in any way that Grushenka could discover. After a very long time she dozed, waking from time to time out of shameful dreams for which she silently begged forgiveness. Then she would lapse into sleep again to find herself lying embraced with Karloff, feeling the heat, the solidity of his flesh against her own, unable to resist the sensations that ran in her body like fire through straw. She would wake again, wondering desperately if she had moaned aloud.

When the little square of sky that was visible through the window lightened to grey, she rose silently and with a sense of relief and after making her morning obeisance and prayers to the icons in the household shrine, she slipped out to the attached barn to milk the two cows and toss hay to the sheep in the fold.

She lingered with the animals longer than was necessary, taking comfort in their warm placidity. For some reason she was reluctant to face even the most trivial questions, even the most casual scrutiny of her family. When she smelled the fragrant pine smoke from the morning fire, she stalled a bit longer, then at last rose and carried the fresh milk into the small annex that served as a dairy room. She had just stepped out into the cold air when she saw her mother, obviously coming to fetch her.

Irena's round face was flushed, her grey eyes wide with some emotion that Grushenka couldn't immediately fathom. "There's a visitor." Irena reached up to smooth her daughter's sleep-disheveled hair. "Grushenka, you must try to pull yourself together some. I think—" Irena suddenly burst into tears. Grushenka tried for a moment to get some explanation for this extraordinary behavior, but Irena would only throw her arms around her daughter's neck and sob speechlessly.

Grushenka gently disentangled her mother and shoved her through the door of the small log house—and felt the next instant as if her legs would collapse from under her.

At their rough wooden table sat the subject of the intense and unwelcome sensations that had troubled her sleep. Baron Alex Karloff was smoking a cigar; he glanced up at her with a faint smile as she came into the room.

Her father also looked up, but he did not smile. His eyes narrowed slightly, suspicious, searching.

"Grushenka, go help your Aunt Sofia dress," he ordered. "Baron Karloff and I have matters to discuss."

Grushenka glanced from one to the other of the men, nodded and hurried through to the sleeping quarters. Sofia was already up, however, and in no need of assistance. As soon as Grushenka came through the curtain, her aunt motioned her to silence, her eyes gleaming in the dim light that came from the small window. The two crouched together by the door, listening to the conversation in the other room. In a few moments Irena joined them, her eyes still damp but her sobbing contained. She gripped Grushenka's hand and listened also.

"I really can't imagine why you would wish to marry my daughter, Baron Karloff," Andrei was saying. "You know we have no dowry to offer. Surely you could find a wife with a respectable *dot*."

"You speak bluntly, Brother Kosnovich," Karloff returned, his tone amused, self-confident. "Let me speak bluntly as well. You must realize that I have no great need of money. I'm thirty-nine years old and there is no other heir to the Karloff estate. I have waited too long to marry as it is. I've spent my last several years in the American colonies and will be returning there as soon as I have gathered a force of men from my lands."

Andrei Kosnovich puffed at his own cigar and then drummed his fingers on the surface of the table. "And so you wish to take my daughter off to the wilderness because a woman of position would not consent to accompany you. No. It is quite out of the question."

"Certainly, I will do nothing against Grushenka's wishes," Karloff said soothingly. "Still, you must realize that her prospects here are severely limited. Whom will she find here in Seeneestakan who is even respectable? She has mettle, you know. Keep her here and you cheat her."

Grushenka listened with a growing sense of unreality. Her father and the baron sounded as if they were discussing some stranger, perhaps even a cow or goat of unusual value.

Andrei snorted and the listeners heard him get up abruptly from the table. "If you will excuse me—"

"I ask nothing of you, sir," Karloff continued, "except

that you allow me to court your daughter. She is, I trust, in good health?"

"She most certainly is," Kosnovich snapped back. "Since I know the question you're really asking, *Baron*, she is completely chaste, as pure as a newborn lamb."

"It would never have occurred to me to question that point," Karloff murmured smoothly.

Grushenka was unable to contain herself any longer. Her ears were burning with rage. She thrust aside the curtain and stood above the two seated men like an avenging Valkyrie.

"How dare you, either of you, speak of me in this way? I am not a thing to be bartered and bargained over. I will never speak to either one of you again."

With that she pushed through the door into the bleak landscape. The frozen fields stretched away to the forest; the air was bitterly cold. She began to run with no idea of where she was heading, heedlessly covering the rough ground and diving among the trees. Even there she continued her wild flight.

She did not stop when she heard the hoofbeats and knew Karloff was pursuing her on horseback. Instead she dodged endlessly. Finally he drew ahead of her and dismounted in her path. Catching her in his arms, he held her against him until she stopped struggling and began to cry in great, gulping, childlike sobs.

"Grushenka," he whispered, "my pretty one, it is not what I said to your father at all. I could not sleep last night for thinking about you. I kept seeing you here like a flame in the taiga. I felt like a schoolboy again. Did you not know that? Did you not guess?"

Grushenka allowed his words to soothe her, allowed herself to succumb to the almost mesmeric effect of the circle of his arms. She looked up into his face, studied it intently.

Still the faint suggestion of mockery, the hard lines around the mouth. . . .

Grushenka remembered the terrifying shot, the hounds, the terror of the buck, Karloff's casual acceptance of the whole matter. *Many men hunt. They do not even think about their prey. Why should they? Deer are pests. The shot was an accident.*

A man of wealth and position wanted her, was entreating her as if she were a princess and he a peasant. To boot, she found him attractive, found her body responding to his physical presence in a way that she had never dreamed of.

He had spoken of the American colonies. She had heard many wild stories, tales of hardship and danger, of Indians and great bears, of bitter climate, starvation, death in a hundred unexpected ways. People came back, though.

There were wolves right here in the taiga, and bears, although she had never actually seen a bear. She also doubted that the climate could be worse than their own, with its endless frozen winters and its too-brief summers.

Karloff continued to soothe her; he streamed sweet nothings into her ears with hot soft breath; he held her and stroked her arms; he brushed her eyelids, her cheeks, the corners of her mouth with his seeking lips.

Sometimes we will come home, even though it is far away . . . the thought ran vaguely through her mind even as little sensations like fire began to course through her. Her lips, as if with a will of their own, moved to meet his.

Then, perhaps, we will go to live in Moscow, the theme ran. This is where she lost: *We will watch the dancers and listen to the beautiful music that Sofia speaks of.*

They were married two weeks later, Grushenka wearing the elaborately embroidered gown that had been Sofia's wedding dress. Both Sofia and Irena had worked on last-minute fittings and alterations, and she would never forget how her mother looked, her mouth full of pins and tears running down her cheeks.

Many times Grushenka determined to call it all off. It was too far from her family—everyone and everything she had ever known. Perhaps she would never see any of them again, she would think, and regret and loneliness and fear passed through her like a physical object, a sword through her vitals. At other times she observed something only suggested in Karloff and the alarm went off in her head again, vague warning of danger and pain.

She quelled her forebodings as the great physical attraction, almost like an addiction, warmed her and blotted out the momentary shiver.

The wedding night was a revelation to her. Karloff was a patient and thorough lover and Grushenka learned at last the meaning of those troublesome and delicious sensations that had begun with her nobleman's kisses.

He gave her pain but pleasure also—a daring, outrageous, perhaps even sinful pleasure that she had previously only wildly imagined, thoughts of which she had sometimes been almost certain she would be condemned to hell for having.

"Nothing is forbidden in the marriage bed," he told her. "Do not be afraid of me, Grushenka. Your body knows what it must do."

After that, of course, there could be no turning back, no possible way to undo what had been done.

Within a week they began the long, long trek across the frozen north of Asia to the ocean on the other side. Beyond that they would journey to another world in company with a band of fur traders as well as with thirty troops Karloff had conscripted from among his serfs.

Chapter 2
In Russian America

Sibir. The land stretches endlessly east. A gigantic plain with few sharp elevations, it slopes generally north to the Arctic Ocean. The taiga is a forest of pine, spruce, Siberian cedar, birch and poplar, one of the major sources of furs in the world. There are found sable, ermine, bear, wolf, many kinds of fox, otter, polar hare, grey squirrel, even leopard and Manchurian tiger.

The land is traversed by mighty rivers: the Lena, the Yenisey, the Amur, the Ob and the Irtysh. For half the year they provide thousands of miles of waterways; the other half they are frozen solid.

Far, far to the east stands a series of massive walls against the Pacific Ocean: the mountains, the Yablonovyy and Stanovoy ranges and finally the great volcanic peaks of the Kamchatka Peninsula.

When Vitus Bering made his voyages of discovery Russia vaulted across the steel-grey salt water to the new continent and founded Russian America. The post of Redoubt St. Michael lay in the far north, Nova Archangelisk—now Sitka—in the forested Alexander Archipelago beneath hanging glaciers. Far to the south Fort Ross was a fur and farming settlement in California, a land claimed by the Spanish.

From the time of Czar Boris Godunov in the sixteenth

century Siberia has been a place of exile for political, religious and criminal offenders, owing in some measure to the extreme climate and the rigorous life.

With the opening of Russian America in the nineteenth century a new kind of exile was established, this for adventurers, explorers, fortune hunters, missionaries and other individuals of relatively unsound mind. Alaska was not a brave extension of the empire, but a fur farm. If troublesome the native peoples were to be exterminated or enslaved. If cooperative they were to be used as native labor for the fur harvest.

Russian men married Eskimo and Indian women and a breed of Slavic Creoles sprang up. Fathers and sons, they were called the *promyshlenniki;* they were fiercely independent hunter-traders of the early years. They in turn were supplanted by the Russian-American Company, administered by aristocratic naval officers who played whist, danced the quadrille and spoke French better than Russian.

June 1854

By the time the Russian-American Company's supply ship reached Redoubt St. Michael, the rude outpost on Norton Sound north of the Yukon River, Alex Karloff was convinced that he had made a serious mistake in marrying Grushenka. It was true that she bore up well under the hardships of the long overland trek across Siberia, enduring bitter cold, rough going and scarce and abominable food. In fact she carried her own weight remarkably well, never voicing a word of complaint. She lost a few pounds, but so did they all.

Then the voyage from the port of Ayan across the Sea of Okhotsk, around the tip of Kamchatka and over the Bering Sea to St. Michael undid her. Every day of the three weeks at sea she was deathly ill, unable to keep down a mouthful of food. She emerged from her bunk emaciated, shaky and so pale that the veins showed greenish through her skin. The surge of sexual passion that began their relationship flickered out completely somewhere on the journey, at least on Karloff's part, and when Grushenka showed signs of being frail as well, he came to look upon her primarily as an annoyance.

Karloff, a man of great physical strength and endurance, was constitutionally incapable of sympathy for weaklings. While it was true that his primary reason for asking her hand was his intense desire for her, it was also precisely true, as he told her father, that he wanted a wife with the strength and endurance of a peasant woman but preferably at least nominally a member of his own class.

As it turned out, Grushenka was a great disappointment on both scores.

Karloff and Grushenka were sitting at dinner in the headquarters building in St. Michael. This unimpressive log structure was the largest of perhaps half a dozen such buildings within a wooden palisade. They sat at a rough-hewn table lighted by whale-oil lamps, for the unpainted wooden interior of the room was dim. The low sun was still above the horizon in these latitudes in May, although it was past ten o'clock, but its light filtered in through only three small windows covered with thin-scraped sealskin.

The meal was delectable. The main course consisted of fresh salmon baked to flaky pink perfection and served by a pretty although apparently cowed Creole girl. There was caviar, white bread made with precious wheat from California and quantities of seal blubber, a native delicacy for which Karloff had never developed a taste and at which Grushenka could not repress a faint shudder, although Count Pieter Dobshansky, their host, ate the oily fat with obvious relish.

Dobshansky even opened a bottle of passable red wine, also from California, in celebration of the arrival of

Karloff and his bride. Alex ate voraciously of everything except the blubber, finding the meal doubly a feast after the long months of the journey with little to eat except dried lentils, hard bread made from spoiled wheat, occasionally a scrap of deteriorating dried meat. Grushenka, he noted, only picked at the food despite the urgings of her host, and she asked to be excused early.

Karloff rose and ceremoniously kissed his wife's hand, admonishing her to rest well, but neither Dobshansky nor Grushenka could fail to detect the annoyance in the hard line of his jaw as she left the room.

"I'm afraid the journey has overtaxed your lady," remarked Dobshansky. His slightly bulbous eyes lingered on her as she stepped through the door, even remained on the door for a moment after it was closed. "Well, it is hard on a woman, any white woman. A pity, *mon baron*. She is quite lovely, Karloff. At the moment she is so thin I imagine her hipbones poke holes in a man's belly, but a little meat on her and I can see that she would be quite a tasty piece."

Dobshansky winked broadly and Karloff set his jaw even harder, gritting his teeth at his superior's crudeness but giving no thought to any retort. There was no point in getting things off to a bad start.

Karloff knew Dobshansky from former years on the frontier, for the count had been with the Russian-American Company from the time he was a young man. He fled to the wild lands early to escape a wife who even at twenty was unbearably pious, although well connected. There was no one to Karloff's mind more thoroughly competent in his work, but Dobshansky was not one he had ever liked. Short, powerful and in his fortieth year running to fat, he had a face that Alex thought vaguely resembled a toad's. The count, recently made acting head of the Russian-American Company's entire Alaskan operation, was given to coarse language and famous for his excesses of women, liquor and brutality to the natives.

Now, as acting head of the company's holdings, he was Alex Karloff's superior. His goodwill was essential both to success with the immediate mission and to Karloff's continued advancement through the ranks of naval service.

"Perhaps we should discuss your plans for Nulato," Karloff said, his voice quiet but his eyes icy. "I understand that you wish to reopen the outpost there and that I am to run it for a time."

"Quite true, quite true. There's not much to discuss. You've already met the half-breed, Ivan Pavloff. He'll be your right-hand man. A simple, honest soul, fairly good with the natives. When the ice is gone from the Yukon, we'll take your men—you've brought thirty, I believe?"

Baron Karloff nodded.

"There's another thirty, mainly Aleuts and Creoles, who can be spared from here for the time being. I would never anticipate any resistance from the Koyukons, you understand, but certainly with a force of sixty armed men there will be none at all. When the ice is gone, as I said *mon frère*, we'll proceed upriver to Nulato. The men will be able to handle whatever repairs or rebuilding needs to be done. After that you're on your own, you and your pretty pigeon—and of course Father Georgi, to keep the two of you honest and the Indians full of religious fervor. I think ten of your own men and perhaps twenty of my Aleuts and Creoles should be a sufficient number for security and to do your trapping, don't you?"

Karloff inclined his head. It wouldn't have mattered in the slightest, naturally, if he had disagreed.

Dobshansky snapped his fingers, summoning the Creole waitress from the kitchen area at the far end of the room. The corner was dominated by a large cast iron stove and a worktable.

"Sabaka," he called, "brandy."

"You call her that?" Karloff asked. "Dog?"

Dobshansky grinned broadly. "She doesn't mind. She is happy whatever I call her. She probably doesn't know what her name means."

The servant set down the kettle, from which she had been about to pour hot water into a pan to do the dinner dishes.

"Brandy?" she asked, glancing up and then back at the floor.

"The brown firewater." Dobshansky handed her a key to the locked cabinet. "She's a stupid slut," he remarked to Karloff, not bothering to lower his voice. "Pretty and obedient, passable on her back, but stupid. She was raised among the Indians and so she is nearly as ignorant as a full-blood."

Karloff glanced at the girl, saw the flush creep up her face as she turned to open the cabinet and extract the bottle, turned back to place it on the table. Karloff noted the pleasant sway of the supple young body in its cotton dress, the full, soft lips, the gentle lines of the round face.

"Glasses, you fool," Dobshansky shouted. "Do I have to tell you everything?"

She stepped to get glasses from another cupboard, and the count grinned his wide, rubbery smile. "You like my little Sabaka, Karloff? Perhaps you would wish to try her out."

At these words the servant looked at Karloff, the briefest sideways glance as she set the glasses on the table and poured some amber liquid into each.

"She's lovely, Dobshansky, but I think tonight, after the long journey—"

"I forget," Dobshansky laughed. "You are newly wed, and to a beautiful Russian woman at that. I don't blame you. I wouldn't mind trading off, but I suppose you'll be selfish."

Then he turned to the servant and addressed her in the

tone of contempt that marked all his communications with the gentle, frightened creature. "Sabaka, *ma petite,* Alex Karloff and I have things we wish to discuss. Leave the cleaning up for later and go to your cabin."

She stepped to the door, silently and with eyes still averted. Before she stepped out, she dropped a curiously formal curtsy.

"And keep your skirts up and your drawers down. I don't want to have to fumble around in the dark later," Dobshansky roared as she ducked out, once again blushing furiously.

Count Dobshansky downed his drink, real French brandy, Karloff noted, more precious than gold in a remote outpost like St. Michael. Karloff sipped at his own, savoring the smooth fire, breathing in the bouquet until his superior urged him to drink up, holding the bottle poised to pour another dollop for each of them. Karloff settled back in his chair and then with a nod raised his glass in salute and drained this one too.

"Filthy savages," Dobshansky sighed suddenly, apropos of nothing. "It's a hard life, Karloff. I almost hope the Indians are on the warpath when we go up to Nulato. It would be such a pleasure to kill them. Did you hear all of what they did to the outpost?" He poured himself another brandy and went on with his story without waiting for Karloff's reply.

"They came in the dead of winter. It was a wild band of Koyukons who apparently were at war with the Ingaliks at the post. They fell upon everyone. Once the blood lust gets up in them, they stop at nothing. It's said that not only did they rape the women of their own tribe who were living with the traders, they roasted the mutilated bodies of the white men and ate their flesh."

He paused to raise his glass again, blinking as if savoring the thought. "Do you suppose they really did that, Karloff? I should think they would have preferred the tenderer flesh of the women."

Karloff studied the count, made particular note of the lines about the mouth. *He looks like a toad with a fat fly,* he thought. *He's competent but a pig.*

Baron Karloff nodded. "I have not observed that any of the natives practice cannibalism."

"Ah, well. I suspected that rumor. The peasants love to tell tales. In any case Deriabin and the others are dead. I sent half a dozen of the promyshlenniki upriver a month or two later to tend to the remains and that's what they told me when they returned."

They spoke a little more of business. Of late years the take of fur seals and sea otters along the coasts had been dropping off, and now even as far north as St. Michael the return from the coastal operations was next to nothing. It was imperative to push inland, where beaver and otter were still abundant, in order to remain competitive with the Hudson's Bay Company and the American independents who were pushing in from the east and the south. With Nulato re-established there was a possibility at least of building outposts farther up the river, perhaps regaining absolute dominance in the market.

The count retailed several bits of gossip, always crude and often cruel. The previous winter a Russian trapper beat his Ikogmiut wife to the point of unconsciousness before passing into a drunken sleep himself. The man awakened later in a storm of pain, his breeches full of blood. By the time he realized his wife had castrated him and managed to stanch the flow of blood, the woman was gone with her family. All the pursuers ever found were the severed genitals, placed with obvious deliberate insult upon a pile of dog excrement.

Dobshansky found the tale thoroughly amusing and roared with laughter as he recounted it. "And you know," he finished, "it's true what they say. Liubov has been much calmer since it happened, much easier to deal with. He no longer wants to get drunk and fight all the time. I've thought castration might not be such a bad idea for all the workers, except that they would get too lazy to move."

"In your cups, Dobshansky," Karloff remarked, "you could make a jackal vomit." He rose and stretched his arms.

Dobshansky guffawed, apparently taking the words as a compliment. "Sit down, sit down," he urged, refilling Karloff's glass. "It's been such a long time since I had anyone of breeding to talk to—other than the governor, of course, but the man's wits are made of lead. Sit down, Baron Karloff. Relax a bit."

Alex returned to his seat and Dobshansky leaned his chair onto its back legs, staring fixedly at the other man. Karloff noticed the glaze of his eyes, the redness of the broad face, the increasing slur in his speech. The chair swayed slightly and threatened to go over; with a thud Dobshansky brought it onto all fours.

"So, Alex," he said, "we have changed estates since the last time we saw each other. We are nearly the same age, and yet you are a newlywed, happy with your beautiful bride, and sadly enough, I am a widower."

"I saw your wife in Moscow shortly before she died," Karloff nodded. "She was a very devout woman, Pieter. I suspect she was ready for heaven."

"She was always ready for heaven," Dobshansky sighed. "She only let me mount her twice in the first year of our marriage. It was her coldness in part that drove me to Kamchatka and to Russian America. It was a marriage in name only. Ah, but I don't need to tell you that. For me she died a long while ago, but still, I'm sorry she's gone, I suppose."

Karloff inclined his head politely, said nothing.

"Well, the juice still flows, you know," the count went on, looking mournful. "But Elizabeth Stepanova,

Lord grant her peace, was the only woman of breeding I ever made love to. Are they all like that? I don't think your pretty woman is cold that way, yet I sense something amiss between you—"

"We have no problems," Karloff said stiffly.

"Well. Perhaps I am wrong, Alex, but I still think you like my dog, my little Sabaka. I will give her to you if you want. You can take her along to Nulato. She can perform whatever menial—" Dobshansky paused, winked significantly—"tasks your lady is not inclined to do. Take her by all means. I do this because I am your friend, because in my way of looking at it we are still equals even though I have been elevated above you for the moment."

Karloff was tempted. He remembered the enticing curve of the girl's bosom, the charming redness that suffused the enchanting face. He would never again be interested in Grushenka, of that he was certain. But pretty Indian girls were easy to acquire, and a gift from Dobshansky, he knew, always had strings attached.

"I thank you for your offer, Pieter," he replied smoothly, "but I'm afraid of offending my wife."

"I'll gladly take care of your wife's doubts," Dobshansky offered immediately, winking lewdly once again. "You just step out the door and go visit my bitch-puppy. I'll speak with your wife."

"Some men would call you out for such a remark," Karloff gritted, "but I'll forget that the words were spoken."

Dobshansky chuckled. "It wouldn't be the first time we've shared a woman."

"Squaws. You're making filthy suggestions concerning my wife, yes, a noblewoman."

"Hah! You've had thirty wives, maybe more. You even have a son, although he will never be your heir in the eyes of the court," Dobshansky said slowly. "He's a fine boy. You even named him for yourself if my memory serves me properly."

"What are you saying? Are you threatening to inform Grushenka of it? By all means, then, feel free to do so. She can do nothing about it."

"Of course not, of course not," Dobshansky grinned. "I'm hurt that you misjudge me so badly. I was thinking about your boy Alexivich the other day is all. He can never inherit from you, but Creoles have gone to Russia to be educated. Why, Father Georgi's place here at the mission will be taken over by a Creole whom I managed to help get enrolled in a seminary. You remember the young man who appeared half Tlingit and half Father Georgi? Anyway, he's just one example of how fortunate Creoles can make their way in the world. It might even be possible with a good word in the right ear for a promising young man to be commissioned as an officer—well, at the lower ranks, of course."

Dobshansky had hit upon what was possibly Karloff's one soft spot. Alexivich was nearly seventeen and was so far as he knew his only son. The mother had died in childbirth, and the boy, the last Karloff had heard, was working as trapper and interpreter at Redoubt St. Nicholas, at the head of Cook Inlet to the south. There were few chances, Karloff realized, for half-breed offspring of even the most highly placed fathers to get ahead.

He thought again of Grushenka and a flash of pity went through him. Frail as she was, he could not turn her over to the gross appetites of a man such as Dobshansky.

The count, watching shrewdly despite his intoxication, saw the other man waver momentarily. "Of course, *mon frère*, it could be that such a young man would be drafted into military service and sent to fight in the Crimea. Unfortunately, I have little control over these matters. . . ."

"To put it differently," Karloff said, rising, "he might be conscripted if you were to . . . nominate him. You're blackmailing me, Dobshansky."

"*Non, non, mon ami*, not really. I'm offering to

return a large favor for a small one, easily given. And I do not think you will find Sabaka so unpleasant for a few hours of diversion. I promise you, Alex, I will treat the baroness with utmost respect. She will not be damaged in any way. After all, I am quite inexperienced at making love to women of breeding, *très innocent.*"

Suddenly Karloff burst out laughing at the absurdity of the entire matter. Of course Grushenka would survive. Women had a remarkable capacity for surviving such events. "You are a pig, Count Dobshansky, an utter pig."

Dobshansky grinned broadly, winked, drank a bit more brandy. "*En verité,* Baron Karloff, what you say is correct, but what is a man to do?"

Karloff shrugged, stepped to the door. "I think I'll take a long walk, Pieter. Don't be alarmed if I'm not back for several hours."

"Yes, yes. The cabin just to your right," Dobshansky called as the door closed behind the other man.

Grushenka had never been a particularly religious person, preferring her own brightly colored fairy tales and daydreams to the rather dull sermons and the monotonous repetition of litany in the church at home. And yet as soon as she escaped into the cool, dim room and was alone after her sumptuous uneaten dinner, the first thing she did was to kneel beside the small, hard bed and try to pray.

Words wouldn't come. What could she ask the Lord for? It would not be right to pray that she could leave her husband and return to her home, and yet that was the only thing she wanted. She leaned her forehead against the rough woolen blanket. What could she pray for?

During the steamer voyage across the choppy Bering Sea all she was able to pray for was land. She lived each day in deathly agony, vomiting everything that she tried to swallow. For days, when there was nothing in her stomach to come up, she had violent dry heaves. She was unable to leave her bunk for almost the entire trip, and yet lying in bed with the world careening around her had been the worst torture imaginable.

When at long last she heard the sailors calling that land was in sight, she mustered all her strength and staggered up onto the deck, voracious for the sight of terra firma. Grushenka clung to the rail, watching eagerly as the thin line on the horizon between the cold grey of the sea and the cold grey of the featureless sky grew larger, closer, more solid.

At last as they sailed into the meager harbor of Redoubt St. Michael the landscape resolved itself into a small, palisaded cluster of log buildings on a low promontory that jutted into the water a few feet above high tide line. Nowhere did she see a tree, a structure beyond the port settlement, anything to relieve the bleak and colorless wasteland that stretched away into the mists. It was just rolling land, tundra, brown and cold and endless.

Grushenka felt in that moment that her anticipated reprieve was a cruel joke, and her heart grew as dreary and barren as the world she had endured during the terrible journey. She would have wept except that she had long since forgotten the respite of tears.

To greet them was a small number of workers, mostly savages of some sort, half-breeds, and Count Pieter Dobshansky, a coarse man with brutality marked upon his face. He made her shudder just by ceremoniously bowing over her hand.

"Dear Jesus, kind St. Nicholas, sweet Mother of our Lord, give me strength to endure whatever may be required of me," she whispered now into the bedcovers, and then she rose stiffly and lay down fully clothed.

Grushenka discovered that after all the weeks of ceaseless motion, her stationary bunk made her dizzy also.

When she closed her eyes, the room spun around her, the familiar lurch at the pit of her stomach returned, and for a moment she was afraid she would have to vomit the little she had managed to eat at dinner.

When she opened her eyes in the twilight, however, and was able to perceive the stability around her, the queasiness subsided. After a time she found she was able to keep her eyes closed without growing dizzy.

Her body was exhausted, but she found that her mind continued to race from memories of the endless trip to useless speculation about her future at the end of the world, the North American colonies. In her innocence she had sometimes thought of Seeneestakan as the end of the world, but now she saw that the warm little house in the taiga and the village with its peasants were crude perhaps, but at least familiar and on the whole pleasant. She longed wholeheartedly for home.

Grushenka was at a low point, her physical vitality sapped by her weeks of illness and her spiritual resiliency shaken by one demoralizing realization after another. It could have been much better, she thought, ashamed of the notion even as she was unable to quell it, if Alex had continued to love me. For a moment she relived parts of the journey, used the force of her imagination to change history.

She was lying in her bunk aboard ship and Alex was leaning over her, bathing her face in cool water, whispering loving words of concern and encouragement. She imagined the two of them holding hands and stepping off the ship at Redoubt St. Michael together into the appalling bleakness, but truly together in a warm bubble of love, insulated against the forbidding world.

Perhaps then it would have been an adventure instead of a disaster, but not so. She was not even certain exactly when Alex stopped looking at her with desire, when he began instead to answer with annoyance when she spoke, to avoid her eyes when she glanced at him with a smile to share. She had not even noticed these small signs at first, still warm and excited in her own love, but before they reached Ayan and embarked for the sea voyage, she gradually came to the realization that Alex Karloff no longer touched her at all.

Once aboard ship she saw that he looked at her, wretched and vomiting, disheveled and frightened, with real loathing. He made all the proper gestures, inquiring every morning after her health, sending a steward with broth every few hours, but he also arranged for separate quarters for himself "to avoid disturbing you."

Grushenka sighed, tried to shut off her thoughts. She was desperate for sleep. She slid beneath several blankets, for the room was quite chilly, as the door closed out the heat from the stove in the other room. She turned onto her side, curled her knees up.

Well, I've seen myself in the mirror. Perhaps that's the whole thing. Her cheeks drew in like an old woman's; the eyes were huge and staring and had dark rings like bruises beneath them; the skin was yellowish. Certainly no man would desire a woman like that.

Grushenka convinced herself by an effort of will that Alex would want her again as soon as she was well. She would regain her weight, the flush in her cheeks, the sparkle in her eyes.

This is your life, whatever you may think of it, Grushenka. Her father's voice was as clear and matter-of-fact as if he were standing in the room. His daughter felt a wave of longing for him, his simple pragmatism, his gift of acceptance, his impatience with self-deception. That's it, Papa, she thought, you'd tell me to stop crying over spilt milk and get on with living. And I will make him love me again. Drowsiness took her and she managed to drift into sleep feeling considerably cheered.

The sound of the door opening only partly wakened her. The room was quite dark and for a moment she was confused at the motionlessness of the bed. She was still trying to sort things out when someone, breathing heavily and smelling of brandy, sat on the edge of the mattress and began fumbling among the covers, running a clumsy hand over her body and squeezing her breast when he found it.

"Alex?" she whispered, half joyful and half apprehensive. "You want me again?"

"Shhh," the figure whispered, working with drunken perseverence to pull the tangle of blankets away from her.

Grushenka felt a chill at the base of her neck. Something about the hissed syllable. . . . She sat up quickly and put a hand out to feel the face of the intruder.

She was shoved back upon the bed and pinned there with one hand as the other went about its rummaging among the blankets.

"Alex?" Her voice rose shrilly.

The man chuckled. "Baron Karloff won't hear you. He has other . . . business . . . to take care of."

Chapter 3
Arctic Poppies

It was not known with certainty when the first Russian Orthodox missionary arrived on the Yukon River, but on February 10, 1845, Innokenty, Bishop of Kamchatka, the Kuriles and Russian America, wrote to the Moscow Synod that he planned to establish a mission on the Yukon or Kuikpak, with Father Jacob Netzvetov to be sent there to take up his holy work.

Netzvetov was a Russian-Indian half-breed, recognized as a boy for his deep and melancholy intellect, much given to dreaming and to reading as well, though under what circumstances he learned this skill is unknown. Nor is it known what happened to his parents.

In due course he was, apparently willingly, sent to the seminary in Irkitsk, Siberia, from which he graduated in 1826. At Atka, an Aleutian island, he translated the Book of Matthew into the tongue of the Aleuts.

In 1846 or 1847 Netzvetov built his mission at the village of Ikogmut, some two hundred miles upriver from the mouths of the Yukon. In December of 1851, according to Bishop Innokenty, "The wooden church built on the northwest coast of America at Ikogmut village was consecrated to the glory of the holy life-giving Cross." The building was topped with a small blue onion dome and three double crosses of the Orthodoxy.

To this day men and women come into the church just before Christmas and the women prepare a feast replete with large quantities of agudak, made of berries, seal oil, shredded whitefish and sugar. The priest orders the lighting of lanterns to burn for four days upon all recent graves. Then the church bells are rung, the flock is summoned and the birth of the Savior is announced. So has it been for a very long time.

In the beginning, however, as afterward reported, "Medicine men openly renounced their craft—polygamists freely offered to give up their wives—murderers confessed their crimes and mothers told of deeds of infanticide that sickened one to hear. Then all earnestly sought for pardon and grace. . . ."

Raven Man sits on a hill beyond the Kuikpak, runs his fingers down the length of his long bill and shakes out his feathers. He knows where the Death Tunnel emerges.

June 1854

Dobshansky.

She recognized the voice immediately and twisted wildly away from the hand that pushed against her chest, lunging off the other side of the bed. Dobshansky stumbled after her, laughing, and fell upon her so that the two of them went to the floor. He held her in place with his weight crushing her upper body. His free hand pulled up her skirts and tugged at the waistband of her woolen bloomers.

"Alex, Alex!" Grushenka screamed: then her voice rose into wordless keening.

Dobshansky laughed once more. "I tell you your husband has other business. Scream if it pleases you, I rather enjoy it."

As he spoke he continued to fumble at her clothing. She kicked hard with both feet against the floor, arching her back and trying to throw him off, but it was like trying to move a tree. His weight was too solid.

"Hold still, damnit, woman. It's been too long since I've had a Russian. You tie yourselves up with Gordian knots."

Grushenka screamed again but felt growing despair. She worked an arm free, felt about on the floor beside the bed. Her hand closed on something solid and smooth. She grasped the rim of a heavy pottery chamber pot and brought it down upon the back of Dobshansky's head as hard as she could.

He grunted and relaxed. She slipped out from under him and scrambled across the bed. Before he caught her she had grabbed the doorhandle and pushed into the other room. The room was still lit by the whale-oil lamps, and Grushenka could see in a glance that it was empty. As Dobshansky caught her around the waist, she called her husband's name again.

The count dragged her back into the bedroom, panting from exertion. He left the door open and pulled her about, trying clumsily to kiss her. "You see? I told you he wasn't there. He's off entertaining little Sabaka, by God. He said you'd be nice to me while he was busy. You're an obedient wife, aren't you?"

He tried to kiss her, but she turned her head away from his wet, wide lips. But the impact of his words—that she couldn't avoid.

Not true, not true. . . . But it could well be true.

Dobshansky threw her onto the bed again, pulling his knife this time and trying to use it one-handed to cut away her undergarment.

My God, he'll kill me. The cunning of desperation came over her and for a moment she went limp so as to avoid being stabbed by the drunken count. She heard the fabric ripping, felt the cold tip of the knife graze the skin of her abdomen. Then he worked her bloomers loose. As he shifted his weight to move between her legs, she drew her knee up sharply toward his groin, felt a sudden hot bolt of pain as her thigh ran onto the point of the knife.

She cried out and simultaneously Dobshansky drew back and delivered a stunning blow to the side of her face. Through a clearing haze she heard him grunt. "So you still want to fight, do you? I don't mind a woman fighting, by Christ, I don't. Only the woman loses, that's how it is."

He struck her twice more, heavy blows, one across the nose so that she dimly felt a warm trickle of blood from her upper lip.

Her vision went vague, with red and black writhing lines. She couldn't see more than dim shapes, nor did her other senses seem to be functioning properly.

Grushenka knew that he had flipped her over onto her face because she felt the rough blanket against her cheek. She felt him lashing her hands together behind her back, felt him raise her up and penetrate her from the rear. None of the sensations was lucid, not even the tearing pain as he entered her.

Far back in her consciousness a voice that seemed quite unattached to her was speaking: *Is this all there is to it? Hardly worth getting your head knocked off, was it?*

She could still feel Dobshansky's thrusts, hear his grunts. A picture flashed through her mind, Alex and the Creole coupling, their cries joyous, intense.

Someone had died. . . . Yes, but she had no idea who it was.

Dobshansky was moving still against her, but he seemed ridiculously far away. She was very tired and not much interested in what was going on. He was not done thrusting and grunting, in fact, when she drifted into warm sleep.

It seemed to Grushenka that true spring came overnight to the tundra. Barren, lifeless hills near St. Michael had seemed locked in eternal winter only a few short weeks ago, enveloped day after day in icy fog or blasted by freezing winds off the grim waters of Norton Sound. Now, however, they were blessed by several days of impeccably blue skies and warming sun, and the days were so long now that there was hardly any night at all.

And it bloomed. The hills had seemed dead, but the brittle brush suddenly leafed out and produced a staggering profusion of flowers, acres and acres of Arctic poppies, cream, yellow, orange, vivid scarlet. Masses of fireweed, or willow brush, along the meandering, boggy streams put forth pale catkins.

It was impossible for Grushenka, still only seventeen, not to respond with a sense of renewed life, even irrational joy, to the burgeoning life around her. She walked out into the fields of flowers every day in the company of Father Georgi, who as it turned out was an amateur botanist and as delighted as a child with spring in the north country. He would exclaim over each new variety of flower he found, make Grushenka kneel on the muddy earth to examine the specimen and have her repeat the name over and over so that she would remember.

The priest stooped and picked a tiny pink flower from a low-growing penstemon, clapping his hands together when she gave him the correct name. Grushenka smiled fondly at Father Georgi, whose round cheeks glowed with pleasure and whose small blue eyes shone bright among their crinkled lines. Even in his robes and his flowing patriarchal beard there was nothing about this man to inspire the kind of awed terror she had felt toward the priests who sometimes came to visit Seeneestakan.

"You have been here for years, Father Georgi. I'd think you'd be used to all this by now," Grushenka laughed, tucking the tiny blossom into her red-gold crown of braids.

"*Nyet,* child," the priest smiled in return. "Every year it is new. Every year I start to worry. Easter is always grey and grim and I start to believe this will be the year winter doesn't go away, another Fimbull Time, as in the old pagan stories. And then when I've all but given up hope, the sun bursts forth and in the course of a few days comes the real resurrection. The land remembers our Lord, but the memory comes late here at St. Michael. It's glorious, isn't it? All flowers, all plants, all birds, all creatures come to life at once, and with such urgency—"

"I'm not sure these are priestly thoughts," Grushenka teased. "First you tell me you lack faith that God will bring the summer back, and then when it comes you turn into a pagan."

"Not at all, not at all," Father Georgi replied, unperturbed. "We love the Father through His creation. That is the message Christ brought us. In any case, Jesus Himself was a pagan, I think. He did not love merely the human multitude, but all things."

"If there is no more to dogma than that, then why do we need the priests to teach us?"

"If you were not such silly creatures, you wouldn't."

Grushenka smiled and nodded. "Is that what they teach you in the seminary?"

Georgi threw back his head and laughed. "You have no respect for me. You think I am foolish because I go into raptures over flowers, because I believe that when a flower blooms it reveals the inner beauty of all things. I'll tell you, I wouldn't feel this way if I didn't have such a bright—and perhaps I shouldn't but will add pretty—pupil. I tried to teach Sergei—Father Matthew—when he was little, but his mind was always on theology. Well, he will be a better priest than I. In truth I never had a head for theology."

"I'm glad. I like you the way you are." Grushenka didn't add that she was a little frightened of Father Matthew, the young half-Indian priest who it was rumored was actually Father Georgi's son. Matthew was a good man, kind-hearted and honest, but he was quiet and intense, and Grushenka had the feeling that he was less concerned with this world than with the next. He frightened her as had the priests back in Mother Russia.

"Ah, Grushenka," Father Georgi smiled, "if you weren't a married lady and if I had not vowed celibacy . . ."

Grushenka grinned, hooked her arm through his and skipped a step, her boots squishing in the sodden earth.

"Dear child," the big priest said, stopping suddenly and facing her, "I think we need to talk seriously for a moment, don't you?"

All Grushenka's gaiety dissolved and she looked down at the ground, her eyes narrowed and her lips pinched. "I will not speak to you about Alex Karloff. I will never go back to him."

"Don't be foolish," the cleric scolded gently. "Very soon we will all be off to Nulato. What will you do then?"

"I don't know. Perhaps I will remain here until a ship leaves for Kamchatka."

"You don't have any money for passage, not unless your husband gives it to you."

"Maybe I will earn the money. At least I know how to lie on my back."

"Ah, Grushenka, you keep saying that, but we both know you couldn't sell yourself to men. I don't know what your husband has done to you because you won't tell me, but he is your husband in the eyes of God. You must soften your heart and forgive him."

"You're a priest. You forgive him," she shot back.

"Look at this." She bent to touch a small purple weed. "What is this called, Father? Let's talk only about pleasant things. This flower is pleasant."

After Dobshansky beat her half senseless and raped her, she awakened with the light of dawn filtering into the room and with the count's body still sprawled across hers.

Her head ached horribly and the cut in her thigh throbbed, but worse than the physical pangs was the terrible psychic desolation she felt, a great blackness and blankness in the hollow of her chest.

She shoved herself out from under the snoring count, who clutched wildly at her in his sleep and then turned onto his side, never awakening. She saw something glinting in the faint light, stooped and picked up Dobshansky's knife from the floor. It was a hunting knife with a heavy razor-sharp blade. She remembered the feel of it in her hand, the good heft. She stood over the sleeping man, knife in tense fist, for perhaps a minute, aching to plunge the blade into the soft skin at the base of his throat. But at last she had realized she couldn't do it, kill even *this* in sleep.

She bent and carefully replaced the knife on the floor. Pulling her clothing about her, she fled outside into air so bitterly cold that her cheeks immediately went numb and she shivered violently in her thin dress.

The need to know with certainty that which she passionately did not want to know prompted her to hurry to the door of the cabin next to the headquarters building. She tried the latch, took a deep breath and pulled the unlocked door open enough to see by the dim light in the tiny room. Two dark heads lay together on the pillow and the fine morocco boots standing beside the bed belonged to her husband.

She softly closed the door and fled away into the compound, but she soon realized she had no place to go. The outpost was sleeping. There was no sound, no smoke rising from any chimney, only silence, pale mist that diffused the light of the rising sun and emptiness that reflected and intensified the emptiness she felt. She could hear the rush of the sea, the grey water dull and cold and eternal, and she thought wildly of throwing herself into it.

But the palisaded settlement could be neither entered nor left before the gates were officially thrown open.

At last she sought out the church. Father Georgi took her in and nursed her back to health as tenderly as her own mother might have done. In the weeks that followed Grushenka returned to blooming good health as her bruises faded and she gained weight.

In the beginning Karloff came courting her again, sending gifts of furs and beautifully made Eskimo boots—begging, through Father Georgi, for a word with her. The priest carried her message of refusal and exhorted the baron to be gentle and to give his wife a little time.

Later Karloff became more demanding. He threatened among other things to have his men march in and take back his woman. Georgi dealt calmly with the threats, assuring Grushenka that the baron would not want such a sacrilege on his soul and that the men wouldn't invade a church in any case.

All along the priest pled Karloff's case as well, trying to persuade the bride to forgive her husband. She was too ashamed to reveal the nature of her grievance, and so Father Georgi assumed that Karloff had beaten her—not a good thing certainly, but not particularly unusual either. Countless women had forgiven their husbands a beating or two.

One day Karloff caught her outside the church and tried to force her to return to him, but she pulled away and swore, "If you make me live with you, I shall kill you in your sleep." Apparently her intensity carried conviction, for after that he stopped coming round.

Karloff subsequently took up living quite openly with the Creole, perhaps hoping jealousy would bring her back where force wouldn't. If that was true, Grushenka reflected, then he did not understand her lack of feelings: his sexual habits were a matter of indifference to her.

She found a friend in Father Georgi, her only friend in this alien land, and she really didn't know what she would do when he left. She preferred not to think about the matter, letting the question go unresolved until the last moment. She passed her days in reading, for the priest had not only several Bibles but a few other books as well. She talked with Father Georgi in the evenings or they played parlor games. She even managed to draw solemn Father Matthew, with his sad brown eyes and stern face, into an occasional conversation.

She bloomed again, finding herself singing at times as she did chores in the mission. Now, with the flowering of the world around her, she knew that the time of decision could no longer be put off. Childishly, however, she could not help wishing that Father Georgi would refrain fom bringing up the subject.

As it turned out there was no more time at all, for when Grushenka and Father Georgi returned to the compound, they found Karloff waiting for them at the church. He informed Father Georgi that Dobshansky had set the following day for departure.

Karloff then bowed formally to Grushenka, whom he had not addressed previously. ''I have taken the liberty of having your things loaded, madame. I trust you will respect your marriage vows and accompany me to the interior?''

Grushenka felt herself beginning to tremble uncontrollably. She had no idea how to reply.

''Certainly she will,'' Father Georgi interposed. ''It's long past the time when husband and wife should forget their grievances and make peace. I have a great deal to do if we are leaving tomorrow. I'll allow the two of you to discuss this matter privately.'' With that he nodded to both of them and turned away.

Grushenka cried out wildly and tried to run after him, but Karloff took her arm and the priest turned and held up one hand. "No, my dear. I can no longer presume to place myself between a man and his wife. I took pity on you because you are so young and were so agitated and so hurt, but I was wrong to allow you to stay so long. I am sure," he said, looking sharply at Alex, "that Baron Karloff will treat you with all respect and consideration, as is fitting."

The priest then put his hands gently on Grushenka's shoulders, blessed both of them and walked away.

Karloff turned Grushenka so that she had to face him. She kept her gaze fixed upon the ground. "Please look at me, beloved," he begged, his voice soft and pleading.

She glanced up and saw that his eyes were fixed on her with a look of such tenderness that she could not turn away again.

"Let's walk out away from the compound a little," he suggested, so Grushenka let herself be led outside the gate again and into a field of poppies. "You're more beautiful than ever. I find myself falling in love harder than before."

"Don't play with me, Alex Karloff," she snapped. "I was a child when we met, but I've grown up since then."

Karloff looked stricken. "I know what happened that night. Dobshansky has confessed the whole thing to me. I should have killed him, but he was so abject. He apologized many times over, saying he was drunk and couldn't control himself. I know that's no excuse, but I swear to you I had no idea that he would do such a thing—and he feels dreadful about it."

"Don't lie to me. He told me you arranged it between you."

"And you believed him?" Karloff cried.

"He also told me you were with the Creole, and I know that was true, because I looked in and saw you in her bed."

"Ah, Grushenka, that was nothing. I felt like drowning myself when I realized what my folly had led to. A man has certain . . . needs. You were too ill. I couldn't impose myself on you. It had been months. Sabaka means nothing to me."

"Is that true indeed, Alex? Then why have you been living with her these past two weeks?"

"What was I supposed to do?" Karloff retorted, beginning to show temper himself. "Remain the laughing-stock of every lout and half-breed in the fort? Do you know that they call you the priest's woman?"

"What?" Grushenka sputtered, her face going scarlet. "They—what? Oh, but that's ridiculous. I never . . . we never imagined. . . ."

"Of course not." Alex took advantage of her confusion to put his arms around her. "I never thought so for a minute. But you see how things can get twisted?"

Grushenka found herself quite literally speechless. Yet again her idea of the world, now based on distrust and disillusion, seemed to be crumbling. She found herself in Karloff's familiar embrace, her face pressed against his shoulder, even the odor of his clothing so immediate to her memory that it was like a homecoming.

Karloff nuzzled her hair. "Many men would leap to the wrong conclusion. It is so easy not to trust, to believe the worst." He tilted her face up in order to kiss her forehead, her eyelids, the bridge of her nose.

"Ah, Grushenka," he said, the words coming out in a kind of passionate groan, "you're the only one I love. I think that you love me also?"

Still speechless, Grushenka wrestled with her thoughts. *I don't know, I don't know anything. Everything has come apart again. Do I love him? Who is he?*

"My darling," he whispered, touching his lips to her face, "my phoenix, my salamander, this is all that matters. We mustn't let evil rumors destroy us or our love. All this time I have longed only for you. You broke my heart, Grushenka, my cruel one."

He kissed her mouth, his tongue forcing its way between her lips. Her body responded at once despite the warning bells still sounding in her mind. Her knees went weak, and his mouth, moving slowly, expertly on hers, awakened a hunger that caused her own lips to open, to bite, to nurse.

He led her away from the settlement after a time, far out into the low hills. He spread his coat over the damp ground and they made love under the clear sky and among the flowers, her own body arching to his, urgently and far beyond her control.

That night both Grushenka and Karloff slept at Father Georgi's mission, for she refused to go back to Dobshansky's quarters and the only other space that might have been made available was the cabin where Sabaka was quartered. By this time of year the nights were so short that they could hardly be called by that name, but they lay down to rest for a few hours before departing for the mouth of the Yukon.

Grushenka slept little, but when she awoke in Alex's arms, she felt refreshed despite her misgivings. Her heart was singing as she went about the numerous small tasks that needed to be taken care of before she was settled into a bidarka, one of the string of small canoes made of animal hides stretched over a wooden frame. In the boat with her were two native oarsmen and a surprising quantity of goods stashed within the covered prow and stern of the long, narrow vessel.

The Ikogmiuts paddled out beyond the breakers and turned west, maneuvering the frail-seeming craft with remarkable ease and swiftness. There were more than a dozen of the boats, strung out like ducks bobbing on the tide. In one of these Grushenka recognized Sabaka.

They rounded the cape and turned south, passing through the strait between the mainland and Stuart Island, and then cut across open sea to the delta of the great river the Eskimos and Indians alike called the Lot of Water, the Yukon, some fifty miles distant.

They reached one of its numerous mouths by late afternoon and turned inland, against the current. They stopped briefly at an Eskimo village and Grushenka was able to step out, stretch her limbs and confront her husband.

"Why is that woman going with us?" she demanded, glancing toward Sabaka.

"She's a gift from Dobshansky," Karloff replied. "I think it's a gesture of apology. He wants you to have her as your personal servant."

Sabaka, noticing their attention, smiled timidly, but Grushenka did not return the smile.

Chapter 4
Nulato

By reason of its charter the Russian-American Company was instructed and committed to the establishment of churches and schools and ultimately to the fostering of agriculture in Alaska. These projects were designed to improve relations with the Eskimos and Indians, who had been in many instances annihilated or enslaved. But the best of intentions availed little, since the Russian officers who ruled the great land behaved much as Russian officers in the far provinces always have.

At times the raw exercise of power proved most effective, while at other times bribery and more subtle forms of coercion did the job. Few of these officers were good businessmen, however, and competition in the fur trade from the British and the Americans was on the increase.

Nicholas I, Czar of all the Russians, had other problems to worry about. His aggressive policy toward the Ottoman Empire in 1853 precipitated the Crimean War; Russian troops occupied a portion of Turkey north of the Danube. France and Britain entered the struggle on the side of Turkey, and the two allies sent a total of seventy thousand troops under Somerset and Saint-Arnaud. They laid siege to Sevastopol, the Russian stronghold by the Black Sea.

This war of attrition would continue for three years and would lead to a Russian defeat. It concluded with the fall of Sevastopol and resulted in the withdrawal of Russian warships from the Black Sea.

A hundred two thousand Russians died. The British and French between them lost ninety thousand men. The treasury of Nicholas I was depleted.

And the stage was set for Russia's eventual withdrawal from its North American colonies. Alaska was to be sold to America in 1867.

July–August 1854

The voyage, more than four hundred miles up the great, swollen river, was exhausting and agonizingly slow. Every foot of headway against the powerful current was won only by prodigious effort on the part of the men, but it was also a blessedly uneventful passage. As they moved into the interior of the country the open tundra gradually transformed into evergreen forests. Grushenka felt much more comfortable among the stands of hemlock, spruce, birch, aspen and cottonwood; even these three deciduous varieties had come into full foliage. The taiga here reminded her keenly of her home, and she felt infinitely more at ease than she had in the tundra.

There were, however, a few moments of genuine difficulty. Two days' travel above the Ingalik village Anvik, some forty miles north of the great bend and the mission of Holy Cross, they came upon a grizzly bear fishing in the shallows. One of the Russian conscripts, excited by his first view of the big North American bear, shot at it with his rifle, not killing the animal but merely enraging it. The grizzly charged the bidarkas, which were not far from the bank, and swam out after them. They were obliged to turn and paddle downstream, out into the swift current toward the middle of the river, letting the flood take them. Finally the bear, discouraged by random shots, gave up the chase and turned back to the bank to lick his wounds.

One of the boats was overturned in the scramble, and although its occupants were all saved, the vessel itself and its contents were lost to the river. They had sacrificed a half-day's laborious upstream travel as well before all was done. When they camped that evening, Dobshansky ordered flogged the men who lost the boat as well as the one who shot the grizzly in the first place. Grushenka was horrified and begged her husband to intercede in behalf of the poor wretches, but he refused, saying that such measures were necessary to maintain discipline.

Later the little flotilla stopped at an Indian encampment further upstream. Karloff discovered a warrior of about fourteen stealing from one of the bidarkas. He drew his pistol and shot the boy dead on the spot, necessitating a hasty departure downstream once again. They lost several miles before they were able to regroup and proceed up the opposite shore.

Grushenka, who witnessed the shooting, was much disturbed, and after the terror for her own and everyone else's life was past, the scene kept returning to her mind—the Indian boy straightening up with a look of utter shock as Karloff fired, the great gush of blood from the center of his chest, the youth's knees seeming to go out as he collapsed much more slowly than natural.

She did not question her husband as to this occurrence, having heard him say often enough that thievery on the part of the Indians must never be tolerated. The only way to gain their respect on this matter was to kill a few of them, he maintained.

Aside from these disquieting facets of Karloff's character, he seemed indeed bent on proving the sincerity of his affection for his wife. In the little time available for such pastimes, he courted Grushenka scrupulously, not making the slightest gesture toward Sabaka. In Grushenka's company at least he was somewhat curt with Pieter Dobshansky and he was at great pains never to leave her alone in the count's presence.

For Sabaka's part, she did not look at anybody, and Grushenka, despite the pangs of jealousy she continued to suffer, could not help pitying the creature. Insisting that she would not have a servant with such an undignified name, Grushenka changed it to Sabrina.

The Creole responded to this news with the first genuine smile Grushenka had ever seen from her. From that moment on Sabrina made a point of following Grushenka everywhere, offering to help her, wanting to do things for her, to the point where it became quite troublesome.

As for Alex, Grushenka still did not entirely trust him, but she tried to convince herself that she had misinterpreted his actions. After all, there was hardly a wife in the world whose husband had not been unfaithful at least once. Most women, she realized, sighed and forgave. Many insisted it was simply the nature of the masculine sex.

The murder of the Indian boy, however, was another matter. She could not forget that, and neither could she find a way of justifying it in her mind. Eventually she simply gave up on pondering the event.

Alex was unfailingly attentive, remorseful, gentle, and the physical attraction was still very powerful, almost irresistible. Her sexual desire, now reawakened, went on almost with a mind of its own, a need precedent to and deeper than any matter of her conscious will. And Alex was her husband.

As to dealing closely with other human beings, she decided, there would simply always be questions that could never be resolved.

* * *

Nulato. Though Dobshansky had talked at length of the necessity of exacting revenge upon the Koyukon Indians for the massacre three years earlier, he realized the needs of commerce were not well served by such a course of action—not here, deep in the interior, far removed from the other Russian outposts.

The men were ready for all eventualities, however, when they approached the village, rifles and pistols loaded, the soldiers on their guard. The Koyukons, however, seemed overjoyed that their *Gossack* traders had returned.

Ivan Pavloff, himself a half-breed Koyukon, was to be the functioning *bidarshik*, chief trader. A man of demonstrated loyalties, or so Dobshansky concluded, Pavloff married the widow of the former *bidarshik* at Anvik and in so doing acquired a ready-made family of five children. Dobshansky saw him as both generous and honest when sober. A short, thickset, swarthy, low-browed man, he became as ungovernable as a mad bull when drunk.

Pavloff was illiterate, but Baron Karloff would tend to the post's accounts. That, in fact, would hardly be a disadvantage. In any case Pavloff's particular charge was that of acting as trader and maintaining good relations with the Indians. Once his wife and children came up to Nulato, Pavloff would become a functioning member of the village, the Indians dependent upon him in a way that they would never be to a white man.

The Koyukons were both friendly and eager to trade. The buildings of the previous post were still standing and in quite good condition. Only one of the locks had been pried loose, and nothing at all had been taken.

"Apparently the savages have been hoping all along we'd come back," Karloff remarked.

And so it turned out to be. The Indians stood about curiously as the Russians moved into the old quarters. They grinned and laughed and ordered their women to bring kettles of soup and boiled caribou meat.

Dobshansky spoke to Pavloff, and the latter invited the headmen into the trading post itself so that they could see firsthand the trade goods that had been brought upriver. The Koyukons nodded, conversed in more or less adequate Russian and were treated to tea and crackers.

Things settled down quickly and Pavloff sent for his family. The Indians brought various kinds of furs in to trade for whatever imported goods took their fancy, sugar being a particularly popular item. Within days the post at Nulato was functioning as though nothing whatsoever had happened three years earlier.

Dobshansky and Karloff, not forgetting the fate of the earlier traders and not failing to take into account the story of cannibalism, ordered that a considerable stockade of upright logs be erected about the entire compound, with sufficient space allotted for Father Georgi's new church, the construction of which would begin as soon as the stockade was completed. The stockade gate would be closed each night and carefully guarded. Never would more than a few Koyukons be allowed inside at any one time.

The Indians themselves were hired to cut and bring in spruce poles, the big fence went up quickly. Karloff and Grushenka moved into the main house; she was able to make do with the furniture already there. One of Karloff's conscripts soon had the cast-iron stove in operation and the house was livable.

No sooner was all this accomplished than Dobshansky and Karloff set off downriver once more to Redoubt St. Michael. Dobshansky was to proceed from there to Nova Archangelisk, and Karloff and half a dozen of his men would bring additional supplies, this time on muleback, two hundred miles across a range of low hills.

Grushenka found herself and Sabrina alone in the large house, while Pavloff and his squaw and five children were all crowded into the smaller quarters. It was a matter of position and birth, as she knew, but the incongruity of the situation bothered her.

As open and friendly as Ivan was, however, Grushenka was always at a loss for words around him—but then, what had they actually to talk about?

She kept the ledgers as Alex had showed her, and Pavloff mingled with the Koyukons and did the actual trading.

Father Georgi came to dinner nearly every evening, and often if business was light, Grushenka and Sabrina together would go over to the old storage building that was serving as a mission.

"The new foundations are laid, my daughter," the priest said, "and already the Indians develop a thirst for Christianity. One of the shamans is skeptical, but the other is curious to know how to read from my medicine book, the Bible. God save them, for all I know they're better off without the message I bring to them. Take monogamy, for instance. If a wealthy man is converted to Orthodox belief, he must give up all but one of his wives."

"That's for the good, isn't it?" Grushenka asked.

"If the wives who are cast out are old," Father Georgi replied, "what are they to do? Can they find other husbands? And what of the children they have borne—the children will then lose all position within the Koyukon tribe. They will be hungry, perhaps even die. No, Grushenka, this matter of bringing the Gospel to these wild children of God is not so simple as one might imagine. I will give special dispensations. That is what Jesus would do, is it not? A river may be diverted, but it cannot be forced to flow back upstream."

"What of such things as Christmas and Easter and the holidays of the saints?"

"Ah," he replied. "The Koyukons will gladly accept our holidays. They are always eager to find occasions for magic and feasting."

* * *

The notes of the first few musical chords hung in the air like birdsong—no, like birds themselves, like wild canaries that burst all at once from a pear tree in the autumn. The sound registered itself immediately upon Grushenka's senses, producing a prickling feeling along the nape of her neck.

A balalaika. . . . Then the music came again, and with it a strong, rich tenor.

"I crossed the marketplace at twilight
And heard the snapping of a wielded whip—
I looked and saw a peasant girl
Whose head was bowed, whose blouse was gone.
She did not cry when the lashes cut her skin
And no one cried in anguished protest
As the riding crop hissed through the air:
'Look!' I cried, 'That is your sister.' "

Grushenka walked to where the group of Koyukons had gathered and were applauding the singer, a big man with a mane of curly black hair. Seated on a bale of furs, he wore a togalike garment of bearskin, moccasin boots, buckskin breeches and a red and white flannel shirt open at the throat to reveal another mat of dark, curly hair.

The singing ceased for the moment and the man seemed intent on tuning his three-stringed instrument.

Beside him stood an Indian who wore a cone-shaped hat of woven cedar bark. His buckskin shirt was brightly painted in symmetric abstract designs—three faces actually, neither human nor animal. The Indian, a powerfully built man of average height, was leaning on a long-barreled rifle. Ivan Pavloff was there, clapping his hands.

"Who are these men?" Grushenka asked.

Pavloff glanced at her and grinned. "A countryman," he said. "Yours or mine, I'm not sure. It's Yuri Borodin an' Red Porcupine, chief of the Tagish. They just come down off the Tanana, brought lots furs with them. Good trading, maybe, eh? Both old friends of mine."

"Borodin?" Grushenka asked. "Ah, I know of him."

Father Georgi had told her about this Borodin, the Minstrel of the North, as he liked to style himself. Half upriver Indian and half Russian, he had been schooled in Nova Archangelisk and subsequently sent to the university in St. Petersburg. There he remained for three years, half-starving and ultimately resorting to a life of petty thievery in order to survive. Apprehended, he was expelled from the university and sent to Lake Baikal, whence he made his way to Kamchatka and ultimately back to Alaska. For the past several years he had lived the life of a promyshlennik, a free trapper, sometimes with his Tagish relatives and at other times alone, but always close by the great mountain that towered in the southeast and that the natives all but revered as a god.

Grushenka pushed her way forward through the throng and stood facing the seated musician and his formidable-looking Indian companion.

"Mr. Borodin?" she asked. "I am Baroness Grushenka Karloff, wife to the officer in charge of the Nulato post."

Borodin smiled, revealing an even set of gleaming white teeth.

"That's unfortunate, *ma chère,*" he replied.

"I don't understand you, sir."

"Of course not. Grushenka, hey? Unfortunate, I mean, that you're married. Otherwise I'd bring you wild roses every morning and sing love songs until you agreed to run away to the mountains with me."

A long silence ensued. The Koyukons, suddenly ill at ease and not understanding what was afoot, shifted nervously. Then Pavloff burst into laughter, and the Indians did likewise.

Grushenka felt herself blushing but managed to hold

her jaw firmly set. "I understand you've brought furs for trade."

"Oh, sure, sure. I bring lots a furs. Me real dumb Injun, by God. This here's Red Porcupine. Him real dumb too. Give us little tobacco, we give you all our furs. Look, Baroness Grushenka—otter, fox, beaver, muskrat. Prime fur, prime fur. Just little tobacco, please?"

"I know who you are, Mr. Borodin. I know you've studied at university. Why are you speaking like an ignoramus?"

"You hear what this little mop of red hair's saying to me?" Borodin asked Red Porcupine. "She thinks I'm human. Maybe she thinks you are too."

"My friend gives in to his Russian side," Red Porcupine apologized. "Do not listen to him, Baroness Karloff. It is true that we have brought furs. It was easier than taking them up to the British at Fort Yukon."

"You speak Russian quite well, chief," Grushenka nodded, concealing her rather considerable surprise.

"I lied," Borodin crowed. "Him smart Injun. Knows little bit Russian, French, lots of English. He's a British spy, to tell the truth."

"Anglos, Gossacks, they're all the same," Red Porcupine said. "Only difference is who pays more, and that's what we came to find out."

"Well, you come to the right place," Pavloff laughed. "Those British, they inside Russian lands. Dobshansky, he's going to go kick them out next year."

"No," Red Porcupine said, his voice taking on a stern tone, "the British are not on Russian lands. They are in the lands of the Tutchones. Big Grayling, he allows them to remain. Russian lands? Nulato is Koyukuk." The Koyukons nodded and muttered their agreement.

"Russians think they own the land," Pavloff said. "Indians, they don't think so. Truth of the matter is nobody owns the land, by God. Maybe Raven Man, he does. That's all."

"Raven Man," Grushenka nodded, not wishing to pursue the matter. This was no time for a political dispute.

"I'll sing you a song, most fair one. What would you like to hear?"

"Something different, Mr. Borodin. I'm not fond of songs about girls being whipped."

"Friend of mine made it up," Borodin said. "Nikolay Nekrasov. The two of us starved together in St. Petersburg. We lost track of one another after the gendarmes gave me a choice between hanging and doing a bit of public service work in old Sibir. How about this one?"

"Grushenka's hair is red gold;
The sunlight gleams upon it,
And when I see her lovely face
My spirit soars, doggone it!
For she's, alas, another's wife,
And I will sorrow all my life
If sure she will not let me hold
And kiss her all night long, doggone it.
Alas, alas, a salmon swims
Down in the dark, dark river."

Borodin ceased playing the balalaika and sat there half smiling.

Grushenka was flabbergasted, could think only to say, "You're quite impudent, sir." She turned immediately, pushed past Ivan Pavloff and walked toward the open gate of the stockade.

His eyes are on me, he's staring at my behind, that rude, rude son of a bitch. She was trembling with indignation as she reached the haven of the post, and she continued toward the safety of her own house.

But even from there she could detect the echo of Borodin's mocking laughter.

In the morning Grushenka discovered an armful of wild pink roses, their stems tied with a red ribbon, lying on the doorstep. Tucked among the flowers was a neatly penned note.

"Your hair is like the sunlight,
Your eyes are the color of summer sky,
Your mouth the red cherries I used to steal
From the markets of St. Petersburg.
Madame, how shall I find the right words?
For these do not reveal my thought.
If they did, they would tell you
That I am smitten. The shaft of Eros
Has pierced this coarse woodsman's heart.
You will throw my note away,
But because lovers hope where there is no hope,
I will wait all morning
Where the big creek runs to the Yukon
Just upstream from the village."

When the music of the balalaika reached her ears, Grushenka looked about, startled, but Borodin was nowhere in sight.

She thrust the note into the bodice of her dress and carried the roses back inside to place them in an old coffee pot, the only vessel she could find close at hand.

Sabrina, preparing breakfast, looked up, noted the flowers and cast a curious glance at Grushenka. "You buy from one of the village boys?"

Grushenka nodded, said nothing and sipped at a cup of tea. *This is ridiculous. How dare he presume such a thing—that I'd actually meet with him off in the woods? I'll have Ivan Pavloff order him out of Nulato.*

She drank the last of the tea and went to peer out the door. Half a dozen conscripts, no longer in military dress, were on their way to work on Father Georgi's new church. They carried axes, hammers, adzes, augers, shovels and picks. Their rowdy talk carried back to her.

Sabrina brought a tin plate heaped with pan-fried fish, potatoes and hard bread smeared with preserves. Grushenka, suddenly quite hungry, sat down to eat.

Of course I would never do such a thing. Does he think I'm some lewd serving girl like Sabaka the dog? When Alex returns, I'll have the man flogged if he's still here at the post.

When she had finished her breakfast, however, Grushenka said, "Tell Ivan I've gone for a walk. No, say I've gone over to visit Father Georgi. I'll be back in twenty minutes, no more than that."

"Something wrong, Baroness?" Sabrina asked.

"Of course not. Why do you ask me that? I'm sorry—I didn't mean to snap at you. Breakfast was very good, Sabrina, it really was. I'll be right back. I must ask the priest a question, nothing more."

Whatever words she intended to scorch his ears with were never spoken, for when she reached the small grassy clearing where the stream tumbled across the footpath toward the river, Borodin stepped from behind a clump of willow brush and held out his arms as though he had no doubt she would fall into his embrace.

"*No!*" The syllable exploded from her throat, but even as she spoke she found herself drawn toward him as though some power far greater than her will had taken control of her limbs. She fell into his arms and began to sob, her face pressed against the rough bearskin of his toga.

He held her tightly, kissed her hair and repeated her name over and over. Then without speaking further he took her by the hand and led her through the spruce woods to another small clearing where the midday sunlight was warm, was almost too warm.

He framed her face with his big hands and then removed the tortoise-shell pins that held the coiled braids in place atop her head. He proceeded to undo the braids themselves until all of her reddish gold hair hung down over her shoulders.

Her eyes were closed and she was trembling all over.

"You come to me," he murmured. "Tell me to stop, Grushenka, unless this is something you wish as much as I do. I will not hurt you, no, I will never harm you as long as I live. I will stop what I am doing the moment you utter a sound." He paused. Getting no response, he removed her light jacket, began to unbutton her blouse.

"You are blushing again," Borodin whispered. "I wonder if you blush all over. Grushenka, Grushenka, you are the most beautiful, most desirable woman I have ever seen. I am the man, I am supposed to be in control, but I can hardly breathe as I look at you."

Her eyes were still closed, and she tilted her face toward him, her lips barely open, the tip of her tongue showing at one side of her mouth.

He kissed her gently, firmly, held tight to her and easily lifted her off her feet.

Her tongue went into his mouth, touched his. They kissed for a long while, mouth devouring mouth, and Grushenka felt trickling fires running all over her body.

"You are wearing perfume," he said. "Did you do that for me, dearest one? All night I could not sleep for thinking of you. Oh, I never thought you would come to me. . . ."

"Borodin, I—"

"Do you wish me to stop, Grushenka? I will do whatever you tell me to do."

"Then . . . lie down with me. I must catch my breath. Yuri? Your name is Yuri Borodin?"

He lifted her in his arms and carried her to a spot in the midst of the dazzling sunlight, where he knelt and set her down. He removed the bearskin and spread it over the grass.

"I ache for you," he sighed. "I can hardly stand it, I ache so."

She pulled him to her and they lay side by side, kissing and touching.

"Take my clothing off," she whispered, hardly able to form the words. Then the sunlight flamed all over her, touched the nipples of her breasts, touched her throat. Flames dripped from the skin of her legs and pooled at the center of her.

"You are beautiful." He laughed softly. "You are perfect, more beautiful even than I imagined."

"Kiss me," she said. As he leaned over her, her hand, as if with a will of its own, reached up and felt the good male hardness between his legs.

Her arms and face and belly itched with the maddening stings of mosquito bites and her buttocks chafed on the coarse fur of the bearhide. She scratched a welt on her forearm and pinched through her clothing at a place just below her left breast.

She giggled as she walked. She felt new soreness between her legs and remembered her first times with Alex. It seemed so long ago it was almost as if it had never happened.

And Borodin? Well, the men spoke laughingly of making love to the grizzlies, and now she had done it herself. She had made love to a half-wild bear-man who nevertheless spoke proper Russian and a graceful smattering of French, who made music and poetry. If Alex Karloff could give her away to a pig like Dobshansky, certainly she could give herself away to a mad poet who chose to live among the Indians.

"In the morning, Grushenka, the sun comes up and bathes Denali, and the glaciers burn crimson, unbelievable beauty. It's like our Father in heaven just created the world all over again, all fresh and new and singing the entire history of mankind." He broke out laughing then. It was afterward, as the two of them lay close together and she breathed in and savored the odors of bear musk and something like tallow and the smell of Borodin himself, and the smell of his essence smeared all over her belly and legs.

"Except that God doesn't care a bit more for us than He does for the salmon or the caribou or the eagle, and sometimes I think He's more concerned about them than about us. Oh, God cares, Grushenka, I swear it, but mostly He just watches and grins. He has grinned now, at us. I wonder if He thinks we have made love in the proper way, you with your legs locked about me, you drawing me in until I touched the center of you? Grushenka . . ."

It was late afternoon when she entered the house; the sun was orange-red and arcing away toward the north, where it would eventually touch the green hills beyond the village of Nulato.

She was startled to find Ivan Pavloff there, seated at the table with Sabrina, and between them one of Pavloff's adopted children. All, the little girl included, were drinking tea.

"I pulled out in time . . . no children will come of this, Grushenka. My darling, my pale goddess, I wish—"

"Ivan," she said, her voice weak in her throat, "what . . . ?"

"Brought you the tally sheets, ma'am, that an' some news. A runner come in this afternoon. Your husband an' a string of mules loaded to their eyeballs is just twenty miles away. Be here by noon tomorrow, I guess."

"Oh, wonderful," she replied, trying to smile. "Yes, that's very good news. I went walking along the river today. It's so beautiful out there that I simply couldn't bring myself to come . . . home."

"Father Georgi," Sabrina said, "he looking for you too. Here, ma'am, teapot's still half full. Sit down. I will get you a cup."

"*Will you meet me here tomorrow? I'll sing songs for you, I'll do whatever you want.*"

"*No, Yuri. I have never done such a thing before. I must not ever do it again. I have to go now. I have to. Yuri? You have already done exactly what I wanted you to do.*"

"Be gettin' back to the war department," Ivan Pavloff said. "Sabaka here's got the list of furs. That's right, Sabrina. The new name you give her's much better, Baroness Karloff, ma'am. I'da got her away from Dobshansky somehow or another if he hadn't give her to your husband. I go now. Good evening."

"Until tomorrow."

Until tomorrow. There could be no tomorrow for her and Borodin, and as this thought came to her she realized a terrible sense of loss, tangible, a dull ache beneath her heart.

Grushenka drank her tea and went directly to her room, sat down on the bed and began to cry. Since she was unable to fight the tears away, she gave in to them and sobbed for half an hour or more.

Sabrina appeared at the door, a look of concern on her features. "Something wrong, ma'am?"

"No," Grushenka managed, "everything's quite all right. I just need to be alone for a time."

When the door was once more closed, she stood up and went to the big wooden steel-banded trunk from

Seeneestakan. She withdrew a fresh change of clothing and the embroidered blanket Aunt Sofia had made for her. She put the clothing onto the blanket along with a few of her personal effects and the loaded pistol Alex had left for her in case of emergency. All these things she tied up inside the blanket, making a neat bundle.

When the post grounds were deserted during the evening meal, Grushenka came out of her room, nodded to the surprised Sabrina and left the house. She proceeded to the stockade gate, waved hello to the single guard on duty and walked on toward the village itself.

"*Gospozha Karloff,*" he called after her, "how long will you be out? I must secure the gate in just a few minutes."

"By all means," she called back.

"*Red Porcupine and I and our friends, we are camped just a mile upriver from here, a good camping spot among the birches.*"

She walked on through the twilight, refusing to think of the inevitable implications of her act. She came to the place where the trail crossed the creek, waded across and continued walking.

An owl called from across the broad Yukon River and close at hand another answered. The river glittered red in the waning light and a soft wind played among the branches of the trees to either side of her. It was almost, she thought, like wandering back into the taiga beyond Seeneestakan. For a moment she felt the keen, burning pangs of homesickness for Mother, Father, Aunt Sofia, even the cows.

Then she smelled wood smoke, and not too far ahead she could detect the music of a balalaika and a male voice.

Borodin was singing.

Chapter 5
The Kantishna River

Yoyekoi is the bearer of Indian tales. Though each village may have its own teller of stories, the great Yoyekoi is everywhere—in the air, the clouds, the glaciers, the waters, the forests and the high, bare granite.

Yoyekoi, himself a god, says that Denali is also a god, sleeping and dreaming beneath his blanket of perpetual ice in the center of the land.

Yoyekoi speaks of animal people, fish people, bird people. Sometimes he speaks from Kutiga, the totem pole: perhaps from the mouth of a panting bear, red-nostriled, tongue lolling, eyes emboldened with black. From his chest emerges the mad-eyed head of a fox or coyote, mouth open, paws touching the bear's knees, ears erect.

Perhaps he speaks of Ugruk, the huge bearded seal, or of Beluga, the white whale, perhaps of wave after wave of migratory birds whose comings and goings punctuate and define the seasons. Thousands, millions of wingbeats and wild songs fill the air; feathered creatures arrive and bask through the brief, intense summers. Two million waterfowl lived on the Yukon delta alone—widgeon, teal, canvasback, mallard, pintail, scaup, loons, geese, grebes.

He sometimes speaks of the vanished ones—woolly mammoths, antelope, bison, mastodon, camel, sabertooth tiger.

A band of caribou stands outlined against a steel grey sky.

A wolf contemplates mice.

A flying squirrel leaps and glides recklessly from tree to tree.

A tufted puffin struts on orange feet, parading heavy orange beak, amber eyes, white face with trailing yellow-white eyebrows.

Orca leaps in the channels.

Dall sheep and mountain goats trample orange and red, grey and green lichens on the rocks.

Far away, far to the south in this year of 1854, Henry David Thoreau publishes *Walden, or Life in the Woods*. Yoyekoi speaks through him too, a philosophy of an individual gaining freedom through nature and by the rediscovery of himself, even though he has never been to Kantishna River, has never looked upon great Denali.

September–November 1854

Late September sunlight lay like a warm hand on her skin, her bare breasts, her belly. She lay with her eyes nearly closed so that all she could see was a dazzle of gold and blue, the leaves of aspens glittering against flawless sky. She could hear the faint rustle of a light breeze among the restless foliage, the gurgling of lake waters lapping at the shore—and the sharper, more distinct splashing of Yuri returning from his swim far out to a flock of geese.

Grushenka had never swum before this summer, and although Yuri tried to teach her, she had not really gotten the knack of it and contented herself with paddling in the shallows. Now, when the water of the lake was noticeably chillier than during the long days of late August and early September, she much preferred to doze in the sunlight and let Yuri carry out the little tests of strength and stamina that he seemed compelled to set for himself.

"He is still half a child," she thought, smiling to herself. The other half was all man, competent, sure, skilled in the wilds, and wiser and gentler beneath his mask of whimsical humor than any other man she had known with the possible exception of Father Georgi.

Grushenka rolled onto her stomach, her skin savoring the sun-warmed softness of the bearskin beneath the aspens. She hugged her secret to herself, smiling again. Soon she would have to share the knowledge with her lover, but not quite yet. For now it was still too delicious to let the sunlight caress her skin, to snuggle her face into the warmth of fur and feel the secret like a small sun, another glow within.

Why had she not yet told Yuri? She wasn't sure, for she really didn't have any doubt about his reaction to the news, even though the baby would certainly present complications. No, it was more simply reluctance to ripple the surface of a time as still and shining as the surface of the lake on a day without wind.

Grushenka felt almost as if she had passed the time in a trance since she came with Yuri Borodin to the little cabin built on a bluff above a lake. Myriad lakes emptied into the Kantishna River, whose sources were high up on Denali. This great white-shouldered giant she could see from her doorstep, Denali with attendant gods flanking it in a long line southwest to northeast.

The long, long days were luminous, the sky was a flawless blue, although at times thunderheads piled up against the peaks and occasionally an afternoon lightning storm reached back down to them. They were not idle, for both Yuri and Grushenka worked hard to get in a store of food for the long winter.

She accompanied him on several hunting trips, sometimes going out with people from the Tanana village on the other side of the lake, at other times the two of them alone. She learned from the Tanana women how to remove the hides of elk and caribou and moose and those of the sheep with the great curving horns, how to slice the meat thin and hang it on elevated wooden racks to dry. She was still very clumsy at the work, so slow that the Tanana women couldn't help laughing at her, but with their help and particularly that of a young woman called Fireweed, who had become Grushenka's special friend, she managed to keep up with Yuri's take of game.

In truth Grushenka worked as hard as she ever had on her family's farm, but this was different. Now when she worked, she did so with a little bubble of happiness in her chest, and sometimes she felt she was moving to a dance step. Even while she was cutting the carcass of an elk, engulfed in the thick odor of blood and covered in blue-black flies, she caught herself humming one of Yuri's tunes.

Sometimes she would laugh out loud. "Here I am," she told her lover one night as she bathed in a big tub in front of the fire, "working my fingers to the bone, and for what purpose? So that I can live in a wilderness more remote than the one I grew up in. I want to live in Moscow, Yuri, that's what I've always wanted. Yet I am happy. Is this love or insanity?"

"Insanity?" Yuri growled, laying aside his balalaika. "I'll teach you insanity, my little savage."

And then he pinned her down in the warm water and plied his other hand on her body in such a way that they both ended up gasping. She tumbled out of the tub still wet, and they coupled immediately and passionately on the sheepskin in front of the fire.

There were many days when they didn't work, though, and it was these times of idleness, she knew, that gave the summer its peculiar golden quality in her memory, days spent eating and making up silly verses for one another, swimming in the lake, making love in the shallows, on the shore, in the tall grass under the aspens above the lake.

Sometimes the sheer physicality of her life at this time almost frightened her.

She would demand of herself, *Is this all it takes to make me happy? Is there really nothing more than sex and this man, a cabin near a spring of clear water, and a great white god soaring into the sky—and work and sex and this man?*

For the most part she thought not at all, but lived like a contented animal day to day, moving through a dream and glorying in it.

She rolled onto her back again, ran her hand down her belly, let the palm rest against her womb. No sign yet—her tummy was still flat, but she imagined she could feel a tiny spark of energy, a mysterious sense of life within.

Her ruminations broke off abruptly when a shower of cold water landed on her warm skin. Her eyes flew open and she sat up shrieking.

Yuri stood over her, grinning, his hands in his thick black hair shaking water onto her. "Lazy wench," he growled, "what are you good for, I ask you? Dozing in the sun and forcing me to attend to the business of swimming after geese—"

"Is it so important that geese be pursued?" she laughed. She saw that he had an erection, grabbed for it as he ducked out of the way. "I'll show you what I'm good for."

"Ah, no," he said, flopping onto the bearskin beside her. "First you must suffer."

And then he was upon her, tickling her until she was helpless, her limbs weak, her breath caught in her throat. He kissed her mouth, ran his lips down the side of her throat and fastened them onto her nipple. His hand moved to the cleft of her thighs, probing until she moaned aloud. A tide of fire seemed to swell within her. She moved to caress him, but he grabbed her hands and pinned them to the ground, running his tongue down over her belly and to the aching center of her need.

She abandoned herself to the sensations, letting her thighs drop open. The tide built in great, rippling circles centered on a point of fire. Her breath came in quick gasps, her pulse beat in her ears.

Her eyes were partly open. Aspen leaves glittered intensely, unbelievably gold against blue sky. Above the shimmer of leaves, high above, a dark form winged, slicing air in wide circles.

I am with him, with the eagle. Ah, it is too intolerably sweet. I will die, I will die. . . .

And then the sensations built higher still, washed over, burst and flooded her with wave after wave of flame, so that her body arched and she cried out pure, incoherent joy.

Grushenka gripped Yuri hard with her thighs, pulled her hands loose and clutched at his hair to make him stop. He tried to wrestle her down and continue, but she couldn't bear any more and struggled free. She gathered herself and rolled over, shoving him back and mounting him, riding him until he, too, groaned and shuddered in release.

Yuri lay utterly relaxed, his hands resting lightly against her abdomen. She loved the look of his face in these moments. His head was thrown back and a faint, inward smile lay on his lips: dark hair curled down over his forehead, one tendril touching the corner of a slightly slanted faun's eye. In a moment they opened slightly, dark irises glinting in sunlight, and he smiled at her, reached up to pull her down against him.

At that moment something wet plopped onto Grushenka's back so that she sucked in her breath sharply, startled. A chorus of giggles and scuffling feet ensued.

Her cheeks flaming, Grushenka rolled off Yuri and tried to wrap the corner of the bearskin around her, while her lover, stark naked, rose with a great roar and ran after the little band of black-haired, black-eyed elves, brandishing an aspen limb and shouting dire threats in both Russian and Tanana.

The children vanished down the beach, still gurgling with laughter, and Yuri came back. Grushenka felt to see what it was they had thrown at her and wiped a blob of mud off her back.

"Rascals! Hooligans!" Borodin muttered, half grinning, half angry. "Children should be against the law, but here there is only the law of Raven Man."

"Are you sure of that?"

"Of course. I am sure of everything I say. Ah, Grushenka, I am not human like other men—don't you know that?"

"Then, my love," she replied, "we are illegal—or we would be if there were laws beneath Denali. Actually, I guess we are anyway, considering our adulterous—"

"What?" Borodin interrupted. "Don't prattle on, Grushenka. Do you mean you're pregnant?"

She nodded, feeling suddenly uncertain at the stern look on his face. He glared at her for a few seconds more and then abruptly let out a great whoop and began dancing her awkwardly around the aspen grove, improvising a tune as he went.

"Grushenka is my woman,
I took her to the wild
And now she up and tells me
She's going to bear my child!
Ya lyoobloo vahs, ya lyoobloo vahs!
I love this wench with honey hair,
I think her most excessive fair—
Especially when she's standing bare-
Ass naked."

Borodin insisted on inviting the entire Tanana village

to a great celebratory feast. This caused Grushenka some mild embarrassment. Earlier in her life she might have been acutely embarrassed, but she had lost a great deal of her self-consciousness, often going bare-breasted as the Indian women did during the summer and lounging about totally unclothed when no one was present but herself and Yuri.

The villagers came, all forty-two of them from Fireweed's new infant in arms to the shaman's mother, who claimed ninety-three winters and looked all of it. The Tananas loved a celebration of any kind, and the fact that none of them would have considered a pregnancy occasion for a feast hardly damped their enthusiasm, for they were more than happy to accommodate the whims of the Gossack couple who were, for all their strange ways, good-hearted and friendly.

Yuri Borodin, after all, half Tagish and half Russian, was close friends with Red Porcupine, the powerful Tagish chief, and it was said that he had journeyed far into the lands of the white men and could read from the Bible as well as the Russian priests or the British reverends. As for Grushenka, was she not the most beautiful woman any of them had ever seen?

Most of the women pitched in to help with the cooking and many men brought haunches and quarters of freshly killed meat, which the women set to roast on spits over open fires or buried in firepits to barbecue slowly. Quantities of salmon grayling were plastered thickly with mud and also set to bake in firepits. The day before Grushenka had baked bread with her precious supply of wheat flour, and this treat, smeared with deer tallow, was a great hit with the guests.

On the whole the celebration was a huge success. The visitors straggled in in twos and threes on the morning of the feast and stayed until well after the sun set. Yuri gave tobacco to all the male visitors and steel needles and mirrors to the women. The Tananas also brought gifts, fur robes and woven cradleboards for the baby and warm fur-lined moccasins for the parents. A number of dances were begun, improvisations from more traditional occasions, and several rather bawdy tales about Raven Man's copulatory exploits were told.

The shaman, a leather-skinned man named Burning Eyes who appeared nearly as old as his mother, insisted on performing a blessing ceremony for Grushenka. As many people as could squeezed inside the Borodin cabin and the rest crowded close outside. The old medicine man, assisted by his mother and his wife, shuffled in place and shook rattles and chanted over Grushenka for what seemed a very long time.

She understood few of the words Burning Eyes enunciated, but the hypnotic rise and fall of his voice affected her strangely. At one point her eyes closed and Grushenka imagined herself wandering in a frozen landscape, alone except for the child she was carrying, searching for Yuri. Suddenly the shaman was there, facing her on the path and looking at her with his hooded ancient eyes. Terrible sadness in those eyes frightened her.

It was at that moment Burning Eyes stopped chanting in the middle of a phrase. Grushenka came out of her near-trance to look questioningly at the shaman. A sudden chill traveled up her spine as for a moment he returned her gaze. She saw the same look, the ancient sadness that she had seen in her brief vision.

Then Burning Eyes smiled at her, spoke a few words of blessing and announced the ceremony was over. "I will continue to pray for you, Sun-haired Woman," he said gently.

"You saw something bad," Grushenka said as best she could in the Tanana language. "Please—tell me what you saw."

"Don't be silly," the shaman replied, smiling as if

nothing strange had happened. "Women who are with child imagine things all the time. I will tell you this. The baby will be strong. I think it will be a girl, and she will travel farther than women usually do. She is someone special. Come, we will go enjoy the celebration."

It was clear that the shaman would have no more to say, and so Grushenka did as he suggested. She tried to dismiss the feeling of heaviness the vague premonition had left her with.

I am being entirely foolish. What would Father Georgi say? Pagan divining, witchcraft, demonism . . .

Fireweed, her infant strapped to her back and her older child, a boy of four, playing among everyone's feet, was delighted with Grushenka's impending motherhood. She was full of sage advice.

"When you start to get big belly," Fireweed explained, "then you mustn't eat no meat from then on. When time comes real close, then your husband, he shouldn't eat meat either. Otherwise baby want to fight all the time, no good. Try not to look at any porcupines so baby don't come out backward. And when he come, first thing you wash him off in cold water. That way he won't be afraid of cold."

The other women nodded, agreed that the advice was good and offered their own bits of lore.

Before the feast was over, Fireweed produced a small leather packet containing some dried plant matter. She handed it to Grushenka, winking.

"I know you don't pay no attention to all those other things we told you, and probably they don't matter for white women, anyhow," she said. "But when your time comes, this really works. Makes pain less, baby come easier. Even old Burning Eyes don't know about this. Only women know."

Grushenka took the packet, thanking her friend. For no reason she could think of tears came to her eyes. Impulsively she embraced the Indian woman.

"Everything will be all right," Fireweed reassured her, patting her back. "Maybe you and Borodin better come with us this year. Pretty soon winter walks down from Denali all of a sudden. We move down on Kantishna to sheltered valleys. Better weather, more game down there. Women to help you when time comes. Not so good up here alone."

"Thank you, Fireweed," Grushenka whispered. "You have been so kind to me. I will never forget you."

"You going to stay here with your husband," Fireweed stated, looking sadly into Grushenka's eyes. "Well, that's what wives got to do. But next summer, then we come back and see your little new one."

Grushenka nodded and tried to smile.

The feast continued late into the night as the dances got sillier and the stories and songs more obscene. Yuri encouraged the revelers, making up a very long, licentious song, which he sang in the Tanana dialect, a torrent of notes pouring up from his balalaika. Thereafter he rose and danced a sailor's hornpipe. To finish off he attempted a Cossack dance, falling back on his rear almost immediately. Grushenka began to suspect that Yuri had been secretly irrigating himself and his male guests with some kind of liquor.

It was well after midnight when the revelry died out. Various groups of visitors wandered back to their own village by the light of a nearly full moon, although several simply lay down in their robes when they got sleepy and didn't actually depart until morning.

Yuri Borodin was in high spirits, drawing Grushenka into a waltz and singing.

"Grushenka, Grushenka, her garden doth grow:
She's as big as the sea
But it's all right with me,
For we reap whatever we sow."

She laughed at him and told him of the various bits of advice Fireweed and the others had given her. They discussed the party, agreed it was a grand success. Yuri had been inside the cabin during the shaman's blessing ceremony, but apparently he hadn't noticed anything strange, and so she didn't tell him of her frightening vision or of Burning Eyes' evasion. Yuri would certainly have made light of the occurrence, for despite his Tagish background, he was not in the least superstitious—owing, no doubt, to the years he had spent at the university at St. Petersburg. But she was unable to bring herself to speak of the matter. Instead she smiled and tried to join in with her lover's happiness.

I am happy, she insisted to herself later as she lay in Yuri's arms, listening to his even breathing. She could feel his heartbeat through his hard chest; the rhythm was both comforting and frightening in its assertion of life and mortality.

"Happiness is very fragile. Laughter before breakfast means tears before bedtime"—her mother's proverb, she remembered.

Grushenka shivered, drew closer to Yuri's sleeping warmth. She touched his cheek with her lips, a whisper of a kiss. He mumbled a question, squeezed her briefly, and relaxed into sleep once more.

She slept, dreamed of a child's face, a laughing, bold dark-haired girl, very lovely. Grushenka could watch, but she couldn't act. The girl was close by a church in a village very much like Nulato. She knelt by a weatherworn wooden cross. Two narrow, bright tracks of tears lay on the young cheeks and she was speaking, although Grushenka couldn't hear the words. She wished she could comfort the young woman, but action was not within her power. And yet in some way that she couldn't understand she herself was comforted by the dream, and she felt a certain joy.

The vision faded and Grushenka noted a raven sitting in a tree. The bird became larger, turning almost human.

Raven Man, the demon god of the north country, was laughing and crying at the same time. Then the black wings beat at the air and the creature flew away to soar high, impossibly high over Denali.

A few days after the feast winter set in like the sudden closing of a door. One morning the sun did not appear. Day came late as an infusion of grey light filtering through heavy clouds the color of tarnished silver. When Grushenka stepped out to fetch water from the spring, she looked, as she always did, south toward Denali. The mountain was invisible; clouds obscured even the nearer foothills. The visible world had shrunk to the lake, the nearby hills and the valley below. The air was cold and still. Grushenka had the momentary feeling of being under deep, chill water.

She was shivering when she returned indoors, glad to find that Yuri had alrady begun to build up the banked fire from the night before. As she cooked breakfast, he sat on the edge of the bed of interlaced willow saplings of his own construction, whistling and oiling the traps that he had taken down from their pegs in the wall.

"Fur-growing weather, my duckling," he explained to Grushenka when she brought him his breakfast. "All the little beavers, all the little foxes, all the minks and otters and muskrats look at each other and say, 'Pretty soon Brother Yuri will be coming for our coats, so we'd better get to work on these pelts.' "

"Poor creatures," Grushenka said. "It seems a shame to make a living this way."

Somehow the entire matter struck her in a way that it hadn't before and she felt like weeping for the animals that would die because humans envied their fur.

"It's one of the very few ways a man can remain free," Yuri shrugged. "I too would rather see a fox pelt on a fox's back than draped about the throat of some dame in Rostov or Moscow. Still, Ikogmiut, Koyukon, Tanana, Tutchone, Tagish—what would these people do without taking furs? The animal people give us their warmth so that we may live in this land."

"If God were kinder, the foxes would wear stoles made of the hair of duchesses," Grushenka replied.

"And the mice and ground squirrels say that if God were kinder, foxes would eat grass," Yuri agreed, scooping up a spoonful of elk stew. "Your Russian god has a hard time juggling this obligation of kindness. Now Raven Man, he doesn't have to worry about it because no one expects it of him. His people don't force him to be a hypocrite. Animal people and human people, we all go scrambling through the Black Bird's tunnel when the time comes; we all find our way out the other side and into the spirit world."

"And what happens there?"

"There? Oh, the same as here. The foxes still don't eat grass."

"You're talking in circles," Grushenka snapped. "I was speaking about animals, not theology. I don't care what God is called."

Confused and perhaps frightened by the tone of her own voice, she found tears welling up in her eyes and she couldn't stop them from leaking down her face. Yuri, seeing that she was genuinely distressed over something, took her hand and squeezed it.

"I don't know why I'm doing this, Yuri," she said, shaking her head to clear away the tears. "I don't want us to argue over silly things. It's only—I feel sorry for the animals."

I saw Raven-Man laughing and weeping at the same time, and it was partly for us. . . . But still she did not mention her vision.

Yuri set his plate down, wrapped his powerful arms about her and stroked her hair. "And I was being flip, a bad habit I got into when they sent me off to St. Petersburg to atone for my sins. But I'm more Tagish than Russian inside me, where it matters. Another season or two, my pretty, and you'll be Indian, just like me. It's the land that does it. Yep, and old Denali up there, higher than the clouds. Just seeing it all the time changes us.

"Red Porcupine, he'll tell you that it's proper to send the animal people back into the spirit world, send them with prayers. That way the animals come back to earth, to this side of the tunnel. Raven Man's got it all figured out. Now I don't suppose things really happen exactly that way, but I still say the prayers. My mother taught my Russian father the correct words to say and he taught me. They're dead, both of them, but I still speak the words when I kill an animal. Grushenka, this is not something I would confess to anyone but you. The whites, they don't understand it."

Grushenka put her arms around him, murmured against the side of his neck, "I knew I was right about you, love."

"How so, my sweet cabbage?" he smiled, squeezing her breast.

"I knew you were crazy all along, ever since that first day in Nulato. That must be what we have in common."

"Humm. Did I tell you what else is good about winter? Except for a little trapping, there is nothing to do but—"

He broke off, kissed her ear, ran his tongue in delicate circles along the whorls. Grushenka gasped, caught Yuri's hand and kissed it.

"I don't know what comes over me," she said, looking into his eyes and having again the odd sensation of falling into their darkness. "Sometimes I'm afraid of being so happy."

"Are you afraid of demons coming to take it away?"

Yuri laughed. "Don't worry, my little mudhen, I am much tougher than demons. I will kill them all. Now hush."

He enforced his last order by pressing his lips against her mouth, sliding his tongue along the parting until she could think of nothing, remember nothing except the insistent fire that was again flickering beneath her skin.

She heard the music of a balalaika, the tune unutterably sweet, compelling. She ran beneath trees, golden sunlight spilling through green leaves that were somehow the same as the music she was following. She was certain it was Yuri, although there was no voice accompanying the instrument. It seemed the melody was the exact song she had heard sometime before she was born and had been searching for all her life. She thought she must find the player before he finished his song so she could ask what it was.

All at once she found herself in a clearing and the trees were blackened, bare, dead or dormant. There was snow on the ground. A great black bird sat on a limb in one of the dead trees, plucking with his beak at a balalaika that was made up of human skulls, hundreds of skulls. She cried out and would have turned to flee, but she was unable to move; her body was rigid, heavy.

The bird saw her and laughed a great wind that blew the snow away so she could see Yuri lying half-propped against the trunk, his eyes open but unseeing, his face white and blank as the snow itself.

She screamed out his name, awoke shivering and gasping for breath. In the cold dark of the room she could still see the glowing eyes of Raven, bright with laughter and sorrow.

Grushenka reached instinctively for Yuri, searched among the bedcovers for a moment until she remembered that she was alone. Yuri Borodin had been away for three weeks to run a trapline on one of the nearby rivers. He had promised her he'd be back in a few days, no more than one week at the very most.

A wind had come up outside, a hard wind that howled around the corners of the cabin and roared through the trees like a thousand angry bears, the very sound she had heard in Raven's laughter. The sense of dread that had been growing within her since Yuri left seemed like a hand knotted around her throat so she couldn't breathe.

"Yuri," she called again into the darkness of the room, her voice catching in a choking sob.

There was no answer, and in a moment of wild panic, a sense of terrible urgency that blotted out reason, she ran to the door and flung it open. Wind struck against her like a tangible, physical body, the force of the rushing air driving the breath back into her throat. Icy particles whirled around her, numbed her in an instant. Grushenka struggled to get the door closed. At last she succeeded in pushing it into place and dropping the wooden bar into its slot when the gusts momentarily subsided.

Shivering violently, she felt her way to the bed and pulled one of the fur robes around her shoulders. She sat hugging it about herself until the convulsive shudders eased. Then she rose, lit a candle and built up the fire. Reason had returned with great force, and it had thrust upon her an inescapable conclusion.

She could do nothing until the blizzard let up. She sat huddled in her blanket for hours, mechanically rising from time to time to feed the fire, listening to the wind roaring like a swollen torrent that carried on its blind and murderous current every green twig of the last golden summer.

She kept seeing Yuri, his face dead white. The faun-slanted eyes were black pools that did not see her but looked steadily and forever at something on the other side of the blackness.

Raven Man played his balalaika and laughed the wind from the north.

Chapter 6
Return to Nulato

At times the Russians had extreme difficulty supplying their Alaskan outposts. In the winter of 1805–06, for instance, scurvy and starvation hit Nova Archangelisk, the center of Russian-American operations.

Nikolai Rezanov, after purchasing the American ship *Juno* and its cargo, sailed south to Spanish California, only to discover that Spanish law forbade commerce with foreigners. In the process of trying to work things out Rezanov fell in love with Concepción Arguello, daughter of the San Francisco commander. She accepted his proposal of marriage.

Now Spanish at least by impending marriage, Rezanov gained a full cargo and set sail for Nova Archangelisk. From there he crossed Kamchatka and Siberia to report to the Czar and to gain permission to marry Doña Concepción. Alas, he met fatal illness in Yakutsk. Concepción waited long, finally took refuge in a convent.

The need for supplies continued. In 1812 the Russians established Fort Ross near Bodega Bay on the California coast north of San Francisco. By 1833 it was a flourishing fur center with personnel numbering three hundred. Seventy of them were Russians.

The primary purpose, farming and raising stock, did not thrive despite the best of intentions. Shipbuilding likewise proved unsuccessful, as the four ships of California oak soon rotted.

The fur take dwindled, and under Kostromitinov and Rotchev agriculture greatly expanded during the 1830's. Some seven farms were in operation by native Pomos and imported Aleuts and Creoles. Even then it was not possible to meet the needs of the Alaskan posts.

When it became possible to buy wheat from Mexican California more cheaply that it could be grown in Russian California, the decision was made to abandon the operation. In the year 1840 the colony was sold to General John Sutter of New Helvetia.

Some eight years later gold was discovered on Sutter's lands near Coloma, and New Helvetia, like Fort Ross, passed into history.

November–December 1854

Grushenka walked through a world of endless white. The snow was dry and powdery, almost like strange, cold dust that clung to everything. It striped the boles of hemlock and spruce, bent boughs, clung to needle fronds. Though the snowfall had ceased, the sky remained uniformly grey.

The fur-lined parka and mukluks Fireweed had made for her were warm, and she felt no physical discomfort as she moved toward the Kantishna River's main branch, where Yuri's elkhide canoe sat on a bank above the water. She remembered suggesting to him that the craft be concealed, but he had laughed and assured her that no one would touch it. "If someone needs the beast more than I, why he's welcome enough. But it'll be here when we have need of it, Grushenka."

She was numb, but not from cold. The temperature, as she realized, was only slightly below freezing. When the skies cleared, that would be the time to worry about the cold, for then with no clouds to hold the heat and daylight only a few hours long, first the little streams and finally even the big rivers would freeze solid. Had winter not wrought precisely the same effect in Seeneestakan? In this strange land the climate was said to be far harsher.

All manner of tracks marked the fresh snow: the looping spoor of Arctic hares, the more precise prints of mink, ermine, martin and fox, the irregular hopping, scratching marks of mice and birds.

As she left the forest and began her journey across the muskeg bogs, she sighted a large band of caribou. The big ungulates were moving slowly, nonchalantly, despite some wolves and a pair of coyotes behind them. The canine tails were actually wagging as the wild dogs leaped, arched in the air and pounced for mice whose burrows had been disturbed by the passing of the caribou.

On a small rise, motionless, perched a big white owl.

"*Lazy as a Frenchman, they are,*" Yuri once said. "*They'll sit for hours waiting for a mouse to come to them. Then the quick claws, ma chérie, the quick claws. The owl, he prefers his prey to join him for dinner.*"

"Yuri," she cried, "why have you left me? I know you would come back if you could. Dearest one, how can I—?" But the question, unfinished, received no answer.

Ahead of her stood a grove of leafless aspens, and in the upper branches were perched three bald eagles and half a dozen ravens. Grushenka skirted the grove rather than pass through it, as she had intended. She could feel the intense, ever-watchful eyes of the birds upon her.

They wonder if I will fall down and die, she thought. *Perhaps they do not expect it, but they wish it would happen anyway. They bear me no malice, but they know I would make them a good feast. Much easier than hunting for themselves. Just like the owl.*

Grushenka moved on ahead, increasing her pace. She

had hoped to reach the main branch of the Kantishna before darkness once more overwhelmed the land, but now, with the landscape transformed by a few inches of snow, she began to wonder if she knew the way at all.

Then it was grey twilight and she took shelter within a small grove of hemlocks that stabbed up like so many knives from a rocky hummock. She gathered a mound of shredded cones, the seeds stripped out by squirrels or marmots, and built a fire. When the small pyramid was burning brightly, she dragged in a heavy pitch-filled deadfall and placed the root end atop her fire. Soon the small roots caught and flared. The pitch within the bole began to ooze and bubble out, hissing and spitting as it flamed and gave off extremely pungent black smoke.

Grushenka was terribly weary from the long hours of plodding ahead through the snow, and her back and shoulders ached from the constant shifting weight of the pack she carried.

She drew the big bearskin robe about herself and huddled by the fire, unwilling to sleep but unable to prevent it.

She startled awake at a sudden sound, realized it was no more than the popping of her banklog and breathed deeply to slow the beating of her heart. Snow, she realized, was falling once again.

With the first hint of morning twilight she folded the bearskin and lashed it to her pack. Eating no more than a few pieces of jerked elk meat left over from her meal of the night before, Grushenka shouldered her pack and started out through the half-darkness.

"How far?" she wondered. Then she grew fearful that she might actually be retracing her steps from the previous day.

More of Yuri's advice came to mind. "The first thing you must remember is never to give in to panic. Do you think I don't ever get turned around? No, the land itself will tell you which way to go, it will tell you through all of your senses together. But you can't hear if your mind's in turmoil; no one can."

Again she breathed deeply, enforced calm upon herself and studied the shadowy landscape about her.

Long darkness ahead held trees. I saw that yesterday just before I went under the hemlocks. Reassured, she began to walk again.

Gradually the world about her became more visible and the snow-clotted trees standing here and there upon mounds of higher earth changed from black and white to dark green and white.

The inch or so of snow that had fallen during the night had effaced all animal tracks, and everything was perfect, pristine white.

She saw half a dozen willow ptarmigans scratching for grass seed on a slope the wind had divested of snow, and the presence of other living beings gave her heart. She felt tears start to her eyes and rubbed her face with one hand, adjusted her load with the other and drove herself to a faster pace.

A mile further she saw a black bear happily engaged in clawing to pieces a rotten downed tree trunk in the hope of discovering fat white grubs inside. It reared up at her approach, woofed twice and moved its head back and forth, curious as to what sort of creature had distracted it. Then, perceiving no threat, the bear returned to its task.

Grushenka gave the big animal a wide berth and continued her trek to the Kantishna landing.

She reached the river just past midday and found the canoe in its proper place, the flat-bladed paddle lying in the empty hull. Grushenka turned the canoe over, batted at the sides with her gloved hands and knocked the snow out of it. Then she righted the craft, and clinging to its side, slid it down to the water. She stepped within, sat down and used the paddle to push herself free of the bank.

Working her way out from the shore, she felt the sudden grasp of the Kantishna's current and pulled the canoe about, stroking the deep green water easily, firmly, not biting too deep, just as Yuri had shown her. "On a downstream run you don't have to do more than just keep her steady. Current does the rest. Upstream, that's a different matter. Stay close to the shore then, work from eddy to eddy."

The craft glided on down the river. Seventy miles more or less to the Toklat's mouth, thirty more to the Tanana. She remembered Yuri's words. Yes, and with luck she would find the Tanana, her friend Fireweed and her husband and children. If not? Why then, she would continue her voyage downriver another ninety miles to the Yukon and the permanent Tanana village where months earlier she and Borodin had parted company with Red Porcupine and his Tagish companions.

The skies remained dull grey and at intervals swirls of snow would drift over the river, the silent spruce woods and the barrens beyond.

As the uninhabited wilderness drifted past her, kingfishers screamed from the leafless willows and loons darted across the water, their wings tipping the surface. A moose, shoulder deep in the shallows, tilted his great rack toward her, snorted and gazed at her from behind dreamy eyes.

On the third day she reached the broad channel of the Tanana River. Its course and that of the Kantishna met almost head on and then flowed away westward. But there was no friendly smoke from lodge fires, no sign whatsoever of human presence.

Grushenka held the paddle in both hands, hunched forward and began to sob to have come so far and to have found nothing.

Chill air bit at her face as she rubbed the tears away. Dipping the paddle once more into the water, she drove the canoe in to shore.

Sitting on the bank and panting a little, she considered her plight. *I will not die here. Yuri is dead. The child of our love lives in me. I must find help, a place where my baby can be born.*

With first light she was under way once again, letting the current take her where it would, stroking ahead where it would not. Her hands, arms, back were beyond even exhaustion and pain.

On the second day down from the forks the cloud cover broke and for a few precious minutes sunlight played over the water and the trees. Eagles drifted high above the grey-green waters of the river and half a dozen ravens came winging upstream, swooping low to where Grushenka sat hunched forward in the canoe. They glided past her on motionless wings, arrogant and at home, mocking her misery.

Then the magic moment vanished as ragged clouds moved in from the west. Within an hour the first drops of rain began to fall. It gradually increased in intensity until Grushenka realized it would be necessary to discontinue her voyage, even though an hour of daylight remained. She drew her craft into a cove defined by the mouth of a creek, pulled the prow of the canoe up onto the mud-and-pebble shore and sought shelter on the lee side of a large deformed half-dead cottonwood.

Even the kindling of a fire was almost more than she had energy to accomplish, and she toyed with the idea of simply wrapping herself in the bearskin and sleeping until the rain had subsided. Better sense ultimately prevailed, however, and close by she found the heaped twigs of a deserted wood rat's nest. The heart of the wad was still dry, and she carried an armful back to the cottonwood and used the flint and steel Yuri had given her to kindle a blaze. Among the winter-bare willow brush she found sections of driftwood left during flood, and with the additional fuel the fire grew large. At last its smoke coiled up through the bare branches of the cottonwood and drifted eastward along with the slant of the falling rain.

When she was once again warm and feeling somewhat better, she brought out the last of her dried meat and ate it greedily, chewing it well, savoring the rich taste. All the food that remained in her pack was perhaps two pounds of coarse-ground flour, which might be mixed with water and formed into cakes that could be crisped over an open flame.

"I'll make it," she said aloud. "Another thirty miles, a day at the most I think, to Tanana. There I'll find shelter and perhaps passage down to Nulato. Alex is still there? Yes, but Father Georgi will allow me to take refuge in his church. Karloff will not want me back and the priest will not leave me to fend for myself."

Only two pounds of flour, but she had one other thing—the cap-and-ball musket that Yuri had left with her, that and a good deal of ammunition. He had taught her to use the weapon, but she had never attempted to kill anything with it. As much as the idea repelled her, a moment's thought told her that she had to feed herself, for starvation would end not only her own life but also the life she carried within.

"A little girl—a girl named Katrina. How do I know that?"

Somehow she was certain, and as she fell into slumber, the face of the baby who would not be born until May struggled up in front of her. The spirit of Yuri Borodin, Grushenka believed, would live on in that child.

When she awoke it was already light and the campfire was burning brightly. She drew the bearskin back away from her face and studied the dancing flames.

That is not possible, she concluded. *It should have burned to ashes long before this time.* Grushenka sat up slowly, looked about, saw no one, but at the edge of the cove there were two canoes.

Her breath came tight and she reached down beneath the robes, slowly, slowly, for the pistol, already fully loaded and needing only its hammer to be drawn back to be ready for firing.

"Are you awake now?" The Russian that did not sound Russian came from behind her.

In a moment she had spun free from her covers and held the pistol out in both hands, aimed at the voice.

A short, powerfully built Indian dressed in a salmon-skin parka, buckskin trousers and calf-high laced leather moccasins stood with hands on hips, staring at her, shaking his head.

"I have come a long way to find you," the Indian said. "Now you are going to kill me?"

Grushenka stared at the man's face—prominent wide-set cheekbones, lantern jaw, penetrating brown eyes. Then recognition came.

"Red Porcupine? It is you."

"Yes, little one. Is it possible for me to persuade you to put the pistol down? I become oddly nervous when guns are pointed at me. These Gossack weapons, sometimes they go off when we do not wish them to do so."

Grushenka shuddered, lowered the pistol and began suddenly to cough, the spasms bending her double.

"Giyeg has come to you as you slept," Red Porcupine said. "The cold rain has gotten to you perhaps. Come sit by the fire, Grushenka Borodin, and I will prepare some gum tea. You will feel better in a little while. Then we must decide what to do."

Borodin, not Karloff? she thought—and in a moment answered herself. *Yes, it is true. The other was long ago. My life began when I heard the notes of a balalaika; my life began where the big creek runs to the Yukon just upstream from Nulato.*

She turned gratefully toward the fire, stood before it, breathed in the pungent wood smoke. When she began coughing once again she steadied herself and breathed in deeply. Red Porcupine poured a small quantity of what smelled like dried mint into a battle-scarred blue-specked coffee pot and then added a powdery yellow substance.

"It will be ready soon," he said. "Are you hungry this morning? Yes, you must eat. Look, I have brought dried currants and some fine salmon cakes. They are fresh one moon past. My wife, Short Day, made them from fish we took at Throndiuk River, the Hammerwater. I have salt too. I will get it."

He strode down to his canoe to rummage through one of the buckskin bags in the prow.

"I did not leave your friend Yuri," Grushenka stammered, pressing one hand against her middle to ease the pain in her chest. "He is . . ."

"Dead." Red Porcupine nodded. "Yes, when we had finished fishing, I sent my people back up the Lot of Water to our village, and then I crossed over to Tanana River, up the Nenana and over to Toklat. You see, I was coming to visit. I hoped you and Yuri would accompany me to Hootalinqua and spend the winter with us.

"That is where I found his body, on the Toklat. I buried him beneath a big mound of river stones so that the skunk bear and the coyote would not find him. He is in the other world now; he has left the lodge of Raven Man's stepmother and has crossed the lake to the other side. One day we will all go there, and then we will see him again. He will be glad to see us when that time comes."

"Buried?" she asked, staring into the fire. "Oh yes. Are you certain it was him? Perhaps I left our cabin too soon. I should have waited for him to return."

Red Porcupine stared at Grushenka's face. Her cheeks were drawn, her eyes marked by dark circles of exhaustion.

He shook his head. "I found him sitting by a waterfall close by the trail the Tananas use between Toklat and Kantishna. He held his musical instrument in one hand and his eyes were wide open. I saw him there and called out to him, but he did not answer. At first I thought he was playing a trick on me, Grushenka Borodin, but when I climbed up to where he was sitting, his flesh was already cold. The Nahoen had come to him, perhaps while he was thinking of you, and took Yeg, his spirit. I do not know what happened.

"Once I saw a black bear sit down and die, all in a moment, and sometimes it is that way with very old people. Yuri had no injury of any kind. It is a great mystery, but one we must accept, for we have no other choice."

"And he is buried?"

"Yes, he is buried. After that I came across to the Kantishna branch where the cabin is. There I found the message you had left and so I came to find you. Why did you not go to Burning Eyes' village? That is where I thought you would be, that is where I thought your footsteps in the snow were leading. Then at Kantishna there were no more steps, and so I knew you had taken a canoe and gone downriver. I borrowed another canoe that had been left nearby and went to the Tanana village, but you were not there."

"The village? I could not find a village. The Tananas were not at the place where the rivers come together, and so—"

"You went on down the Tanana River. You were only a mile from Burning Eyes' village, Grushenka, not more than that. Well, it does not matter now. I have found you. Here, the tea is ready. You must drink some. It will make you feel better."

He poured the steaming liquid into a hard leather cup and handed it to her.

She sipped, coughed, spilled some of the mixture onto the ground. "Strong. It tastes like—"

"It has a strange taste," Red Porcupine nodded. "You must eat some of the salmon."

Grushenka did as she was told, chewed, swallowed and once more sipped at the medicinal tea. "He is gone, then? You were his friend, you loved him too."

"Yes."

"I am not weeping, Red Porcupine. I have done that already. I knew when he left to go trapping; part of me knew. And then the waiting . . . Sometimes I would go far up the trail he had taken and call his name over and over. I—"

"Each loved the other, and now the one we loved has gone away from us. It is very hard to accept, but that is what we must do."

Grushenka sipped again at the tea, caught her breath, and said, "Part of him is within me. I must guard the child."

She wished to go to Father Georgi at Nulato, and Red Porcupine agreed to accompany her there. As she sat huddled in the rear of the young Tagish chief's canoe, Grushenka's sickness grew progressively worse. Grey sky or sunlight on the water, it made no difference, for the two were alike.

Sometimes when she looked up, she was certain that Yuri Borodin himself was guiding the craft, and she spoke his name. Then the truth returned long enough for her to realize that her mind was not right.

Dreams came, waking dreams punctuated by fits of coughing that left her exhausted. Though she clung desperately to consciousness, sometimes it deserted her.

* * *

Then there were people around her. She was being helped out of the canoe and carried.

"Send for my husband," she mumbled, "send for Yuri Borodin. Tell him I have his baby, and then he will come for me."

She was taken into a lodge in the earth. Was this the tunnel Yuri had laughed about? She looked for a man with feathers over his shoulders, the body of a man, a grotesque raven-head mask with plumes and rings of bells and feathers about calf and ankle.

Warmth; a fire burned. Its draft helped expel musky smells of bear grease and human skin, lamps burned and then there was darkness.

It was a beautiful darkness like a whirlpool, and she was slipping into it; the current was drawing her down. She wanted to resist the spinning water, but she was unable to do so.

When she awoke Red Porcupine was seated beside her next to another Indian, a young woman she at first mistook for Sabrina.

"Where am I?" she asked, trying to sit up. Red Porcupine's big hands restrained her.

"You have wandered a long way, little sister," Red Porcupine said, smiling at her. "The village shaman said you were already gone, but White Poppy has nursed you back. You are going to live, Grushenka. You will live to bear your child. *Paglan,* welcome back."

Her vision cleared and her eyes took in the shadowy outlines of the interior of the kashim where she lay.

"Where am I?" she repeated. "Are we in Nulato, Red Porcupine?"

"No, no, we are still a long way from there. This is the village called Nuklukayet. When you have regained your strength, I will take you to Nulato if that is what you wish."

"Yes," she replied, closing her eyes for a moment. "Father Georgi will help me. Then I will go home, back to Seeneestakan. It is a long way, but that is where I will go."

"I do not know where that place is, little one, but I will do whatever you say."

"White Poppy?" Grushenka asked, gazing upon the face of the woman beside Red Porcupine. "A beautiful name. You have nursed me?"

"She does not understand Russian," Red Porcupine said, "but she can see that you are grateful. I will tell her what you said about her name."

Grushenka smiled, lifted her hand, and placed it for an instant upon the Tagish chief's forearm. "I am still very sleepy. I must rest some more."

"Yes. You have had the lung disease. A number of people died in my own village, several winters ago. A good spirit has been with you. Sleep again, but when you waken once more, then you must eat something. After that your strength will begin to come back."

Two weeks passed before Grushenka was ready to continue her journey. The time of the short day was near and temperatures were falling to zero Fahrenheit and even colder each darkness, rising to little more than that during the brief intervals of low sunlight during the days. Many of the small streams were already frozen solid, and Red Porcupine was fearful that further delay would see the Yukon itself iced over and water travel impossible.

Grushenka embraced White Poppy and gave her a small silver locket from Russia. Then Red Porcupine helped her into the canoe. He pushed out from the landing and dipped the paddle deep into the river to drive the craft to center stream.

Plates of ice drifted with the current, sections that formed along the banks during the long hours of darkness and broke away under the influence of the weak winter sun. The world to either side of the river seemed dull, grey, nearly dead.

When the low sun touched the hills far to the south of the river, Red Porcupine continued the rhythmic dipping of his paddle into the water, first to one side, then to the other, using both the great river's current and his own strength to keep the canoe sliding ahead over the rippling surface. Even when the stars appeared he did not cease.

"After a while the moon will guide us," he said. "Sleep while you are able. Later I will find shelter in a cove. Then I will build a fire and rest."

Grushenka dozed fitfully. Always when she woke it was the same, the strokes of the paddle, the hiss of water, a strange world of shadows gliding past.

The northern lights poured up in a huge arch across the sky, yellow and green and crimson-violet in pulsing bands, a great pathway through the heavens.

Only when the first hint of twilight touched the sky and the glow of the aurora had long since vanished did Red Porcupine guide the canoe in to shore. He built up a great fire against the deepening cold and the two of them shared a quantity of dried caribou flesh and a pouch of nuts.

They lay close by the fire, side by side, with all their blankets about them, and Red Porcupine slept. Grushenka could not sleep, not with someone other than Yuri beside her, even if he had been Yuri's close friend and had certainly saved her own life.

At noon on the fourth day they reached Nulato. A handful of curious Koyukon Indians stood by as Red Porcupine drew his canoe ashore, and one of the men greeted him.

"Is the priest still here? The man called Father Georgi?"

The Koyukon nodded and pointed toward a half-completed structure within the stockade yard.

Red Porcupine assisted Grushenka ashore and then, half supporting her, began to walk toward the open gate to the compound yard. "The woman's belongings are at the front of the canoe," he said. "One of you bring them."

A few minutes later an astonished Father Georgi recognized and welcomed into his quarters the woman he had supposed he would never see again.

Ivan Pavloff, seated at the priest's table, cigar between his teeth, rose and greeted Red Porcupine. "You boys done with her?" he grinned.

The muscles in Red Porcupine's face hardened for a moment and then he shrugged. "Yuri Borodin is dead. I have buried him near Toklat River. His wife wished to come here, to the Russian church."

Chapter 7
The Yukon Freezes

The problem of supplying foodstuffs to the Russian-American posts was severe and seemingly unsolvable.

Raven Man, patient as always, watched from the trees.

Archimandrite Joseph of Kodiak declared his intention "to start the raising of potatoes, cabbage and other vegetables here, but the main obstacle is that nobody knows anything about it." The promyshlenniki were not inclined to farm, and their offspring could no more be taught agriculture than could wild birds.

Shelikhov believed that ". . . within a short time it will be possible to train and use volunteers from among the Indians in agriculture, shipbuilding and navigation," but his vision remained unfulfilled. Aleuts were set to raising cattle, but this attempt did not prosper ". . . owing to their untidiness, laziness and perhaps disinclination. Through negligence or ignorance most calves died." Even the half-breed Creoles handled livestock so badly that the cows in their care gave scant milk and as often as not perished.

The Tlingit Indians did well enough with such agriculture as suited them, and they sold quantities of potatoes to the company. For some reason or another, however, Raven Man laughed, they did not like these Russian Gossacks. In 1802 the Tlingits—Koloshes, as the Russians called them—destroyed Nova Archangelisk and in 1806 the settlement of Yakutat.

Nova Archangelisk was regained in 1804. Rezanov reported that ". . . our men do not go to the shipyard nor to the forest to cut timber or burn charcoal without loaded guns. At all other kinds of labor similar precautions are taken." Some claimed American sea captains were inciting the Indians and even providing them with pistols, rifles and ammunition.

The Tlingits were discovered to be excellent marksmen, and as late as 1861 it was reported that ". . . no Russian dared to go fifty paces from the fort of Nova Archangelisk for fear of the Koloshes. We cannot even let our pigs feed in the woods."

December 1854

"Is Alex still in Nulato?" Grushenka asked.

Father Georgi glanced at Ivan Pavloff and replied, "Yes, my child, your husband is here. He will leave soon, next week I think it is, to go overland to Redoubt St. Michael and on to Nova Archangelisk. We expect him to return with our shipment of supplies early next summer. That is what I understand."

"*Da, da,* I will stay here," Pavloff grunted. "Karloff will bring trade goods upriver at midsummer."

"Will you allow me to stay with you, Father Georgi? I have no intention of going back to Alex Karloff. When we walked together among the fields of flowers at St. Michael, you told me that you would remain at Nulato only until the new church was built. Is that still true? You're returning to Russia?"

The old priest made a vague gesture with his hands. "Ah, Grushenka, the mother church makes these decisions, not I. I believe that is what will happen, for that is what the bishop has said. Baron Karloff presented me with the letter containing my orders when you and he arrived from Okhotsk, and I have had no further communication since then."

"I formally request sanctuary within the church in that case. I ask you as a servant of God as well as a friend to take me with you when you leave Nulato. I cannot stay here."

Father Georgi glanced once more at Pavloff and then at Red Porcupine. The latter leaned on the cast-iron stove against the wall of the old storage building the priest had been given for temporary quarters.

"The church grants sanctuary to all who require it," Father Georgi said, "but you must not ask me to deceive Baron Karloff. I am honor bound to inform him that you have returned to Nulato. In truth we all long since supposed you dead, though rumor had it you went away with Borodin and his friends."

Pavloff nodded. "I will tell the baron. Sabrina, she stayed away last night an' Alex got drunk. Still asleep when I come over here. Alex, he don't have good luck with women sometimes."

Pavloff winked at Grushenka, nodded to Father Georgi and Red Porcupine and strutted out of the building.

"I do not wish to see him," Grushenka exclaimed. "My marriage to that man never existed, not after the night we reached St. Michael."

"Whatever happened that night, Grushenka, you two were reconciled afterward. Indeed, you seemed happy enough until— You were married in the holy church and in the eyes of God. Alex Karloff did not desert you, no matter what you may have thought. No, he merely went back to the redoubt for additional supplies. When he returned and you were not here, he led a group of his men in search of you.

"My daughter, I think you are the one who has wronged him this time, wronged him most gravely, I should say. Oh, I cannot be angry with you even though I should be. And yes, I will help you in any way I can. But would it not be possible to claim the Indians kidnapped you, took you away against your will, and this gentleman, Chief Red Porcupine, assisted you in escaping? If something of the sort is indeed true, then appearances might be maintained and—"

"Pavloff knows what happened," Red Porcupine said, moving to the table where Grushenka and the priest were seated. "He knew Yuri Borodin ever since Yuri came back from the Russian school. What he remarked when we came in—Pavloff thinks like a coyote. I know him too. Months ago he said, 'Don't worry about her. She's gone off with the singing man. You'll never see her again.' "

Father Georgi drummed his fingers on the surface of the table. "Dispensations must be made. I will say that I have received your confession—that you told me you were taken against your will and that this chief has slain the man who abducted you and has brought you back to Nulato. That will account for everything, and Karloff will have to take you back."

"Why would I kill my best friend?" Red Porcupine demanded. "You are Grushenka's friend and a Gossack shaman, but I will kill you if you say such a thing."

Father Georgi rose, gestured wildly, shook his head. "Listen now, both of you. Red Porcupine, I have heard the men of Nulato speak of you and I know you are an honorable man. I would only say the words, not believe them. Grushenka has chosen to return and we must find a way to make it safe for her. You're Tagish? What would you do if your wife ran away with another man—with a man from another tribe, let's say? If she came back to you would you accept her?"

Red Porcupine shook his head. "I could not do that."

"Aha! Neither can Baron Karloff, not unless we present him with a story that he finds acceptable. Do you understand now?"

"I understand that it would be said I killed my best friend in order to bring a Gossack's wife back to him. What would my own people think if they heard such a tale?"

"You listen to me, Father Georgi," Grushenka demanded. "Am I an old bone to be taken from one man and given to another? All of this is beside the point. I have no intention of returning to Karloff. Don't you understand? I am pregnant to Yuri Borodin and I went with him of my own free will. In the eyes of God we were man and wife, we loved each other, we . . . Do you understand?"

Father George breathed deeply and once more sat down at the table, his round face a mask of resignation, his blue eyes clouded with age-old sadness. "It will be as you say, then Grushenka. I am an old man; what do I know of these things? And yet I was young once. Well, Alex Karloff will be here directly. His pride will require him to make a show of authority. I think he will demand that you return to his house, and after that—"

"After that my death," Grushenka finished. "I will not go with him. If I am forced to go, I will kill him before he has a chance to harm me. Will you not give me sanctuary, Father Georgi?"

"I have already granted it. Red Porcupine, you have played angel of the Lord and I thank you from my heart. Now for your own safety you must leave. The baron has twenty armed men and he will order them to shoot you, as likely as not. You must get out of the fort as fast as possible. Go and Godspeed, my son."

Red Porcupine smiled and shook his head. "This Gossack shaman is very strange," he told Grushenka. "I can see that he cares for you and will not allow harm to come to you. Yes, I will go, for one man is not the equal of twenty. Not unless his medicine is very strong and theirs very weak. I will go, but not far, not yet. When I believe Grushenka is safe, than I will begin the long journey back up the lot of water to my own people."

With these words he was out the door, striding toward the stockade gate. There he turned, stared back at the priest's dwelling and observed a tall man in uniform emerge from the trading post with Ivan Pavloff a step or two behind him.

Alex Karloff pounded at Father Georgi's door, straightened his hastily donned military jacket and impatiently thumped the wooden door once again. His eyes ached dully from the previous night's overindulgence and he was in no mood to be kept waiting.

At first he merely laughed at the news Pavloff delivered to him, half supposing his bidarshik to be engaging in some sort of preposterous lie, though the telling of such tales was absurdly out of character. Then Pavloff supplied details and insisted that he was speaking the truth. Alex sat up on the edge of his bed, demanded coffee and began to pull on his clothing. He cursed his boots, his lack of authority within the hegemony of the Russian-American Company, Sabrina and Grushenka Karloff.

Ivan Pavloff warmed the nearly empty pot of hours-old coffee and brought a mug of it to his chief in command. Karloff sipped at the stale brew, cursed again, spit on the floor and groped into the closet for his jacket.

Now the damnable priest was refusing to open his door. Was this whole thing after all some sort of perverse jest that Ivan had inexplicably decided to play? But at length the door did open partway.

"Pavloff tells me you've got Grushenka here. If he's lied to me, I'll have him flogged senseless. Well?"

Father Georgi nodded to Pavloff and then replied, "Yes, Baron Karloff, your wife is inside. For reasons best known to her she has requested sanctuary within the house of the Lord and I have granted it. I must tell you, Alex, she does not wish to speak to you or even to see you. I would say she's in shock having just been delivered back to us by a virtuous Indian to whom she owes her very life. She has been very sick and I advise you to give her time to compose herself, my son."

"The devil take you, you old hypocrite. If my wife's in there, I demand to see her. Now open the door and let me in or I'll have you flogged, by the sacred blood of Christ."

"It would not be wise, Baron Karloff."

Alex stared at the priest's wrinkled face, grinned and drew out his service pistol. "I will be the judge of wisdom. Get out of my way."

"Come in then, by all means. I believe you know this lady?"

"Not me," Ivan Pavloff said, turning away. "Don't want no part of this." The bidarshik strode back toward the trading post.

"Thank you," Father Georgi called out after the retreating Pavloff and then closed the door.

Grushenka was seated at the table, a half-finished bowl of rolled oats in front of her.

"So the whore of Babylon has come crawling back to her husband," Karloff said, his speech slow, the words clipped. "How many of the bucks did you manage to bed, Grushenka? Ah, maybe it got cold out there—or did the savages get tired of you?"

Grushenka met his angry glare, did not turn away. "I have nothing to say to you, Alex."

"Nothing to say? By God, I'll give you something to say, you piece of baggage, daughter of a cow farmer. Perhaps I'll have you shipped back to Andrei Kosnovich and let him tend to you. A bit of disgrace there, eh? Life in Seeneestakan wouldn't be worth much to him then, would it?"

"For the love of Christ, baron," Father Georgi cut in, "wouldn't it be wiser to learn what happened to your wife?"

"My wife?" Karloff asked, breaking into laughter. "Well, Grushenka, what sort of wild tale have you prepared for me?"

"She was kidnapped, taken off against her will," Father Georgi said. "And now she has been returned to you unharmed."

"Your . . . *health* is good, is it?" Karloff demanded, not even glancing at the priest.

"As a matter of fact, Alex," she replied, "I've been quite ill. The Tananas nursed me back to life, so perhaps you can blame them for having to look upon me again. But I am much better now, thank you.

"I loved you once—I loved you dearly. Then you lost interest and gave me to that pig Dobshansky. After that I gave in to your pleas for understanding because not wisely, I still loved you. But it was never the same again, was it?

"What I have just said—it's something I have never told anyone, not even Father Georgi. That was our filthy secret, wasn't it, Alex? But you can't hurt me any more. I have known more honest love—"

"She's raving," Karloff said to Father Georgi. "There's so much guilt and hate in her that she'll say anything. Where's this savage that brought her in? I want to reward him."

"He's vanished back into the forest," Grushenka said. "Send all your men out if you like, you won't find him. Besides, he's not the one. The man I loved is dead. He was the father."

"A child?" Karloff asked. "You're pregnant? Then it will be born with my name. Hah! It better not look like an Indian. I believe you like the savages better than me."

"Believe what you wish. It is of no concern to me."

"Both of you," Father Georgi implored, "I ask you to calm yourselves. Baron Karloff, one of our own has miraculously returned from the dead, and . . . I begged you not to force your way into the house of God. All that has been said may still be unsaid. No word of this will ever pass beyond these walls. I am not perfect, no, I am not even worthy of my calling, but I am nonetheless the agent of the Lord. His mercy is open to both of you, and will be freely granted, requiring of you only that you both repent of these words spoken in the heat of anger.

"Baron Karloff, please calm yourself and sit down. Grushenka, you have suffered through a terrible ordeal and yet you are still alive and well. All things happen according to divine plan; that is something I come to understand more and more with each passing year. There is a purpose to everything, and as children of god we are capable of learning if only we will. All that has happened to the two of you as man and wife may still be made right."

Yuri, how could you leave me? Dearest, I know you never meant to; I must not blame you. I think you read my thoughts, I think you know everything in my mind. Will we once again be together? I would crawl a thousand miles over ice to find Raven Man's tunnel, the one that leads to where you are. I am Christian, but that makes no difference. If there is another realm, another world, even if it is a place forever beyond the reach of the Almighty's blessed grace, I would choose that in an instant to be with you.

Our summer of love passed into nothingness, and we did not know it, never even wildly supposed it. We thought only of our life together and of the child. Being so in love, we never dreamed of death. Warm tides bore us onward, yes, and the long, pleasant days and the talking together and the lovemaking.

I will come to you, Yuri Borodin, I promise that. But

we must both be patient, for I must still bear the child who joins us and who came of our joining. It will be a girl, Yuri. Did I tell you that? I nearly saw her face in a dream, but the vision blurred.

I will rear her myself somehow. I will never again lie in the embrace of any other man. Oh, I hear you strum a sad chord on the balalaika and shake your head, but I speak from my heart, and the passing of years will not change me or weaken my vow. Having drunk fire, how could mere water ever slake my thirst?

You say I am still very young, I will soon forget, but I am far stronger than you can imagine—I have learned much in a very short time. I will be true to you always.

An inner voice told Red Porcupine his business in Nulato village was not yet finished, and so he remained a few days even though his own lodge was nearly a thousand miles up the great river and even though with the year at its close the journey by dogsled would be beset by fierce storms and terrible cold. It was a journey only a madman would undertake, and yet he had no doubts as to his capacity to confront the elements. Storms and cold could be waited out, and he was not without friends in the villages along the river. Under the best of conditions the trek would require a full month and under the worst, perhaps two.

The young Tagish chief took lodging in the kashim of Blind Wolf and his wife Slippery Otter. The two of them, now both in their sixties, had befriended his own father, who brought Red Procupine to Nulato as a young boy. From Blind Wolf he was able to borrow a team of six malemute dogs and a sled and harness that required only minor repairs. These he would return the following summer at trading time, either personally or via his tribesmen.

Blind Wolf had a son, a tall, good-looking young man named Moon Hides, a bachelor who as it turned out had eyes for the young Creole woman who lived with Baron Karloff. The two of them were meeting secretly and in fact planned to run away in summer to Huslia, a village on the Koyukuk River.

It was from Moon Hides that Red Porcupine learned the cause of the antagonism between Grushenka and her husband. "Sabrina told me the story," Moon Hides related. "First she belonged to the Gossack killer Dobshansky, who called her Dog. He gave Sabrina to Karloff. And for what? I will tell you, Red Porcupine. Dobshansky wished to lie with Karloff's wife. The Ikogmiuts, they do this sort of thing, but Sabrina says the whites do not—and yet it happened. This was at Redoubt St. Michael early last summer. Dobshansky beats his women. He enjoys them more that way. Sabrina has told me he used to strip off her clothing and tie her hands and legs and use a leather belt on her. One day I will find a way to kill him."

"You think this Dobshansky did such a thing to Grushenka?"

"Yes, and after that she went to hide in the church with the same priest who is here in Nulato. Now she is with him again; that is where you left her."

Red Porcupine idly drew out his steel-bladed skinning knife, used the point of it to tease at a half-healed cut on the back of his left hand.

"She is gravid," he remarked. "I took her to the priest because that is what she asked me to do. What now? Do you suppose she will return to her Russian husband?"

Slippery Otter brought in a hide bowl full of fish broth and poured out portions for her son and for Red Porcupine. "I am old," she said, "but I can still hear. Yes, and I will tell you the answer also. If this Gossack woman has Borodin's baby in her belly, then Karloff will lure her back to him and have her murdered before she bears it. Gossacks are crazy about these things. That is what I think."

"He would not wish to rear the child?" Red Porcupine asked.

"Of course not," Slippery Otter said. "But I am only an old woman. What do I know?"

"What sort of man is this Karloff?" Red Porcupine asked.

Moon Hides shrugged. "He has not been cruel to Sabrina—not until now. When he did not know we were meeting, everything was fine. But now he suspects and yesterday he hit her with his fist and made her eye swell."

Red Porcupine returned his knife to its case and stood up. "Perhaps it is time for your people to kill everyone at the Nulato post once again," he said. "These Russians pay better prices for furs than the British do, but they cannot be trusted. It is much easier to deal with the British, for they are very stupid, even though they cheat us when we trade with them. Well, I suppose we need some white men. Pavloff, he's a good man."

"Yes," Moon Hides agreed. "Ivan Pavloff is just like us."

On Christmas day the Yukon River was a solid sheet of ice, low in its bed with the winter ebb and shining like polished pewter in the weak sunlight.

Outside the stockade gates Father Georgi had assembled a replica of the manger in Bethlehem, complete with Mary and Joseph, the Christ Child, the three Magi and some angels. He had brought the figurines upriver with him from the mission at Redoubt St. Michael. Behind the tableau the old priest erected a cross of hand-hewn wood, the adze marks still visible despite the brassy paint Father Georgi so carefully applied to his rood.

The Koyukons were curious, highly interested. After a time two of the headmen grew bold enough to inquire as to the meaning of the display.

Father Georgi explained quite patiently. He used as

much of the Koyukon dialect as he had been able to master during his half-year in Nulato and filled in with Russian phrases, most of which were relatively well understood by the natives. When the explanation was complete the priest gave his blessing and rang the hand-held bell that signaled the beginning of the feast. Then he looked up and was startled to see Red Porcupine standing just a few feet away alongside the Indian known as Blind Wolf. The Tagish chief was wearing a pistol and had a percussion rifle cradled across his forearm.

Red Porcupine said a few indistinguishable words to Blind Wolf and then stepped forward as though to confront the priest. The Koyukons to a man withdrew a few steps and stood watching in a semicircle, waiting to see what would happen next.

"I thought you had left us," Father Georgi said, uncertain and cautious because the Tagish chief was visibly armed.

"Grushenka Borodin," Red Porcupine asked, "is she well?"

"Oh yes, quite well, quite well. She owes her life to you. All of us are genuinely grateful. You have done a very brave and selfless thing. Yes. She would be pleased, I know, to see you again before you leave to return to your own people—but you must leave your weapons outside the fort, Red Porcupine. I will arrange for the meeting, my son, if that is what you wish, but first I must bless the food the women are bringing in for the celebration of the Lord's birth."

Red Porcupine shook his head. "Will she be forced to return to Karloff's house?"

"Forced? No, of course not, but she and the baron are married, you know. I do not know the customs of your people, but if a woman is married to a man, would that marriage not be respected by all others? And if a woman ran away for a time, would she not be expected to return to her husband?''

The semicircle of Koyukon men drew closer. Father Georgi, despite the authority of his robes and the calm face he managed to maintain, felt a shudder of fear run through him as echoes of the tale of the Nulato massacre rang in his ears.

''Do you love the woman Grushenka?'' Red Porcupine asked.

''I am old,'' the priest replied, ''and I have taken vows that prevent me from having any woman, if that is what you are asking. In the grace of God I do love her, yes, as a man loves his own daughter. That is why I have granted her the protection of my house.''

''She needs this protection from the man who was once her husband?''

''Who is still her husband. No, she does not need protection from Baron Karloff.''

''Then why did she ask for it?'' Red Porcupine demanded.

Father Georgi stared into the other man's eyes. His mouth came partway open, but he was unable to find words with which to reply.

Red Porcupine nodded. ''Now I understand.'' He turned and walked away from the priest and the Koyukons gave way before him.

The Christmas sun, above the horizon for only a few short hours, slid off toward the southwest and hung low above a rising cloud of thin mists and particles of ice along the Yukon River. The sun showed itself ovoid and huge and seemed to produce light without heat. Its deep redness suffused the mists and caused what appeared to be the glow of a huge fire such as the one that had raced through the taiga near Seeneestakan years earlier.

A lifetime ago, Alex Karloff mused. *A lifetime and many vanished dreams . . .*

The big river, open only here and there, formed a single ribbon of ice that ran nearly two thousand miles from deep in Canadian territory to the grey wastes of the Bering Sea. The river and the mists would glow for a time during the lingering sundown, then quiet to a long twilight, gradually deepening into profound darkness. The temperature, near zero during the Christmas festivities, was already dropping and might well reach thirty below this night.

In Seeneestakan as well and throughout much of Russia and Russian Siberia such temperatures were hardly uncommon, and in the far north of Siberia there were vast regions where the sun never rose at all for nearly three months at a time. But somehow the same conditions here were far less tolerable, bleaker, almost malign.

No place for civilized humanity, he thought. *We walk barefoot along the edge of a sword. One slip and the wilderness cuts to the bone—yes, and we ourselves turn savage. That has long since happened to Pieter Dobshansky, and perhaps I have not remained so sane as I would like to think either.* Ya oosta, ya bol'noy . . . *I am tired, I am ill.*

Something in Karloff was frozen hard and cold as the Yukon. It was not that he regretted his service with the Russian-American Company; indeed, he preferred it to life even in Moscow or the great European cities. But the barren stockade at Nulato was a far remove from the warmth and conviviality of such a place as Nova Archangelisk even, to say nothing of Petropavlovsk in Kamchatka. *Fort Ross and Bodega in Mexican California—that was the good time,* his thoughts ran. *Fat young Indian girls wandered about all summer with their breasts bare, willing sex partners, and their bucks hardly jealous at all.* Fort Ross was only a memory; the redoubt was sold to a half-crazed Swiss-German determined to build an empire for himself. The Russians had pulled back some fourteen years earlier, and now the beautiful land of California lay under the dominion of the Yankees.

It was all a long time ago. I was a young man then, in my twenties, and things were still new to me.

Karloff studied the surface of the darkening Yukon. In his mind's eye he could envision a shallow-draft steamer coming upstream, stopping at Nulato to take on firewood and continuing as far as the river remained navigable. There would be other posts and greatly increased fur trade, a whole new realm of forests capable of producing a bounteous harvest of furs. The Yukon River and Nulato in particular would provide the key to it all.

If only he, Alex Karloff, could persevere, his reputation would grow greatly. The prospect of one day being Pieter Dobshansky's superior was indeed an appealing one.

Karloff spat tobacco juice onto the rounded stones at his feet, could imagine the heat vanishing, the liquid freezing to a brown glaze over the rocks.

Like a damned fool, he thought, *I took a poor man's daughter to wife, only to have her grow sickly and repugnant. When she recovered she turned willful, disobedient; she ran away and came back disgraced. Kidnapped by savages, was she? The mouths of priests are crammed with lies. I dreamed of a son to inherit my lands, a strong woman beside me. Instead I am saddled with a slut who disappears for six months, comes back pregnant and has not even the decency to kill herself and atone for her shame.*

Father Georgi, for all his sanctimonious bravado, had no authority to keep a man, particularly a baron, from his lawfully wedded wife. It was debatable, in fact, whether the domain of Jesus even extended to this savage portion of the world, missions and missionaries notwithstanding. Father Georgi eventually would be obliged to turn Grushenka out, and in any case summer would see the last of the old man at Nulato, or so Dobshansky said.

There would be time—and time as well to see how soon the birthing took place. It could not be his, of course; six months along she would show a lot more. But it might be passed off as a seven-month or even six-month baby if it was not too big, if it was a boy, and most important, if it was emphatically not a Creole.

If the baby had an unfortunate complexion or was a girl, the mother and child would die of complications and nobody would even be much surprised, considering the hardships. Otherwise Karloff might elect to keep his heir and free himself from ever having to consider marriage again. If the child was particularly pleasing—say it looked for all the world like a Karloff—he might even allow the mother to live for the first year or so as a means of keeping it healthy.

The last red fingernail of the visible sun was gone now, and Baron Karloff slapped his gloved hands together three times. He turned and began the short walk back to the fort, his attention on appropriate measures of discipline to be taken against Sabrina—Sabaka; her original name was far more fitting.

"Karloff, I have brought you a present." The words of the unseen speaker were in Russian but had a strangely dissonant quality.

"Come out into the open." Karloff used his most authoritative tone of voice. "I can't see you. Who speaks to me in this fashion?"

A rather short, stocky figure emerged from the shadows, his faintly discernible costume immediately identifying him as an Indian.

"What do you want?" Karloff demanded.

"I am Red Porcupine, chief of the Tagish. I wish you to know my name. We will have a potlatch now, Gossack. I will give you something and then you will give me something far more valuable in return."

"Do you intend to rob me?"

"No. I have no need for anything that belongs to you, Karloff. I wish only the safety of one who is dear to me."

"Am I to assume it was you who brought my wife back to Nulato? If my guess is correct, I have a reward for you, Red Porcupine of the Tagish. Come with me to the fort and I will give it to you." Karloff took a step forward, reaching for his service pistol.

Gunpowder flared a blue red directly in front of him. Baron Karloff never heard the noise, did not feel the stones rushing up beneath him as he fell. He knew only scarlet mists, as though the sun had risen once more above the long, frozen Yukon River—and then there was nothing.

Chapter 8
Borodin's Daughter

During the years 1826–1830 perhaps as much as sixty percent of the fur seals taken from Alaskan waters were bartered to the Americans in exchange for supplies. The Americans paid less than half what the skins were worth in Russia. The company became alarmed, for soon there were no longer enough seals for both the home market and the Americans.

Governor Chistyakov defended his trade policies by arguing, ". . . throughout my governorship . . . many of the most important items for the colonies—such as sugar, rum, tea . . . sent annually via Okhotsk . . . have despite the promises of the head office been either missing or . . . in negligible quantity. . . . I am forced . . . to resort to buying these articles from foreigners. [If we] supply the colonies . . . with all possible needs via Okhotsk, the number of fur seals exported to Russia will, of course, [increase accordingly.]"

A decade later, in 1840, Governor Etholen wrote, "I have fully noted the will of the head office 'not to place any orders or to make purchases from foreigners other than the agent of the Hudson's Bay Company,' which will be faithfully observed during my administration. . . . In the future during my five-year term absolutely no goods whatever will be bought here from foreigners, except those delivered here by the Hudson's Bay Company on contracted terms."

By then the fur seals and the sea otters had all but vanished due to indiscriminate slaughter, and Yankee sea captains with whales on their minds were directing their attentions to other waters.

January–June 1855

At the settlement of Nulato—except for shouts through the still air, the ring of axes cleaving firewood, the barking of dogs and the rare rifle fire when a Russian spotted a stray elk or moose—the world had been silent for a very long time. Wild animals and birds either holed up or were gone away and all the running water was locked in ice. It was a world of white and grey and somber blackish conifer green.

Grushenka would go for short walks outside the compound accompanied by Sabrina or Father Georgi during the brief but ever-lengthening hours of daylight. She must escape the dreary monotony of life in small rooms with too many people, often confined to her bed. On these walks she would remember the much longer walks of her girlhood—really only two years past.

She remembered her fairy tales. Her favorite was the one about a land gone dormant through its long winter, motionless and dead. The princess lay dreaming in her tower in a sleep like death, all things suspended, waiting for a magic kiss that might never come. She thought of Yuri as she had seen him in her dream, as Red Porcupine had described him, pale as ice, his eyes open on oblivion, waiting for her in the spirit world.

As the long winter drew on she began to find it difficult to imagine spring and even more difficult to believe she would live to see the return of warmth and life.

Sometimes she woke up screaming from nightmares she couldn't remember. At such times Sabrina, who slept in the room with her, would pad noiselessly to her bed. Grushenka would feel her weight settle as the Creole sat on the edge of the cot and took her hand. It was then, because of the weakness let in by the dark and the horror from the vague dreams, that Grushenka would confide her morbid thoughts to her friend.

"You talk silly," Sabrina would say, patting her hand, smoothing the covers back over Grushenka. "You see. You have a fine baby when flowers bloom, and then you go back to Mama and Papa in the great western land. Maybe I come with you if that big fool Moon Hides don't ask me to marry him pretty soon. We used to talk about running away together, but now he don't say much."

Grushenka nodded, smiling sadly. Some of the men, vaguely aware of the young man's meetings with Sabrina, immediately suspected Moon Hides of the murder of Alex Karloff; had not Ivan Pavloff intervened, the Koyukon's life might well have been forfeit. The bidarshik pointed out that Moon Hides had no pistol, and it was unquestionably a pistol ball that had been dug out of Karloff's throat.

Red Porcupine, the other chief suspect, had left Nulato, and no one, even the Russians, was interested in giving pursuit. Baron Karloff was put in cold storage in a tool shed, the body to be transported back to Redoubt St. Michael when the weather permitted.

Usually Grushenka tried to maintain a cheerful front for Sabrina and Father Georgi. She knew they were worried about her, for the pregnancy was a difficult one, troubled with bouts of bleeding and sometimes such intense pain that Grushenka thought she was losing the baby. For days at a time she would be confined to her bed, afraid even to move for fear that she would trigger a miscarriage.

Before the first of February the bleeding ceased for good, and Grushenka found it possible to smile genuinely. She had grown quite round, and she would often press her hands to her belly. As her figure burgeoned, the life within became more real to her, and she began to sing to it, sometimes lullabies, sometimes verses from Yuri's nonsense songs. She still grieved deeply, felt sometimes such keen longing that it seemed unbearable. Unthinkable that he would never see this creature, the product of their joy together, but she began to feel rather than merely know that there was purpose and a possibility of joy in life.

Even though the crisis was past, both Father Georgi and Sabrina saw what Grushenka herself didn't notice, that as the baby grew, Grushenka's legs and arms and face grew ever thinner. Her cheeks hollowed and dark circles formed under her eyes. Although her spirits were improved, even short walks exhausted her, and Father Georgi called a halt to these excursions, relenting only after he realized she became increasingly listless and fretful when confined.

In fact Grushenka became a subject of concern to the entire settlement. Ivan Pavloff and his wife often stopped by; they had at Grushenka's urging taken up residence in the main quarters and were completely in charity with her. The Indian wives of several of the trappers, none of whom had been overfond of Karloff in the first place, vied with each other to bring the widow nourishing and particularly taste-tempting dishes. Their initial shy gestures of friendship, when met by Grushenka's melancholy warmth, turned into good-natured bullying.

"You got to eat," a scolding would go. "How you gonna take care of that baby if you all bones like this? How you make milk out of bones? You eat."

Grushenka responded with a soft smile and a polite sampling of the food, her manner tender, slightly amused, always somehow remote, other-worldly. The women went away shaking their heads and as often as not blamed Father Georgi for filling her with notions of saints and angels so that she dwelt unhealthfully upon the hereafter. Koyukon, Ingalik, Ikogmiut—they all shared the conviction that Nulato on the Lot of Water was superior to Father Georgi's heaven or even the spirit world on the other end of Raven Man's tunnel.

Father Georgi was not guilty of these charges, however; he devoted a great deal of time to the attempt to interest Grushenka in things around her. He tried everything from jokes to games of cards to exasperated shouting, but nothing seemed to stir her good-humored but essentially unreachable heart.

For her own part, once the pains and bleeding ceased, Grushenka found a nearly magical way of cushioning reality. She was perfectly well aware of everything that happened, but none of it concerned her very much. Her real life was devoted to a warm and comfortable inner existence where she felt her baby grow, spoke to it, even spoke often to Yuri. She could never quite see him except in her dreams, but frequently she felt he answered her.

She passed months in this bubble of silence while the world outside was also silent. This lasted until the day she began to hear little gurglings and tricklings in the earth one sunny afternoon out walking with Sabrina. At first she glanced at her companion, uncertain where the sound could be coming from, it had been so long since she heard running water.

Sabrina listened also, and then a broad grin spread across her round face and she clapped her hands like a child and hugged Grushenka.

"Spring coming," she chortled. "Things start to melt, water runs under snow, under ground. Pretty soon flowers come and the ice goes away. After that your new little one comes. The boats will get here from St. Michael then, and you will go home across the sea."

* * *

Grushenka was oddly disturbed by this first tiny manifestation of spring. That night she was seized with new pain, a gripping tightness that cramped the base of her spine so that she could hardly rise from a sitting position. She felt as if her bones were being pulled apart, and she found that her comfortable, sheltering bubble had disappeared and she was once more fully in the world of other people, of pain and death and change.

As the days passed other signs of summer began to appear. Tiny flowers materialized in sunny places where the snow was gone. One day a flight of geese passed overhead, sounding down their wild cries, so stirring Grushenka found herself in tears. Every day new growth appeared, willow catkins, aspen buds, tiny glimmers of green here and there.

The waters gathered; springs ran from every bluff and hillside; the ground was sodden underfoot. The great river, still frozen but inundated by these new flows, developed a band of muddy water along either side of the unbroken strip of ice in the center. Men came up the Yukon on dogsleds but floated downstream in bidarkas and canoes.

Grushenka went on wildflower walks with Father Georgi once again, her gait awkward from the pain at the base of her spine and from the unwieldy weight of her protruding abdomen. Despite her discomfort she was once again happy, keenly at one with the season as she carried her own burden of new life. She picked wildflowers and imagined the features of Katrina, dark brown eyes like Yuri's, glossy black curls, smile habitual joy.

There were a few days of wet, soft snowfall, a few days of drizzling rain, many days of sunshine and sky a blue that seemed newly invented. The Yukon ice was rotten, marked by holes and spongy areas. No one traveled on it, for it was weak and treacherous. Grushenka grew accustomed to the eerie creak and moan of shifting stresses as the ice began to move on its bed of water. Sometimes it sounded like the drawn-out groan of a grizzly bear or a man making love, sometimes like a woman giving birth, sometimes like a great crowd of people speaking softly.

The Yukon was rising with its spring flood, lifting the ice upon its back.

One afternoon a tremendous roar awakened Grushenka from her nap. She sat up, heart pounding, and waited briefly for the pain in her back to subside. Then as quickly as she could she went outdoors, thinking perhaps the powder magazine had exploded. She was certain she would find a scene of devastation, maimed bodies and splintered buildings. She heard excited voices when she stepped out, but it sounded like cheering and the settlement seemed to be as before.

The earth-shaking sound repeated and was followed by a vast grinding screech. Grushenka followed the voices and discovered nearly the entire population of Nulato gathered outside the palisade on the low bluff overlooking the river.

A great sheet of ice was standing nearly vertical, wedged upright, the whole pushed onward by yet more ice, so that in a few minutes the first sheet crashed forward and another rose behind it with a drawn out thundering boom. The great Yukon ice ribbon was folding and buckling, folding and buckling as the winter melt tried desperately to obey the law of gravity. It sounded like war in heaven.

Father Georgi was ecstatic. "There is the work of the God I serve," he cried, gripping Grushenka's arm and pointing as another massive slab of ice toppled. "Would anyone dare not serve such a one?"

Grushenka stood speechless. The skin at the back of her neck prickled with awe and terror and peculiar exaltation. The priest too saw it as a rampage on high, but why was the gentlest man she knew reveling in such destruction?

"Do you not see the beauty, the grandeur of it? Of that—" he waved both arms at the rending, screeching Yukon—"and of this as well." He swooped to pluck a frail pink crocus and handed it to her. She gaped at him and accepted it.

He bowed grandly at the mob of trappers, traders and Indians, then smiled and touched her abdomen. "They and we and this one are all the same in Him. Look on *all* His works and worship."

Grushenka tried to envision this god. Perhaps he had a stern face and a long beard such as the priests wore. He made a broad gesture and broke the ice in the Yukon. Another sweep of the robed arm and an avalanche ripped over and buried a village; a tiny, delicate gesture and flowers grew and babies were born. Somewhere a great impassive bearded Father conducted the entire drama like the master of an opera.

She remembered her vision of Raven Man sitting in the dead tree and playing on his instrument of human bones, laughing and weeping and dancing. She shivered. Almost she saw what Father Georgi spoke of, the beauty of the vast scene, but she thought of Yuri beneath a tree near a waterfall, his eyes wide open, and she could not put aside her feelings.

The noise of the breaking ice continued through many days, a deafening sound that became almost like silence as Grushenka grew accustomed to it. Sometimes when she awakened at night it seemed the earth was coming apart, being reshaped and put back together. The sound was surely the song of creation.

Sometimes massive torrents of water rushed down, flooding over the banks and carrying everything away after an ice dam broke upstream. Trees floated down, and the bodies of moose and caribou. Once a major jam developed below the village. Russians and Indians alike watched anxiously as the water rose behind the impasse, fearful that the post and the Koyukon village would be inundated. When at last the dam broke, the earth shook with the thunder of water and ice. The children danced and mocked the ebbing danger until the shaman stalked out of his lodge and put the fear of the gods into them.

It was while this overwhelming noise, this roar of destruction and creation pounded the air and shook the earth around her that Grushenka awoke in the black of night. She was gripped with shuddering pain, a dreadful, clamping ache as if a huge fist were squeezing her middle. She cried out aloud with it and drew up her knees. After an eternity it subsided and she realized that both Sabrina and Father Georgi were at her side. The priest held a whale-oil lamp; he was hanging it on a hook over the bed.

Sabrina wiped the perspiration off Grushenka's face with the corner of a blanket and the priest took her hand and peered closely into her face. "Is it your time, my dear child? I'll go for old One Ear in the village. She's ugly as death, but the Indian women swear she is the best midwife in the world."

"I don't know, I'm not sure," Grushenka murmured, overpoweringly drowsy now that the agony had passed. "Probably it is nothing, a little pang." Her voice faded and she drifted into a doze. Sabrina still sat on the edge of her bed, holding her hand.

When the next pain woke her, the lamp still flickered but she was alone with Sabrina. The Creole gripped her hand tightly as she cried out with the new spasm. An elemental crash and a long, grinding creak from the river drowned out her voice.

"Do like this," Sabrina said when Grushenka could hear her again, opening her mouth and breathing rapidly, shallowly. "Pant like a dog. It helps—that is what the old women say."

Grushenka tried the technique briefly, found that she couldn't sustain it—as the squeezing ache forced her breath into a groan and then into a wail.

"Long time to go yet," Sabrina said when the paroxysm had subsided again. "Long time from the first pain to this one. Pretty soon One Ear will come back with Father Georgi. Then you be all right. In Nulato they say One Ear knows everything."

Grushenka saw that Sabrina's eyes were wide and frightened. "I'm a terrible baby, I think," she whispered. "I know the Indian women don't carry on this way."

"You holler good and loud," Sabrina ordered. "Shows you got plenty of strength."

Grushenka smiled, squeezed Sabrina's fingers, dozed again.

When she next awoke, a huge grey-haired old woman was pulling the covers back and lifting her nightgown, apparently unconcerned that the priest was in the room. His face shone scarlet in the dim light from the lamp as he stared fixedly at the far corner of the room.

"Wait, wait," Grushenka said, sitting up and trying to cover her legs again.

The old woman paid no attention, but pulled the cloth out of her hands and forced her knees apart. Another pain took Grushenka and One Ear pulled her up into a squatting position on the bed.

When the pain had passed, she allowed Grushenka to lie down again and continued her examination, ordering Sabrina to bring the light close and probing into Grushenka in a way that the young Russian woman found extremely embarrassing, although Father Georgi had left the room by now.

"Long time yet," One Ear muttered when she had finished. "Robe Man come for me way too soon. Robe Man fix One Ear cup of tea," she called through the doorway. "Plenty sugar."

As the midwife turned to waddle from the room, grumbling to herself about being awakened unnecessarily, Grushenka noticed that her left ear was only a stump of cartilage.

She breathed deeply then, felt tension go out of her limbs, dozed.

Raven flew up from a shrieking old woman, the ear clutched in his beak. A loud crack from the river turned into a shot and the bird went plummeting to earth in a shower of black feathers that seemed to catch fire as he fell. In a moment the black form rose up from the flames again, still laughing like thunder.

She awoke again and again to terrible, wrenching agonies. All sense of time was gone and all that remained were intervals of physical pain worse than anything she had ever imagined. Her torment increased as the old midwife insisted that she squat for the duration of the contractions, which were interspersed with sleep, half-sleep, dreaming. Eventually it came to seem that there were hardly any intervals between the spasms and the world shrank down to the circle of light in the room, the inferno of her labor. She made dreadful efforts to push, to expel the source of her suffering, but the child wouldn't come.

Grushenka became aware at some point that the square hide that covered the window had grown light. Later, after what could have been minutes or decades, it grew dark once again. She was too weak to sustain the squatting posture, too weak to push with more than a feeble effort against the contractions.

Eventually she drifted away from the torment. She was in some dark place far down in her mind, warm and safe. Now she could observe the activities in the room, the broad-faced old woman shouting "Push! Push!" as if she were the one in labor. Sabrina's face was tear-stained and her eyes glistened wide with fear. From time to time Father Georgi appeared in the doorway, his own face anxious, his lips moving in prayer.

She thought she should comfort these two and tried to speak to them. She couldn't make herself heard over the sound of someone moaning aloud. It was her own throat issuing the moans; she grew aware again of the pain, but from a distance, as if it really had little to do with her.

Above her whimpers and the murmurs of the others rose the voice of the Yukon River, shouting aloud that spring was here.

"Baby comin' backwards," said the old woman. "Can't turn him."

These voices didn't really matter. What mattered was that she was walking in a meadow dotted with flowers in colors like gemstones. Sitting beneath a tree not far from a white drapery of falling water, his eyes open and sparkling with invitation and humor, holding the balalaika and singing, was Yuri Borodin.

As she moved toward him she heard from far, far back in the distance a tiny, piercing cry that called her back to the room, the lamplight and the old woman holding a tiny dark-haired shrieking bundle.

Grushenka smiled and reached out.

"She's losing too much blood," the old woman whispered, but Grushenka heard her clearly, although the words didn't seem to have any particular import except that she wasn't stepping forward with the baby.

Sabrina, tears still streaming down her cheeks, snatched the infant away from One Ear and put it against Grushenka's breast. Grushenka smiled, placed the little mouth against a nipple, felt the sucking keenly, piercingly. She touched the fuzzy head, savored it with her fingers.

"Katrina," she whispered. "She is a girl."

It was a statement rather than a question. Sabrina nodded.

Grushenka smiled and held the infant for another moment.

She drifted away again, back to the meadow where the sun shone like pure amber through the delicate, glittering leaves of aspens. Yuri walked toward her through the light and shade, his hand stretched out, smiling. The pure sky was alive with birds. She could no longer hear the thunder of the other world, but Yuri's voice came clear. He was singing the song he made up for her that first time they lay together.

She laughed aloud, reached to embrace her lover, laughed again for pure joy. The laughter fell from the sky like birds swooping, catching, rising up again.

Near the end of June Red Porcupine and nearly fifty of his men came down the Yukon in a flotilla of canoes and bidarkas, bringing with them a good deal of peltry for trade as well as six malemute dogs and a well-worn dogsled. The Tagish had come to trade with Ivan Pavloff, but they were curiously well armed, many with pistol or rifle, relatively new and of American or British manufacture. Ivan Pavloff concluded that the Tagish had good connections with the Hudson's Bay Company—or else they had simply overrun a post and had taken whatever they wished.

Red Porcupine declined to enter the stockade, demanding instead that Pavloff bring out his trade goods.

If there had previously been talk of revenge for the baron among Russians from Karloff's lands in Siberia, there was no such talk at this time. The prospect of doing battle against a superior force so heavily armed appealed to no one. Ivan Pavloff was well pleased to note how the stick floated, for in any sort of a showdown it seemed certain to the bidarshik that the Koyukon men would side with the Tagish, and the result could hardly be other than a second massacre.

Red Porcupine returned the dogs and sled to Blind Wolf and Slippery Otter and neglected to remove a bale of beaver pelts first.

"My old friends," he said, embracing first Blind Wolf and then his wife, "where is your son Moon Hides? I have this old rifle I wish to give him."

"Ah," Slippery Otter replied, "our son has run away with the half-breed woman who belonged to the Gossack you killed."

"I killed?" Red Porcupine asked. "Who dares to say I killed the man Karloff?"

"Then how did you know his name, my friend?" Blind Wolf asked mildly.

"I just knew. Birds fly far along the Lot of Water, and sometimes I listen to what they say."

"Have your birds told you that the Russian woman is dead? Yes, she passed to the other side as she was giving birth to a daughter. She is buried behind the new church."

"The girl? Did the daughter survive?"

"Oh, yes," Slippery Otter said. "She is nearly two moons of age now and grows rapidly. Several women of the village go to the church to give her suck, but soon she will leave."

"What do you mean?"

"The Robe Man, Father Georgi, he is returning across the water. He has been mother and father to the child, so he will take her with him."

Red Porcupine scratched his chin and shook his head. "No, that is not right. Both parents were my friends, Yuri for many winters, Grushenka for a short time. It is not right that their child should be taken across the grey water."

Red Porcupine and a dozen armed men entered the stockade; Ivan Pavloff gave no order to bar their way. In a cluster they walked directly to the church and entered.

Father Georgi looked up, nodded. "Red Porcupine, I hoped you would come to see me, though I did not expect you to bring an army. I have a child in the other room, and she is a great problem to me. How would it look for an old priest like me to return to Russia with an infant? I'm afraid I would never be able to explain it."

Red Porcupine stared into Robe Man's blue eyes, searched for some hidden meaning. "Do you offer her to me, then?"

"Exactly, if you will promise to take her as one of your own. She's in the next room, but leave your army here. I would not wish to frighten her until after she has met her father."

Red Porcupine, having come to claim the child by force, found himself at a loss for words. This particular Gossack, he concluded, was quite different from the others, probably beyond understanding.

"I have two young sons," he said at last. "They will be pleased to have a sister and my wife will be pleased to have a daughter."

Father Georgi pulled back the veil from a squat handcrafted crib and Red Porcupine looked down at the sleeping infant.

"Katrina," the priest said. "That is the name Grushenka gave her. She's got a temper like a fury, but she's healthy as a horse. Quite a handful, I'm afraid. You'll need a wet nurse, Red Porcupine. I believe one of the women here in the village might be persuaded to go back upriver with you. Indeed, I have promised to pay her well for that service. I will be gone when the woman returns to Nulato, but Pavloff can be trusted, and I will take care to let it be known among the Koyukons the nature of our bargain."

For the first time Red Porcupine was hit with the implications of this undertaking. A resolute man, he nodded and said again, "I will raise her as my own."

"Will you make me a solemn promise?" Father Georgi asked.

"Yes, if it is honorable. I will swear on your medicine book if you wish me to."

"Not necessary, not necessary, I shall accept your word. I know something of the ways of your people, Red Porcupine; at least I presume your traditions are much like those of the Koyukons and the Ingaliks. When a woman marries, she is purchased for a bride-price, is that not so?"

"Yes, that is true."

"And the woman may not have any choice in the matter?"

"Sometimes that is so."

"And it is almost that way among my people, the Russians—except that the bride-price is paid by the woman's father to her new husband. Nonetheless, the result is the same."

"I do not understand that, but what is it you wish me to promise?"

"This: when Katrina is ready for marriage, you must allow her to choose for herself. You must not make her marry a man she does not want. Grushenka's marriage was arranged and it ended very badly."

"I am told Karloff fell in the river and drowned," Red Porcupine said.

"Yes, it was something of that sort. Will you give me your word, Red Porcupine?"

Katrina awoke. Her baby-colored eyes stared up, became aware of the unfamiliar face above her. She squinted, puffed out her cheeks and began to scream. There were, Red Porcupine noted, no tears in her eyes at all.

"The yeg in this little one is very strong, I think. Could a man force such a woman to marry against her will? I do not think I would wish to try."

"Then you give me your word?"

"Red Porcupine, Chief of the Tagish, gives his word."

The two men shook hands, and little Katrina, still screaming her lungs out, studied the face of the man who was to be her father.

Book Two:
PRINCESS LUDMILA

Chapter 9
The Wreck of the *Loire*

Denali, frozen god of the north—his glacier-hung shoulders hide in clouds; his brow rises above them. He is so huge that those who see him are stunned with disbelief.

An autumn storm passes, drenching spruce forests. Clouds swirl; twilight glitters on a still lake, burning its surface. Above, beyond, strange lights gleam from ice fields rising peak beyond peak to the massive giant still partly obscured by drifting mist trails.

Glacier-fed streams gush out and down, endless cascading ribbons of light. More ice forms as the mountain drinks air, sucks moisture, chills both with its cold hard granite bones.

Dall sheep with forward-curved amber horns stir and sniff, nervously crop brown grass on the rocky slopes below the snow zone.

A cow moose, shoulder-deep in lake shallows, dips her blunt nose to the water. Her two young, close together, stand disconsolately nearby, and a bald eagle, dark against Denali's scarlet glow, glides to a nest in a broken-top spruce.

Somewhere far away an American president is slain and outsiders decide to call the mountain by his name, but the magic word Denali will not die.

April 1867

Back home in Rostov, Princess Ludmila Andreiovna thought, *the daffodils are blooming along the garden paths and the cherry trees are covered with blossoms. The clouds float fat and white and the sky is delicate blue, the grass still as fine as kitten's fur.*

At Petropavlovsk-Kamchatskiy, where she stood, the sky was the color of old pewter, the air bleak. A chill wind from the dull sea bit at her face but could not get through her fur cap or her heavy cloaks.

Hers was a small-boned, slender figure, but no one thought her fragile when she put up her chin. Banishing daydreams, she did so now, and looked around at the last-minute loading of the steamship *Loire*. The vessel would take her to a new life as the wife of Count Pieter Dobshansky in the outpost of Nova Archangelisk on the coast of a strange, rough land across the sea.

Well, she assured herself, *I have always said I wanted an adventure, that I would not spend the rest of my life drinking tea and growing stout, discussing French literature with whispery ladies. This must be an adventure. Still, it would be nice to have an adventure where the flowers are blooming and the sun shines occasionally. Instead I've come thousands of miles to marry a man I've never even met.*

Ludmila pulled her collar up more tightly around her chin, thrust her hand back into the warm hollow of her muff.

The men loading the ship were clad far too lightly for the climate, she thought, wearing only rough woolen trousers and tunics, and yet they seemed to be perspiring as they wrestled the boxes, bales and heavy trunks up the gangway. They cursed in Russian, English and French, and in another language spoken by the short, muscular Kamchatkans, who had golden skins and slanting eyes.

A trunk she recognized as her own went on board, carried between a Mongol with a wispy beard on his chin and a red-faced, red-haired peasant youth. The hide-covered brass-bound trunk contained her precious Sevres china. The peasant boy stumbled and Ludmila involuntarily sucked in her breath. Her china, her few small items of furniture, her Paris trousseau were her last tenuous thread to civilization. She had not understood until now how intensely she cared about her treasures.

The peasant righted himself in time and the loading proceeded.

A trio came from the Russian-American Company's headquarters; Ludmila watched them with interest. They were dressed in rough leathers, and all were heavily armed with knives, pistols and hatchets. Their hair was below their collars and two of them wore beards that did not at all resemble the carefully groomed facial hair popular among the Russian officers, but were untrimmed, uncombed, unwashed. One was a giant, a head taller than anyone else. The third man, the darkest of the three, had only a shadow of mustache above his mouth.

In contrast even to the stevedores and the frontier officers these men, Americans as she gathered, seemed wilder than any she had seen from Rostov clear across Asia to the end of the world.

The men moved aimlessly toward the dock and watched the loading, speaking rather loudly a very different version of English than she had learned from Mme. Olga Bohmer, her governess and companion.

"Thievin' Russki bastids," one was saying. "Them coons'll sell our furs for twenty times what they give us, an' no frostbite, neither."

"Calm down, Charley," laughed the tall one, whose beard and hair were dull sandy gold. "No matter what, we came out all right."

"I reckon," Charley grumbled. "Even at Kamchat

prices two thousand gold rubles will buy us a drink of their damned vodka. What do you say, boys? This lad's so dry the wind could blow him clear to Sitka, sure as your brown bear shits in the woods."

"Wind's the wrong way," the beardless one observed. "Long John, don't you think we'd better be gettin' on board this French potboiler? Amigos, we don't want to find ourselves sittin' here come November, an' no way out of the Russkis' howlin' wilderness."

"Taos is right, Charley. There's likely a drop on board a fancy steam blower like the *Loire,*" Long John pointed out. "You do want to get back to civilization, don't you?" The other two laughed loudly and they threaded their way up to the gangway.

Ludmila observed the strange trio, caught between amusement and horror. Back home even the peasants who worked her father's fields would not be allowed to go about looking so wild and ill-kempt, and yet there was something about the Americans, particularly the tall, light-haired one. She watched as he sauntered up the crowded gangway, studied the unself-conscious grace of his movements. He moved more like a great cat than a man; his most casual motion suggested hard, fierce strength, unquestioning confidence in himself.

"*Qui sont les sauvages anglais, Nikolai Ilyich?*" she asked the young officer of the guard who had been sent to escort her to her wilderness kingdom. She tilted her head sideways and smiled up at him, knowing the charming little dimple in her left cheek peeped out to advantage from the frame of sable.

"You know I do not speak French well, your highness." The lieutenant's round, serious face blushed red. "My family's holdings are near Uralsk, out in the provinces. We are plain people."

Ludmila knew, of course, since she had goaded him to this same earnest explanation several times during the journey eastward. It was wicked, she new, to take such delight in teasing the gentle, awkward young man who was so obviously smitten with her, but the demon in her could not resist.

"Forgive me, lieutenant," she said softly. "I asked—"

"You asked about the English savages, I believe," he interrupted, blushing even harder.

"Why, yes. You see, Nikolai, you are a man of culture, despite your modest protestations." She smiled, winked at him. *Really,* she thought, *he is so lovely. He has beautiful strong shoulders and he adores me.*

Ludmila cut off the unworthy thought. Her fiance, whom she had never met, was an older man. Fifty-two, her father had explained, very rich and powerful, but fifty-two. Still, she did not consider herself a light-willed coquette, a type she had encountered all too often in the society to which she was accustomed.

"They are not English but American, I believe," Lieutenant Ilyich was explaining, "fur trappers, I would guess. Americans are not very genteel people, and these trappers are probably the worst of the lot. The tall man is named Emerson—I know little more than that."

Ludmila nodded solemnly and glanced toward the wagon—no carriages in this outpost—in time to catch a disapproving glance from Olga Bohmer, once her governess and now her chaperone and companion.

"I suppose I shall now hear about the impropriety of a young lady of birth consorting with an officer of the guard," she sighed aloud.

Nikolai looked alarmed, then drew himself to attention. "We were not consorting, your highness," he stammered.

"Of course not," Ludmila smiled, "but you don't know Mme. Olga as I do."

"I suppose not, my lady," Nikolai Ilyich agreed, his speech now very formal and proper.

Ludmila sighed again, realizing that Lieutenant Ilyich

had put up his wall, as he did when she teased him too much, and there would be no drawing him out for a time. Perhaps the worst part of the journey was that there was no one to talk to. Mme. Bohmer had been worse than useless. Mostly she wept for her lost home in Rostov. When that palled she reiterated that if only Ludmila had been less impulsive, more ladylike, there would have been a prince or a count, perhaps even in Moscow, to wed her and so spare herself and her governess exile to a godforsaken wilderness outpost.

Even now, as Ludmila climbed back into the wagon and settled beside the older woman, Mme. Olga's eyes were red from weeping and patiently reproachful. The governess made a great point of speaking not a word of Ludmila's unladylike conduct. "It is quite chilly here, is it not, my dear princess?" the portly governess remarked.

"Quite," replied Ludmila, adding then what Mme. Olga refrained from mentioning. "No doubt the lilacs are blooming in Rostov. I suppose we would be there now had I behaved more like my cousin Marya—taken tiny steps and sipped my tea daintily and adored an adorable lap dog."

"I have never said such a thing to you, Ludmila." Then the governess clutched her handkerchief against her eyes and went off into another fit of delicate sniffs and sobs.

It was nearly noon when the *Loire* finally moved out with the tide. The sky was still leaden, but the wind was perhaps a touch less frigid. Captain Mirabeaux, a short, stocky and very courtly Frenchman, insisted that the ladies have his own cabin for the duration of the voyage to Sitka.

"I will hear of nothing else, *princesse et madame*," Mirabeaux said, despite Ludmila's protest that they did not wish to turn him out of his quarters. "We do not often have such distinguished passengers on the *Loire*, for we are primarily a merchant ship—in the tea trade, as you know. And never do we have such distinguished lady passengers. My own cabin is the only place that would be suitable. Please, you must not shame me." So they were installed forthwith in the captain's quarters.

When Ludmila later inspected some of the other accommodations on board, she found the best to be no more than four feet wide and barely long enough to contain two stacked bunks and a washstand. Then she began to appreciate Mirabeaux's generosity.

Lunch was brought to them shortly after they got under way, while the women were still settling in; even the captain's cabin was somewhat cramped and Spartan. After lunch Ludmila proposed that they go up on deck, but Olga insisted that she was tired and that both of them should rest their eyes for a time. When Ludmila asserted that she would go by herself then, Olga sighed in resignation.

"I have no say over what you do, princess, as you are my mistress. I do not know how I shall hold my head up, though, if you go parading about among all these rough sailors by yourself. Well, there is probably no one of breeding aboard, and so there will be no one to say I have not taught you properly."

Ludmila smiled and nodded, knowing when she was fairly beaten, and lay back on her bunk, obediently closing her eyes to rest them. The sea was rough and it seemed necessary to brace herself somewhat to remain on the narrow pallet, so she found it difficult to relax. She opened her eyes and looked at the lacquered wood of the walls and ceiling and at the brass lamp swinging on its chain. She thought wistfully of her own room, her yellow chiffon curtains blowing gently in a soft April breeze, her pretty French wallpaper, her soft bed.

From the other bunk came the sound of Mme. Bohmer's restrained sniffling, and Ludmila clenched her teeth. She willed herself not to weep and she remained dry-eyed, but Mme. Olga, she thought impatiently, made up for both of them.

By midafternoon the governess was deathly sick, and after losing her lunch was unable to do anything but lie on her bunk and moan. Ludmila called the two soldiers who had stationed themselves outside the cabin door to come in and tend to her and took advantage of her chaperone's indisposition to escape to the deck.

She made her way to the foredeck, which was largely deserted, and stood at the railing, gazing out at the uniform chilly grey of water and sky. The horizon was so indistinct that she could imagine herself, the ship and all aboard to be in the center of a great colorless cold sphere. She shuddered and looked back to the west, where the dark green hills and high, snowy mountains of Kamchatka were still faintly visible.

The *Loire's* short, cross-braced stack belched grey-black smoke, the result of burning both wood and coal, as Ludmila supposed. The tall, double masts were under full sail as well, the canvas sheets irregularly discolored from smoke. At either side of the ship the big, clumsy-looking sidewheels implacably turned forward, pushed and lifted the sea so that water and foam poured down off the aft blades.

Rigging creaked as the hawsers tightened or went slack with the wind, and the sails billowed and flapped by turns. A crewman was climbing the rear rigging; he hung there like a spider against the intricate webbing of rope, seemed to be making some minor repair.

From nowhere Nikolai Ilyich appeared and stood unobtrusively near her, not speaking but obviously guarding her. Ludmila sighed and began to descend to the main deck, where she perceived all the activity to be taking place.

Nikolai, still not speaking, followed.

* * *

Long John Emerson and his companions, Taos Danny and Charley St. Francis, booked passage for deck space only, not for reasons of economy but because none of them could abide the tiny, claustrophobic passenger cabins. The trappers rigged their canvas tarpaulin in a comparatively wind-sheltered corner of the deck. While Long John stretched out, leaning on his bedroll and smoking his pipe, Taos Danny Vasquez, the half-breed Irish Shoshone, got a hand game going with a group of sailors and two of the Russian soldiers who were escorting the princess to her digs in Sitka.

"Don't think you ought to do 'er, Taos," Long John muttered out of the side of his mouth when he saw his friend bringing the marked pebbles out of his pocket. Ignoring him, Taos prepared to make the elaborate passes of the Plains Indians' gambling game.

"John's right," Charley agreed softly. "Ain't one of these boys without an Arkansas toothpick in his belt, an' most of 'em's got scars."

"Figger you two coons can handle things if the goin' gets rough," Danny whispered cheerfully.

Then he raised his voice. "Now, gents, I'll show you how the game goes a couple of times. Simple, see? I makes a few passes, thus, an' I sing a leetle song to give you some extry entertainment. Then you choose the hand. Hell, I'm flush, I'm easy. Now then, who wants to take my money?"

None of the men responded, so Danny made a few more passes, moving his hands slowly, keeping up his patter. After a short time one of the Russians, a stocky, dark man with a big mustache, laughed and reached into the purse at his belt.

"I try that," he said. "How much my money you want to take, *americain*?"

"Ai, ai," Taos Danny laughed, "the Russki knows

how to talk *muy bueno*. Hokay, then, let's give 'er a try. . . ."

Danny let the Russian win the first round, as his companions knew he would, and then passed the bones to his opponent. He also lost the next few rounds, and gradually all but one of the spectators joined the game.

Then, as Taos began winning, both Charley and Long John sat up, watchful; it was only a matter of time before a brawl developed.

Suddenly Emerson blinked, pushed his hat to the back of his head and stared. Sure enough, it was the little princess, her small figure almost entirely muffled in glossy furs, sauntering right toward the group of men and shadowed by a lanky soldier. The Cossack stuck close to her heels and scowled like a big, stiff-legged watchdog. Long John poked Charley with his elbow and St. Francis' mouth came open in surprise.

"Dog my cats," Charley muttered. "Didn't know they allowed royalty to mingle with the common folk." Taos Danny glanced up and went on with his patter and his passes with the bones, not missing a beat.

The princess and Nikolai drew up to the little group of men. Ludmila watched closely, her dark eyes sparkling with interest, but the lieutenant, when he saw what was going on, grasped the two Russian soldiers by the arm and ordered them back to their quarters.

"I should put you in chains," he raged. "You men are supposed to be performing your duty, but instead of guarding Princess Ludmila, you're out here wasting your money."

"Oh, Nikolai," Ludmila pleaded, "let them have their fun—" but the two guilty guards had already saluted her and slunk away.

Long John Emerson rose to his full height of six and a half feet. He bowed to the lady as gallantly as he was able, sweeping his battered hat half-mockingly across at waist level. His eyes, Ludmila noticed, were almost the same cold grey as the sky, but several shades lighter, and they remained fixed on her face, the corners wrinkling slightly in amusement.

"Please," the princess said in English, "tell your friend to go on with the game. I am interested in how this is done."

"Proceed, Taos Daniel," Emerson said, affecting a grand tone.

But the eyes of the entire group remained fixed on Ludmila and no one moved. The intense male scrutiny seemed almost able to penetrate the furs and examine the female flesh beneath.

"Name's John Emerson, ma'am—your highness. The boys call me Long John. That's because—I guess it's my height."

Despite herself Ludmila was charmed. The huge man babbled like a schoolboy, she observed, but his grey eyes remained as steady and amused as ever.

"I'd be mighty honored if you'd have a seat right here on my bedroll, ma'am, since you're interested."

Taos Danny laughed inexplicably, yipped twice and stared up into the overcast sky. Nikolai stiffened and Ludmila noted that the lieutenant's hand moved toward his scabbard. She also saw Emerson's cool eyes flicker to the officer and back to her.

He went on talking without a break. "It ain't much, but you're welcome. An' if any of the boys spits or cusses, I'll personally kick the livin'— I'll see to it he's severely reprimanded." Emerson glanced at the glowering Ilyich and reached out to take Ludmila's elbow. "If you'll allow me, ma'am—"

Drawing his sword, Nikolai stepped between the princess and the trapper. In a movement too quick for Ludmila to see a long-bladed gleaming knife appeared in Emerson's hand and was weaving back and forth like the tongue of a serpent.

Nikolai raised his sword.

Ludmila caught her breath and deftly moved between the two big men. "Nikolai, put up your sword, you fool. This man does not intend to harm me. No, no, do as I say. I have been protected far too much in my life."

She turned. "Mr. Emerson, I do not wish you to make holes in my guard. He is too zealous, perhaps, but I like him."

Nikolai Ilyich stepped back, his face flushed red once again, and slowly slid his sword into its scabbard, but he continued to glower at Emerson.

Long John grinned and sheathed his own weapon. Only then did Ludmila notice that both the trapper's companions were also on their feet, St. Francis with pistol drawn and Taos Danny's knife in hand. They followed Emerson's lead and put up their weapons.

Ludmila's mouth was dry and she was shaking. Feeling the eyes of the men upon her, she turned abruptly, not waiting for Nikolai, and strode off to her quarters. Ilyich glared at the Americans for a moment longer and then hurried off after his charge.

"Hell, Johnny, you can cut his throat later, then pitch 'im overboard. Lots of time between here an' Sitka. C'mon lads, this Irish Injun's got more gold pieces to lose."

But the interlude of near-violence had brought the French sailors back to their senses, and they shook their heads and drifted off. Taos shrugged, glanced at his bones and slipped them back into his pocket.

"By God, Long John," Charley St. Francis said after a thoughtful silence, "princess or no, that's one honest-to-bearshit woman."

"Lightnin' in 'er eyes," Taos agreed, "thunder in her voice."

"I suppose," Emerson nodded, glancing skeptically

after Ludmila and her guard. "Cain't say I care much for the company she keeps, though."

"Gov'ment issue," Charley shrugged, "find 'em everywhere. No foolin', though, you see the way she stepped right in between you two big ol' red-faced males? By God, an' her no bigger'n an ounce of cat piss."

"Tell you what, Charley," Emerson laughed, "you figger out a way to get her away from the King of Alaska or whatever he is, an' you can take her off to an Injun shack an' marry her."

"King of Alaska?"

"That's what one of the Frenchies told me just after we come on board this steam boiler. She's fixin' to marry Dobshansky, the company man in Sitka—an' she ain't never even met him before. Russians is peculiar people for a fact."

"You sure it ain't the governor she's plannin' to hitch with? Dobshansky's supposed to have squaws from St. Mike to Ketchikan. Anyhow, I wasn't thinkin' of myself precisely, Long John. Me, I'd take an Injun gal every time over one of your overbred white females, princess or no."

"First thing you know, she'd be hangin' lace curtains in the earth lodge an' making you go outside to spit," Taos laughed.

"Damn right," Long John agreed. But the image stayed with him—small face, all color drained away, eyes alive with courage, voice strong and amused, denying fear.

Princess Ludmila spent the remainder of the afternoon at loose ends. She couldn't bring herself to stay in the cabin with the wretched Mme. Olga, nor, since she couldn't shake Nikolai loose, did she wish to venture onto the lower deck again. She tried to occupy herself with some embroidery in a deck chair the lieutenant set up for her on the upper deck, but she had never had much patience with fine sewing.

Eventually, since she couldn't get rid of Nikolai Ilyich, she amused herself by helping him to improve his French. He was almost pathetically attentive but a tediously slow student.

When Nikolai did leave her for a few moments to see if there was anything he might do for Olga Bohmer, Ludmila gazed out across the darkening ocean, noted the deep banks of fog lying directly in the *Loire's* path and observed the hundred or so gulls and cormorants in the steamer's wake. A sea bird occasionally settled on the ship's railing, cocked its head and directed its amber eyes at her.

She went to bed early following the evening meal. After lying in her bunk for what seemed like hours listening to Olga Bohmer's moans, she fell into a half-sleep.

She found herself in an almost featureless wilderness, a land of snow and ice with a few wind-tortured trees lost on the plains. She was alone, frightened and strangely exhilarated by the solitude and bleakness of her surroundings. Some great secret lay just out of sight, something she could discover but perhaps at deadly peril. Snow swirled around her, obliterating everything farther than a few feet away and strange shapes seemed to emerge from the swirl.

Suddenly someone appeared out of the whiteness; she recognized the American savage, Long John Emerson. A great wave of gladness swept over her. He spread his arms toward her and she was about to embrace him when she awoke furious with herself but unable to rid her mind of the curiously intense dream-longing.

The days passed tediously for Princess Ludmila Andreiovna as the *Loire* moved east through heavy seas and seemingly endless fogs. Mme. Olga continued to be violently seasick.

When the weather cleared briefly and the sun came out, Ludmila persuaded her governess to come up on deck for some air and was shocked to see that the stout figure had wasted so that her voluminous dress hung loose on her. Olga managed to sip a bit of clear broth and then sat back in her chair, weeping weakly. Ludmila was overcome with remorse; she had neglected her companion, who had, after all, devoted a number of years of her life to the young princess.

Ludmila lost track of the number of days they had been at sea. Sometime after that a violent storm blew up, apparently out of nowhere. Howling winds and sheets of rain intermixed with sleet and snow; high seas heaved the *Loire* about. Captain Mirabeaux ordered all sheets down and the ship steadied.

All passengers were forced to remain below decks, and Mme. Olga's illness returned with renewed force. Confined to the cabin or the dim and stuffy corridors, Ludmila thought she would lose her hold on sanity. At last on the second morning she could stand no more. She borrowed a slicker from one of the guards and climbed to the deck.

Rain and wind struck her in the face with force she had not imagined possible, taking her breath away completely for a moment.

Nikolai, at her elbow, had to shout to make himself heard. "You really must not do this, princess. You must go back below. You may be swept overboard."

Ludmila pushed him away and struggled forward against the wind. She was clinging to a bulkhead when suddenly the *Loire* reared up like a great stallion. She put her hands out, found herself sprawled flat. The next instant the bottom seemed to drop out of the world entirely as the ship came down into a trench between huge waves, the deck tilting wildly. Ludmila felt herself sliding, snatched blindly for something to hold onto. The next instant a vast avalanche of water rolled over her, tumbling her loose from her handhold and washing her up against a railing.

She gasped for air, coughing salt water, and struggled to get to her knees, clinging to the railing with one hand and wiping hair and water from her eyes with the other. The deck was a blur of activity. Sailors rushed frantically, shouting. Where was Nikolai? Ludmila got to her feet, staggered along the railing, fought against the lurching of the deck beneath her.

"She's going to founder."

"Takin' on too much goddam water. Pumps can't handle it."

"*Enfant de Dieu.*"

"Mme. Olga," Ludmila thought, "I have to get her out. We're going to sink. My God, we're going to sink. Olga!"

Her mind did not seem to be working right. She struggled to move along the railing, intent upon the fixed and frantic thought of rescuing her companion, but she realized she had no idea where the cabin might be. Everything was turned around.

Another sheet of water swept over the side of the *Loire* and Ludmila hung on desperately against it, continued moving blindly.

Suddenly Nikolai was beside her once again, holding her and guiding her in a different direction.

"Mme. Bohmer," she shouted, "we must get her out." She struggled to free herself from Ilyich's grasp.

"I will get her, princess, but first you must go over here. Mirabeaux has ordered that the dinghies be lowered."

Ludmila was immensely grateful for the assurance, the sense in Nikolai's words. Nonetheless, she yelled, "Mme. Olga," again, staring urgently into his eyes to make certain he understood.

"Yes, princess," he agreed.

Without noticeable transition someone else was holding her—another of her soldiers, she realized. Nikolai was battling his way back across the deck. The guard placed her bodily into a dinghy that was about to be lowered, even as she struggled against him, still thinking only of the governess. The soldier held her down as if she were a child and she found herself staring stupidly at the streaming black hairs of his mustache. The dinghy began to descend, its guide ropes whipping back and forth and then going taut.

Ludmila saw Nikolai lurch across the deck, half carrying Olga. She waved and called out to them. Just then the *Loire* gently settled sideways and the dinghy took a wild swing upward. It paused high above the ship and the sea and then it crashed back down and splintered against the side of the steamer.

The world dissolved in a dreadful, rending sound, and the next moment Ludmila found herself engulfed in frigid water. Her hands found something large and held it.

Her head came above water. She was clinging to a seat of the dinghy. She drew herself further up onto the wood, gasping as another wave broke over her head. Her heavy skirts dragged at her, but she could not free herself of them without letting go of her float.

All was confusion about her. As she maintained her hold on her unsteady raft she made detached mental notes of everything, but she could make no sense of any of it. Screams rose above the deafening thunder of waves and wind; she thought they were human but could not be sure. Objects bobbed in the heaving water: pieces of wood, dark round shapes that could be human heads.

Surprisingly far away the foundering ship reared against the mists, listing grotesquely. Even as she watched, the *Loire* settled deeper into the ocean.

Another boat dropped over the side; this one rode all the way down. She thought of releasing her hold on her own flotsam to swim to the dinghy, but it was so far away she couldn't even see who was in it.

A deafening noise rendered the roar of wind and water nothing and the *Loire* blossomed with flame and smoke. A portion of the side bulged, ripped away, disintegrated. The next instant a huge wave hurled Ludmila and her plank into the air and crashed down over them.

Water pounded over her. She clung savagely, desperately to the seat. Splinters dug into her hands. She held her breath; there was nothing else she could do. While she waited for her body to demand air and suck in seawater to drown her, she tried kicking but her skirts fouled her legs.

The current threw her up. Blinded and gagging, she still held to her perch. When she was able, she looked back at the wounded steamer. It was much farther away than it had been, and little spurts of flame grew up from place to place. Not more than half the body of the vessel was visible above the ocean. Small figures jumped from the rapidly sinking ship in the last desperate moment.

Ludmila closed her eyes out of weary reflex and began to shiver uncontrollably. Her arms and hands felt like sticks of wood or ice. They no longer seemed to belong to her, but clung with a will of their own, the muscles clenched, the fingers flexed like hooks.

Periodically waves washed over her head, but she hardly noticed. She willed herself to fight off a greater enemy than the water; the cold, which was rapidly sapping her remaining strength.

Her fingers slipped and her nails broke as they scraped over the water-soaked wood. She screamed when she felt her raft slip away from her, felt the water come up around her.

She gasped for air, thought she heard a voice. At first she did not trouble to open her eyes, but at the second call she raised her head, tried to swim, looked around. There was no sign of the *Loire,* although the waves were littered with bits of wood, floating boxes, bottles.

She turned in the other direction, fighting against the drag of her clothing. A dinghy was drawing very near, and the inhabitants were attempting to reach her, calling to her.

The small vessel was only a few feet away and Ludmila made a frantic motion to launch herself toward it even as a voice cried out to her to wait. She made two floundering strokes through the water and felt her heavy skirts dragging her down. Her head sank beneath the surface. A tiny voice inside her own skull whispered, This is where it ends . . . and *it doesn't matter very much after all.*

She felt herself mysteriously drawn up, pulled out of the ocean. A distant pain suggested something tugging at her hair and the next instant she was pulled by the wrists over the side of the dinghy. She looked up briefly, saw the water-darkened sandy beard of Long John Emerson, the American. For a moment she thought she must be in another vivid dream, and then as she thudded against the bottom of the craft all consciousness departed.

When Ludmila awoke it was dark. A strong arm was holding her head over the side of the dinghy and she was vomiting water.

"Calm down, now, princess, you're gonna be all right. Just don't go jumpin' back in the drink. Had enough trouble fishin' you out the first time."

Emerson's grip didn't relax until she did. Finally she turned, sat up in the boat and pushed her wet, fouled hair out of her face.

Ludmila stared at Emerson, decided that she was not hallucinating and glanced at the others in the craft. Their faces were only partly visible in the nearly vanished twilight.

There were Taos Danny and Charley, and slumped against the rear lay Olga Bohmer, only half conscious. Between the seats lay Nikolai Ilyich. He had a large discolored lump on the side of his head, and as she stared more intently at him, Ludmila discerned a thin trickle of blood from his partly open mouth. She turned to the Americans, unable to frame the question she so desperately wanted to ask.

"Found 'em floatin' on a piece of the railing after the damn ship blew," Charley St. Francis explained. "Reckon your maid or whatever she is will pull through."

"And Nikolai?" Ludmila whispered.

"Don't look to me like the big guy's gonna make it," Taos Danny said quietly, shielding his eyes against the wind and rain, which continued unabated.

"Course, Meskins are wrong most of the time," Charley added.

Taos Danny glared at his friend, muttered an obscenity and spat to lee. Wind-whipped spray from the crest of a wave danced across the open dinghy and Mme. Bohmer moaned.

Ludmila began to weep and terrible, gasping sobs ripped at her throat. Emerson's arm tightened around her once again, and she found herself crying against his wet, odorous leather shirt, grateful for human comfort.

"Take your hands off her, you beast," came Mme. Olga's weak, hoarse voice from the rear of the boat. "She is a princess. How dare you fondle her?"

At that Ludmila's sobs turned into giggles and the giggles into uncontrollable laughter.

They drifted all night in the unrelenting storm. Shortly before dawn Lieutenant Nikolai Ilyich died. Ludmila said a prayer and the men lifted the Russian officer's body to the rail and let the form slip into the water. Ludmila began weeping once more.

"He died because he tried to save my life," Madame Olga whispered "He should have saved himself. I am an old woman."

Ludmila hugged her governess. "I should never have

teased him the way I did," she said brokenly. "I think Nikolai was worth twenty of me."

"Could be I've got to reassess my own feelings about the poor bastard," Long John said. "I'm mighty sorry you lost your soldier, princess, even if I did think hard about sticking him a few days back."

The storm was dying away at last, and with full dawn the three men and two women who were still alive found themselves adrift on a featureless sea, still heaving under the first wisps of gliding fog. No one of them felt much like speaking, and they shared the last of the fresh water and munched on a few soggy biscuits Charley St. Francis produced from the pockets of his buckskin jacket.

"Well," Taos Danny said at last, "I reckon we're somewhere. Meanwhile, I got me a pack of cards here in my possibles sack. Not too damned soggy, though it's a wonder. Anybody care to while away the time?"

"If you ladies need to relieve yourselves," Emerson said, not looking at either of them, "me an' the boys'll turn the other way until you're finished. Guess we got to do things proper somehow, even out here."

Olga Bohmer flushed. Ludmila stared fixedly at the single oar that had survived the tempest.

"Just don't stick your tails out too far," Taos grunted. "We all been in the drink enough already."

Chapter 10
Gift from the Sea

The Aleutian Islands curve some twelve hundred miles from the Alaska Peninsula southwest and then a little northwest toward the Kamchatka Peninsula. They benefit enormously from the warm Kamchatka Current, which flows up the coast of Asia and saves the archipelago from total barrenness. The price of life-sustaining warmth is eternal fog, formed minute by minute as warm water meets arctic air; nothing in the Aleutians is ever really dry.

The islands are members of the Aleutian Range; their peaks separate the Bering Sea from the Pacific Ocean and nearly link North America to Asia. Many are active volcanoes; many more sleep only fitfully.

Steam drifts from the cone of Shihaldin on Unimak Island. Fog drifts ceaselessly across the grey-green water of the Fox Islands, the Andreanof Islands, the Rat Islands, the Near Islands.

Thickly scattered reefs are a major danger to navigation. Many of the islands are not inhabited, though a few Aleut villages have stood for a very long time. These peoples were discovered by Alexei Chirikov and Vitus Bering in the year 1741.

The lands bore gulls and cormorants, walruses, fur seals and sea lions. The few trees, all stunted growth, punctuated abundant grasses.

Aleut men in garments of waterproof gutskin used kayaks to travel the seas, navigating by the stars and using a primitive compass. Their poisoned harpoons arced in the salt twilight as the men hunted the great whales.

Their women loved bright colors and especially favored seal-lion-gut clothing trimmed with bits of fur, dyed sealskin and feathers and long-visored hats, delicately carved and painted and decorated with sea-lion whiskers and bits of ivory.

Enslaved by the fur-traders, slain at random, they diminished in numbers and their culture died.

April–May 1867

The dinghy rose and fell as endless fog formed in the wake of the storm. The vapors coiled across the waters like creatures of dream, taking momentary shapes or near-shapes and then dissipating in the steady wind.

Long John Emerson squinted at his companions. Taos and Charley huddled together on one side of the small craft, the princess and her nanny opposite in an almost identical posture; altogether they looked like a set of bookends.

The third night was ending. A low suffusion of silver light began to penetrate the mists.

Hungry, Emerson thought, *more thirsty than hungry. A man can put up without grub for a time, but water's a different matter. The little gal—we'll be settin' her adrift pretty soon, I'm afraid. By God, it's a bitch-kitty, a cave an' no way out. Nothing to do but* esnaih, *as the Ingaliks say, just keep movin' till we cain't.*

Beaver-Man's thirsty and he says to himself, "What am I goin' to do? Guess I better make some water so we can all take a drink."

Emerson's thoughts turned to Red Porcupine. The Tagish chief once found him exhausted and half-frozen on the Pelly

River, fifty miles up from Fort Selkirk, without a chance in hell of making it to safety. Emerson lay in the snow feeling strangely warm and freezing to death. Several hours later Red Porcupine found him, warmed him, fed him and took him back to the Tagish village, where he remained until the spring thaws.

Now Emerson spoke aloud. "You crazy old witch doctor, where the hell are you? Don't think you're going to pull Long John out of this scrape. Guess I won't be marryin' that daughter of yours when she grows up after all. Kate, child, you're goin' to have to find yourself another gringo trapper, I guess."

The light was gaining rapidly now. Emerson, his hand shading his eyes, stared out into the fog and shook his head.

"Amigo," Taos Danny muttered, "have we reached Seattle yet?"

"Not yet, compadre. And if we had, a man wouldn't know it."

"Didn't think so." Taos stirred and woke Charley St. Francis in the process.

"Cain't let a man sleep, you damned Meskin?" St. Francis growled.

"You call me that again, I cut your heart out. I never been to Mexico in my life."

"So you've said once or twice," St. Francis grinned. He was weak though, and he dozed off again.

Suddenly Emerson's shade hand stiffened. He was the last man to kindle false hopes, but the furthest, foggiest swell on the horizon seem not to heave. He knew better than to stare directly at a distant object he wanted to see; he shifted his eyes around and around the vague grey-blue shadow. The more he tried to make it go away the more it stayed.

In spite of everything he hoped a little. He stopped

preparing himself for death and sat up a little straighter, squinted a little to test if the shape would stay for steady eyes. It did; he nearly whooped for joy.

It was too soon to celebrate, of course; land in sight was a far cry from land underfoot, but Emerson was already working out whether they would get there. He felt the wind, eyed the waves, listened for shore birds. His heart rose a little further.

The change in him was remarkable. Five minutes ago he had been lolling in the stern, elbow on the gunwale, head resting on an indifferent hand, legs stretched before him and crossed at the ankles. Now he sat forward; his feet were planted on the bottom of the boat, his knees at shoulder height and his hand formed a plane over his brow, the thumb at a strict right angle. His back was rigid, his head cocked, his look eager.

"What is it?" Ludmila demanded. "Have we found land?"

Emerson nodded. "Land of some sort or another, ladies an' gentlemen. Look—look straight ahead."

"Goddamn, I knew it," Taos laughed. "You boys don't have enough Injun in you. Johnny, the Raven's gonna let us die on land."

"If he don't drown us on the way in. It's not just some rocks, mates, there's a whole island attached, even some wind-blasted trees. Seattle or not, it's by God beautiful. All of you now, hang on to your ass with one hand and the scow with the other. Pardon me, ladies, but I don't think we're goin' to be able to just float on in—damned waves are hittin' the rocks pretty hard. Charley, best you grab hold of Ludmila—an' Taos, you grab Miz Olga."

"Hang on, you old biddy," Taos laughed. "Charley's always had the good luck, an' me, I get the leavin's."

He squeezed one of Mme. Bohmer's breasts, laughed again and ducked as she slapped at him.

"Capsize us here and we're all dead," Emerson shouted. "Hang on, you blue-nosed fools."

The rocky beach was much closer now, and the next wave lifted the little craft, spun it about and set it hurtling down the face of shining water. Its crest curled in on them and half-filled the craft with bilge.

Olga screamed and Taos gave a war whoop. Ludmila pressed her face to St. Francis' chest and held to him. Taken unawares, Emerson lunged for a grip, fell and clung to the plank seat. The rushing water momentarily submerged him.

The dinghy wallowed in a trough between waves, turned sideways to the next rushing wall of water, tilted to one side and capsized. Emerson fought for the surface, sucked air and shouted, "Swim! Goddamn the lot of you, swim for it!"

Another wave hit them and sent the dinghy spinning away from all the grasping hands. Ludmila, her mind strangely calm, saw the black face of death before her. No, it was a rock, and the water was pinning her against it. Then an arm grasped her waist, pulled her sideways and shoreward.

She felt solid land beneath her feet and then another wave poured over her. She fought to free herself not only from the water but also from the hard masculine arm that was locked about her. She sucked water, gagged, coughed and gasped for air.

"Hang on," a male voice commanded. "Damn you, don't kick me." Emerson's arm spun her and sent her reeling forward so that she went to her hands and knees. The water and foam rushed past her; pebbles of the beach scraped her knees and half-numb hands.

"This one is trying to drown me," Taos Danny shouted. "Dammit, Long John, give me a hand!"

Emerson plunged back into the sea. He grabbed the

governess by one arm and the two men dragged her up the beach.

"Where's Charley?" Emerson demanded.

"Damn fool must've gone under. I didn't see him after the boat went over."

"Where's the dinghy?" Emerson scanned the foggy beach, saw the form of the overturned boat. Charley St. Francis rose beside it bent at the middle and painfully rejected a great deal of sea water. Then Danny was at his side and put his arms around the larger man. The two of them stumbled drunkenly up onto the shingle away from the hissing yellow foam.

The little island rose like a dark tooth. Heaps of fractured stone lay jumbled above a bench where grass was profusely speckled with small blue flowers. A line of wind-blasted spruces grew along one rim; the land was so far devoid of other life. Soggy brown grass lay in mats between clumps of green. "Got to get a fire going now," Emerson said. "Let's see what we come through with."

He unstrapped his possibles sack, untied it and withdrew some watersoaked twists of tobacco, a number of lead balls, a Haley's patent fire-striker and a canister of black powder. He prized off the canister's top, pinched wet powder between thumb and forefinger. "Check yours," he nodded to his partners.

"Same here," Taos said.

Charley St. Francis grinned, coughed for perhaps the hundredth time and scratched at his damp beard. "My powder's dry, boys. Send the squaws up to get firewood."

Mme. Bohmer voiced momentary indignation, realized St. Francis was chuckling and relaxed.

"What do you want me to do?" Ludmila asked. "I'll go cut wood—just give me a blade."

Emerson motioned for her to sit back down.

"Hell," Taos Danny grunted, "I'll be the squaw—

but just for wood-cuttin'. You hear me right, St. Francis?" With that the Irish-Shoshone half-breed scrambled up over the boulders toward the line of trees, broke off several dead limbs and slung them back down to the beach.

Emerson examined the silver-grey wood, picked up a section, scraped the lichens away and began to carve long slivers into a pile. Charley examined each of them, now placing one aside, now another.

Taos made his way back down, stood watching. "Who has to sleep with Olga tonight?" he asked.

Mme. Bohmer hissed indignantly and looked away.

"Keep your Meskin mind on important matters," St. Francis said.

Emerson squinted at his two partners, glanced at Mme. Bohmer and Ludmila, shook his head. "Damned striker's too wet," he said. "Cain't get a damned spark."

"Keep at it," St. Francis shrugged, arranging the slivers of wood and sprinkling powder next to them.

At length the magic of flint and steel began to work and the gunpowder started to sizzle and flare up, igniting the carvings. A small flame darted, threatened to go out and then rose once more. The men huddled over it, using their bodies to shield the flame against a sudden gust of air, feeding more slivers to the small but growing blaze.

"We got 'er, Johnny," Taos laughed. "By God, we got us a fire. We may die of thirst an' empty stomachs, but by heaven we're goin' to go out warm."

Emerson broke sections of deadwood over his knee and criss-crossed them into a small box-shaped structure about the gaining flames. Then that caught too, and sap began to ooze and bubble along the weathered cracks and seams.

"Olga and Ludmila," he said, "get over here. We'll get you two dried out a bit first. Charley, you stay here with the ladies. Danny and I'll go see if we can find us a spring—rainwater caught in a rock basin—anything drinkable. Get that taken care of, and maybe we can find some clams or mussels or something. We'll eat crickets and worms if we have to. Folks, I've thought the matter over. Not sure how, but we're goin' to make it some way."

"Figure there's worms out here on North America's big toe?" Taos Danny asked.

Emerson and Danny found an ooze on the grassy slope beyond the line of twisted spruces, dug out a hollow in the black, grainy soil and watched intently as the water accumulated. One after the other they greedily drank the muddy water. Then, with a bit of ingenuity, they coaxed a quart or more into Long John's empty possibles sack.

"She's leakin' a mite," Danny observed. "I told ye to use more bear grease on 'er."

"Fill yours, damnit. I'll get this one back down to the others."

"Should have built the fire up here—"

But Emerson was already gone, loping away downslope, the water bag in his fist. Minutes later Danny's sack was also bulging with fluid, and he too jogged off toward the thin line of smoke that was barely visible in the fog.

The women drank first. Mme. Bohmer closed her eyes but did not otherwise protest at the muddy liquid. Then she pulled Ludmila back to the fire and huddled next to it.

Emerson turned and started back toward the spring on the hillside above. He stopped again when Ludmila asked, "How long can we survive here, Mr. Emerson? Tell me the truth now, is there any chance of anyone finding us?"

Long John turned back toward the sable-haired young woman with the penetrating dark eyes. He shrugged and gestured with his palms up. "The truth?"

"Please, Mr. Emerson."

"The truth, then," he answered. "Little lady, I'd say we've got just about the chance of a snowball in hell. On the other hand, there's something I learned a long while back. You play the cards that Raven Man gives you and you don't quit playing until Blackbird calls in the chips. We're still alive and our feet are on more or less dry ground. We got mud to drink an' a fire to stand next to. With luck we'll find shellfish or some damned thing to eat. In other words—"

"In other words, the Blackbird, as you call it, hasn't called in all the chips yet. Do I understand you correctly?"

"That you do, pretty one. That's it exactly."

Taos began laughing. The rest all turned to stare at him. "Weak in the head," St. Francis shrugged.

"I was thinkin'," Danny managed between spasms of laughter, "that we could kill Olga and eat her. We could eat for a month. Dibs on her left titty."

The governess looked horrified, half certain Danny was serious.

"Sure ain't enough on your skinny bones," St. Francis said, running his tongue over his teeth and spitting.

The tide dropped, exposing considerably more of the gravel-strewn beach, and Emerson dragged the dinghy some yards back onto the littoral, beyond the high-water mark. Cold fog was blowing in from the south, and already the mists were beginning to take on the crimson of the lengthening northern twilight.

His prized Freeman .44 freshly loaded with dry powder from Charley's canister, Long John set out hunting. He had no hope of finding deer or even rabbits, for it was common knowledge in the north country that there was no animal life on the Aleutian Islands, where Emerson presumed they were. But with luck, he supposed, he would happen on a seal or sea lion—perhaps even a walrus. The .44, heavily loaded, could take down a grizzly with three or four rounds; in all likelihood it would handle a walrus as well.

It was nearly time for the sea mammals to return to their rookeries to bear young and to mate again.

Emerson stalked the water, his eye keen for the slightest motion, his ear tuned for telltale barking and bellowing. All he found were the gulls and cormorants and a cluster of pelicans perched on a reef a hundred yards out and oblivious to any danger from the single human.

Within an hour he had managed to encircle the small island without luck. He met Charley near the dinghy, made an open-handed gesture of futility. The others were still huddled about the fire, the women side by side and Taos Danny sprawled out, hugging the ground and apparently sleeping.

"Mussels," Charley said. "I've gathered some—it's not much, but better than stewed grass, I reckon."

"Some tide pools down that way." Long John pointed. "Maybe we ought to take a look in them."

The efforts of a few minutes netted the two men a pair of big Dungeness crabs, though not until after Long John and Charley managed to soak themselves to the waist once again.

"Bastard damn near took my thumb off," Charley growled, cracking the crab's shell with a stone.

Bubbles appeared in the pebble-strewn mud of the beach.

"Clams, goddamn it," Emerson chortled. "Charles, we've spent too much of our lives inland. That's what they are, sure as hell. Start diggin', old friend."

They drew their knives and began to plunge them into the mud wherever the bubbles appeared, but not until his sixth attempt did St. Francis give a victory whoop. "Got one!" he yelled.

"Damn things dig faster than we do," Emerson complained. "You must have caught an old fellow."

They continued their labors, more intent now, and by

the time the light had grown too dim to discern the bubbles, they had collected nearly a dozen of the big clams.

"Don't suppose we've got us some pearls to boot, do you, John?"

"Not unless our friends here have picked up oyster habits."

Charley pried open a clam, cut the meat out with his knife and thrust the whole morsel into his mouth. "Damn things have sand in their gizzards. You suppose they'll taste better if we roast 'em?"

"You'd gripe if you were hung with a new rope," Long John mumbled, prying open a clam of his own and following St. Francis' procedure.

"Chow's chow when a coon's starvin' to death," Charley nodded. "Don't suppose these bastards are poison, do you?"

"What difference? Let's get on back and poison the rest. If we're goin' to die of the ptomaine, we might as well have company."

The meal of shellfish was eaten down to the last chewable shred. Danny hauled down a deadfall spruce half his own size, with Taos stumbling and cursing his way through the darkness; down the scree at the foot of the rim, where the twisted spruces clung to the earth, Emerson fashioned a bank log, packing damp earth over a portion of it to slow the flames. Thereafter the two women and finally the three men, lying as close to the fire as possible and doing their best to ignore the cold, wind-blown fog, fell into deep and welcome sleep.

With first light Ludmila awoke. One side of her body, not having the warmth of Olga's back, was nearly numb with the damp cold. She rose, moved closer to the remains of the fire and began to feed it, but with little success.

Emerson rose, squatted silently beside her and used his knife to dig up some glowing coals. He nudged

Ludmila's framework of sticks onto the hot spot and blew gently until a small flame appeared.

Within a few moments the fire was dancing happily. "Where's the coffee pot?" Emerson asked.

Ludmila squinted at him and for a moment wondered if the American were fully awake.

"Be good to have some right now, wouldn't it?" Emerson persisted. "Or are Russian princesses allowed to drink coffee? Maybe we could brew some spruce-bark tea in the clamshells. You want to try it, ma'am?"

Taos Danny moved in his sleep, cursed under his breath, and then began to snore.

Ludmila smiled, glanced toward the beach, noted the thin crimson glitter of water over the mud. "Look," she said. "There's an animal of some kind."

"My God," Emerson laughed, "old Raven Man has sent us a present—a fur seal, sure as hell. Dead, an' the tide washed him up. Tell you what, princess, if he's not too far gone maybe we've got us some steaks. Let's go take a look."

At the water's edge Ludmila and Long John stood staring at the creature. The big body was still slick with water, lying on its side. "It's dead?"

"Yep, but not for long. Maybe even seals drown sometimes, I don't know. We're goin' to have honest-to-God meat for a while, anyhow. An' the hide'll make us a blanket maybe—maybe even a sail for our schooner. I'm thinkin' we might find a way off this rockpile yet."

Ludmila watched as Long John drew his knife and began to butcher the seal. She was slightly repelled by the opening of the paunch and the withdrawing of the entrails and the strange, wild, but not altogether offensive odor of the viscera.

Emerson cut out the liver. Ludmila was horrified to see him hold it up, wink and take a bite of it. "Good," he said, "damned good. Here, princess."

She shook her head. "Shouldn't you cook it first?"

"Maybe, but civilized folk cook their meat too damned much—that's what the Injuns an' Eskimos tell me. That's how come your Russki sailors get scurvy; don't like raw meat. Injuns don't get 'er, an' they eat nothing but meat all winter. Never heard of limes an' such."

Ludmila was doubtful, said nothing, continued to watch as Long John Emerson proceeded to skin the seal. He cut away the blubber and placed squares and oblongs of it to one side next to the intestines and stomach, whose contents he had squeezed out.

"Moose and elk intestines are tasty as hell," he remarked. "A real delicacy among the Tagish. Roast 'em on the coals, or else they stuff 'em with meat an' berries an' whatnot."

"Sausage," Ludmila nodded, "of course."

"If enough live seals come in to visit us, princess, we can take enough meat to get us through the whole damned winter, most likely. We'll build us a lodge of some kind, an' by God we'll just set up our own kingdom. Could be Raven Man's decided to give us another chance. Hell, you an' Charley could get married proper an' raise us some little ones. We'll form us a new tribe. I suppose your nanny's past breedin' age, ain't she?"

"You're being vulgar, Mr. Emerson . . ." Ludmila said austerely. "Surely a ship will pass by, we must be right in the sea lane. If we keep a big fire going, someone will see the smoke and rescue us."

"Never did believe in the Tooth Fairy," Emerson grunted.

He rolled the seal carcass over. "Ain't never butchered a seal before, but the devil's not much different than a deer or a hog, when you get right down to it—nor a man neither. Grab hold of some of that meat, ma'am. We got to get everything up away from the water. We'll set up some dryin' racks. Cain't waste nothin', got to use tongue, bone marrow, brains, all of 'im. One way or another we'll keep body an' soul together, for a spell, anyhow."

Another indeterminate passage of time was marked only by discernible lengthening of the period of daylight. The sun rose higher in the northeast, swinging to meridian, and then drew around in a great arc and disappeared high in the northwest quadrant.

Three men and two women worked their way along the beaches between outcroppings of rock, searching the tide pools and muds. The hide of a fur seal, scraped clean and stretched taut over a trench between lava boulders, made separate quarters of sorts for the women but scant protection from the chill mists and occasional downpours.

A fire perpetually blazed at the foot of an overhang of stone; each day its feed had to be dragged in from farther away.

Taos Danny, sucking on a crab's leg, casually suggested that Mme. Olga be killed and her clothing used as a sail for the dinghy so that the rest might drift down to Seattle.

Olga, growing used to the banter, made a formal request to borrow Long John's knife so that she might breakfast on her antagonist's manhood. All laughed uproariously, including Taos, who then proposed that Mme. Bohmer should marry him, inasmuch as he believed she would be most comfortable to sleep on.

On the first clear day Emerson climbed to the island's high crest, a volcanic cinder cone, eroded and trenched. The tall man standing atop the only world he possessed gazed in all directions, but he saw no vessels on the broad glittering ocean. There was, however, another island to the east, a considerable peak rising through the haze. Its crown was tipped with snow.

* * *

Ludmila met him on his way down, at the upper reach of the sloping meadows beyond the line of stunted spruces. He saw her and came loping down the last few yards.

"Island to the east," he grinned, "a fairly good-sized one—twenty-five miles long, from the looks of it—however you Russians calculate distance. Anyway, a big island. Maybe it has a village. I think we can make it there. Charley's got that new oar carved now, and we can rig something, fit our seal hide up for a sail."

"Land?" Ludmila asked. "How far is it . . . John? Do we really have a chance to make it?"

"Seventy-five miles off, maybe a hundred, maybe a little farther. With wind from the west and two men rowing—by God, yes, we'll make it, ma'am."

Ludmila laughed, delighted with the news and impulsively flung herself into Emerson's arms. At first the surprised trapper, uncertain what to do, touched only his fingers to her back, feeling awkward, uneasy. Ludmila held fast to him, pressed her head against his chest.

He lifted her with both hands, spun her easily and placed her back on her feet.

Her eyes gleamed staring into his. Her lips parted slightly. A strand of dark hair trailed over her nose.

He touched the strand, then ran the tips of his fingers over her face. And she did not draw away.

"Ludmila," he said, finding it suddenly very difficult to speak at all. "Princess Ludmila, ma'am, I sure would like to kiss you."

"Do it, then," she answered—but didn't wait, grabbed hold of his beard and pulled his face to hers. You great hulking clod of a savage, can't you tell I want you, that I have chosen you—yes, chosen you. Take me just as the bear takes his woman, growling and snarling and biting. I am crazy to have your mouth pressed to mine, to have your hands upon me, to have you hurl me down on this godforsaken island.

You are all but indifferent to me; you ignore my presence. I thought I had power over all men, and I will have power over you too, John Emerson.

I am acting crazy, I cannot control my mind, my emotions. I do not know what is happening to me—it is a burning. John Emerson, help me, please know what to do. I do not know—but I do not want to die without knowing. I am all on fire and I do not know what to do next. . . .

She could feel his manhood pressing against her. He was lifting her, carrying her. The smell of dew-wet grass, the smell of salt air, the soft sensation of the wind rising from below caressed her.

His lips were at her throat; his big hands squeezed her breasts. The nipples tingled beneath her clothing. It was difficult to breathe.

Her skirts were pushed up, her legs spread against damp grass, scratching her calves and thighs.

Please help me, even if there is pain I must have it. Pressing into me, sacred Jesus, go slowly, slowly. He is into me, oh—not all the way yet? John, John, what is happening to me, you cover me like an eagle with beating wings, I cannot breathe, I feel it coming, soon, soon, quickly, quickly now because I cannot stand it any longer, give me your seed, give me. . . .

They lay together quietly for a time, and finally Emerson pushed himself up, took his weight from her. She sucked in deeply, her mouth wide open, her eyes still closed.

"Ludmila," he said, his voice near to stuttering, "I . . . princess, I didn't mean . . . did I hurt you, Ludmila?"

"I am not hurt," she whispered.

"I'm sorry, little one, my God but this child's sorry. I never meant for it to happen, I swear it—"

"It is not your fault." Ludmila opened her eyes and

stared up at him. "I could not stand to die without— Do you understand me, John . . . Emerson?"

"I guess so, ma'am. Me neither. I've wanted you ever since I saw you the first time, wanted you bad, but I never meant to do it. You're a princess and another man's woman. An' I never had the right even to think about— It's like your friend Nikolai read my mind that day an' saw me for what I am, ignorant an' a damn barbarian. I never meant to hurt you, Ludmila. Please don't hate me, I mean that."

She sat up, smiling foolishly and knowing it. "Hate you?" she laughed. "You have been my teacher, Emerson. How could I hate you for that? But we must never allow this to happen again, not even if we both should wish it."

Chapter 11
East to Nova Archangelisk

Cold fog hung low to the steel-grey waters that day in August 1728. Vitus Bering, a Dane who sailed for the Russians under Peter the Great, nosed his ship northward and passed between what is now called Seward Peninsula and the easternmost tip of Asia, but he could see nothing more than two small islands; even then he did not know with certainty that Asia and America were not a single vast continent.

Thirteen years passed before Bering was able to confirm his surmise. Explorations along the coast of Kamchatka, the Sea of Okhotsk and northern Siberia occupied the intervening period.

In 1741 he sailed from Petropavlovsk along the Aleutian Islands and the Alaska Peninsula until he sighted the outline of a snow-mantled giant against the north. This was not Denali, the great one he had heard of in Eskimo legend, but another, Mount Saint Elias, a huge presence fronting the ocean.

On July twenty-ninth he landed on a cape below the glacier that now bears his name, then removed to Kayak Island to prepare for his return to Kamchatka.

A sea, a strait, a glacier and finally an uninhabited island were eventually named after him. His storm-driven vessel, the *St. Peter*, was wrecked on the island and there Bering died a month later.

His men built a new vessel and in good spirits returned to their home port with a cargo of furs trapped on the island, a hundred thousand dollars' worth in all.

May–June 1867.

They had exhausted the clam beds near their campsite, and so Long John, in search of a new food supply, made his way around the island's tip to a series of mud and rock beaches he had earlier noted as being promising. The tide was on its way out; as Emerson strode along the shore, the telltale bubbles seemed to be rising everywhere.

He stripped off his buckskin jacket and shirt, made note of the pale whiteness of his skin after the long winter on Kamachatka and the chill mists here on the island. This day the sky was clear and light sparkled in the gently undulating waves out beyond the last jagged reef. He decided to take advantage of the warmth.

"One of the things this island's got is no damned mosquitoes," he mumbled. In summer literally clouds of them hung above the marshes along the Yukon River, above the long, wide muskeg basin the trappers called Yukon Flats.

Emerson got down on his knees, knife in hand, and began to dig. The first eluded him, but then his luck improved and within an hour he'd accumulated a full three dozen big clams.

With shirt and jacket as bundles, the arms knotted securely, Long John made his way back toward camp, sometimes through the shallows at the base of cliff rocks and sometimes over shelves of eroded lava. From a rim he stared down at the hidden inlet where the women sometimes went to bathe.

The princess was frisking along the water's edge,

now dashing forward a few steps, now slowing to a walk once more.

"Beautiful," he whispered.

She was naked as a jaybird, her long dark hair down over her shoulders. Light seemed to shine from the whiteness of her thin legs and arms, her slightly jiggling buttocks.

"If this don't beat all," he murmured. "Like a damned goddess come up out of the ocean."

Cormorants drifted in the air above and behind her, wheeling as Ludmila reached the boulder-strewn limit of the beach and turned about. She came walking back, her small, shapely breasts moving slightly with each step she took. The motion was hardly discernible from where Emerson crouched.

"If this don't beat all," he repeated. He could feel the intoxication of desire begin to run through his veins.

"Maybe I'd best just head on back to camp," he thought; without question that was what intended to do when he rose to his feet.

Instead he called out her name and held up the two bundles he was carrying. "Clams for dinner," he shouted.

For a moment she was motionless, her eyes searching the rim. Then she saw him, ran and slithered into the water.

Long John stood there feeling awkward and foolish, uncertain what to do next.

"You've been spying on me," she cried out from the shield of the water.

He could think of no answer.

"Come down," she said. "I want you to swim out to the reef with me. There's a pole jammed between the rocks. We can make a mast of it for the dinghy."

Emerson squinted out at the reef and saw what she was talking about. Since the idea almost made sense, he shrugged and climbed down to the sand.

"Come on, then," she shouted, her voice rich with challenge.

Bewildered, Long John sat down on the sand, pulled off his Russian-issue high-topped boots and wet wool socks, felt the sand beneath his feet. He rose, uncertain what to do next, and then walked slowly toward the water.

"Not fair," Ludmila objected. "Take off your trousers too, so we're equal."

"Don't seem right, ma'am," Emerson called back.

"You've seen me. Now I want to see you, that's all."

Emerson's breath was coming short and he was getting an erection. "That's what you want, Ludmila?"

"Yes. Hurry now. Together we can get the mast for our dinghy so that we can sail to that island of yours."

Still Long John hesitated, tried to will his erection away, was unsuccessful. He turned from her, slipped off his leather trousers and ran for the water, fully hard and bobbing as he moved.

He splashed hard into the cold water and was pleased to go soft on contact with it.

He swam toward her, tossing his wet hair back out of his eyes, and gave a whoop. "All right," he said, a few feet from her. "You sure you can swim good enough? She's fifty yards or more out there."

"I'll race you, John Emerson," she laughed. Like quicksilver she slipped beneath the water and darted forward like a dolphin. Surfacing, she began to stroke toward the reef, her face in the water.

Emerson, proud of his skill at swimming, drove along after her, head up, but was surprised to discover that catching her was no easy matter. Male pride was on the line, however, and a few yards short of the reef he drew up behind her, grasped her ankle and pulled. He surged ahead to touch the mast and was astonished. A furious windmill of limbs hauled up next to him and fought the race to a draw.

"Here," he laughed, "let me give you a hand."

"Don't touch me," she snarled. "I'd have beaten you except that you cheated. I'll stay in the water. You climb up and get the pole."

A wave of modesty came over him and for a moment he remained waist-deep in the sea, clinging to a ledge with one hand. Ludmila gave him a bright, steady stare. "You're stronger," she pointed out.

"Up to you, I guess," he grunted. He pulled himself from the water and scrambled on hands and knees to the cleft and the ten-foot-long nearly straight sapling that was lodged in it. He ignored her, knowing she was watching him intently, and within a few moments he dislodged the wooden shaft and hurled it into the water. Then he dived, surfaced, shook the water out of his hair, ran his hand over his eyes and forehead.

"You're strong," Ludmila admitted. "I tried to get it loose earlier and couldn't do it."

"You come out here by yourself?"

"Of course. Fifty yards is nothing. I wished to see you and to win a race, though. I learned in the Sea of Azov, of which my family owns a portion. I can easily swim a mile if the water is warm, which this is not." She shivered. "Let's go back now. We'll take turns pushing the log ahead of us." She struck out shoreward.

At the beach Ludmila said, "You go ahead, John Emerson. I'll stay here while you get dressed."

Emerson didn't question her command. He was getting cold, little as he wished to admit it. He strode from the water, the spruce pole in his arms, and tossed it onto the sand. Then he moved quickly, shivering somewhat, toward the spot where his boots stood beside his scrupulously folded leathers.

Before he reached them Ludmila was beside him, too tempting . . .

They embraced; their mouths joined, their bodies, slippery and chilled, pressed together. Without a word they were lying together on the warm sand, kissing and shivering. Her hands glided over his back and down to his hips; his fingers tangled in her wet hair.

Ludmila felt him growing hard against her. She hesitated and then reached down to touch his maleness.

He groaned, whispered, "Oh, princess, sweeting, my God how I want you."

The princess turned onto her back, her eyes closed to the orange-red glow of the sun. She guided him into her, heard herself making a strange little animal quaver as he moved his hips forward.

Now I have known it twice; he is surely mine. How can I ever let go of him?

When it was over his body shuddered and he gasped for breath. She felt wonderfully used, and yet she was capable of much more. She had not wanted him to stop, had been almost ready to explode, but the burst and the surge had no chance to come. Finally her own tide ebbed, the glorious sensations abating only slowly. Then when she was calm the name Dobshansky formed in her mind.

At Ludmila's insistence they returned to camp separately. "You don't know what a time I had getting away from Olga in the first place. I was getting crazy, having her breathe on my neck all the time." The princess laughed shakily. "I guess we both know what she's scared of, don't we? And she's so right, of course. Still, if she didn't badger me so much I would never have sneaked off in the first place."

Emerson went first with his clams, and the princess followed half an hour later. Taos and Charley had just returned with firewood when Long John appeared swinging his bundles. The sleeves were joined so that he could sling the makeshift sacks around his neck, drag the pole and still have a hand free for balance and the unexpected.

He was whistling and he chuckled again and again at his friends' account of the difficulties of bringing fuel from so far off.

"Why cain't we move the damned camp, that's what I'd like to know," Taos grumbled.

"Ain't no point, that's why," Long John said mildly.

"There damned sure is a point," Charley insisted. "Else you haul in the kindlin' tomorrow, and by God we'll go dig up the clams."

Emerson chuckled again and shook his head.

"Does anyone happen to know where Princess Ludmila is?" Olga Bohmer asked. "She's been gone for a long while, not that any of you is interested in anything but himself. What if she's been killed by a bear?"

"Won't need to bury 'er, then," Taos Danny said.

"Ain't no bear on the island, ma'am, else we'd have eaten him awhile back." Long John looked bored.

"Are you quite certain of that, young man?"

"Problem with you, madame," Taos growled, squinting at her, "is that you're just plain iggerant. If they was bears, they'da come in by now an' eaten your titties. That's what these here polar bears love best in the world, for a fact."

"Vulgar savages," Olga scowled. "If none of you is man enough to go searching for the princess, then I'm going to go by myself."

"No need," Emerson said, untying his bundles. He used his knife to scoop out a hollow in the sand beside the embers, then placed the clams in his cooking pit. "Ludmila . . . the princess'll be in shortly. If not, then I'll go rescue her from the polar bears—give you my word on it." Again he chuckled. His weathered face split into a grin and Taos and Charley exchanged glances.

"Don't you realize it's your duty to see to her safety?"

"By God, she's right," Danny laughed. "There's a new law in Utah Territory what says so. But first we ought to give you what you're astin' for, Mrs. Olga, that's what I think."

'And what would that be?"

Taos winked at her, licked his lips and turned to spit. "It's a known fact that mares need breedin', an' the older ones need it more than the younger. So me an' Charley agreed that he'd stick you in the front, an' I'd stick you in the tail. But then ye'd probly start yippin' an' carrying on, so maybe Johnny here could stick ye in the mouth at the same time. That'd about solve the problem, I reckon."

Despite themselves Emerson and St. Francis began to roar with laughter. Olga, beet red with indignation, abruptly turned away from the trappers and strode briskly off to the sealskin-covered women's quarters.

Emerson shook his head and wiped his eyes. "Weren't no real need to say that, Dan. Seems like she's honest to God worried about Ludmila—the leetle gal's been her whole life for quite a few years, as I gather. Besides, this whole thing's been a mite out of her range of experience, so to say. I know Miz Bohmer's a trial, but—"

"Kinda out of our range of experience too, I'd say." St. Francis shrugged and broke sections of deadwood over a rock before he added them to the fire.

"Din't mean nothing," Taos said. "Truth is, lads, I wouldn't mind beddin' the old gal. Guess I been away from squaws an' she-bears too long. Damned if Olga ain't got a nice pair of tits on 'er anyway. A mite long in the tooth, but hell, that don't mean nothin'."

The conversaion ended abruptly as Princess Ludmila walked into camp.

Directly after the evening meal Mme. Bohmer complained of a headache and returned to the women's quarters to lie down. The trappers smoked a pipeful of their soggy, salty tobacco, passing the pipe around and agreeing, as they did every night, that it was likely a tad better than dried seaweed—only a tad, mind you. Emerson even offered Ludmila a puff, but the princess declined. Their eyes met for a long moment before she turned to stare at the stretched sealhide covering, beneath which her chaperone was probably already asleep.

The meeting of eyes did not go unnoticed by Taos and Charley, both of whom felt suddenly uneasy, as though they had inadvertently intruded on something.

"I'd best go now," Ludmila said, her voice half a whisper.

She rose and marched away from the fire through the gradually reddening May twilight to the makeshift shelter.

Olga was not asleep; on the contrary, she was weeping again, as she had not done for a number of days.

"What's wrong?" Ludmila knelt beside her governess.

"Les américains," the companion sobbed. "My dearest, those men are beyond redemption. What terrible sin has one of us committed that we should be trapped here with them? Oh, how I wish we had never left Rostov. Ludmila, even if God somehow helps us to leave here and find our way to Nova Archangelisk, how do you know that your Count Dobshansky is not one of them? Of course he's of good blood, educated, highly regarded by the czar, but it's also true that he's lived in this forsaken land for a long time. This emptiness, this wildness, it's inhuman, no place for a gentle noblewoman. Oh, my dear, why could not you have encouraged Valery Vladimir? Not rich, not very old . . . Or Ilya Pansky? Very rich, very old . . ."

"Calm yourself, Olga," Ludmila commanded. "Perhaps the Lord is testing us. Perhaps everything will turn out well for us. John and I found a mast for the dinghy today—"

Mme. Bohmer's head came up. "You and John Emerson. He was with you today?"

Ludmila flushed violently. Turning to stare out toward the sea . . . she hoped that the rose of twilight masked her embarrassment. "Yes," she babbled, "I saw a pole out on the reef, and so I went to fetch him where he was digging for clams. When I told him what I had found, he came immediately and swam out to get it. Now we will be able to fit up a sail for our boat and make our way to the next island. You remember, he told us he saw another island that day when he climbed to the top of this one. He hopes for a village over there. If not, at least it's more likely someone will stop to take on firewood or hunt for seals. This is their mating season and—"

"He did not try to touch you, did he, Ludmila?"

"Of course not, Olga. Why must you always think the worst of everyone? J—Mr. Emerson has always behaved toward me like a perfect gentleman."

Olga sobbed again for a moment, then cleared her throat. "You should have heard what that Danny one said to me tonight before you got back. I dare not even repeat it."

Ludmila lay rigid in the grey semi-darkness, unable to sleep. Soon, she thought, it would be fully dark, and then perhaps . . .

The episode at the hidden cove played itself over and over in her mind. The image of John Emerson, splendidly naked, wet and gleaming as he strode ahead of her through the sunlight, would not leave her, nor would the hot sweet frustrating union that followed.

Chill, misty air soughed up from the beach. Mme. Bohmer next to her was sound asleep now.

Ludmila was perspiring. *He would come to me if I called him. He would come if he thought it permissible.*

She wanted desperately to turn over, press against his strength, know he was there. A terrible feeling of guilt possessed her also, and for long minutes she toyed with the notion that she was damned.

Tears came to her eyes; she did not wipe them away but took solace in the dim awareness of their hot pressure against her eyelids. At length she reached for the little gold locket at her throat, an inlaid miniature of the madonna and child. "Little Jesus," she whispered, "can you still hear me? I know you must be everywhere, but can you hear me now? This is Ludmila Andreiovna, Jesus, and I have to speak to you."

She clutched the locket with both hands and lay very quiet, listening. In spite of deep concentration she heard only the soft rhythm of Olga Bohmer's breath and the insistent sound of the ocean. The tide was reaching to full now; the waves hissed over the rocky beach and spurted up against the solemn stone faces to either side of it.

She dared speak no more. *Can you hear me, little Jesus? I have to confess, for there is no priest and I have sinned. I am no longer a virgin, sacred Jesus. I did not wait for my husband-to-be. Perhaps now he will not even want me. I have never met him, but I have wronged him. Even now I do not know how to repent of what I did.*

I love him, even though I know that I must not touch him again. I plead for your understanding, Jesus. Something inside me deprived me of my reason. I was afraid I would die here and never know what it was to be a woman.

That is no excuse—I know, I know. All along I was heedless and gave in to my body. I am ashamed but cannot bring myself to repent.

In some way, today was different. What happened was good, though I cannot explain it. Until today, the second time, I but played with fire; but now the fire has burned me, and I am different for it. The second time was like waves running over me, like an eagle's wings beating above me. I cannot repent because my conscience tells me it was right. Am I cursed? Am I possessed? I will myself never to do it again. I will marry Pieter Dobshansky and be a good wife to him. I will do all he requires of me if only you will let me go to him now.

Ludmila breathed deeply, listened to Olga's breathing and the ocean ceaselessly gaining and withdrawing along the island's rough edge.

"Amen," she whispered.

The darkness grew thicker at last, but for a long while Ludmila was unable to sleep.

The figure of Jesus appeared, the face demonstrating extreme pain, the head crowned with great, sharp thorns. A gilt cross was suspended as if from heaven behind the altar in the great cathedral at Rostov.

The Christ wore the wings of an angel and the wings were changing color, darkening to jet black.

The Lord's face pinched out and formed a beak; the thorns were gone.

A huge raven was nailed to the golden cross. Then the cross itself vanished, and the raven's wings fanned gently, gently, extinguishing the candles along the altar rail. Trickles of incense drifted up into the half-light and blended with the smell of the sea, of kelp along the beach, of the sea water dashing itself against black fangs of stone.

The beak moved and the throat produced the cry of a raven, "*Krruach, Krruach, kor-kor-kor!*"

Morning came clear again, and Emerson and St. Francis went to work to fit the dinghy with a mast. One section of the spruce pole they hewed off and laced crosswise with strips of leather cut from the sleeves of their shirts.

"I don't see no way of setting the damned thing in place," Charley said. "How we goin' to do this, John?"

"Charles, Charles," Emerson laughed, "ain't we walked across half of Alaska on snowshoes, for hell's sake? Sure we're not goin' to let a leetle problem stop us now. Let's say it's a hundred damned miles to the next island. Okay. Two of us row and the other one holds up the rotten sail for whatever push we can get from the wind. Now you got that other oar carved out, we can make it even without the sail—as long as another typhoon don't hit us. Besides, we got Olga for ballast. We'll make 'er, old friend."

St. Francis sheathed his knife, stood up. "Let's go get the sealskin, then. You figure on settin' off today, eh?"

"See any point in waitin'?"

"Guess not. Let's do 'er, then. Got to do somethin', even if it's wrong."

Long John stood up, glanced out over the sea and stiffened. "For hell's sake look out there."

A craft, maybe three miles out, was coming in.

"By God, Johnny, they've seen our smoke. But what the hell is it?"

"Don't know for sure. Let's get our tub into the brine an' row out to meet 'em. Our medicine ain't played out yet, no sir."

The strange-looking craft took Emerson and St. Francis aboard and trailed their dinghy from a light hawser. It found its way in through the reefs and cast anchor a few yards from the beach. Flat-bottomed with a high-raked transom stern and a low, pointed bow, it was rigged with a double lugsail to allow it to ply the high seas. The fishing sampan was greeted by loud whoops from Taos Danny and by polite, enthusiastic cheers from Princess Ludmila and Olga Bohmer.

Darakusha was painted across the bow in half-recognizable English letters. She was the dwelling and livelihood of a Japanese fishing couple of the yeta or peasant class. Musi was in his early twenties and Okime was a hardy and intelligent woman nearly twice her husband's age.

They had been fishing north of the island of Hokkaido when the same storm that sent the *Loire* under drove them far out to sea. The winds bore them north to Komandorskije Island and the small Russian outpost there. The Russians treated them graciously and showed them their position on a chart. Thereupon the irrepressible Musi, against Okime's strong objections, concluded that they must cross to Alaska, where there would be far less competition to supply fish, seal and dolphin meat to the cargo ships that passed south to America or west to Kamchatka. Both spoke English surprisingly well, a consequence of relying upon Yankee merchantmen for a good portion of their meager living.

Musi and Okime came ashore, bringing a quantity of dried fish as well as some bottles of poor-quality pickled caviar, a flask of Scotch whiskey and a straw-covered jug of sake, rice wine.

Musi stepped from the dinghy onto the beach and held up the whiskey. He was grinning and he waved Taos Danny and the two women forward.

"Good drink, good drink," he crowed. "We pick up castaways, yes? You pay us and we take you to Alaska. But first we must eat and drink. You are all my friends and we will celebrate now."

Long John attempted to assist Okime ashore, but she pulled away from him, indignant that she might be supposed helpless.

Princess Ludmila, gleefully concluding that perhaps Jesus had indeed heard at least part of her prayer, could not fully control her emotions; she flung herself into Long John Emerson's arms to hug him tightly, then let go and stepped back.

Emerson, uncertain how to respond, glanced at Charley and Taos and shrugged. Olga stared at Ludmila and shook her head.

"Let us go up to your fire," Musi suggested. "You Mericans can drink whiskey. Okime and I will drink sake. After that we all go to Alaska. But you pay us something, *hai?*"

"You going to make us pay you for rescuing us?" Taos Danny wailed. "Ain't you never heard about the good Samarium? What makes ye think we got any money at all?"

"Your friend *Nagai* John said so," Okime smiled patiently.

"You tell 'em that, Emerson?"

"Only way I could get the thieves to come in an' take us aboard. Figgered we was all getting a bit tired of it here."

"I am Princess Ludmila Andreiovna. My father is the Duke of Rostov—a Russian duke, do you understand me? I was on my way to marry Count Pieter Dobshansky, the commandant of the Russian-American Company in Alaska. Count Dobshansky will pay you whatever you wish if you will deliver me and my governess, Mme. Bohmer, to him safely. Do you understand me?"

Musi turned to Emerson. "Roossia?" he asked. "Me, I am king of Roossia. This woman is full of words. You have *tomi,* hai? I am not a child. Musi and Okime must live also. Tomi, gold?"

Taos burst out laughing. "These slant-eyed niggers don't believe you, your highness. Looks like us pore common folk is gonna have to buy you an' big-bosoms over there your tickets to the opry. Ain't that somethin'?"

"Two hundred rubles in gold, you understand?" Emerson offered.

Musi and Okime glanced at one another. "Don't trust Roossia," Okime said, waving her arms. "Those people trying to take away northern islands. You pay us more."

"Two hundred in gold when we get to Sitka," Long John repeated with exaggerated patience.

"Just two hundred for all of you?" Musi sniffed. "Not enough. You pay three hundred in advance."

"Tell them to go back to their boat," Ludmila exclaimed. "They're nothing but money-grubbers."

"Go back, hell," Emerson snorted. "Much as I'd admire to stay here with you a leetle while, ma'am, right now this here's the only railroad in the North Pacific and I'd like to leave sometime. All right, Musi, two fifty, not a damned kopeck more."

Musi showed his teeth in a rather alarming grin. "In advance."

"Oh, all right, half in advance."

Okime gave her husband a nudge. Obligingly he held up the whiskey and sake to signal a deal. Long John grabbed the Scotch and took a deep swig from the bottle, then disappeared behind the rocks to a private place where he deemed it safe to take off his money belt.

"Is this craft seaworthy?" Olga asked, staring out at the strange-looking sampan.

"Good ship, good ship," Musi insisted. "Much better than French steamer."

"He's got a point, John," Charley said. "The *Loire*'s on the bottom an' the what's-its-name here is still afloat an' looking pretty good to this coon. What's that name you got painted on the scow mean, anyhow?"

Okime shrugged, touched the long black braid that hung over her shoulder. "*Bad One*. Your Commodore Perry named it fifteen years ago in Uraga when he came aboard. Means reprobate. I was young woman then, still with my first husband, Hiron. Musi was a boy, no parents, living on waterfront, stealing things. Hiron liked him, took him aboard. After that Hiron drowned, so Musi and I sailed *Darakusha* together. When he grew to be a man, we were married."

Musi nodded. "It is good for the wife to be older."

Emerson laughed and pounded the much smaller Musi

on the back. "Give me a pull on the whiskey jug and I'll see if I can find our gold stash."

As the group climbed from the beach to the still-smoking fire, Ludmila drew alongside Emerson. "Do you actually have the money, John?"

"Two thousand rubles in gold coin," Emerson assured her. " 'Bout twenty-four hundred American. Had it in a canvas belt around my middle when me an' the boys took leave of Captain Mirabeaux an' his steamer. Gold's one thing a man don't turn his back on with a cutthroat crew like that one."

By midafternoon the *Darakusha* was under way, its sails billowing nicely in a westerly. All save Olga were in high spirits; the unfortunate governess was once more seasick. Musi sang as he tended the rudder and Okime counted the gold several times, then rolled it up in a sash and tied it around her waist under her clothes. She came on deck and squatted beside her husband. Her long hair, unbraided now, blew back from her head.

Emerson and Taos Danny stood together at the bow and watched the waves curl past the sampan's wooden hull.

"Don't mean to be blunt," Taos said, "but you an' the leetle princess got somethin' going'? If this coon's wrong just say so, John, but it sure took you a long while to dig them clams, an' then when she come in, there was light glintin' in her eyes just like a mare after the stallion's been on her. No offense, now."

Emerson stroked his beard and was silent for a long moment. "Don't know what you're talkin' about, Taos old friend."

"That's what I thought. Well, then, you thinkin' about hangin' on to her? An' what you gonna do about her an' the King of Alaska when we reach port? I was sort of thinkin' that mebbe we just ought to head on down to

Seattle instead. Fine farmland out in Utah Territory, an' the Mormons is good folks even if they are touched in the head. A coon could do a lot worse, Johnny. Hell, the bunch of us could put together a damned fine cattle ranch. There's more'n one way of strikin' it rich, you know."

"An' take Olga with us?" Emerson asked, grinning and winking.

"Come on, John. Truth is, I wouldn't mind beddin' her, though. Just once, to see what it was like."

Chapter 12
Arrival at Sitka

Drifting plates of ice break off from the big glaciers that flow miles wide from the coastal mountains. The bergs float and twist in blue-green waters at the heads of fjords and in the channels from the myriad islands of the Alexander Archipelago north and west to Prince William Sound.

Bering Glacier, Mendenhall, Aku, are dwarfed by great Malaspina, a living river of ice that runs from the heights to the sea. It is larger in area than the state of Rhode Island.

Countless waterfalls spill over cliff faces to the heaving salt water below. The ages have cut channels deep and shallow where walrus, sea lion and seal drift through the surges, surface for air, submerge again or slither and waddle up onto boulders and ledges to sun themselves alseep.

Orca the killer whale, largest and most powerful carnivore ever to live on this planet, haunts the Alaskan deeps. Fearsome and beautiful creatures of astounding symmetry in black and white, they are revered and honored as deities by the natives. What are even the biggest bears to such beings?

Dense forests of spruce rise to ice-choked ranges. Bald eagles swarm on Admiralty Island, which holds more bears than men.

Mud flats, grass flats and lakes—Tustumena, Skilak, Kenai—support water lilies, scarlet firegrass, wild poppies, yellow skunk cabbage. Loons float on breakwater ponds and lakes, laughing insanely or mimicking the cries of wolves and coyotes. Light flickers from their unblinking orange-red eyes, jeweled flame of some primeval conflagration.

June 1867

Neither the owners of the *Darakusha* nor any of the shipwrecked group knew the date when they pulled into Sitka harbor. It was a brilliant blue day and the sun sparkled on water and gleamed off the snow atop the mountains. The highest peak in particular impressed the two Japanese, who thought it greatly resembled their sacred Fujiyama.

The town itself was a collection of log and plank cabins within and without a stockade fence. The whole was situated on a slope above the harbor at the foot of the precipitous peaks. On an eminence above the main part of the settlement rose the imposing structure of the governor's mansion. Presently occupied by Prince Makustov, his wife and his various retainers, it was a plank and stave structure designed in the fashion of the great Russian estate houses.

At the southern verge of the town stood a second large house, not so fine or large as the governor's mansion but nonetheless quite impressive by Sitka standards. This was the dwelling of Count Pieter Dobshansky, as Ludmila immediately surmised.

Between these two rose the Cathedral of St. Michael, not a rival to the great structures in Moscow or even Rostov, but grand enough with its familiar gleaming onion towers topped with golden crosses. In all her first impression of Nova Archangelisk was sufficient to cheer Ludmila considerably.

On the whole, she reflected, while the town's nickname of *Paris of the Pacific* represented considerable optimistic hyperbole, neither was it the rude and roughshod frontier outpost she had expected. There were at least the rudiments of civilization.

As they sailed into the mouth of the big harbor, Mme. Olga suddenly flung herself into worried activity. "Ah, what shall we do, my princess?" she fussed. "What will Count Pieter think of us, and Prince Makustov? They will surely think we are savage Indians. Your fiance will turn us away as imposters."

Gazing down at the badly torn and filthy remnant of what had been a fine Paris gown, Ludmila shrugged. She had not thought of her appearance since the shipwreck, she realized with some surprise. Was it so very easy to neglect the amenities of civilization? She glanced involuntarily at Long John Emerson, remembering the almost animal passion on the island. She blushed and placed one hand on the gold locket containing the representation of the madonna and child. Her pledge to Jesus was clear in her mind and her will was strong. She would keep her word.

Emerson returned her glance and winked, almost as though he supposed himself able to read her thoughts.

"And so our new life begins, Olga," she said as the older woman worked at her hair. Using a comb borrowed from Okime she braided it and pinned it with a couple of bone skewers from the same source. "Does it not seem strange to you? Soon it will be as if our adventure never happened. We will soon be drinking tea in a parlor set with mirrors and we will tell it all as a story. Perhaps you will meet a handsome Cossack and marry again and leave me."

"Ha," snorted Mme. Olga, ineffectually running a damp cloth over the stained fabric of Ludmila's bodice. "Adventure—and the rest doesn't matter, because the count will send both of us to the back door and put us to work scrubbing pots and pans."

Taos Danny, who had sidled up to the governess, grunted. "Don't you worry about it, Olga," he offered. "I done told you I'd marry you. Hell, if your count or whatever turns up his nose, I'll even marry the princess too. Ol' Charley here ain't the marryin' kind, and Long John's still got a passel of she-bears waitin' for him out on the Yukon River."

"The Meskin here is always ready to make the ultimate sacrifice," Charley added, having come up alongside the others. "Besides, who says I ain't the marryin' kind? Hell, I been married more times than the rest of you put together, with the possible exception of Olga here."

Mme. Bohmer ignored the banter and turned her futile grooming efforts to her own person.

Long John Emerson approached the rail to stand a little apart from the others; he did not join in with their joking. Ludmila moved over beside him. Both stared ahead at the cluster of buildings to which the *Darakusha* was drawing ever closer.

She searched for something to say. "Will you accompany Olga and me to Governor Makustov's residence?" she asked. She could think of nothing else.

"Not to Dobshansky's place?"

"My father instructed me to present myself to the governor first. I cannot go unwed to my intended's own house."

"You want me to sort of give the bride away, only to the governor an' not to the coon she's marryin'." He heard an unexpected edge of bitterness in his voice. "Sure, why not?"

Silence descended upon them again.

"I will not forget you, John Emerson," Ludmila said softly.

"It'll be good to know there's an honest-to-God princess rememberin' me somewhere. Sure you don't want to chuck it all an' go live in an Injun hut with me?"

"I almost think I would do that if you were really asking me."

"Figger you'd last about a week, Ludmila. Best you stick with your own kind." Then he turned to face her and the sarcasm suddenly dropped from his manner. "I'm sorry, pretty little Roossian princess. You don't deserve my orneriness. Guess I'm taking it out on you. Damnit, gal, I'm goin' to miss you something terrible and there's not a blessed thing either one of us can do about it."

"You were my first, John," she said, looking away from him and feeling the color come to her face.

"Know I was." He nodded at the sea. "I know that, Ludmila, an'—"

"I would kiss you if we were alone," she whispered. He glanced over and found her gazing steadily into his eyes, a small smile touching the corners of her mouth despite the painful lump in her throat. "The island, that was our Eden, yours and mine. All any of us wanted was to get away, but now I wish we were there again."

There were a number of trading vessels in the port, both steam and sail, the larger ones at anchor. Musi and Okime skillfully tacked among these and slid up to a pier. Musi tossed a line, jumped easily from the prow to the dock and secured the hawser, then hopped back aboard.

The group said its farewells to the Japanese couple, thanking them over and over for the rescue. The two smiled and bowed politely, accepting their due. As the group made to go ashore, however, Musi spoke up. "Emerson-san, have you not forget something?"

Emerson stopped in his tracks and slowly turned. "What would that be?"

"Small matter of large reward."

"Oh, that. Yeah. Well, er, okay. Have to step into the cabin a second, though. Excuse me, folks."

"Pardon me, Musi," Ludmila said sweetly. "I take it all back."

"Take it back all what?" Musi demanded, much puzzled.

"All the nice things I just said to you." Ludmila turned her back and stared at the highest mountains until Long John reappeared.

As Charley St. Francis and Long John Emerson assisted the two women off the sampan, Okime called, "We stay right here two, three days. Maybe Mericans want to go fishing? We share part of our catch, sell to English schooner."

"Good-bye, please," Ludmila called back.

Long John, Taos and Charley escorted the women to the Russian-American headquarters on the waterfront, where a clerk, upon hearing the story of shipwreck and survival, offered to accompany them to Prince Makustov's dwelling.

"You ladies will understand if I don't tag along the rest of the way to the palace?" Long John said, addressing both women but looking only at Ludmila. "This fine gentleman here will take good care of you, an' me an' Charley an' Taos got us some business to conduct with the company. Get some of our Russian gold changed into paper dollars, so to speak. I'd like to lose a little weight before we head south to Seattle."

Ludmila stared at Emerson, her eyes widening with disbelief. The parting, then, was to come even sooner than she had expected. She had been anticipating some final moment alone. She had also, she realized, half-hoped the parting would not really occur, that somehow it could be delayed forever. Suddenly she felt betrayed, abandoned. She felt like weeping.

He is right, though. What would be the point of prolonging it? Besides, we are not really so much to each other—just a meadow and a beach. We will both forget in time.

No, I will not forget. There is new life within me.

She straightened her back and held her hand out to Emerson and the other two trappers.

"Good-bye, Mr. Emerson, Taos, Charley. You all have my thanks and Mme. Olga's. Mr. St. Francis, Mr. . . . Danny." Taos was staring at Olga, licking his lips suggestively, and Olga was pointedly looking at the floor.

Ludmila inclined her head to the clerk and followed him out the doorway without looking back, her bearing regal indeed, despite the tatters of her dress. She was childishly satisfied to have detected a flash of hurt in Emerson's eyes in response to her cool and formal farewell.

The trappers' business with the Russian-American Company was over fast. It consisted of an exchange of American currency for gold and the purchase of half a dozen bottles of vodka from the young soldier who acted as clerk in the commissary. Charley opened the first bottle while Long John was still paying. The group's communal funds converted to about two thousand dollars after they paid for the spirits. "Feels good around my waist," Long John said, stretching.

"You got objections if we just set over here on these bales of skins while we take the edge off our thirst, friend?" Charley asked the clerk, offering the man a pull on the newly opened bottle.

The young soldier shrugged, grinned, took a healthy swig of the proffered liquor.

"Hear tell you boys make this stuff from rotten potato peelings an' the like," Taos Danny said. "That right, compañero?"

"Potatoes, da. *Kartofyel*. Damn good, eh?"

"Personal, I like good Kaintuck sippin' whiskey, but this ain't half bad after a two-month dry," Charley said, retrieving the bottle and taking his own draught. He coughed slightly as the raw alcohol burned its way down his throat.

Long John took his turn, nodded without speaking.

"The goddamn human spirit's amazin', ain't it?" Taos observed as his turn came round. "I mean, you think about a pile of old rotten potatoes and you just about cain't think of a thing seems more useless on the face of 'er. Human spirit's a wonderful thing. Next you know, they'll be makin' liquor out of horse droppin's or some such."

Charley St. Francis nodded solemnly, but the young Russian's mouth began to tighten and his ruddy cheeks grew redder.

"No offense, friend," Long John said quickly, passing the bottle once more to the soldier. "My buddy here's just waxing philosophic. Gets carried away on his own invention at times. Me an' Charley have got to the point where we don't pay much attention."

"What's this?" Taos cried. "Did this man think I was insultin' him or his rotgut? No, amigo, compañero, quite the reverse. I was admirin'. I was commentin' upon the grandeur, so to speak, of human ingenuity. Come here," he continued, leaning across the counter to slap the bewildered clerk's shoulder. "Come on over here an' set with us on this bale of furs. Come on, there ain't nobody in the damned store anyhow. I'll explain to you what I meant so's you won't have your feelings disarrayed. The goddamn Russkis an' the Americans ought to be friends. Rumor has it the U.S. Gov'ment's buyin' Alaska itself from you coons. Heard that in Kamchatka, sure as the pope piddles in the woods. Or were it a bear?"

"Grandeur of human ingenuity," Charley snorted. "Shouldn't never send a goldanged Meskin to school."

"Ain't no Meskin an' I ain't been to school 'cept that one time a couple of months when my leg was broke an' I couldn't get away."

"Shouldn't teach a damn heathen Injun to read, then," Charley insisted. "Nothin' good can ever come of it."

"Easy, lads," Long John put in. "Don't want our potato-squeezin' friend here to get no wrong ideas about us Yankees."

"At least dumbhead Charley's gettin' closer to the truth," Danny shrugged. "Come on, my Russian friend—what's your name, anyhow?"

"Me, I am Ivan Popovich Borofsky," the young Russian responded, taking another pull at the bottle and moving unsteadily around the counter to join the trappers.

Almost immediately Danny produced his water-stained deck of playing cards and started a game of poker. The stakes were that each player should start with a full bottle of vodka and that the losers of each hand had to buy a round.

Ivan Popovich, whom Charley and Danny both called Pop, submitted to the game good-naturedly, listening to Danny's instructions both as to the general rules and the strategy. Borofsky grinned, although it was soon apparent that he hadn't understood more than half of it.

"Speaks good English, by God. What do you say, Pop? I see your bottle's empty already. Want me to stake you to another round?" Danny offered, having trouble shuffling the battered, still somewhat sticky playing cards.

Ivan Borofsky leaned back and held his hands out, palms forward, shaking his head and laughing.

"Nyet, nyet. You . . . how you say it? You fleece me like a damn sheep."

Long John cleared his throat and Danny and Charley laughed and tilted their bottles to their lips. "Okay, then, Pop the Russki, you got to provide the entertainment." Charley insisted.

"Enterten-a-ment?"

"Yeah," Danny said. "You know any dirty songs?"

"Da, song. I know song. Not dirty, though; very sad. Good drinking song. Russians drink, sing, cry very much. Is very good way to spend evening. Handsome soldier goes away to war and sweetheart thinks he is dead, marries brother—''

''Marries her brother!'' Charley interjected, scandalized.

''Nyet, nyet, not her own brother, *his* brother. Then he comes home, soldier. Kills brother, kills sweetheart, feels very sad, is going to kill self, oobevaht.''

''Sounds like a real upliftin' tale. Let 'er rip, Pop.'' Taos grabbed the bottle and took a deep slug.

The young soldier had a remarkably good baritone voice and he boomed out the lugubrious melody strong and true despite his considerable liquid fortification. By the time he had finished the melody the first time through, he was weeping copiously, although his voice remained steady. Taos Danny and Charley joined him on the chorus the second time through, humming and mumbling to go with their lacerated version of the melody.

Long John tried to join in the spirit of the impromptu celebration but found he couldn't. More than anything he wanted the liquor to free him from the vague ache that had haunted him since Ludmila marched away to her own people to await the man she would marry. But the drink had not had the desired effect. Rather, he found that his depression deepened as the vodka stripped away his internal defenses. He found himself, as the absurdly sentimental song began a third time, with a lump in his throat. At the same time he was becoming hugely annoyed with his companions, who were, after all, only doing what he wished he could do himself.

Danny suddenly broke the sad drone of the Russian's song and began singing one of his own, an amazingly obscene ditty. The others had just taken up this rollicking tune when the door of the commissary burst open and two silver-buttoned officers strode into the room.

Ivan Borofsky tried to scramble upright, stumbled, fell back upon the bale of furs. The officers dragged him to his feet and spoke to him harshly in Russian, giving him what the Americans could tell was a thorough dressing-down.

Charley, Danny and Long John glanced at one another and all three rose unsteadily. Emerson caught hold of one officer's sleeve, began trying to persuade him to go easy on their friend. "Ivan here was just tryin' to make your customers feel at home."

The officer glared at the huge American, pulled his arm free with a muted snarl.

"An' we're mighty good customers, too," Charley added, gripping the same man's other arm.

"Damn right," agreed Danny, his right hand dropping to his Bowie knife. "You goddamn Russkis cain't treat our friends this way."

The second officer made a quick survey of the three Americans. "You are indeed good customers," he said. "Now go sleep off the vodka you've drunk or you will find yourselves in the stockade with Private Borofsky here."

"I done told you not to mistreat our leetle friend," Danny growled, taking a wild, looping swing at the senior officer.

"Nyet, nyet," Ivan whispered urgently, but Taos was not to be discouraged so easily. Missing with his first blow, he wound up for another. The officer ducked and called loudly out the door.

Half a dozen soldiers materialized and surrounded the Americans. "You go quietly now," said the senior officer. "You are good customers, that is right. Outside the palisade, third cabin from gate. You take your bottles there. Pretty girls, *prostituées*, they help you to celebrate."

"We want to take Ivan here with us," Danny insisted, preparing yet another assault upon his several potential antagonists. Two soldiers immediately pinned his arms. Taos managed a good kick at a third before he was clubbed over the head.

Charley and Long John felt honor bound to defend their partner, and a brief wild skirmish ensued. Emerson laid out two of the Russians before superior numbers managed to quell him. The three trappers were efficiently subdued, however, and within seconds they found themselves pushed by main force through the heavy plank door, which was then barred behind them.

They sat slumped in silence for a brief time, each privately assessing his own damages.

"Guess we didn't win that one," Danny ventured.

"Naw, but we give an honorable showing, bein' as it was three to one, almost," Charley reflected.

"My head hurts a mite," Danny added. "Wasn't fair, that son of a bitch pullin' a club on me."

"Hope they don't do nothin' too bad to the kid," Emerson said, rubbing at the bruised side of his face.

"Might have been better if I hadn'ta tried to help," Taos Danny admitted.

"Ain't your fault," Charley said, blinking his eyes against the bright sunlight. "Dumbass Meskins ain't expected to figger things out too good in advance."

"Code of ethics," Taos insisted. "Some of us by God live by a code of ethics."

Charley didn't reply, and the three men sat in silence again for a time. Danny took a long swig from his open bottle, which had somehow come through the scuffle without losing a drop.

"Third house from the gate, did he say?" the half-breed asked at last.

Bruised, dirty and drunk as they were, the three companions set off in search of the place the officer had mentioned. The directions, as it turned out, were redundant. The cabin in question, along with several others nearby, was conspicuous for the candle in a red glass holder prominently displayed in the one small window.

When Taos Danny knocked at the door, it was answered by a nearly pretty Indian girl in Russian garb. Behind her stood two more girls, peering over her shoulder at the men and giggling. None of the three appeared to be more than sixteen.

Long John Emerson suddenly felt cold sober and infinitely depressed. His teeth ached and his stomach was unsteady. He turned and walked away, mumbling, "See you back at the sampan."

"Come back, come back, big boy," called a feminine voice. "You think I not pretty? I show you good time."

"No, ma'am," he felt compelled to answer. "I think you're real pretty. Just . . . my mood ain't right, is all."

Charley followed his friend for a few steps. "Look, you want some company, Johnny? I reckon you're havin' a hard time gettin' that little princess out of your craw. I ain't much in the mood myself, come to think of 'er. We'll go find someplace an' finish off our rotgut an' get morose an' throw up an' have a hell of a good time."

Emerson waved him off. "Naw, it ain't that. You know I ain't one to brood over women, Charley. You go have yourself a good time for me. I'm a mite tired an' my teeth are startin' to hurt. Guess I'll just go turn in. Don't suppose Musi an' Okime will mind."

St. Francis hesitated, watching Emerson carefully for a moment, then shrugged and went back to the whorehouse, where the girls were still holding the door and beckoning.

Governor Prince Makustov, having overcome his initial incredulous surprise, received Princess Ludmila and Mme. Bohmer most hospitably. He had what he supposed Ludmila must certainly see as bad news. Count Pieter Dobshansky, having learned of the sinking of the *Loire* from Russian-American headquarters in Kamchatka, supposed her drowned.

Word of the *Loire*'s fate had been borne to Petropavlovsk by a handful of survivors who drifted aimlessly until picked up by a Dutch frigate on its way from Alaska to Kamchatka. As a consequence, the governor said, Dobshansky had swallowed his grief, it being by then nearly a month since the *Loire* left port, and sailed to Redoubt St. Michael on the Bering coast near the mouth of the Yukon River.

Less than certain but in all probability reliable, word had reached Sitka that the sale of Alaska to the United States was imminent, if indeed the transaction had not already been consummated, and so Dobshansky had gone to St. Michael to ready it for evacuation. When the count might return to Sitka was a matter of some conjecture, though Prince Makustov believed it would be soon.

He ordered that comfortable quarters be prepared, separate rooms for the princess and her attendant, and he sent his servants to borrow suitable clothing from the women of his household, his own wife and the wives of his aides.

So for the first time since leaving Petropavlovsk, Ludmila found herself that night in a proper bed, a soft, wide down mattress in a carved wooden frame, even a damask canopy and hangings. She wore an embroidered linen nightdress, very nice although borrowed and a little large, and lay between linen sheets and beneath two quilted comforters.

She had a long, warm bath carried in by the servants, and when her toilette was complete, she had a pleasant dinner with Prince and Princess Makustov. The governor-prince, a handsome man with silver-threaded hair and point-trimmed beard, proved himself a polite and skilled conversationalist. He made a point of remarking quite favorably upon Dobshansky's good reputation as chief agent for the Russian-American Company.

Now, having spent the afternoon and evening in the governor's mansion in the familiar and comfortable pastimes of society as she had known it all her life, she was unable to sleep. Ludmila drew back the hangings on her bed, padded to the dormer window of her room and opened the curtains. She stared out at the small lantern-lit town of Nova Archangelisk. A half-moon, riding down toward the mountaintops to the northwest, illumined the settlement and laid a sheen across the calm water of the harbor. Nothing moved in the shadows of the buildings and only a very few people appeared to be in the streets. Leaning down and looking up through the tall window, she could see the seven bright stars of the Great Bear, even higher the curved tail and small cup of the Little Bear.

Without thinking she began to hum a tune she remembered from her childhood, then stopped abruptly when she recalled the words, about a young girl waiting for her love to come elope with her. Ludmila glanced down at the still, dark forms of the wooden buildings of the little settlement. She detected some movement close beneath her window, leaned her forehead against the glass as she stared intently into the moon-shadows. A dog trotted into the light on its own business, paused to urinate against a verandah post, moseyed on.

"It is only nerves," she assured herself; nerves were the popular European malady of the upper classes. "It is natural. Soon I will meet Count Dobshansky. I wonder what he's like?"

Prominent against the sky on an eminence only slightly lower than Prince Makustov's was the dwelling of Count Pieter Dobshansky, her husband-to-be. She stared at its indistinct dark outline, trying to discern from it some clue to her fiance and the life they would share. Ludmila attempted to picture the man, older, powerful, wealthy. It would be the sort of life she had expected to live, but she found she could form no image of either the man or the future.

Instead, unbidden, her inner eye focused on the face of Long John Emerson, unkempt sandy beard, cool gray eyes, weather-etched lines in the skin. It seemed his eyes closed, his face tensed and then relaxed, utterly given over to her in the moment of passion. Beyond them the white gulls slid over the ocean; above them a dark wing-form—a hawk or perhaps an eagle—

"No!" Her voice rang startlingly loud in the intense silence of the room.

She rose abruptly from the window seat, paced back and forth across the soft rug. The chill of the night was beginning to seep into her consciousness and she shivered.

Perhaps a cup of tea, she thought, and pulled on the silken bell cord. After a minute or two an Indian called Irena tapped softly at the door before she entered.

"Madame have trouble sleeping?" she asked, her voice soft and kind despite the obvious fact that she had been roused from slumber.

Suddenly as she looked at the servant, who was really no more than a girl in a plain bathrobe and dark hair around her shoulders, Ludmila felt embarrassed, as if she had no right to demand service, no right to arouse her from her own rest, even to tend to the needs of a Russian princess. It was the first time such a thought had ever occurred to her, and the idea was momentarily disquieting.

"I . . . uh . . . I'm sorry, Irena. I shouldn't have awakened you."

"Is all right. Is what I am here for. You want something, perhaps tea? Maybe a little vodka in it to help sleep?"

"I don't know," Ludmila answered. "Maybe I had something of the sort in mind. To tell the truth I think I was just lonely. Why don't you go back to bed? I shouldn't have awakened you."

"You want me sing you song?" Irena asked. "I comb your hair if you like. Sometimes ladies like me to comb hair."

"No, thank you. How old are you, Irena? How did you come to be in this house?"

"Not sure, Princess Ludmila. Maybe thirteen, fourteen winters."

"Shouldn't you be at home chasing the boys at your age?"

"No chase boys. Priest take me three summer ago. Father dead long time, mother die. Hungry then, lots of bad times. Now got plenty food, warm place. When I die I go live Jesus."

Ludmila studied the girl, the dark planes of whose face were half-revealed in moonlight, half-hidden in shadows.

"What about Raven Man?" Ludmila asked. "I have heard that your people worship Raven Man."

"Raven Man no good. Priest tell me. Raven Man, him devil, devil got my people. That why men get drunk all the time, not hunt, baby cry."

On an impulse Ludmila embraced the servant and kissed her cheek.

Irena looked startled, then smiled shyly. "You want me to bring you hot tea now?"

"No," Ludmila whispered. "You go back to bed now. I will sleep."

Irena hesitated a moment, then nodded, made a small curtsy and backed out the door, shutting it softly behind her.

"Irena—" Ludmila started to call out, moving toward the door. Then she stopped realizing that what she had wanted to say would not only be useless but possibly hurtful.

She still thought it though: *You are wrong about*

Jesus, about the white priests. It was not Raven Man but the white traders, who brought the liquor that makes your men waste themselves. The prince has not done you a favor, but enslaved you. Jesus is your enemy . . .

Ludmila put her hands to the sides of her head as if to keep it physically from coming apart. Blasphemy! "I am a Christian, I have spoken to Jesus. What has happened to me?" she whispered.

She lay down on the bed again, her thoughts more troubled than before. Why had she asked the serving maid to talk? The conversation left her confused, frustrated and curiously empty.

Did I want to hear that life is free and good in the wilderness, that these are children of nature, somehow inherently noble, uncorrupted? Why would I want to hear that? There is nothing out there for me. This is my world, where people know how to be comfortable, how to speak pleasantly and amusingly. There is no idyllic cabin in the woods where one goes and lives in peace and harmony with a bearded trapper. I learned that at sea, on the island. Nature is not the friend of any man.

Ludmila lay staring into the darkness above her and reminded herself again of the blissful comfort of clean linen, of a soft, warm bed. She resolved on the morrow that she would give herself no more idle time to waste on fruitless speculation. She would go to Musi and Okime, she would hire them to take her directly to Redoubt St. Michael. There would be no further delay. She would be married, and once and for all that would put an end to her foolishness.

Feeling that she had in some way gotten things once more in control, with her resolve firm in her mind, Ludmila drifted into sleep, dreamed.

A Christ-figure like the one in her own church in Rostov, a tortured, emaciated body, hung from a cross, the face twisted with agony and exaltation. Suddenly the eyes opened and the figure spoke.

"The hell with this. Time to cut bait, by God."

Then the Christ-figure grew wings, big black wings, and flew away from the cross, circling up and up, laughing, croaking. The raven laughter fell back like thunder, and she stood near the empty cross and wept.

Ludmila awoke crying out, "Wait! Raven Man, Long John, wait; I want to go too; Don't you understand, you great fool? You are giving up your own son."

Chapter 13
The Raven Mutters

Offspring of Raven Man practice esnai, keep moving about. We hear his cry in the wind, see his black wings in drifting snow. In the summer, when there's no darkness but only twilight, that's his breath making the long, hot days. Twilight—that's when the sun hides in the north, comes up again, makes a long circle through the sky.

Clouds of mosquitoes drift over Yukon Flats. Grayling, pike, whitefish, inconnu—they dream under the water.

Yukon, Old Lot of Water, is always muddy, seems like. Eats the land, keeps moving it around.

Only in winter it gets smaller and freezes over, when it's dark and twilight is all we have besides the cold.

Each year the salmon come. We catch a lot of them, dry out the red meat, make *ukali*. All winter we eat ukali.

Salmon people live in three villages under the water, one village for each kind—king salmon, dog salmon, silver salmon.

Salmon have yeg, spirit, just like people. They wear fine parkas, take them off when they go upriver for a potlatch.

Esnaih: all animals do it. All fish and birds do it, just like people. Raven Man told us to do it long ago: keep moving. Otherwise we die when the cold comes up out of the ground and the sky is dark, with only stars and a little twilight in between darks.

We stay in the kashim then, try to stay warm, tell stories that last a long time. Salmon oil burns good, lights the meeting lodge. Tastes very good also.

Denato created this world, but he is not responsible for everything. Raven Man created death, but Giyeg causes it; he feeds on us when our spirits wander from our bodies. The Nahoen, whose hair streams down to their feet, help Giyeg.

Yes, Raven Man created death, but he is our father. We all belong to him.

June 1867

He was chasing an otter, a light, glossy otter that had escaped from his trap. He followed the creature across a beach, up through spruce trees, almost catching it several times. Always it darted away, glancing back over its shoulder and seeming to laugh at him, its brown eyes glittering. It seemed to him vitally important that he catch the animal, as if that were the only thing in life that mattered.

He suddenly realized he had chased the otter right into a well-appointed parlor and that a number of handsomely dressed people on settles and chairs had all turned to gaze at him. He became conscious of his crude clothing, of his muddy boots upon the pale carpet. He felt awkward, bearlike. The otter vanished.

He saw Ludmila seated next to a man in uniform. She watched him with the others, but it seemed to him that she was laughing as the otter had laughed, the brown eyes glinting before she turned to embrace her companion.

He shouted aloud in rage and pain and leaped across the room, intent upon killing the uniformed man.

* * *

John Emerson awoke with his own war cry ringing in his head, although he was not certain whether he had actually shouted aloud. He sat up confused, blinking to clear his vision. Almost nothing was visible. The structure of the mast disappeared into greyness above him, and on the deck only the coil of rope upon which he had lain might be discerned. For a moment he thought he must still be dreaming until he sucked in a deep breath, tasted the sea-dampness and became aware of a clammy chill against his skin.

"Fog," he muttered. "Damned near always fog along the coast in the morning. That's where we are. Made 'er to Sitka yesterday, by God, and here I am, still on the sampan."

Emerson ran his tongue around the inside of his mouth, which tasted foul and gritty. He winced when he touched a puffy cut on his lip. His head felt slightly enlarged and his eyes ached vaguely, but the sensations seemed to him appropriate to the fog.

He felt a certain grim sense of fitness. *Got drunker'n a damned fruit fly in a bottle of port, an' I didn't even have a good time.*

He'd shared his remaining bottle of vodka with the Japanese couple after he left his companions at the whorehouse, he remembered, and when that bottle was done, Musi had produced some of his seemingly endless supply of sake. Emerson could remember very little of the conversation with the fisherman and his wife, except that there had been a great deal of it and that he'd done most of the talking.

"A man's gotta do what a man's gotta do." He remembered repeating that phrase with considerable solemnity several times, and he was certain he had discoursed at length upon the differing natures of man and woman, in the process trotting out every scrap of folk wisdom he could recall. With regard to most of his assertions, Musi had nodded wisely and in properly inscrutable Oriental fashion, but Okime disagreed again and again.

"Woman don't need silk carpets, all that stuff you say," she snapped. "You look at me, Long John. I need fancy house, someone to take care of me? I got good man, good life. Woman wants same thing man does, but every man except Musi too ignorant to figure that out."

"Some women's got a more delicate nature," Emerson drunkenly insisted, at which remark Okime snorted contemptuously.

"Some women live on little bare island for weeks, still come out okay."

Musi started to laugh.

Emerson shook his head, groaned at the recollection. "Ain't no harder to figger out than fresh tracks on new snow," he mumbled, pushing the fragments of remembered conversation away and rising to his feet. "Dumbass coon. Just like the dream—she's got to me, that's what. Time to get to Seattle, get the hell away from this place."

He steadied himself against the mast, prepared to move to the little cabin where Musi and Okime slept. He'd attempt to persuade the Japanese couple to transport him and his compañeros to the southern port, or if that failed, to make arrangements on whatever vessel he could find in Sitka harbor. Surely some ship or another was heading south.

Already the fog was beginning to lighten. Rays from the low sun illuminated the mist and nearby boats and the pier itself were emerging from obscurity.

Emerson blinked, rubbed his eyes, stared at the human figure that came walking out of the mist like a lingering dream-wisp. Ludmila's small, dark figure, a fur cape hugged about her shoulders, shone in the strange light. Long John blinked again, once more involuntarily rubbed his eyes, half expecting her to disappear.

By now she was standing directly across from him on

the grey-white planking of the pier, a seagull scuttling behind her in the hope that she might drop a crumb for it.

"John?" She spoke hesitantly, as if there were some doubt of his identity. "I didn't know you would be here. I want to see Musi and Okime. I need to ask them something." She paused, uncertain how to proceed.

Emerson roused himself out of his daze. "Good morning, princess," he said. "I'll give you a hand on board. I . . . I was just about to leave. Truth to tell I wasn't expectin' to see you again."

Ludmila accepted his hand to steady her as she crossed the narrow plank that served as a gangway, and he grasped her at the waist as she jumped down onto the deck. They stood awkwardly for a moment, looking at each other without words, like strangers caught in an unexpectedly intimate encounter.

"Ludmila . . ." Emerson began, and then he realized that he didn't have any words ready. Her physical nearness and the tactile memory of her body, awakened by the feel of her waist between his hands, combined with his odd formality and overwhelmed him. Suddenly his arms were around her, pressing her small body against his chest, holding her with fierce possessiveness.

Ludmila wrapped her own arms around his waist for a moment, pressed her cheek against his chest, seduced by the good familiar feel, the beloved odor of him.

This is right. Yes, this is where I belong, inside these fierce arms, this is how I will stay because this is where I must stay . . . the thought rose into her mind but lacked precise words.

I promised Jesus, she told this vagrant part of her mind—and pushed herself gently away, resisting the embrace until Emerson dropped his arms.

"I've made a vow, John," she explained, watching his eyes, seeing her own tiny black reflection. "I've come to ask Musi and Okime to take me to Redoubt St. Michael.

That's where Count Dobshansky went. I . . . we should be married right away. I am not very strong. I keep thinking about you in ways that I shouldn't. The island was a different world for both of us." After many hesitations and false starts her voice trailed away and the two were left looking at one another again.

"Yeah," Emerson said after a time. "Well. I guess we all do what we have to do. If you're commandeering the sampan, princess, I guess I'd best get scramblin' an' find a ride to Seattle for me and Charley and Taos." He turned quickly and stepped up onto the gangplank, his mouth set and his eyes cold.

Without thinking what she was doing, Ludmila caught hold of his wrist. "Wait, John, please. I must explain. I . . . I don't think I can bear your anger. I have been having dreams. Please, come back and listen. I have been dreaming about your Raven, dreaming about Jesus turning into this Raven Man and flying away. I am coming apart. I don't know what anything means. Come down and tell me what I am to do."

Emerson heard the edge of hysteria in her voice, saw the glitter of tears in her eyes. He stepped back into the boat and took her shoulders, struggling not to be moved by her distress. "You've got to get a grip on yourself, princess."

"John, I think I am in love with you. I know I am, but it's wrong. I feel lost. I have always been a Christian; I have never even had to think about it before. But in this wild place, on our island, even here where there is a church and priests, Christ does not seem to be very strong here. No, that is blasphemy. Everything is coming apart—"

"Don't know what you want this child to say, Ludmila. I don't even know for sure what you're talkin' about. I never had no strong religious streak. I really got nothin' to offer you—"

"That is not what I asked," she cried out.

"Well, damnit, what did you ask?" He looked at her. Her eyes were wide and shining in the strange foggy sunlight. Again it seemed to him that she was an apparition from some other realm and that her eyes fixed on him were demanding something that neither of them could define. Then her demeanor suddenly changed. She seemed to shake herself and her expression closed, became both decisive and resigned, her jaw lifting and her mouth firming.

"That is why I must go to St. Michael," she said. "I will be married at once, and then this floundering will end. Everything will be fixed and determined."

Emerson forced himself to look away from her, off toward the fog-shrouded town of Sitka. "Well, this child don't think you ought to go runnin' off to what's his name clear up to St. Mike. I figger you ought to set here where you're safe until he gets back."

"I'm afraid I'm losing my mind," Ludmila cried. "Don't you see that, John? It must be done soon. I cannot . . . bear . . . *freedom*!"

Emerson was stunned by this last assertion, chewed on it, noted a pair of gulls swooping away toward the town and disappearing into the mist.

"Why you tellin' me this, Ludmila? What do you want? Do you want me to marry you? Carry you off to the woods and make you live like a squaw? I love you, girl, right enough, but you know you'd hate the life. Count Dobshansky will give you a nice house, a comfortable life. If us Yanks are buyin' Alaska, you'll be going back to Russia most likely, and you'll have your artists and whatnot."

"Didn't I say that? Didn't I say that?" she demanded. "I did not ask you to carry me off to your *woods*. I said I was going to Redoubt St. Michael to meet my fiance."

"Right enough," Emerson nodded, "that's what you said. You just don't seem altogether convinced, I guess."

Ludmila shrugged Emerson's hands away from her

shoulders, becoming once again the princess. "You are very arrogant, Mr. Emerson, to presume that I would wish to marry a *sauvage*. A person of my birth has certain social obligations, shall we say? I would not wish to embarrass my family. Be so kind, please, as to forgive my . . . momentary lapse."

"Shee-it," Emerson bellowed, frustrated. "What in hell brought this on?" He glanced toward the cabin. Musi and Okime had emerged and were watching the scene with obvious interest. A half-smile drew the corners of Okime's mouth toward the corners of her eyes. Long John's outrage was such, however, that the mere presence of others was not enough to quell him.

"You've had a couple of *momentary lapses*, haven't you, your majesty? Go off to Redoubt St. Mike, damnit. Maybe you'll catch your fiance in between rendezvous with twelve-year-old Injun gals, if you're lucky. Your King of Alaska's got half-breed bastards growin' up all along the coast—but you didn't know that, eh? Well, everyone else does. So go to St. Mike or go to hell, you won't catch me romancin' no damn phony princesses, by God, not while there's a good honest squaw or a damned grizzly bear, for that matter, left in the woods."

"Good morning, princess," Okime called brightly when Emerson had finished his tirade and was stalking away. "Good morning, Long John. You want nice hot cup tea? Not good to quarrel in morning without nice cup hot tea."

"Naw," the American growled, looking directly at Ludmila for a moment. "I'm gonna go find me that whorehouse where Charley and Taos wound up. Mebbe they got a mornin' shift. I could use a decent lay, damnit."

Ludmila blanched dead white and Long John stepped up onto the gangplank again and hurried to the dock. *Serves her right,* he told himself, but he could not quite keep hold of his sense of triumph, not thinking about the shocked, small face, the eyes like the big, dark eyes of an otter caught in a trap.

Woman's touched in the head, though, and that's a fact. High-strung is what they call it. No kind of a female partner except mebbe for some dumbass count what ain't got nothin' better to do than keep her in silks and suchlike. The King of Alaska's found his match, I'm thinkin'. . . .

The sun had dissipated the fog completely by now, and Emerson stood idly watching the waterfront activity: the lighters being loaded before they were rowed out to the big steamers at anchor in the bay, a supply ship being offloaded, men shouting at one another in a variety of languages. In the midst of all of it the clouds of seagulls wheeled in on their big wings to alight on and engage in noisy and passionate battles over the feast of garbage in the bay and on shore as well.

He found Taos Danny and Charley St. Francis as he was walking toward company headquarters to make inquiries for the next ship to Seattle. The two approached him with slow, uncertain steps, their hands and faces lined with dirt and something decidedly hangdog about their bearing. Neither seemed to be willing to look Emerson directly in the face when he greeted them.

Long John shook his head and laughed. "You look like you been et, digested, and deposited by a sow grizzly, an' then a flock of ravens went over what was left. Now just don't go tellin' this coon any bad news, on account of I got enough to keep me mad already."

"Right you are, Long John," Taos Danny agreed, glancing up at the big man. "By God, we won't tell you, then."

"I'm on my way to find us a ride to Seattle, get us out of this stinkin' Russki hole," Emerson said. "Get back to the states and out of trouble, spend our money on somethin' worthwhile."

"Well, could be spendin' that money ain't so much of a problem as you mighta thought," Danny hedged.

"Dumbass Meskin," Charley growled.

"Oh Christ," Emerson groaned. "Tell me you dumb bastids ain't gonna say what I'm startin' to think."

"Wouldn't never happened if the stupid greaser here hadn'ta decided he could beat the thievin' Tlingits at the hand game," Charley said.

"Well, you wasn't hogtied, dumbhead," Taos shrugged. "You coulda knocked me cold or somethin'. An' you shouldn't never give me your stake when I ask for it."

Emerson grimaced, rubbed his eyes. "So how much you feeble-minded coons got left?"

"Well . . . I was thinkin', so I saved back enough for a stake. We'll make 'er all back in one more winter's trappin'," Charley said hopefully.

"Yeah," Taos said, "but that was before we went back to the damned cathouse. Them gals cleaned out the rest, fair an' square."

"Oh, hell." Emerson was utterly disgusted. "That's it. I've still got most of my tin, and I'm heading back for the states. The two of you can set here until you rot. Blew your whole damned pile in one rotten day and night."

"Look, Long John, I know you're a mite put out with us just now," Danny offered. "I can even see why. Guess mebbe I'd feel the same. But by God, I would never desert a friend in a bad fix, no sir."

"Truth is," Charley added, "we can't stay here in Sitka or the Russkis'll throw us in the stockade."

"Them coons give us till today to disappear," Taos agreed. "See, after we lost all our money we was feelin' pretty low, and they was some soldiers that got ornery, an' one thing led to another, an' . . ."

Emerson drew a deep breath, and the other two men lapsed into surreptitiously watchful silence.

Long John, for his part, passed through fury, disgust

and then despair as he realized that the two years of grueling work in the frozen forests around Kl'uci were down the drain. They had nothing to show for two winters of freezing and starving and breaking snow to get to traplines, two winters of abject exhaustion, of shipwreck and near-death. All was gone in one night.

"An' I didn't even get to be in on the fun," he said aloud.

"Huh?" Charley asked.

The absurdity of the situation was beginning to overpower Long John, and he began to chuckle. "A two-fucking-winter night an' I didn't even get to be in on it." Emerson roared with laughter, bent double with it. Taos and Charley looked at one another, smiled uncertainly.

"More'n a thousand dollars between you two bastids," Emerson managed between spasms of laughter. "She musta been one hell of a party, lads, an' all I was doin' was sleepin' an' moonin' over a highfalutin piece who just by God told me in no uncertain terms what I am." He laughed more wildly than ever, and his two companions began to chuckle, but with growing unease.

Emerson pounded the two of them across the shoulders. "I'm a goddamned sauvage, boys, that's what I am. What the hell? Old Raven Man has his fun. Go find yourselves a boat to save you from the vile Gossacks. I guess this child'll go wrestle him a grizzly for a while."

Emerson proceeded through the mudhole streets of Sitka, still not certain what to do but very sure he did not want the company of his friends. He bought some smoked salmon and a bottle of vodka at the commissary, and then on impulse a jar of brandied peaches. He considered making good on his threat to visit the bordello outside the stockade wall, but as he approached the collection of ramshackle huts with their quagmire yards and a gaggle of ragged, shrieking children chasing each other, he found that he had no appetite for human companionship of any sort.

He turned his steps toward the hills and climbed rapidly up into the quiet spruce forest. Within a very short time he felt far from human concerns. Not even a whiff of smoke from the morning fires of Sitka reached him. He breathed deeply as he worked his way upslope under the darkness of the woods amidst the luxuriant fern. He noted a bald eagle perched at the edge of its nest and fanning its big wings.

Chicks, he thought. *Daddy, he's guarding the nest while his woman's off fishing. Dumb birds have got the whole thing turned around—or maybe they don't.*

Emerson toyed with the idea for a moment and then allowed his thoughts to drift elsewhere. Now, alone for one of the few times since he and Taos and Charley came down out of the Kamchatka forests, he began to feel immeasurably better.

"Human critters is what it is. Just bein' around 'em awhile, you can't seem to help gettin' dragged into all their craziness, an' you don't even know it's happenin' to you till you get away to breathe for a space."

He moved more slowly now, falling back into the easy rhythm of the woodsman, the hunter. He figured that if a deer or a bear came and tapped him on the shoulder, maybe he'd take a shot at it. But mostly he was enjoying his solitude.

He spent the morning tramping toward the interior of the island, climbing ridges and descending drainages. He saw no game except a small band of elk feeding in a meadow far below his vantage point on the shoulder of a mountain. At the edge of the trees near the little herd a pair of wolves lay merely watching the ruminants, apparently not hungry but sitting with their tongues lolling out at the big deer. Emerson fancied the wolves displayed a certain proprietary pride in the herd.

Eventually he made his way to a rocky promontory on one of the highest peaks. It was not more than four thousand feet high, he knew, and yet it gave the illusion of much greater elevation because of the steepness of its rise and the commanding view from the top. High up the snow still lay to a depth of several feet in shadowy areas, and from his vantage point Long John could see clear across to the great peaks of the mainland, gleaming white, row after jagged row of them soaring into the haze. He chewed on his tough, salty salmon and picked peaches out of the jar with his fingers, savoring the tangy sweetness of the fruit. It had been months since he'd had such a treat.

His vodka bottle remained unopened.

A Steller's jay came and perched on a low branch of a dwarfed tree nearby; the dark, tufted head turned one way and the other as the bird watched the man eat. From time to time the jay uttered a loud squawk, as if demanding food. Emerson bit off a piece of salmon and tossed it to the ground beside the tree. The bird dropped gracefully to retrieve the morsel and then fluttered back to its branch. It eyed the man cautiously as it tested the food in its beak, biting rapidly several times before dropping the scrap of fish and flying off in a series of outraged shrieks.

"Guess he don't like ukali," Long John said aloud and then lay back, laughing, possessed of a great feeling of well-being.

"By God," he said to the blue sky, "ain't no woman in the world can make a man feel really bad as long as he can get off by himself to somethin' like this. Hell, I don't want to drift down to the States, do I?"

The statement was partly bravado, and he knew it—knew it by the hollow space inside him, but he could put the feeling away a little now, look at it from a distance. "I been lonely before," he concluded. "They's lots of things worse, even if bein' a castaway ain't."

* * *

It was late afternoon when he returned to the village of Sitka, and the sun laid a dazzling path of light across the water in the harbor. The sense of well-being, of newly rediscovered sanity, was still with Long John as he headed for the docks. He noted the lazy huskies and malemutes lying about, some of them half-starved, some fat. They brought to mind the wolves he had seen earlier and he drew certain comparisons, concluding that the wolves, dependent upon no one but themselves, had by far the better life.

Emerson figured that if he didn't find Danny and Charley at the Japanese fishing vessel, at least Musi and Okime were likely to have an idea where the two would be. As he neared the vessel's mooring place, however, he became aware of loud shrieks in Russian, Japanese and English—the latter the unmistakable tones of Taos Danny and Charley St. Francis.

Long John broke into a run and leaped across onto the deck of the *Darakusha,* where he found a scene of wonderful confusion. Taos Danny was straddled on the midsection of a short, barrel-chested Russian soldier. His hands clutched the man's hair and methodically banged the head against the deck.

Charley St. Francis had the soldier's arm and hand stretched out above his head clutching a pistol. Backed up against the railing of the boat was Olga Bohmer, both hands pressed against her broad bosom and her mouth wide, wailing and crying. Okime was leaning over the three combatants, shouting at them shrilly with a string of Japanese invectives, and Musi sat grinning hugely on a coil of rope.

"Goldang it, Ivan, let go the gun," Charley was shouting. "We don't want to have to kill you, you dumbass horse fucker."

"Like hell we don't," Taos grunted, continuing his assault upon the soldier's head. "I'm gettin' downright tired of goddamn sojers jumpin' on me all the time. I ain't done nothin' to any of 'em, not yet. Now I wants to pull the bastard's scalp."

"Ye oughta keep your ignorant tater-hole shut," Charley snapped, still struggling to disarm the Russian.

"Well hell, cain't I just be friendly, pass the time o' day with Miz Boomer? Dang it, 'twere a compliment on 'er. I like a woman with bazooms like great mounds o' biled squash."

The Russian soldier gave a convulsive thrust with his upper body, got one hand free and grabbed for Danny's throat. "I keel you, Yankee dog," he roared.

Emerson stood above the group, his revolver out and trained on the stranger. Mme. Olga leaped forward and clutched Long John's gun arm, still shrieking. "Don't let them hurt him any more, Mr. Emerson," she cried. "He was defending *mon honneur*. Please, you are the sane one—do something."

"Will everybody just shut up?" Emerson bellowed, shaking the startled companion off his arm. "By God, I'll murder the lot of you."

A sudden silence fell over the group at this demand from a new quarter, and Long John managed, with Mme. Olga's help, to persuade the Russian sergeant to release his weapon on the condition that Taos and St. Francis should cease battering him.

The sergeant, a powerfully built man of perhaps fifty and the owner of a large, fierce mustache, had leaped to defend the governess' honor against the trappers. As Long John restored a somewhat calmer atmosphere, Mme. Bohmer sought to soothe the still-bristling soldier, explaining to him in Russian how it was with American barbarians. One could not take seriously most of what they said; she had learned that it was not necessary to take offense at what the savages probably could not control.

"What the hell they all doing here?" Emerson asked Musi, who was sitting beside him hoping for more action.

Musi shifted position on the coil of rope and said, "Princess-san offer us plenty money to take her north to man she marry. I tell her that not a very good idea, but she sure want to go. Bohmer-san tell her not to go, sergeant here tell her. She not listen to nobody, Emerson-san. Ludmila-san give us thousand dollar when she come back, she say. Thousand dollar—Okime and Musi maybe buy another boat, maybe buy little house in Shiranuka when we go back to Japan—"

"But what are *they* doing here?" Long John interrupted. "It ain't my business what Ludmila does."

"They come bring princess' things for trip. We leave in morning, by golly. You ready to leave in morning too, Long John?"

"Hell no," Emerson answered. "I ain't going to St. Mike."

"Wal, actually we are," put in Charley St. Francis, who had edged over to hear what Emerson and Musi were discussing. "I woulda discussed the notion with you, John, but you was gone all day, an'—"

"Ain't going," Emerson repeated. "You an' Danny go if you've a mind to, but I just got a few things settled to my satisfaction an' I ain't goin'."

"Thought ye might have strong feelin's concernin' the matter," Charley said, "but the truth is—"

"No, damnit, I ain't going."

"Truth is," Charley continued blithely, "Danny and me ain't got much choice. One steamer out there's heading back to Kamchatka, an' one is bound for California, which we ain't got the money to take. Ain't any others for a week or more. You know me and the ignorant Meskin cain't stay around here that long. We're pure poison to these sojers. We'll be in the slammer if we're here past tomorrow."

"See?" Taos Danny was explaining to the Russian sergeant, "I like Miz Boomer here. I wouldn't say nothin' to offend her, not for the world. Hell, I done saved her life. Ain't that right, Olga?"

"You do not call her by her first name, nyet. I stick a knife in you." The Russian started for Danny again.

"Nyet, nyet," cried Mme. Olga. "It is like the words of children. They really don't know any better." She put her hand upon the arm of the stocky sergeant, glanced up at him shyly. He turned to her and their eyes met for a moment before both looked away, reddening.

"I still throw them in stockade," he blustered. "Da, by damn."

"Nyet, nyet," Olga repeated. "It is best to ignore these. They are not like us, Dimitri."

"See what I mean?" Charley St. Francis whispered to Emerson. "We gotta get that dumbass Taos away from here before he gets us into a stew we cain't climb out of."

Emerson unsnapped his money belt, pulled out the remainder of their Kamchatka profits. "Here," he snapped, pressing two hundred into Charley's hands. "You buy passage for the two of you. Better get your outfit tonight if you're sailin' in the mornin'. Me, I've had it with the whole lot of you. I'll make out. I'll go live with Red Porcupine and his crew again. Swim to Dyea if I have to, an' then mosey on over the High Grease Trail."

He wheeled and strode off the sampan, ignoring both Charley St. Francis and Taos Danny, who called after him to come back. He headed away from town, back into the hills, and fashioned a sleeping place for himself of spruce boughs under the trees.

The late sun vanished into the glowing sea to the northwest, leaving the sky brassy yellow from horizon to horizon.

He uncorked the bottle of vodka that he had carried

with him all day long. He took a long shuddering swallow of the volatile liquid. The equanimity he had gained during his day's walk up into the mountains vanished. As the first stars appeared, Ludmila's image rose in his mind. He recalled vividly her odor, the feel of her flesh under his hands.

He raised the bottle, swallowed, shuddered again. "Women," he muttered.

A raven flapped in to roost on a tree above him, croaked loudly when it saw him.

"Naw, it ain't just women. It's people," he told the raven.

The black bird croaked again.

"An' I know you're tellin' me to get lost. You don't think much of humans either, even though Red Porcupine says you created 'em. But the fact is, you're either goin' to have to put up with me, my fine bird, or move out."

The raven shuffled back and forth on the branch but didn't speak again.

"Standoff," John muttered. He lay back and stared up at the sky as it gradually darkened and more stars appeared.

"What the hell," he said at length. "Redoubt St. Mike it is, I guess, then across to Anvik an' up the Yukon. Trap my way clear up to Red Porcupine's village an' winter with 'em. Ain't nothin' back in the States for this child anyhow."

He took another swig from his bottle. "But by God I ain't speakin' to any of them thieves, an' that includes her majesty the princess."

The raven muttered irritably from the growing darkness.

"Ain't even speakin' to you," Emerson growled.

Chapter 14
Ludmila's Wedding

Old Raven Man, he lit in a spruce and looked around, but at first he couldn't see anything very clearly because everything was still changing. Red fire streamed down the sides of Denali, the great one, and there was so much dust in the air that it fell like snow.

Raven Man was patient. He waited a long time. He saw the Yukon River, but there were no human people along it, not even a single small village.

Then Camp Robber flew into the tree and sat beside Raven Man. "Is there anything to eat?" Raven Man asked his friend.

"I have nothing," Camp Robber replied. "I never eat. I live on the wind—just open my mouth. What about you?"

Raven Man cleared his throat and his cry echoed off across the ash-covered landscape. "I just wander around," he said. "Sometimes I catch fish. I'll bet there's some grayling over in the river. Any people where you come from?"

"Not many," Camp Robber replied. "Denato the Creator has killed them all, but you could make new ones. I'll bet you could do that if you wanted to."

"Perhaps I will," Raven Man said. And so he flew away and went down the Yukon River, the Lot of Water.

When he came to a high bank where a thick stand of spruces grew, Raven Man lit again and fanned his big wings. "Should be a village here," he croaked.

From a cottonwood tree he took some bark and used it to form the arms and legs and body of a tiny man. He had to be careful with the penis because it was so small. Then he took more cottonwood bark and formed the body of an even smaller woman. He had even more trouble with her. Then when he was finished he struck the two of them into the earth on a high bank facing the Lot of Water. He put them close together, belly to belly.

Raven Man laughed and once again fanned his wings. "When I come back up the river," he told the two figures he had formed, "I want to find a lot of people here. That's why I've stuck you together this way. You know what to do next."

June 1867

Emerson rose when the sunlight woke him. Mosquitoes were singing about his face and had already bitten him several times when he came fully awake. He slapped at the insects, cursed under his breath and got to his feet.

He made his way back to the sampan, where he found Musi and Okime already hard at work preparing for the departure. Taos Danny and Charley St. Francis had gone ashore to purchase traps, rifles, ammunition and such other supplies as were necessary for a winter's trapping along the Yukon.

The Japanese couple greeted him warmly, Okime insisting that he sit down in the cabin and have a cup of tea and some boiled fish and rice for breakfast.

"I know you come back," she said, nodding wisely. "I tell your friends to get supplies for you, too, so you don't need do nothing until they come."

"Well," Long John said, accepting the proffered tea

gratefully, "I couldn't just let Taos and Charley go off by themselves. God knows what they'd get into if I wasn't around to keep an eye on 'em."

"That's one reason," Okime agreed, smiling at Musi and winking.

"It's the only damned reason," Long John snapped.

"Musi and me, we hear little bit of you arguing with Princess Ludmila yesterday. Thought maybe you want to finish argument."

"Love very strange thing," Musi nodded. "Nobody can fight like two people in love. *Shikari, aisuru—ai, koi, aijin*—all different kinds love. Makes people act like they hate, *nikumu*."

"Talk English, damnit," Emerson growled. "You know I don't ken that jabber of yours, not enough to say so. Love's a pile of horse dung, pardon the expression, ma'am. An' it ain't got a blessed thing to do with me."

"You not looking forward even little bit to seeing pretty Russian, then?" Okime smiled.

"You two keep this up an' I might just stay here in Archangel after all. Hell, the two of you are bein' matchmakers, and you know Ludmila ain't free even if we wanted each other, which we don't."

"Sometimes things turn out different than you think," Okime shrugged, pressing her shiny black hair back away from her eyes.

"Sure," Musi added cheerfully. "Maybe husband-to-be sink in ship to Redoubt St. Michael. Maybe already drowned."

Emerson burst out laughing in spite of himself. "By God, you're right. Always look for the brighter side of life."

"That's what I say," Musi grinned. "I always say so. Isn't that true, Okime?"

* * *

Taos and Charley returned with outfits for themselves and for Long John as well. Emerson had already finished eating, and the *Darakusha* was in sailing order. Neither Ludmila nor anyone from her party had yet appeared, and as Charley hastened to explain, none of them would.

"Dobshansky's back," he said, tossing a rifle to Long John without a word of greeting. "Come in last night after the moon rose, so I guess they ain't much point waitin' for the leetle princess."

"Damn shame, if you ast me," Taos Danny added. "I was lookin' forward to havin' the lovely Olga around again."

Despite his own resolve and his protestations to the Japanese couple Emerson felt as if he had been hit in the lights—hard. He saw Musi and Okime glance at one another and then at him, sympathy in their expressions, and he hastened to speak for fear they might start to comfort him.

"Well, that's good news. That means we don't have to go to St. Mike at all. I propose we dock at Dyea an' saunter over the High Grease to see the Tagish. We can winter with Red Porcupine, an' I'll get a chance to see how that daughter of his is shapin' up. Little Kate, by God, she should be half a woman by now. Another year or two an' by heavens I'll marry her. Turn Injun, pure an' simple."

"Likely more fur farther down on the Yukon," Charley said. "Maybe we ought to head for the Redoubt anyway."

"Wait a minute, *dozo*, wait a minute," Musi interposed quickly. "Who is going to pay for trip now? Princess was only one with money."

"Aw, come on, Musi. We thought you was our friend," Danny cried.

"Yeah," Charley added. "You folks don't wanna see

them Russkis lock me an' the Meskin away, now do you?''

''Sure, you friends,'' Musi agreed, ''but what about Musi and Okime, eh? You think Musi and Okime eat air. Now you want us to starve to death. We lose thousand dollar.''

They continued to debate the matter for several minutes, the discussion growing so charged that none of the group noticed the small figure of Irena the Tlingit servant slip on board. She glanced nervously in their direction and then addressed Okime, who was standing to one side and impassively watching the conversation.

Okime listened to Irena and then lifted up her hands and called out, ''All right, all right, that's enough for now. We talk this over later. This Indian say she come from Princess Ludmila, brings message.''

The men stopped talking and turned to stare at Irena in her neat dark gown. Her hair was braided and coiled about her head in Russian fashion, but the planes of her pale bronze face clearly attested to her heritage.

Taos Danny let out a long whistle. ''Gotta admit she's a hell of an improvement over Olga,'' he said aside to the others. ''Thunderin' rainclouds, this Irish Injun's goddam well in love—''

''Meskins don't know what love is,'' St. Francis snorted, arching one eyebrow and staring.

Irena cleared her throat nervously and began to speak in a barely audible voice. ''Princess Ludmila say she not go on boat. . . .''

''You gotta speak up, purty thing,'' Taos said, rising and going to put an arm about her shoulders. ''You ain't got no call to be scairt of us, ain't—''

Danny didn't get a chance to finish his sentence; the timid creature suddenly turned at the touch of his arm on her shoulders, backed away a step and slapped the trapper across the face with a blow that sent his hat flying.

"Do not touch Irena," she snarled. "I am good Christian. You sit down there, listen to what I say."

Taos Danny closed his mouth and sat down immediately, while Charley St. Francis stifled a snort of laughter and Okime turned her head aside, one hand over her mouth.

The Indian continued, this time in a much stronger voice, all her fear apparently overcome in her burst of indignation. "She say she not going because Count Dobshansky came back last night. They be married right away. Count say for men who save princess, also owners of boat, come to his house right now. He wishes to give reward."

"How big reward?" Okime asked.

"Thousand dollars American."

"Thousand each?" Charley asked.

Irena shrugged. "Count only say thousand. Don't know no more."

Her message delivered, Irena left, making an obvious point of ignoring Taos Danny. By now he had recovered from his shock and was attempting to wheedle her into staying so that she might convert him to Christianity.

"Do your soul good, an' mine too," he called to the rapidly retreating back. "All Christians want to save some pore sinner. Most points you can get, gal, just ast your priest."

"Give it up," Long John laughed. "I'd say that Injun gal ain't all that impressed with you. Tlingits have got spunk, just like I've always told ye."

"Tlingit, is she? By God, she will be, one way or another," Danny insisted. "This child's in love, Long John. By the great blue Jesus it's true," he added, a note of genuine surprise coming into his voice.

"Despite the romantic swoons everybody seems to be sufferin'," Charley St. Francis suggested, "I'm for going over there an' pickin' up whatever tin the King of Alaska wants to give us.''

''And I'm for gettin' the hell out of this place,'' Emerson said. ''My instincts tell me the less we have to do with this count feller, the better off we're going to be.''

''You gone snowblind and bush-mad?'' Charley howled. ''The Injun said a thousand dollars, and she weren't even sure whether that's apiece or not. One way or the other we stand to profit a heap.''

''I'll bet you that Andy Johnson's done awready bought Alaska from the Russkis, just like them rumors we heard in Petropavlovsk when we come down out of the hills,'' Taos Danny put in. ''So now the count an' Governor Prince Makustov wants to reward us for savin' the princess. We're by God goin' to be the recipients of an act of international goodwill—that's how this child's got it figgered. Use your noodle, Long John.''

''Taos and Charley right,'' Musi agreed. ''We all Mericans. You not want to go, you stay here. We bring your money back to you, Long John.''

''Hell, no,'' Danny said. ''He's gotta go with us. He don't, sure as God's green balls, we'll end up with the whole Russki army on our backs, one way or another.''

''Meskin's right for once,'' Charley agreed, ''much as I hate to say so. He'll open that big flytrap of his and—''

''It's lucky for you I'm in love an' at peace with the world, dumbhead,'' Danny grumbled, ''otherwise that would be the one time too many you called me a damn Meskin an' I would cut out your liver an' feed the damned thing to the seagulls.''

''Don't go divertin' the subject, now,'' Charley insisted. ''The subject is that Long John here has got to go with us, an' if we have to hit him over the head an' drag him along—''

''All right, all right,'' Emerson shouted, throwing up

his hands. "I'll go along just to get you two jackasses out of my hair."

Count Pieter Dobshansky was only of average height, but he was powerfully built, the shoulders broad, the arms muscular, the paunch well cushioned with fat. The face was also broad, coarse, the mouth wide and heavy-lipped, the eyes slightly bulbous, the nose purple-veined from heavy drinking. He wore a ruffled shirt, a bright green cravat and several medals on his coat. The dandyish clothing emphasized rather than disguised the general crudity of his features.

Long John Emerson took an instant and violent dislike to him, whom he had known heretofore by reputation only.

Ain't gonna do anything foolish, though, he decided. *Just gonna take the money that Charley and Danny and the Japanese folks want so bad and then be on our way, no fireworks, no nothin'.*

"I really must apologize for the state of my house," the count was saying in his unctuous slightly accented voice. "As you probably know, I got back from a long journey only last night, and servants being what they are, well . . . Mostly we use the local Indians, and I am afraid that when the master is away, they prefer to spend their time drinking and playing the hand game. Gambling's in their blood."

Long John studied Dobshansky's face—a mask, as the American supposed, that only partially concealed the cruelty for which Dobshansky was known among the various Alaskan Indian peoples. He was both sophisticated and utterly ruthless; at his orders half a dozen or more Indian villages had been annihilated.

Out of the corner of his eye Emerson noted Danny's hand start toward his knife, saw Charley grab Taos' arm and twist it behind his back. Emerson fought back his own urge to spring at the Russian's throat.

This pig an' Ludmila in bed, him slobberin' over her an' God knows what else. Maybe I'll figure a way of putting a round or two into his carcass.

"Please be seated, gentlemen, uh, madam," Dobshansky continued as the group entered a small parlor crowded with upholstered furniture, lamps, shelves full of knickknacks and half a dozen leather-bound books. Emerson perched on the edge of a damask-covered wingback chair, tried to keep his mind off the image of this grotesque, toadlike man with Ludmila, beautiful Ludmila.

"My fiancee has told me how you all were instrumental in saving her life," the count went on, "and naturally I want to extend to you all a token of my immense gratitude—"

"That a thousand apiece or a thousand for the five of us?" Charley asked abruptly.

"What?" the count demanded, half-startled, half-indignant. Then he began to laugh. "You Americans are always so direct. Considering the fact that the three of you spent a month alone on an island with Princess Ludmila, I'm not sure you shouldn't be paying me. But my fiancee has assured me that you were all perfect gentlemen, and of course I have implicit faith in—"

Suddenly Long John found himself on his feet, irrational rage boiling inside his skull. "Caught you any good Injun fillies lately, count?" Emerson heard himself drawling.

"*What?*" Dobshanksy jumped up and reached for a nearby bell cord.

"I ast if you've raped an' tortured any Injun women lately, you damned ugly sissified Frenchified leetle squat toad. Rumor has it that's what you take special pleasure in."

Out of the corner of his eye John noted that Danny and Charley were poised, ready for a brawl. "You stay out of this, lads," Emerson commanded. "Me and the King of Alaska's gonna settle matters by ourselves."

"Not so, my barbaric friend," Dobshansky purred, yanking on the bell cord.

Emerson heard the quick rush of feet on wooden floors, knew that within seconds he would be surrounded by Russian troops, very likely shot, certainly thrown into the stockade. "What the hell," he muttered. Picking up a heavy oak chair, he leaped at the count, bringing the piece of furniture down as hard as he could on the man's head, feeling intense satisfaction as he observed Dobshansky crumple.

Then the door burst open and he himself felt a heavy blow to the back of his head, a sense of pressure that expanded into a rush of darkness as the floor rose to meet his face.

Princess Ludmila peered over the shoulder of Prince Makustov, with whom she was dancing, scanning the crowded room. The few ladies wore their most colorful gowns and such jewelry as they had; the men without exception had on some form of military dress. Music was provided by a single young officer who played the balalaika and a half-breed Russian-Tlingit who sawed enthusiastically on an old fiddle. The combined sounds were marvelously tuneless but somewhat engaging despite the inexpertise of the musicians. This was roughly a waltz, and as the prince dipped and executed a turn, the bloated face of Count Dobshansky came directly into her view. The face was made even more grotesque by the swollen, purplish lump on his forehead and one blackened eye.

Ludmila giggled at the sight, thinking how much the great Count Pieter looked like a peasant farmer after a night on the town. Then she had to repress a shudder as it came to her for perhaps the twentieth time that this man, Dobshansky, was now her husband. Just a few hours earlier she had exchanged the most sacred of vows with him.

"You are gay this afternoon, my dear," Prince Makustov said, hearing the giggle but apparently missing the shudder. "I suppose it is natural that a young woman should be so on her wedding day."

Ludmila hiccoughed, missed a step and stumbled against Makustov, a move for which he smoothly corrected so that it appeared never to have happened.

"Yes, very nat—natural," Ludmila agreed. "I am married to the man of my dreams." She paused, peered across the room again. "I have always had nightmares, you know," she added, and went off into another round of uncontrollable giggles.

"Ah," smiled the prince, "you are ever the little jokester. I know that you will be very happy in your new life. That life will not be lived here, of course, not in Alaska, thank heaven. We are expecting word any day. The Russian Empire has completed its business in North America, and soon we must leave it, mud, ice, and disease-ridden natives, to the Americans. They themselves are hungry for empire, and this godforsaken land will suit them for a time. Count Dobshansky and I, with luck, will be summoned back to Moscow and honored for our long years of labor. My wife Emily speaks of nothing else these days, as you know. I gather she has spent some time bending your ear as well as my own."

Ludmila stumbled again, felt a sudden rush of nausea. "I think," she mumbled, "I think maybe I'd best sit down, prince."

Prince Makustov helped Ludmila to a chair, leaning above her solicitously and speaking soothingly.

Dobshansky came over immediately, but she waved both men away, stammered something about needing fresh air, and found herself being ushered outside to the verandah by Princess Makustov and Olga Bohmer. The older women scrutinized Ludmila keenly after putting her into a wicker chair.

"I will send Irena with a cup of tea, my dear," Princess Makustov said. "I hope you won't mind my saying so, but I believe that you are not used to drinking champagne."

Ludmila nodded apologetically and felt the world beginning to spin once more. She put a hand over her mouth, hoping fervently that she could avoid being sick at least until she was alone. Olga rushed to her with a series of clucking sounds, put her cool hand against the princess' forehead, smoothed her hair.

"My poor *byonka*, my little one," she crooned—slightly more than tipsy herself. "My byonka is married today. Ah, I taught her to walk, her first steps were to me. Princess Makustov, I taught her to read and not to throw her food at table. She is always my precious, and now she is leaving her Olga."

Mme. Bohmer was by now sobbing, and tears streamed down her ruddy round cheeks. Ludmila smiled despite her nausea and found herself hugging the broad shoulders of her lifelong companion, serving as comforter to the one who would give comfort.

"Oh, madame," Ludmila managed, "you must not take on so. Why, you will not be alone in the world. I will be happy if you remain with me, but I think that handsome sergeant—Dimitri is it not?—I think he may have other plans for you before long."

Olga blushed even more redly than before. "I do not know what you are speaking of, Ludmila. Sergeant Dimitri has been kind, but then, he is a gentleman."

"Ah, Mme. Olga, I too have seen the way his eyes follow you. He is a fine man," Princess Makustov said, her voice fluttery and possibly even sincere. "Well, I will go find that Irena. I'm sure a cup of tea will do us all good. It has been an exciting day, has it not? I remember my own wedding as if it were yesterday. . . . Well, you don't want to hear that story. I will go find Irena."

The chunky little woman hurried inside and Ludmila sat hugging her governess for a few more moments. "Perhaps you should return to the party, Olga," she suggested, feeling an almost panicky need to be alone for a few minutes. "I will be fine. I'll just sit here for a little while, and I am certain the fresh air will revive me completely. I think Sergeant Dimitri misses you already."

Olga snorted. "How you talk on your wedding day. Still, perhaps I should go see to it that everything is in order at Count Dobshansky's house. One cannot trust servants without supervision. I must make sure that your trousseau has been sent over, such as it is. Soon you will be able to order your own things and not have to rely on hand-me-downs. Are you quite confident that you'll be all right here, my precious?"

Ludmila nodded and managed a wan smile. Soon Olga departed—toward the ballroom rather than the front hall.

The fresh air and the solitude after the noisy, stuffy room began to revive Ludmila. Sunlight slanted in across the water of Sitka harbor, creating a broad, shining path too bright to look at directly. The light fell amber-colored across the rough buildings of the settlement, the almost painfully dark green slopes of the hills.

It seemed to Ludmila that the afternoon had gone on forever, started in some dim time before she became truly conscious and would stretch uncertainly and incompletely until long beyond her death.

"My wedding day," she muttered, trying to bring a sense of reality to it all, but failing. "Princess Ludmila Andreiovna, Countess Dobshanksy . . ." Her voice trailed off.

She thought of the man she had married, his coarse, ugly face, the suggestion of both sensuality and cruelty in the heavy configuration of lips and nose. She shivered again, an involuntary response, and tears came to her eyes. I will be a good wife, she swore. I will do my Christian duty.

She had only first laid eyes on her husband two days previously, when he returned from Redoubt St. Michael. She remembered his words of greeting. "You are far more beautiful than I had even dared to hope, Ludmila" At the same time his prominent, pale eyes ran up and down her figure like unclean hands.

And then came the dreadful incident, with John Emerson breaking a chair over Pieter's head. The count remained unconscious for some time, and upon coming to was in a fearful rage, ordering Emerson to be taken out of the stockade and shot immediately. Makustov remained aloof from the matter, not wishing to alienate Dobshansky, and so it was only with the most circumspect intercession that Ludmila herself managed to persuade the count to spare the life of her savior. She felt constrained not only to employ all her feminine wiles, but to argue very carefully in doing so to avoid letting Pieter Dobshansky suspect her own interest was more personal than the abstract service of mercy.

Two days later, when Dobshansky's physician determined that his patient was sufficiently recovered, this very day at two o'clock in the Sitka afternoon, the count and Princess Ludmila had become one.

Long John Emerson still languished, along with his two American companions, in the stockade. The thousand-dollar reward had been sent by courier to the Japanese fisherman and his wife, for they were accounted guiltless in the outbreak of violence. And now, sometime later on this very night, Ludmila would be in the arms of a man of whom she could not think without the greatest revulsion, no matter how she tried to persuade herself otherwise or what words she whispered to the icon of Jesus in her locket.

She had indeed drunk far too much champagne. She had been by turns hilarious and active, flirting outrageously with every young officer at the reception in Prince Makustov's mansion, laughing noisily, and at other times somber, withdrawn, dreading what the end of the party would bring, moving through a haze of unaccustomed tipsiness and unreality.

Irena slipped noiselessly onto the verandah to stand beside Ludmila and hold out a cup and saucer to her. Ludmila took the tea, sipped automatically at it, studied the quiet-faced Indian. "Does it seem to you, Irena," she asked, "that something has happened to time?"

"I don' know what you say," Irena shrugged.

"I think I am probably a little drunk," Ludmila explained, "and that might be why it is. But it seems to me that this afternoon has stretched out forever."

"Summertime," said Irena, nodding knowingly. "Sun only go down for a little while. Come up early, go down late. That what it is."

"No—yes," Ludmila answered, smiling in spite of herself. "I guess that's part of it. I was hoping it might be something magic, that it would remain afternoon forever, and tonight . . ."

She left the thought unfinished, realizing how improper it would be to express what she was thinking, particularly to a servant. She felt horribly alone. There was no one, no one in her whole world to whom she could confide her fears, her pain, her perverse desire for Long John, which her marriage had done not a thing to mitigate, as she had half-hoped it would. Quite unexpectedly she burst into tears.

Irena stood by uncertainly, reaching out a tentative hand to lay it upon Ludmila's quaking shoulder. "You scared?" she asked softly.

"I guess I am," Ludmila gasped. "I'm sorry, I shouldn't—"

"You scared of man-woman thing, you and count tonight?"

Ludmila looked up, startled.

"Russian womans, they scared of that, talk about it in whispers, not like man-woman thing. Womans in my village say it pretty good. I don' know which one right. Sometimes I think maybe Russian womans lie a little bit. I don' think you need to be scared."

Ludmila stared at Irena, dumfounded by her blunt speech, and then began laughing. Irena looked puzzled as the princess continued to laugh.

"Irena," Ludmila said, standing up and hugging her, "you are very good for me. Will you come with me tonight, when I go to my husband's—my—house?"

"You ask Princess Makustov," Irena answered, "but I don't think count gonna want servant around house this night."

Ludmila glanced toward the sun, which she had to admit to herself was dropping imperceptibly nearer to the water to the northwest, then shuddered again.

Three candles burned in an elaborate silver holder on the mantelpiece of Count Pieter Dobshansky's bedroom. The count himself lay back in an overstuffed armchair, his short legs sprawled wide before him, his head tilted back, his prominent eyes half-closed as he watched Ludmila. She sat before the long mirror over the marble-topped dresser, nervously dragging a brush through her unbound black hair. She wore a white lace pegnoir over a heavy satin nightgown, Princess Makustov's best set, which had been cut down by the servants in the mad rush to prepare things for the wedding.

In the mirror Ludmila could see Dobshansky. *My*

husband, she thought. She felt a knotting sensation in her gut, as of ice forming.

He raised the glass, took a long drink. His eyes never moved from her, and his expression of almost reptilian blankness never changed. She had stalled the moment as long as she could, pleading to send for a servant to fetch some trifles from the prince's mansion, and then locking herself in the bathroom for a long bath, not emerging until her husband pounded rudely on the door and insisted that she come out.

She had spent perhaps the last hour feigning various mysterious toiletries, but now, her hair brushed at least three hundred strokes, her face dabbed and patted, her person bathed and perfumed, she could really not think of anything else to do. She continued to bring the brush up to her scalp, mechanically stroking it through the length of her hair.

"Take your clothes off, Ludmila," Dobshanksy suddenly drawled into the intense silence of the room.

Ludmila felt the blood drain from her face. She raised the brush once more. In the mirror she saw the count rise from his chair, stumble slightly. She turned quickly. "What was it you said, my husband?" she asked. "My mind was elsewhere, I'm afraid."

"I said that you should take your nightdress off. I want to see you."

"I . . . I can't do that," she pleaded, using a tone of modest embarassment to disguise the repulsion she felt. *I will blow the candles out, and it will happen in the dark. It will be over quickly.*

"You are my wife," Dobshansky said, the voice cracking like a whip despite the slurring caused by drink. "You will do as I tell you."

"I am not used to the idea yet," she whispered. "Please, let me . . ."

Without finishing the sentence, she stepped to the

fireplace and blew out two of the three candles. Before she could extinguish the third, Dobshansky took her arm and whirled her around, shoving her onto the wide bed.

"You do not understand, do you, my dear?" he growled. "You think of yourself as a princess. Perhaps you even find me repulsive. But you are my wife. You belong to me now as much as my furniture belongs to me, as much as my cattle belong to me, as much as my servants belong to me. You are here to do my bidding."

As he spoke, he half turned and lit the two candles from the third. "Now," he continued, coming to lean over her, his breath redolent of alcohol and wafting directly into her face, "now that you understand your position, that your personal tastes do not matter and do not even interest me, you will disrobe. Otherwise . . ." He thrust a hand into the bosom of her nightdress, pinched a nipple, then ripped the fabric down from the neckline.

"There are many other things that I can do that you may find unpleasant," he said. "Perhaps you will obey your husband and I will not need to resort to them."

Ludmila struggled to rise from the bed, trying to clutch the torn clothing about her breasts. Dobshansky shoved her back upon the mattress. Instinctively she slapped his face, tried to rise again. Dobshansky swung his own hand back and hit her with a blow across the cheek, stunning her. She crouched on the bed, holding her face, staring in horror at the man to whom she had pledged her faith that very afternoon.

"You are mad," she whispered.

"No, Ludmila, my lovely. I merely know what I want. I am quite capable of beating you senseless if that becomes necessary, but considering that I am your husband, I should think that you would see your duty."

Ludmila closed her eyes and drew in a deep breath. *Sweet Jesus, help me now. Are you testing me? Are you doing this because I have sinned? Help me to be strong.*

With her eyes still shut she pulled the pegnoir and gown over her head, lay back passively and waited. She could hear the breath whistling through Dobshansky's nostrils, could feel, she thought, his gaze traveling over her body like something that crawled from breast to belly to the secret place between her legs. Glass clinked on glass as Pieter poured himself another drink; clothing rustled as he disrobed.

The bed creaked as he lowered himself beside her. He pinched her nipple between his fingers once again, hard, so that Ludmila cried out in pain. Her eyes opened involuntarily upon the grotesque, nude form of Pieter Dobshansky leaning above her, his face contorted in a grin. She saw that his manhood was not erect, felt a faint stirring of hope that perhaps he had drunk too much to perform.

Suddenly he pulled her legs apart, thrust two fingers into her, withdrew the hand and delivered another stunning blow to her face, this time with his fist closed. "Slut," he shouted, "you are no virgin, Ludmila!"

He struck her again and again, punctuating his words with blows. "Whore! You pretend to be too modest for your own husband, and all along you have been spreading your legs for someone else. Who is your lover, *ma fille*? Who? Who?"

Each time he shouted *who,* he struck her again. His voice had grown distant, the blows distant as well. Ludmila lay half-conscious and listened to the words that had no meaning she could discern.

Suddenly he grabbed her shoulders, pulled her upright, shook her until her eyes opened.

"Please . . . ," she mumbled through lips already swelling. "Please, Pieter. I . . . I had an accident when I was a girl, riding horses. . . ."

Dobshansky interrupted her with another blow across the mouth. "Hah," he roared, "*malaya vada,* the tide is out. Of course I believe you. Tell me the man. Was it one of the Americans? Perhaps the soldiers who rode with you across Siberia—perhaps all of them. I think you opened your pretty legs for all of them, you whore."

He continued to beat her as he spoke and she saw that he had attained a full erection. *Is this what he needs, he must beat me first*?

"I should throw you out with the other prostitutes," he shouted, slapping her again, "but your looks please me, Ludmila, so perhaps I will keep you for a time, then have you killed. Ah, Prince Rostov, it was sad. My heart nearly broke within me when she died of the cholera. So beautiful, so pure she was, yes, like the first snow of winter. We have both lost someone who was very special. Did you love your daughter? But no, Ludmila. Perhaps I will keep you and beat you every night. What? You have nothing to say, do you, whore?"

Ludmila whimpered, attempted to put her hands in front of her face to defend herself. She could not seem to think clearly, saw that her field of vision had narrowed, darkened.

Perhaps I will die now. Jesus, am I strong enough for what comes next? Long John, Raven Man, I love you. If I live, I will bear your child, our child. But he will grow up to be Pieter Dobshansky's son. I will love you through him, Long John. Why do I think . . . ?

Dobshansky rolled Ludmila over onto her belly and proceeded to sodomize her. Sharp pain wrenched her back to consciousness, the tearing pain that went on and on until she did not think she could bear it any longer. She cried out in anguish, screamed again and again, but her cries served only to increase the vigor of the count's thrusts.

"Maybe this opening is virgin, you pig," he grunted. "You slut, filthy whore. You got any other holes that haven't already been used?"

Dobshansky repeated the words, seeming to excite

himself with the obscene litany. At last he groaned, shuddered, fell heavily on top of her. By inches she moved her ravaged body from under his weight.

He didn't waken.

When she was at last free, she crept from the bed. She stood for a long moment, staring at the coarse, naked form of the snoring man, and the thought of murder was strong within her.

But she turned and walked from the room, pulled her wedding dress on and stepped out into the night. The sky was already beginning to pale with approaching dawn. Streamers of fog drifted among the ghostly forms of the buildings of Sitka, only half visible. Fog lay heavy over the bay. Not so much as a single mast projected above the mists.

Chapter 7
High Grease Trail

Raven Man followed the Lot of Water clear to the ocean, stopping again and again to make people out of cottonwood bark. He made so many that finally his stick-knife wore out and he had to fashion another one. This happened several times, and that is why there are different tribes who all speak a little different.

When Raven Man reached the Yukon Delta, he turned around and started back up the river. When he came to a village, the people all stared at him. "Don't you know me?" Raven Man asked.

"Never seen you before," they replied.

"That is because I made you. If I hadn't done that, the world would sure look funny."

So he taught the people to make bows and arrows and spears and pots from birch bark, parkas from the skins of salmon. He taught them to catch fish with nets and traps, to dry and smoke the meat for winter, to hunt for deer, elk, moose and bear.

"Remember what I have shown you or you will starve to death when the Yukon freezes and the sun hardly comes up at all. Make lamps so you can burn the oil of the salmon, warm your kashims, give light."

So Raven Man left and went on upriver. At each place where he had left the dolls of cottonwood bark, there was a village with lots of people in it. Lots of people and lots of houses, the underground kind.

Different places had different kinds of game, different kinds of plants that grew in the summer. He explained to each of the peoples how they could live best, what was the best way to hunt, what was the best way to fish.

He took the red fire down from the sides of the great one, Denali, and he spread it out in the meadows where there were no villages, but it didn't burn anything. Instead it became red-orange flowers, what we call fireweed.

June–July 1867

Long John Emerson awoke. The big sergeant who served as stockade guard was kicking him persistently, although relatively gently, in the ribs. Emerson came to his feet, ready to fight although not yet certain of his surroundings. The sergeant laughed and held him off until the big trapper regained full consciousness.

"Easy, easy, American barbarian. Da, I come with good news for you and yet you try to kill me," the guard boomed.

"Good news?" Emerson asked.

Taos Danny Vasquez stirred, sat up. "What's goin' on? The Russkis finally gonna take us out an' shoot us or what?" he mumbled.

"Coffee," St. Francis croaked. "Gotta get some coffee in this here joint. It's unhuman, damnit. Been here three, four days, an' you potato-bustin' bastids ain't once had the goddamn grace to give us no coffee in the morning."

"Shut up, you dumbass coons," Emerson interrupted, "an' give the sarge here a chance to speak his piece. Man says he's got good news. Don't know exactly what that means to a vodka-swillin' Russki, but I'd like to find out."

"*Shto vi hateetye*?" the Russian asked. "What would

you like? Freedom maybe? Da, that is what I think. Good news is you get out, Yankees."

All three trappers let out ear-splitting whoops as the sergeant stood back with folded arms, grinning.

"What the hell happened?" Emerson asked when the three of them had quieted down a bit. "Thought sure we'd rot in here half our lives for what I done."

"Prince Makustov's orders this morning," the soldier shrugged. "He did not tell me why, but I think is because Alaska has been sold to you Americans. Not official, not yet. The Russian double eagle is still flying from the governor's mansion, but word came in with a freighter this morning that the czar has sold our colony to your President."

"Hoorah for the States," Taos shouted.

"By God, George, you been the best guard I ever had," Charley added exuberantly.

"Nyet, my name is not George. My name is—"

"Don't tell me again," St. Francis interrupted. "It only makes my head hurt. What I was gonna say is that bein' as you was such a good compañero, my friend Long John here is gonna give you a leetle reward. Ain't that right, Johnny?"

"Got a real penchant for spendin' other people's money, ain't you?" Emerson growled. "Hell, I was gonna give him something," he added, noting the disappointment on the sergeant's face. "Just wanted to do it on my own hook is all. But everything we got is on the sampan, so I'll have to pay you a bit later. If Musi and Okime ain't sailed back to Japan, that is."

The guard shrugged, grinned and opened the stockade gates for the three happy Yanks.

"American territory or not," Taos Danny said when they had picked up their belongings and were out of earshot of the Russian installation, "I think we'd best shake the dust immediately. Boys, we ain't exactly the most popular niggers in Sitka."

"My thoughts precisely, Daniel," Emerson agreed. "We'll find the *Darakusha*, if it's still here, an' see how much the Japanese thieves want to ferry us to Dyea."

"You figger that's far enough away?" Charley asked.

"Don't figger they'll want us especially. Ain't any good to 'em now that the whole rotten gang of Russkis'll be fixing to go home. In any case I thought we'd saunter up over the High Grease an' get on over to Red Porcupine's country, maybe down to Fort Selkirk or Fort Yukon, see if the British are interested in hirin' us on. Get some tin in our bag. Look for gold when we ain't got nothin' else to do. Been rumors about that ever since I first come north. Skookum Jim, Red Porcupine's kid, he's got a lump the size of your fist. Used to carry it around for a good luck token. Wouldn't tell me where he got it, though."

Musi and Okime were more than happy to take the trappers away from Nova Archangelisk. To Long John's surprise they didn't even haggle over the price of passage.

The three trappers made one last trip ashore to purchase additional supplies, mainly goods to give as presents to the Tagish Indians, with whom they planned to winter. The Japanese couple urged them to hurry, explaining that owing to tides and prevailing winds it would be necessary to depart as soon as possible.

"Somethin' sorta strange about the way Musi and Okime are actin', wouldn't you say?" Charley observed.

"Who knows?" Emerson shrugged. "Main thing is they're bein' peculiar in a way that goes along with what we want anyhow. No point questionin' good luck, I guess. Hell, I'm surprised they didn't make off for parts unknown an' take our share of that damned reward with 'em."

"Reckon," Charley agreed. "Always makes me a mite uneasy, though, when someone acts in a way that seems unnatural to 'em."

The three made their purchases quickly and Long

John left a ten-dollar gold piece for the guard at the stockade, for the man had indeed dealt with his American prisoners quite kindly. Then they returend to the *Darakusha,* where the Japanese fisherman and his wife greeted them with obvious relief, casting off from the pier in Sitka harbor almost immediately.

The sampan cleared the harbor, its sail billowed nicely, and they rounded the tip of Chichagof Island to make the trip to the inland passage. Okime scanned the expanse of choppy waters carefully, even climbing up the mast and surveying the water and shore by means of the brass-cased telescope mounted near the top. At last she descended, apparently satisfied, and opened the door of the cabin, which had remained inexplicably locked until that moment. She spoke to someone inside and then turned to Long John, her eyes sparkling and a secretive smile wrinkling up one of her cheeks. Okime stepped back with the gesture of one presenting an honored guest, swinging the door wide as Emerson watched in total mystification.

The first figure to emerge was the Indian, Irena. Immediately following her came Princess Ludmila Andreiovna Dobshansky.

"Well, I'll be dipped in . . . the blood o' the lamb," Charley St. Francis breathed slowly.

For his own part Emerson was certain his mouth was hanging open. He couldn't think of a thing to say until he saw that Ludmila had a scarf wrapped around her head in such a way that most of her face was not visible. There was something about the way she stood too, a certain hunched quality, tension in the shoulders, that convinced him the princess was hurt.

Emerson moved to her without a word. He pulled the scarf away from her face and saw that her lips were swollen and cut. One eye was black and nearly closed. She had a gash on one cheek and she would not raise her gaze meet his.

He felt the breath leave his body as though he had been kicked hard in the stomach. Without thinking he drew her into his arms, held her tenderly against him until the rage began to build in him and he knew he intended to kill.

"Dobshansky did this to you?" he asked, moving her slightly away from him but still holding her shoulders.

Ludmila did not reply but raised her eyes to look directly into his.

"That shit-eating son of a bitch," he exploded. "Musi, turn this goddamned tub around. I'm headin' back to Sitka an' a little unfinished business."

"You gonna fight the Russian Army again?" Taos Danny asked. "Didn't turn out so good last time, as I recall."

"You'll get your chance, Johnny, sure as old griz pisses in the woods," Charley said. "Hell, you think the King of Alaska's gonna let us get away with his bride an' not even come lookin' for us? If the winds stay with us, maybe we'll have a chance for a leetle scuffle up on the Chilkoot Trail. Up there we got a chance, even against the czar's damned army. I say we keep headin' for Dyea."

Taos glanced at Irena, then back at Long John. "They's two of us got somethin' to fight for even if Miss Tlingit spits in this child's face. She's with us now an' I'm guessin' she don't want to go back to Sitka, no sir."

"Stupid men," Okime scolded. "Ludmila-san don't want to hear all this killing, all this shooting, bang-bang. Come on, pretty one, you get back into cabin, lie down some more, rest. When men get through talking stupid, then Emerson-san can come in."

Ludmila let herself be propelled by the energetic Japanese woman without resistance. She was still somewhat numb from the events of the night, her husband's unexpected brutality, her flight to Prince Makustov's residence after Dobshansky had fallen asleep.

* * *

Irena opened the door for her and put her to bed in her old room, and Ludmila sobbed out a half-coherent recounting of the night's events, words that she could not now recollect.

Irena conveyed the story to Princess Makustov and to Olga Bohmer. In the morning she came in to inform Ludmila that the prince would go to see Dobshansky after breakfast to arrange a reconciliation between the newlyweds, this over Princess Makustov's strong objections.

The latter bustled into Ludmila's room as soon as her husband left the mansion. "Can you dress yourself and travel, my dear? Men are such fools. The governor does not wish to 'interfere in the private affairs of a man and his wife,' as he puts it, but I would not send a wild beast back to that devil. Irena will bring you some clothing. I have ordered her to get you on board a ship, any ship that is leaving immediately. She has money for your necessities. Return to Petropavlovsk and take refuge there. Dobshansky will not follow for a time. He will be quite fully occupied with company business for a while, I think. The governor has just received definite word that the czar has sold the North American lands to the Americans."

Princess Makustov broke off, hugged Ludmila, touched her hair. "Good luck to you, my dear, and may the Lord be with you. I wish I could do more."

Olga came into the room with Irena and helped Ludmila to dress, her eyes red with weeping and her shoulders shaking the entire time.

"I will go with you. My little one, will I ever see you again? To have come so far only for this to happen—I must go with you," she sobbed, hugging Ludmila to her big bosom.

"No, Olga, you must stay here," Ludmila insisted. "I don't know where I will end up, but I promise I will let you know somehow. You have a chance for your own life now."

The two embraced and kissed emotionally, and Ludmila finally persuaded the governess to stay behind. The argument was cut short when Irena took Ludmila firmly by the elbow and tugged her toward the door.

"We go now," she said in a tone that allowed for no argument.

Even at present, lying on the hard straw mat that served as a bed in the sampan's cabin, many miles already from the settlement and her husband, Ludmila could not bring a sense of reality to bear upon anything that had happened since the wedding. She felt as if she had been moving and still moved through a hazy dream, and she did not really have the energy to fight off the feeling. She let her eyes drop shut and fell into a troubled sleep.

When she woke, John Emerson was on the floor beside her, looking as if he had been there for some time.

"Long John," she murmured. "I really did not expect to see you ever again. I did not know—"

He shushed her gently by putting two fingers to her lips. "No need to talk just yet. We got plenty of time for that. Okime's cooked up this stuff, some kind of fishhead broth or whatever, with all kinds of magical herbs and powders in it. Says it'll make you good as new. Smells more like it'd kill you outright, but maybe you better try some anyway." He helped her to sit up and held the cup of broth to her mouth.

She swallowed a mouthful of warm, nauseating liquid, grimaced horribly and pushed the cup away. "If I must die, I think I will die unaided," she said.

Emerson and Ludmila looked at each other and began to laugh with the sheer pleasure of being together once more.

"Oh, do not make me laugh," Ludmila cried, trying

unsuccessfully to stop. "It hurts, it hurts. Quick, Long John Emerson, tell me something sad."

Long John gathered her into his arms and held her against him, rocking her slightly. "Ludmila, leetle princess, you know I ain't got a blessed thing to offer you, but seein' you like this—by God, I can't let you go off by yourself again. We'll make it together, princess, somehow."

She leaned against his chest, breathing in the familiar odor of her man, and slow tears began to come.

"Unless," Emerson added, drawing back slightly to look into her battered face, "unless you want to go back to your folks—your ma and pa in Rostov. If that's what you want, why I'll see to 'er somehow. Not much I can do until next spring, but Red Porcupine's people'll treat us all right, hide us from that bastard Dobshansky an' his trained dogs. Come spring I should have a stash o' plews, an' I'll take you back to Rooshia personal . . ."

Ludmila shook her head. This time it was she who shushed Emerson. "You great fool," she whispered, "we will go live in an Indian hut. We'll build a nest out of branches or whatever you do. You are mine, John Emerson, if you'll have me after all this. I'll make a good squaw—is that the word? Do you think I would let the father of my child abandon me in this condition?"

Emerson stared at the princess for a time, not really comprehending.

"Ludmila, you mean—you're already? Why the hell didn't you tell me? That makes, let's see, she's the last day of June now, an'—"

"Our baby will be born in February," Ludmila said, laughing again.

"By God, princess, I'll build you a castle, I swear I will. Might take a while, but what with royalty runnin' rampant in the family, why—"

Ludmila touched Emerson's face, his beard. "We've been fools, haven't we, John Emerson?"

"Prob'ly still are," he agreed.

"No, now we will be wise together," Ludmila insisted. Her voice was beginning to go blurry with sleep again. "I think there must have been something in Okime's broth, something strong. Will we really have a castle, John? That would be nice, but it doesn't matter. . . ."

She lay down with her head against Emerson's leg; her eyes fell shut.

He gently touched her hair, ran the tips of his fingers over her swollen face. She was asleep again.

"Family man in spite of myself," he muttered aloud, shaking his head and trying to let the sense of things sink in. "I'll be damned. I'll be damned."

The *Darakusha* reached the head of the fjord known as Lynn Canal several days later. This narrow arm of the ocean extended north a hundred miles, with rich forests of fir and hemlock growing on either side and extending up to timberline on the precipitous glacier-mantled mountains east and west.

The sampan docked just below Dyea, near what is now Port Chilkoot and Pierre Grayfish, the half-French, half-Chilkoot owner of the rough log trading post, came down to greet the inhabitants of the peculiar-looking vessel even before they could debark. He immediately recognized Long John Emerson as well as Charley St. Francis and Taos Danny. He had known Emerson for years and met Taos and Charley in Sitka two years earlier, when the three men were preparing to depart for Russian Kamchatka.

Pierre Grayfish greeted the Americans effusively, his language an odd mixture of guttural Chilkoot tones, Russian harshness and the French melody all blended into a species of English that was entirely his own.

"Hey, Slim Jeams, where you find this kind of tub? *Moi*, I never seen nothing like dat," he called out. "You come, eh? Have drink with Pierre, you and Sharley and

Danny. Bring friends *aussi*. You stay few days here, we talk big bunch, eh?''

Emerson laughed, jumped onto the dock to shake hands with Grayfish, then turned to help Irena and Ludmila ashore.

''Eh, you got pretty sows wit' you. You been beating on dis white woman, Slim Jeams? You never been like dat before, eh? She do somethin' *mauvais*?''

''Naw, damnit, Pierre, I ain't been beatin' her,'' Emerson growled. ''But the son of a bitch what did is likely to be comin' after us—Dobshansky himself. Afraid we can't even take time out for that drink you mentioned. Plannin' to head up over the High Grease Trail if you an' your cousins don't object. Got to get over to Tagish country before the whole damned Russian Army catches up to us. What you got in the way of mules, my old compadre?''

Pierre's mouth fell open, but for a long moment he did not speak. ''Dobshansky?'' he asked finally. ''Mon ami, dis is real bad. Goddamn Rooshians kill you, non? They know where you come? Goddamn bad. Maybe I go up the High Grease wit' you.''

''Only authority Dobshansky's got is however many Cossacks he brings with him,'' Emerson said. ''News ain't reached you yet? The whole damned Alaska from Yukon Delta to Canada, it's American now. Pierre, you're a genuine gringo, by God. Course it don't change much for us. You see, this lady's Dobshansky's wife, and—''

''*Merde de Dieu! Enfant de grâce*! Nyet. nyet, Slim Jeams—you gone crazy or what? Dobshansky, he's mean son of bitch, goddamn.''

''Yep,'' Emerson grinned, ''an' that's just part of the problem. Irena here, she's Makustov's servant. Four mules, Grayfish—I need four mules.''

''Goddamn,'' Pierre Grayfish said. ''You goin' see Red Porcupine? He supposed to come here two weeks ago. Supposed to bring in lots furs—foxes and beavers and that kind. Maybe somethin' happen, I don' know. You get to village at Tagish Lake, you tell old Porcupine Pierre needs furs. Prices good. I pay him good too."

Within less than an hour the seven companions, outfitted with four mules—at an outrageous price—set out from the tiny port settlement and were on their way to Sheep Camp. This was the base of the treacherous route called the High Grease, the main trade route employed by Chilkoots and Chilkats alike in their dealings with the Indian peoples of the interior. The route was known to very few whites, only men such as Long John Emerson who enjoyed the protection of the Tagish.

Musi and Okime were frantic. Okime spotted a three-masted ship coming in from fifteen miles or so down the Lynn Canal and recognized it as the same vessel that had conveyed Dobshansky back from Redoubt St. Michael. The couple unceremoniously entrusted the *Darakusha* to the care of Pierre Grayfish and prepared to flee. If the approaching Russian ship indeed brought Dobshansky and his troops, they surmised, they stood little chance of escaping with their lives. Suddenly the prospect of an unknown wilderness seemed infinitely preferable to the wrath of a Russian count. Any attempt to flee by water appeared doomed to failure.

The group moved as quickly as it could manage, not pausing at the deserted base camp. They drove their laden mules ahead up the narrow, steep, twisting path, which clung impossibly hundreds of feet above boulder-strewn ravines. They traveled mainly in tense silence, aware that in all probability Dobshansky and an unknown number of Russian soldiers were only a few hours behind them, possibly closing the gap. Their only chance, as Long John saw it, lay in continuing their march through the long twilight, getting well beyond Sheep Camp and up onto the back of the mountain above the timberline, into the zone where the snow in many places still lay deep and the Russian pursuers would be clear out of their element.

Fifty miles beyond the pass, more or less, lay safety—Red Porcupine's village on Tagish Lake—a place unknown to the Russians, who had wisely chosen to respect the Indians' property rights.

Emerson, in fact, had made the assumption—perhaps merely a hope—that Dobshansky would not pursue them beyond the crest of the mountains, would not venture down into the unknown realm beyond.

They were less than ten miles from Dyea when Ludmila began to wonder how she could go on. The breath already burned in her lungs; her legs were lead. And yet she went on, struggling to keep up the forced pace set by the trappers. After a small eternity she forgot the pain and just moved her legs in a mechanical and endless rhythm. Her brain after a time did not function at all except to keep her body moving: one step, another; avoid that loose rock, that root; one step, another.

So long as Irena and old Okime could continue, she could too.

At early twilight they reached Sheep Camp and she supposed Emerson would call a halt, but the march continued. The trail was quite steep now, and doglegged its way toward the pass.

Jesus, I am trying, I am trying. Do you hear me? I cannot go even a step farther without your help.

Somehow her feet kept moving. Irena stayed close to her, helped her up over muddy embankments, saying nothing.

Darkness closed about them. The far mountain crowns burned a thin crimson and a full moon rose in a sky with only half a dozen stars as yet visible.

Ludmila paused and fought for breath as the men, cursing and shoving, attempted to get a mule up yet one more slippery embankment. The animal kept getting lamer, and Ludmila watched as the four men unloaded the beast and attempted to assist it up the incline.

One leg gave way and the mule, braying in terror, went over sideways and pitched into the dark emptiness below. She heard a series of muffled thuds then rock itself gave way and slid and a torrent of stone hurtled into the ravine.

Dawn found them far up the mountain, two thousand feet or so above Sheep Camp, which was dimly visible far below at the head of the canyon. They had slept for no more than an hour when Long John roused them, and then they were moving once more, crossing snowbanks, pushing the three remaining mules along. The four men took up the load from the lost mule and trudged along drunkenly.

After the sun rose above the crest of the mountains Emerson climbed to a projecting point to scan back down along the trail. He could see the harbor from his vantage point, could see the tall triple masts of the ship in port. He pointed, calling to Charley St. Francis and Taos Danny.

No more than half a mile distant by straight line and perhaps three miles by the twisting High Grease Trail were a dozen, no, thirteen figures moving along single file in the distinctive red jackets of Russian soldiers.

St. Francis climbed to where Emerson stood. "Gotta give the bloodthirsty bastard credit," Long John said. "He kept his boys marchin' all night, too."

"Don't think we're gonna make 'er," Emerson said under his breath, not wishing those below to hear. "Ludmila's on her last legs—that beating took a lot out of her, an' she ain't used to this kind of thing anyhow. Okime, she's limpin' and so's Musi, What do you figger, Charles?"

"Thirteen of 'em?" St. Francis mused. "About time for a leetle selective bushwhackin', I'd say. Think maybe we ought to fort up somewheres?"

"It'll take 'em a few hours to catch us. They're gaining, no question, but we're damned near to the top. You been over this way before, Charley?"

"Nope. Haven't had the pleasure until now."

"Big rubble of boulders just over the crest. Cain't touch us there, but we got no water—not unless there's some snow left in the crevices. If there is, we could hole up for a week or more an' just kind of potshot the Russkis."

"Grayfish said Red Porcupine's bunch was overdue," Charley suggested.

"Cain't count on that, but it's true, if old Raven Man's in a good mood there's a bare chance we might meet up with 'em somewheres along the line. Just one way to get from Tagish Lake to Dyea, an' that's the road we're on. Even so, we'd still better figure some way of solvin' this problem on our own."

Taos Danny climbed up beside his fellow trappers and muttered a single word: "Shee-it."

"We get across the pass and we're goin' downhill and the Russkis are still climbin' up, maybe we'll make it." Emerson shrugged and Danny nodded.

Ludmila noted the men conversing hastily in low tones and guessed the nature of the trouble, but she didn't speak; she resolved to push her exhausted body harder. It seemed as if they had been walking through water or thick mud, and in fact in places they had been. The energy it took was enormous, the gain agonizingly slow.

Emerson shared the unwelcome news with Musi and the women, and the group moved ahead, grimly determined to escape.

The hours passed and the slow-motion chase continued. The Russians had sighted them by now, but Dobshansky's men, trained though they were, stumbled and occasionally came to a halt, no doubt also at the edge of exhaustion.

The sun had passed the meridian when the fugitives

crested the summit. Taos Danny let out a triumphant whoop and the rest felt cheered. The ascent was over, the trail downhill from this point.

"Dumbass Meskin," Charley snorted, "You want the whole goddamn Russian Army to hear you?" But he too was grinning.

Long John did not seem to share in the general elation, however. By his calculations the Russian troops, temporarily out of sight, should be very near. "Don't slack off now. Take advantage of the terrain. If we can keep ahead of 'em a couple more miles, we may just have a chance. You holdin' up okay, princess?" He winked at her, squeezed her shoulder.

"I am fine," she panted. She caught her breath, looked keenly into Emerson's eyes without slackening her pace. "You think they're going to catch up to us, don't you, Long John?"

He hesitated, then nodded.

"Is there any way to escape them?"

"Not sure. Maybe."

"If I were to go back to Dobshansky, the rest of you would be safe. His quarrel is with me, not with you—not with Danny—not with anyone else."

"Well, the feelin' ain't mutual. Whatever the odds, this here's my turf now. If there's a way, we'll find 'er. For a princess you say dumb things, by God. You know that? There's no way I could let you go back to that ugly puffed-up bastard. Now let's save our breath an' move."

A mile beyond the pass the Russians came once more into view, the distance between the two groups having shrunk considerably.

"There they be," Charley called out. "Damnit, Johnny, where's that rockpile you was talking about?"

"Due east, young feller. You get the folks up into 'er, clear to the top. Mile to go, more or less. Me an'

Taos, we're goin' to provide a leetle delayin' action. You up for 'er, Dan?''

''*Sí, sí, señor.*''

''What I been sayin' all along?'' Charley muttered, raising one eyebrow.

The rest of the group moved ahead as Long John and Taos Danny took cover behind a snowbank. The two of them were grateful for the respite. They waited until the Russians had approached to within about four hundred yards, and then they began to fire, reload, fire again. Dobshansky and his men were beyond effective rifle range, but the red-coated Russians scrambled for cover nonetheless and began to return fire.

''Not much room for the boys to spread out,'' Emerson noted, ''and I 'spect they're not too damned eager to come straight ahead. Few more rounds, Daniel, an' then we run like hell—if we're still up to 'er.''

''Find another snowbank and try it again?'' Taos squeezed off another round.

''Exactly. St. Francis needs maybe ten minutes to get everybody up into the rocks. Shouldn't be no trouble givin' him that.''

''You sure we gotta run like hell?'' Danny asked. ''Maybe we could just sorta walk like hell, huh?''

''Whatever works,'' Long John grinned. ''You ready to pull back, general?''

''One more shot. Maybe I hit somebody this time.''

The group struggled up the scree and into the pile of precariously balanced boulders above that. St. Francis immediately took position, pistol in hand.

Emerson and Taos were running for cover, turning, firing back at the pursuing soldiers. St. Francis noted Dobshansky was keeping well to the rear, shouting orders nonstop.

When Long John and Danny reached the scree, Charley began to fire at the Russians, though the troops were still out of range. The shots were ineffectual, but the soldiers were taking cover, for the moment a bit less intent upon pursuing the two men who were climbing the rockpile.

Behind him the mules were snorting and thrashing. "Goddamnit, Musi, get them beasts tethered up to somethin'. Cain't you see I'm tryin' to concentrate?"

Then Emerson and Taos lurched in amongst their fellows, threw themselves down and struggled for breath.

As the Russians approached rifle range they advanced more cautiously, taking advantage of whatever cover they could find, firing from behind rocks and ragged brush. Some of the shots sang among the boulders where the little group was sheltered. The two parties exchanged rounds for a time, neither side scoring on the other.

The hours passed slowly, tediously. The trappers fired only occasionally now, waiting for a soldier to attempt to work his way up the steep slope of broken rock.

Late sun still lingered on the western slopes of the peaks beyond them, but night was coming on and it was evident that a standoff had been reached.

Finally Dobshansky himself emerged from his cover and approached the boulders, a white handkerchief waving from the tip of his upraised sword.

Long John Emerson, his rifle barrel aimed through an opening between shelves of stone, observed the short, powerful figure through the sights of his Enfield rifle. He carefully aligned the front blade with the rear notch, both centered on the count's chest just to the left of his silver buttons. Emerson's finger tightened on the trigger.

So easy; dead center him now and the rest will panic. So easy, just think what the bastard did to Ludmila, what he's done to the Injuns. Who the hell says we have to play by army rules?

Dobshansky approached to within fifty feet of the

base of the rockpile and stood staring directly toward the protruding barrel of Emerson's rifle. He knew it was centered on his heart, but he showed not a sign of fear.

Emerson relaxed his finger on the trigger, lowered the rifle. "Shit," he muttered, and then yelled out, "What do you want, you murdering son of a bitch?"

"Is that you, Mr. Emerson? I have a proposal to make. May I come in closer?"

"We can hear you fine from where you are. What's your proposal?"

"Mr. Emerson, I believe that your party has kidnapped my wife. You know very well that you have no chance of escaping alive. We also know that we will lose some men in taking you. I'd prefer to avoid such unnecessary bloodshed."

"Talks real purty, don't he?" Taos Danny growled. "Watch out for 'im, Long John."

Emerson glanced over his shoulder, saw that Ludmila had risen. She was quite pale but had the lift to her chin that he so admired. "Don't go thinkin' anything noble, Ludmila," he said. "I ain't gonna let you do it."

"Mr. Emerson," Dobshansky called out, "I think you know my terms."

"Sure, now," Emerson replied. "We send the princess to you so's you can beat her up some more, an' you let the rest of us go. That about it?"

"You need not concern yourself for my wife's welfare, but yes, Mr. Emerson, those are my conditions. Not one of you will remain alive otherwise, even if you do succeed in taking some of my men with you."

"I will go," Ludmila cried suddenly and clambered past Long John. Emerson managed to grab her by the arm and swing her back behind him, holding her pinned as she struggled against his strength. "John," she shouted, her face flushed and tears streaking her cheeks, "this is madness.

You will all die, just as the count says—and I will either die or be taken back anyway. I can't let you do it."

"Ludmila, you ain't got enough faith. Charley, Danny, damnit, grab hold of this hellcat. You just shut up, princess, an' let me handle this. Ain't just you now. You got somethin' of mine, an' I ain't lettin' go without a fight. Even goddamned American *sauvages* has got rights, you know." He kissed her hard on the mouth and then released her to Taos Danny, who pinned her about the waist.

She had already ceased struggling. *It is a bad dream. This is not really happening. Jesus, let me wake up now.*

Another voice, not her own, answered, *No, Ludmila. Jesus does not answer the prayers of those who persist in vice. To persist willfully is to beg for damnation.*

She tried to place the second voice even as the normal order of life fell apart round her. Perhaps it was the priest, stern old Father Josephus at church in Rostov.

Irena knelt beside her and held her hand, trying to give comfort even though she too was horribly afraid.

"We be okay, princess," the Indian whispered. "You see soon. I pray too. You good woman. God don't say you got to stay with husband who hurts you bad."

Ludmila squeezed Irena's hand and fought back two contrary impulses, the one for more tears and the other for laughter. "I think that's exactly what God says, Irena," the princess whispered, breaking into an incongruous giggle.

"Then God no damn good," Irena shrugged, "and I start praying to somebody else."

Emerson, meantime, had climbed down from the rocks and stood at the foot of the scree a few feet in front of Dobshansky.

"Here's your chance, old friend," Long John grinned. "These are my terms. Tell you what. You ain't gettin' the princess back while I'm alive, an' that's just the way things stand. But I'll fight you here and now, man to man.

You like knives? I got a nice pair. You put me under, the princess goes back with you an' my friends go free. I win, your soldier boys head back down the mountain nice an' peaceful. You up to the skirmish, or do Rooshian dogs only chew up helpless women?''

Dobshansky drew himself stiffly erect, spat on the ground near Emerson's feet. ''I have killed at least a dozen men in duels, as I'm sure you know,'' he snarled, ''but a gentleman does not dishonor himself by dueling with one who is so far beneath him. Your terms are not satisfactory, Mr. Emerson. I trust that you will not shoot me in the back while I return to my troops?''

Long John narrowed his eyes and nodded. ''Figgered you for a coward all along,'' he observed. ''Shootin' in the back sounds about right. I'll have to think on 'er.''

But he turned, climbed back to his perch among the rocks, disdained even to watch the straight figure as Count Pieter Dobshansky walked slowly down to where his men waited.

''Looks like we're back to the original terms,'' Charley St. Francis remarked.

''Odds don't look too good,'' Emerson agreed. ''Right sorry I got all of you into this. Prob'ly the rest of you could get away without too much trouble. Ain't you he wants, it's me an' Ludmila.''

''I been through eighty-below cold with you, John, an' lost at sea, an' we've damned near starved together more than once,'' Charley said. ''An' you've saved my bacon a time or two. Ain't nowhere I'm of a mind to go just now. How about you, Meskin, old buddy?''

''Too far to walk to Seattle, amigo. Guess I'll stay here an' kill me some Russians.''

The Japanese couple murmured somewhat less enthusiastic agreement and Irena continued to sit by Ludmila, holding the princess' hand and not speaking.

''Hell, Long John,'' Charley added, ''we been in

spots that looked a sight worse. Never know what old Raven's hatchin' in that mean little head o' his. 'It's a good day to die,' that's what old Jimmy Beckwourth said when Chivington pulled a gun on 'im an' forced 'im to guide us into Sand Creek. Well, I come through that one an' one or two others, so I'm not figgerin' on goin' under just yet.''

Long John nodded. ''Then we got to find a way to whittle down the odds a mite,'' he said.

Chapter 16
Blood on the Snow

No one understands everything Raven Man does, but at first no one died. Then Raven Man changed that too.

Old Raven decided his mother-in-law was much better looking than his wife, but how could he get rid of the daughter? Besides, since no one died, there were getting to be too many people; all the good places to set fish traps were taken and lots of people were going hungry. Little children tended to be all bones and great big eyes.

Raven Man thought about the problem and at last he knew what to do. He decided to go away.

"Where you going?" his wife asked.

"Out."

"Where?"

"Someplace."

"You coming back, Raven Man?"

"Oh yes, maybe by dinnertime. Only there's nothing to eat."

He was gone for two years. He was digging a long tunnel that came out on the Yukon bank far from his village. At the end of it he built two summer houses of cottonwood bark.

When he returned to his village, his pretty mother-in-law was sick, and that was good. She stopped eating and looked like a ghost, like a yeg that was trying to get out of its body.

When the mother-in-law tried to get away, her daughter grabbed her, but it was like she was made out of air. Raven Man was watching, and now he guided his mother-in-law to the tunnel entrance. Both of them went inside. Four days later they reached the two houses. The woman was all pretty again and Raven Man invited her to share his bed. She wanted that too, so they made love for four days. They got stuck together, the way dogs and wolves do.

Then Raven Man told her to move over to the other house. "If you want to sleep with me, then you can come to this house. If I want to be in bed with you, then I will come over there. We are dead now, and I have you and also plenty of places to put fish traps. The others will come along later, but there will always be plenty of room here in the spirit world."

"Will my daughter die also?" the first dead person asked.

"Yes, but by then she will have a new husband and won't want to bother us any more, even when we are trying to make babies."

July 1867

"There's no way the count an' his soldier boys can get to us," Emerson said. "But at the same time, they ain't no way we can get away from 'em, neither. It's a standoff, pure an' simple."

"What if they rush us all at once?" Ludmila asked, peering down through the waning darkness to where the red glow of a night watch fire faintly revealed the figure of one of the Russian soldiers. "There are thirteen, counting Pieter, all of them trained marksmen. We are only seven. Perhaps Okime can shoot, but Dobshansky will not give up. If he takes you prisoner, John, he will have you shot. He will destroy anyone who has opposed him. Perhaps after all he will kill me also. He threatened to do that when—"

Emerson put his hands to either side of her face and gently kissed her forehead.

"Hell, I been in lots worse scrapes. You too Ludmila, you've been in worse. Like after the *Loire* went down, for instance. An' later, when we was stranded on the island. Somethin' always turns up. Remember how we found that dead fur seal? Naw, it ain't time to go under just yet, not time to go wanderin' off with the gods of the Tagish an' the Tutchones. Haven't heard Taos singin' no death chant, have you? That time comes to all of us soon or late, but I still figure there's a way off this rockpile. Just haven't figured out what it is yet, is all."

Ludmila pressed close to Emerson's chest, taking comfort from his bearlike strength. She closed her eyes and breathed in the familiar wild odor of his buckskins.

"Irena," she said softly, "Irena was chanting something earlier tonight. At first I thought she was speaking in her sleep."

"Prayin', mebbe," Emerson responded, stroking Ludmila's hair. "It don't hurt none to pray, whether it's to Denato or Jehovah. By God I pray sometimes. Never can tell when the Old Man is listenin' and has a mind to help out a bit. Anyhow, Irena's still a kid, not much more than that. Your Russian priests, they get to as many of the Injuns as they can, whether for good or bad I don't know. But Irena's got that string o' beads, an' they give her comfort I guess. Probably prayin' for protection against Giyeg, askin' Jesus to protect her."

"What is Giyeg?" Ludmila asked, her voice whispered and dreamy.

"Well, probably the Tlingits don't worry about it anyway. Hell, they got old Orca out there in the water, old

Killer Whale, an' that's a god that demands believin', so to speak. Giyeg, he eats people's bodies when their minds go wanderin'. That's how folks grow old and worn out. Like a whirlwind, the Ingaliks say. Others say he's a withered old man, an' others say he travels underground, only his shadow glides along on the surface. There's lots o' magic things a body can do to ward Giyeg off, but he gets everyone at last. Got helpers, too—the Nahoens. Bastards have great long fingernails, as I understand the matter. Eat a pair o' human eyes, Ludmila, an' ye'll turn into one of the Nahoen, sure as hell. I've got that on the best authority."

"What strange things to believe in," Ludmila whispered, clinging to Emerson and staring downslope toward the campfire once again. "Irena's people and all the others must be like children."

Emerson chuckled. "Is it really stranger than all your saints and devils an' the like? I recollect a story about Jesus casting demons into some poor pigs an' drivin' the beasts over a cliff—somethin' like that."

"You've been to church, then?" Ludmila asked. "You've read the Bible?"

Emerson laughed, hugged her tightly.

"You really got me figgered for an outright savage, don't you, girl? Sure, I been to church an' I been to school, though neither place ever really caught hold of me. We got churches down in Idaho Territory where I grew up, Roman Catholic an' Protestant both. The missionaries came early to civilize the Injuns there, just like you Russkis been doin' here in Alaska. My pa actually had an old Jesuit, a renegade who'd tossed off his cloth, working on the cattle ranch for two, three years. Learned more from him than I did in church, truth to say. Loved to talk, he did. An Irishman who'd come over from the old country, had a thing goin' with a Shoshone woman an' left his calling. He finally left us an' turned pure Injun. Married his squaw an' took up life with 'em."

"What's it like in Idaho? Will we go there, John?"

Emerson cleared his throat, petted the princess' hair once more. "Same as here," he said, "only the days don't get so long in summer or so short in winter. Mountains, woods, rivers an' a big valley along the Snake River. Cold in the winter an' hotter'n blazes in summer. She's a good land, but I guess I like the north better. Besides, I've sort of gotten out of the habit of herding whiteface cattle around. Mebbe sometime—mebbe. But first we got to get down off this rockpile an' get shed o' your husband an' his soldiers. Dawn's coming, Ludmila, big twilight, an' I expect we're going to have some real excitement before this one's finished."

Long John set cap to nipple on the old three-band Enfield muzzle-loader Taos and Charley had purchased for him. He nodded and studied the movements of the Russian soldiers, who peered back from little more than three hundred yards downslope of Emerson's basalt slab.

"Temptin'," he said. "With the advantage of height, I just might pick one of 'em off. Bastards are cookin' breakfast, by God."

"They'll come up to visit after a bit—that's what I'm thinkin'," St. Francis replied. "They'll play hell takin' our rockpile, but maybe ain't even Russkis dumb enough to come chargin' up through them boulders."

"Could be they figure to camp for a week an' starve us out," Emerson said. "Only my guess is they didn't take time to haul much in the way o' supplies with 'em, bein' in a hurry to catch us an' all. Could send a couple of men down to Dyea, commandeer mules and tote supplies back up the way we done it, I guess. Naw, Dobshansky ain't got that kind of patience. It's the nature of dumbass Russians to try some kind of frontal assault, an' when they do, I'd say we stand a fair chance of whittlin' away the odds a bit.''

''They got needle guns, breach-loaders,'' Charley responded. ''They can get off maybe two shots to our one.''

''An' we got rocks to hide behind. They've got to run and hide and shoot all at once. I figger not more than half a dozen of 'em will still be kickin' by the time they get up into pistol range. If that's what happens, I'd say we'd have things pretty much our own way. Was Danny awake when you come down here?''

''Awake? I don't think the Meskin slept at all, just sat there makin' eyes at leetle Irena most of the night.''

''Dumb son of a bitch,'' Emerson growled. ''Middle of the firefight, an' he'll decide he needs to take a siesta. Maybe you're right, Charles. Maybe he is a Mex.''

''Whatever he is, I'm glad he's with us on this one. He's a damned fine compañero, even if he does have more guts than brains.''

Emerson laughed. ''There are times when I get the feeling all three of us are a tad short on brains. But if we put our noodles together, I'd say we've still got an advantage over the King of Alaska down there. By god I'd like to get my hands on that feller, just me an' him. Seems like there'd be a good way of killin' him real slow, now don't it?''

''Look there, Johnny. The count's linin' 'em up an' givin' 'em orders. Think you're right—I'll bet they are goin' to rush us.''

''You think Musi can handle the extra rifle?''

''I imagine. There's lots of things a coon can do if he's pressed to it. If not he can load for one of us. Okime too, I'm thinkin'.''

''Best if we keep the women out of it,'' Emerson said. ''If worst comes to worst, Dobshansky's not likely to hurt them, not unless they been shootin'. So I guess it's you an' me an' Taos, just like always. Hell, St. Francis, we're up to it, ain't we? Go get Dan, will you? You hear my Enfield pop, you'll know she's started."

Charley St. Francis climbed over the rim and dropped down to where the mules were tethered. He nodded to Ludmila and the others, who huddled about a small fire Musi had managed to make of some thin ropelike roots. St. Francis knelt by the bundles off the mules and began to root. Suddenly he pounced on a saddlebag and grinned fiercely. He had laid hands on the explosives, the new-fangled dynamite that Danny on a whim bought when they were getting their gear together in the post at Sitka.

The clerk explained briefly the method of using the wax-paper cylinders—how to fit the cap, attach the fuse. "Good for moving boulders. With enough of it we could move half a mountain, da. Very strong."

St. Francis stared at the ten sticks, nodded, rummaged further to find the caps and fusing. Johnny wants to whittle down the odds, as he puts it. Mebbe there's a way yet. Hell, he don't even know we got this stuff, he mused.

"What you into, Charley?" Taos called out.

St. Francis held up the package of dynamite. "Thought you was crazy to waste the money at the time," he called back. "Mebbe now we make a leetle present for the Roossians?"

"Don't bring it near the goddamned fire, you dumbhead," Taos bellowed. "You want to kill us all?"

"Fire don't do nothin' to it," St. Francis replied, coming closer. "Don't you ever remember nothin'?"

"What is it?" Ludmila demanded. "Those look like Chinese fireworks."

"Might say so," Charley nodded, "only these is Swedish; that's what we was told, anyhow. Swedish firecrackers."

"Let me see," Musi demanded. "Big ones, huh?"

"Anything cookin' yet down below?" Taos asked. "Maybe we better get up on the rim with Slim Jeams, eh?"

"Not enough guns for everybody," Okime said. "What we gonna do?"

"First off, the bossman says the women stay here," Charley answered. "You too, Musi. Long John's orders. Keep low an' stay out of the fight. The three of us can handle 'er, an' if we cain't, then maybe the King of Alaska'll leave the rest of you be."

Ludmila started to protest just as Emerson's Enfield rifle sang out.

"Time's a-wastin'," Taos said. "Come on, Charley, let's get our tails up there."

The men scrambled through the boulders, and after a moment's hesitation Ludmila set out after them.

The Russians, moving upslope all at once, had begun their assault. Four men in the rear halted at the foot of the rockslide, crouching among the rubble and covering those ahead of them.

Emerson's first shot missed, and now he sighted down carefully, got the bead he wanted and squeezed off his second.

A red-jacketed Russian bent backward at the knees, twisted slowly, and rolled several yards downslope.

"That's one," Emerson muttered, reloading as rapidly as he could, fitting another brass cap to the nipple. Then Taos and Charley were beside him, and each fired without success.

A moment later Ludmila leaped down from above, half-stumbling, and crouched beside Emerson.

"Goddamnit, ma'am, I said stay back with the others. Charley, didn't you tell 'em to stay where they was?"

"He told me. I didn't listen. Give me your pistol, John. This is my fight, too. Do you think I'm helpless?"

She didn't wait for a response but pulled Long John's Colt revolver from its holster.

"You know how to use it?"

"We royals must be good at everything. I have learned."

She pulled back the hammer, aimed downslope and fired. "This thing fires high left," she snorted.

Taos Danny flattened himself against the stony rim, took aim and squeezed off his round. "Got me one," he bragged. "One's makin' it to the base, John. Can you git 'im?"

Emerson drew down and fired. "Three," he said, ramming a new load home. "Charles, what the hell you doin'?"

"Tryin' to whittle them odds," St. Francis replied, holding up a stick of dynamite, which he had fit with a primer charge and a foot-long fuse. "Thought we might try a leetle selective excavation."

Ludmila fired again, and this time her bullet found its mark, striking a Russian soldier in the shoulder and sending him howling and tumbling down the rocky slope.

"Good work, gal," Emerson cheered, firing again at almost the same time but missing. "Charley, what is that thing?"

St. Francis, fumbling with his fire-striker, lit the fuse, stood up and hurled the dynamite down at three soldiers who had taken momentary cover behind a broken sheaf of stone.

"Use your rifle, damnit," Emerson shouted.

St. Francis peered over the edge, looking disappointed. Then the blast ripped off, hurling fragments of stone and sending up a blue-black cloud of smoke.

"What in the Jesus," Emerson bellowed, "a goddamn bomb?"

"It works! It really works," Charley sang out, "just like the leetle clerk said it would."

When the dust cleared, it was evident that three more Russians lay dead on the slag at the foot of the boulders. In the aftermath of the blast the remaining soldiers lost heart and began plunging down the slope. St. Francis, laughing with glee, lit the fuse to a second stick of dynamite. He leaped to the rim, caught his balance and hurled the charge as far out as he could.

Then a moment before the blast Charley St. Francis suddenly sat down, one hand clamped to his throat.

"Charley, get back down here," Emerson yelled, his words half drowned by the explosion.

St. Francis struggled to turn. Blood was welling out between his fingers. "Damnit, Johnny," he managed, "I guess I got carried away with myself. Like a kid—" He slumped backward, twisted over and fell heavily at Taos Danny's feet. The hand flopped away from the neck and blood spurted from the gaping wound; the torn arteries pumped and pumped.

Taos made a frantic effort to stanch the flow with his hands, but in a moment it was all over. "He's gone." Taos rose and stared down at his own red slippery hands. "Just like that he's gone."

Ludmila knelt beside the dead man, her hands drawn to the sides of her face. Then she stared up pleadingly at Emerson.

Long John shook his head, laid down his rifle and dropped to his knees. "Charley, goddamnit," he groaned, reaching down to touch St. Francis' face.

"Dead," Ludmila whispered. "John . . ."

"You saved our bacon, Charles, do you know that? Goddamnit, lad, it weren't supposed to happen this way. They's more damned furs down in Tagish country than you've ever seen, an' mebbe gold too. We coulda found 'er, you an' me an' Taos."

Emerson lifted the dead man in his arms and made his

way back over the rocks to the shelter area where the mules were tied.

"Dobshansky's still got four men whole an' another wounded if I counted right," Emerson said. "His troops have been cut up pretty bad, an' I guess he wasn't expectin' the explosives: I know I wasn't. Taos, why didn't you tell me we had that stuff?"

"Guess I forgot. I woulda thought of it soon, but Charley beat me to it. Where we gonna bury him, John?"

Emerson glanced at his dead friend and shrugged. "Not up here. Down to Red Porcupine's village, if we ever get there. Charley'd want to have folks he knew around him for a time, an' after that it don't make no difference. We all go where he's gone, soon or late."

"I'll carve a cross for him," Taos said. "It didn't matter if he called me a Meskin. I never minded, not really. You think he knew that?"

"Only did it to get your goat, Dan. Liked to get a rise out of you. Yep, I think he'd feel honored. He'd like that, I know it."

"I'm very good at carvin'. Not as good as the dumb-head Injuns, mebbe, but I'll take my time and do a good job."

"Charley good man," Okime said. "Gentle. That's good thing in a man. Like Musi—that's why I marry him."

"Hai, so she can tell me what to do alla time."

"Will he try to ambush us, then?" Ludmila asked. "My husband?"

"Do I have to slit the bastard's throat before you'll stop callin' him husband, Ludmila?" Emerson asked. "You're my woman an' I don't give a damn about some words spoke by a priest. You're mine just like I'm yours."

"Don't be angry with me, John. This is terrible. We're all in shock. I can't believe he isn't still with us—just sleeping or gone away for a little while. It's my fault, though, isn't it? If it weren't for me—"

"No, princess," Taos said, "it was his time, that's all. Men like me an' Long John an' Charley, we live this way because we have to. We don't fit nowhere else. No laws up here, just fate, an' it don't matter if we live a month or ten years or—"

Emerson nodded. "We choose what happens. Charley chose an' you've chose too, Ludmila. Irena, don't know whether she's chose or not—she's just gettin' to be a full woman. Danny, he's dumbass in love with 'er, but she's gonna have to think about it for a time. Then maybe she'll break his heart. But first we got to get down off this rockpile, an' Charley's comin' with us. Out there's Dobshansky, an' I don't think he's give up yet, so he's chose too. It's strange how all of a sudden I don't even hate him anymore—or else I hate him so much I cain't feel it."

"*I* hate him," Ludmila said softly. "Before I was just afraid of him, as I was afraid of many things. Perhaps more than anything else I was afraid of my own feelings, didn't trust them, didn't think I had the right to them. On the island that fear left me until we reached Nova Archangelisk. He treated me badly but no worse than many women are treated by their husbands. I can even forgive that, but I will never forgive . . . Charley was always just there, John, almost like part of you. I didn't know him, and yet I knew him very well. I . . ."

"I'll carve a beautiful cross for him," Taos said, uneasy in the long silence. "His name was Christian, even if maybe he lost faith after what he had to do at—"

"Sand Creek," Emerson put in. "He told me the whole story two, three times. It was a damn preacher led the slaughter. Hell, it wasn't real people, just Injuns, wasn't it? An' after that old Charley deserted, come north into Canada, signed on with Hudson's Bay. That's how we got hooked up together."

"Damned fine compañero," Taos Danny mourned.

"Damned fine," Emerson agreed.

"He love both of you," Musi said. "Me and Okime, we go with you to place where Charley gets buried, maybe stay awhile. Maybe fish for *sakiero,* salmon, in big lakes you tell us about. After that we go back to get *Darakusha.*"

Emerson toyed with the idea of pursuing Pieter Dobshansky, decided the matter could wait unless the count himself pushed things and turned the little group north once more. They continued downslope toward the headwaters of the Yukon River and the Tagish village on the long, narrow three-pronged branch of Tagish Lake, which connected with the main body of water from the south.

The group moved more slowly, half numb with exhaustion. Taos Danny trailed them, scouting the terrain for any sight of Dobshansky and his remaining troops.

At midday, within sight of the upper end of the lake, Emerson called a halt. Musi built a fire and Okime found some mint at the edges of the rivulet and used the green spears to brew a respectable pot of tea.

They were drinking the tea and eating hard bread and dried fish when Taos Danny came loping into camp. "Company's comin'," he yelled. "Johnny, they be friends of yours, an' they've got some coons with 'em that ain't friends to none of us."

"What in hell are you talking about?" Emerson demanded.

"Injuns, that's what. Old chief named Scarlet Hedgehawk or somethin'. Got his kids with 'im, an' forty warriors, mebbe more. *An'* Dobshansky an' his boys, tied up as neat as can be. Musta caught 'em dozin', by God. Wasn't a shot fired, so the chief says. They'd been down to Klukwap on the other arm o' the Lynn, then back over to Dyea.

Pierre Grayfish told 'em what was afoot an' they struck out after us."

"Red Porcupine? An' he's got Dobshansky prisoner. Well, now if that don't beat all. Raven Man's tryin', I guess, but he didn't get things worked out quite right. A little sooner an'—"

"I was thinkin' the same thing," Taos agreed. "Charley might still be alive. But they's no way of knowin' that either."

"Leetle gal, not quite Irena's size, wanted to know if you was all right."

"Kate," Emerson said. "You hear that, Ludmila? You've got a twelve- or thirteen-year-old rival named Hammerwater Kate. I told you about 'er."

"Pieter Dobshansky is a prisoner?" Ludmila had already placed Long John's revolver in the inner pocket of her coat. The long barrel was awkward there, but the hard pressure of gunmetal felt comforting and purposeful.

She rose to stand staring upslope in the direction from which Taos Danny had come.

Pieter Dobshansky's face was red and contorted with vexation and rage. "I will come back with two, three hundred soldiers," he threatened. "I will burn your village to the ground, Red Porcupine. The *volk*, the wolf, will raise her cubs in what remains."

The Tagish chief shrugged. "Roossa soldiers come into our lands, we kill them all. Always your men cheat my people at trading, pay us only half, so we trade with Pierre Grayfish or with the British at Fort Selkirk instead. Besides, I think maybe you will go back across the ocean now. Your warriors and church shamans will all leave. That is what I have heard. Am I right, Long John?"

"That's the news," Emerson agreed.

"So what do we do?" Red Porcupine asked. "I think we should kill these men. We could cut off their heads and stick them up on poles outside the village. That will keep Giyeg and the Nahoen away from us, and after a while the smell goes away. Just nice white skulls then, something for the children to throw stones at when they have nothing else to do."

"Ludmila Andreiovna," Dobshansky said, "you are my wife in the eyes of God even though you have fled from me. I have come to bring you back, just as any husband would do, nyet? I am not afraid to apologize for what I did. I beg your forgiveness, but you must come with me now. We return to Mother Russia soon. I will give you a mansion and servants, as befits your honor and my fortune. It is not fitting to discuss such a matter with my soldiers listening and these barbarians as well, but I am willing to respect your bed. I will never come to it unless you have honored me with your request. What more would you have of me?"

"I do not think so, Pieter."

"Think, Ludmila, think! What life will you lead with your barbarian? All that has happened has robbed you of your senses. After a time your reason will return to you, but by then it will be too late. Will you live in a hole in the earth among the savages? You are a woman of nobility, educated, refined. I apologize for my own actions and forgive yours entirely. Even your tall friend here must realize the folly of what you are doing. Even Americans are capable of reason. No, let him find a squaw and live as he will. This wilderness is no place for you, Ludmila."

Ludmila stared at the count for a long moment and then turned and walked away.

"Now I kill him and cut off his head, Father?" Skookum Jim asked.

Red Porcupine's face was without expression as he looked at his tall, powerfully built son, twenty winters of age now and nearly a match physically even for Long John Emerson.

"No, I will fight him to the death," Tagish Charlie, the younger brother, insisted. "I am the one who took him prisoner, so he is mine to do with as I wish."

"I will stick a knife into his belly," Hammerwater Kate offered. "He has slain Long John's friend and so he must die."

"Quiet, pup," Red Porcupine said to his daughter. "Next time I will leave you home. That is where you belong, with the women. Perhaps they will eventually be able to teach you to prepare salmon skins properly. All this time I have hoped that Long John would return and take this little wolverine off my hands, just as he once said he would, but now he returns with another woman. Well, two women in one lodge is not the worst thing."

Kate glared at her father and the Tagish warriors began to laugh.

"The fate of these Gossacks is in your hands, Long John Emerson," Red Porcupine said. "What shall we do with them?"

"The soldiers have done only what they were ordered to do. They are poor things, not worth killing, but they have very good rifles. The Tagish chief will wish to keep them. Send the men back across the High Grease. If they make it unarmed they deserve to live. Dobshansky here, he owes me somethin'."

"Has he cheated you at trading also," Red Porcupine asked, touching the tips of his fingers to his chin, "or is it true, my friend, that you have stolen his wife?"

"He beat her," Emerson explained, "and so she left him."

"Why should not a husband beat his wife if she offends him?"

"May a Tagish woman not leave her husband if she wishes? Hell, I remember when—"

"It is true," Red Porcupine nodded. "She may even bar him from the kashim if he fails to provide for her and her children. Then he must move in with his relatives and not bother her again."

"Figgered so," Emerson said. "So Ludmila left 'im of her own free will, an' she hid away on Musi's boat. Me an' the boys didn't find out about 'er until we was out to sea."

"Ugly little boat in the harbor?" Red Porcupine asked. "I would not wish to go to sea in that. The waves would tip it over." Again the warriors laughed.

Musi folded his arms across his chest.

"Perhaps it is a good boat," Red Porcupine admitted. "Maybe your friend will take me for a ride on it one day, but I will make prayers that Orca does not come up and bite us in half. Now you must decide what to do with the leader of these Gossacks, however."

"Put a bullet in 'is head an' be done with it," Taos Danny grunted.

"I'll give ye a chance for your life, Dobshansky," Long John said, spitting on the ground. "Like I offered before—with knives. If it's still beneath your dignity then I guess I'll let leetle Kate here slit ye open. I owe 'er a present. She'll tie ye up to a tree with your own gut."

The Tagish warriors muttered their approval.

"You confuse honor with bravery, Mr. Emerson," Dobshansky said. "Since I have little choice in the matter, I'll happily dispatch you to whatever god you revere. Tell this young lout to unbind me, and let's get on with it."

Skookum Jim, glancing from Long John to Red Porcupine, proceeded to untie Dobshansky's hands.

The count massaged his wrists, straightened his military jacket. "May I have a knife, please?"

Long John borrowed Danny's blade, held up the weapon alongside his own, and then tossed the two knives onto the ground.

The Tagish warriors drew back a step or two to increase the size of the combat area.

"So," Dobshansky grinned. "First I kill the sauvage Américain and then the Tagish kill me and my remaining soldiers. Ah, it is all in the spirit of old Roman times. Friend Emerson, would you care to dance?" With that Dobshansky bowed from the waist, stepped forward, and selected one of the knives.

"Your men go free," Emerson said. "Ye put me under, you go too."

"And the charming Ludmila? Will she be allowed to accompany me?"

"Think ye've had your answer to that question."

"If you would be so kind, then, as to pick up your blade, I suggest that we commence."

Long John, half expecting a sudden rush by Dobshansky, snatched up the weapon, Danny's, for the count had chosen the other. Maybe I'll saunter into the spirit world stuck with my own Idaho toothpick. Damn near could swear I hear a raven cacklin'.

The two men, one tall and dressed in buckskins, the other shorter but powerful in his uniform, circled each other, their blades weaving back and forth and glinting in the sunlight.

Emerson feinted once, twice. He was surprised at Dobshansky's nimbleness. Bastard's got a reputation for killin' men. Maybe it's not jest all rumors, by God.

The Tagish, quiet at first, began a kind of low yipping chant, and above that sound, Long John could hear Taos Danny yelling encouragement.

Dobshansky, pretending to stumble, lunged forward, growling like an angry bear, his eyes narrowed, the civilized side of his nature vanished.

Long John stepped to one side, twisted about and deftly delivered a kick to the Russian's ribs. Dobshansky winced but made no other sound, turning nimbly and drawing back his lips in a grin of rage.

Again they circled each other.

"My God," Emerson hissed. "it scares this child half to death jest lookin' at ye. You are without a doubt the ugliest-lookin' monkey I've ever seen. About done playin' now, are ye?"

"I am ready to kill you now, da. Smyert'—death."

Half turning away, Dobshansky raised his knife, bellowed and rushed forward. Emerson ducked, and rammed his head into the Russian's mid-section. Straightening, he flipped the count backward.

The blade flew from Dobshansky's hand and he lay fighting for breath.

Long John knelt beside him, held Danny's knife to the Count's throat, hesitated, rose, and shrugged. "Didn't even give me a good tussle, Dobshansky. Ye want to try 'er again? Hell, this child's got all day."

"Finish 'er, John, ye damned fool," Taos yelled out.

The Tagish warriors were yipping and clapping at the same time now.

Dobshansky rose slowly to his feet, looked about for his weapon.

"Here," Emerson said, tossing Danny's knife to his adversary. "I don't guess I even need a blade with you. This way the odds is kind of evened up a bit."

Dobshansky, still struggling for breath, nevertheless made a halfhearted bow, picked up the weapon and squared off once more.

"You are very certain of yourself, Mr. Emerson," he said, "but you have just made a terrible mistake, I think. Have it your way, however." The count's eyes narrowed and the blade flashed out.

Long John parried the thrust with his left hand and drove his right fist full into Dobshansky's face, dropping him on the spot.

The Tagish were yelling for the kill, but Emerson stared down at the fallen man, seemed almost bemused, and then turned away.

Dobshansky, on hands and knees, lunged for Emerson's legs, missed, rose to one knee. He stared about at the painted faces of the Tagish men, made momentary eye contact with little Hammerwater Kate, her own knife clasped in her hand, and then turned to Ludmila, who had stepped forward.

"Will you not intercede in my behalf, princess?" he asked.

"Yes, Pieter, I will do that for you," she answered. So saying, she withdrew the Colt pistol from within her coat, leveled the weapon and fired.

The shot tore into Dobshansky's crotch and he tumbled forward, howling in pain. Her next shot ended it.

Chapter 17
In the Tagish Village

When a man dies, the yeg is freed from his body and he sits near the entrance to Raven Man's tunnel and is sad. Then he finds a bowl of fish oil and he dips his fingers into it and eats.

He hears the mourning chants begin and he enters the tunnel. Bowls of food have been left along the way. His wife and relatives see to this by throwing scraps of food into the cooking fire during the four days required for him to make his way to the spirit world.

At the end of four days the man emerges from Raven Man's tunnel. Two sticks flare up in the fire of Raven Man's mother-in-law and the pot of water sitting over the fire comes to a boil. The mother-in-law has grown old, but when the water boils, she jumps in and emerges young-looking and beautiful once more. After that she sleeps with the newcomer for one or two nights, depending on how attractive he is to her.

If the dead person is a woman, then two sticks flare up in Raven Man's fire. Raven Man meets her at the door to his lodge. He is still very handsome, for the passing of time does not affect him at all. He takes the woman into his arms and makes love to her for one night or two, depending on how pretty she is.

When it is time to leave, a big meal is prepared for

the dead person, and then Raven Man or the mother-in-law tells the person to be on his way.

The dead one flies away to the riverbank, and there he is welcomed by people who have come in canoes—many people, many canoes. They will take the dead to their village in the spirit world, and life there will be just as it is here on earth except that there is no more death and no more hunger.

If not enough people come through the tunnel, then Raven Man and his mother-in-law will shake the stone pillar that Denato the creator has placed between the two lodges. That will cause an earthquake, and more dead people will come through the tunnel.

February 1868

Charley St. Francis, native of Missouri and unwilling participant in the Sand Creek massacre, deserter from the Union Army, north-country trapper and close friend to Long John Emerson, was buried near the shores of Tagish Lake just below Red Porcupine's village. After a time the makeshift cross that marked his grave was replaced by a far more elaborate one, hand carved, decorative, with his name on it.

Charley St. Francis
died '67
buried here by those what loved him

Long John and Ludmila were married by Chief Red Porcupine. After some discussion with regard to propriety it was decided that a bride price might be paid to Red Porcupine and his wife Short Day; the goods would be put on display before the chief's lodge. Included were a number of Russian swords and seven needle-action breech-loading rifles.

There was also a beaver cap with silver and gold braid that had once belonged to Count Pieter Dobshansky. The hat was the subject of one or two quarrels between husband and wife, but at length they compromised and wore it by turns.

John and Ludmila were given use of the marriage lodge for a time. The other newcomers managed to find sleeping room in the chief's large kashim. A new totem pole was erected with the others at the southern entrance to the village. It depicted in part Emerson's knife victory over the Russian as well as his death, which brought Ludmila much honor in the village.

Emerson, with the help of Taos Danny and Musi, began construction of the promised "mansion," a large British-style log cabin that would have an onion tower of sorts at either end of the roof and a cinder-and-mud short-stack chimney in the middle. The latter would be no more than an ornate smokehole to accommodate the open fire below.

The work went slowly, however. The men found it essential to spend a good deal of time hunting and accompanying the Tagish far downriver past the Tagish and Tutchone village of Hootalinqua at the confluence of the Yukon and Teslin. They traveled below Lake Laberge and on by canoe to the Hudson's Bay Company post at Fort Selkirk. Ultimately they reached the Klondike the Throndiuk River, the Hammerwater, generally considered the best salmon stream of all the Yukon's tributaries, and incidentally young Kate's namesake.

Summer waned and the days rapidly grew shorter. The first heavy frosts and rains came just about the time daylight and darkness were equal. Willow and cottonwood turned yellow, bush maples burned scarlet and waterfowl vanished from tarn and marsh.

Back at the Tagish village Danny renewed his courtship of Irena, annoyed at times that she seemed to prefer boys her own age. Relentless Danny ultimately gained her full attention and even extracted from her what almost amounted to a promise that she would consider marriage next summer, when she would be fifteen years of age.

Musi and Okime, out of sight of the ocean for the first time in their lives, discussed again and again the return to the *Darakusha*, the North Pacific and Hokkaido. At the end of September they made their farewells to their own party, to Red Porcupine and his family, to sundry Tagish friends and finally to the grave of Charley St. Francis.

When no one remained to whom they might bid good-bye and with Skookum Jim and Tagish Charlie as guides, they left the village to cross the High Grease to Dyea.

A week and a half later they got back to the Tagish village just as the first snow of winter began to fall.

"Not good time to go back," Musi explained to Long John and Ludmila. "Bad omens."

"*Seikakuni,*" Okime agreed, "exactly. Bad omens. Too much ice in water. Pierre Grayfish help us to get *Darakusha* into drydock. He take care until next summer."

"Omens?" Long John laughed. "Don't know that icebergs ever bothered you before."

"Welcome back, both of you," Ludmila smiled. "We have missed you."

Sometimes snow fell, and sometimes rain, and sometimes freezing rain. Finally when the skies cleared the heavy cold of the interior set in and the temperature fell below zero.

Snow flurries continued through the month of November and the days shortened until by the solstice the sun rimmed the southern horizon for a little more than two hours only.

One morning the lake was frozen nearly across. The

mansion, mantled in white, stood iced over and unfinished. Hunting grew difficult.

Ludmila, seven months pregnant, grew despondent at times and could not help recalling the words of the man she had slain. Thoughts of Mother Russia came to her, memories of music, gaiety, festivities, the good, crackling heat of the big fireplaces in her parents' palace, choric voices in the cathedral.

When Emerson was away hunting and trapping, the depression was almost more than she could bear. Even Red Porcupine's big kashim was miserably cramped. Though Skookum Jim, Tagish Charlie and Kate were sleeping in the lodges of various relatives, they still spent much of their time in their parents' home.

Gale-force winds sang down from the mountains, driving blinding whiteness before them, and the temperature, Long John surmised, sometimes dropped to forty, fifty, even sixty below zero.

A black bear came into the village, whimpering and demanding entry into one of the lodges, but it was finally persuaded to take up sleeping quarters in an abandoned and half-caved-in kashim near the edge of the village. The bear, moaning pathetically, allowed itself to be herded into the old lodge, found the quarters satisfactory, curled up and slept.

Wolves wandered into the village at times. The camp dogs, barking furiously, would back close to lodge doorways and allow their wild cousins to pass.

The days grew noticeably longer, but the cold showed no signs of abating. The people stayed inside during bitterest cold, kept on their heavy clothing and huddled close to the fire. The old ones told tales of Beaver Man and Raven Man, Bluejay and White Wolf. The small children listened, clinging to their mothers and fathers and uncles and aunts, to how the mysterious Giyeg glided soundlessly beneath the surface of the snow and the Nahoen stole children who wandered away from their villages.

In February the first cracks appeared in the ice of the lake. Even though these froze solid once again during the nights, Red Porcupine puffed at his pipeful of native tobacco and confidently predicted that springtime could not be too far distant. "Ice breaks up pretty soon. Don't worry, days gettin' longer all the time."

Ludmila knew that her time was near. She had long since lost count of the days, but she was certain it would not be long.

The men were gone more frequently now, trapping for the winter-prime fur of otter, beaver, white fox. In these periods, as before, Ludmila was subject to brooding. She did not regret her decision to cast her lot with Long John, for she remained deeply in love, but in the darkness, cold and forced inactivity she sometimes could not help dwelling on life in Rostov, impossibly distant now.

She had to admit that everyday existence in Red Porcupine's semisubterranean kashim was not particularly difficult. The Tagish held a monopoly on trade between the coastal and interior tribes so they were quite well provided with material comforts, the chief's family most of all.

The lodge, constructed of wood and well insulated with earth, was kept warm by a fire that was never allowed to go out. The larders, large, elaborately carved painted wooden boxes, were well stocked with an abundance of dried salmon, venison, elk, moose and mutton as well as camas flour and a variety of fruits and vessels of oil. Short Day even had a gallon jug half full of vinegar, brought upriver from the British post at Fort Selkirk, and two bags of wheat flour, which Skookum Jim had hauled up over the High Grease from Dyea.

The women's life Ludmila found almost unbearably tedious. They spent their time weaving, preparing food and gossiping. This round of chores and amusements, once the novelty had worn off, was in fact drearily similar to the traditional pursuits of women in Rostov. At home, though, there were horses to ride, books to read, pleasant green hills and garden paths to walk, educated and artistic friends to converse with.

In addition her pregnancy was not an easy one. Violent bouts of nausea in the early months were replaced by dreadful, grinding pain in her lower back, heartburn every time she ate and increasing clumsiness. She loved and wanted her baby with every fiber of her being, but she had long since decided she hated pregnancy.

When the men were absent, her main companions were Short Day and the twelve-year-old hoyden Hammerwater Kate, otherwise known as Throndiuk.

Irena remained both attentive and devoted, while Okime and sometimes Musi provided comfort and good conversation. Short Day could be quite an amusing companion when she was in a mood to tell stories. She had a seemingly infinite hoard of variant editions of the Raven, Eagle and Beaver tales the men told as well as stories of things that had happened to her personally. Occasionally in the long evenings Short Day and Okime would get into an undeclared story-telling contest. Each sought to top the other, speaking broken English and matching one another yarn for yarn from their vastly different traditions and backgrounds. These were some of the most enjoyable evenings for Ludmila—when the men were absent.

Throndiuk, the twelve-year-old, remained unmoved by all Ludmila's attempts to befriend her. Ludmila felt a sort of kinship for her; she was a rebel against traditional expectations just as the princess was. Indeed, Kate was herself a princess in the reckoning of the Tagish. For the most part she was polite but distant, a result, Ludmila understood, of infatuation with Long John.

One day all the men had been absent for several days when a snowstorm blew in. Winds howled around the corners of the lodges and raised blinding waves of powdery snow.

Short Day decided to have all the women of the village in for a feast. "Mens not the only ones can have feasts. They think so, but they not. Womens get tired sittin' round, nothin' to do. We have everybody come over here. I got plenty stuff, lotsa frozen fish, lotsa *olachen* oil. We whip 'em up good with soapberry, even got some salmon been sittin' in a box from last year, all nice an' ripe now. We have sing, women dances. Womens don' have to sit round, wait for mens to have good time."

The women in Red Porcupine's lodge got to work immediately. Short Day sent Kate to all the houses in the village with the invitation, and the rest buckled down to cook and prepare the house. Okime contributed a keg of brandy from the ship's stores. Irena worked cheerfully with Short Day, and even Ludmila got caught up in the older woman's excitement and broke out a large sack of dried apricots that Long John had brought from Fort Selkirk and that she had been hoarding jealously.

The guests began arriving just after sunset; many of the women also brought some special dish. Right from the beginning the party was a huge success. There was not enough brandy to get anyone drunk, but enough to loosen tongues and brighten spirits.

At first they sang. A few women performed tunes that were theirs by right of birth, others sang general property songs. The younger women danced a women's dance, and then, carried away by the spirit of frivolity, Short Day and several of the older women did a daring parody of one of the men's hunting dances. This performance made the

Tagish women shriek with laughter, although most of the satire was lost on Ludmila.

She was persuaded, with much pressure from Short Day and Irena, to sing some of the songs that she remembered from her homeland. Irena translated the Russian lyrics for the others.

Ludmila started out with ballads and finished with an extremely bawdy drinking song in English she had learned from hearing Taos Danny. The performance was a hit.

Everyone ate enormously except for Ludmila, who used her pregnancy and accompanying digestive problems as an excuse not to sample some of the delicacies she found most repugnant, such as the frothed fish oil and the decomposed salmon cheese. Okime apparently felt no such compunctions, tasting everything and finding it much to her liking. Only young Kate had the cheek simply to refuse food. She was quite fond of whipped fish oil, but when it came to the strong-smelling aged salmon, she held her nose and made a face. She had never liked the dish.

The women stayed late into the evening, telling stories until the fire burned low and the children began falling asleep. Everyone departed in a glow of good feelings, assuring each other that they would do it again soon.

They all retired shortly after the last guest left. Ludmila was not yet asleep when she heard Irena moaning. The princess rolled onto her stomach and began to push herself up, the only way she could rise from a prone position these days. Before she had completed the tedious maneuver, Short Day rose and built up the fire with twigs.

Outside the lodge the unfortunate Irena was bent over retching. Ludmila and Short Day looked at each other in puzzlement and concern. Kate, sleeping at home in the absence of the men, was up as well.

"Maybe Irena eat too much," she shrugged.

"Maybe," Short Day agreed. "I go out, bring her back inside."

Before the older woman gained the door, she too suddenly stopped short, doubling over in pain. Okime awoke with a great cry, staring wildly and groaning a few syllables in Japanese. She did not make it to the door, but puked into a kettle.

Irena returned, her forehead damp, her face ghastly pale. Ludmila rushed to her and took her hand. "What is it, Irena?" She smoothed a strand of hair away from the pinched face.

Irena shook her head, unable to speak, and Ludmila helped her back to her bunk. The young Tlingit almost immediately turned onto her side and doubled up with retching again. Ludmila grabbed the closest vessel, a large wooden bowl, and placed it before her, then turned to check on Okime and Short Day. Their features, contorted in the dim light of the single fish oil lamp, suggested they were in equally bad straits.

Of the five inhabitants of the kashim, only Hammerwater Kate and Ludmila Andreiovna remained untouched by the strange and sudden affliction. The two were desperately busy for a time, emptying reeking vessels outside, wringing cloths in cool water to put on the foreheads of the sufferers. Ludmila and Kate worked side by side, and Kate's usually confident and even cheeky expression changed until her face appeared small and frightened, for the three ill women seemed to be getting worse, not better.

"Does your mother have any stomach remedies, Kate? Any roots or powders that you know of?"

Kate went to Short Day's medicine box and withdrew a packet. "I think she give us this for belly troubles. She mix 'em up in water, make us drink. All I know about."

"Let's try it, then. We've got to do something."

Ludmila managed to get Short Day to look at the powder and nod. Kate mixed the potion and they administered it to Okime, Irena and Short Day.

Hours passed and eventually the violent vomiting and

diarrhea eased, but all three women gradually lapsed into semiconsciousness. Their foreheads were damp and clammy, their skin pallid.

"Going to die?" Kate whispered, her eyes wide and panicky as she stared at her mother.

"No," Ludmila reassured her, patting her gently on the shoulder. "There was something in the food, I'm certain that's it." But she thought, *smallpox, bubonic plague, diphtheria, scarlet fever, spotted fever. . . .*

"Since we are the only ones who are well, Kate, we'll have to care for everybody." Kate nodded.

They spent the remainder of that stormy night and most of the next day making their rounds from house to house. Except for several small children who shared Kate's distaste for aged salmon, everyone in the village was ill, some less severely than others. Stick Woman, the old shaman, was ill but remained conscious. She was able to direct Kate and Ludmila to give treatment, producing medicines and explaining their preparation.

"Not so good without chanting," she grunted, "but maybe good enough. I be better soon. Then I go around, pray for people. I pray right here for everybody, but it not so good. The Nahoens, the mad ones, they fly about in the wind, their voices drown out mine."

"I am certain," Ludmila said gently, "that even praying here in bed will be helpful. Everyone says your spirit is very powerful."

Stick Woman nodded weakly, her mouth a tight line.

By late afternoon it was apparent that the ill would recover. All were fully conscious, although very weak, and it fell to Kate and Ludmila to keep fires burning in the lodges and to see to it that those who were able to take food were given nourishing broth.

* * *

The storm abated somewhat and the fierce winds died down. Thin flecks of snow continued to drift down and the temperature was still near zero.

Toward sunset Ludmila went down to the lake alone to chop out the ice hole in order to draw the night's supply of water. As the sun sank to the horizon it broke through the cold, grey clouds and the sky, the lake and the snow-covered hills briefly glowed blood-crimson. On impulse she walked toward the glow of red to the southwest, going farther and farther out onto the ice until the village was out of sight among the slopes. As she walked the glow faded to red-violet, then to dull maroon purple.

Nothing moved; no sound of life, no bird song, not even a breath of wind. The light faded entirely, leaving her in deep blue dusk illuminated only by the faint reflection of the white world around her. She felt alone as she had never felt before. As she breathed in she seemed to breathe the dimly perceived whiteness of lake and mountains, the brooding sky, the solitude and the growing dark.

I could walk on across the lake. I could walk toward where the sun went down. I could walk forever in any direction and no one would ever find me. Perhaps I would eventually come to the southlands where lilacs bloom and a warm sea whispers over the sand.

The odor of lilacs was strong in her memory, as if she were suddenly smelling them here and now.

Rostov, that is where I was a girl. This is where I am a woman.

A sudden gust of wind lifted a swirl of snow powder from the surface of the ice and spun it around her. In the darkness the cloud of snow took on vague forms, dancing half-human shapes.

Ludmila remembered Short Day's stories of people who wandered off into the winter night and were never seen again. "Sometimes somethin' strange happen. People go out, they get like in a dream, they keep followin' somethin'. Funny things out there. Some say Giyeg gets them, sucks out soul. Not good to wander alone."

Ludmila thought of Jesus, and the long-ago vision reappeared to her for an instant. It had been months, she realized, since she thought at all of the religion she had been raised in.

"Ain't certain," Long John had once said, "whether Jesus ever even heard of this place. Could be he stays down to Sitka."

With inward sadness Ludmila caressed the locket containing the image of the Christ-child as if she were caressing an outworn but much loved garment. Then along with the memory of lilacs and the sun-drenched gardens of Rostov she put the thought away, dropped the small locket back inside her clothing. Perhaps someday, when Long John took her away to the south, when they had a real home, perhaps then. . . .

"In Raven Man's eye then," she whispered, looking around her at the faintly gleaming hollow of darkness. "Here we dwell in your eye, Raven Man."

Ludmila shook her head, trying to bring back some sense of the normal. "I am not thinking right," she said aloud. "I am tired. I must get back to the village."

Then the pain took her, a strong wave of intense, cramping agony in her midsection, doubling her over and rendering her unable to breathe until it passed.

"My God," she gasped. "Labor? My time? No, not here, not alone on the frozen lake!"

When she was able to walk again, she headed back toward the village and was hit midway by another convulsion. By the time she reached Short Day's lodge she was trembling and damp with perspiration. As she entered, she bent over with another pang, gasping until it had passed.

Short Day perceived the problem immediately and began to walk Ludmila around the lodge.

Kate returned to the kashim soon afterward, and with

Short Day instucting her in what to do, she tended to Ludmila. Okime occasionally put in advice completely contrary to Tagish methods.

As the pains came closer together and more intense, Ludmila lost track of everything around her. Kate gave her a bitter potion to drink, something supposed to ease the pangs and hasten the birth, but even so it seemed that the agony went on forever with strange jumps in time, so that Ludmila was not even certain whether hours or days had passed.

Hammerwater Kate tended her gently and patiently, squeezing Ludmila's hand when the pains gripped her, face tense with sympathy. At some point in the eternity Ludmila woke out of a half-doze that had lasted a few seconds between contractions and saw the serious, boyish face watching her with concern.

"You do like me after all, don't you, Kate?" Ludmila whispered, smiling weakly.

"I always like you," Kate began defensively. "Never say anything mean to you." Then she broke into a sudden grin that transformed her features. "You one pretty tough *cheechako*. You be all right."

The child did not come until dawn. Ludmila, assured that the new arrival was a boy and in good condition, fell into a deep, exhausted sleep, the infant at her breast. She could not stay awake long enough to drink the broth that Kate had brought her.

When she awakened, Long John Emerson was sitting beside her, holding her hand and grinning. Kate, on the other side of him, held the newborn.

"My God," Emerson whispered, "you're a beautiful creature, Ludmila."

"So are you, my husband. I'm afraid I'm dreaming. When did you return? Your son John, do you like him?"

"Homeliest leetle rugrat I ever seen," he grinned,

"but if you don't mind I'd kind of like to name him Charles. For old Charley, you know."

Ludmila nodded. "That's a fine name and he was a good man, a good friend. Charles Rostov Emerson. Is it all right to have Rostov to remember my home and my father?"

"Sure thing," Long John agreed. He studied her for a long time and then cleared his throat. "You ain't gonna go runnin' off there on me someday, are you? Every now and then I start to wonderin', I mean about how this ain't what you're used to, that you must miss—"

"Hush, John. Rostov in our son's name is all I need." She held her arms out for the baby, smiled and winked at Kate. "Naw," Ludmila drawled in imitation of the trappers, "you ain't gettin' rid o' this child so easy. This here is one pretty tough *cheechako*, ain't that right now, Hammerwater?"

Taos Danny, sitting across the room beside Irena, looked up and guffawed. Kate giggled and Emerson, glancing at them, began to smile. Then he chuckled and the chuckle grew into full, booming male laughter.

She slept.

Book Three:
HAMMERWATER KATE

Chapter 18
Hootalinqua Princess

The *Yukon* was a stern-wheel steamboat twelve feet wide and fifty long. She looked like a little cow barn set up on a scow.

In June of 1869 she was lowered from the deck of the *Commodore* into the waters of Norton Sound. Boiler hissing and whistle screaming out her name in short, high-pitched bursts of sound, she found her way to the Apoon Channel of the Yukon delta.

There she grounded, was extricated and proceeded up the Lot of Water. She was good for ten hours between firewood stops if she carried five cords stacked up on the decks.

She entered the delta on July fourth with Captain Charles P. Raymond, United States Army, on his way upriver to persuade the British to abandon Fort Yukon, something the Russians had never been inclined to do.

"When all is finished," the Hudson's Bay commandant grumbled, "the Russians may advance when they damned please."

Indians along the Yukon River were amazed, for what had they known of civilization beyond flintlocks, glass beads and steel knives?

"The Yukon appeared to them a huge monster, breathing fire and smoke," Captain Raymond noted.

The British left without a fuss, and Parrott & Company placed Mercier and Westdahl in charge of the post. After that the Alaska Commercial Company took over, and for years the little steamer plied the great river, at last with Leroy Napoleon McQuesten at her wheel.

"The Yukon," he said, "is very old and liable to blow up at any time." So she was hauled into a slough near Fort Yukon for protection against the crushing strength of the river's ice, but a flood the spring of '80 brought floes to batter her.

"Finished," McQuesten shrugged. He wasn't worried. ACCo had ordered a new vessel that awaited assembly at St. Mike.

April 1880

It was time for her to find her man. Well—past time, and she knew it. At twenty-five she was the oldest unmarried woman in her father's village. There was no lack of suitors. Many young men courted her, and some even went so far as to bring sleds full of presents to Red Porcupine's lodge. But the Tagish chief, though he often urged her to marry lest the fading of her youth find her still without a husband, nevertheless respected her wishes; he held up his hands crosswise and shook his head.

"I would be pleased to have you as my son-in-law," Red Porcupine said more than once, "but my daughter would not make you a good wife. She would rather hunt and fish with her brothers than marry and have children. I do not understand her. I do not understand her at all, but long ago I promised the Russian priest, Father Georgi, that I would respect her will when she grew to womanhood. If she were of my blood, I would accept what you bring me this day."

It was the year Long John Emerson returned to the Tagish village with Ludmila Andreiovna, his wife, that

Kate learned of her birth. Red Porcupine and Short Day told her shortly after she emerged from the women's lodge following the onset of menstruation.

"Yuri Borodin, Baroness Grushenka Karloff," she said softly, savoring the sounds of the strange names.

It made little difference, of course. A number of others among the Tagish were adopted, some orphans, a few from down the Lot of Water or from Dyea or even Sitka. In all ways that mattered, she was indeed the daughter of Red Porcupine and Short Day, and when she married, the man she took for a husband would eventually become the chief of the Tagish, for that was the way of things.

Red Porcupine was eager to have his successor so that he could guide the younger man and teach him what a chief must know.

How, she wondered, did her father feel about her present and most persistent suitor, Big Grayling, chief of the Southern Tutchones and nearly Red Porcupine's age? Such a marriage would reinforce the casual alliance between the Tutchones and the Tagish; the union would be politically wise. Nonetheless Kate suspected that Red Porcupine was less than enthusiastic with the prospect of a son-in-law of his own generation, even though he and Big Grayling had been friends for many winters. Kate had come downriver, partly to escape the dogged gestures of the Big Grayling for a while.

She stood up, pushed her way through the willow thicket and gazed down to the slough, where the men were at work trying to revive the damaged riverboat, the *Yukon*. The Japanese couple had suggested the idea, and Long John, after scoffing for a time, finally began to take the notion seriously. At length he grinned, clapped little Musi on the back and said, "By God, old friend, mebbe we can do 'er at that. Let's drift down to Fort Yukon an' see if McQuesten's willing to sell his junkpile."

The ACCo agent shrugged and agreed. ''I doubt you'll ever get 'er out of the mud, Johnny.''

''Got 'er all figgered out,'' Emerson grinned. ''Sky hook.''

McQuesten hawked and spat tobacco juice. ''Whatever you say.''

''So what's the barge worth?''

''Not much, that's sure. You gonna pull the boiler an' set up a still, or what?''

''Hadn't figgered on it,'' Emerson replied.

''Fifty dollars. That's enough to keep the company happy.''

''A hundred,'' Emerson said.

''How's that?''

''A hundred—an' you throw in whatever you've got in the way of tar, oakum, varnish, spare parts an' the like.''

''You're not thinkin' to get 'er floatin' again?''

''Course, Leroy. Gonna turn 'er into the Hootalinqua-to-St. Mike express, drive the Alaska Commercial Company clean off the river.''

''A fool an' his money,'' McQuesten sighed.

''Gold, my friend. Genuine north-country gold—right here in this pouch.''

''So you've been findin' somethin' after all up at Forty Mile,'' McQuesten grinned. Then they weighed out the nuggets.

That was two weeks past Kate reflected, and now Leroy Napoleon McQuesten was gone downriver to St. Michael to take possession of the new and larger stern-wheeler being assembled for trade on the river.

Emerson and the others, working with ropes and pulleys, managed to get the half-sunk steamer up onto the muddy bank of the slough and were hard at work replacing the broken-in sections of the hull. The oddly dissonant odors of burning spruce logs and fumes from the big pot of bubbling tar drifted up to her. She walked down to where the men were working.

"Katie," Long John called out, "toss me that doublejohn on top of the coil of pump hose, will you?"

He should have waited for me to grow up. It would only have been a little while. As the thought formed she felt a twinge of guilt, for immediately the image of her friend Ludmila came to her—kind, gentle, beautiful Ludmila, the most beautiful woman Kate had ever seen. Yes, and the inevitable image of young Charles Emerson rose as well. The boy was twelve winters old now and had been her faithful companion on more than one hunting expedition. He was frighteningly like herself in many ways.

Perhaps I will wait for the son, then.

"Hurry up, Kate of the Klondike. I can't hold this damned plank in place all day."

"The White Horse should think ahead, perhaps," she yelled back, tossing the hammer to Emerson. He caught it by the handle, nodded and winked at her.

Musi grinned. He held the whiskey bottle filled with slough water in his right hand, raised it above his head and smashed it across the keel of the rehabilitated stern-wheeler.

"*Hootalinqua Princess,*" he announced. Then he bowed in formal Japanese fashion.

Okime applauded, but Long John bellowed, "That ain't what we was goin' to name 'er, and you know it too, you slant-eyed thief."

"*Yukon Pisser* not good name." Musi shook his head solemnly. "Lot of work to make her go again, and that name not dignified. I told you that, John. We all told you. Boats need proper names."

"That's why we always had trouble with *Darakusha,*" Okime agreed, "bad name. This name honors Ludmila. We will have good luck from that. She is not pretty like your wife, Long John Emerson, but now we will always think of her when we are far down the big river. I will paint on the name myself."

"I guess Ludmila won't mind," Emerson growled, squinting as he studied the lines of the ungainly craft. "What do you think, Katie my girl?"

"Ludmila will be proud," Kate nodded, "but maybe we shouldn't name the boat until we see whether it sinks again."

"Right," Emerson agreed. "Skookum Jim, hang tight to that winch wheel now. Taos! Easy on 'er, easy, easy. If she goes down the mudbank too fast, she'll stern-wheel right to the bottom, sure as bearshit."

As the ropes began to ease tension, Musi leaped aboard, his jaw set, as if preparing to go down with his ship.

The *Hootalinqua Princess* slid a few feet and then stopped, the blades of her paddle wheel barely touching the water.

"Down the mudbank too fast, my tail end," Taos Danny howled. "She's had enough of the water an' she knows it."

"Loose the lines, Jim," Emerson called. "Katie get back. Damned scow's stuck on somethin' is all."

Kate glanced at Musi, who was clinging to the deck house in an attempt to maintain his balance, and smiled. "Perhaps we will have to wait for a flood, John Emerson," she yelled.

Then the *Hootalinqua Princess* slid sideways, nearly pitching Musi to the mudbank. Skookum Jim tried desperately to pull back on the lead line, his powerful arms straining against the makeshift winch.

The rope snapped. As the boat plunged toward the waters of the slough, the other two lines went as well. The stern of the *Princess* dug into the water, sending spray twenty feet into the air, and then the craft bobbed up like a great, ungainly cork and slowly drifted across the narrow channel to bump gently against the far bank.

"She floats," Musi exulted. "She is launched. Good boat, very good."

Emerson shook his head, then nodded. "Let's fire 'er up, by God," he yelled back. "See if that boiler's gonna hold."

The shipbuilders boarded their raft and poled across the silty water of the slough to where the *Princess* lay motionless against the mudbank. They climbed aboard and began to pound one another on the back.

Musi and Okime, captains of their own craft once more, did a kind of jig across the deck, kissing one another all the time

"No time for smoochin'," Taos Danny yipped. "Come on, boatwrights, let's get this tub to snortin'."

"Danny's right," Emerson said. "She's a thousand miles to Norton Sound an' St. Mike. Let's celebrate when we're sure we got somethin' to shout about."

Kindling wood flared in the burner and armloads of spruce sections went in after it. The furnace roared and the rusty steam pressure gauge began to register.

Kate, standing between Long John and Skookum Jim, watched intently. She knew well enough that the burning wood heated the steam that drove the engine that turned the paddle wheel, but she was not at all certain the magic would work for anyone but McQuesten.

"We got power now." Musi moved the throttle slowly forward. The paddle wheel's spindle groaned and the blades began to cut slowly through the water.

A cheer went up and Emerson yanked the cord that activated the steam whistle, sending a high-pitched yelp out across the water of the slough and the taiga beyond. In the moment of silence that followed a nesting eagle screamed back.

The *Hootalinqua Princess* began to make her way along the narrow channel toward the broader waters of the Yukon River and the silver-white piers of the old dock in front of the trading post of Fort Yukon, the one-time Hudson's Bay trading center at the confluence of the Porcupine River and the Lot of Water.

Long John Emerson, Taos Danny and Skookum Jim returned upriver to their gold mine. It lay not far from the tiny settlement of Forty Mile among the beds of auriferous gravels. Working the mine was difficult, inasmuch as even during the hot days of summer the earth stayed frozen no more than two feet below the surface in most places. The long hours of midsummer sunlight were barely sufficient to thaw the bottom of the pit so that the gold-bearing gravel and sand could be hoisted up and placered out by means of a flume and riffles and running water.

For five years there had been rumors of gold strikes all along the upper reaches of the Yukon, but very few had proven sufficiently rich to pay. Emerson's digs were among the best, but the mining of gold, Long John concluded, did not provide easy riches. On balance trapping and hunting were a far more certain way of acquiring the necessaries and of putting a little away for the time when he, Ludmila and young Charles might wish to head south to the outside.

The worst part of it, without question, was that the working of the mine kept him four hundred miles away from the village of Hootalinqua and his wife and son. From April until the first of October, while he was mining, he would be able to make only one or two brief visits home. They made the long summer months almost—but not quite—tolerable—good times to be spent with his wife, always foolishly pleased with the small amounts of gold he brought, and with his son Charles, who was growing like a river weed.

The *Hootalinqua Princess*, meanwhile, was drifting westward, belching steam and smoke, as she moved downstream along the Yukon River on her way to the Apoon Channel, Norton Sound and Redoubt St. Michael. She would pass through the broad, mosquito-infested wetlands of Yukon Flats, then past Beaver, over the narrower, swifter waters to Rampart and Nuklukayet and Tanana—these villages close to the mouth of the Tanana River—and ultimately to Fort Hamilton.

The great river was high and muddy with the spring floods and the currents were treacherous in many places. Since Musi and Okime fled across the High Grease Trail with Long John and Ludmila they had had a number of opportunities to traverse the river. Several times they took the *Yukon* herself and once on the only other steamer on the Lot of Water, the Western Trading and Fur Company's vessel the *St. Michael*.

Though they were both fascinated by the art of river voyaging and paid close attention to all that transpired against the time when they might get their hands on a river boat, this first venture at the wheel of the *Hootalinqua Princess* proved trying indeed. The river did not remain the same, but constantly changed its channel, even shifted its bed in places, eroding away banks and creating new ones, depositing and then washing away sandbars, hiding treacherous logs and boulders beneath its impenetrably muddy surface.

Just above Rampart in an extremely difficult stretch of swift water a main valve jammed shut. Musi was able only with great difficulty to pilot his craft into a gently swirling eddy and set anchor by means of looping his main hawser about a big gnarled cottonwood.

Kate watched intently as Musi fumbled with the maintenance tools, disassembling the valve and discovering a broken spring. "There are others in the big wooden chest Emerson got from McQuesten," she said. "I think they are all the same kind."

"This one should be our mechanic," Okime observed. "She is always watching how things are done."

Musi was unimpressed. "Where are these springs?"

"I'll get them for you," Kate answered, jumping down from the high bench where she had been sitting cross-legged.

Within an hour Musi gave a blast of the whistle and the *Princess* moved once more toward center channel.

On the seventh day downriver from Fort Yukon the *Hootalinqua Princess* pulled in at the mixed-race village of Nulato, in the vicinity of which Tagish Charlie had spent the winter trapping. The Koyukons came out en masse to greet the old stern-wheeler, all of them astonished to find the craft afloat again.

McQuesten had stopped there two weeks earlier and explained that winter ice had caved in the river craft's hull. Long John Emerson and his gang, the pilot said, were scrapping the *Yukon,* intending to build a whiskey still with the parts from the old boiler.

McQuesten did some trading, taking what pelts aboard his make shift bidarka he could. He visited briefly with Francois Mercier, temporarily the resident agent at the ACCo post in Nulato. Then he pushed back out into the muddy Yukon waters bound for St. Michael, where Moise Mercier's men were in the process of assembling a new and much larger craft, already dubbed the *St. Michael,* for the company's operations along the river.

A young Koyukon was paid to proceed up to the big loop on the Koyukuk River to alert Tagish Charlie that Musi, Okime and Kate had arrived. Musi began garnering trade. He took on a modest cargo of furs and paid in United States currency until his money ran out. Then he drafted the commoner notes of trade, the IOU's that were standard tokens of value along the Lot of Water.

An hour or so before twilight, after assisting Musi and Okime to load their cargo aboard the *Princess,* Kate walked through the muddy little village. There she spoke briefly with a young woman of her own age, a Russian-Koyukon whose Christian wedding Kate had attended three years earlier while Deacon Robert McDonald, the Anglican, was evangelizing at Nulato. The woman, Carolyn as she was now known, looked far older than her years. She had put on quite a bit of weight, and her eyes were dull with despair. The newborn child in her arms was doing well enough, Carolyn said, but her twins, now two winters of age, suffered from a chronic malady of some sort, something that the village shaman had been unable to dispel. He blamed the sickness on the fact that she and Tom Wounded Wolf had been married by the British Gossack rather than according to the traditional rites of the Koyukon people. The children had been unable to gain weight and they often suffered from fevers and dysentery.

Kate walked on, passed the Russian Orthodox church, now being used as a storage building by the ACCo traders, and then turned back. She wandered around to the small cemetery behind the log building with its strange cross-topped onion dome. There she found the mound of white stones and the bleached wooden cross upon which could still faintly be traced the carved letters spelling out the legend *Grushenka Karloff, d. 1855*.

Close by were the rotting spruce slabs that stood above the graves of Deriabin, Bernard and Bulegin, said to have been murdered by the Koyukons and roasted for a feast during the harsh winter of 1850–51. Other markers as well dated from the time of that same Koyukon massacre. The newer graves belonged mostly to Indians who had died during McDonald's tenure at Nulato but also included that of the trader's wife Mary Bean, murdered by Koyukons up on the Tanana River and buried at Nulato in 1878. Mrs. Bean had been the first American woman to live and die along the Yukon River.

But Kate was not interested in any of these, nor in the old house where Alex Karloff had lived with Grushenka. What was Karloff to her? Red Porcupine often told her of the Russian trader's cruelty, how he drove Grushenka straight into the arms of Yuri Borodin, her own father. Red Porcupine spoke as well of the time he found Grushenka half dead and took her to Nulato. He placed the baroness in the care of a priest named Father Georgi and later shot this Karloff through the throat.

Hammerwater Kate stood before the weathered Russian cross that marked her blood mother's grave. She knelt at last and laid her lips on the faintly decipherable letter *G*.

"I have come again, Mother I never knew," she whispered. "It is Katrina. Do you remember me, Mother? Do the dead remember the living at all? It has been two years since I came last, just after they buried Mrs. Bean."

As Kate knelt, a raven drifted over the old church, came low to the ground, circled and then flapped away toward the river.

"I am well, Mother. I am still living with Red Porcupine and his wife, Short Day. They have been wonderful parents to me—but I have told you all this before. I am Kate called Hammerwater. Do you remember me at all?"

Faintly from the distance came sounds of laughter. It was Koyukon children batting a moose bladder filled with dried grass, shouting, yelling at one another.

"I am well," Kate continued, "but I am not happy. I am twenty-five years old and I have no mate. I have not yet found the man with whom I wish to spend my life. There has been one, but he is married to another and she is my friend. She came from the land to the west, your land, my mother. She was a princess there as she is here. Princess Ludmila was a child when you married the man called Karloff.

"I wish you could have known her. She has been like a sister to me for a long time now, and I would like to look like her and be like her. She is the most beautiful woman in the world, I think. All the men in our village say so.

"She has even taught me how to read from books. She has told me many stories about Russia, about the great buildings and the wide streets and how the men and women ride about in carriages. Perhaps someday I will be able to go there with her, for sometimes she talks about that. But if I went with her, how would I know what to do?"

A mouse poked up its head, contemplated the kneeling woman for an instant, and then disappeared back among the heaped stones at the foot of the cross.

"I am wretched," Kate whispered, traces of moisture starting to her eyes. "It is wrong for me to go on dreaming about what it would be like to lie with Ludmila's husband. Sometimes I dream about it and wake up trembling. I have been having such thoughts for more than ten years, and sometimes I believe that my mind has gone into the other world, that I have lain with Raven Man during my sleep. But now I have begun to dream differently."

Kate took a deep breath, stood up and looked about her to see if anyone might be watching. "Grushenka," she whispered, "I have begun to dream of a man who has no face. He does not act like a white man nor the Tagish either. He opens his breeches and shows his manhood to me, but it is not like a man's at all. It is red and stiff like a crazy malemute dog's. I take it into my hands and kiss it. Then I wake up and cannot go back to sleep again.

"Is Giyeg feeding on my flesh while I sleep? I do not want to have dreams like this, Grushenka. You are in the other world. Will you say prayers for me? I think it is a Nahoen Giyeg sends to me so that I will spread my legs to him."

"Katie."

At first Kate thought Grushenka had actually answered her, but then she recognized the voice and whirled.

"Okime?"

"Little Kate, I thought you would be here. Koyukon scout has come back. Tagish Charlie, he was bringing furs in to Nulato. Very good catch this year. He is on board the *Hootalinqua Princess* now."

Kate nodded, cast one backward glance at Grushenka's grave and turned to follow the Japanese woman, whose hair these past three years was noticeably streaked with grey.

On down the Lot of Water they rolled, sometimes drifting with the current, sometimes stoking the furnace so the paddle wheel of the *Princess* would dip steadily and powerfully into the silty flood. Past the village of Kaltag and the low Kaiyuh Mountains to the east the Yukon broadened. It ran a mile to two miles wide and was punctuated by a long succession of islands; the channel was deep and contained far fewer hazards. Onward drifted the *Princess*, past the Ingalik village of Anvik, first visited by Andrei Glazunov during the winter of 1834.

Glazunov was the discoverer of the river as Ludmila told the story to Kate. Hearing her, Red Porcupine grunted, squinted at the fire in the stone fireplace Emerson had constructed, and commented, "Is it not strange that my people lived here so long and never saw the river? Ah yes, it took a Gossack to show it to us."

Then Holy Cross and Ikogmut, where the larger Russian church stood, and on to Marshall and Fort Hamilton and finally out into the slate-grey waters of Norton Sound, where the river passed out of the taiga forest and into the desolate brush and heather country of the delta. These were the lands inhabited by the Eskimo peoples.

As the *Princess* passed through the strait between Stuart Island and the Mainland, rounded the cape and made the final few miles to Redoubt St. Michael, Musi blared the steam whistle every five minutes. Kate and Tagish Charlie had long since counted out the pelts of fox, otter, muskrat and beaver and calculated the likely prices the winter's take would bring. Now they were happily engaged in a game of blackjack, using bits of stick as counters, while swapping stories.

Okime stood close by, occasionally winking or shaking her head. "That one is not true, I do not think." She smiled. "One of McQuesten's men told Katie that, and he heard it from a Tutchone who is known to lie very much."

Chapter 19
Enter George Washington Carmack

Was it a great bargain or Seward's Folly? Whatever the folks in the States thought, the payment of $7.2 million dollars by the United States to Russia made little difference to anyone in Alaska, white or Indian. The province was ruled first by the army, then by the navy, but there was little ruling to be done. Some of the Russians stayed on, including the old believers of Ninilchik, those who clung to tradition and found freedom under American hegemony. But for the most part the people continued to live as before, unconcerned whether the distant entity called government resided ultimately in Moscow or in Washington, D.C. The soldiers, if they came at all, wore different uniforms, and perhaps they acted a bit more decently—but perhaps they did not.

A few came north from California and other such places, but seldom did anyone stay.

There were rumors of gold, of course, a madness that had begun in California and spread throughout the Western states and territories. Still, the bitter cold of the Alaskan interior, the huge mountains and vast taiga and tundra, the permanently frozen earth, the great bears and the astounding clouds of mosquitoes were sufficient to keep the Americans at home.

Then Joe Juneau and Dick Harris found "color" in a

stream they called Gold Creek. That led to the discovery of quartz gold and the founding of hard rock mines, the Treadwell and the AJ, both along the Gastineau Channel. The boom towns of Harrisburg, later called Juneau and Douglas sprang up, and all around the land was claimed as the miners came in from California, Oregon, Montana and Colorado.

May 1880

George Washington Carmack, a big burly man, round-faced, and short-necked, climbed out of the dory and went ashore at Redoubt St. Michael. He stood on the weather-beaten dock and ran his fingers over his Manchu mustache. He turned, squinted and stared back across the choppy grey waters to the lean form of the *Seattle Sojourner*, a five-masted double-rigged steamer that had brought him north from San Francisco.

He had intended to stop at Harrisburg, but neither the Treadwell nor the AJ had been hiring, not even experienced hardrock men like himself. Carmack further ascertained that every likely rockpile within miles of the settlements on the Gastineau Channel had long since been claimed. Such being the case, Carmack had but two choices: to return to California or to head for the Alaskan interior to find the gold whose presence burned its come-hither into his brain.

The first option represented an admission of failure. The second was little more than a great question mark. His money, saved up over four years, was nearly gone, but there remained enough to provide him with a small grubstake. By God, he would take a chance to see what was out there along the Lot of Water past the great mountain called Denali.

If it was bigger than Shasta, Carmack concluded, then by heaven it was worth seeing.

More than that, he *knew* there was gold in the interior, knew in his bones, and maybe more gold than California had ever dreamed of. It hid undiscovered in a wilderness twice the size of Texas.

Once reality had been clearly confronted, Carmack chose the obvious option. He booked passage with the *Sojourner* once more for the remote fur post of St. Michael, whence, he had been told, he might be able to catch a paddle-wheeler upriver clear to Fort Yukon on the Arctic Circle.

So here he was, standing on the bleached white dock at St. Mike, halfway to the end of the world. He sized up the village—a scattering of huts. Half a dozen log cabins of uncertain vintage were blasted by incessant winds and freezing fog. Round-faced, dark-skinned Eskimo children ran about in good spirits and utter abandon, parents nowhere in sight. The old stockade, one wall somewhat sagged in, originally a Russian outpost, was now the warehouse for the Alaskan Commercial Company, the virtual owners of the interior, powerful enough to embrace and entertain their competition for the fur trade along the river.

"Somewhere out there," he muttered, gazing inland toward the low, faintly visible hills that rose beyond the tundra, "my fortune is waiting for me."

He was twenty-eight and strong in the arms, strong in cunning and determination as well. Possibly he had come to this place not only for the lure of uncertain gold but also to repossess the innocent wildness that had been the heritage of his mother's people, the Maidu Indians, in the days before the California gold rush.

A half-breed, he had never been fully at home in the white man's world, and without worrying the matter excessively, he sensed that his own native California foothills and mountains, even the great Sierras themselves, had suffered under the heavy boots of the Americans for too long. A railroad crossed those mountains. He was seventeen years old when the rail connection to the East was made.

What, after all, was his heritage? His Maidu mother, a Digger squaw in the eyes of the whites, was ten years dead of consumption. And his father, Jean Carmack? In Colorado the last he'd heard—a restless, wandering man, no more able to deal with civilization than was his son.

"Like father, like son," Carmack sighed as he walked toward the ACCo post. "Drifters, both of us, goddamned aliens wherever we go."

Even the name was suspect. Jean was in California at the time of the Coloma gold discovery and shortly thereafter took an Indian wife. He claimed Scots ancestry, but his English was heavy and broken. Young George Washington Carmack took that burden with him to the small white clapboard schoolhouse in Chicago Park within whose single room during the next few years the grey-haired, spectacled schoolmarm was at great pains to get him to talk "like a white man."

"You're very intelligent, George. You have a good mind, yes, and a chance to make something of your life. Now try again."

Was his father really Russian? Had the name actually been Karmakski? His father might well be one of those who deserted from the Russian outpost at Fort Ross, came inland and cast his fortunes with John Sutter at New Helvetia. Thus he would have been among those present at Sutter's Mill the day John Marshall found something amazing in the millrace.

"One day I'll track the old dog down," Carmack mused, "and make him level with me. No danger of the czar's troops finding him now and court-martialing his ass."

Before turning upslope toward the stockade Carmack stopped to gaze down at the knot of men at work assembling a paddle boat. The project obviously was near completion. He spotted the foreman immediately, a big, slope-shouldered fellow who was sitting with his back against the foredeck railing, smoking a pipe and occasionally bellowing instructions to his fellows.

Carmack raised his arm in greeting. "I'm looking for gold," he yelled. "Can you tell me where to find it? Big nuggets, now. The little ones ain't worth my time."

"Stranger," the foreman shouted back, "you're crazy as a by-god shithouse rat. Get back on the steamer an' head south, that's my advice."

"That's what my pa always told me."

The foreman stood up, tugged his beard and adjusted his beaver. "Figgerin' to head up the Kuikpak River?" he asked.

"No," Carmack answered, "I'm going up the Yukon. When's your riverboat going to be ready?"

"Damn outland fool," the foreman snorted, "Yukon is the Kuikpak. Another week or so an' I'm takin' 'er up to Fort Yukon. Passage ain't much if you're good with an axe. Lot of wood to split between here an' there."

"Who's in charge at the post, friend?"

"Mercier—Moise Mercier. An' tell 'im McQuesten says to send down a pot of beans an' a kettle of hot coffee. Tell that dumb bastard I'll cut 'im a new bunghole if me an' my boys ain't fed soon."

"Good to meet you, McQuesten. My handle's Carmack. I'm figuring to take over around here before too long."

McQuesten pulled his nose and then bellowed with laughter, joined by the audience of workmen, who had turned to stare at the mustachioed figure on the bank above them.

The stranger laughed too, as richly as the rest, then called, "Won't be long a-tall."

"Ye don't say?" McQuesten responded, raising one fist and shaking it at Carmack.

* * *

Carmack took lodgings within the post, accepted employment from Moise Mercier to assist in transferring firewood to the *Seattle Sojourner* and to assist in the tallying and baling of furs taken in trade from the Ikogmiut villages round about. He ate his meals with the Merciers and McQuesten and his St. Mike woman, a strong-looking Tlingit named Red Finch. He asked all manner of questions concerning the vast land out of which the Yukon flowed. In particular he wanted to know about regions where mining was going on or where there were rumors of gold finds.

"Lots o' placer," McQuesten said, "an' plenty of color, but they's damned few that ever makes a fifty-cent pan. Truth is, a gold strike that'd be profitable in the outside just ain't up here. Not with the cost of everything a man needs to live with."

"Oui, mon frère," Mercier added, "and the placer, it is all frozen beyond a foot and a half down, *glace* and gravel, glace and gravel. *C'est impossible* to dig very much at a time. Very slow process."

"If there's gold," Carmack grinned, "I'll find it. Got a nose for that sort of thing, gents. But what's this stuff about glace? You're not telling me the ground's frozen down below eighteen inches, are you? No, I get it. She freezes down to a foot and a half. Hell, that's no problem. The long summer days up here ought to take care of the problem."

McQuesten laughed and Red Finch and Mme. Mercier exchanged amused glances, sipped at their glasses of Russian vodka. It was just in from Petropavlovsk a week.

"Hell's bells and gingerbread, you thick-headed Californio, what Moise here is tellin' you—it's permafrost, froze down to the center of the earth, most likely. Ain't nobody knows how deep she be cause nobody ain't never dug that deep. Some places there's beasties froze solid down in the muck, Goddamned elephants an' tigers. Shake you head all you want, but you'll find 'em too. Got washed up the Yukon with Noah's flood, most likely, an' then got covered over and friz. Ain't that right, Mercier?"

"*Enfant de grâce,* I have never seen no tiger, non. But elephants, oui, many of those. Mr. Carmack, the ivory, it washes up on the beaches after the storms. The Kinugmiuts and the Malemiuts, they find it or trade for it from *les esquimaux* further north. Some seasons we make a lot of money, other years not so much. It is *très intéressant.* I have even seen sections of palm trees frozen in the muck where the Kuikpak has cut away its banks. During the time of Eden, *peut-être,* who knows? Many strange things in the world."

Carmack teased his mustache, first one side, then the other. "I've seen bones and such uncovered in the hydraulic diggings in California, but—"

"Russkis tell us the same thing," McQuesten said. "They find 'em out in Siberia. A sea captain told me the Eskimos over there sometimes digs out whole frozen elephants an' eats 'em."

Carmack sipped at his own vodka and laughed. "By the pope's pizzle, you don't look gullible, McQuesten. You must think I am, then. You boys are just funning me, right?"

Moise Mercer rose, leaned over and bit his wife's neck, then whispered something in her ear, bringing a blush to her cheeks. He straightened up, rubbed his fingers on his mouth and said, "All the time men come here from down below, and many wander off into the taiga and we never see them again, *jamais.* In the old days some of them were roasted and eaten by the Koyukons. Others just disappeared. Alaska, it is the great land, but it is very hard on those who do not understand it. I wish you great luck, George Washington Carmack, but now I must go to bed. My lady, she wishes me to do some little thing for her. It has ever been that way. The women, they wish for a thing, and their men must provide.''

''Shameless, this one,'' Mme. Mercier smiled, rising to stand beside her husband. ''He is like a child. He never listens to the words that pour out of his mouth. But the earth is frozen, Mr. Carmack. I have been up to Kaltag during July, and I watched the Indians digging out their earth lodges. As for the ivory, we have more than a ton of it in the storehouse right now. Perhaps Moise will show it to you tomorrow if he has time.''

''I am drowsy, wife,'' Mercier said. ''If you talk longer, I will pass out on my feet, en verité.''

''Not for a while yet,'' Mrs. Mercier smiled. The two of them disappeared into their quarters.

''Could be you don't have to wait for my boys to get the new paddle-wheeler together,'' McQuesten said. ''One of the Ikogmiuts what just come in by kayak says my upriver friends have patched up the old scow I been guidin' up an' down the Yukon since God was born. The *Yukon,* we called 'er, but they've daubed a new name on the prow. She was at Fort Hamilton day before yesterday, so she should show up tomorrow if she don't sink in the meanwhile. Long John Emerson, he bought 'er from me last month. I figgered he was gonna junk her, otherwise I wouldn't a took his money. Now I got competition as long as she holds together. Emerson, he's minin' gold up around Forty Mile, but I think it's just sort of a hobby with 'im. Mostly he traps fur; always has.''

''And there are others along the Yukon?'' Carmack asked.

''A few, a few. I spent a time lookin' some years back an' made a strike or two, but nothin' to get excited over. Six years ago an Injun brought in some coarse gold to Nukluroyit Station an' we all got riled up for a time. Art Harper, he checked it out—didn't find a damned thing. Truth is, Carmack, the real gold of the Yukon's in furs, an' mostly a man gets them by tradin' for 'em. ACCo could use a man like you, that's what I'm thinkin'. Put in with us, an' in a couple of years, mebbe Francois Mercier, Moise's brother, he'll set you up in a post of your own.''

Red Finch, Carmack noted, was getting quite drunk. He watched as she poured yet another glass of vodka, but McQuesten seemed oblivious.

''Lots of gold on the Gastineau Channel,'' Carmack insisted.

''Sure, sure,'' McQuesten said, refilling his own glass, ''but that's a whole different world down there, south of the mountains that separate the Lot of Water from the rest of the world. Anyhow, your mind's made up. You take passage on Emerson's tub an' he'll take you clear up to Fort Reliance, mebbe. I'm the one what founded the place—first white man ever to sail that far up the river, by God. Long John, he's married to a Roossian princess—no shit, Carmack, it's the damned truth. Lives clear on up to Hootalinqua with old Red Porcupine an' his Tagish bunch. Good Injuns, so long as you don't cross 'em.''

''Russian royalty?'' Carmack asked, raising one eyebrow. ''Must be a story there. Maybe I ought to turn writer and make my gold that way.''

''Sure, sure. An' Emerson's got a Japanese couple that works for 'im as well as the Injuns. They're a clan, sort of. Taos Danny an' his wife, Skookum Jim an' Tagish Charlie an' Kate. Now there's a woman for you, Carmack. That gal can outhunt, outtrap, an' mebbe even outfight most of the men in the North. An' her brother, Skookum Jim—once he kilt a grizzly bear with an unloaded rifle. Clubbed the griz to death with his rifle barrel an' come back to camp with all his clothes tore off. I figger Jim's the only man on the river what could whip Long John in a fair fight, but mebbe not. Emerson's close to seven feet tall.''

Carmack nodded, expressionless, but he had the distinct feeling he was being had. If McQuesten didn't pass out soon, he reflected, the elephants down in the frozen ground would still be alive and the Queen of Sheba would be out there somewhere, living in an ice palace and dining on edible emeralds.

Red Finch, he noted, had already passed out.

Carmack studied the ACCo charts of the Alaskan interior and for lack of a better plan concluded that he would follow the Nenana River, tributary to the Tanana, upstream to its source. The company chart indicated Denali and its estimated elevation of twenty-one thousand feet; it showed the mouth and the lower reaches of the Nenana, but the upper portion of the river's course was indicated only by a dotted line marked *probable*.

Nuklukayet stood at the point where the Tanana joined the Yukon, some seven hundred fifty miles up the big river. That place, Carmack decided, would be his debarking point. Somewhere out in the vast expanse of unexplored territory there was gold—a fortune in gold, and each fist-sized nugget had his name engraved upon it.

Gold, the conscious mind said, but the unconscious said something different: wilderness, hunting and fishing and wandering. Carmack imagined innocent wildness, a life difficult, dangerous and pure, uncomplicated and probably short. That vision as much as anything else had brought him to the north country.

The *Hootalinqua Princess* came in to Redoubt St. Michael, its engine throbbing and belching steam and smoke, its whistle shrilling across the gull-cluttered water. As soon as the little vessel pulled to dock, Carmack jumped aboard. Confronting Tagish Charlie, he demanded to know when the paddle-wheeler would return up the Yukon.

"Just got here, you damned fool," Charlie replied. "Got business, got furs to sell. You talk to Musi. He'll tell you when we leave and how much it will cost.'' Charlie pointed to the little Japanese in the wheelhouse and cast a hawser ashore.

It was then that George Washington Carmack caught his first sight of Kate. She was dressed in man's clothing and had her hair tied behind her head. Her ample breasts strained at the fastenings of the heavy moosehide jacket she wore.

It's her, the one McQuesten told me about—a by-God Amazon, and a body like—

He was in love; he was lost and he knew it. His better judgment told him to look away, but his eyes refused the command. His mouth fell open and one hand automatically came up to smooth his mustache.

Kate's eyes met his and for a long moment the man and the woman stared at each other. ''You're ugly,'' Kate said. ''What is it you want? Go tell McQuesten and Mercier we're here.''

''And you are beautiful,'' Carmack replied. ''Will you marry me?''

Kate laughed. ''Maybe, maybe not. Did McQuesten send you to help us unload?''

''Yes,'' Carmack said without a moment's hesitation. ''He told me to speak with your captain.''

Musi came out, glanced at Kate and the stranger. ''Who this guy, Kate?''

''Keep away from my sister,'' Tagish Charlie warned, coming over to stand next to Kate. ''We are Tagish, not Ikogmiut. Maybe you better get off our ship, white man.''

''White man, hell,'' Carmack drawled. ''Can't one Indian tell another when he sees him? What I want is to buy passage up the Yukon River to Nuklukayet. Then I'll be off your ship and out of your way.''

''Buy ticket?'' Musi asked, suddenly smiling. ''We take on our first passenger. Kate and Charlie, you be nice to this man. He's customer.''

"First we got to unload and do business and take on supplies," Tagish Charlie grumbled. "Then we go upriver. You going to help us or not?"

"Why not?" Carmack grinned. "The sooner we get this old relic turned around, the happier I'll be."

The *Hootalinqua Princess,* with her new cargo and five cords of firewood, set course for the Yukon Delta and the Apoon Channel. Thence she struggled upstream past Fort Hamilton and on into the main channel of the Lot of Water, puffing and hissing against the current. She chugged through the low tundra and into the interior, coming at last to a stretch of river lined with stunted spruces that gradually spread out from the river and up onto the low rises beyond the island-dotted main channel.

Carmack soon made friends with Musi, Okime and Tagish Charlie, talking with them at great length and good-naturedly assisting the crew. When the *Princess* pulled in to shore to take on firewood, Carmack demonstrated himself to be adept with a double-bladed axe. He tried as well to engage Kate in conversation, but her answers to every question were brief to the point of rudeness. In short she ignored him almost totally.

At times Carmack felt humiliated sensing the benign amusement of the Japanese couple and Tagish Charlie, but he kept his temper and continued to smile, fingering his mustache as he did so. Kate stayed in the wheelhouse with Musi or sat cross-legged on the prow, searching the muddy current for snags, sand and mud bars.

As the *Princess* approached each village in turn, Musi would yank on the whistle rope, and by the time they reached the landing, a small crowd had inevitably formed at the landing site.

Musi sold what goods he could spare, taking United States money in return, and even did a bit of bartering for dried fish and jerked moose and elk meat, as well as for half a dozen finely crafted salmon-skin parkas, the specialty of the women of Anvik.

The ever-lengthening days passed, and when the *Princess* reached the village and trading post of Ruby, some six hundred miles from the river's mouth, there was hardly more than an hour out of twenty-four when the stars came visible. Even during this interval the darkness was little more than that of the twilight hours of evening and morning that Carmack had been used to.

From the ACCo chart, of which Musi had a copy on the wall of the wheelhouse, Carmack determined that they were no more than two hundred miles south of the Arctic Circle. Fort Yukon, four hundred miles farther up the river, was almost on the Arctic Circle. And at that latitude, Carmack knew, the midsummer sun would not set for at least one day of the year, and there would be no real darkness for several weeks, but at present the long days brought with them no real warmth.

June and July temperatures in the far north, as McQuesten had told him, occasionally drifted up into the nineties, sometimes even past a hundred, but these late-May skies were often cloudy. Sometimes hoarfrost formed on the railings of the *Princess* during the brief twilight, and the woodpile gleamed as if snow-covered for several hours past sunrise.

Carmack, genuinely smitten with the young Indian woman who hardly looked Indian at all, apart from her mode of dress, made repeated gestures of friendliness toward her, but she either ignored him or brusquely suggested that she had no interest in his words and that in any case he talked altogether too much.

Tagish Charlie, however, warmed to Carmack and ultimately offered to play hand game, the nearly universal Indian gambling mode. The two men played for hours on end, using chips of firewood as tokens, and the gestures that accompanied the guessing game were elaborate. After three days of more or less constant play they found themselves dead even.

"You're pretty good for being only part Injun," Charlie growled.

"Not bad yourself," Carmack shrugged. "You had enough? Maybe we ought to try poker."

Musi sounded the whistle as the *Princess* approached the little village called Ruby, and Tagish Charlie grinned, displaying a mouthful of even white teeth. "Later. First we have to cut lots more firewood for the furnace. This old boat's been on the Yukon so long it's a wonder there are any trees left at all. You good with that axe too, Carmack, make very good woodcutter. I think Musi and Okime hire you permanently, that's what."

Carmack shook his head. "It's gold I'm looking for, Charles, old man. Out there somewhere there's rich diggings. I can feel it in my bones."

"Long John got a good mine," Tagish Charlie answered. "Not many others, though. Lots of gold down on the Gastineau. No need to come way up the Kuikpak."

"I want my *own* gold."

"Well, lots of places to look, anyway."

"When I find the gold," Carmack said, "then I'll come back and marry your sister. Pay any bride price your daddy wants."

"Hammerwater? You better forget her, Carmack. She could marry anybody she wanted but she don't want to. Always has been that way."

Carmack stroked his mustache. "I've got no business asking this, but what the hell. She's your sister, but she doesn't look like you—not at all."

Tagish Charlie glanced toward the wheelhouse, where Musi, Okime and Kate stood together. He leaned forward and spoke in a half-whisper.

"She's my sister, but not my sister by blood. Red

Porcupine, he brought her to lodge when she was still a little baby. It's no big secret, I guess. Everybody knows. That way with lots of people. In her blood she's a white woman mostly. Borodin, her father, he was half-breed Gossack, and her mother, she was Russian. Kate goes to visit her grave sometimes when we stop at Nulato; she's buried on the bluff behind the old church. But that's only her blood, Carmack. Other ways she's all Tagish, just like me and Skookum Jim, my brother."

"Russian," Carmack mused. "I'll be damned."

Charlie laughed. "Nahoen, he gets you then."

Chapter 20
''Now I own you.''

Four hundred miles upriver from Fort Yukon stands Fort Reliance, established in 1874, just six miles from where Dawson would eventually rise some twenty-three years later. Leroy Napoleon McQuesten founded the post.

''As it was the first time the steamer had been on that part of the River, we had considerable trouble in keeping the channel, which necessarily delayed us some. We had only about three ton of merchandise aboard and a Whale boat in tow. We selected a location near Thrundeck. . . .''

Mercier called it ''Clondik,'' from the Indian word Throndiuk; later it was known as the Klondike.

Leroy McQuesten was a long way from his home in New England, drawn there by the love of wildness, the possibility of making a fortune by trading with the Indians, by the lure of gold.

''Gold?'' McQuesten was to scoff later. ''Leave that to damn fools like Art Harper an' Long John Emerson. Half the time you find it where it aren't.''

Then the Indians ran Harper and Mayo out of Fort Reliance and McQuesten set the prow of the Yukon upriver, intent upon restoring order. During the absence of the traders three Han women died of poisoned flour from the abandoned post.

''There was one blind girl about sixteen years old

who got poisoned—her father said she was a great deal of help to her mother. He had taken one of our dogs to replace the girl, but if I would pay for the girl he would return the dog. I told him I would think the matter over and let him know later on. Finally I told them the girl's Mother could keep the dog, so that settled the matter and that was the last I ever heard about the poison." That was two years earlier, in '78.

Now he was heading upriver in a new steamer, the *St. Michael,* intending to spend Christmas at Fort Reliance. With him were Art Harper and his friend Bates; the two of them intended to prospect south from Emerson's claim along Fortymile River.

"They's gold an' be damned, me lad," Harper insisted. "Long John's found 'im some, an' we figger to find more yet."

May 1880

On a low rise above the post at Ruby stood perhaps a hundred acres of dead spruce. Fire had burned there a year earlier and would no doubt have continued to roar through thousands of acres of the taiga had it not been for a major thunderstorm that doused the blaze before it fairly took hold. To this place the crew of the *Hootalinqua Princess* went to cut firewood, at Tagish Charlie's suggestion, for the riverbanks were rank with mosquitoes. A team of borrowed mules and a wobbly-wheeled wagon would get the cordwood down to the steamer. Musi and Carmack worked together to sling the six-foot blade of the misery whip, while Tagish Charlie preferred his double axe.

The sky was clear and the day quite warm. Carmack at length stripped off his buckskin jacket and chambray shirt. He stood in his red flannel undershirt, flexed his heavily muscled arms and let out a whoop.

Tagish Charlie laughed. "Bad idea. Pointy-noses will

come, suck out all your blood. Don't bother Injuns, just white men."

"Well, hell, I'm half Indian," Carmack said. "Mosquitoes never have bothered me." But within a few minutes he was obliged to put back on both his shirt and jacket.

"Goddamn *kaya,*" Musi complained. "They have found us. Sometimes get big enough to carry off wolf cubs, you know that, Carmack?"

"You mean there's more like the one that just bit me?"

At length even Charlie found himself slapping and cursing the bloodsucking insects. Then he began to gather limbwood, piled it high and lit a big fire.

Carmack nodded. "Better too hot than sucked dry."

By mid morning the mosquitoes had vanished, and after that the work went far faster. Finally Okime and Kate came up the hill, bouncing along on the seat of the buckboard and yelling all manner of threats at the balky and ill-matched mules, who firmly held the opinion that they were being put upon.

"You ladies bring the whiskey and chow?" Carmack demanded.

"Good whiskey," Okime assured him, "Just what doctor ordered."

"Toss me the jug, sweet Kate."

"This one's for you," she responded. "I put the poison in myself."

Carmack nodded, took the bottle, drank and passed the container to Musi. "Hits the spot."

"Maybe better load some wood before we drink," Musi suggested. "Take five wagon trips."

They ate lunch—a big loaf of hard bread, cold venison and some cakes of dried salmon. Carmack took another slug of whiskey, licked his lips and winked at Kate.

"It was slow poison," she said, staring back at him.

* * *

Carmack, Tagish Charlie and Kate had taken the mule team up for the last of the firewood and were on their way back. The mules had to struggle through a swampy meadow near the Yukon River; all of them were exhausted from the day's labors. Charlie was whistling and Carmack was explaining to Kate how things were going to be after the two of them had gotten married. She shook her head from time to time and in general attempted to ignore him.

Charlie stopped whistling. "Maybe you should marry Carmack after all," he said. He kept his face blank except for the distinct twinkling of his brown eyes.

"First he must make love to a grizzly bear," she sniffed.

"How about a moose?" Carmack asked, pointing across the meadow to where a cow moose and her calf were half heartedly grazing at some swamp grass. "If that'll satisfy you, I'll do it right now." He leaped down and began stalking across the meadow toward the cow.

"Crazy son of a bitch," Tagish Charlie cried, "that one is worse than the grizzly."

"Stay away from her," Kate called out.

"By God," Carmack whooped, "I believe the little lady's actually jealous."

The calf, until now oblivious to the humans and mules, looked up, stared nearsightedly about and half in play and half in fright frisked stiff-legged away from its mother, cutting across Carmack's path.

The cow sensed enemy, a threat to her young one, and charged Carmack. He saw the danger and came to a standstill, waved his arms and shouted a string of curses at the onrushing moose.

This tactic, he reasoned, always worked to frighten off black bears. But the cow moose only lowered her head slightly and continued her charge.

Carmack attempted to leap out of the way at the last

moment, but the moose swerved and thumped him heavily to the wet ground. Then the enraged creature turned with astonishing agility and three times belabored his back and sides with a forehoof before settling in to trample him to death. He hid his face in his arms and tried to kick back.

Then the moose was away from him and he pulled himself to hands and knees and looked about.

Kate was lashing the cow with a long branch. The big ungulate drove at her. She in turn leaped nimbly out of the way and began a mad dash for the Yukon River, the cow in immediate pursuit. Kate dodged into a willow thicket, reversed direction and emerged once more as the cow got half-mired in the mud and interlaced branches.

Once more she ran for the river, and once again the big cow gave pursuit. The desperate race ended only when Kate leaped down into the swirling, silt-laden water

On the bank above the cow wagged her head back and forth and stamped her forehooves on the rim.

Three pistol shots rang out, and the cow, as if suddenly remembering the cause of her rage, turned and lumbered off after the calf. Both finally disappeared into the thick stand of spruce upslope from the marshy meadow.

Carmack held onto his sides, hugged himself to subdue the pain and rose unsteadily to his feet. "Jesus Christ, Charlie, can Kate swim? That current'll take her away."

"Swims like salmon," Charlie said, reaching Carmack's side and assisting him back to the buckboard.

"Why didn't you shoot the beast? That damned cow could have killed me and Katie both."

"Too far for pistol shot," Charlie answered. "Besides, she don't do nothin' wrong. Only damnfool white man would ever get between a moose an' her calf. The moose, she's tougher than even a grizzly. Once I saw a cow kick holy hell out of a bear, by God. Chased him half a mile. You pretty dumb gringo, you know that, Carmack? You go fuck a grizzly sow if you want, but leave the damned mooses alone. Next time maybe you not have my sister to save your ass."

Carmack climbed slowly into the buckboard, still grunting and holding his sides.

Kate struggled up the bank from the Yukon, soaking wet and all over with mud. She glared at Carmack, climbed onto the buckboard and sat down half turned away from the man whose life she had just saved.

"Thank you, Katie," Carmack managed.

But she would not answer.

Back at the trading post at Ruby, however, in front of Musi and Okime as well as agent Uncle Bill Savage and Lulu, his Koyukon wife, Kate proceeded to give Carmack a severe tongue-lashing, her words punctuated with every bit of profanity she had ever heard from the white men along the River.

In the midst of it all Carmack broke out laughing, gritted his teeth against the pain of his aching ribs, groaned and continued to laugh uncontrollably.

"You empty-headed jackass," she snarled, "stop croaking. Have you lost your mind completely?"

"I love you, Katie," the Californian wheezed, closing his eyes and shaking his head. "By God, I love you and I want to marry you."

"Gimme whiskey, Uncle Bill," Tagish Charlie said. "This crazy cow-humper don't even bother to stump-break 'em. I can't listen to no more of this an' stay sober, by God."

Bill Savage shrugged and brought down the bottle.

Kate stopped in her tracks. Her mouth hung open, her breath held in check. Finally she exhaled, nodded to Bill Savage and tapped on the counter. "This American is a very stupid man," she said slowly. "He cannot tell a grizzly bear from a cow moose with a calf. I have already told him I would marry him only after he has stuck his thing into a sow grizzly's behind. Then perhaps I will think about it. That's why he went running after the moose."

"This is good man, maybe," Okime said. "He does everything you tell him, even if he does it wrong. He will give you pleasure, *tanoshimi*."

Carmack glanced at Okime, winked and grinned at the still-livid Kate.

Musi guided the *Princess* on up the river another hundred twenty-five miles. This part of the Yukon was wide and contained an occasional island, some more or less permanent and overgrown with mats of red willow, others composed of sand and silt, deposited and then washed away by the restless flood. To the south of the river lay the muskeg bogs of the flood plain, and to the north, the low blue undulating wall of the Kokrines Hills. This earth-swell gradually increased in height to the north and east, culminating in the mile-high rims of the Ray Mountains beyond the Tazitna River.

Then the wide Tanana River, as broad as but less swift than the Lot of Water itself, joined the greater stream from the south. The five-hundred-mile-long tributary's upper course so far remained unexplored by the white men, though McQuesten held the opinion that its headwaters were close to those of the White River among the massive ice fields of the Wrangell Mountains. The highest peaks were estimated to stand at least sixteen thousand feet, making them the highest mountains in the north country with the exceptions of the great peaks of the St. Elias Range and the astounding mass of Denali and its subordinates.

Carmack listened carefully to McQuesten's words, though in his own mind he had resolved to take everything with the proverbial grain of salt. "On a completely clear day, if they ever is one, a man can see Denali itself from just below Nuklukayet. She looks like thunderheads way off to the south."

"How far is it?" Carmack asked.

"God only knows. Hundred fifty, two hundred miles, I figger."

"Maybe it was thunderheads you saw, McQuesten."

"Thunderheads, hell. This coon knows a goddamned mountain when he sees one."

"How high you say it is?"

"She's big enough for God an' Raven Man to set on both at once, that's how high she is. Mebbe four, five miles I guess. You keep your eyes peeled, Carmack, that's all."

As the *Princess* approached the mouth of the Tanana the sky was overcast, slate grey, and a cold drizzle was in progress.

"You ever seen Denali from here on the river?" Carmack asked Tagish Charlie.

"Sure, lots of times."

"You telling me the truth, Charles?"

"I'm not damned white man."

"That's why I asked if you were telling the truth."

Tagish Charlie spit into the river. "When you make love to that grizzly sow, then you find out all about truth."

Carmack laughed. "Charlie, if it's the only way there is for me to be your brother-in-law, then I've got to do it, just like one of the knights in the old stories."

Tagish Charlie squinted. "Night did that? Some dumbass white man's story, huh? I'll tell you secret, Carmack. First you find real lonely grizzly, then lift her tail an' tickle her, just like with any other woman. Use tongue on her little bit. After that she'll be ready for you. That's the whole secret. White men don't know it, an' that's why they always gettin' killed when they try. You do like I say, though, an' then maybe Kate marry you."

Charlie thought about what he had said for a moment and then roared with laughter.

Carmack shook his head and spit into the river; then he too began to laugh.

The *Princess* stopped at Nuklukayet to take on more firewood and to deliver supplies to the post at the Tanana village. Musi had received this consignment in light of the fact that no one knew for certain when McQuesten and his new steamer would make their wåy up the river. Lenardo Hovanski, the Creole trader at the post, had promised ready-cut firewood as partial payment for the supplies, and the big Ingalik-Russian was as good as his word. The specified five cords were neatly stacked alongside the dock.

"Can't stay to help you boys, nyet," Hovanski said. "The Kutchins are here, Dying Salmon and his band of thieves. Is it raining still? Well, the wood will burn, the wood will burn. I come back when Dying Salmon leaves. Musi, what I still owe you?"

"Bad Indians," Musi nodded. "Katie, she already over at post? Okime, maybe you better go see, huh?'

Okime nodded and followed Hovanski toward the post as Carmack and Tagish Charlie began to play catch from dock to boat with sections of still-green spruce logs.

They had just finished loading when Okime returned. "Can't find your *shimai* anywhere, Charlie. Don't know where she's gone. She have friends here in Nuklukayet that I don't know about?"

Hovanski came ambling down to the dock as Tagish Charlie and Okime were discussing Kate's possible whereabouts.

"Kutchins are gone. I see you got the wood all loaded; good, good. Now we have little drink?"

"Dying Salmon is gone already, and we can't find my sister," Charlie said. "You don't think—"

"Katie?" Hovanski chuckled. "Why would she?"

"No," Charlie answered, "why would *he?*"

"Damn bad Indians," Musi said, wringing his hands. "You think they made Katie go with them?"

"I don't understand." Hovanski sputtered. "Here in my village? Even Dying Salmon is not damn fool enough to make off with Red Porcupine's daughter, even if he is renegade."

"Two years ago in Nulato," Charlie pointed out, "the Kutchin chief tried to persuade Kate to marry him, offered many gifts to Red Porcupine. Hammerwater Kate spit in his face that time. Dying Salmon was very angry."

"Where do these Kutchins live?" Carmack asked. He spoke quietly but he looked like thunder and lightning.

"You passenger or Charlie's friend?" Hovanski asked, as though fully aware of Carmack's presence for the first time.

"They come over from the Koyukuk?" Charlie asked.

Hovanski nodded. "On foot. Hochandochtla Trail, I think. Da, that is what he said. John Graywing must have ferried them back across the Kuikpak. He will know if Kate was with them."

"Downriver to the Tozitna, then across the Kokrines?" Charlie demanded. "Yes, yes. Where is Graywing? Let's go find him, Lenardo."

Three of Hovanski's best riding mules were induced aboard the *Hootalinqua Princess,* though not without difficulty. Carmack and Tagish Charlie stoked the furnace as Musi guided his craft back out into the brown current of the Yukon and set course, full steam ahead, for the village of Tanana a dozen miles back downriver.

John Graywing had indeed transported Dying Salmon and his Kutchins across the Yukon nearly two hours earlier. Yes, he admitted, just such a woman, not at all friendly and indeed given to cursing, was with them.

Halfway across the river Dying Salmon, growing weary of the woman's sharp tongue, grabbed her about the throat and thumped her head against the side of the dory with such vigor that Graywing feared the Kutchin chief might injure her permanently. But after all it was not his business, so he said nothing. Women could be difficult at times, and most men agreed it was the husband's right to discipline his wife in any way he saw fit. This woman spoke like a Tagish, however, which was why Graywing made note of the occurrence.

Two hours brought the *Princess* to Tanana. Leaving Okime aboard the steamer, the three men made immediate inquiries. They learned that the Kutchin band had passed through the village no more than an hour earlier and proceeded on up the Hochandochtla Trail. Charlie already had the mules' saddlebags filled with supplies. The mules, despite their objections, stamped down the gangplank and onto the pier, and Charlie, Musi and Carmack set out at a brisk pace in pursuit of the kidnappers.

"Old bastard Dying Salmon knows we are following," Musi said. "Damned bad Indian, steals dogs and women. That's what I have heard."

"Moving at a forced march," Tagish Charlie agreed. "Must figure once they're across the Tozitna they're home free. Their own country lies beyond that, and Dying Salmon must be sure he'll be able to lose us."

Carmack, a tight knot in his stomach, kicked his heels into the mule's ribs and said nothing.

They reached the Tozitna, a tributary from the Ray Mountains, running clear in late May. Its wide shallow waters gleamed silver-white in the afternoon sun, a band of brilliantly reflected light bounded on either side by the dark green of spruce forest.

They found footprints in damp earth, tracks into which the water was still oozing.

"Close," Charlie nodded. "They are running now.

Maybe left one man back as a trailer and he spotted us coming."

The three men urged their mules ahead and Carmack reached to his side for the reassuring solidness of his Colt revolver.

"How many Kutchins are there?" Carmack asked Charlie, the issue of numbers coming into his mind for the first time.

"Dunno. Dozen, maybe."

"They got guns?"

"Sure, three or four, anyway."

"So—what? We're going to have to shoot it out?"

"Money," Musi said. "We pay as much as Dying Salmon wants. Otherwise Red Porcupine, he have to bring warriors clear down to Dying Salmon's village. That maybe a thousand miles, very long trip. And Kate, she might be pregnant by then, too late. I got enough money to buy her back."

"If the Kutchin's willing to sell," Charlie added.

"He want her so much he won't accept money, you think?" Musi asked. "Katie don't make very good wife unless she wants to. Must be he understands that already. He better be careful or she castrate the bad Indian."

Tagish Charlie pointed ahead half a mile distant to where a pair of bald eagles were winging upward and away, then circling back.

"Our friends are close," he said. "They've disturbed the big fishing birds—maybe thinking about crossing the Tozitna."

The three men kicked and swatted at their mules, who responded by picking up the pace a little.

Dying Salmon was not interested in selling back his new wife, even though Kate, with her well-armed allies at her back, resumed her stream of invective against him, promising to slit his throat as he slept if he forced her into a marriage lodge.

"Kutchin men smell like rotting fish," she proclaimed. "They get drunk and piss all over themselves."

Dying Salmon ignored her and seemed unconcerned as well that Tagish Charlie and his two companions had been able to overtake him. With a body of his own men about him the threat of three, however well armed they might be, did not seem to pose any great danger.

"Tell Red Porcupine I will send him a bride price, maybe this autumn before the cold weather comes back. First I must see a child in her belly, then I will know how much she is worth. Tell the little man to take his steamer on up the river. I don't want to kill nobody. No reason for anyone to get shot. This bad-natured woman belongs to me now."

"Nobody owns Hammerwater Kate of the Tagish. I will turn you into a woman-man with a high voice if you do not allow me to leave with my brother."

A few of Dying Salmon's men began to chuckle; the Kutchin chief cast them a baleful glance. "I have spoken. You have heard my words. You are this one's brother; then tell Red Porcupine his daughter is now wife to the chief of the Kutchins."

Carmack listened to the heated exchange, sized up the situation and concluded that the Kutchin men were not eager to exchange shots. While their numbers would almost certainly ensure victory, the matter could not be settled without several of them being either wounded or killed. Their chief's amorous whim did not provide sufficient cause, but whatever their feelings, they would stand by him if forced to do so.

Dying Salmon himself was a short, powerful man, thick-necked, round-faced and somewhat overweight. While his bearing suggested a good deal of confidence in his own physical power as well as in his control over the men with him, he was, after all, most likely in his midfifties and quite possibly neither so agile or so strong as he had once been.

"Tell this fat little fool I'll wrestle him," Carmack said to Charlie. Tell him that if I win, then Kate comes with us. If he wins, then his men may kill me."

Tagish Charlie stared at Carmack, but he did not speak, only shook his head.

"Tell him he is very ugly. Tell him I said Kate is right—he smells like rotting fish. Isn't that what she said?"

"I know goddamn English," Dying Salmon responded, now turning his full attention to the man with the mustache. "You, what? Goddamn Gossack Roossia? You insult Dying Salmon—Dying Salmon going to kill you, cut off your cock if you got one, throw it in Tozitna."

Carmack grinned. Quite deliberately he removed his buckskin jacket and handed it to Musi, and his Colt revolver as well. Then he dismounted from the mule and approached Dying Salmon.

"Tell the crazy one to get back," Kate called to Tagish Charlie. "This does not concern him at all, only us."

"Bad idea, Carmack," Tagish Charlie said. "You a long way from home to get buried. You're bigger than him, but—"

"Toss the stinking bastard a knife or something then," Carmack laughed. "Katie's my woman, not his."

A number of the Kutchins were now chuckling happily. The prospect of white man's blood, the thought of his severed genitals floating down the Tozitna . . .

"*Hakkyo,*" the stunned Musi finally called out. "Don't do this, American George. This very badass Indian."

Dying Salmon, his eyes narrowed, drew his steel-bladed skinning knife, hissed something indecipherable through his worn, yellow teeth and lunged at the Californian.

Carmack let out a loud whoop, stepped to one side

and delivered a terrific kick to the onrushing Kutchin's ribs, sending him to the ground. He was amazed to see how fast the Indian was back on his feet, his lips drawn back in a demonic grin, the glinting steel blade once more waving before him.

"Going to make me humiliate you in front of your men, old man? Well, have at it then."

Dying Salmon, now enraged, leaped forward, slashing with his knife. Carmack, parrying the thrust, drove a big fist directly into the Indian's face, twisting at the hips and locking muscle and tendon in his right arm just at the moment of impact so as to put the full force of his bulk into the punch.

Blood spurted from Dying Salmon's nose as he staggered backward, blinking and wiping his face. Then Carmack was on top of him, heaving him to the ground. One knee pressed across the Kutchin's throat, choking off his air, and both hands clamped about the wrist of the Kutchin's knife hand.

Dying Salmon struggled to throw the weight off his throat and in the attempt was obliged to drop the skinning blade. Then Carmack got it, twisted about and placed the tip of the blade just above one of Dying Salmon's eyes.

The Kutchin men were astonished, but now they gave a murmur of angry disapproval. Carmack heard it, laughed loudly and leaped back to his feet.

"The Gossack has won," Dying Salmon muttered in English. Then he too got up. "He has spared my life, even though I would have killed him if I could. This woman has been very bad luck from the beginning. She is evil medicine to me, like some creature Giyeg has sent, and she has also become very ugly. I no longer wish to marry her. Take her back to her father. Go in peace, white man. I have grown old and weak and now my people will choose another in my place. Go before I change my mind. I do not wish ever to see this ugly woman again."

* * *

Dying Salmon and his Kutchins crossed the Tozitna without so much as a backward glance and within moments had disappeared into the darkness of the thick-growing spindly spruces beyond, heading north into the Kokrines Hills.

Kate embraced both Musi and Tagish Charlie and then stood facing Carmack. "You are a crazy man, but you are also brave," she said at last. "How did you know the Kutchins would not kill you even if you did defeat Dying Salmon?"

"Just knew."

"You did not know that at all."

"Well," Carmack said, stroking both sides of his mustache with thumb and index finger, "I figured that if I could humiliate the leader, the other boys wouldn't be of a mind to risk their hides for him. Once I got the knife away from him, he must have come to the same conclusion."

"Not be leader much longer, I think," Musi agreed. "Very bad to be shamed in front of one's inferiors. Maybe he will commit suicide."

"Or maybe the bad-medicine idea will wear off and they'll swing back to ambush us," Tagish Charlie suggested. "I think we better head our mules back to Tanana, get aboard the *Princess*."

"Admirable idea, Charles," Carmack said. "Katie, you ride my animal. I'll trail along behind and keep an eye out." They moved away fast with Carmack on foot bringing up the rear.

The mules were already aboard the stern-wheeler when Carmack came running in long, easy strides past the trading post and down to the river.

"No Kutchins in sight," he asserted as he bounded up the gangplank. "By God, fellows, we did it. Let's head on up the river."

Tagish Charlie pulled in the hawser and Musi gave a

blast on the steam whistle, sending a flight of geese aloft far across on the opposite shore of the Yukon. The paddle-wheel rolled in the muddy water and the *Hootalinqua Princess* moved out into the main channel.

Kate approached Carmack, and stood before him uneasily. "I did not thank you for saving my life."

Carmack grinned, then sobered. "A fat old Kutchin isn't the same as a grizzly," he said slowly, "but among my mother's people if one person saves another's life, then the one who's saved belongs to the one who did the saving. It's the same with your people, isn't that so, Hammerwater Kate?"

"So now you think I should belong to you? Is that what you think, George Carmack?"

"Something like that."

"But I already saved your life, and so—"

"And so I figure we belong to each other. Don't see any way out of it, Lady Kate."

Kate glared, then abruptly turned away.

Chapter 21
Carmack meets Long John

Ursus arctos horribilis, otherwise known as grizzly, silvertip, or big brown bear—when standing upright the creature may be eight feet tall. An adult bear weighs four hundred to a thousand pounds or more and fears no creature alive, including the human being, with the possible exception of an enraged moose or a particularly grouchy wolverine.

Shovel-faced with a meaty hump over the shoulders, grizzlies often give off a skunklike smell, not musk but the result of their propensity for rolling in carrion. Their fur is usually quite shaggy, the color ranging from dark gray to amber, but long guard hairs give a grizzled appearance.

When angry the bear gives a fierce bawling cry, at other times a low, rumbling growl, often in conjunction with barks, coughs and grunts.

This creature is omnivorous. A full-grown grizzly is able to take down an elk or deer but generally feeds on roots, grubs, nuts, grasses, succulent plants, carrion, fish and berries. The bear will drive all comers away from a favored berry patch.

The grizzly is said to be totally unpredictable, particularly when hungry or when plagued by abcessed teeth. A sow defending her cubs is most dangerous of all.

There is no point in attempting to outrun a grizzly, for the beast can travel up to thirty miles per hour. Since grizzlies cannot retract their claws and since they often weigh too much, they are poor tree climbers. For these reasons the agile prey may wish to retire to a tree.

Men who have been out in the bush for extended periods and hence have been denied the companionship of females of their own kind are specifically cautioned against attempting to copulate with these ladies of the forest, whether or not there are cubs about.

June 1880

For more than a week George Washington Carmack made every possible effort to charm Kate, but all efforts failed. Even an admiring comment on the red highlights in her hair, most evident in bright sunshine, got him little more than a nod and a faint smile.

Then the *Hootalinqua Princess* pulled in at Forty Mile. Carmack, after assisting Musi and Tagish Charlie to get yet another five cords of wood aboard the steamer, bade Musi and Okime farewell. He packed up his gear, shouldered it and strode down the gangplank to where Musi stood talking to a cluster of Han Indians.

"Where'd Charlie and Kate get to, Musi?" Carmack asked. "I wanted to say so long before I head up Fortymile River and on over to the Tanana. I sure hope it's where it's supposed to be. When the season turns maybe I'll mosey upriver to Hootalinqua and spend the winter with you. Another three hundred fifty miles upstream from here, you say?"

"Hai. You know which village is the right one because *Hootalinqua Princess* is there."

Carmack nodded. "Like to meet that gen-u-ine Russian princess. You be looking for me, Musi. But where'd her ladyship and Charles get to?"

"Oh, they head up to Long John's mine, going to bring him and Skookum Jim back down to *Princess*. Then we all going up to Hootalinqua together. Maybe Long John strike it rich, who knows? You going up Fortymile, you meet them again for sure."

"They got a head start on me then. I've heard so much about Long John Emerson it seems like I already know him. He'll give me some advice, I guess, on where to look for gold."

Musi grinned and nodded several times. "You good man, Carmack. Maybe we see each other again, okay. Good luck to you."

Carmack shook Musi's hand, adjusted his shoulder straps, picked up his rifle and strode off through the little village toward the river trail beyond.

According to the chart inside Musi's wheelhouse Carmack was some ten to fifteen miles inside Canada. Musi had pointed out the boundary cairn on a rim above the Yukon shortly after the *Princess* passed by Eagle, a village downstream from Forty Mile. Geopolitically he was now in Yukon Territory, but, he reflected, the boundaries of nations were all but meaningless in the vast sprawl of this northern land. On the Alaskan side of the cairn ACCo agents acted the part, quite unofficially, of minor United States bureaucrats, their authority minimal in the eyes of the Indian peoples through whose lands the winding Yukon River flowed.

And up the river on the Canadian side? Two hundred miles and more to the Royal Mounted Police station at old Fort Selkirk, a trading post and the residence of a single ranger. The officer was seldom called upon even to settle minor disagreements between Indians and white prospectors.

Carmack, full of a sense of freedom, adjusted his pack and continued happily along the river trail, passing through dense stands of white-barked aspens interspersed with clusters of birch and poplar, paused at moments to stare across at the nearly clear waters of Fortymile River, feeding down from mile-high hills to the west and southwest out of Alaska.

He rounded a bend in the river trail and passed under a dense covering of fir, the spindly trees so closely grown that their branches all but obscured the sunlight. A horned owl, startled, took wing in a sudden explosion of plumage and glided silently away, weaving through the thicket.

Carmack realized he was sweating and his hands trembled. He laughed, cursed, laughed again. "I've wandered the woods all my life," he said aloud. "Why should a damned owl take my by surprise that way?"

Lost.

"Hell, no, I'm not lost. I know exactly where I am, maybe five, six miles up from the Yukon, maybe another ten miles to Long John Emerson's damned gold mine, depending on whether it's in Alaska or Canada."

Emerson himself didn't know that, or so Musi claimed. What difference did it make, after all?

Carmack left the trail and scrambled down the gravel of the river's bank. He stopped and studied the alluvial formation. He used his Bowie knife to prize out a clump of sand and clay. He spread it on the palm of his hand, poked at it and detected a small bit of gold, a nugget no larger than a pinhead.

"Look at this," he said, grinning. "Maybe I ought to do a little panning right here."

But the lower run of the Fortymile, he was certain, had already been prospected for all it was worth. Emerson himself wouldn't have gone a dozen or so miles upriver to dig if—Perhaps the river had eroded back the gravels and exposed some new layerings as yet untested.

Carmack dug out another quantity of sand, ran ran it over his hand, found nothing. He shrugged, picked up a rounded stone and tossed it out into the current. He took a cigar out of his big coat pocket, snapped a match with his thumbnail and lit the stogie.

A white-necked kingfish darted from across the river, clung to a trailing spruce bough and shouted outrage at the unwanted human presence. Then it streaked off downriver, a dull smear of blue against the green of the forest.

"Didn't mean to disturb you, bird," Carmack chuckled. He rose, laid his cigar to one side, and slipped the metal pan out of his packsack and used it to scoop out a quantity of sand and pebbles from the bank. His cigar between his teeth once more, he strode to the water's edge. Kneeling, he dipped water into the pan of earth.

After a few minutes of careful work he examined the leavings, tossed a few small white pebbles aside and ran his forefinger through the mixture of yellow and black sand.

"A few colors," he nodded, puffing at the cigar. "Could be that bank's got possibilities, all right."

It was nothing to get excited about and he knew it. He rose, replaced the pan in the packsack, shouldered his load and climbed back up the gravel bank to the river trail.

There he saw a weathered totem half hidden beneath the spruces. Hawk's head, stylized wings, the bird's feet clamped into the hair above a more or less human face. The eyes were far too large, the mouth wide and expressionless. The whole was carefully painted blue, red, yellow and black, but years and storms had removed nearly all of it to show the grey-white surface of the wood.

"Funny I didn't catch sight of you before, old fellow," Carmack muttered. "Must have been sleepwalking."

He was sweating and once again his hands were trembling. "Edgy as any damned greenhorn, like a kid too far from home and scared. Come on George, let's get things together here. It's not a damned grizzly after all—no, and not a riled-up cow moose either."

By the base of the totem, half covered with duff and a litter of twigs, lay a pile of round stones, obviously placed there by human hands. This was somebody's grave, the totem set in place as a marker.

Great country, Carmack reflected. *Big enough for each man to have his own graveyard. Probably a lot of these one-man cemeteries around, if that's what it is.* Don't suppose it's trying to tell me something.

Carmack hurried back onto the river trail, puffed resolutely on his cigar and strode west toward Long John Emerson's mine. Tagish Charlie and Kate the Terrible would be there when he arrived, and he wished to say good-bye to both of them. That, at least, was what he told himself.

It was a new experience for George Carmack, for he could not remember since he reached full manhood having felt small in the presence of another man. But here was John Emerson, half a legend in Carmack's mind, the "Slim Jeams" he had first heard of in Harrisburg, reputed to be the first white man to cross the Chilkoot Trail to the interior. Whether true or not, that hardly mattered, for he was, if anything, larger in the flesh than any of the stories that circulated about him. At six foot six or so, the older man's whole aspect radiated strength and absolute confidence and forest cunning. The very tone of his voice, the half drawl of a mountain man, was sufficient to induce belief in whatever he might have said.

Skookum Jim, reputed to have beaten a grizzly to death with his unloaded rifle—even Skookum Jim, rawhide and bone, seemed strangely dwarfed beside Long John.

Carmack shook hands with both men, then glanced at Kate whose gleaming eyes betrayed a definitely proprietary sense with regard to both her older brother and Long John.

"So you're the coon that saved leetle Katie," Emerson grinned cordially. "George Washington Carmack. That's quite a handle, the kind that a man's got to live up to. Not Irish, are you?''

''Californian,'' Carmack replied. ''My ma was Maidu Indian and my pa was a wanderer. Maybe Scot, maybe Russian, I'm not sure. He was never around long enough for the subject to come up.''

''Californio,'' Skookum Jim nodded. ''I got into a fight with some Californios in Sitka last summer. Didn't look like you, though.''

''Probably not relatives then.'' Carmack shrugged.

''This Carmack, he's brave man,'' Skookum Jim said to Emerson. ''Takes real man to go chasin' after a cow moose. Fightin' Dying Salmon, that was brave too.''

''Prob'ly saved all our lives,'' Tagish Charlie put in.

''Wal, we're owin' to you, George Carmack. If those Kutchin boys had managed to make off with Katie, Red Porcupine would have marched all his Tagish warriors an' most of the Tutchones over to Koyukuk country, an' a lot of men wouldn't see another winter. I'da been right with 'em, too. This leetle hellcat's like my own daughter she is. I promised to marry 'er when she was just a shavetail, an' she's never let me forget it. Like my own family, Carmack, an' by God I'm grateful. You ever need friends, me an' Jim here are for you. A man don't forget that kind of thing.''

''He's a good man,'' Kate agreed, ''but crazy in the head. I think he sleeps naked in the moonlight.''

''Kate's grateful too,'' Emerson said. ''She don't insult nobody unless she likes 'em. You're lookin' for gold, as I take it?''

''That I am,'' Carmack replied.

''Lots of gold but hard to find it,'' Skookum Jim remarked.

''It's true,'' Emerson agreed. ''Half of the rivers'll let

you see color, but the problem's in finding a placer that'll make you as much as takin' furs.

"Permafrost's another problem. Even in midsummer a man digs down a couple of feet an' he hits frozen ground. Then it takes twenty-four hours to thaw out more gravel so's you can get it out of the hole to work it. A couple of times me an' Jim have burnt our holes out to speed things up, but she's a slow process no matter how you cut it.

"A couple of months diggin' an' washin', and then the season turns. Everything freezes solid as hell. She's a good way to spend the summer, though. We'd do better if we didn't get so damned lonely. When we cain't take it no more, we high tail 'er back upriver, like right now, then come back for a few more weeks."

"You're married to a Russian princess," Carmack said. "That's what I've heard, anyhow."

"Ludmila? By God, that's what she was once. Kate an' Charlie told you, I guess. It don't seem too likely, I know, any more than I know why she ever took to an old woods bum like me in the first place, but I'm a lucky nigger, I'll tell you. She gave me a son, too, twelve years old. Fortunately he takes after Ludmila a lot more than me. Charles Rostov Emerson—an' by God that's a handle almost as fine as the one you've got, Carmack."

Carmack grinned and glanced at Kate once again. For the briefest of moments their eyes met, and then Kate turned away. Carmack wasn't certain whether she was smiling or frowning.

"You got no mule," Skookum Jim said. "You going to carry all that stuff clear over to the Tanana? That's what my brother told me."

"The Tanana?" Emerson asked. "Follow the south fork to its head an' then keep on goin'. You'll get to 'er after a spell. Then what? You goin' to make a bullboat an' float on down to Nuklukayet? Word has it you'll be havin' some company over that way as soon as McQuesten gets his new potboiler put together. Harper an' Bates told me last winter they was goin' to do 'er. Skookum Jim here's been all the way down the Tanana, but I never heard no white coon done it."

"Other direction. Upriver along the Tanana—that's what I was figuring on. Your friend Musi invited me to spend the winter in Hootalinqua, so I thought I'd find out where the Tanana comes from and then move east, back to the Yukon."

Emerson and Skookum Jim glanced at Tagish Charlie and then at each other. "Bad country," Skookum Jim said. "Mountains to cross. Long way on foot, Carmack."

"I made a copy of Musi's map, gents. I'll find my way to Hootalinqua, all right."

"Prob'ly four hundred miles across." Emerson shook his head. "You talkin' about that old map in the captain's shack? It's more wrong than right, I'll tell you. Maps get drawn up by coons what ain't never been to most of what they put down. The Tanana comes down from the Wrangells all right, but not where the map says it does. Then you'll have to cross to White River an' then back down to the Yukon an' then upriver to Fort Selkirk at the Pelly Mouth an' then on up to the Teslin Branch. Ain't that the best way, Jim?"

"Best way is down the Tanana to Nuklukayet. Better way yet is don't go."

"I got to," Carmack said

"Why? There's gold here on Fortymile, good gravels just upriver from where we are now. You lookin' for gold, Carmack, or somethin' else?"

"That too," Carmack replied. "It's a long way from California just to sit down and start digging. Besides, I've got to find a sow grizzly that's already stump-trained."

Emerson pursed his lips, wiped his beard and laughed. "That your idea, Katie? I've heard this leetle gal use that line on coons before. Take my advice, lad, and leave the damned grizzlies alone. Now look. If you're determined, at least take my extry mule. I've got three an' don't need but two. It's the by-God least I can do for havin' you save Katie's pretty behind."

"Damn you anyway, Long John," Kate howled, "I didn't need this crazy person to save me. I'd have slipped away that night and made it back to the *Princess*. I'm not helpless and you know it."

Emerson grinned and rubbed his eyes, clapped Carmack and Skookum Jim both on the back

"She's right, lads, damned if she ain't. Tell you what, Carmack. Since you're figgerin' on comin' up to Hootalinqua, just borrow the mule. If you bring the beast back, fine. If not, why I owed it to you anyhow. Come on into the shack now. We got a big pot of hot coffee, an' I'll show you our collection of nuggets an' dust. There's gold, all right, an' one day there's gonna be a gold rush up here that'll put what happened in Californy to shame. It'll happen, Carmack. You just remember old Long John's words."

He took the mule, a creature named Timothy. Half of its left ear had been torn away, or so Emerson said, by an angry badger that old Tim had gotten too curious about one summer day five years earlier. He had also accepted half a sack of red beans and the advice to follow the north branch and bear left when the river forked just below some considerable mountains.

Another thing Carmack took with him upriver was his final vision of Kate. She was wearing a crimson tuniclike garment, elaborately decorated with yarn embroidery of blue, grey, orange and white edged in black. Over her breasts was the design of a face, though of what kind of creature one could not be certain. An owl with teeth? A sad-faced bear with a human mouth, the eyes closed? The eyes lay on her breasts, so that as she breathed the being appeared to be nodding its head. Beautiful Katie wore her long red-tinted hair braided to either side of her head. Her eyes were deep brown with flecks of near-silver, her face round, its structure distinctly Indian but the skin no darker than Long John Emerson's or his own. She was tall and finely proportioned, her narrow waist accentuated by a black sash. Sturdy peasant stock, perhaps, her Russian heritage?

As he led old Timothy back into the forest away from Emerson's digs, the farewells already said, something made him turn around. She was waving good-bye. Then, realizing that he saw her, she turned quickly.

At no time during the voyage upriver had she worn anything other than men's buckskins and a furlined parka during bad weather. What was the significance, then, in the brightly colored garment she wore on the day he left? Could she possibly have dressed up for his benefit?

And she did wave farewell, even if she had not meant for him to see.

At the end of what he judged to be ten miles Carmack tethered Tim alongside a rivulet that crossed the river trail. He withdrew hand pick and pan from the packsack, slapped the mule across the rump and strode whistling down over the gravel banks to the river's edge.

Floods earlier that year had somewhat altered the course of the Fortymile, taking down a stretch of overhang nearly a hundred yards long and revealing the alluvial deposits of some far earlier time.

Carmack pulled at the right side of his mustache, nodded and clucked his tongue.

"Looks good," he said aloud. "Now then, let's see what the water shows me."

He used the pick to pry loose a hanging section of earth held in place by a large root some ten feet down from the rim. The sand and gravel slid into a crumpled mass at his feet, and from this pile he half-filled his pan, then made his way out onto a projecting shelf of rock that extended into the swift-running river. He crouched down on one knee and dipped the pan, swirled the contents, watched as water took a long trail of mud downstream from where he worked.

At length he examined the results.

"Two bits' worth," he grumbled. "Nothing to get excited about."

He rose and returned to the overhanging bank, selected another spot and drove the pick into a seam of red-yellow sand, this time perhaps fifteen feet down from the rim.

The pick lodged against something and Carmack pried up on the handle. The close-packed sand broke free, sliding to his feet, and left a black object protruding from the bank. Carmack stared at the stone for a long moment before he concluded that it had not been shaped by the natural forces of running water and grinding silt.

"What in hell?" He grasped the black object, twisted it, pulled it loose from the hard sand surrounding it. It was a pipe, a stone pipe. Its bowl, composed of a second piece of stone of pale amber color, fitted tightly into the main portion. On the heavy end, beyond the bowl, clearly evident once he had brushed away the grains of clinging sand, was the stylized face of a killer whale, its small, jagged teeth finely incised into the black rock. The opposite end tapered to a flattened bit and the whole thing was perfectly symmetrical, proportioned and executed without flaw. It had, Carmack realized, taken many hours to produce. But could such a thing have been done without benefit of cold steel?

"Amazing, amazing," he whispered. He carried it down to the river, dipped it into the water and carefully cleaned its surface. He used his skinning knife to prize out the sand lodged in the mouthpiece and the bowl, then washed it once more and rubbed it against the heavy flannel of the green plaid shirt he wore beneath his buckskin jacket. He held the object up into the sunlight and admired it.

"I'll be goddamned."

After a moment's hesitation he drew the whale-pipe to his mouth, set his teeth on the bit and blew out through it. It resisted at first and then a blob of wet sand popped out through the bowl and the pipe was clear.

I hear voices all around me, the voices of the ancient ones, those who lived in this land long ago. They are chuckling; I think they are laughing at me.

From upstream beyond a long vee of white water a loon cried out. Carmack had heard it many times in his native Sierra Nevada, the strange, high-pitched shriek of the bird with the voice of a woman, and for a moment he vaguely recalled the tale of Loon Woman, who fell in love with her own brother and haunted him until he slew her. His Maidu mother told him the tale when he was very small.

A pair of coots, hidden until this moment beneath the thick fronds of willow overreaching the river on the far shore, took wing, beating at water and air until they were high enough to streak downriver.

He stood up and glanced at the silver disc of the midday sun. Then he held up the pipe in both hands, shielding his eyes with it, so that the object seemed to pulse and glow before him like something magic. "This is my *sila,*" Carmack chanted. "This is a gift that *Peheipe Oleli,* the Coyote Clown, has given to me. This object gives me strength over myself and over others as well. It gives me strength over the *kakini busda,* the spirit within me. I am whole now, I have come home to myself."

Then he was aware of the wind against his face and he turned. Hearing the loud croaking of a raven, he looked about and saw the bird at last, perched in a stunted cottonwood, studying him.

"Raven Man, is it you? Tagish Charlie told me about you. Are you the one, then, who has made me this gift? Am I a stranger to you, old fellow? I'm George Washington Carmack, a man split in half—half one thing, half the other. Now I am whole. I will always remember this moment. I will remember it every time I smoke the pipe you have given me."

The big black bird cocked its head, slowly fanned its wings and took to the air. He dived within twenty feet or so of the startled Carmack and then winged away downriver, following nearly the same flight path the coots had taken.

Carmack shook his head. "Half a day out in the bush," he muttered, "and I've lost my wits already."

He thrust the pipe into his jacket pocket, strode back to the gravel bank and reached for his pick and pan. Then as if the thought had just occurred to him he studied the spot from which he had dug out the pipe. How long had it been hidden there?

He studied the exposed formation of gravels and sands and made a wild guess of several thousand years.

Or maybe the alluvium was deposited here just a century or so ago, then earthquakes raised the land, and the gravels began to erode away. Musi says there are earthquakes all the time, though I haven't felt one yet. Twenty thousand years, perhaps more . . .

Carmack laughed at the idea and in his mind's eye saw the imprint in Roman letters: Manufactured in Boston. He laughed again, pressed his right hand to the lump inside his coat pocket and began to climb up the bank to where Timothy the mule was no doubt grazing and waiting patiently.

He pushed ahead another ten miles. In a camp by the Fortymile Carmack built a good fire of pitch knots, which more or less kept the mosquitoes away, set a pot of coffee in against the flames and ate a meal of elk jerky. He had with him food enough for a week or more, so there was no need as yet to do any hunting. But when the time came, Carmack was certain, his own good eye and his trusty 50-caliber Centennial Winchester rifle would provide him with fresh meat.

Once he had finished his meal he pulled a blanket about his shoulders and leaned back against the trunk of a dead spruce. It was late, nearly eleven o'clock by his watch, and yet the sky was still dim blue with faint sunlight glittering from the aspen groves on the high hills off to the southeast. The year's longest day was near, and Carmack imagined a midnight sun at Fort Yukon, some two hundred miles to the northwest on the Arctic Circle.

Seward's Icebox, he mused. *A damned strange land it is, but maybe not so different than up in the Sierra. No permafrost up there that I know of, but the snow doesn't melt out until April or May, and it comes again in November, just like here, from what they tell me. Gets colder here by a long shot, but it doesn't snow as much. Farther south and this land might be just like Nevada—dry and windy and damned few trees.*

He lay back finally and pulled his blanket over his face to fend off the occasional mosquito. He closed his eyes, shifted about to get comfortable and relaxed completely.

At length he slept and dreamed of a woman in a red toga, a black sash at her waist, wearing high-topped fur-lined boots decorated with beads and quillwork. She was waving to him as he led the mule away.

Then she was in his arms, her face against his naked chest. He was on fire to have her, but she alternately clung to him and then pushed him from her.

Katie, goddamnit anyway, I want you, I want you. But she pulled away, stood unclothed before him. And when he moved toward her, she turned into a silver grizzly.

* * *

Startled, Carmack awoke. The sky was dark, nearly dark at least, and a few stars burned above him. He steadied himself by staring at the heavens, surprised once more that the polestar should be so close to the center of the sky.

He sat up, fumbled for the stone whale-pipe in his jacket pocket and ran his fingers over it as though through the sense of touch to unlock its secret.

Timothy, tethered just a few feet distant, began to bray. Carmack leaped to his feet, grabbing for the Winchester rifle leaning against the old dead spruce behind him.

The mule brayed again and Carmack levered a cartridge into the firing chamber and fired off a single shot in the direction of the opposite canyon wall. He went to the mule, rubbed its bad ear and gave the animal a few words of reassurance.

He returned to his fire, now little more than a bed of coals, and placed more wood on it. Flames began to lick up at the edges of the chunks of limbwood.

From the bottom of his packsack he produced a pouch of tobacco and filled the whale pipe. He lit the contents with a twig and puffed several times.

A mile or so away, faintly audible above the muttering of the swift-flowing river, a coyote yowled—or was it a wolf?

Carmack listened for a repetition of the sound, but it did not come again. "Whatever kind of beast it be, I feel like I'm by-God at home. Timothy, keep your fool yap shut now. It's time to sleep."

Chapter 22
Big Grayling Courts Kate

Beaver and Porcupine went everywhere together, but when Porcupine visited Beaver's house, he left quills scattered about. Beaver did not like it.

One time Beaver said, "All right, I will take you out to the lodge on my back," but instead of taking his friend home, he took him to a stump in the middle of the lake. "This is my new house. Do you like it, old friend?"

Then Beaver went ashore and left Porcupine snorting and coughing, stranded on the stump in the middle of the water.

At last Porcupine thought of what he could do to save himself, for porcupines hate to swim. "Let the water be frozen," he sang out. "Let the water be frozen so I can walk over to Wolverine's place."

The lake froze solid and Porcupine went to visit Wolverine. At that time he wanted nothing more to do with Beaver. But later the two made friends once more, and once more they began to play together.

"Come on, now," Porcupine said. "It's my turn to carry you on my back."

So Beaver had to get on Porcupine's back. He was very careful to press down the quills in the direction of Porcupine's tail so as not to get stuck, very careful not to move about.

That was when Porcupine realized he had a chance to get even for the time Beaver had left him out in the middle of the lake, so he climbed to the top of a very tall tree and left Beaver there.

Beaver did not know how to get down. Instead he clung to the tree top and screamed—hissing, barking, squealing, mewing.

Porcupine sat at the bottom of the tree and laughed at his friend, but finally he began to feel sorry for him. Still, there was nothing he could do to help.

"Climb down, Brother Beaver," he called out. "You can do it."

"You know I'm afraid of being up high," the Beaver squealed again. "You have played a very bad joke on me." After a time he got hungry and managed to climb back down and the two were friends once more.

Raven Man had been watching, however. Beaver had scratched the bark of the spruce, and so now all spruces have rough bark. And Porcupine is the one who causes the lakes to freeze.

June–July 1880

When the *Hootalinqua Princess* reached Fort Reliance, McQuesten and the *St. Michael* were already there—no great surprise to Musi, Emerson and the others, for the *St. Michael* had passed Forty Mile, stopping briefly, as Musi and Okime waited for Long John and Skookum Jim.

"By God," McQuesten roared, "we'll have us a boat race up to Fort Selkirk. Old tub with a new pilot, new tub with an old hand at the wheel. You don't have a chance, boys. The *St. Mike*'ll outrun the *Yukon* by two, three knots an hour."

"No more *Yukon*," Musi said. "You call *Hootalinqua Princess* by her right name or Skookum Jim will cut off your hair."

"Right you are, my friend. The *Princess* she be. Long John, I got some news that'll surprise you. Ladue come downriver in a canoe an' I talked with 'im at Ruby. Tells me the U.S. Army's been across the Chilkoot Trail—a Cap'n Beardsley an' twenty regulars."

"The Injuns didn't object?" Emerson asked. "Well, that's a surprise all right. They wantin' to do some surveying or what?"

"Survey hell. They escorted a score of prospectors, accordin' to Ladue. A guy named Ed Bean was the leader of the group—no relation to Jim, whose wife's planted down at Nulato. Nope, these boys was fresh up from the States, gold hunters. I guess the cap'n sort of impressed the Tlingits. Brought a damned Gatling gun along an' demonstrated it to 'em. After that they let the soldiers an' the prospectors through, no questions ast."

"Well, Leroy, we're just waitin' for a gold rush to happen. The gold's here, it's just a matter of findin' it."

"You ain't struck it rich yet, have you?"

"Truth to say, no. But Skookum Jim an' me, we've done all right. You know Carmack, of course—fella with the mustache. He's gone up Fortymile River, an' we met Harper an' Bates as we was coming back down to the Yukon. Get enough prospectors rummagin' around the land an' the gold'll turn up or else ye can call me skunk-bear."

McQuesten clapped Emerson on the shoulder. "Always did call you that, Long John, me lad. So Carmack's gone off by hisself? Well, the wolves chew 'is bones. It's no country for a damned greenhorn to be wanderin' about in alone. If the Raven don't shit on 'im, maybe Art Harper an' his buddy'll run into 'im and lead 'im back down the Tanana before the snow flies."

"I loaned him old Tim. That dumbass Californian was on foot, loaded down like any pack animal."

"Your one-eared mule? That's last you'll see of him, Johnny."

"Bean's bunch, they all greenhorns?"

"From what I hear. Ladue, he don't talk much. I figger the boys'll get discouraged directly an' head back to Harrisburg or Juneau or whatever they're callin' it now. Might be gold enough to say so on the Gastineau, but they ain't here, an' I don't care what you say."

"Look at this, then. It'll make a believer out of you."

Emerson produced a pouch half full of nuggets and fines. McQuesten poked at the gold with his finger and shook his head.

"Jesus, I thought you told me . . . Must be six, seven hundred dollars' worth here, John."

"Just a dab," Emerson grinned. "We ain't got to the good stuff yet."

The *Princess* passed the post at Fort Selkirk and continued up the Yukon—a first, since no steamer had ever been east of Selkirk.

In places the current was difficult, requiring the full limits of Musi's skill. At one point it appeared they might have to moor the craft for the winter and continue by muleback and on foot to Hootalinqua, some fifty miles upstream. However, Musi was able to tack into the current, then away, into it and away again. After several hours of minimal progress they entered wider, more placid waters.

When the craft slid sideways and turned with the current, threatening to founder, Emerson's two mules began to stamp their hooves and bray in panic, but Musi pulled the craft around. Kate let out a whoop. Musi, grinning, yanked the cord to the steam whistle; the shrieking sound sent half a dozen snow geese beating their wings into the air.

As they finally approached their home village, a gang

of young boys began running along the bank, yelling and cheering. Three of them stripped off their clothing and plunged into the river to swim out to the *Princess*

"Will you enter the village naked?" Kate demanded. "Swim back and get your clothes. Musi will be glad to have you help when we bring the boat ashore."

More of the villagers, Tagish and Tutchones alike, were assembled by the time the *Princess* drew up into the backwater channel just down from Red Porcupine's lodge, and the young men of both tribes were childishly pleased to assist with the unloading.

Kate, Skookum Jim and Tagish Charlie greeted their parents, Red Porcupine and Short Day. Ludmila and Charles Rostov Emerson came scrambling aboard to welcome Long John home. They knew his visit would be short; he would soon be away downriver to the gold mine and would not return to Hootalinqua until the turning of the season.

When the initial excitement passed and hurried preparations for a feast were under way, Red Porcupine addressed his daughter. "I must tell you, Big Grayling has offered me a very large bride price for you. Does this man meet with favor in your eyes? You have been gone for several months and have had much time to think the matter over."

"No more than he ever did," Kate answered.

"And yet he is a very powerful man, the chief of the Tutchones and my friend. How shall I be able to tell him that my only daughter does not wish to marry him?"

"I would not make him a good wife. You know it and he knows it too. Have I ever encouraged him in any way, Father? No, I have told him bluntly that I do not wish to marry him. He has two wives already, and I will not be the third. Besides, I feel nothing for him."

"I understand your words," Red Porcupine said. "You do not need to explain further. I was obliged to tell you of the offer he had made me. You would have high position with such a marriage, high position within both our tribes. In all practical ways—"

"I do not have a practical heart, Father. And long ago you promised—"

"Yes indeed, I promised. But you are not growing younger, Kate. It is not natural for a woman to remain unmarried as long as you have. Soon you must select a lover, a husband, a man who is able to protect you and provide for you."

Kate laughed. "You know I can do those things for myself, but still perhaps soon I will choose. As you say, I have had much time to think things over. If Raven Man smiles upon me, I will still be able to present you with some grandchildren. My heart is open to the right man."

Twelve-year-old Charles Rostov Emerson came running into the house and the heavy cross-bolted front door swung wide behind him. "Born in a barn, was you?" Long John asked, not looking up from sharpening Ludmila's prized steel kitchen knives. "Close the damned door, you young heathen."

Charles, dressed in buckskins and only vaguely distinguishable from the Indian children of the village, breathed out a sigh of protest and turned back to close the offending door

"What is it, Charles?" Ludmila asked. "From the looks of you you've run from one end of Hootalinqua to the other."

"Taos Danny says he's going up to Lake Laberge to hunt, and—"

"And you want to go with 'im."

"Yes, Father."

"There's quite enough for you to do here, young man," Ludmila said.

"He's only going to be gone a week," Charles protested. "I'm not a little kid anymore. The Tagish boys are always going off somewhere. I'm the only one who has to stay home."

"You spend half your time hunting as it is," Ludmila insisted.

"Red Porcupine says Charles is the best shot of all the boys," Long John said. "Ludmila, they ain't no harm can come of it. Cain't keep a healthy young animal in a cage, you know."

"How far is it to Lake Laberge?"

"Thirty miles, mebbe. Charles, who all's goin' besides Taos?"

"Then I can go?"

"Didn't say that, son."

Emerson looked at Ludmila, who in turn looked at Charles.

"Is Irena going along?" she asked.

"Yes, ma'am. Irena's going and so is Kate. It'll be just the four of us and Danny's two mules. I sure wish we still had old Timothy—like last year, when I went down to the Fortymile mine with Pa. You think that guy will ever bring him back, like he promised?"

"Mebbe," Long John nodded. "Mules an' gold-diggers, they got a way of turnin' up. You know the difference between a greenhorn an' a grizzly, Charles? McQuesten tells me there's a bunch of white men lookin' for gold up above Laberge somewhere, an' I wouldn't want you poppin' a round from that Remington carbine I give you into one of 'em."

"Then I can go?"

"Well, why not?" Ludmila asked. "If my husband isn't going off somewhere with Leetle Katie, then my son is. Better my son than my husband, I suppose. What am I to do?"

"Ain't no harm in Katie," Long John grumbled. "She's been good for the boy. He's learned more about huntin' an' the like from Katie than he has from me, to tell the truth."

"Well," Ludmila said, her hands on her hips, "I just wish she'd be sociable with somebody's men other than mine for a change, that's all."

"So I can go?"

"Sure," Long John said, touching his thumb to the edge of the knife he had just finished sharpening, "I reckon, if it's all right with your mother. They's loaded cartridges in the back room."

The boy let out a whoop and was out the front door before any further words could be spoken, and once again the door stood wide open.

Emerson handed Ludmila the knife and rose to close the door. "Lad's growin' up."

"Yes, I know, and he's growing up wild, just like the Tagish and Tutchone boys. How does one say this? Perhaps we should think of sending him outside to school. He's already read every book we have in the house, John, maybe twice or more. He's so intelligent it frightens me at times. Surely there are good schools down in Seattle or San Francisco, and—"

"Takes after you, Ludmila. And mebbe they'll come a time when that's what he'll choose, mebbe not. We got a good enough life right here an' they ain't a white boy in the world that wouldn't be a red Injun if he had the choice."

"That's how you were, anyway," Ludmila laughed, but there was trouble in her eyes.

It was thirty miles upstream from Hootalinqua and the mouth of the Teslin River to Lake Laberge. The lake was up to ten miles across and fifty miles long. Its green waters lay between folded ridges of fir, spruce, hemlock, birch, aspen and cottonwood. It was named for Mike Laberge, who came upriver from Fort Selkirk in 1867, but called Long Water or Lower Lake by the Tagish.

Between Laberge and the Teslin mouth the Yukon is a different river, a surging stream of twisting switchbacks and sections of white water. The river comes down from the ice fields of the Coast Mountans and lingers in the flooded valleys of the various branches of Tagish Lake below the mountains, then plunges on through Miles Canyon and Whitehorse Rapids to another long meander through Lake Laberge.

Its shores harbor bald eagles, bufflehead ducks and scoters, wild pink roses and blue lupines. It gets twenty hours of sunlight at the summer solstice.

The long ears of a cow moose sweep forward, her large nose wrinkles, she stops chewing a half-eaten willow branch. Black bears and grizzlies tolerate one another and clamber over the tangles of driftwood at the lake's lower end in search of fish, termite logs, ants, perhaps a honey tree. Ospreys perch in spruce branches.

The bull moose rubs his antlers free of velvet and destroys several small trees in the process.

A campfire on a grassy bench above the lake warms four people. A fifth person hides not far away, cautiously observant—Big Grayling, the Tutchone chief.

A pair of king salmon, netted from one of the creeks feeding down into Laberge, were spitted and slowly roasting above the flames. The flesh dripped oil.

Across the lake as twilight came on wolves began to howl, joined almost immediately by what sounded like a hundred or more coyotes, though there were no more than ten or a dozen. The sounds carried, echoed, drifted back and forth along the lake

Irena sat next to her husband and Kate and Charles sat across the fire from them, perhaps a yard apart.

"Look what this child's got," Taos grinned. He produced a flask of whiskey.

"Why did you bring that?" Kate asked.

"Bring 'er? Why, me an' Irena, we like to have a swig before we—"

Charles Rostov knew what Taos had been about to say, though the thought of people as old as his own mother and father actually *doing it* bothered him somehow. Though he knew better, he preferred to pretend that Long John and Ludmila no longer did that sort of thing. Long John and Danny, after all, were over forty years old, Ludmila more than thirty, Irena somewhat younger—actually not much older than Kate.

It wasn't that he had any objections, it was just that such activity seemed to him more appropriate for young people. Why this was he couldn't say.

He sometimes dreamed of things like going swimming in the nude with Katie, just as he sometimes did with the boys and girls of the village. But when he had such dreams, Throndiuk would look at how he was still hairless between the legs and laugh at him.

Nonetheless, Charles was beginning to have occasional difficulties beneath his breeches. Erections came upon him at the most unpredictable and embarrassing moments.

"You want a nip or two, Katie?" Taos asked.

Kate considered the matter for a moment. "Yes. Let me have some."

Taos winked at Irena and passed the wiskey. Kate tilted the bottle to her mouth, sipped, blinked her eyes and shook her head. "Each time I expect it to taste better than it does."

"Ain't supposed to taste good," Danny laughed. "It's supposed to put a leetle fire into your blood. An' it does, too, don't it, Irena?"

"Yes," she smiled, "it puts fire into Danny's blood, anyway. If he drinks enough, he will wish to spend all night squeezing my breasts." She laughed and glanced at young Charles.

"Lad," Danny asked, "you want a snort? Ludmila's not here, an' Long John'd be all for it. Just a mite, now."

Charles nodded and took the bottle. He swallowed too much. His eyes watered and he began to cough.

"Powerful, ain't it?" Danny chuckled

"Yes," Charles replied when he had caught his breath once more. He handed the bottle back to Kate, who took another drink.

"I think the fish are ready now," Irena said, poking the crisp skins with her knife. "It is time to eat. Tomorrow the hunters will go off and I will be all alone here in the camp. Perhaps a handsome young man will come out of the forest to visit me."

"Let's hear none of that kind of talk, by the green tongue of God. I'll lock ye in a chastity belt if I have to."

"Give me your plate, Danny. After you've eaten your dinner we'll talk about chastity belts. I've seen you making eyes at that young Tutchone woman."

"I ain't neither, an' you know it. Swimming Muskrat don't interest me at all, no sir."

"Then how did you know which one I was talking about? You don't need no second wife, Danny."

"True enough," Taos agreed, taking his plate from her hand and spearing a chunk of salmon with his knife.

"I will stay in camp with Irena," Kate said suddenly. "You and Charles go. Let the men hunt. The women will stay together and spend the day talking and sleeping in the sunlight. Irena and I have some things to discuss. Then the next day maybe we will go hunting and you two can stay here and take care of the camp."

Danny chewed a mouthful of salmon, swallowed, shrugged. *She's got that marriage look in her eye, but who's she got in mind? Sure it ain't that Carmack fella that come upriver an' then took off with Long John's mule. She'll never see that one again, that's what I'm thinkin'.*

Who is it, then? Well, Irena'll tell me the whole thing when I get back. Or am I just dreamin' this up?

With Danny and Charles away Kate spent the morning talking with Irena about married life, but not once did she mention the name of any possible suitor. Irena, for her part, did not pry into the matter.

The two gathered gooseberries, plunged them into boiling water, removed the skins and ate them with leftover salmon for lunch. When they had finished eating, a long silence ensued.

Then Kate said, "I have met a man I like. Perhaps I will never see him again, so it does not matter. Irena, I'm asking for help, I guess. I know I must marry soon, for my father tells me that all the time. But I have never been with a man before. I never know what to say, and so instead I act like I'm not interested."

"Is that what you did with this man you like?"

"I'm afraid so. He wanted me, too. Even after I was very rude to him, he still liked me. At first I thought he was simply a fool, a man from outside with no brains in his head. He did everything he could think of to impress me. He even went chasing after a cow moose and nearly got killed."

"This is the one who saved your life?"

"Yes. That's what he thought he was doing, at least. And he risked his own life to help me."

Irena nodded. "A man only does that when he loves a woman. Years ago, Taos Danny acted very foolish around me. He is foolish anyway, but he did everything he could think of so that I would marry him. I was just a young girl, but I knew how much he wanted me."

"But what did you do to let him know you were interested?"

"Didn't have to do nothing," she grinned. "The

woman don't have to do nothing, but she got to do it right."

Kate studied Irena's face for a moment and then began to laugh. They both laughed.

Kate went alone to a cove. She stripped off her clothing and stepped to the water's edge. She squinted at her own reflection in the clear green water, then closed her eyes, felt the good warmth of the summer sunlight upon her flesh, felt the soft stirrings of air as they moved over and about her. She studied the reflection once more.

Carmack insisted that she was beautiful. Was it true indeed? She was taller than the other Tagish women, stronger in the arms and legs, faster. Perhaps after all she looked more like a young man than a woman.

Men, she concluded after a moment's thought, did not have large breasts, nor were their hips shaped like hers.

Foolish, foolish. You have had many suitors and rejected them all in one way or another. Is it any wonder that they no longer come to visit Red Porcupine's lodge? You have driven them all away.

McQuesten had said something about a Canadian Mounted officer coming to Hootalinqua the following year, setting up a post there. For a moment she toyed with this idea, envisioned a man in a red jacket, fur cap, pistols at his sides, thumb and forefinger stroking a mustache.

"Carmack," she said aloud. "Carmack in an Anglo uniform." She shook her head, disgusted with herself. She waded out into the cold water, lunged forward and swam. When she began to grow tired she floated, drifting on the lake's surface, moving her feet slightly and staring up at the sun. The surface of the water gleamed about her, a million needle points of light darting from the undulating surface of the lake as a breeze passed over it.

Dreamlike, I have passed through Raven Man's tun-

nel and emerged into a world that is nothing but dream. . . . She turned and began to swim back to shore.

She stood in the sunlight and allowed the heat of the day to dry her skin. She ran her fingers through her long hair and shook her head. Then almost grudgingly she dressed and started up away from the cove and back to the campsite where Irena was waiting.

Her thoughts were elsewhere, so it took her a long moment to realize that Big Grayling was standing on the path in front of her. He was wearing the elaborate clothing that denoted his position as chief, and his arms were folded across his chest. She immediately recognized the flaming red cloak over his shoulders, the intertwined arm bands of shells and wolves' teeth and eagle claws.

But the eyes staring directly at her were not Big Grayling's eyes. They were huge, round, deep-set, the pupils fixed within circles of intricately carved yellow-stained wood. The flattened nose had a hook on its end and the mouth was set in a hideous grin, revealing a double row of small white pointed teeth.

Above the eyes were broad dark red arches that represented brows. Human hair projected from the forehead in small tufts.

Even knowing who this specter most certainly was, Kate momentarily had to fight for breath.

He did not speak. Her eyes played over him. The genitals were exposed, the limp penis painted red.

"I claim you as my wife," the specter said at last.

At this assertion, Kate frightened though she was, burst out laughing. "You look ridiculous. Take off that mask and cover yourself up, Big Grayling. My father has told me of the bride price you offered, but I do not wish to marry you. I told you that months ago, and I have not changed my mind. You are a powerful man and a good man, but you already have two wives. No, I am not the one for you. I do not wish to be married at all."

"I claim you, Hammerwater Kate. I am chief of the Tutchones and I have come here to claim you."

She did not answer him this time but instead stared down at the earth, the gesture of a woman who has declined a man's offer. And then, still looking downward, she stepped forward to go back to the campsite, carefully circling Big Grayling.

But the Tutchone chief moved toward her, reaching out.

> "Whu, Bear,
> Whu, whu!
> You are a woman.
> You do not know
> Your own mind.
> I am the grizzly.
> You are my mate.
> I will force you
> To lie with me now."

He grasped her, one hand at her throat and one hand on her breast. Kate backed away, but Big Grayling, roaring in imitation of a bear, lunged at her.

She tripped and fell backward and he was upon her. His face pressed upon hers and one hand struggled to pull loose the rawhide drawstring of her breeches.

She twisted, freed one hand and grasped the ceremonial mask, pulling it away from his face.

> "Whu, whu, whu!
> Now I will have you!"

We'll see about that, she thought, and yanked up her knee. Big Grayling groaned with pain, arching away from her.

She leaped to her feet, spun as he crouched there,

panting and moaning, grabbed for a willow switch and began to belabor him with it across the shoulders and head.

This new pain caused Big Grayling to forget his other discomfort. He turned away from the whipping, scrambled to his feet and sought to move out of range of the burning lashes she was delivering. Kate enraged that the Tutchone should have attempted to force himself on her, leaped after him, bringing down the switch with both hands again and again.

Big Grayling, now in full retreat, began to run toward the lakeshore. Kate screaming like a she-eagle protecting her nest, was right after him, pausing only to set herself and lash once more.

The Tutchone chief, seeing no other escape from the fury that beset him, leaped into the still, green water of the lake, his red cape fanning out upon the surface, and the ceremonial mask, moored by its lacings, floating to one side of his head.

"You are not the bear," she shouted down at him. "You are only the turds of the bear. I will kill you if you ever touch me again—I will take a knife and cut off that thing you're so proud of."

Then she dropped the lash and began to laugh.

Big Grayling, struggling to tread water because of his bulky clothing, cried out, "Hammerwater Kate, Red Porcupine's daughter, forgive me! I have been wrong, I have been wrong. Let me come back to shore or I will drown."

"Will you behave yourself?" she called out between fits of laughter.

"I promise I will." He struggled to shore, panting heavily. Standing knee-deep in the lake, he held out his palms in supplication.

"I have slain grizzlies," he said, "but you are more powerful than any of them. Forgive me for being a foolish old man. The cold water has brought me to my senses. You have cured me of my desire for a young wife. I beg you, do not—"

"Speak of this to anyone?" she laughed, finishing his sentence. "No, I will never tell all of what happened. Go back to Hootalinqua, Big Grayling. Tell my father that you withdraw your offer. Tell him that it is best to allow his daughter to find her own husband if that is what she wishes."

Chapter 23
Carmack's Bad Luck

It was the year of the tenth decennial census. The total number of inhabitants in the United States, including Alaska, was set at 50,189,209; the Union was composed of some thirty-eight states plus the territories.

Thomas Edison was granted a patent for the incandescent electric lamp. On March thirty-first the city of Wabash, Indiana, began to light its streets with electric lamps.

The Supreme court ruled it unconstitutional to bar Negroes from service on juries and George Railton and seven women workers established a command post in Philadelphia for the Christian Mission, an organization ultimately to be known as the Salvation Army.

At their convention in Chicago on the thirty-sixth ballot the Republicans nominated James A. Garfield for President and Chester A. Arthur as his running mate. In Cincinnati the Democrats nominated Winfield Scott Hancock and William H. English.

President Rutherford B. Hayes, meanwhile, was serving out his single term, desiring no second one. He planned to return to Ohio and work for the education of freed slaves in the South.

Election day 1880 saw Garfield win in a close contest, with a popular vote difference of just over nine thousand out of nearly nine million ballots.

News of the gold strikes on Auke Bay, Alaska, spread rapidly, and the waterfront in Seattle was buzzing as thousands headed north in search of riches near the town called Juneau after old Joe Juneau, who had found pay dirt.

Most Americans presumed the great gold strikes were over, and in any case Alaska remained but dimly registered in the American consciousness. It was just a huge, empty, nearly frozen wilderness to those who bothered to think about it at all.

People joked about selling iceboxes to the Eskimos.

November 1880

The sub-Arctic winter descended over Hootalinqua as the days rapidly grew shorter. With ropes and a hundred Tagish men to tug on them the *Princess* was pulled from the water and rolled up on spruce poles clear of the crushing force of ice, for Musi and Okime were determined that their big plaything should not suffer the fate that had overtaken it at Fort Yukon the previous winter.

Terrific cold set in, freezing first the smaller streams and finally the Yukon itself as well as the lakes and marshes.

Geese and ducks had vanished several weeks earlier, and blizzard-force winds began to drive down from the Big Salmon Range and the Pelly Mountains to the east. They brought with them the first real snow, only a few inches on the ground, but a blinding whiteness as it was whirled about by the winds

Not even the heavy fur-trimmed parkas were sufficient to protect the people who ventured out into the screaming storm. One man, in search of firewood near the village, did not return but was found frozen to death a week later within half a mile of his own lodge.

The Tagish and the Tutchones remained within their earth lodges and ate and talked, making the best of nature's early ferocity. Not even the Emerson mansion, a large log cabin with a pair of small onion towers set awkwardly atop it, was really sufficient to keep out the cold. The temperature dropped to fifty, then sixty and finally to seventy degrees below zero.

Ludmila expressed concern about the animals of the forest, a problem she brought up each time a great blizzard hit.

"The U.S. Gov'ment's give 'em all leetle coal-oil heaters, darlin'." Emerson shuffled the cards and dealt to Musi and to Charles Rostov. "Next year I figger the boys in Washington'll give us human critters heaters too. Mark my words, Ludmila."

"Ah," she replied, "this government of yours, you have great faith in it, but I think all governments are the same. They line their own pockets and don't care at all what happens out in the provinces. They hire bureaucrats whose job it is to make them rich, and when the underlings abuse the common people, they look at the other way. In this country at least some of the people are allowed to vote, to choose which criminals they wish to be led by. But when will Red Porcupine's people be allowed to vote? And when will I be allowed to vote? Or you, John? That is supposed to be the great difference between Russia and the United States, but I do not see much difference at all."

Emerson studied his cards and then raised two white chips.

Charles gazed at his father's face, trying to determine whether or not Emerson were bluffing, and finally pushed two of his own chips forward. Musi did likewise.

"How many you need, gents?" Emerson asked, taping the deck. Musi and Charles signaled for one card each.

"Well," he said, "I'm thinkin' it's a real big difference, for what it's worth. An' the boys on the outside have chose 'em a new president just last week, though we prob'ly ain't goin' to hear about it until after the ice breaks next spring. Besides, even if Alaska was a state, which it prob'ly ain't never goin' to be, it wouldn't make no difference to us. We're a hundred an' fifty miles into Canada one direction an' a hundred the other. We're by God Canadians."

"I know that," Ludmila said, "and our government consists of one man in a red coat at Fort Selkirk. But you certainly don't think of yourself as Canadian."

"That's 'cause I ain't. We're all of us citizens of the Republic of the Yukon River. Charles, you've got a pair of aces showin'. Your bet, son."

Charles pushed forward two red chips and glanced first at Long John and then at Musi.

"Too much for me. No luck with draw." Musi pushed his chips to the center of the table, rose and walked across the room. Okime was sitting by the fireplace, knitting a pair of gloves out of bright red yarn.

"I'll call," Emerson said. "Let's see what you've got, lad."

Young Charles displayed his hand, fanning the cards out. "Two pair, aces and jacks."

"Beats me," Long John sighed, pushing the stack of chips toward his son. He slid his own cards under the chips without displaying them and got up. "Winner gets to put 'em back in the rack."

Charles counted his winnnings, and grinned. When his father's back was turned he checked to see what kind of hand Long John had been holding. He blinked in surprise at a full house, fives over tens. He started to say something, then shrugged and put the chips and cards away.

"Danny and Irena have been gone for a long while," Ludmila said. "Do you suppose they're all right?"

"Prob'ly with Red Porcupine an' his gang," Long John replied, pouring himself a cup of tea from the pot by the fire. "Think maybe I ought to go check on 'em?"

"Perhaps," she replied. "Did Charles actually win this time, or did you—"

"Of course he won," Emerson snorted, "fair an' square. The lad's got a real talent for cards."

Ludmila yanked her husband's beard. "I shouldn't let him gamble at all, even if it is for fun. What he really needs, John, is more books."

"Likely you're right," Emerson caught Ludmila by surprise and planted a kiss on her mouth.

"Maybe tonight?" she whispered, then cast a glance at their son.

"Good idea. Once they all get to sleep. Think you can do 'er quiet, so's not to wake the whole house?"

Ludmila laughed. "I'm not the one who makes all the noise."

The cold spell persisted in the wake of the storm. Skies stayed clear during the ever-shortening days and northern lights poured across the star-rich heavens at night. The long, slowly changing bands of shimmering blue-green seemed to rise from the earth and to arch to midsky and beyond, and with them came trailing veils of violet, red, pale yellow.

Past midnight the temperature plunged to minus fifty and lower and by noon it had failed to rise above the zero mark.

Food in Hootalinqua had begun to run short. The Tagish and Tutchone men, some armed with rifles and some with bows and arrows, fanned out from the village to either side of the frozen Yukon River and had some luck at bringing in moose, caribou, elk and even a couple of black bears.

Emerson decided to mount an expedition, for the early cold had cut short the time he usually spent hunting. All were in much the same fix, and the frigid air held forays to a minimum. But with dog sleds, Emerson reasoned, he would be able to be gone a week or more without great danger and so get to areas where game was more plentiful. Long John, Taos Danny, Skookum Jim and Kate set out on snowshoes, taking three teams of sled dogs with them.

When Emerson talked of the plan to Ludmila, she seemed unaccountably hesitant, bringing up all manner of objections to the idea of an elaborate hunting venture. "It ain't the huntin', Ludmila," he said, "it ain't that at all. Come on, gal, out with it. What's botherin' you?"

Ludmila folded her arms across her breasts and stared into her husband's eyes. "Why does *she* have to go along?"

"Kate? Damned good hunter, an' you know it."

"What is she hunting this time, John Emerson?"

"Jealous—is that what you be? Ludmila, you know there's no harm in Katie. She's been like a daughter to both of us, just like one of the family. You don't think I'd—"

"Polygamy is not uncommon among the Tagish," Ludmila insisted. "Are you quite sure Kate doesn't still have it in mind to— She ought to be married by now. I'm content to live among the Tagish, John, and I respect their customs but I'll not have you taking a second wife. I simply won't have it. You belong in my bed, not in anyone else's."

Emerson embraced Ludmila, felt her go rigid in his arms, ignored it and laughed softly. "You're right about Kate needin' to get hitched. Big Grayling's been moonin' after her for quite a spell, but I gather that's finished now. She damned near beat him to death and drowned him to boot, from what Danny says. She's a strange one, an' she needs to find her a buck, that's for certain. Ludmila, you know you can trust me. Damnit, I ain't never had no one else on my mind since we got on board the *Loire* together, an' it's been what, thirteen years now. Once Long John Emerson makes up his mind on somethin', he don't change an' you know it, too."

"You're not thinking about a younger wife, then?"

"Ludmila, I swear to God, for someone who's smart enough to teach half the Injuns in the village to read, kids an' grown folks too, you're dumb as any post. I love you, don't you know that now?"

Ludmila relaxed in his embrace. "Yes, I know that. And Katie is like a daughter. But she's so attractive, and . . . Do you still find me attractive, John?"

Emerson chuckled. "Didn't it seem that way to you last night?"

She hugged him them. "Yes, it did seem that way. Nevertheless, White Bear of the North, maybe I should come hunting too, just to be sure."

"Tell you what, Ludmila. When we get back, mebbe you ought to have a talk with Katie. Tell her how to go about trappin' her a husband, just like you done."

Now they were moving west through the frozen lake country, toward the Niordenskiold River. The land was white and undulating, barrens alternating with areas of thick forests of stunted spruce. Already the hunting had been good.

Thirty yards ahead Skookum Jim and Kate rode the lead sled. The two figures in heavy parkas and doubled leathers were virtually indistinguishable. Emerson nodded, recalling Ludmila's words.

"Caribou downslope," Taos Danny shouted from behind. "Amigo, we take five, six of 'em mebbe."

Emerson called to Skookum Jim and all three dogsleds came to a halt, the malemutes and huskies glad for a rest.

Kate lay in her heavy robes. Sleep would not come this night. It was colder than before. How much colder she did not know, but her restlessness derived from some other undefined source.

To either side of her lay a man, one a brother, the other the big white man whom she had loved almost as long as she could remember. Even now, at the age of twenty-five, she was no more than a child to him. He was her friend and in his clumsy way he loved her, but he belonged to another woman, also her friend. For perhaps the ten-thousandth time she warned herself against indulging her fantasy of him

Male strength lay close on either side of her. She was one with them, a hunter, and yet she was a woman.

"I should have been a man," she thought, but the words rang hollow in her mind. In truth she had no desire for any other identity. She reveled in her woman's body, her woman's way of perceiving things. For all practical purposes, she firmly believed, women were more intelligent than men, more capable of seeing things as they are.

She thought of the white man beside her and of his wife. The White Horse overcame difficulties by means of sheer strength, badgerlike persistence and blind determination. Ludmila, quick-witted, sensitive, perceptive, understood the magic of books and generously shared this magic with them. Her people who had been exposed to the British missionaries talked of saints capable of protecting and guiding, persons who did the work of the God they called Jesus and who were granted special powers by the Divinity.

If there were such persons, was Ludmila Emerson not one of them, whether recognized as such or not? She knew the Christian stories and would tell them if asked, would read aloud from her Bible if asked, and seemed to know all of that thick red-covered book. She delighted equally in the stories and legends of the Tagish people and was compliling her own book of the myths and tales of the beginnings of things. If she revered Christ, Kate had long since concluded, she revered Raven Man as much.

Once Kate asked Ludmila what god she believed in, and the princess smiled and reached out to stroke her hair. "Jesus of Nazareth would never have seen our northern lights," she said—and spoke in such a manner that Kate did not realize until later that Ludmila never answered the question at all.

I love you, Ludmila. I have been wrong, very wrong to think that I might one day possess the man you love. I was only a child and I believed what he told me. The yeg within me listened and believed when it should only have listened and laughed. I have been foolish and wrong; will you forgive me, my sister? I am only a daughter to him, a younger sister. You are the only one he cares for in the way of a man and a woman.

Kate pulled the heavy bearskin back away from her face and felt the sudden rush of cold on her eyes and mouth. The air burned in her lungs as she breathed. For a moment she toyed with the idea that the world might get so cold that everything and everyone would vanish. All that would remain would be blackness—that and perhaps the northern lights, alone in space.

She pulled tight on the drawstring of her parka so that the double-lined leathers and the fur came up over her mouth. Blinking against the cold, she stared up into the sky beyond the wind-bent hemlocks in the boulders on the other side of the fire.

Curtains of red and violet showed this night, yellow-green tracings to either side. Cascades of magic lights slowly, slowly swirled across the center of the sky, obliterating the great star Emerson called Polaris. Waves of light shimmered and in the midst of all hovered the outline of a gigantic black bird.

"Raven Man," Kate whispered, "have you come to call me this night? I am not ready yet, I am not ready."

Even as she stared upward, the form changed, transformed itself, came to look more like a hand rimmed in crimson.

Frozen clouds streamed against the lightfalls, ever changing.

Kate rose from her robes, held her hands beneath her arms and stepped to the glowing, red-orange bed of coals —all that remained of their fire. She tugged at one of the big pitch-filled root knobs Skookum Jim had pried from between the boulders at twilight. The dry wood was inexplicably frozen to the chunk that lay beside it. She wrenched the two apart, then placed them side by side on the bed of coals.

After a few moments flames began to lick up, and soon after that the pitch began to heat and bubble and hiss, oozing down the sides of the dead wood and flaring.

The warmth touched her cheeks and forehead and she muttered an indeterminate *thank you*. Then Taos Danny was standing beside her, clapping his gloved hands together and whistling between his teeth.

"Katie, no need for you to get up. Old Dan woulda tended the fire. *Frio, frio,* God's beard itself has frozen this night, pretty one. I'da woke up soon an' took care of 'er. Go on back to sleep, now."

Kate shook her head. "Sleep deserts me this night. Something troubles me, but I do not know what it is. I thought I heard someone calling me."

"Pore old lonely wolf that's got run out of his pack, most likely. I heard 'im yellin' out there too. He'd come in an' set by the fire if he had nerve enough. Long John figgered the worst of the cold snap was over before we left Hootalinqua. I've been doin' whatever that big bastard says for years now, an' I never think about questionin' his word until it's too damned late. It's got me into more trouble'n I could tell you about in a week of talkin'. The Big Coyote musta dealt me short on brains, or by the Virgin's hot box I'd a got it figgered out by now. It's just that he always sounds so certain, you know what I mean, Katie?"

Katie nodded and playfully punched Danny's shoulder.

"Let's don't go gettin' physical now," he laughed. "You know I don't never fight no one I cain't whip."

"We head back tomorrow?"

"Have to wait an' see what the lout tells us to do, I reckon." He winked at her and squatted down to push the solidly frozen coffee pot in against the coals

They followed the Niordenskiold northward, taking the sled dogs out onto river ice where it was smooth and moving down one bank or the other when the ice was tumbled and broken.

Near the fork of the river they came upon several hundred caribou. The ungulates were feasting on the twigs and bark of an extensive stand of young aspen, poplar and cottonwood, the moisture-loving trees having grown up in the wake of a great bog fire of thirty or forty years earlier.

Not even the approach of men and dogs was sufficient to drive the caribou away from their feeding area. The animals stared out from the thick growth of winter-bare saplings, and a couple of the larger bucks pawed restlessly at the frozen snow as if contemplating an attack.

"Coyotes must have told the caribou people we already finished our hunt," Skookum Jim grinned. He pointed across the white surface of the meadows to where three adult coyotes and four half-grown pups were sitting together in a line, pointed ears alert, watching.

"You'd think they was Eskimos and that was their herd," Taos Danny laughed. "The song dogs, they follow the caribou, whose hooves break the snow. That way the coyotes can get to the mice without having to dig for 'em. They's probably a couple dozen more scattered out all round the goddamned herd. Everybody is looking for *alimento*."

"Be nice if they'd come into graze on the aspens close to Hootalinqua," Emerson growled. "Woulda saved us coons a hell of a lot of travel time."

"Maybe that's what they wished to do," Skookum

Jim said, "but the coyotes told them not to. Coyotes can be very insistent at times."

The sled dogs whined and growled deep in their throats as they labored in their traces, dragging the meat-laden sleds down through the meadows, but the coyotes did not move. Only a few of the caribou, becoming nervous, shuffled back a bit further into the stands of grey and white saplings.

The coyotes laugh at our dogs," Kate said. "They laugh because they have freedom and the dogs do not."

"Maybe," Emerson nodded, "but our mutts get fed an' the coyotes don't. Bein' hungry's the price of freedom, I'm thinkin."

"Sometimes they get fed, an' sometimes they get et—if times are tough," Taos Danny Vasquez added. "An' I call that the price of civilization. Just like with dumbass people. They get 'em a government to protect 'em, an' then when things gets sparse, the government eats up the people. That's the truth, John, an' you know it too. Take your Civil War, for instance. Et up thousands an' thousands, mebbe millions for all I know. An' for what? Let the dogs fight an' eat up what's left. Charley St. Francis, he figgered that much out, an' that's why he come north. Couldn't stomach no more after Sand Creek. Just got sick of the whole damn thing an' headed for the Yukon."

Emerson nodded again, pursed his lips and spat into the cold air. "Good man, real good man. I still miss that son of a bitch. Charley, he figgered out that you was a damned Meskin long before I did."

"*Chinga tu madre,*" Taos exploded. "You know I ain't no Meskin. That was just Charley's way of rilin' me."

"Worked, too," Emerson chuckled.

At that moment a mournful braying sound echoed

across the bleak white landscape. "What in hell?" Danny asked.

Emerson rubbed his mouth, breaking away the bits of ice that had formed on his beard. "Unless this child's mistaken, that there's my old friend Timothy. He's the only mule I ever heard that yelled with one lung at a time."

George Washington Carmack's luck had gone sour. Taking his hand-drawn map and Long John Emerson's advice, he followed Fortymile River to its source and crested the mountains on a bright, almost perfectly clear day. To the southwest rose huge, ice-mantled peaks—a hundred miles away but nevertheless massive in aspect, no larger than Shasta certainly, but big. Far beyond these mountains, phantomlike and nearly transparent against the horizon, stood a white dome that could be one mountain only—Denali.

He spent the night under a tangle of hemlocks. He built a grand campfire and roasted a haunch of mountain goat he had shot earlier in the day. With the first light of morning he searched the horizon once again for the great and mysterious mountain, but it was no longer visible, for running clouds rimmed the big peaks to the southwest, obscuring all behind them.

From that point on the goddess of good fortune deserted him. Timothy went lame and Carmack was obliged to shoulder at least half the load. The gravel beds he tested were all barren, and when he did find color, the amount was so small that he realized he could have done better by panning any of the neighborhood creeks in California.

When he reached the big river he presumed to be the Tanana, he slipped down a muddy bank and lost his patented fire-starter. It was more than a week before he was able to find a ledge of flint good enough to make reliable sparks.

He prospected the Tanana River while Timothy's

cracked hoof was mending and then decided to work his way downriver toward the Yukon. Where the Tanana widened into a considerable lake some miles in length he met Harper and Bates, McQuesten's friends. The two had come upriver with McQuesten and crossed over to the Tanana along the north branch of Fortymile River. They showed him samples they had taken from a north branch placer—a flask of fines and small nuggets of gold.

He remained with Harper and Bates for a week or so and then decided to explore the upper Tanana to where it fed down from a gigantic range of mountains to the south. Their peaks were he concluded, considerably higher than his beloved Mt. Shasta. These mountains, the Wrangells, kept their entire massif covered with glacial ice.

The days were growing shorter. Carmack decided to cross over to White River and up its tributary the Nisling, which Arthur Harper had assured him fed down from a range of hills beyond which lay the Yukon basin and Red Porcupine's village.

He found his way to the White and then to the Nisling but followed the wrong branch of this river. Carmack came to doubt that Harper even vaguely knew what he was talking about. Still, he took it upstream for what he estimated to be a hundred and fifty miles, arriving at length at a long, twisting lake and Kluane, a settlement of Tutchone Indians. The people at first were friendly to the white man with the strange mustache but later attempted to murder him, so that only a desperate flight astride the faithful Timothy saved his life.

He crossed high barren ridges, sometimes went hungry for days at a time. When he was able to take game, he rested, gorged himself and then moved on. He found another large lake between walls of mountain and another Indian village; this one he avoided.

He was crossing yet more mountains when the snow and the terrible cold hit, and he and Timothy huddled together beneath any cover they could find. At last next to the Niordenskiold he ran afoul of another moose, this time an ill-tempered male that charged Timothy. The beast's rack caught Carmack across the leg and broke it.

He crawled to the mouth of a cave near the river, and with old Tim following curiously, his bad ear flopping forward, Carmack managed to gather firewood and light a blaze at the cave's mouth. He tried to set his leg by means of a coil of rope lashed to a broken spruce but passed out from the pain and awoke some time later quite numb with cold. The fire had died down to nothing and Timothy was nuzzling at his face, no doubt wondering if the man was dead.

Every movement sent streams of fire through his broken right leg, but Carmack doggedly pulled himself about, gathered more wood and managed to keep a fire going. He wrapped himself in blankets, chewed jerked elk and sucked on handfulls of snow and ice. For several days the mule stayed close, but finally it wandered off to search for food.

Carmack was running a fever and at times his mind wasn't right. Ghost-like beings swirled around him and he would awake shouting. Finally, when he had grown too weak even to keep the fire going, he knew his end was near. "It's been a great adventure," he said, gazing out through the darkness at the astounding display of the northern lights, "but goddamn it, I don't want it to be over yet. Still don't seem to have much choice."

He was still alive when the morning twilight came, and with a last desperate exertion he managed to use his rope to pull in a deadfall and was able to get one end of it burning.

Then there was nothing left and he lay back to die. He did not even have the energy to compose a death chant in the manner of his mother's people. Darkness spun about him and he no longer felt cold, but was alert enough only to know that the end must be near.

Then something was nuzzling his face once more. He opened his eyes to discover Timothy's big grey head and floppy ear hanging over him.

"Come to say good-bye, did you?" he asked. Then he began to cry, not even certain at first they were tears of joy. "Not time to go home yet?"

The mule fluttered its gray, bristly lips and Carmack forced his right arm to move, his numb hand to reach toward the mule and rubbed the nose. "Got to move, old Tim. Got to get the fire burning again. Raven Man or whatever he's called is slow, goddamned slow. Might as well try to be comfortable while I'm waiting."

Carmack drew on resources he had never suspected he had and somehow managed to move the unburned portion of the deadfall into what the bed of coals. Hacking at the wood with his knife, he finally managed to coax the slivers into flames.

Exhausted then, he rested for a time as Timothy shifted uneasily and began to bray. Carmack was startled awake, saw that the fire was burning nicely and fumbled in his leathers for the whale-head pipe and his nearly empty tobacco pouch. He managed to fill the bowl and light the tobacco, and then he lay back and stared at the blur of light beyond the cave's mouth. He puffed a few times and closed his eyes once more.

Chapter 24
Buried Alive

I was hidden from everything, from everyone. The outside world ceased to exist. Where I was only pain mattered. Raven Man himself could not find me, I was so well hidden; I could not even find myself. Nonetheless, somewhere, I knew, the gleaming black-feathered wings and the great beak and the huge eyes were moving toward me.

The spirit inside me was not ready. It could not accept what had happened to me. I had come a far way to this place, but why had I come?

I have seen the bones of vanished creatures projecting from eroded floodbanks. I have seen great eagles soaring on currents of wind. I have heard the river singing of the gold I have not been able to find.

A conclave of grizzlies met on the Tanana. Twenty-three of the beasts milled about and slapping tall-finned graylings and cohos and chinooks up onto the rocks. I have seen wolves of white and black and silver grey. One night a pair came to sit just at the edge of the light circle of my fire. I talked to them for a long while, and they listened closely.

I have seen moose splashing in shallow ponds like so many huge four-legged children. They paid me no attention.

I have walked through shadows thick with crimson fireweed, paintbrush, cottonweed, Arctic poppies of yellow, red and white. I have felt the wind of the northland on my face and have seen it touch the leaves of quaking aspens and make them dance in frenzy.

Mountain sheep have paused to stare at me; I waved my hat to them. Far peaks shouldered above rivers of glacial ice and glittered in sunlight and then vanished in bandings of cloud.

But all that was before this time of cold, before pain was all that mattered, before I was so well hidden I could not even find myself.

November 1880

"Timothy, you old thief!" Long John Emerson hugged the mule, which was eagerly nibbling at his pockets, hoping for a bit of tobacco or even something sweet, honeycomb or sugar. "What have you done with Carmack, Tim?'

Skookum Jim pointed at the wisp of smoke rising near the cutbank a hundred yards ahead. The hunters left their sleds behind and moved ahead as rapidly as their snowshoes would permit. They found the cave easily enough and stood at the mouth staring into it at the form of a man. His leg was twisted and a ceremonial pipe warmed in his hand; smoke was still curling upward from its bowl.

"George Carmack," Emerson demanded, "are you alive then?"

Kate pushed past her brother and Taos Danny to kneel beside Carmack. She placed one hand on his shoulder as if to rouse him from sleep, but without success.

"He breathin'?" Skookum Jim asked.

"I don't know. Maybe. Yes, maybe he is."

"Leg's bust," Danny said. "Had 'im a last smoke from the looks of 'er."

"You, crazy man," Kate wailed, shaking Carmack

more vigorously, "wake up. Come back from wherever you've gone."

Emerson pulled off his leather gloves so he could touch his hand to the face. "Lost a lot of body heat. Could be he ain't comin' back, Katie."

"Get more wood for the fire," she commanded. "Long John, boil some coffee. I'll make him wake up."

Emerson obeyed and Hammerwater Kate continued to shake the comatose George Washington Carmack. "Wake up, crazy Southerner. Think I want to explain this to your ancestors?"

Emerson found a slide area where enough loose stones of the right size might make a burial cairn for the heavy-set Californian. However, due mostly to Katie's persistence and sheer force of will, George Carmack came crawling back out of Raven Man's tunnel and entered once more into the world of the living.

Emerson set Carmack's leg. The muscles had drawn in so tightly, that it took a good deal of manipulation and the combined strength of John, Skookum Jim and Taos. The terrible pain revealed itself clearly on Carmack's face, but he uttered no sound other than a few suppressed groans.

At last the bone was set, splinted with a pair of carefully halved hemlock branches and wrapped with five layers of caribou hide. Everyone secretly thanked Raven Man for breaking somebody else's leg instead of his own.

After that Carmack slept for a time. Once more Emerson supposed the man had drifted away toward the spirit world, but when the dim light of morning showed, Carmack moaned, opened his eyes and tried to sit up.

"Still with us, are you?" Long John asked, handing Carmack a cup of steaming coffee well laced with honey.

Carmack blinked, stared, nodded and grinned. "Hell of a way to treat a man. First you lend me a damned mule that's afraid of mice, and then you spend an hour or so grinding my leg bones together. That's torture to a fellow who can't fight back—''

Emerson laughed. ''Still tryin' to hump a brown bear, was you, lad?''

''Naturally,'' Carmack answered, ''but the beast took a hammer and broke my leg.'' He glanced at Kate, pulled his mustache and winked at her. She bit at her lip and glared at him.

''Goddamnit,'' he bawled, ''aren't you even going to say you're glad to find out your future husband's still alive?''

''You are still too ugly. Here is something to eat. I killed one of your totem animals yesterday and cooked it for you. When I saw that you were still breathing, I even warmed it up so that you would wish to eat it.''

Taos Danny and Skookum Jim exchanged glances and Danny chuckled deep in his throat. Carmack reached into the small hide container he was offered and took a chunk of meat, put it into his mouth and began to chew. He closed his eyes for a moment and swallowed. ''Klondike Kate,'' he said, ''that's the worst-tasting stuff I've ever eaten. You soak it in boiled bearshit or what?''

''Skunk bear—carcajou.'' Carmack pushed the hide container away. ''Nobody eats wolverine. Why'd you decide that was my sacred animal? I sure as hell never said so.''

Kate shrugged, glanced at Long John. ''Very grumpy, not afraid of anything, smells terrible. You didn't have to tell me. The skunk bear, he's just like you.'' Emerson slapped his leg, rose and strode to the mouth of the cave.

Taos Danny and Skookum Jim laughed. ''Eat some more,'' Skookum Jim said. ''Very strong meat, Carmack. Give you lots of strength.''

''All right, all right. Hell, I'll eat anything. Kate, are you sure this is good for what ails me?''

She offered him the container and he took another chunk and chewed. "Ugly and dumb too," she concluded.

The following day the cold broke and temperatures rose above freezing, so that the flow-ice draperies about the cave mouth began to drip. Long John could see that Carmack was still in no condition to be moved, certainly not fifty miles or so back to Hootalinqua. However, if a warm snap set in it was altogether possible that the dog sleds would become useless, the hard-won supply of meat would be lost and the sleds themselves might have to be cached until more snow fell.

With these things in mind, he insisted on an immediate return to the village. Danny, he suggested, could stay with Carmack and bring him in when it was possible to do so.

Kate said otherwise. She herself would remain with Carmack. Emerson was to return to the cave as quickly as possible with mules or dogs to bring them home.

Long John was somewhat doubtful, but Kate insisted. At length Skookum Jim convinced the tall white man that his sister would not be in any danger. The three men and their dogs, old Timothy trailing behind, set out across the lake-dotted barrens, frozen swamps and evergreen forests toward Hootalinqua.

Carmack, though his roughly splinted leg was bothering him considerably, responded to care. His appetite was voracious. Kate brought in fresh meat, a caribou's hindquarter, leaving the remainder of the slain animal for the coyotes and wolves.

Within three days Carmack was up and about, using a pair of spruce branches bound with hide for a crutch. The frostbite had gone out of his hands, feet and face; his spirits were greatly improved.

The warm snap passed quickly. When light came the

second day after the departure of the others, the flow ice about the cave mouth was no longer inclined to drip.

Long John, Skookum Jim and Danny had pledged themselves to a swift return, and for the moment everything was under control. The men left a considerable supply of firewood near the cave as well as more than half their remaining coffee beans.

Kate and Carmack, getting along fairly well now that the others were absent, talked at length. Carmack told stories of his boyhood in California and Kate listened intently, only half believing his accounts of a land where snow did not fall even during the winter and where the summers were endlessly hot and blue, almost totally without rain. She listened intently and despite herself found she was drawn to this outsider who claimed to be half Indian and who professed that desire to become wholly so. He wished to live in the wild lands, he said, just like his mother's people before gold was discovered and the American's came to their lands in astounding numbers.

"There are not that many people in the world," she insisted.

Carmack shrugged and lit his whale-head pipe, which Kate had examined carefully. Having been told how he found it, she shrugged and said, "The old ones left it there."

"How long ago—how old do you suppose it is?"

"I do not know, but long ago my people lived where the sea comes in over the land, where the great glaciers break off into the water. Short Day, my mother, told me this story.

"It was the time when Eagle Claw and his wife were fishing in the sea. She caught a strange fish and asked her husband what to do with it. He told her to gut it and cut it up for drying, and that's what she did. After that the whale god Orca caught her and dragged her down under the water, but Eagle Claw realized what had happened. He lit a pitch torch and went down under the water after her, for in those days the fish could come up land, and men could go under the water."

"A long time ago, then," Carmack mused, vaguely remembering some of the strange tales his own mother had told.

"Yes, but Eagle Claw could not find where Orca had taken his wife, and so he asked Shark to help him. Shark led him to a great lodge where Orca and his family lived and they found out that Orca intended to cook Eagle Claw's wife for dinner.

"There was a great fire burning and already the water in the pot had begun to boil. Shark wished to help Eagle Claw, so he pretended to stumble. He knocked over the other kettles of water and the water spilled onto the fire. Then the lodge was filled with steam and smoke."

"Quick," Shark cried, "take your wife and flee. Climb up the High Grease Trail and go to the Yukon. You will be safe there."

"Orca will catch me and eat both me and my wife."

"If he follows I will fight him. I will fight everyone in his family if that is what I must do."

"Eagle Claw fled, hearing a great noise behind him. Shark was fighting with all the Whale People, biting them with his sharp teeth and scratching them with his rough skin. Eagle Claw and his wife got away and they did what Shark told them.

They came to this land and here they met the old ones, who were all dying. They told their story and the old ones taught them to make smoking pipes like the one you have found. Red Porcupine has one too, smaller than that one but almost the same. After that the old ones all died and went through Raven Man's tunnel into the spirit world."

"How do you suppose the pipe got so far down into the gravel bank? Looks to me like it had been there for thousands of years."

"Thousands," Kate mused, "that would be a very long time. Maybe it just fell down into a hole in the ground and the river uncovered it."

Carmack nodded, puffed at the pipe, said nothing. Kate stirred the coals, put more wood on the fire. "Would you like to smoke, Kate? Is it permitted among your people?"

"Yes," Kate answered, "and no." She reached for the pipe and he handed it to her.

At last they retired to their blankets and covered their heads against the increasingly bitter cold. Kate did not sleep. Her heart was beating too fast, and she was feeling different than she ever had before. She thought about the things they had spoken of and even toyed with the idea of the two of them living together in their own lodge of split spruce. The front would be brightly painted in designs of animals and men designs of red, white, yellow, brown and black.

Then she was in the lodge. A fire was burning and children were playing with a stack of wolf bones; they were her children.

She whispered a soft *no* and closed her eyes tightly, but something like a thin flame played about the nipples of her breasts and the same kind of flame tickled between her legs. She reached down under her heavy clothing and discovered that she was hot and slippery and wet.

She laughed softly at herself and tried to focus her mind on other things, the time when the salmon came up into the stream for which she was named, how her people waded out into the current and set willow nets to catch them.

The salmon will swim up into the Hammerwater . . . Then she realized she was not thinking about something different at all.

Later, when she supposed Carmack to be asleep, she

rolled over against him, moving very carefully so as not to jar his broken leg.

George Washington Carmack pretended not to waken.

Grey twilight had not yet come when they felt the first shock. Carmack came fully awake as the floor of the cave shuddered and heaved beneath him. A slab of limestone just to the right of the smoldering fire split open and sagged sideways, grinding, then settled once more.

The smell of fractured stone, the smell of released energy, the easing of strain in the earth . . . "That was either a hell of a dream," he said, "or we've just had an earthquake."

"Raven Man is digging in his tunnel again," Kate whispered.

"Think maybe we ought to get out of here?"

"The earth is still again. It happens often, but there is usually no damage. Once when I was a child the earth shook. The Kuikpak turned back on itself and some new islands came up out of the river. One is still there, about five miles below the village. Red Porcupine says that is how the lakes were formed long ago, but I do not believe him. No, I think we are safe now, Carmack."

George Carmack was less than convinced. Earthquakes were not so rare in the California foothills, and he had never before felt anything like the temblor that had just ran through the rock beneath him.

"You sure?" Then a far more massive jolt hit them. It shattered several already truncated stalactites further back in the cave and made the slab of stone that had moved earlier tilt over on its side, breaking in half in the process. Ash spurted up from the firepit and there was a terrible grinding, almost screaming noise far down in the rocks.

Then came the third jolt. The very hillside itself momentarily forgot about gravity and inertia as rock was flung loose from the cave walls. Then they heard a great hissing and muffled rumbling and dust and particles of ice filled the air about them like a strange heavy fog.

In the moment it happened Carmack rolled over, using his own body to shield Kate, ignoring the pain in his broken leg, moaning in spite of himself but placing his hands about her head and drawing her to his chest.

When the sounds of breaking and falling rocks had ceased, he released her, rolled over onto his back and lay gasping for breath.

Kate did not move for a long while, then sat up. "Is it over?"

"It happens often." He forced himself to laugh. "There is usually no damage."

"This is not funny, crazy person. I cannot see anything, but I think the entry to the cave has slid down. I think we are trapped inside."

"Trapped?"

"Unless we can find a hole to get out of. How can I tell? I'll build up the fire so we can have some light."

"Don't, my dear. If we're sealed in a fire will use up all the oxygen, the air we breathe, and the cave will fill up with smoke and suffocate us that way."

"I know what oxygen is; do you think I'm stupid? When the oxygen is gone, then the air is worn out. But there is always plenty of good air in caves. It comes out of the rocks."

Carmack adjusted his position slightly so as to ease the pain in his leg. "Okay, okay. You want to die warm. Do whatever you think is best."

"You're right about the smoke," she admitted. "We need to make just a little fire, a torch. There are some pitch knots if I can find them in the dark. I'll get one of those burning in the coals and then we'll be able to see what's happened."

She crawled away into the darkness and returned

within a short time. She placed the pitchwood in the bed of coals, stirred until a few small flames came up and cast a pale glow across the litter of broken rock that lay scattered upon the floor of the cave.

She waited until the pitchy knot had caught fire before she spoke. "We are trapped, Carmack. I tried to find a way out, but there is none. Half the hillside must have slid down. There's no way out."

Carmack thought about things for a moment. "Buried alive, are we? Well, luck's been no friend of mine for weeks now. If it's time to die, I guess I can handle that. I hate like hell to have you trapped in here with me, though. No way to move the rocks and dig our way out?"

"I don't think so, but maybe there is. Some of the rocks are very big, though. Maybe—"

"Tell you what, Kate. Crippled up this way, I'm not going to be much help. With one leg broke half a man's strength is gone. Can't carry things, I mean, but I'll do my best. Put that coffee pot on and heat 'er up. After we've had a swig or two let's do our damnedest. No sense just sitting around and waiting for death. Raven Man has either got it in for me or else he's just damned well forgotten about me. You wouldn't have any kind of magic that might help us, I don't suppose?"

"I have my own two hands, George Carmack. We both do. And Long John promised to come back for us as fast as he could. He'll see what's happened and figure out a way to free us."

"Put the coffee on, Katie. I've got a powerful dry, as your tall friend says. You think he'll have the foresight to bring along a pry bar or two?"

"Emerson will move the mountain with his hands if he has to," she replied. "He loves me."

"That's two of us, then. If we get out of here alive and I get healed up again, don't tell me I'm going to have to fight that overgrown horse before you'll have me?"

''Here's your coffee. What makes you think I'd have you no matter what happens?''

Carmack sipped the warm coffee. ''Because you're falling in love with me, that's why. Women always do once they get to know me.''

''I do not wish to talk this kind of foolishness. I am going to start digging.''

Carmack laughed, then whistled softly. ''You thought I was asleep when you curled up against me last night. I wasn't though. I knew what you were thinking about.''

''Close your mouth, Carmack. A little warmth is better than none, and if I manage to get out, I'm going to close up the hole behind me. When Emerson comes I'll tell him you're dead.''

''Love it when you get mad,'' he chuckled.

For hours they struggled in the dark, moving big stones aside, dragging them, pushing them to one side, and using their hands to scoop away dirt and smaller broken stone that had come down with the slide. Carmack wormed along on his good side, devised ways to use his good knee as a lever so that he could bring the strength of his arms to bear upon the rocks.

Kate found a green pole among the wood that had been heaped inside the cave and Carmack used his Bowie knife to notch it so she could use it as a lever. They worked together in silence, speaking but rarely, patiently and determinedly. Finally the lever pole broke and Kate sat down, fighting back tears.

''It's no good,'' Carmack said. ''Every time we get one of the brutes out something else comes down in its place. I never had much steam in the first place, and what I had has just about run out. Tell you the truth I really haven't been feeling so well lately. Could be your damned mosquitoes have done me in.''

"I thought you said it was a moose that broke your leg."

"Might have been, might have been. It's hard to tell the critters apart some times."

"We have to keep digging," Kate insisted.

"You noticed the cave isn't filling up with smoke? Seems like it's drifting back into the hole. Why do you suppose that would be?"

"Not much fire, not much smoke. Just enough to keep it going."

"Sometimes caves have more than one entry. There's one like that just south of Auburn."

"What are you talking about, Carmack?"

"California, that other world you don't know anything about."

"Where you say it never snows?"

"The very place. Only it does snow in the mountains—I've seen it when it was twenty feet deep, by God."

"Do you wish to keep on talking or shall we search for another way out?"

With the cave sealed off the temperature slowly rose past the freezing point. An ice formation between fractures in the stone began to melt. Carmack hacked off the ice, using his knife as a hand axe. They put the portions into the coffee pot, melted them and drank deeply of the lukewarm water. "Hits the spot," Carmack said. "You got any more of those pitch knots?"

"One more, but not a good one."

"Well, light 'er up. Then the goddess and the crippled kid'll go cave exploring. We'll just follow the smoke out into the daylight, by heavens."

"It's night again by now."

"Into the brilliant starlight, then. There we are, it's burning. Onward, Katie. Lead us out of here."

They slowly moved back into the depths of the cave.

At times they came into large rooms that lay littered with the remains of fractured draperies; at others they must inch their way through narrow passages that eventually led out into other rooms.

"Glad you know where you're going," Carmack muttered, "because I haven't got the slightest damned idea how to get back to the campfire."

"We will remember if we have to."

In one high wide room the light of their torch revealed a hole in the ceiling—or what appeared to be a hole—a patch of darkness against the pale shiny stone. Kate held up the torch and the two of them observed that the black smoke from the sputtering flame rose straight up.

They glanced at each other and Carmack shook his head. "Wherever it goes there's no way to get to it. Too high."

"Maybe we'd better go back and wait for Long John. What if he digs in and we aren't there?"

"You've got more faith in old Long John than I do."

"You should trust in him also. He saved your life. He heard the mule and came looking for you."

"And he was fixing to bury me when I came to. That was about the first thing I heard when my mind began to clear."

"We all thought you were dying."

"Yep, I thought I was too. As a matter of fact a part of me wasn't all that happy about being dragged back. By the time the boys got my leg splinted up I was firmly convinced, you might say, that I'd have been better off dead. There's no pain down there, Katie. It's a pure and perfect release."

"Yes, a release from everything that matters."

Carmack ran thumb and forefinger over his mustache and nodded. "Guess you're right about that."

They began to move again, back the way they had come. Sometimes they had to stop and discuss their route, and once they took the wrong way and ended up in a room with no outlet.

At length the torch sputtered out and after that they felt their way. Luck was with them this time. After a few more wrong turns and what seemed like a very long time indeed they caught the odor of smoke and knew they were close.

Back in the main room they piled a small amount of wood on the faintly glowing bed of coals, and Kate, on hands and knees, blew at the embers until they flared up and took hold of the splintery end of a piece of dried spruce.

They melted more ice, drank thirstily and ate slices of cold meat. With food for only another three to four days, they knew their chances for escape were slim indeed. When the meal was finished Carmack, exhausted, lay back and closed his eyes. He could not control the rhythm of his breathing, though he tried. Kate herself approaching exhaustion, moved back to the blocked entryway and once again began to work at the heaped stones, which by now were largely frozen in place.

"Rest, Katie. Save yourself. I think you're right. The only hope we've got is that old Tall Timbers will show up with Skookum Jim and Danny and they'll dig us out. If not, hell, I've just about gotten used to the idea of death. It's not so bad, I tell you. This leg of mine has got lightning in it. The bindings are way too tight—she's swollen up from climbing around the cave, I guess. Think maybe I'd better loosen them."

"I'll do it for you, Carmack." She was beside him, tending him as though he were a child. He wanted to resist, to take care of matters himself, but he was just too tired.

Once the splint was adjusted Kate lay down beside him. When he reached over and placed his hand on her arm, she did not object nor move away.

"Guess that debt you owed me has been repaid a couple of times over."

"What debt?"

"You know, when old Stinking Salmon, or whatever his name was caught you. Anyhow, I guess I don't own you any more. Maybe you own me now, truth to tell."

"You're my slave now?"

"Suppose so. I'm willing to die with you. Isn't that what a good slave's supposed to do?"

Kate laughed softly and placed her own hand over Carmack's. "If we get out of here alive, then I will allow you to be my slave. You will come live in my father's village and we will allow you to gather firewood for us."

"Can't do that, not unless you'll marry me."

A long silence ensued. "Why would I wish to marry a man with a broken leg?"

"Won't be broken forever."

Chapter 25
Kuikpak Requirements

Aurora borealis, northern light; aurora australis, southern light; aurora polaris, polar light. The luminous atmospheric phenomenon occurs most often in high latitudes but is also seen in other parts of the world.

The aurora consists of rapidly shifting patches and dancing columns of colored light. Extensive displays appear to be accompanied by disturbances in terrestrial magnetism and are associated with interference in radio, telegraph and telephone communications. Maximum and minimum auroral intensity are said to follow almost exactly the sunspot cycle.

John Muir first journeyed to Alaska in 1879 and described one such display of the northern lights: "My bed was two boulders, and as I lay wedged and bent on their up-bulging sides, beguiling the hard, cold time in gazing into the starry sky and across the sparkling bay, magnificent upright bars of light in bright prismatic colors suddenly appeared, marching swiftly in close succession along the northern horizon from west to east as if in diligent haste, an auroral display very different from any I had ever before beheld. . . . But in this glory of light, so pure, so bright, so enthusiastic in motion, there was nothing in the least cloudlike. The short color bars, apparently about two degrees in height, though blending, seemed to be as well defined as those of the solar spectrum.

"How long these glad, eager soldiers of light held on their way I cannot tell; for sense of time was charmed out of mind and the blessed night circled away in measureless rejoicing enthusiasm."

On another night he spoke of aurora "as novel and wonderful as the marching rainbow-colored columns—a glowing silver bow . . . right under the zenith, or a little to the south of it, the ends resting on the top of the mountain-walls. And though colorless and steadfast, its intense, solid white splendor, noble proportions and fineness of finish excited boundless admiration. In form and proportion it was like a rainbow, a bridge of one span five miles wide and so brilliant, so fine and solid and homogeneous in every part, I fancy that if all the stars were raked together into one window, fused and welded and run through some celestial rolling-mill, all would be required to make this one glowing white colossal bridge."

November 1880–February 1881

The fire had gone out. It was not the cold that woke George Washington Carmack, but throbbing pain in his broken leg. He had rolled over on it as he slept. He shifted closer to Kate and once more pulled the blankets up over his face.

It would be morning twilight outside by now, he thought, but what was the point of rising? Whether the temperature was thirty below or thirty above, freezing was of no concern—not to him, not to her. They had sufficient food for another day or two, but the firewood was gone, hope with it.

Was that more rocks falling? He concentrated on the sound for a moment before he was able to assure himself that the muted, clinking sounds were as regular as though someone was working with a pick.

Emerson's back, by God, just like he said. Carmack reached over, gently stirred the sleeping woman. She muttered something. He shook her again, more vigorously this time. His movement sent fire surging through his bad leg.

"How can you make love to me if your leg is broken?" Kate mumbled.

"Katie, wake up, damn it! Get your mind off your urges and wake up. I think Long John's trying to dig us out. Give a listen."

She sat up, eyes wide in the darkness, and heard the tapping. "I knew he would come to save me."

"Hope he's planning to take me out of here too," Carmack said. "I've just gotten to the point where I like your company."

"Us, I meant us. We must give him some kind of signal so he'll know we're alive."

Then she was scrambling across the cave, feeling her way until she reached the barrier that sealed them away from the outside world. She grasped a fist-sized stone and began to hammer upon one boulder and then another.

Silence fell on the other side; then came an answering tattoo. Carmack as well pulled himself across the cave and began to thump at the rockslide and shout.

"He cannot hear our voices, but he can hear when I tap the stone. Perhaps we will not die here after all, Carmack."

Two hours later a thin trickle of light shot into the cave. From beyond came the voice of Long John Emerson. "Hang on, leetle Kate. Me an' Charlie'll have you out in a bit. Stay back away from the slide. This whole mess could come slippin' down any old time."

"Tagish Charlie," Carmack called through the small opening, "are you out there, you damned red devil? I challenge you to the hand game, by God."

"Get back away from the rock slide, Carmack," Charlie answered. "Do just what Long John says."

"I will, I will," Carmack answered. "Everyone else does and I'm no different. Hurry it up, Emerson, or by heavens I'll whip you good, crippled or not."

After a moment of silence, "Katie," Long John called, "drag that damn fool back into the cave, will you? I want my hands on him alive."

A thin snow was falling as the small procession made its way into Hootalinqua. Long John and Tagish Charlie rode their dog sled, the huskies and malemutes straining and wimpering in their traces and glad for the journey to be over. Kate sat astraddle Timothy the mule and Carmack lay behind, drawn on a travois.

A gang of Indian boys, their round brown faces all but hidden within the furred rims of their parka hoods, stamped along to either side of them. A number of adult villagers came out to greet them as well, mostly out of curiosity about the strange outsider of whom Musi, Tagish Charlie, Skookum Jim and Okime had told such funny stories.

Carmack, enjoying the attention, grinned, waved his fur cap and puffed on his whale-head pipe, an object he was sure would be recognized for the ceremonial artifact Kate said it was.

Even the Tutchone chief Big Grayling was there, standing to the rear of the assemblage, his arms folded. Kate had told Carmack the story of the Tutchone chief's ill-fated courtship of her, and Carmack immediately guessed the man's identity from his red cape.

When the party drew up in front of the Emerson house, Big Grayling strode forward, arms still folded, and stood next to Timothy as Kate dismounted. "I was worried about you."

Kate nodded, glanced back at Carmack. "I am well. There was no danger at all."

"She's sort of forgettin' to tell you about gettin' buried alive an' one or two other things," Emerson said.

Then he turned as both Ludmila and Charles Rostov came bolting out of the house. Emerson grabbed his son, lifted him off his feet and set him down again. He took Ludmila in his arms and kissed her full on the mouth as some of the Indians averted their heads in mild embarrassment.

"Buried?" Big Grayling asked in his own dialect. He turned to the man who lay bound to the travois and said in English, "So you are the one our Kate has chosen. She never told me that, but I knew it anyway. You are welcome to our village, George Carmack."

"I have chosen no one, Big Grayling," Kate insisted, "and you are wrong to say such a thing. I will choose when I am ready and not before."

The Tutchone chief ignored this and went on speaking to Carmack. "You have a broken leg, but if Long John Emerson set it for you, then it will heal straight and strong. You will not even limp afterward. The year grows short now, but soon enough the ice will break on the river. By that time you will be walking as well as anyone. Then it will be time for a marriage feast. The Tagish chief's daughter has already waited too long to take a man. I am very glad for you."

Carmack stole a glance at Kate. Her cheeks were touched with color and she was was staring at the packed snow. "I am pleased to meet you, Big Grayling. I call you by your name because I know you can be no other. Tagish Charlie has told me of the time you killed the great one-eyed bear armed only with a salmon spear. Only a great hunter could have done such a thing."

"Tagish Charlie told you of that?" Big Grayling was obviously pleased that the newcomer had heard of his prowess. "That was a long time ago, however, and now I am an old man. My people continue to listen to me only because they are in the habit of doing so."

"Nothing but a fish spear," Carmack said, extending his hand as he allowed his voice to trail off. The Tutchone chief hesitated only for a moment and then accepted the handshake.

Red Porcupine and Skookum Jim pushed through the throng. The older man embraced his daughter, held her back at arm's length and then brushed the tips of his fingers against the side of her face.

"It is good to have you back, Kate. You have done a brave thing and Raven Man has fanned his wings over you in blessing.

"So this is the white man who came from far away. Once you are settled, Carmack, I will send the shaman to you. If there is evil in your leg, he will coax it out." Again Carmack extended his hand.

Ludmila moved to the side of the travois. "All of you stop talking now. Help me remove the bindings so I can get him into the house and warm him up. He must be half frozen. Mr. Carmack, I am Ludmila Andreiovna Emerson. You must stay here in our home until you are well again."

"Mrs. Long John?" Carmack grinned. "I've heard much about you, ma'am, and I'm most pleased to make your acquaintance. Leroy McQuesten told me about the beautiful Russian princess, but you're far lovelier than I dared to imagine." He took her hand, kissed it softly and smiled up at her.

"How are you? Oh, you speak with a pretty tongue for one who has lain at death's own doorway. John, assist Mr. Carmack into the house, will you?"

The dark of the year came and passed. The Tagish and the Tutchones joined to heap up a great pile of firewood. They lit it at the time of the long darkness and held a feast of roast elk, caribou and black bear, along with various delicacies fashioned of salmon flour and dried roots and berries. There was even diluted whiskey to drink, it having been brought inland across the High Grease Trail. It came from one of the stills operated by enterprising Chilkat Indians along the shores of the Lynn Canal, near Haines, Klukwa and Dyea.

In the Emerson household, however, a different sort of ritual was observed—with Christmas tree and Yule log, a few candles in cups of colored glass and strung bolls of cotton grass. A few presents were exchanged. This potlatch was not fully understood by Red Porcupine, Big Grayling and their peoples, but nonetheless they accepted it as one among the many strange customs practiced by the huge white man and his beautiful, strange-mannered wife.

A few, of course, did understand after a fashion, for they had gleaned a great deal of information about the world outside when Ludmila taught them to read. Others had the rudiments of the Christian religion indirectly from relatives downriver who knew the priests of the Russian churches or directly and more recently from the Anglican missionaries who visited their villages and maintained a church at Fort Selkirk.

Such a notion of religion, however, was still generally regarded with suspicion. The people continued to rely on the shamans and to revere the deities of Beaver, Porcupine, Raven Man, Bluejay, White Wolf and Giyeg, though some, with relatives among the Tlingits, held that Orca, the Killer Whale, was indeed the most powerful of the spirit beings.

Carmack fashioned himself a set of crutches, assisted by Charles Emerson, who proved himself quite adept with the carving knife and who brought in just the right spruce branches.

The swelling diminished and the infection vanished. The weight Carmack had lost during his incapacitation he quickly regained. Ludmila fed him up on broth and various mysterious concoctions of meat, fish, parched roots, salmon oil and honey. She was nurse, mother and scolding aunt all at once. At times she would order him to lie down and rest, at others insist that he be up and about. Did he not know he would never regain his strength if he didn't force himself to get exercise?

At times Long John, Taos Danny, young Charles and Carmack whiled away the hours with the deck of cards and the rack of poker chips. Ludmila would let it be known, none too subtly, that she considered such activity a waste of time and possibly a bad influence on her son. Her concern was not utterly unjustified either, given the Tagish predisposition for gambling of all sorts, a vice that had caused more than one man to be obliged to leave the village in disgrace. Having made her feelings known, Ludmila would retire to the opposite end of the main room, taking Irena with her, and the two of them would indulge themselves in long conversations, sometimes of the need for education among the native peoples and sometimes of the martial felicities and difficulties that were being gossiped about in the village, an area in which Irena had far more sources of information than had Ludmila.

At first Kate came to visit each day, and as the other members of the Emerson clan viewed the matter, the two of them appeared to be getting along famously.

"Old George, he's bit by the love bug. Call me hog if I'm not right." Long John winked at Ludmila.

"Perhaps, beloved one," his wife returned, "but I'm not so certain about our Katie."

"Her too."

"Is that a fact, now?" Ludmila asked. "And why am I to suppose that you're such an authority, John?"

"Got a good eye for suchlike, an' you know it. Take us, for instance. Princess, I knowed you was head over heels in love with me from the first time you laid eyes on me."

Ludmila stared at her husband and absently touched her chin. "You knew it well before I did, then. Even later, little did I know you intended to bring me here, to this howling wilderness you're so pleased with. You promised me a mansion, John Emerson. And many times you've promised me that you'd take me to see *les Etats Unis*, your land of free men and captive women."

"Come on now, Ludmila, we been happy, ain't we? We built us this house an' everything. Besides, we'll get down to the outside yet, I promise you."

"Ah well," she replied, "a woman has no say in such matters."

"What you grinnin' at me for?" he asked.

"Grinning? Oh, I was just thinking about poor George. I suppose. Look at the two of them over there, conspiring like thieves. What if she decides to marry him? What will happen to the unfortunate man then?"

"What'll happen? Well, he'll most likely end up bein' the first by-God outside American that's ever been chief of the Tagish Injuns—unless the boys pass them a special ordinance."

Ludmila glanced over at Carmack and Kate. They were whispering and obviously involved in a discussion of particular import. "That's true, isn't it?" Ludmila mused. "The women have no real authority, but the chieftainship passes from the father through his daughter to the son-in-law."

Emerson reached out and placed his big hand over his wife's.

"Yes?"

"You got any plans for tonight after all the others is sound asleep? I was thinkin' that—"

"You make me blush, sir, but yes, as a matter of fact there is a certain thing I'd like you to do for me."

* * *

After that Kate's visits became less frequent and finally ceased altogether. Carmack grew moody and restless, untalkative, all but despondent. Nevertheless, he managed to clatter about the house on his crutches, and sometimes in the long, cold nights Emerson and Ludmila vaguely knew he had risen and gone out into the night.

"Gonna take a tumble an' bust that leg all over," Emerson grumbled. "Now I've got to stay awake until he decides to come back in. Got to be thirty, forty below out there."

"That's why he won't be gone long," Ludmila answered.

Always within a few minutes they would hear the heavy wooden door open and close, would feel the blast of frigid air that came in with George.

One day late in January at dinner Carmack blurted out in apparent reference to nothing at all, "I walked without the damned crutches today. I guess I'll be headin' back downriver when the ice breaks. Musi, will you sell me a ticket to Nuklukayet?"

"Don't need ticket, George," Musi answered.

After that Carmack lapsed once more into silence, finished his meal and promptly retired to his sleeping pallet. He walked slowly, carefully, but without the crutches.

The following day Emerson and Skookum Jim left on a brief hunting foray, taking advantage of clear skies and a moderate temperature, scarcely below freezing.

When he returned, the dog sled was laden with two caribou and a dall ram. Emerson unloaded the meat, hung it in the freezing shed and told Ludmila, "I've got some business with Red Porcupine, princess. Fix me some supper, if you will. This child'll be right back."

The meal was prepared, but Long John didn't return until several hours later. "Got to talk to George in the mornin'," he said. "Sorry to be so long, but—"

"I'll forgive you, John, if you'll tell me exactly what you and Red Porcupine were talking about. Hurry now."

Charles Rostov was standing there, his eyes wide, his curiosity up.

"Son," Emerson said, "why don't you go see if George Washington's interested in a card game. Tell him it's either that or he's got to arm-wrestle the old man."

"Big secret, huh? I wish I was grown up." He turned, albeit reluctantly, and walked across the room to where George was reading.

Carmack was massaging his bad leg with one hand and puffing at his whale-head pipe.

"Big medicine?" Emerson asked. "Mind if I join you?"

Carmack looked up, nodded and handed Emerson the pipe. John puffed a couple of times and returned the artifact to its owner.

"Here's how I see it," Emerson said, sitting down on the floor next to Carmack. "You're dumbass loco in love with leetle Katie, an' you've got to the point where you don't know what to do next. Ain't that right?"

"She's no concern of mine," Carmack said stubbornly.

"Figgered all along you two was in love. All right, then. Now you claim to be half Injun, an' I ain't doubtin' your word. Back before the gold rush, if a buck had eyes for a gal, what would he do? Start visitin' her pappy, ain't that right? An' start bringin' presents."

"Something like that."

"So why do you just set here broodin' all the time? It ain't like you, George, damnit. I swear, you're drivin' me an' Ludmila to the nuthouse, if they was one on the Yukon."

"I'm not very good company, I know it. I appreciate all you've done for me, you and Ludmila, by God I do. I'll figure some way to pay back part of it, anyhow. Another two months and I'll be off downriver, prospect up the Tanana. There's gold out there somewhere, I can feel it in my bones. And when I strike it rich, John—"

"If you want to pay us back, I got a lettle job for you. That new Winchester lever-action rifle of mine? I want to potlatch it to Red Porcupine, only he might not take it from me. I want you to take it over there an' give it to 'im. Bolt of blue cloth for his wife, too. Short Day, she's powerful fond of blue. Ammunition for the rifle, of course, an' I got ten strings of dentalium shells. I want to give 'im this stuff, but if I do it, he'll feel honor bound to give me back somethin' that's worth even more. An' he ain't got nothin' I want, if you see what I'm gettin' at."

Carmack studied Emerson's bearded face, a faintly suppressed smile at the corners of the mouth, the eyes gleaming. "You want me to offer a brideprice for Katie? John, that's something I'd have to do on my own, and the truth is, I'm awful close to being out of tin. Won't be able to do it until next fall, and then only if the Raven winks at me."

Emerson chuckled. "George, I hereby potlatch you this here stuff I'm takin' about. An' they's only one way ye can get shed of your obligation, an' that's by potlatchin' it onto Red Porcupine. After that it's his problem what to give you in return."

The full February moon was still low in the sky the night George Washington Carmack approached Red Porcupine's brightly painted vertical plank lodge, leading old Timothy the mule, laden with cloth, blankets, ammunition, strings of shells and a '76 Winchester sheathed in fancy leather scabbard.

Skookum Jim admitted Carmack into the lodge and led him to a seat by the lodge fire across from where Red Porcupine sat.

"Emerson said you might wish to visit me," Red

Porcupine said. "Short Day, bring me my pipe. I wish to smoke with my guest."

The entire clan was present, Skookum Jim and his Tutchone wife, Tagish Charlie, Kate and a young boy and his sister. Their parents had died shortly after the terrible cold spell of three and a half months earlier, and the children were now more or less officially adopted by Red Porcupine and his wife.

Kate said nothing, as was proper, but Carmack was aware of her eyes upon him. For his part, he pretended not to notice her.

Red Porcupine lit his medicine pipe, puffed three times and passed it around the fire to Carmack, who puffed in turn and handed it back to Tagish Charlie.

"I bring presents to the Tagish chief."

Red Porcupine nodded. "Are these your own presents, or do you bring them for someone else?"

"They are mine and I bring them to you."

"Short Day and I have wondered why you waited so long. Well, what have you brought us, Carmack? Bring these things inside so that we may look at them."

Charlie rose and accompanied Carmack outside, helped him to carry the objects into the lodge. Timothy, unloaded, trotted briskly off into the darkness.

"He knows his way home," Charlie grinned, clapping Carmack across the shoulders. "He is a smart mule, does not wish to stand here in the cold."

The gifts were placed to one side of the lodge, and Red Porcupine and Short Day examined each thing carefully but without comment, their faces impassive. "This is a strong potlatch," Red Porcupine said when he had returned to his place by the fire. "And yet perhaps it is not strong enough. Is there not something else that you wish to give me?"

Carmack stared at the Tagish chief, suddenly ill at ease and uncertain what was expected of him. Then he nodded. "Yes, I nearly forgot. I have something that once belonged to the people you call the old ones. I found it in a gravel bed along Fortymile River. It has great magic, but I have not learned how to use the magic, and so it is of no use to me. You must take this, Red Porcupine, for I think you will understand it."

Carmack produced the whale-head pipe from within the pocket of his buckskin coat and handed the gleaming black stone object with the amber-colored bowl to Red Porcupine.

"It is beautiful, Carmack. I think perhaps it is very old indeed, and Raven Man smiled upon you the day he showed you where it was hidden. Now your potlatch is very powerful, and so I must give you that which is most precious to me. I will give you Hammerwater Kate, my daughter. Will you accept this present from me or shall I be shamed in the eyes of my people and be obliged to leave them and go to live in a miserable hut in the mountains?"

Carmack glanced at his beloved and saw that her jaw was set, her eyes flaring. She said nothing, however, but sat staring into the lodge fire.

"I will gladly accept your daughter, Red Porcupine, but only as my wife."

"Kate," Red Porcupine asked, "shall I be allowed to complete this transaction, or will you shame me as you so often have before by protesting that you do not wish to marry yet?"

Kate glanced up, stared at her father and then looked directly into Carmack's eyes. Their gazes locked for a long moment. "I will marry this man, even though he is very ugly and has a silly-looking mustache," she said. "I know that I have shamed my father in the past and I do not wish to do so again."

"Will you be happy with this man?"

"Yes, I will try to be happy."

"Do you love this man, my daughter?"

Carmack held his breath as he waited for Kate to answer her father.

"Will you ask him if he loves me?"

"Certainly," Red Porcupine said. "I will do that. Carmack, I wish to know if you love my daughter. How will you answer?"

Carmack grinned, unconsciously put thumb and forefinger to his mustache and said, "By God, I do love her, and that's the truth."

Skookum Jim and Tagish Charlie began to roar with laughter but ceased when Red Porcupine cast a reproachful look at them. "He says that he loves you, Kate. Now you must answer my question."

"I love him also," Kate replied, her voice strangely soft.

"Then the two of you may now be man and wife," Red Porcupine said. He filled the whale-head pipe with tobacco, lit it and puffed carefully three times. Then the pipe went to Skookum Jim, next to Tagish Charlie and finally to Carmack.

"I wish to smoke too," Throndiuk said.

"How did I know our daughter would not be able to do this thing right?" Red Porcupine asked Short Day. "Well, if I honor her request, I must swear all of you to great secrecy. Carmack, I think she acts this way because her blood mother was Gossack. Here, you are her husband now. You may allow her to smoke if you wish."

Carmack held the pipe in his hand, and once again his gaze locked with Kate's. "Does my wife wish for this?" he asked.

"If she is to be your wife, she does."

Carmack was uncertain what to do next. He knew that among the Tagish, at least as a matter of public appearance, the women were not allowed to smoke a medicine pipe.

Yet Red Porcupine had seemed to be about to allow it, then had passed the responsibility for making the decision, to him. Under the circumstances, what was proper?

"I am Maidu," he said at last. "My mother's people once controlled all the lands from the *Cosumnes* River to the snow-covered fire mountain far to the north, from the great valley of the *Nem Seyoo* to the high mountains the white men call Sierra but the Indians call *Inyo*. Yes, I am Maidu, and among my people it is permitted for the women to smoke the ceremonial pipe. Kate is my wife now, and so I will grant her the rights of my mother's people."

With these words he passed the pipe. If Kate was momentarily surprised, she did not show it. Instead she placed the bit of the pipe to her lips and puffed, in imitation of the men, three times.

Red Porcupine nodded, seemingly satisfied. Then when he held the pipe again, he said, "Short Day, escort our daughter to the wedding lodge. Instruct her to prepare herself for her husband. Tell her he will join her in a little while."

Short Day rose, took Kate by the hand, and led her into the separate room at the rear of the big lodge. The two women entered and closed the elkhide and lath door behind them.

"You have chosen a headstrong woman," Red Porcupine said quietly to Carmack. "I think she will destroy you unless you are very careful and very wise. But now you are my son-in-law, and I accept you as my heir. It is good that my sons are your friends. Perhaps you have already learned of the ways of our people? Well, you will have much to learn. But one day when I am no longer here, you will be the chief of the Tagish; it will be expected of you if you remain among us. I will teach you all I know so that when the time comes the people will accept you."

"Red Porcupine is still a young man," Carmack said. "I will have much time to learn."

"No, I am not young, even though I am still healthy and strong. When the Lot of Water freezes two more times, I will have seen sixty winters, and that is the age when a man's strength is said to fail him. But that is later. Now you must go in to your wife and honor your marriage. I do not have to caution you to be gentle with her because you have already said you love her, and that makes a man gentle. She has waited a long time, and she has chosen you. You must go to her now, but first I would ask a question."

"I will answer, Red Porcupine."

The chief glanced at his sons and asked, "Among your people do the women truly smoke the medicine pipe?"

"The whites moved into our lands in great numbers, great numbers," Carmack said. "Some of my people became like white men themselves and forgot the old ways. Most of the others were killed, for they could not stand up to the whites. My father was a white man, and I was sent to the white man's school. And for these reasons I do not know the answer to that question."

Red Porcupine nodded, clucked his tongue. "You have spoken wisely, both now and before. Go to your wife, my son. Short Day will pour the flaming oil from two lamps into yet a third lamp, and after that she will leave the room and we will all pretend that you and Kate have gone away for a time. Perhaps you will beget a grandson for me this night."

Book Four:
TAMARA ROSAVI

Chapter 26
Lying George Finds Gold

Magma cools, grano-diorite forms and pure quartz is deposited in its fracture planes. Threaded through the quartz here and there is a small amount of gold.

The magma, some millions of years ago, bulged up beneath the overburden that became the Rocky Mountains, and through subsequent erosion the quartz seams were exposed, chipped, cracked and abraded away. The gold, thus liberated, joined the till carried toward the Bering Sea.

The rivers are restless. They change channels. Mountains rise and fall, landslides and mudslides cover, expose cover once more. Sand and gravel deposits, fined by the movement of running water, contain placer gold.

Put two shovelfuls of gravel into a miner's pan, add water, agitate the mixture in a swirling motion. Mud washes off, sand spins out, larger pebbles fly away. Gold, nearly twice as heavy as lead, remains in the pan.

The discovery of gold at Juneau led fortune seekers up the Chilkoot Trail and on to the upper reaches of the Yukon. Throughout the eighties and into the nineties they came. A few found gold, but most did not; they returned to the outside.

Leroy McQuesten was carrying miners' supplies aboard his stern-wheeler, taking them above Forty Mile to Fort

Reliance to supply mining operations at Chapman Bar and Steam Boat Bar.

Boswell, Frazer, Poplin, Ladue, Franklin, Williams, Madison, Hess were all there the summer of 1885. By the following summer they had taken out eight hundred dollars per man in fine gold.

The next summer McQuesten and Art Harper, now seeking his gold by means of trade abandoned old Fort Reliance and set up again at the Yukon-Stewart confluence. The new currency of trade would be dust and nuggets from the miner's pouch, and not merely beaver, mink, fox and marten pelts.

In fall of 1886 Franklin and Madison struck a minor bonanza in the frozen muddy placers along Fortymile River. Art Harper, damning his luck, was alone at the new post and could not leave, for McQuesten had gone south to San Francisco. Harper sent Williams across the Chilkoot with news, but Williams' luck went sour and he died in Dyea without speaking his message.

Word got out nonetheless, but the real gold remained hidden and would stay that way for another ten years.

July–August 1896

More than fifteen years had passed since that night in the lodge of Chief Red Porcupine when George Washington Carmack and Hammerwater Kate Borodin lay down together as man and wife. They did not beget the grandson Red Porcupine requested, but that night—or some night during the weeks following—a girl-child was conceived, born in November of that year, and named at Kate's request by Ludmila Emerson, acting as godmother, Grafenya Groza Carmack. The name later was transformed to Graphic Gracie, for Leroy Napoleon McQuesten and Long John Emerson were of the opinion that the Russian name was too hard to say.

The night of Grace Carmack's birth was marked by a terrific storm, complete with generous doses of thunder and lightning; hence the name Ludmila gave to the child: Countess Thunderstorm. This name, as the years fled by, proved to be highly descriptive, for Grace had inherited all of her mother's willfulness and sudden shifts of temper.

Two days later another child was born in the village of Hootalinqua, for Ludmila Emerson herself gave birth to a boy, John Daniel Emerson, called John Daniel, as he would not tolerate less. "Little John" particularly enraged him from the time he understood the words.

George Carmack and Long John were from the beginning of the opinion that the two children should probably marry one another when they reached adulthood, though the mothers had some reservations.

Life along the Yukon River continued much as it always had, not governed by the calendar of the outside world and in most ways little affected by the happenings in the United States, in Russia or in Europe. More and more prospectors came from the outside in search of gold. Change was indeed in the wind, and the Indian peoples grew ever more dependent upon the white traders for implements of hunting, trapping, cooking and so forth. Stone knives, bows and arrows and spears took on the guise of tradition rather than utility.

As time went by, however, a reverse process seemed to have taken hold of George Carmack. With each season he appeared to grow more Indian and less white. McQuésten dubbed him *Siwash George*, the Squaw Man. McQuesten's own wife was Indian, as were the wives of most of the traders and miners, so the nickname apparently had little to do with that, especially since those who knew Kate knew also that she was far more Russian than Indian. No, it was that Carmack, for reasons of his own, had become Indian.

Carmack and Kate were drifters. Along with Gracie, Skookum Jim, Tagish Charlie and sometimes Charles Rostov and John Daniel Emerson as well they wandered about, now attempting one thing, now another. Their luck at finding gold had been minimal, and their other enterprises, including running a trading post and mining coal, had similarly amounted to little. Carmack's enthusiasm for his adopted far north never waned, however, and he remained confident that the gold was out there somewhere and that he would eventually find it.

Musi and Okime continued to operate the *Hootalinqua Princess*. The ancient craft held together by "spit and cussedness," as Long John put the matter, though Okime, still spry and energetic, was approaching her seventieth birthday and Musi was in his fifties.

Emerson himself, now nearly sixty winters, remained an imposing specimen of manhood, but he had several years earlier given up his diggings on Fortymile River. With a hundred-odd miners working here and there in the muck along the river's main branch and several forks, the place was getting "too damned civilized for this old coon." So now everyone else was mining gold. Emerson, Taos Danny and Charles Rostov Emerson twenty-eight and still unmarried, turned once again to trapping. The "mansion" he had long ago promised Ludmila was complete and well furnished with all manner of fixings from the outside, and the Emersons, Taos Danny and Irena as well were, according to the standards of the world they lived in, comfortably wealthy—upper class citizens in an Indian village.

Ludmila, apparently immune to the passing of years, remained the legendary beauty of the Yukon. She had convinced Long John and Red Porcupine both that a school was essential to the Tagish and Tutchone peoples, and thus a one-room structure had arisen and was well attended by the children of the village; sometimes by the adults as well. Times were changing, she said, and if the Indians did not master the elementary skills of literacy, they would fall victims to encroaching forces from the outside. An

Anglican church now stood in the village as well, and Ludmila attended, with or without her husband, despite the fact that the rituals were in many ways different from those she had known as a girl in far-off Rostov.

In 1895 Carmack placed a note on the door of his trading post at Five Finger Rapids: "*Gone to Forty Mile for grub.*"

Even then he probably knew he did not intend to return. There was coal in the bluff behind the post and he had tried his hand at mining it and taking it downriver to be sold as fuel for stern-wheelers and miners' stoves. But the margin of profit was slim. Further, running a trading post didn't really appeal to him, and it appealed to Kate even less.

With his clan in tow he made the trip to Forty Mile, prospected for a time along the southern branch of Fortymile River, missed the *Hottalinqua Princess* on her upriver voyage and made it to Hootalinqua on muleback shortly before the Yukon winter set in.

Countess Thunderstorm was happy to be reunited with Little John Emerson and the other children of the village. With negligible reluctance she settled down to a winter of study near the tutelage of Miz Emerson.

Kate and George spent the winter trapping with Long John, and Charles Emerson and Taos Danny. They did well enough, but Carmack was once again thinking about gold.

When the Yukon ice broke that spring and Musi and Okime were happily directing other, younger people to ready the river-worn *Princess* for the venture down to St. Mike, Carmack began to get itchy feet.

"I don't want to go looking for gold anymore," Kate told her husband.

"Damnit, Katie," he replied, "this is *the* year. Can't you just smell it in the air?"

"Air doesn't smell any different to me. What good's gold anyway? We got everything we need right here in the village."

"Where's your sense of adventure, woman?"

"Went off with a crazy man years ago," she replied. "All right, Carmack, where we going this time?"

"What's your name?"

"You don't know yet? I should have waited for Charles to grow up. Now I'm too old and he don't want me."

"The Hammerwater," Carmack crowed. "Got a hunch. Nobody's ever prospected that one much. If we don't find a good claim, hell, we can always cut timber for the mill at Forty Mile and float the logs downriver. After that we can go fishing for salmon."

"That much makes sense. The Hammerwater's a fishing river, not a gold-digging river. Long John decided that years ago. He tried the Hammerwater before he started digging on Fortymile."

Carmack kissed Kate on the forehead and grinned. "Might have missed something, though. Maybe on some of the side creeks."

Skookum Jim and Tagish Charlie had just brought in a string of mules loaded with supplies for John Healy's trading post at Dyea. With the promise of good weather ahead they were eager to join Carmack in his venture. Charles Emerson too was ready for adventure and demanded to be included in the party.

Gracie, it was determined, would stay in Hootalinqua. As much as she might have wished to accompany her parents, her close friendship with Little John Emerson was sufficient to salve her displeasure at being left at home.

"Not sure those two should be encouraged to spend so much time together," Kate said. "You and Long John have always said they'd end up marrying each other one day, but they're still a bit young. I'm not ready to be a grandmother just yet."

"What you talking about, woman? For God's sake, they're only ten years old."

Kate shook her head. "She'll be fifteen when winter comes, and so will he. Your own child and you don't even know how old she is?"

"Guess I did not notice she's starting to get a nice set of titties, just like her old lady," Carmack admitted.

"Other girls her age have already spent their time in the women's lodge, for heaven's sake."

"Come on, Katie, where's your sense of humor? Of course I know how old she is."

"All right, then," Kate muttered.

"Want to know why I decided on the Hammerwater?"

Kate shrugged.

"I took this cheechaco silver dollar and flipped it, that's how. It came down tails and that means downriver. Then I flipped it again, and it came down heads. And that means the Klondike, by God."

"Why does it mean that?"

Carmack grinned, kissed her silver dollar and slipped it back into his pocket.

"Secret Injun medicine. It's not something I can just explain to every white woman who comes along, you know."

Kate stared at her husband. "Tonight while you're sleeping I'm going to cut off your manhood and throw it into the river."

"Make a hell of a splash. Wake up the whole damned village if you do."

Kate smiled. "Very little splash."

The party canoed down to the mouth of the Klondike, a three days' venture, and encamped a mile or so up the tributary stream. Charles Emerson, trying out his new

Winchester-Hotchkiss bolt action carbine for the first time, brought down a young elk.

That evening Skookum Jim built a big fire and the prospectors roasted a full hindquarter. Carmack opened a jug of whiskey after they had eaten their fill and passed it around. Full stomachs and hard liquor fueled their enthusiasm for the new venture, and conversation ran on and on until finally everyone burrowed under the blankets. The day had been quite warm, nearly eighty, but the night came cold, and frost formed shortly after twilight fell.

Carmack dreamed he was sitting on a bank beside a milk-green creek that poured down through a series of rapids. Graylings worked their way upstream, their tall fins breaking the surface of the water. Then the fish began to scatter and two huge king salmon came shooting up the creek in a frenzy, spun in the foam and stopped directly below him.

Beautiful, he thought, *beautiful fish, but something's wrong*.

They had no scales. The bodies were textured unevenly, all of inlay of gold nuggets, and the eyes were twenty-dollar gold pieces.

Carmack remembered reaching down for one of the golden salmon but awoke with a death grip on his right ear.

He got no more sleep that night. He tried to rouse Kate, but his wife muttered an obscenity and pulled her robes up over her head. Jim and Charlie, he knew, were invariably in a foul mood if he woke them before they were ready, so he turned to Charles Emerson.

"Charles, lad," he said, nudging Emerson's shoulder, "get up and have some coffee with me. Raven Man's whispered in my ear and told me where the goddamned gold is. Come on, young fellow, wake up."

Charles Emerson sat up, rubbed his eyes and involuntarily reached for his Hotchkiss-Winchester.

"Ain't nothing to shoot, Charley. I've dreamed of gold—it's a fair sign."

"Carmack, you crazy bastard, won't it wait until tomorrow?"

"Tomorrow's passing us by. Sun'll be up any minute now. It's gold, I tell you, more than you and your pa ever dreamed of over on Fortymile. There's a creek around here somewhere that's got fish in it covered with the stuff."

"George, you're still drunk, damnit. All right, I'll fix the coffee. Pile some squaw wood on the campfire and let's hear what the blackbird's told you. Truth is, I think you've got the curse of Art Harper on you. You and him—always dreaming about a bonanza and never finding a color. You're two of a kind. Fishing and cutting wood—that's the only part of this wild goose chase that makes any sense at all. Where'd you hide the coffee beans?"

Carmack reached into his gear bag and tossed Emerson a fat leather pouch. "Already been ground, lad. Get the chip off your shoulder. Honest to God, I don't know why I pal around with any of you bad-natured heathens. Get you a woman, Charles. It'll do wonders for your disposition."

"You mean a permanent woman?" Emerson asked as he poured a quantity of coffee into the big pot and filled it with water. "Now why would I be wanting to do that?"

"A man can't spend his whole life diddling around in the willow brakes. The winters up here are just too long."

What Raven Man had whispered into Carmack's ear was received with less than enthusiasm by the other members of the expedition, and so they turned to the primary orders of business: they set their nets into the river. Two days of labor produced a respectable take of king salmon, big, plump fish, purple-skinned and certain to provide good quantities of oil. The fish were split open and the orange-red flesh went on racks for drying.

Charles Emerson and Skookum Jim ventured up Rabbit Creek in search of salable timber, found some stands close by the water and made a point of panning a bit here and there along their way. When they returned to the camp at the mouth of the Hammerwater, they were without any great hopes despite the fact that in one or two places they had produced fifty-cent pans or better.

Carmack winked at them as though he had a great private joke. He seemed to have forgotten about his dream of gold and cut timber with uncharacteristic enthusiasm. After all, the sawmill at Forty Mile was paying twenty-five dollars per thousand board feet.

One by one the logs came floating down Rabbit Creek to the Klondike, where George and Charles formed them into a series of rafts in preparation for the run down to Forty Mile.

At length they were ready and the bindings were cut, the rafts in turn urged out into the flood of the Yukon. Tagish Charlie and Charles Emerson, each in his own canoe, accompanied Carmack down to the mill. They collected their money from McQuesten's foreman and immediately began the return trip to the Klondike.

"Three hundred to the good," Carmack sang out as they worked their way back up the river, "and now it's time for the *real* business to get under way."

For the first two weeks of August Charles Emerson dutifully followed George Carmack and his Tagish family over ridge and down canyon, through stands of stick spruce so tightly grown that even the midday sunlight could not penetrate, and across muskeg swamps above which hovered grey-white clouds of mosquitoes. Bob Henderson, the Nova Scotian, had found surface prospects on a stream he dubbed Gold Bottom Creek, but he gave Carmack and Emerson to know that he didn't want any damned Siwash Injuns staking claims close to his.

Charles Emerson's blood boiled, but Carmack remained calm. He was particularly impressed with Gold Bottom Creek; he even promised Henderson to let him in on whatever lode the group might turn up.

They continued up Rabbit Creek a few miles and made camp. George, Kate and Tagish Charlie prospected a tributary while Skookum Jim and Charles went hunting. After missing one moose their luck turned and they brought down a barren cow. They butchered the creature and hauled as much of the meat as they could back to the camp beside Rabbit Creek. Charles built a good fire and Skookum Jim set a quarter to roasting.

Carmack and the others were late returning, and Emerson and Skookum Jim decided to eat. Emerson was discouraged with the Klondike adventure and opined that prospects might be better over on one of the branches of the Pelly. Skookum Jim, who didn't really care whether they found gold or not, nodded obligingly, though without conviction.

At length the big Indian, a chuck of half-cooked moose meat in hand, got up and wandered over to the creek to get a drink. "Emerson," he called back, "come take a look at this."

Charles rose and walked to where Jim was standing.

The creek bed was studded with gold. Nuggets the size of a man's thumbnail lay about like drifts of pebbles.

Charles waded into the creek, scooped up a fistful of sand and nuggest, held one between thumb and forefinger, bit down on it. "Skooks," he said, grinning from ear to ear, "I think we've just stepped into Lying George's dream. All we need is a couple of fish to stick some of these onto."

"Big surprise when Carmack gets back. Maybe we ought to let him eat dinner first? Show him what we've found too soon and he'll get the stomach disease."

Emerson and Skookum Jim returned to camp and

Charles placed his five nuggets in Carmack's prized glass ashtray, which lay conspicuously beside George and Kate's bed roll. The two men then, quite pleased with themselves, cut off additional portions of meat and sat down to enjoy their meal.

The sun was low to the rim when George, Kate and Charlie came in, discouragement clear on their faces.

"Eat and you'll feel better," Skookum Jim said. "Then maybe we drink some more whiskey."

"Not a good night for a celebration," Kate replied, filling her plate with roast.

"Maybe, maybe not," Skookum Jim shrugged. "Me an' Emerson, we think Pelly River's a good place to look. Start out tomorrow, by God."

"I *know* there's gold on the Klondike somewhere," Carmack insisted. "Just haven't found it yet, that's all. It's here, I tell you."

"Good placers on the Pelly," Emerson grinned.

"Ain't no placers worth a damn and you know it. You and Long John spent a month over there two summers back. If you found anything, you sure as hell didn't let anybody else in on it."

"Well," Emerson purred between mouthfuls of meat, "take this creek, for instance. Barren as a mountainside. Look for yourself, George."

"Maybe so, but the gold's here somewhere. I know it as sure as I know my own name, and nobody's going to change my mind."

"Go check out the creek, then," Skookum Jim said, wiping the grease from his mouth.

"I will, I will. This pup and every other pup along the Hammerwater until I find the right one. Can't you just hear the gold whispering to us?"

"Don't hear nothin'," Skookum Jim said. "Kate, you hear anything?" Kate glared at her brother and continued to eat.

At length Carmack stood up, pulled a cigar out of his coat pocket, used a flaming twig to light the stogie and strode over to get his ashtray.

"What's this?" he demanded. "Where in hell'd you boys find these?"

"What are you talking about, Carmack?" Emerson asked.

"You goddamn fools, I'm talking about gold nuggets. One of you put 'em here. Where'd you find them?"

"Just mud from the creek, by God," Skookum Jim grinned.

"Which ewe-humping creek are you talking about?"

"How many creeks around here?" Charles scoffed.

Carmack studied the faces of Skookum Jim and Charles Emerson, dumped the nuggets into the palm of his hand, puffed on his cigar and then stubbed it out. He walked to the creek, stared down at the formations beneath the clear-running water. After a moment he stepped into the water, reached down to elbow depth and brought up another half dozen nuggets. He held one to his teeth and bit down on it.

Tagish Charlie, pan in hand, came running, stumbled on the bank and fell into Carmack's arms.

"By God, gold," Carmack shouted. "You sons of bitches, I told you it was here. Gold, goddamnit, gold! Katie, come look at this. It's just lying here thick, like cheese sandwiches. It's all over the place."

Then, suddenly, four men and one woman were knee-deep in the creek, bringing up fists full of nuggets, shouting and leaping in what Carmack was later to describe as "a combination war dance composed of a Scotch hornpipe, Indian fox trot, syncopated Irish jig and a sort of Siwash hula-hula."

Then came the shovels and pans. As if possessed they worked until the twilight was so dim that they could no longer see what they were doing.

Finally Skookum Jim laid down his shovel and stood with arms crossed. "Maybe we drink some whiskey now?"

The following morning Carmack posted his claim notice on a spruce tree.

> TO WHOM IT MAY CONCERN
>
> I do this day locate and claim, by right of discovery, five hundred feet running upstream from this notice. Located this seventeenth day of August, 1896.
>
> G.W. Carmack

The other claims were also duly marked, and when they were finished, Carmack cut a piece of birch bark and penciled on it, I name this creek "Bonanza." He attached the bark to a stake and drove that into the bank next to Skookum Jim's discovery.

When all of this was done, the band set off downriver for the town of Forty Mile. It was time to announce to the world what lay in the creek bottoms and in the placers along the Klondike and its tributary streams.

As Officer Hayne of the Royal Canadian Mounted Police put it, George Washington Carmack "would never acknowledge himself beaten, but always endeavored to present his fortunes in the most advantageous light." This was to put the matter nicely. Other men tended to think of Carmack as Lying George.

Now the discoverers entered Bill McPhee's Saloon, where a number of miners had gathered. McPhee was tending bar. Carmack, looking neither left nor right, marched directly to him and said, "Set 'em up, William. Me and my family have worked up a powerful thirst."

McPhee obliged. George and Kate, Jim and Charlie

and Charles Emerson lifted their shotglasses in a toast to one another and drank.

"You boys look like you just been walkin' through fire," McPhee said. "No offense, Katie. You too."

"That we have," Carmack laughed, signaling for a second round.

"That's to say we've had some good luck for a change," Emerson added.

"So it appears, so it appears. Good fishin' upriver?"

"Tell him, George," Tagish Charlie grinned.

"Katie, why don't you do the honors?" Carmack suggested.

"Let Charles. I want another drink."

"Charles, hell," Emerson said. "Get on with it, Carmack."

George finished his drink, sprang up onto the bar and called for attention. He stared out over the smoke-filled lamp-lit saloon and took note of those present: Bill Haskell, old Jay Whipple, Charles Constantine, the Canadian Inspector of Claims—the very man with whom Carmack had business—Frank Phiscator, Charlie Anderson the Swede, Louis Rhodes and a dozen others, many of whom Carmack did not know.

"Where's old Jack McQuesten and Art Harper?" Carmack demanded.

"At Circle City, an' you know it, too," Jay Whipple yelled back. "You gone loco, Carmack?"

"Sure enough, sure enough. I was just testing you boys."

"Say your piece and get down off my bar," McPhee said from behind.

"Hold on, Bill, just give a man time. That's all I'm asking."

"Out with it, Siwash George," Charlie Anderson boomed.

"Why'd you have to bring Kate along with you?" a

female voice sang out from the back of the room. Carmack and Charles Emerson both recognized it as belonging to Maggie Laimee, one of Forty Mile's resident professional ladies.

Kate looked across, glared at the gussied-up female and decided to ignore her.

"Boys," Carmack intoned, "I've got some good news to tell you. There's a big strike up the river. Just wish McQuesten and Harper was here, that's all."

"Strike, hell," Anton Stander growled. "Carmack ain't never found gold in his life. An' if he did, it'd turn into lead inside of a goddamned hour."

The men of McPhee's Saloon whistled, hissed and applauded all at once.

"Some of you call me Lying George because you can't tell truth from God's own falsehood." Carmack laughed. "I figured you might not believe me just at first. So I've brought along a little, what would you say? A convincer."

From his coat pocket Carmack drew out a brass cartridge casing and tapped the contents out onto the bar.

"Fines from just *one pan* washed out of Bonanza Creek."

This gesture caught the attention of the miners and they crowded around, inspecting the little pile of dust. "This don't prove nothin'," Anton Stander declared. "How'd we know it were just one pan?"

"You got a point," Carmack conceded.

Then Kate held up a leather pouch, loosed the drawstring and poured out a pound and a half of nuggets of varying sizes. "Now you bastards believe us?"

"More gold than you ever saw in your lives," Charles Emerson added, "and it's lying around in plain sight."

"Where's Bonanza Creek?" Swede Anderson asked. "I don't know of no Bonanza Creek."

"Named it myself," Carmack said, doing a little jig on the bar.

The men, crowding forward more tightly, stared in amazement at the pile of yellow metal.

Old Jay Whipple picked up the largest of the nuggets, bit it and placed it almost reverentially back onto the surface of the bar. "Carmack," he said, "I've knowed you since '88, and I've never heard you lie to a white man or a Siwash. I guess I can lick any hootch-guzzling, salmon-eating son of a bitch what says you lie now. But say, old man, if it ain't askin' too much, just where in hell is this Bonanza Creek, or ain't you goin' to tell us?"

"Drinks for the house," Carmack called out. "Hell yes, boys, I'm going to tell you. Truth is, that's what we came all the way down here for. Bonanza Creek, it's on the Klondike River. And there's gold for every mother's son of you."

Chapter 27
Frisco Rose

Robert Henderson's claim on Gold Bottom Creek would amount to little, though he hoped that when he reached bedrock the gold would lie solid like the streets of the New Jerusalem; hence the name he bestowed upon the creek. It wasn't so, and Henderson, like many another, wandered on in search of better prospects, a victim of the continuing ailment known as gold fever.

The government of Canada did eventually award him a pension of two hundred dollars a month for life, honoring him as the discoverer of the Klondike gold fields. George Washington Carmack, the actual discoverer, never got a pension and never needed one, for the holes he dug and the placers he worked provided genuine riches.

The gold field proved to be more than seven hundred fifty square miles total, some three hundred miles of creeks in all. By Canadian law each claim was five hundred feet in length. This allowed for something over three thousand claims, many of them barren or nearly so, like Henderson's. Beyond these there were many bench claims on the hillsides, squares a hundred feet on a side where with luck a man might put down a vertical shaft and reach the till of an ancient streambed. Or he might find nothing at all, having hewn the shaft through permafrost to no avail.

It was hard country though from the point of view of

the Tagish, the Tutchones, the Hans and the Nabesnas the land was bountiful along the Hammerwater.

Outsiders, however, struggled to adjust to winter twilight, darkness and cold. Mercury turned solid at thirty-eight below, strong whiskey froze at fifty-five below, kerosene went at sixty-five. Perry Davis' Pain-killer was good to minus seventy-five. The steel head of an axe, left outside, would get so brittle it shattered when used.

And in summer, so the miners swore, they could not without difficulty distinguish between golden eagles and mosquitoes.

September 1896

By September virtually the entire population of Forty Mile and the surrounding mines was camped in the basin of the Klondike River, including Maggie Laimee and her three working girls. Word found its way downriver to Eagle, Circle City, and Fort Yukon, so that a number of miners, trappers, rivermen and Kutchin Indians either had already arrived at the Hammerwater or were on their way. That included Leroy Napoleon McQuesten and Arthur Harper in the *St. Michael*, huffing and whistling and dragging two whale boats of supplies in tow.

George Carmack and Charles Emerson considered it wise to stay with their claims and to work them through the winter. Burning out the permafrost Carmack concluded, would work through the winter as well as summer and fifty below be damned. True, the diggings pile would freeze again at once, but when spring came, it would thaw and be ready for washing.

Long John had toyed with the method years earlier over the Fortymile, and others had picked up the idea and used it for winter workings. However, the scheme required supplies, and McQuesten's prices were subject to sharp increases once he and Harper realized the extent of the gold deposits.

"You and Charlie tired of digging?" Charles Emerson asked Skookum Jim.

"Tired before I began," Jim replied. "Charlie too."

"Good," Emerson said. "George and I have talked it over and—"

Skookum Jim cast up his eyes. "What is it you want us to do?"

"Take the mules over the High Grease Trail to Dyea, then catch a boat to Sitka if you got to. Buy all the supplies the mules can carry and get them back to Hootalinqua. Then raft the lot of them down here. And bring my pa and Danny and anyone else who wants to come with you. George and Katie and I are going to spend the winter here. Come spring we'll be rich, all of us. Unfortunately, without a load of supplies at coast prices McQuesten, Harper and ACCo will end up with all the tin. George and I figure prices are gonna get real high around here after the rivers freeze. Supply and demand, I guess you could call it."

Skookum Jim glanced at Tagish Charlie and saw that his brother was grinning. "We take some extra gold, have a little fun in Sitka?"

"Hauling supplies, that's hard work," Tagish Charlie agreed. "When we work for John Healy and Pierre Grayfish, they pay us. We need some good reason for crossing the Chilkoot again."

"Been there once already this year," Skookum Jim nodded.

"Plenty of gold for whatever you want." Charles Emerson grinned at them. Both of them were approaching fifty years of age, though they were as lithe and powerful as most men of half their years—and still quite taken with the idea of paying occasional visits to Sitka's whorehouses.

"We'll leave in the morning," Tagish Charlie said.

"New lady in Sitka. She's Russian, came up from California. Got a bunch of nice girls, too."

Skookum Jim lit one of Carmack's cigars and puffed on it. "White women ain't no different." He winked at Charles. "But they wear lots prettier clothes. All the same after they undress, though, at least the ones that ain't scared."

"With you two," Emerson laughed. "I wouldn't think there was anything left to be frightened of. I bet you both wore out years ago."

Skookum Jim wrinkled his brow and puffed determinedly on the cigar. "Charlie," he said, "this kid don't know nothin'. Still thinks women get children by rubbing noses."

"I defer to your wisdom, Big Jim. How long will it take you to get back up to Hootalinqua?"

"We walk that, hey, Charlie? Ten days, maybe less. Another five days to Dyea if we can keep the mules going. We'll be back here before the river freezes; you don't need to worry."

"Damned right," Tagish Charlie added, grabbing the cigar from his brother's hand and puffing away in a manner most authoritative.

Without question Sitka, once Nova Archangelisk, had looked much better the night before, for then it had been a place of exciting prospects and the lure of professional ladies. Now Tagish Charlie's head was pounding from the previous night's excesses, his mouth tasted like pine pitch and his ears were ringing. He didn't feel good at all.

An amazing thing happened.

Charlie stared, his mouth half open. A slender young woman with hair such a pale blond that she seemed to have come from another world swung her arm back and with astounding force slapped the pretty, doll-faced buxom redhead one, two, three, four times. The redhead lost her defiance, screeched and wept but offered no resistance. "Ow, please, mum, I won't do it again, I swear. It's 'alf his own bloody fault, anyhow, bandyin' about that great bag of gold as 'e was—"

"It's a certainty you won't do it again in my house, Janie Thoms," the other cut in, her voice as sharp-edged and as cold as a sheet of thin ice breaking. "You knew the rules when I took you in. There's no stealing from the clients here. Samuel, Boston Bob, will you be so kind as to see to it that Miss Thoms packs her belongings and is on the street within fifteen minutes?"

The one tall man was muscular, lean and dark, obviously part Indian; the other was massive and brown-haired with a fearsome beard. Minutes before they had politely but irresistibly restrained Charlie himself; he had entered like a thunderstorm, hell-bent on dismantling the Sitka Rose stick by stick following his discovery that he had been relieved of his pouch of nuggets during his night in the company of pretty Janie.

The previous evening was mostly a blur punctuated by a few bright spots from the time Charlie and Skookum Jim decided to follow the enthusiastic advice of their local Tlingit acquaintances. This was to try out Sitka's newest and by all accounts finest entertainment palace, the whorehouse they heard about but did not patronize when they were here three months earlier. Charlie remembered being astonished at the opulence of the big log building. Rose having somehow contrived to import red plush draperies to cover not only the one small window in the main bar and gaming room but half the wall from floor to ceiling as well. There was a chandelier with glass prisms, a huge plate-glass mirror adorning the length of the wall behind the bar and a baby grand piano.

He had also been pleasantly surprised at the girls, half a dozen of them, all much prettier and younger than the usual run of such ladies in frontier outposts. Charlie recalled losing a few nuggets at card games and very nearly getting into a fistfight with a brash young gold seeker on his way to Juneau. The disagreement was neatly averted by the commanding presence of Skookum Jim and by the intervention of the proprietress, her pleasant but adamantine manner defusing the opponents and greatly impressing both Charlie and Jim.

He remembered that the ladies had done a dance on the small stage at one end of the room, kicking their legs high in the air and turning around at the conclusion to flip up their skirts and revealing rounded posteriors in scanty bloomers. That spectacle caused a pleasant warmth to spread in his groin and soon led to his weaving up the stairs in the company of Janie, whose soft, full bosom was barely covered by her low-cut bodice and whose high-coifed hair glowed red as flame in his imagination. To his chagrin most of what happened after that was a blank in his memory, and he had a nagging suspicion that he had passed out on the bed before anything happened. When he awakened some time later, he did not even think to check for his pouch. He staggered out of town to camp, for neither he nor his brother relished the idea of sleeping inside a building in Sitka.

It was only when he awakened at dawn with the nagging sense that something was amiss that he realized his gold had been taken. He was too ashamed of his folly to call Skookum Jim, who was sleeping off his own excesses. Charlie slipped away back to town, his heart full of rage and the need for revenge. He vowed to murder not only the wily redhead but the smooth blond madam as well.

Once Tagish Charlie had been restrained from destroying the place and persuaded to speak his complaint coherently, the proprietress dragged the redhead from her room and forced her to return Charlie's property. Now she was in the process of firing her prettiest employee. Tagish Charlie was impressed despite himself.

Tamara Rosavi, locally known as the White Rose or Frisco Rose or simply Mme. Rose, ignored Janie's shrieks and protestations as the two musclemen carried out their orders. She turned her full attention to the outraged client before her, giving him a smile that warmed the pallor of her high-boned face. It reminded Charlie for all the world of the first rays of sun striking a snow field. It transformed the frosty skin and ice-blue eyes with pale gold lashes into something breathtaking.

"Please accept my apologies and my thanks, Mr. . . ?"

"Everybody calls me Tagish Charlie."

"Do you prefer that name?" She fixed her eyes on him as if it was very important.

"It works okay," he said gruffly, still miffed and hungover. "Long John Emerson, him an' McQuesten started calling me that when I was a boy, long time ago."

"Yes," Tamara Rosavi nodded, "I've heard those names. I half supposed they were legends. You and your brother brought in news of the gold strike, didn't you? Well then, I hope you'll have a drink on the house, Tagish Charlie. What would you like? And of course last night's entertainment is on the house as well."

She was smiling. She looked, Charlie thought, almost like a picture of an angel in one of Ludmila's books.

"Don't think I need any more drinks, ma'am," Charlie returned, shaking his head gently. "Just my gold back's sufficient, thanks."

"Now, Charlie," Tamara Rosavi said, putting her hand on his arm as he turned to leave, "I can't let you go without doing something for you. My reputation as a businesswoman is at stake. It's against my policy to let a client leave without being completely satisfied. Anything you want, Tagish Charlie. I'll go wake up any of the girls you might have a fancy for, have Rosita cook you breakfast, anything else. . . ."

Charlie grinned broadly as he considered the thread of suggestion the White Rose left dangling at the end of her offer, the inexpressibly delicate but sly smile that accompanied the words. In the early morning light slanting in through the frilly white undercurtains, her face scrubbed free of rouge and mascara, her hair combed out, pulled back and tied with a blue ribbon Mme. Rose looked more like a young girl than a madam. She spoke English with a trace of an accent, an intonation that reminded Charlie of Ludmila somehow made her language seem mysterious and elegant. She was Russian, all right, just as he had heard.

No question, she's a beauty, almost like one of those white angels Ludmila has in her picture books. Truth to tell, though, it makes a man a bit unsettled, all the whiteness, like someone who's come back out of Raven Man's tunnel.

"I thank you kindly for the offer, ma'am," he said, inclining his head politely. "Fact is, I ain't really up to anything much this morning."

"Ah," Tamara Rosavi nodded gravely. "You are—how do you put it?—over hung? Hung over? You must wait just one second. I have the best remedy for that. This was my papa's recipe, back in Mother Russia. He liked to celebrate, my papa. Sometimes he would celebrate from the time the grain was harvested until the time the ground thawed in the spring, so he had to have a good cure for the overhang."

As Tamara chattered good-naturedly, she busied herself behind the bar, whipping together eggs, what looked to be horseradish, a dash of salt and pepper and a generous dollop of vodka. When she was finished she handed the foamy mixture to Tagish Charlie, coming around the bar to sit at the table across from him.

He held his breath and swallowed the nostrum in one gagging gulp, mainly to avoid hurting the lady's feelings.

"A toast to your health. There, you feel better now, don't you?"

Charlie tried to assess the state of his ravaged body and decided that at the very least the liquor had numbed the worst of the symptoms, although it hadn't done much to help the grogginess.

By the time Skookum Jim came to the Sitka Rose to find his brother, Charlie had consumed two more glassfuls of Madame Rosavi's *hangover* cure and was in a considerably more optimistic frame of mind. Jim found the two of them conversing as if they were old friends. The beautiful Russian invited Jim to join them, arguing the nearly magical qualities of her home remedy, even inviting both brothers to stay and enjoy the hospitality of her establishment—free—that evening. But Jim had awakened in a foul mood, and finding his brother gone from camp only increased his annoyance.

"God's truth, Rosie," Charlie advised her as he prepared to leave, giving in to the insistent Skookum Jim, "you ought to bring your girls right now and head over to the Throndiuk—the Klondike. I tell you, come spring the word'll be out everywhere and the men'll be thick as fleas on an old busted-tooth wolf. They'll dig more nuggets than you ever seen; you could end up a rich woman without ever layin' hand to a shovel. There's more gold on the Hammerwater than anywhere else in the world."

"Damn, you got the big mouth, Charlie," Skookum Jim growled. "You're still drunk, don't know what you're talkin' about."

"Perhaps you should listen to your brother's advice," Frisco Rose said. She winked at Charlie, a tiny smile tilting up one corner of her mouth. "But it seems to me there were two men in here last night flashing nuggets. At any rate I thank you for the tip. I am here on business, so perhaps when the gold hunters start pouring through Sitka on their way to your fabulous river, maybe then you'll see my ladies and me with them."

"I tell you," Charlie insisted, "you better come now, get the jump on your competition. Maggie Laimee and her girls, they're already over there. You can stop off in Red Porcupine's village—he's our father, old as the rivers an' as tough as the two of us put together. We even got a real Russian princess there, *Kenyagienya Ludmila*. You talk a little like she does. You two'd probably get along like a pair of—"

Tamara Rosavi laughed. "You know some Russian. I almost believe you."

"Yeah, and you get those girls up there for the winter, Charlie, an' nobody'd see any more work out of you," Skookum Jim interrupted. "My brother an' me thank you for your hospitality, ma'am, but we got to be going now."

"Perhaps next year, not now. If you see us, Skookum Jim, it won't be until spring, along with the rest of the migratory flocks. For now I shear the sheep that graze here in Sitka."

Tamara tried to prevail upon the brothers to stay for one more evening and enjoy the hospitality of her establishment. She considered it good business to efface any negative impression that might linger and be passed on. Besides, she liked Charlie and felt certain she could bring his suspicious brother around as well, given a little time. But Skookum Jim was impatient to be off, and so she wished them continued luck in their prospecting.

As they were rising to leave, Rosita brought in a package of sandwiches Frisco Rose had asked her to make. Charlie took the food and nodded. "*Spaseebo*," he said, "thank you."

Tamara smiled, her eyes twinkling. "You are very

polite, very proper," she answered. "Good morning, gentlemen."

By the time the two Tagish Indians had departed, it was nearly midday, and rather than returning to catch the sleep she had been roused from too early, Tamara dressed in old clothes and helped the Mexican-Californian Indian serving woman to finish straightening up the barroom in preparation for the afternoon's opening. She had brought Rosita with her from San Francisco—a short, silent, unsmiling woman nearly as wide as she was tall, but with a heart full of fierce devotion to Tamara.

"And that's a street that goes both ways," she thought. She glanced with affection at the squat figure standing, it appeared, permanently in place behind the bar, polishing glasses and stacking them in glittering rows on the shelves in back.

Tamara remembered her first sight of that square, grim-mouthed face nearly six years before. It was shortly after she, Tamara, jumped ship in San Francisco and was raped, robbed and left semi-conscious in an alleyway by a gang of waterfront thugs. Rosita found her and took her to her own apartment, a tiny, dark place over an opium den. The room was plastered with cheap pictures of Christ and the saints as well as several crucifixes. Tamara came out of her stupor in the room full of icons. Rosita was bending over her to force hot chicken broth between her lips, murmuring gentle but incomprehensible words and phrases. It occurred to Tamara for a wild moment that she had died and that this was what angels looked like—squat and dark and worried, rather than tall, golden, winged.

At that time Rosita lived with one Leon Tiburcio, a hard-faced, brutal man, also of Mexican and Indian extraction, who beat her viciously and taunted her with her unattractiveness. He sold her sexual favors for liquor money and drank away what little she was able to earn by doing laundry and odd chores for the denizens of the city's slums. Rosita stayed with Leon, as she explained to Tamara when they had learned to communicate with one another, "Because he just keel me if I leave, and anyway, then I am all alone. Woman got to have somebody."

This fatalism Tamara Rosavi failed to understand, although she had seen it often enough among the peasant wives in her own village near Kursk, in European Russia.

When her own fortunes began to rise, Tamara solved the problem by simply buying Rosita from Tiburcio. She insured her purchase's security by suggesting that any attempts to coerce or terrorize Rosita, in fact any hint of his presence near her, would certainly result in serious damage to his person. This would be administered by Boston Bob, the large bearded man she had recently hired as a bodyguard. Boston Bob spoke the kind of language that Leon Tiburcio understood very well.

Besides her own mother and father, Tamara occasionally admitted to herself, Rosita Tiburcio was the only person she had ever loved in her life. Although Tamara Rosavi herself never dwelt upon the fact, the world had dealt her very few high cards.

She was the only child born to a peasant couple in the village of Katrinkov near the River Seym. Her family worked a small farm that year by year produced a smaller and smaller crop from the rocky soil, although the landlord's share remained the same. In order to make ends meet her mother had worked as a seamstress, her father as a cobbler during the winter months. Tamara had been given a needle and thread and taught to sew by the age of five. By the time she was six she was also out working in the fields in the summertime, hoeing and pulling weeds and helping to gather the cut grain at harvest time.

Even with all their combined efforts there had been evenings when supper was no more than a couple of turnips or a bowl of thin barley gruel. Once when she was very small, she asked for more and saw the look of pain on her mother's thin face as she explained that there was no more. After that Tamara decided that an empty belly was easier to bear than the hurt in her mother's face, and she never questioned or complained again.

The summer she was ten a terrible sickness swept through Katrinkov, and by autumn a third of the village's population was dead, thirty-two in all. Among them were both of Tamara Rosavi's parents. She was grudgingly taken in by her only remaining relatives, a cousin of her father with a wife and a half a dozen children to feed from his own poor farm.

The following summer, shortly before her eleventh birthday, Tamara's guardian persuaded his landlord to take the child into service at the big house in Kursk. This provided Tamara with her first glimpse of a manner of living she had never before imagined, a life of spacious rooms, beautiful furnishings, soft, refined speech and music, for the lady of the house owned and played a magnificent grand piano.

Tamara became something of a pet to the lady, and although she slept in a windowless cubbyhole beneath the back stairway and ate leftovers from the dining table, Mme. Kyrillic often contrived to have Tamara sew a comparatively easy task. In spare moments she also taught the daughter of peasants the unthinkable refinements of reading and writing and playing a few simple tunes on the piano.

For a time the child nearly worshipped the elegant Mme. Kyrillic. The lady of the manor was everything a poor child could imagine a true aristocrat to be—gentle speech, erect posture an aura of gentility as strong and sweet as her French perfume.

Tamara strove very hard to please her mistress, emulating her manner and learning her lessons very quickly, as well as doing her assigned tasks to the best of her ability. She worked so hard and so eagerly, in fact, that it became necessary for Mme, Kyrillic to delineate quite clearly the borderline between family and servants, however well treated.

"You are quite an adept student, my dear," she said one day over Tamara's lessons. "I only wish my own two girls were as conscientious. Ah, well, they had their friends and their parties, I suppose, and they both married well, so it doesn't really matter. For a person such as yourself, however, this is much more important. You are fortunate. With your skills you should have no trouble finding a place as a governess. You will be able to better your lot substantially."

Tamara lowered her eyes and said nothing, but the words stung like a blow across the face. She continued after that to pursue her lessons relentlessly, for her pragmatic soul already realized knowledge was always valuable, but she ceased to idolize Mme. Kryillic. She also resolved that no matter what, she would not live her life as a servant to the rich. No, she herself would finally possess the beautiful trappings of wealth.

Frisco Rose straightened the floral-patterned throw on the settle in the parlor, a small area partitioned off from the barroom and furnished with several pieces upholstered in red plush. The room had its own fireplace, and she laid kindling and logs ready to light later on.

There were men in Sitka, as in San Francisco, Mme. Rose had learned, who preferred the more intimate feeling of such a room. These were usually the ones who had ambitions to be recognized as of the local aristocracy, and she fully intended to accommodate this class.

Hers was the only whorehouse to boast a parlor. She had taken care to provide it with a number of small luxuries, including a magnificent bearskin rug, a silver candlestick, a small Venus de Milo in real marble and a large gilt-framed nude above the fireplace.

Tamara Rosavi smiled wryly to herself and walked back out into the barroom, where Rosita was polishing the big plate-glass mirror, stepping back from time to time and tilting her head as she squinted at the glass and then rubbed vigorously at some tiny smear she had discovered.

"Over there to your left, Rosita," Tamara teased. "I see something. You see it? Yes, that's what it is. Some mosquito has walked there with muddy feet."

"*Donde está?*" Rosita asked, immediately applying her cloth further to the left. "Where is that thing? Oh, you just joke me. Is important to keep nice things pretty, clean." She looked miffed and Tamara laughed at her affectionately.

Rosita adored the luxuries she lived among. Here in this frontier town, where such trappings were scarce, she took pride in her surroundings that would have been objectionable were it not so innocent.

Red plush drapes and gilt-framed nudes, even the big mirror behind the solid oak bar—Tamara had shipped it all from California at a cost many would consider a subtantial fortune. The result was a far cry from the discreet elegance of Mme. Kryillic's drawing room, but in a town like Stika it was the height of luxury. Moreover, the White Rose took a certain pleasure in knowing that she could buy and sell Mme. Kyrillic's whole estate without blinking. Since her standards of comparison had broadened, she recognized that the genteel landlord's holdings were not much except in contrast to the poverty of the peasants who worked the meager land.

Tamara poured herself a cup of coffee from the big pot that Rosita always kept on the cookstove in the kitchen, walked back out, and sat at a table in the barroom, sipping the black, strong brew and watching Rosita lovingly wax the shining surface of the baby grand.

"At least Mme. Kyrillic would appreciate the piano," she thought, smiling. "As for me, I am only a peasant. What I own is vulgar, but what I own I have earned."

Chapter 28
Enter Edouard de Vris

The mosquito is the acknowledged though unofficial bird of the North.

"Apparently no larger than the ordinary mosquito of lower latitudes, they are several times as venomous. One may hurl a blanket through a cloud of them, but ranks are closed up and the cloud is again intact before the blanket has hit the ground. They rise in vast clouds from the peculiar moss along the banks and creeks, and their rapaciousness knows no limits. They have been known to drive men to suicide, and the sting of a few dozen will make a man miserable for days. I have seen tough miners sit and cry."

The moss is sphagnum, muskeg. In many areas it covers the ground a foot or two in depth. In summer it thaws, providing a perfect breeding ground for the insects.

Below the sphagnum lies the permafrost, a thousand feet, perhaps two thousand feet deep in places. This the miners were required to penetrate if they wished to do more than pan the creeks for dust and nuggets, for the real gold of the Klondike rested on bedrock, some fifteen, thirty, even fifty feet down. Fire-setting melted out the frost, and the miners dug down toward hoped-for riches, cutting lateral drifts along the streak when bedrock had been reached. These shafts required no timbering, inasmuch as frozen earth supports itself quite nicely.

As the news spread and more and more claims were taken up along the Hammerwater, on creeks called Bonanza and Eldorado, the mining area came to resemble an ever-expanding zone of hot springs and fumaroles. Stands of spruce, hemlock, birch and cottonwood vanished into the fires in the holes.

At the confluence of the Hammerwater and the far greater Yukon, a town would spring up—first merely a camping area, then a village, then an actual city that would a year later have a population estimated at some twenty-five thousand. Joe Ladue and Art Harper, looking ahead, bought a hundred-and-seventy-eight-acre townsite from the Crown. Once the area was laid out in plats and quads and the gold of the Klondike began to accumulate in men's pouches and kegs and suitcases, the price of real estate rose to five thousand dollars a running foot along the main street of Dawson.

November 1896

The days were rapidly drawing shorter and rain had been falling, with few respites, for the past six weeks. The streets of Sitka were quagmires barely usable for horse- and mule-drawn carriages and wagons. Two major snows melted almost immediately, but Mount Edgecumbe, a sentinel above the busy little port city, already wore a deep mantle of white. The same was true of every hill over a thousand feet high on Baranov Island. Thus far, as the year drifted toward its close, the temperature had but rarely dropped below freezing, but with incessant wind and rain driving in from the Gulf of Alaska, the sensation of cold was nonetheless quite real.

Tamara Rosavi remembered the keen, dry cold of her native Russia, but even those extended periods of below-zero weather were somehow preferable to the bone-chilling damp of Sitka.

The waters of Sitka Sound had changed from blue to steel-grey. Whaling ships, American, Japanese, Russian, Brithish and French, made Sitka a regular port of call, as did countless fishing ships. The crewmen, though rowdy at times, made excellent clients, easily pleased after extended periods at sea.

Ships' captains, like the gentry of Sitka, required more elaborate service. Some liked to be bound and whipped, tormented at length before sexual release. One Frenchman, insistent on being manipulated and prodded by three women at once, suffered a fatal heart attack and was borne back to his freighter in an expensive coffin, polished cedar inlaid with ivory, to be buried at sea with full nautical honors.

Another preferred being tickled with a feather duster as he smoked his pipeful of opium and observed two women rolling on the bearskin rug, kissing and fondling one another and gradually removing each other's clothing. Yet another wished to sit naked on the toilet, masturbating while Tamara herself, dressed as a schoolmarm, read to him from *Ecclesiastes*.

The variety of men's sexual preferences, Tamara knew well enough, was virtually limitless and usually harmless. She attempted to provide whatever service was requested, drawing the line only at any practice that might injure or prove painful to a member of the house. If a man wished to abuse a woman he was obliged to seek his pleasure elsewhere.

Frisco Rose rang the ship's bell, a present from a doting sea captain, and within a few minutes the ladies began to drift into the main room from their bedrooms, still drowsy-eyed and disheveled, some in carelessly tied robes, others in nothing more than chemise or corset. Tamara couldn't help chuckling at them as they made their way individually to the kitchen, returning with hot coffee.

They looked, she thought always, like rumpled, disgruntled birds emerging from their nests to hail a rainy morning.

She greeted each in her turn: blonde, big-busted Jacqueline, brown-haired Susie with her frail waif look, Sadie, a real beauty with black hair and blue eyes. Sadie's determination to better her lot was clearly visible in the firm set of her jaw; Tamara silently applauded the ambition. Sadie was the only one of the group who had combed her hair and put on a neat robe before coming out of her room.

In addition to these, all of whom had chosen to travel with Tamara when she moved her operation from San Francisco, there were Rebecca and Maggie from the nearby Tlingit village. Rebecca had come to Tamara asking for a job in order to escape a marriage she detested; Maggie's own father had sold her while he could still be sure she was a virgin. Tamara offered Maggie, just fourteen years old, her freedom—but Maggie chose to stay.

As always, Frisco Rose gave a mild lecture about grooming. "What if one of our gentlemen should show up here early, break down the door and see you all looking this way? My reputation would be ruined and we would all starve to death, that is what would happen. I am here on business; you must remember that."

As always, they laughed at her. As they began to wake up, they started swapping funny stories about their "dates" of the previous evening.

Then someone began to pound at the rear door. "There, you see?" Mme. Rose exclaimed. "Rosita, please go tell our over zealous patron to be patient. Do you not hear the knocking? We will open in one hour, no sooner."

Rosita glanced at Tamara, nodded, stalked out to the kitchen. "You go away," they heard her say a moment later, shouting through the closed rear door. "One hour you wait, *por favor*."

"Rosita, you fat slug," came the voice from without, "let me in, damnit. This is Edouard de Vris."

* * *

De Vris was the reason Tamara had left San Francisco. A wealthy lawyer, he was given to elaborate schemes of all kinds. He had found her in an opium den, purchased her services and took her to his own rooms in a carriage and four. He gave her champagne and black Russian caviar, explained what he wanted as calmly as a man going through a cargo invoice, kissed her behind the ear and slipped a hundred-dollar bill into her hand. Then he led her to his bathroom, elaborately done in marble and gold-plated fixtures, and instructed her to bathe. He turned on the tap tested the temperature and set the big tub to filling. He poured in a quantity of perfumed green soap crystals and stood back, rubbing his hands together.

"Undress and get in. I'll watch for a time and then I'll join you in the tub. We have all night, and there will be no disturbances."

Confused and at that time only half-able to communicate in English, she turned to him and gestured awkwardly. De Vris grinned, shrugged and suddenly ripped off her blouse and undergarment.

Tamara covered herself with both hands and de Vris roared with laughter. Then he lifted her off her feet, bit her throat and set her down, skirts, laced boots, and all, in the bubble bath.

"I won't hurt you," he said in Russian. "I'll never do that; you may trust me. But I simply will not be argued with. If a man is willing to pay for what nature intended as a gift, the woman must be willing to oblige."

She was surprised at de Vris' Russian, but there were, she found out through the course of their relationship, quite a number of other surprises as well. His sexual eccentricities were not really among them, however, for she was by this time an adept. Her experience was sufficient that nothing surprised her about the male animal at all.

His power over other men surprised her. It was composed of cunning, of intellect and of manipulating situations to his own benefit. It amazed her that he was able again and again to emerge the winner in financial dealings that would have defeated anyone else.

The range of his acquaintances astounded her, for he knew, it seemed, half the members of the state legislature. He was involved in deals and swindles with many of them, having become a millionaire several times over through real estate dealings in the Los Angeles and San Diego areas.

His success in defending extremely questionable but wealthy clients was a legend in San Francisco, and earlier that year he argued a case before the Supreme Court of the United States and prevailed. Further, he assisted in gaining the establishment of Yosemite as a national park; he claimed to be a personal friend of Grover Cleveland, President of the United States; and he backed William McKinley in his successful bid for the nomination of the Republican Party on the grounds that the protectionist tariffs that were part of McKinley's scheme of things were desperately needed.

Tamara was also surprised to learn that much of the opium traffic in San Francisco, as well as up and down the coast, was controlled by de Vris as well. Further, he provided backing for several of San Francisco's more successful and elaborate bordellos and he owned a great deal of stock in railroads.

For a time she was his private whore, enjoying all the trappings of a mistress. On more than one occasion she even accompanied him to civic functions.

She gained his confidence as she learned to accommodate his highly irregular tastes in lovemaking, if, indeed, that was the proper word for it. De Vris was fond of giving gala parties for visiting businessmen and dignitaries. These functions were invariably staffed by the professional ladies from his establishments. Orgies were the order of the evening, and the activities of unsuspecting legislators, ambassadors and businessmen were recorded by means of hidden cameras placed at strategic spots behind false walls in the boudoirs. After a time Tamara was taken out of the parties so she could operate the cameras instead.

At other times she photographed de Vris himself as he romped in the nude with prostitutes costumed as angels, devils, animals and children, as well as with boys wearing elaborately coifed wigs, open-crotch panties and prosthetic breasts.

His sex sessions with her were often preceded by the two of them drinking, smoking opium and going through one album or another of de Vris' *galerie d'amour*. After that he was especially fond of being massaged with spicy oils of one sort or another, spanked as she talked dirty to him, and then sucked to climax. At other times he preferred direct entry into her rear door, as he called it, and occasionally he would wish her to strap on a painted rubber dildo, bind him hand and foot, gag him and plumb him in the rear, massaging his penis until he came.

He kept his word and tried never to hurt her more than she wished to be hurt. He would back away from any practice if she objected. At such times he would grin, wink and ask, "What then would my lady wish? Ah, we have missed the boat."

It was impossible to remain angry with him, but her own ambition told her that it was necessary to gain some power over him, to make herself independent of him—even if she did continue to be his consort. And so with information regarding his various business dealings and with a roll or two of film she had taken on the sly she was able at last to confront him.

"Blackmail, you Russian vixen," he chuckled. "I see you've learned to use what's inside that pretty head of yours. All you had to do was ask, Tamara the Rose. What is it you want? Your own bordello? It's yours."

Tamara nodded. At this moment the world lay before her, and she knew it. "Yes, Edouard. That is exactly what I want—that and a hundred thousand dollars in exchange for my photographs and of my vow of silence."

De Vris squinted at her and lit a cigar. "And how much next month?"

"Your friendship, Edouard, now and always."

"And I'm to believe you? Tammy, I would have given you anything you wanted. I understand. But blackmail? Perhaps it would be better for me simply to have you killed. I could do that easily enough, you know."

"Yes," she replied. "But would you ever again find anyone to please you the way I do? I don't think so. I love you, but I must look out for myself. What if something happened to you? Where would I be?"

De Vris puffed contemplatively at his cigar. "Yes, of course. Don't say you love me, though. Lying ill befits you. All right, then, it's a deal. You pick the place and I'll have my people set it up for you in any way you'd like. Go to Wells Fargo tomorrow afternoon—you'll find an account set up in your name. I won't have you murdered just yet."

"Thank you, Edouard," she purred, reaching down to press gently at his groin.

He smiled and nodded. "Will you whip me tonight, then?"

Tamara touched her tongue to her upper lip.

So it had begun and so it had gone. Within a short time she was Mme. Rose, the proprietress of one of the most succesful whorehouses in San Francisco. Edouard kept his word in all things, and Tamara Rosavi was a wealthy woman, a businesswoman who within a few months managed to double the hundred thousand de Vris had put in her account.

Her connection with the lawyer and ultimately her dependence upon him continued to bother her. Edouard was sexually obsessed—completely infatuated with her, crazy to be with her and crazy when he was with her. In his own way he was totally dependent upon her for the satisfaction of a variety of needs, both emotional and physical. But how long could it last? And when his compulsive ardor cooled, what then?

I won't have you murdered—just yet.

She seized her chance when de Vris decided to go east and work for McKinley's nomination. She saw him off on the train from Oakland and rode the ferry back to San Francisco deep in thought. De Vris would likely enough be gone until after the election some three months hence.

She didn't count on it, though. Wasting no time, she sold her establishment, cleaned out her accounts and ushered about half her ladies aboard a steamer for Sitka. Three weeks to the day after she put de Vris on the train San Francisco faded from her view and she felt free at last.

When de Vris returned to California it would be possible for him to track her down, of course, but she did not think he would do that. There would have been a span of months for his heat to cool. In all likelihood he would in the interval have found another young woman to his liking and brought her back to California with him.

Wrong again. Now he was here, in Sitka.

The one trump life had dealt to the little orphan girl was her extraordinary angelic beauty, but it wasn't until nearly three years after Mme. Kryillic took her in that she had any inkling of this gift. Certainly she had been aware of adults in the village cooïng over her, calling her little angel when she was very small, but she subsequently went through a gawky phase when the odd angles of rapidly growing limbs, clumsiness and extreme shyness served to override the perfection of her face, the delicate rose-alabaster complexion, the moonlight color of her hair.

By the summer Tamara turned fourteen all the elements of her physical attractiveness seemed to come together almost magically. She herself had no real idea what happened; she looked in her bit of cracked mirror and saw only Tamara Rosavi, with her hopeless background and her secret intense flame of determination.

But the Kyrillics noticed. The baron, who had until that time taken no more interest in the gawky servant than in the arrangement of furniture, suddenly became jocular, avuncular. He took obvious pleasure in Tamara's presence, although he tried nothing untoward. As for *madame la baronne*, the change was in the opposite direction: a tangible chill in her manner, sharpness in the orders she gave. She entirely lost interest in the lessons, and as her husband's fondness for Tamara became more apparent, madame came to treat her more and more like the servant she was.

Relations grew strained and Tamara began desperately to wish for a way out. She even approached Mme. Kyrillic with that lady's suggestion from earlier years, asking her if she had any friends to whom she might recommend Tamara as a governess.

"Really, my dear," the lady laughed, "such grand airs you have taken on. Knowing how to read and write a smattering of Russian and French does not make a governess. Perhaps Countess Marovna has need of a scrub maid. I will ask if you like."

And so Tamara stayed, simmering within. She had nearly reached the point of simply running away to the world outside, of which she had only the vaguest notion. In wild moments she considered murdering her mistress caught herself wondering if the lady would notice the taste of rat poison in her custard. However, Tamara's memory of earlier kindness and her gratitude for the gift of literacy prevented her from seriously considering truly desperate acts. Unfortunately, it seemed true that now Mme. Kyrillic had a fiendish obsession with making Tamara's life uncomfortable.

Into this atmosphere of tension came Prince Revennik, a high-ranking officer in His Majesty's Navy and owner of a fleet of ships that plied the profitable trade routes between Siberia, China, Japan and the west coast of North America. He was well over fifty years of age and his trade had made him a very wealthy man, richer by many times than his old friend the baron. From the moment he first saw the lovely blonde servant the prince made no attempt to hide the fact that he was smitten.

Tamara didn't really mind the attention. The prince wanted no one but her to serve him at table or run his errands. When he learned that she played the piano a little, he was not satisfied until he had made her play and sing for him each evening during his stay. His hostess graciously acceded to these demands, but the icy looks she cast at her servant made Tamara shudder at what she knew would follow Prince Revennik's departure.

The prince persisted, including Tamara in his conversation as if she were an equal. He was a cultured and witty gentleman, and Tamara was pleased to be included in these exchanges. He was a handsome man, although not in the way that appeals to fourteen-year-old girls. He was large and florid-faced and he wore great mutton-chop whiskers sprinkled with grey. But most of all he was kind, and he treated Tamara as if she were important, something her soul had hungered for, it seemed, forever.

She was not really surprised when he caught her in a hallway one afternoon and kissed her on the mouth, grasping urgently at her buttocks, pulling her against him. She backed away and said, "Stop that," but she didn't really mind much.

He released her immediately but stood smiling an odd little smile, as if they were conspirators. He reached out and fondled her small, perfectly formed breasts; this time she did not draw away, but felt a peculiar shivery sensation at his touch, a stirring of desire even though she did not find him particularly attractive.

His smile widened. "I want you very much."

"Then marry me."

"I'm afraid that's not possible, but I will give you anything else you want. You are lovely, Tamara. It would be a pleasure to me to give you beautiful things."

"Then will you take me with you?"

"You can't stay here, that's for sure. I've taken care of that quite neatly."

When Prince Revennik left the following day for his home in Moscow, Tamara and her few belongings in a small box rode on the carriage seat next to him. It was the first journey she had ever taken in her life, and she kept parting the curtains to stare out the little isinglass window, even though she couldn't see much for the dust and the imperfections in the semitransparent substance of the glazing. The prince, whose first name she discovered was Anton, took delight in her undisguised excitement, calling her "my little girl" and continually fondling her as the vehicle bounced and rattled over the rough roads.

He particularly enjoyed running his hands up under her skirt, exclaiming with joy when he discovered she wore nothing beneath her petticoat. At one point a short while after they left the Kyrillic's estate, he unfastened his trousers and attempted to have her by taking Tamara onto his lap, but the experiment was a failure because of the bumping of the carriage and the awkwardness of the seat.

Revennik gave up and had Tamara kneel in front of him, showing her how to caress him with her hands and her mouth until he shuddered and clutched her to him in orgasm. In a moment he passed her his handkerchief, but Tamara, upon finding herself with a mouthful, simply shrugged and swallowed it.

For her part she was much more interested in what was outside their conveyance than in Anton's caresses, but she understood from the outset the nature of the bargain, and she fully intended to keep up her side.

Sex was no great mystery to her, no more than it was to any peasant. There had been no privacy in the little hut she shared with her mother and father, and what she couldn't figure out from the muffled gasping and rustling of blankets in the dead of night, she could easily observe among the animals by daylight. She cheerfully cooperated with Anton's wishes.

Upon their arrival in the great city, though, she insisted upon rolling down the isinglass so that she could look out and marvel at the buildings, the hordes of people and conveyances in the streets. Prince Revennik's mansion was set back from the side street on a long, curved driveway, surrounded by a park containing several formal flower gardens in full summer bloom, and groves of great chestnuts and elms and maples. The house itself was like a grand ornate bauble in the center. Tamara felt as if they were driving into the heart of the fairy tale. She was afraid for a moment that she would waken to find she had been dreaming.

She found herself set up in a guest cottage on the grounds, small by comparison to the mansion, but to Tamara marvelously spacious and beautiful. For the first few months she was delighted with her new life, playing with her new quarters as if it were a doll house.

Prince Revennik was kind in every way and very generous. He provided her with servants of her own and insisted that she furnish the house in any way she pleased. She tried several experiments, picking out the most exquisite and expensive watered silk for her curtains, showing it to him beforehand for his approval. He merely smiled, nodded and kissed her on her hair as if she were truly his child. She picked out several pieces of Louis Quinze furniture and an antique Chinese jade horse with an astronomic price tag. Again Revennik smiled and shurgged. "Money is worth nothing but the pleasure it can bring."

At this point she stopped asking for approval and furnshed the house as it pleased her. She also bought a few very fine jewels to keep against the time when her fortunes would change. She knew Anton would grow tired of her in time or even perhaps die, although his health seemed excellent. Tamara already knew that only fools expected good luck or bad to last and that the wise ones did not worry about rain but carried umbrellas.

What was required of her in exchange for this new luxury was, she found, ridiculously small. The prince lived in the mansion with his wife, a pathetic invalid. Over the past few years the princess had lost her memory and by this time was unable to speak, feed herself or control her bodily functions. In the evenings after dinner and after he had spent some time visiting with the poor creature, reading or talking with her although she showed no sign that she understood a word, he would come over to Tamara's bungalow.

Anton Revennik particularly delighted in dressing Tamara up as a little girl with a white dress and a wide sash. She leaned to speak with a childish lisp that he loved, calling him Uncle Anton and contriving to bend over or sit sprawled in a chair in such a way that he could look up her dress as if by accident. When under some elaborate pretext he finally exposed himself, she would pipe, "Ooh, Uncle Anton, what is that great big thing?" The prince would shiver with delight and carry her to the bed. Sometimes he explained to her that she had been naughty and spanked her, and she would sob and promise to be good.

At other times, however, he would bring a buggy whip and horse collar for her to put about his neck and make her tie him in a kneeling position to the bedpost. He liked for her to wear only riding boots and cap and a leather belt for these sessions when she would whip him as he begged for mercy. The first time this particular fantasy was played, she stopped abruptly when she saw welts appearing, but he insisted she go on until his back and buttocks were criss crossed with red marks.

This last was the only thing he asked for her that she really disliked, but at least he didn't want it often. There were plenty of other fantasies. Sometimes he would pretend to be an animal, growling or whinnying and taking her from the rear; sometimes he wanted to watch her masturbate herself; sometimes he dressed her as a boy.

Tamara thought most of Anton's games silly and not very interesting, but she performed them with all her skill and invention. The prince continued to adore her, and she was fond of him. Occasionally he wanted to do nothing but talk.

She encouraged him to tell her about his business, how money could be used to make more money, how the trade routes worked, what it was like in the various countries he had visited. She carefully filed all this information away against the future. What use it would be she wasn't certain yet, although she was certain it would eventually come in handy.

Gradually, however, her situation began to wear on her. After a few months the novelty of luxurious living lost some of its glitter, and Tamara began to feel more and more that her situation here was as confining as her life in the peasant village or the Kyrillics' home had been. Here the surroundings were beautiful, the life easy and pampered, but she had almost no contact with the outside world. Her company mostly consisted of Anton Revennik and her servant. She came to feel that in the most benign possible way she was being held prisoner.

When Tamara learned the following year that the prince planned to make a journey on one of his trading vessels, she begged him to take her with him. At first he was reluctant, citing the dangers of the long voyage and assuring her that he had made ample provisions for her in his absence. But she persisted.

"What of dangers?" she snapped. "What if you don't come back to me, Anton? Would I wish to live then?"

She resorted to her little girl's voice to plead and her whipmaster's voice to order. At last, very deliberately and slowly, she took off her clothes. Revennik burst out laughing and agreed that she could go. Then he fell upon her, growling deep in his throat.

When she packed for the voyage she bundled all her jewels into a pouch. This she kept on her person or beneath her pillow during the months-long voyage. They steamed from Odessa on the Black Sea through the Sea of Marmara into the Aegean, across the Mediterranean, through the Suez Canal and the Red Sea and out onto the waters of the Indian Ocean.

They called at Bombay, Rangoon, Singapore, Hong Kong, then crossed the great Pacific Ocean to Guayaquil by way of Honolulu. Then it was north to Acapulco, to Mazatlán, to San Diego.

When the ship docked at San Francisco, Tamara secreted her jewels beneath her clothing and quietly left the vessel while Revennik was ashore. Her heart was pounding as she walked up the wet pier. A fine drizzle of rain was coming down, and as she stood for a moment, trying to decipher the jumble of strange and slightly menacing waterfront establishments, she whispered with real regret, "Thank you, dear Anton, for the world."

The next moment as she stepped into an alley rough hands grabbed her and covered her mouth. She felt a sharp pain, saw a burst of red inside her skull before everything went blank. The next thing she saw clearly was Rosita's kind, square face. Her umbrella, her reticule and her little pouch of jewels were gone.

She was obliged, then, to start this new life with nothing, as naked of possessions and defense as a newborn. Something in the realization made her laugh with genuine mirth, even a sense of joy. She had indeed entered a new world.

She opened the door herself and stood looking up at the grinning face that belonged to Edouard de Vris.

"Tammy the Rose," he said, "what's a nice girl like you doing in a place like this? You going to let me in or not? It's wet out here, *tres mouillé, ma petite chérie.*"

"Come in, Edouard. I'm surprised to see you, to say the least. Yes, come in by all means."

"Now it's the Sitka Rose, eh? Bill Hannigan wired me when you pulled up stakes and left the city—thought I'd want to know. I'd have come sooner, Tammy, but we had to get McKinley elected. How about some hot coffee for your benefactor?"

De Vris took off his slicker and hung it on the coatrack. He glanced around Tamara's establishment, nodded approval and said hello to the people he had known in San Francisco.

"Rosita," Tamara called, "coffee for two. We'll be in my boudoir."

"Brandy in mine," de Vris called as he followed Tamara to her suite at the rear of the building.

"Not a bad move, Tamara," he said. "The potential of this land is immense. "There'll be states up here eventually, probably two or three of them. When I found out where you'd gone, I started doing some homework. Timber, fishing, mining, maybe even agriculture in a few places. The potential's virtually endless, and the climate isn't even all that bad. Hell, it's colder than this in

Washington, D.C. right now. Not even any snow on the ground.''

''No shortage of rainfall, either,'' Tamara agreed.

De Vris laughed. ''It's not San Diego, I'll grant you that, but there's money to be made, lots of it. I'll bet you're doing a good business here, but there's more to life than running places of entertainment for gentlemen. You need to branch out, invest in a few things. It's just a rumor, but I've heard of an honest-to-God major gold strike along the Yukon River. Have you picked up anything about that?''

''The Klondike River,'' she nodded, ''yes. They talk of a rush when spring arrives, but I'm not convinced. We hear of new gold strikes every week or so, and usually they come to nothing.''

''And furs. The fur trade isn't dead, Tammy, just sleeping for a time. I'd guess the Alaskan interior will prove to be a treasure trove yet, and that's why I've already done some investing of my own—in the old Alaska Commercial Company.

''Met a man named McQuesten in San Francisco about ten years back. He'd come south to purchase a shipload of supplies for the company—a sourdough, I guess you'd call him, but quite right, shrewd as hell. He tried to talk me into investing, but I declined. Six months later word came in about the gold deposits along the Yukon—Fortymile River, as I recall—and I kicked myself. But I've been thinking about it ever since.''

''So your man is to be president?''

''Yes,'' de Vris said, winking at her. ''For a while I thought we'd made a mistake when he staring talking bimetalism, but he came around. McKinley has an astounding capacity to anticipate which way the wind's going to blow. Bryan stumped the nation and we kept McKinley at home. A little pressure here, a little there. Hell, New York City was talking about withdrawing from the Union, for

God's sake, if Bryan got elected. But now the people have spoken. McKinley carried California, I'm happy to say, and most of the East and Midwest. We'll have something over two hundred seventy votes when the Electoral College meets. The gold standard's safe and populism is dead."

"Your American politics makes no sense to me. Edouard, why have you followed me to Sitka?"

De Vris grinned. "My blond-haired Russian angel," he crooned. "I've had a stiff cock for months now, and there's only one woman in the world with sufficient skill to cure my malady."

Tamara Rosavi smiled and shook her head. "All right, then. I know just the thing for you."

She rose, walked to the big hand-carved dresser opposite her bed, opened a drawer and withdrew a riding crop and a set of menacles, held them up questioningly.

"I suppose I'd better have three or four drinks first," he laughed. "Will you send for a bottle of good vodka?"

"Of course, Edouard," she purred. "You drink and get yourself ready. I'll put on something a bit more appropriate."

Rosita brought the vodka and two glasses.

Tamara disappeared into her bathroom and de Vris quickly downed two shots of liquor. He breathed deeply, wiped his eyes and then unbuttoned his trousers, revealing an erect and swollen member.

He had another drink and then lay back on the bed, "You undress me," he called out.

Chapter 29
Ladies on the High Grease

The unofficial motto of the Russian-American Company and of its American successor, the Alaska Commercial Company, taken from the records of the two concerns, might have been phrased, "Get in, get it and get out." Indeed, the hegemony of the United States in Alaska was in many ways no improvement over the Russian example, for the land continued to be mined of its resources without regard for the future. The slaughter of fur seals continued on the Pribilofs until the extinction of the species was in sight.

Most of the outside believed the great land to be worthless, and the government in Washington was all too ready to dismiss the proper needs of "Seward's Icebox," the "Duchy of Walrussia."

But July of 1897 saw the steamer *Portland* dock in Seattle. On it was a band of miners bearing in excess of two tons of gold from a new town named Dawson at the mouth of the Klondike.

It was no longer a matter of rumor. The great rush to the north was under way immediately; more than sixty thousand men took passage on whatever vessels could be made to float.

Attempts were even made to reach the Klondike from the post of Edmonton in Canada and from Yakutat Bay across the gigantic Malaspina Glacier and the Saint Elias Range, with tragic results.

Forty thousand reached Dawson and discovered that the best of the claim sites had been taken in the immediate aftermath of Carmack's discovery. Dawson, rising from the mire, turned from town to city, but most of the men who had ventured north returned to the outside, while others, driven onward by gold fever, continued their search, bringing in new strikes in Fairbanks, in Nome and elsewhere.

The great land was explored, its huge dimensions and its astounding potential slowly perceived.

April–May 1897

Throughout the winter the rumors grew in the port town of Sitka. The stories got wider and wilder, like streams tumbling together to form an unstoppable river of words. Whether fable or truth Tamara Rosavi had no idea, but well before spring she heard too many tales of the richness of the tributaries of the Klondike. Gold was said to glitter from holes burned through permafrost to bedrock, to be so abundant that a few pans from a day's digging served to cover one miner's payroll of a hundred fifty dollars. She heard of a man paying for a sack of salt in the new town of Dawson with its weight in gold. There was talk of little else in the stores and bars and brothels of Sitka.

By spring many ships lay abandoned in the harbor, the sailors and fishermen having struck out for the mainland to cross the Chilkoot Trail even while the land lay locked in ice and the treacherous pass would certainly claim many of their lives. Stores, bars, stables, every sort of establishment soon came to be short handed; the bustling port by April was reduced nearly to a ghost town.

Also by April Frisco Rose had decided it was time to move her own operation. Edouard de Vris departed in

March to attend to some scheme of his in southern California, promising to return by midsummer, but Tamara did not trust him to remain gone for that long, and she felt it imperative to disappear before he returned.

In the confined world of Sitka throughout the winter his sexual obsessions seemed to grow stronger and more erratic. He took more and more of her time away from her business, and his fantasies grew more sadistic, even to the point of frightening Frisco Rose, the one for whom life held no surprises.

"Do you know," he whispered one night, the tone of his voice wistful in a way that chilled Tamara to the bone, "I have never killed anyone. That is the one thing I haven't done."

And then quick as a striking snake his hands were at her throat, thumbs pressing painfully against the larnyx. She was unable to speak, to move, watched horrified as his face twisted into a cheerful, even affectionate grin. "Tammy the Rose, my angelic whore. It would be so easy, wouldn't it?"

For a few seconds his hands remained locked about her neck, applying no more pressure but not loosening, a few seconds of eternity in which she listened to her own heart pounding in her ears. And then he let her go, laughed and gave her a playful swat as she rose shaking from the bed.

"Tammy, you bought it," he grinned. "Come, tie me to the bed, my sweet. Would I break my prettiest toy?" He smiled softly, stroked her hair. "Don't run off on me again, Frisco Rose. Promise now."

On a late April morning just two weeks after de Vris' departure Tamara Rosavi informed the girls that they were leaving. They would follow the steady and steadily growing stream of men heading over the Chilkoot Trail to the headwaters of the Yukon, thence down to the mouth of the

Klondike and the settlement of Dawson, named for George Mercer Dawson, head of the Canadian Geological Survey Office.

Stories had begun to reach Sitka that when the spring thaw set in and the miners began to work their gravel piles, frozen all winter, it was soon discovered that the deposits were even richer than the prospectors had dared to hope. They were so rich, the story went, that many miners were in a stupor, able only to run wildly from camp to camp, showing off their handful of nuggets.

Tamara was still not entirely convinced of the veracity of the rumors, but she was certain that it was a good time to leave Sitka. There were many arrangements to be made. She sought the advice of such trappers and Indian traders as had made the journey across the High Grease about provisioning, guides, packers and the like. She gathered and saw to the packing of supplies both for the trail and in order to set up an establishment in Dawson.

At the beginning she envisioned, a simple tent business. Her prized furnishings, she decided, would come by steamer up the Yukon, this operation to be overseen by Rosita. Rose would trust these possessions to no one else, and in addition she was uncertain how Rosita several years older and pounds heavier than the girls would bear up under the rigors of the difficult trail over the mountains.

Thus it was the first week in May when the entourage of the notorious Frisco Rose set out upon their journey, a day of soft rain interspersed with patches of blue sky. Tamara had had considerable difficulty in even finding a boat to take them up the Lynn Canal to their debarkation point, but she at last managed to make arrangements with a tight-mouthed fisherman who remained skeptical about the gold hysteria. The man felt it obligatory to express his disapproval of Satan's angels, as he called Mme. Rose and her company, before finally agreeing to ferry the party to the mainland for an astronomical fee.

They debarked at Dyea. The cove was so shallow at low tide that it was necessary to unload their supplies onto flat-bottomed barges for yet another fee. The Chilkoot ferryman, Boston Bob and Sam performed this chore while the fisherman and his son stood with arms folded and watched, the father puffing on a pipe, his face impassive, the son smirking openly.

Slender Susie with her soft brown hair and her wistful brown eyes cursed the pair in language that would put a sailor to shame and gave each a quick, vicious kick to the shins just before she darted over the side to the waiting barge. She was out of range and standing between Sam and Bob before her victims had time to react other than by grabbing at their injured legs. Tamara and the others, already on the flat-bottomed craft, laughed delightedly at the spectacle of the two men standing one-legged and clutching their shins as the impassive bargemen quickly poled through the shallows toward the littoral.

"You owe me for that, you cussed hoor," the fisherman shouted.

"Pay you when I see you in hell," Susie called back, "you pig-faced peckerless boy-humping old thief."

At this remark even the stone face of one of the Chilkoot barge tenders broke into a broad grin, and he gazed admiringly at Susie. She returned his stare with a broad, curving smile.

"Pretty good mouth on that one," the Chilkoot remarked to Sam. "Too bad she's so skinny, bones sticking out. How much you want for her?"

Dyea was nothing more than a scattering of Indian shacks and a surprisingly large population of prospective miners whose tents and piles of provisions littered the area around the cove. It was a ragged-looking regiment indeed preparing to scale the Chilkoot Pass and press on into the interior. John Healy and Old Pierre Grayfish, the two resident traders, nevertheless looked upon them with some degree of genuine pleasure. Never had business been so good; the single difficulty lay in obtaining sufficient supplies from Sitka to supply the gang of deserters, thieves, fortune hunters and other misfits.

When they debarked Tamara's party was immediately surrounded by a sizable number of rather menacing-looking Indians, all offering their services as packers over the trail that had been their private trade route until recently. Tamara selected a group of six, not troubling to barter with them over the prices they asked. She added a seventh when the Chilkoot bargeman, apparently quite smitten with Susie volunteered to go along, insisting that they needed his services because the others, even though every one of them was his cousin, would be sure to lead them over a precipice. He, Salmon-mouth Jack, was the only man who really knew the trail.

They camped there for the night and set out early the next day. The packers carried astoundingly large loads on their backs and strode easily up the slope for the first few miles. The day was grey, cold, drizzling. Despite their heavy men's clothing everyone was wet and miserable within the first hour.

"Ain't it about time to stop for lunch or somethin'?" Jacqueline complained. "I feel like we been goin' all day already, and I know I got blisters poppin' up like toadstools. Damn boots."

"Yeah, Rose, how about it?" Susie asked. "You know we ain't much used to workin' on our feet all day."

"Ah, my little mattress-backs," Tamara replied calmly, "take heart, lambs, the worst is yet to come."

"Easy part here," Rebecca agreed. "Bad part comes tomorrow. Then we go straight up to the clouds, so," and she made a vertical gesture with one hand, "back down, whiss!"

"I needed to hear that," Jacqueline muttered.

"Just fix your minds on gold," Rose counseled. "Gold is very heavy, but the thought of it will make your hearts light and the way easy. Just look at Lucinda. You don't hear her complaining."

"Lucinda ain't even human," Susie teased. "My guess is she's got invisible darkies carryin' her along on their shoulders, and she's drawing up plans for the old plantation. Isn't that so?"

Lucinda turned, smiled placidly back over her shoulder. "I am thinking nice thoughts about rich bachelors, honey, perhaps even a gentleman of cul-chah with a poke full of nuggets," she said in her soft Georgia drawl.

"One who just might be interested in buying you a mansion like your grandmama had back before the war," Susie added, mimicking Lucinda's accent.

"It's my heritage, darlin', and my destiny. What's yours?"

Several hours later they stopped for a midday meal at a spot just before the trail became steeper and more difficult as the canyon of the Dyea River drew together. They huddled beneath dripping fir trees and ate the bread, cheese and cold meat Rosita had packed for them. They did not linger in their miserable resting place despite their aching feet and exhaustion because it was equally unpleasant to sit still in the damp.

They had passed several great piles of gear along the trail. These caches were waiting for groups of gold-seekers, whom they also passed frequently, returning to pack another load a little further along the trail. This was the alternative to hiring native workers.

Most of the men seemed to be in high spirits despite their drudgery, already spending in their heads the vast fortunes they expected to amass. Without exception they were gallant, some awestruck by the group of professional ladies making the same difficult trek that they themselves were undertaking. All offered words of encouragement, and many whatever assistance they could render, although it was clear they had all they could handle with their own journey.

By midafternoon the cold drizzle had turned to wet snow and footing on the steep trail became more difficult. More than once various members of the party stumbled and fell to hands and knees, and Susie set up a steady stream of cursing.

Salmon-mouth Jack laughed and called back from his place ahead of them. "By God, I love the way that woman talks. She is like Kuschta, the otter. Her little teeth are clicking all the time. Susie Kuschta, I'm going to marry you so you can cuss at me the rest of my life."

"In a pig's ass, you goddamned savage," Susie yelled back. But she grinned as she said it, and Salmon-mouth's delighted guffaw echoed across the canyon and bounced back from the stony rims.

They reached Sheep Camp, an amphitheater at the base of the sharp ascent to the pass, shortly before sunset. Perhaps twenty prospectors had already set up their tents in the sparse wind-shelter afforded by rock outcroppings and the scraggly, stunted clumps of conifers that grew there.

The snow had slacked off and then stopped altogether, but the group hardly noticed in the continuing cold misery of their trek up-canyon. Now as the Chilkoots and the other two men put up the pair of large tents and chopped a few sticks of the scarce firewood that remained in the area, the clouds parted and a broad ray of light blazed in from the west like a beacon, illuminating the nearly vertical climb that lay ahead of them.

"Shitfire," Susie gasped, her eyes wide and fixed on the awesome boulder-strewn wall of the mountain. "I hope I'm wrong, but I don't see any way over this son of a bitch except straight up."

"Bad part next," Rebecca said, nodding. "My mother take me over to visit relatives one time when I was just little. I remember this."

"That does it," Susie said. "Tomorrow mornin' I'm headin' home, and I don't mean Sitka. I've had enough of this godforsaken hellhole, and that's the truth. Sorry, Rose, but I don't figure there's enough gold in all of Alaska and Canada together to justify this."

"Looks much scarier from here than it is," Rebecca put in by way of comfort.

Tamara put her arm around Susie's shoulders and squeezed. "We'll think about it tomorrow, *ma petite*." She was trying to sound more confident than she felt. "I know we can do it together. What, a little mountain? Pfui. Right now we need to think about a good fire and hot food, and then we'll sleep soundly and things will look much better in the morning. It's always better in the morning."

The men, with the help of a good quantity of gunpowder from Sam's pouch, managed to get a smoky, smoldering fire going. Lucinda took it upon herself to prepare a quick meal. She sizzled chunks of bacon in the bottom of a big pot and then added water and cornmeal to make a thick gruel. They all found this concoction wonderfully good after their hard day's labor.

"Maybe this is the one I marry instead," Salmon-mouth Jack said, grinning. "Or maybe both. This one to cook, that one to cuss, both to . . ."

He let the sentence trail off suggestively to guffaws from all the men. Susie glared and Lucinda looked icily indifferent. The rest of the women were too tired to respond at all. Several of the miners had drifted over to their fire, attracted by the novelty of the women. These were men who had spent the day or a portion of it resting before making the final ascent, and they tried hard to engage the ladies in conversation, but with little success.

As soon as they had finished their meal, the entire female contingent disappeared into their tent, where they slept with bedrolls overlapping, huddled together for warmth. Despite their best efforts they spent a wretchedly uncomfortable night. Much of the bedding was damp and the cold from the ground crept up through the blankets beneath them. They slept fitfully despite their exhaustion, waking when whatever side of the body was against the ground had become thoroughly chilled, turning and seeking a warmer position, sleeping until another portion was numbed and the process needed to be repeated.

They awoke in the morning to Salmon-mouth Jack's strident and infuriatingly cheerful calls, rising slowly with groans and curses, leaving the moderate cold of their bed to stumble out into the true cold of the grey morning. Tamara's body felt beaten all over with heavy bludgeons, but she made the effort to tidy herself, unpinning her hair and smoothing it before she repinned it, brushing as much dirt and mud off her clothing as she could before she stepped outside.

The sky was still overcast, although the clouds appeared not nearly so dark and heavy as they had been the previous day. The Indian guides chatted and laughed among themselves, but the rest of the group huddled in silent gloom around the small cooking fire, all looking as grey and lifeless as the weather. But the big coffeepot was beginning to steam at the edge of the flames, Tamara was happy to note, and Lucinda was stirring yet another pot of cornmeal mush.

"Well," Frisco Rose said with mock cheeriness, "good morning, sunbeams."

Six pairs of eyes turned balefully in her direction. Only Lucinda met Tamara's smile with an ironic grin. No one spoke above a vague mumble. When the mush and coffee were ready, they ate and drank mechanically. To break the oppressive silence Tamara addressed the Chilkoot, who had become the unofficial leader of the packing team. "Tell us what to expect of the trail ahead, Salmon-mouth Jack. It's quite disheartening to look at from here."

The broad-shouldered Indian shrugged, swallowed a mouthful of coffee. "Not too bad. Not half as bad as it looks. My grandfather, he talks Gossack. Used to kill Russians when they tried to come up this trail. Anyhow, not half as bad as it looks. It's only three, four miles from here to the top, and after that it's easy all the way down to Kuikpak River at Lake Bennett."

"Except them three or four miles appear to be straight up," grumbled Boston Bob.

"Not quite." Salmon-mouth Jack laughed. "The last mile's pretty steep, though, up through a chute in the rock. Most people make it through. I been over the top fifty, sixty times, so it can't be all that bad."

With considerable pushing and nagging from Mme. Rose the girls repacked their gear and set out immediately after breakfast. The sun had risen above the rim of mountains to the east and was visible as a faint silver disc through the overcast above the ice fields, a sight that heartened Tamara considerably.

But the path was steep and the footing complicated by several inches of slushy snow. As Salmon-mouth predicted, the last mile was by far the most difficult; the way up to the summit was a stony defile where unmelted ice still lay thick. In places they climbed steps cut into the slippery surface by Klondike venturers who had gone before them. These were so steep that one had to cling with the hands to the steps above, and often the body remained vertical in this operation. By what Tamara considered a bona-fide miracle they all made it without loss of life or equipment, although Lucinda slipped perhaps a third of the way up the icy chute and fell rolling and sliding a dozen yards before she came to a stop against a heap of snow-hung boulders, wrenching her ankle in the process.

Within the few moments that it took Tamara to climb down to the prostrate Lucinda the ankle began to swell, and Lucinda's face was white with pain. Tamara couldn't tell whether the joint was broken or merely badly sprained. She unlaced and gently pulled off the boot to find that the flesh was mottled with dark blue and purple and already nearly twice the size it should have been.

Boston Bob, upon hearing her cry, without a word laid down his own pack beside the trail and slid back down to her aid. At a nod from Tamara he took Lucinda upon his wide back, instructing her to wrap her arms and legs around him tightly, and carried her all the way to the summit, where he set her down and returned for his abandoned pack.

When he returned, struggling under his heavy load and fairly gasping for breath, the injured woman summoned a smile to her pain-drawn face. "Boston Bob, you're a true gentleman. It's God's own pity you aren't rich."

The big man touched a hand to his woolen cap as if to tip it, and the first grin that Tamara could ever recall seeing parted his brown bush of whiskers. "Who knows?" he said. "Maybe when we get down to Dawson, I can pick me up some of those nuggets that are supposed to be lying all over the place. I've got good eyes, by God."

With these words he shouldered his pack once more and moved ahead to where Sam, Salmon-mouth Jack and the other packers were resting. Tamara chuckled.

Lucinda, moving to settle herself and jarring her ankle again, gave a little cry of pain.

"Wish to hell I'd a thought of breaking my damn leg," Susie grumbled cheerfully. "It's gotta be easier than climbing this bastard."

* * *

It was midday by now, and Tamara and the others considered resting at the summit until the next day in order to give Lucinda's ankle a chance to mend. But a wind had come up and the sky once again threatened snow.

The guides assured Tamara that they would be able to make Bennett Lake by nightfall. There would be shelter and firewood and they would lay over for a few days at an old Tagish village while the men built boats for the water portion of their journey.

Rebecca and Maggie prepared a poultice, chewing into a mash some of the native medicinal herbs they always carried with them. This concoction was intended to bring down the swelling and alleviate pain; they wrapped the injured member tightly with bands of woolen cloth. Sam and Boston Bob rigged a blanket stretcher and carried Lucinda between them.

The party reached Bennett Lake shortly after sundown and made camp near the half-deserted Indian village. Salmon-mouth Jack hoped to find shelter in one of the abandoned kashims, but to his chagrin he found that every board and log, every scrap of cut lumber had been stripped away and used as firewood, apparently.

After a quick meal the exhausted band retired to their tents and slept in profound oblivion that even the cold couldn't affect.

By light of morning they discovered the actual fate of the wood from the buildings, for they were awakened by a resounding chorus of hammering, sawing and chopping. There were well over a hundred men camped along the shore of the lake, and all were engaged in boat-building. The prospective Klondikers attacked every straight tree within a mile of the shore, hewing away with axes, dragging the carcasses in and putting together a heterogenous collection of rafts, barges and buckets.

"Damn fools," Salmon-mouth muttered as he and the other Chilkoots set to work cutting slender saplings.

They camped at Bennet Lake for several days while the boats were under construction. As the miners discovered there were women in camp, they began to drift over to visit in twos and threes, finding excuses to rest from their labors, and in the evening a large group gathered near Frisco Rose's camp. One man produced a harmonica and several brought out bottles of rotgut whiskey they had stashed among their necessaries. Mme. Rose was persuaded to sing and all the women except Lucinda whirled into rough dances by one man after another.

One by one Tamara noticed that the whores were disappearing, slipping away from the light of the fire with their dance partners. Susie had been dancing provocatively close against a big man with several days' growth of blond beard on his face. When the two of them began to slip away from the crowd, Salmon-mouth Jack, who had taken several long pulls at one bottle or another, rose swiftly and advanced on the couple, lurching slightly but with a deadly expression.

Tamara saw the glint of a knife in his hand. *Sweet Jesus* she thought, *not a fight*.

She rose hastily, hoping to avert disaster, but by the time she made her way through the crowd, Salmon-mouth had already put his hand on the blond man's shoulder and was talking earnestly with him, gesturing with his knife. The man nodded, backed on and handed Susie over to Jack.

"Hell," he was saying as Tamara came within earshot. "I didn't know she was anybody's woman. Sorry there, partner."

Salmon-mouth Jack looked at the man for a long moment as if still debating whether to run his knife into him, and then shrugged and put the instrument away. Susie began cursing him roundly. He glanced at her, shook his head and picked her up. He threw her across his shoulder and walked away, Susie still shouting and pounding at him with her fists.

The watching miners broke into spontaneous cheers as he carried her out of the firelight.

Tamara hurried after them, thinking it was time to educate Salmon-mouth in the more civilized ways of dealing with white women, but she lost them among the trees when Susie's cursing stopped. A short time later from someplace close by she heard a giggle, a long pause, another giggle.

Tamara made her way back to the fire. She was shaking her head and smiling.

The boats that the Chilkoots made for them were of hide stretched over a sapling framework, the bidarkas the Russians had adapted to the Yukon trade many years earlier. They were much lighter and easier to handle than the clumsy rafts most of the miners preferred because they were easier to construct. When the craft were ready, the Chilkoots left for Dyea, with the exception of Salmon-mouth Jack, who explained that he thought he might go try his own luck in the diggings. As he said his piece, he smiled beatifically at Susie.

"I ain't your woman, no matter what you think, Jack," she muttered, glowering at him. "One little trip into the woods don't make me anybody's woman."

"Maybe that's true," he said. "Maybe you just dumbass woman and only know how to sell what's between your legs, I don't know. Maybe you don't know how to give it away because you like it too."

"You ignorant goddamned savage, what gives you the right to talk to me that way after—"

"Rose's other girls prettier anyway," Salmon-mouth grinned. "Okay, everybody. Bidarkas all ready to go.

Let's get everything aboard now. Long way down to the Klondike."

The sun was shining warmly as they set out with their little string of hide boats, three in all, each carrying three passengers and a quantity of equipment. The journey to the lower end of Bennett Lake went easily enough, forty miles of smooth water and then out onto the larger body of Tagish Lake, the Taku Arm, where they camped for the night.

The second day they reached the lower portion of the lake system, the point where the Yukon River poured out into a series of rapids. Here the river compressed into a narrow trench of rock and its current roared like thunder. They beached their craft above the awesome channel and discussed their alternatives. Tamara favored a portage past the trench, but Salmon-mouth Jack assured her that he had vast experience on this particular stretch of the Yukon and that he personally would ferry each boat through the danger.

A portage, Tamara could see, would add a full day to their travel time, so with considerable misgiving she agreed to Jack's proposal.

The first order of business was to instruct Boston Bob and Sam in the proper procedure: Just try to bounce off the rocks and keep her headed downstream. Then the first of the craft set off, hanging on the brink for an instant and then shooting down into the maw of the trench with terrifying speed. The women climbed up onto the rim of the canyon to try for a glimpse of the boat, but it had already vanished. They headed downstream, straining their eyes into the sunless depths of the rocky gorge, but they saw no sign of the men or the boat.

Half an hour later Jack, Bob and Sam came walking back up-canyon, wet and grinning, heading upstream for the second of the bidarkas.

Susie insisted on riding the next shoot of the rapids. Tamara tried to dissuade her, but Salmon-mouth Jack argued that it was as safe as sledding downhill and would provide the thrill of a lifetime. Tamara remained on the rim and watched this boat drop into the canyon and catapult past her and out of sight with the speed of a runaway locomotive.

When Salmon-mouth Jack returned for the third craft, he would have it no other way but that Tamara should ride with him. "Nothing to it," he boasted. "It ain't right that the lady in charge should walk. Best damned ride you ever had," he added with a wink.

Tamara couldn't help laughing. "All right, all right. I'm a fool, but you've convinced me. How much does the tour cost?"

"Just your life, that's all," Salmon-mouth Jack shrugged. "Come on now."

With heart pounding, kneeling on the hide bottom of the bidarka between Jack and Boston Bob, Tamara rode into the mouth of the trench. As the current caught them, they leaped forward with a bound that made her feel as if her vital organs had been left behind. The walls of rock sped past so quickly that details blurred. They rode straight as an arrow, the men just touching the water with their paddles to keep the vessel with the current.

Bone-chilling spray needled over the craft's sides, dousing her, but she could see ahead to where the canyon opened up again and the current slowed. She took a deep breath. Another minute or so and it would be over and they would be safe.

In the next instant the craft wrenched violently sideways across the current. The men frantically plied their paddles to right the bidarka. Time seemed to slow down and Tamara had plenty of opportunity to see what happened and to think quite clearly.

What she thought was, "I can't swim." Then the boat was tilting, ever so slowly, into the rushing current of the Yukon.

She was in the water. The icy shock of cold knocked the breath out of her and the immense weight and strength of the current pulled her down. Her head went below the surface. She tried to turn her face up, tried to force her nose up to the air. She kept her eyes open and could see the dazzling light of the sky through the skin of the water, but there was no way for her to reach that goal.

The current pulled and tumbled her downstream and the leaden weight of her wet clothing forced her farther and farther below, away from the moving, glittering brilliance that played upon the surface above her.

Tamara saw a dark form through the green haze of the water and realized it must be the capsized boat. She stretched her arms toward it and kicked, but she couldn't force her way across the short distance that separated her from this salvation. Her lungs ached with the need to draw breath and darkness began to form behind her eyes.

I am going to die. The words formed clearly in her mind and were followed by other words, entirely unexpected: *And I have never even loved a man.*

It seemed, somehow, to be the greatest unfairness of all.

Chapter 30
Charles Rostov Emerson

With the election of McKinley, even before the inauguration, prosperity returned rapidly to nearly all sectors of the American economy. This trend would continue with the increasing supply of gold, and business interests manipulated Congress toward the passage of protectionist tariffs.

The press, meanwhile, was busy enlisting public support for insurrection in Cuba, with consequent increases in circulation by the more successful papers.

Phoebe Hearst and Alice Birney founded The National Congress of Mothers, an organization that would eventually become the PTA.

In Carson City, Nevada, a different kind of struggle took place, with Ruby Bob Fitzsimmons defeating Gentleman Jim Corbett for the heavyweight championship via a knockout in the fourteenth round.

Simon Lake built the first really workable submarine, a cigar-shaped craft thirty-six feet long, driven by a gasoline engine. He called it the *Argonaut*.

The summer brought a shipment of three quarters of a million dollars in gold to San Francisco from the Klondike River basin. An eight-hundred-thousand-dollar shipment reached Seattle and the frenzy to venture north increased, carrying with it gamblers, speculators, lawyers, clergymen, actresses, prostitutes and an indeterminate number of damn fools.

In the Bering Sea, separated only by a narrow channel of fog-shrouded water the color of steel, two deserted and apparently worthless islands stared across at each other, Big Diomede and Little Diomede, the former Russian, the latter American. Islands don't stare—fishermen may, but those on neither island were much concerned with matters of which distant nation owned the barren ground they stood on.

America had a new president, and three years earlier Russia had enthroned a new czar, one Nicholas II, a well-intentioned but weak despot, a believer in autocratic principles but easily dominated by others. His wife Alexandra would bear him four daughters and a hemophiliac son. It was to find a cure for the czarevich that Grigori Efimovich Rasputin, a giant monk from Siberia, was brought to court.

Count Leo Tolstoi, dressing and laboring like a peasant, renounced his masterworks, having come to believe that evil derived from ambition, property and selfishness. All such barriers, he now held, must be brought down. Men were to follow the precepts of Christ and not resist violence.

May–June 1897

When spring came the gravel piles thawed out and Emerson and Carmack began to wash out their winter's diggings. It dawned on them then that what they possessed was not a small fortune, but one of almost unbelievable magnitude. For a time the shock of this realization virtually paralyzed the operation. After each shovelful of gravel and sand was cleansed in the rocker and the take of nuggets and fines collected, all were subject to prolonged periods of hysterical laughter or near-catatonic staring. After that it would be necessary to check on nearby claims to compare takes; the whole process at times delayed the next shovelful for several hours.

After a couple of weeks of gold fever Carmack and Kate settled down to the daily work required to collect their fortunes, but Charles Emerson and Kate's two brothers continued to act like children. Siwash George finally filled a large bag with gold for each of them and suggested that they go spread the news to Hootalinqua, after which he and Kate were able to operate with some degree of efficiency.

Thus Charles Rostov Emerson was in high spirits when he and his companions approached the village in late May. He was a twenty-nine-year-old man with a fortune in his saddlebags and the sun warm on his back. Wildflowers pushed up from the soft earth everywhere and the intoxicating odor of spring nearly overwhelmed him, so that he was forced to break into song from time to time.

The white man and the two Indians spontaneously broke into wild shrieks and whoops as they rode their mules into the village; they spurred their mounts into a short gallop that scattered the dogs and children who came running. Charles drew up his mule with a dramatic flourish in front of the one-room schoolhouse, for this was where he expected to find Ludmila teaching her afternoon lessons.

Instead when he flung open the door he saw to his bewilderment that the entire room had changed. Half a dozen cots had been set up around the walls, and on two of these very pretty Indian women sat sewing. They were dressed in expensive white woman's clothing; neither face was familiar. At the big table in the center of the room sat a tall, broad-chested Chilkoot and two more attractive young ladies, both of them white. Charles' younger brother John and the Carmacks' daughter Gracie were at the table as well. Everyone appeared to be engaged in a game of draw poker with buttons for counters.

"What in hell?" Charles began.

Tagish Charlie, pushing into the doorway behind him along with Skookum Jim, interrupted. "By God," Charlie laughed, "they come after all. Look at 'em, Jim. It's the hoors from the Sitka Rose, sure as I'm the richest son of a bitch on the Yukon."

"Whores from Sitka?" Charles asked, confused. "What the hell are they doing here? They planning to set up a cathouse in my mother's schoolroom?"

Skookum Jim shrugged and Tagish Charlie stepped toward the strangers, grinning an enthusiastic greeting. "Do you know that's my kid brother you're corrupting?" Charles demanded of the girls, suddenly becoming indignant. "And my niece? Does my mother know you're here?"

"Who the hell are you, sonny?" one of them asked; it was the slender one with big doe eyes. "If I knew that, I might admit to knowing your mother. You mean the princess? Sure, she's a nice lady. I ain't so sure about her son—her elder son, I mean."

She smiled and winked suggestively at young John, who beamed while Gracie glowered.

"Will somebody please explain what the hell's going on?" Charles Emerson boomed. "Johnny, I think you ought to go on home now, and Grace too."

"Don't worry, big brother, he ain't gonna get the clap from playin' cards," laughed the second white girl, a round-faced blonde with tendrils of curly hair falling over her ears. She had, Charles noted, a very prominent bosom. "His mama knows what he's up to. Listen," she added, rising and stretching out her arm to shake hands, "my name's Jacqueline, and this is Susie, and that's Rebecca and Maggie over there. And that's Salmon-mouth Jack—you gotta watch out for him if you want to make eyes at Susie. You're Charles Emerson, am I right?"

"Correct," Charles agreed, still confused.

"I remember you two," Jacqueline added as she smiled at Tagish Charlie and Skookum Jim. Pretty dimples appeared in her cheeks. "One of you got his nuggets aced by Catmeat Janie, but I don't remember your names."

Tagish Charlie stared innocently across the room, while Skookum Jim fixed him with a hard stare, for it was the first Jim had heard of the theft.

"Where's the White Rose?" Charlie asked to change the subject. "She's the one, young Charles. Too white for my taste, with all that blond hair an' everything, but you, Emerson, you're goin' to fall head over heels."

"Likely," Emerson grumbled.

"Well, that's mostly why we're here," Jacqueline explained. "She's over at the little castle or whatever you call it. Isn't that exciting?" she interrupted herself. "Imagine, a genuine princess way out here."

"Forge ahead, Jackie, for chrissake," Susie urged. "He knows that part of the story; he's her son. We had a little accident up at Miles Canyon," she continued, not waiting for Jacqueline to take the tale up again. "Our boat tipped over—one of our boats. We lost everything aboard, including Boston Bob. Almost lost Frisco Rose too. When Salmon-mouth here hauled her out, she wasn't even breathing."

"Salmon-mouth Jack saved her life," Rebecca put in, her voice soft and solemn.

"Yes," agreed Maggie. "Salmon-mouth Jack was a hero that day, but Susie still won't look at him. I think that's very sad."

"If Salmon-mouth was as good a river pilot as he claimed, Tamara would never have gone into the drink an' needed saving," Susie retorted. "Besides that, we still don't know if she's gonna make it."

"Damn all of you," Charles Emerson shouted. "I still don't have any idea what the hell's going on. I'm going over to talk to my parents. Long John and Ludmila still in their house? That hasn't been turned into a whore-house yet, I trust?"

"Very good people," Salmon-mouth Jack said, gesturing helplessly, his big hands like paddle blades, in an attempt to placate Charles.

"Mama's there," Johnny said. "Pa went down with Musi and Okime on the *Princess*. Going clear down to St. Mike, they said. How come you didn't meet 'em, Charles? Did you really find as much gold as everyone says?"

"Hang on to this sack, little brother. It's not for your card game."

Charles tossed a heavy leather bag of nuggets onto the table, grinned as his brother's mouth formed into a circle, and said casually, "There's more of that stuff in the Klondike placers than we know what to do with. But don't be giving away any free samples."

With that he turned and walked out of the schoolroom, most of his good humor restored. He was, after all, a young man with a fortune, and the odor of spring was like wine in the air. He laughed and tossed his beaver cap into the air.

Tamara Rosavi was walking along a path through broad green meadows. The earth of the path was reddish and every shadow on the damp soil, every pebble and insect stood out with wonderful precision. To either side and in broad washes throughout the meadow flowers bloomed, flowers of such jewellike beauty that she felt she would cry from looking at them. The world seemed alive with expectation.

This is what it is to feel young, she thought. *I have never felt young before.*

She came to a gate, a pretty thing of wrought iron painted white, and looked beyond. Inside the fence was a formal garden, and at a round table beneath an arbor covered with grapevines she recognized her mother and father, smiling and chatting with each other. The woman was dressed in a lovely flower-printed dress, the man in a light suit. They looked much happier and healthier and younger than Tamara had ever seen them.

She called out, her heart leaping with love and joy at the sight of them. "Mama, Papa, I thought you were dead. How did I think that? May I have some of the tea you're drinking? It smells delicious, but I can't open the gate."

They turned and saw her, but instead of appearing overjoyed, they looked concerned. Then her mother spoke, the voice gentle and sad and so exactly as Tamara remembered it that she wanted to weep again. "No, darling, you can't come in. Your room isn't ready yet. Be a good girl and go back for now."

Tamara awakened to a sharp familiar odor, a disagreeable smell that seemed to have plagued her forever. She tried to turn her head away from it, but it followed her. Eventually she opened her eyes and found the face she always seemed to find when she slipped out of her dreams for a few moments. She vaguely remembered calling the woman Mama at times, although she could see clearly now that there was no physical resemblance. This one was dark threaded with gray, while her own mother had been fair. This one had a beautiful, nearly unlined face, while her own mother was old before she was thirty. It must have been something in the tenderness with which her nurse spoke to her in her native tongue, the sweet concern apparent in the lines around the brown eyes, which somehow seemed filled with light. Tamara searched in her scattered fragments of memory for a name to put with the face.

"What can I do? You are awake again," Ludmila crooned in Russian as if she were speaking to a sick child. "That is good. Would you like a drink? You must drink this, my pretty one, for it will make you strong again. This was Short Day's best recipe for lung fevers, and I know it works. Here, one tiny sip."

Tamara held her breath and put her lips to the cup that the older woman held, drank briefly, fought to control the gagging response to the horrible taste. "Princess Ludmila," she whispered, the name coming to her suddenly from nowhere, "that is who you are, is it not?"

"*Da*," said the other, "*moyo eemya Ludmila*," a smile illuminating her features. "You are beginning to remember things now; that is very good. Now you must take one more little taste."

"I remember everything," Tamara insisted. "It is just that I have been dreaming a great deal."

"Yes, I know. One more sip and then you may sleep again."

Tamara sipped the bad-tasting liquid. "Spaseebo. Does this help?" she asked, trying to smile. "I remember the waters closing over my head and I died. It was very cold and I was sorry I had never loved a man. After that someone—perhaps it was the Indian, I don't know—someone made me breathe again, but the river was still in me and it wouldn't let me breathe very well. It kept me terribly cold for a long time. Then I was here, and now I am burning hot, and you make me drink this tea and won't let me take off even one cover—"

The long speech sent her into a fit of coughing and pain at the center of her chest seemed to squeeze her heart.

"Yes," Ludmila said calmly through the paroxysm, stroking Tamara's hair. When the spasm had passed, she added firmly, "You have been stalling. Now you must take a good big drink instead of a little sip, and then I will stop tormenting you."

Tamara Rosavi raised her head and drank, then lay back against the pillow. Her eyes closed and her awareness of her surroundings drifted into the soft blur of semiconsciousness.

* * *

"My God." A new masculine voice spoke softly. "Tagish Charlie was right. A white angel . . ."

Tamara opened her eyes and saw the tall man who stood at the doorway. His eyes were the same light-filled brown as Ludmila's. She smiled, a trace of her old humor resurfacing. "No," she said hoarsely, "not yet. They wouldn't let me in. Perhaps my reservation had been lost." Then she closed her eyes and fell immediately and deeply into oblivion once again.

At her son's voice Ludmila turned and uttered a soft laugh, for she had been given no warning of his coming. Not finding her downstairs, he had come up looking for her at the direction of two more strangers, a beautiful dark-haired blue-eyed woman with a southern drawl and a hard-muscled, slightly dangerous-looking and in Charles' estimation oily male. These, he assumed, were additional members of the notorious Mme. Rose's entourage, who had apparently taken full advantage of his mother's generous heart.

Ludmila pushed her son out the door and then fell upon him, hugging him and scolding him at the same time. "Charles, you demon, you make your mother grow old before her time. First you go off into the wilderness so that I waste away with worry, and then you creep up on me and give me such a turn. I'm getting on, you know. Do you wish to give me a heart attack?"

"You fraud." Charles playfully pulled the pins out of her hair so that her long braids fell over her shoulders. "You're fifty, you look twenty and you'll live to be a hundred."

"Hah," she returned. "I'm beginning to think I will never live to see my grandchildren. Well, come downstairs and I'll get you something to eat. Lucinda has made a beautiful cake. You look thin, darling."

"Lucinda—that the blue-eyed belle downstairs? Who's

the greasy fellow with her? Ma, do you know what you've gotten yourself into?"

Ludmila looked at him sharply. "They are my guests." She used the quiet voice that had always meant *end of discussion* and *proceed at your peril.*

Downstairs he sat at the kitchen table while Ludmila prepared tea in the silver samovar bequeathed her by her mother's mother. She chatted with him the while, catching him up on happenings in the village—a few births, a few deaths, a scandal over an important man's wife running off with a miner.

Musi and Okime, as he knew, were still operating the *Hootalinqua Princess.* They had set out on their first run of the spring a few days before, with Long John aboard as well as Taos Danny, who planned to open a trading post in the village to accommodate the growing stream of gold-seekers on their way down to the Klondike. Danny and Irena's son, who had been fascinated by the riverboat since he was barely able to walk, was serving as the Japanese couple's crew and understudy.

When the tea was ready and the spice cake had been sliced and set before Charles, Ludmila sat down across from him and asked him about his venture with the Carmacks on Bonanza Creek. When she heard about their astounding success, she laughed aloud and clapped her hands together delightedly.

"Ah, Charles," she cried, "now you will be able to travel, to study. You can go to a university."

"Probably not, Ma," he said absently. "I haven't really got used to the idea of being rich yet. Don't know what I'll do with it. How'd you like to take a trip back to the old country?"

"Nyet. I think it is too late for that. I have no one left in Rostov. My life is here with your father."

Charles reached across the table, took Ludmila's hand and kissed it. Nonetheless his mind wasn't really on the conversation and had not been since it began. The vision of the woman upstairs, so beautiful she seemed unreal, with her pale gold hair spread across the pillow and her white cheeks flushed with fever, had registered on him with a power that he had not imagined possible. Despite his attempts to dismiss the image, to distract himself with his mother's conversation, he found that he was only half listening.

"Is she going to die or what, Mama?" he blurted suddenly.

"I don't know," Ludmila replied. So her son was stricken at last! "I do what I can and I pray for her. She is very strong, even though she looks as if she's made of moonbeams and fairy dust."

The princess took a sip of tea and patted her son's hand. "You're taken with her, aren't you, my dear?" Ludmila continued. "I don't blame you; she is lovely. But perhaps you need to understand a little bit about her."

Her words were hesitant, a little shy in discussing this matter with her son.

Charles laughed. "Mother, there's hardly anyone from Juneau to Dawson to St. Mike who hasn't heard by now of Tamara Rosavi, the notorious Mme. Rose, late of Sitka via San Francisco, apparently now headed out to mine the gold fields, or rather the miners. Tagish Charlie's been talking about little else all winter. I'm not the type to fall for a professional lady, so don't fret."

His words, however, displayed considerably more confidence than he felt.

"Ah," Ludmila nodded. "Then next I would tell you not to judge so hastily. Tamara has said many things in her fever, and I would not repeat many of them, but I can tell you that she has not had an easy life, Charles. Her soul is good, despite what she has had to do."

Charles smiled, rose from the table and went around to stand behind his mother. He stooped and kissed the top of her head. "At least I know you have a good soul, my shrimp, despite all the evil things you haven't done. I had better go over to the schoolhouse and see what the gang over there is teaching Gracie and the kid."

Despite his brave words to Ludmila, Charles Emerson found himself unable to shake or ameliorate what amounted to an obsession with the exquisite creature lying so desperately ill in the guest bedroom.

"Temporary insanity," he told himself. "They say it happens to all men sooner or later. Been lucky to put it off so long. Once she wakes up and starts talking, it'll all disappear."

It was more than Tamara Rosavi's remarkable beauty that consumed him. It was the momentary spark of humor, of tenacity and vitality, that shone out when she roused herself to joke about dying. The bravery in the lopsided, ironic smile, her beauty and her painful weakness all together made him for the first few days want nothing more than to hold her, to help her battle against death.

He was terrified that she would die. He found himself slipping up to her room several times a day. Sometimes he was afraid to open the door for fear he would find her dead, but in the end he was always unable to resist the compulsion to turn the knob, to stand in the crack, not breathing until he was sure she still breathed.

When she began to recover and was awake for several hours each day, Charles would find time to read to her or to bring her soup, taking an enormous and unexpected joy in watching her eat. He found that contrary to his expectations she was a charming talker, apparently educated and with a whimsical and sometimes ironic wit that was razor-sharp but somehow without a trace of bitterness.

When it became apparent that she was almost fully recovered, Charles found that his emotional state was so tangled that he really felt he might go mad. That she was well and gaining strength, that she would live, produced a heady euphoria, a sense of lightness, as of a terrible burden having been lifted. At times he would catch himself nearly bounding rather than walking, out of sheer joy.

At the same time he knew that in a short while she would leave to continue her interrupted journey, and when he thought of this, he felt as if a lump of lead were lodged in the center of his chest. Now that she was part of life rather than on the edge of death, he began to be tormented by thoughts of the many lovers she had had. He was unable to stop envisioning her with one man or another in various attitudes of depravity, for Mme. Rose had the reputation of indulging almost any whim for a client.

Tamara had long since invaded his dreams, and now those dreams became more and more sensual. In several of them he murdered faceless men whom he found using his beloved's body. In others he and she were together and the sensations were intoxicating, overwhelming.

It was impossible for him to hide his condition from those close to him, and Tagish Charlie and Skookum Jim ribbed him mercilessly. Ludmila, on the other hand, tried to approach the matter delicately, warning him of the dangers of falling in love with Tamara even as she defended her patient from criticism.

At last on a day when Mme. Rose and her entourage were obviously preparing to go, Charles decided in sheer desperation to approach the matter forthrightly. He found Tamara alone in her room, packing. Her back was turned to him. She wore a simple dark blue dress and her shining hair was tied back with a ribbon so that it hung below her shoulder blades.

"Tamara," he said, his voice cracking like a schoolboy's.

She turned to look directly into his eyes, as was her habit. He noticed again the darker band of color that circled the pale blue of the iris, noticed the light catching in the golden lashes. He swallowed, suddenly furious with himself.

"Damnit, Tamara, I love you and I don't want you to leave," he nearly shouted.

She didn't answer immediately, but stood staring at him. Her eyes got very wide and lines appeared in her forehead as if his words had given her real pain.

"I know that," she said slowly. "Charles . . . I don't think that it's a very good idea—"

"It's not a fucking idea," he growled, pushing past the lump in his throat. "I said I love you."

"I'm sorry," she replied, reaching out and taking his hands. "I didn't mean . . . Maybe I love you too. I'm not sure what it feels like. But there's nothing to be done about it."

"Of course there is. Tamara Rosavi, I'm asking you to marry me." She nodded. "That's the part that's not a good idea."

"I know what you're thinking," he said in a rush. "I don't care about the other men. Tammy, I'm a rich man. I—"

"No," she interrupted, "don't tell me that. If I married you, it wouldn't be for money. I've never done that. Charles, there are men who marry prostitutes, but you aren't that kind."

"I said I didn't care. I would never mention your past. It doesn't matter." He felt as though he were arguing for his life.

"You are willing to forgive me for having many lovers," she retorted, a certain harshness coming into her voice. "Has it occurred to you that I may not feel the need to be forgiven?"

He stared at her, at a loss for words. He felt devastated, as if he had fired his ultimate shot and still failed.

Tamara's face softened and she reached up to stroke

his cheek, moving closer after a moment and pressing herself against him, pulling his head down and kissing him on the mouth. Her lips were exquisitely soft, pliant, warm against his. He groaned and pulled her into the circle of his arms, running his hands along the length of her body.

She thrust the tip of her tongue between his lips. His body responded with furious urgency and he turned to push the door shut with his foot, trying at the same time to guide her toward the bed.

She pulled away, and he noticed that her cheeks were flushed. She too seemed out of breath. "Let's go for a walk," she whispered. "Somewhere we can be alone. Not here, not in Ludmila's home. . . ."

They slipped out of the house quietly by separate doors, arranging to meet downstream on the river. By the time they had found each other they were comfortable again, laughing together like conspirators. Charles showed her the blanket he had managed to bring as though it were a great trophy.

He led her to a spot hidden in a willow thicket a mile downriver from Hootalinqua, a place where no one from the village would have any reason to be. They spread their blanket in the dappled light and shade, the June sunshine warm on their skin.

She undressed for him, slowly, looking full into his eyes and smiling as she removed each garment. At last she stood before him unashamed, slim and lithe and white as ivory. She lay down, still smiling, and opened her arms to him. He felt as if he couldn't breathe, as if he had never made love to a woman before.

When Charles didn't move, Tamara reached over and began to unlace his clothing, laughing delightedly at his erection and bending forward to kiss it before she finished undressing him.

He moved onto her, fastened his lips to hers again,

savoring the delicious merging of mouths, holding back his own urgency until he felt her moving her hips against him, a soft moan in her throat. He entered her and immediately his hips tightened. He could not hold back his orgasm.

"Damn," he muttered when he could breathe again.

Tamara laughed aloud. "That's one," she said.

After they had rested in each other's arms for a time, she began slowly to tease him with her hands, her lips, the whole length of her body. They explored each other slowly, lingeringly, kissing and touching every wonderful secret place. At last they joined, she on top this time, riding him while he tangled his hands in her long hair, pulling her throat into a beautiful white arc. He held back this time until she shivered and gasped and fell forward against his chest, and then he rolled her over and thrust hard, letting the ancient rhythm take him to the point of ecstasy and beyond into happy oblivion, holding her still against him and drifting into a blank, warm sleep.

When they awoke the sun was low and they were both covered with mosquito bites. They dressed quickly, laughing despite the agony of the bites and slapping wildly here and there.

Tamara hurried back to the mansion, but Charles for the sake of discretion decided to spend the night at the lodge of his old friend Red Porcupine. He proceeded to get very drunk with his Tagish companions, not telling them what had happened but unable to prevent their guessing at the source of his happiness. He was certain now that Tamara, who had been as moved by their lovemaking as he, was his no matter what she had said earlier, and that it would only be a matter of time and some patience until she agreed to marry him.

When he awoke again it was late. The sun of the long June day was far up in the sky and Red Porcupine's lodge was deserted. Charles dressed hurriedly, feeling hung over but happy and eager to see Tamara again. He walked quickly to his parents' house. He kissed Ludmila a cheerful "good morning" and then headed for the stairs.

"Son—" Ludmila called. He stopped short. Something in his mother's voice had caught him like a sliver of ice thrust into his chest. "She's gone," Ludmila said quietly when he turned.

He stared at her, certain he had misunderstood.

"They all left early this morning," she explained. "Tamara asked me to say good-bye."

He did not say anything, could think of not one word that made sense.

"Charles," Ludmila began. She finished helplessly, "I'm sorry, my darling."

He nodded at last, turned and walked up the stairs. He opened the door of her room as if to assure himself that it was indeed true.

The room was neat. The blue coverlet matched the curtains, which were pulled back so that the sunlight streamed onto the carpet. A handful of daffodils stood in a red vase on the little table. It was a pretty room, orderly and inviting—and utterly, unspeakably empty.

Charles returned downstairs. The front door stood open and Ludmila was nowhere in sight. He strode across the big room, saw a number of villagers hurrying toward the river landing, Ludmila and John Daniel among them.

The distinctive note of the steam whistle on the *Hootalinqua Princess* sounded from downriver, though the old stern-wheeler was not as yet visible.

Long John, Musi, Okime and Taos Danny Vasquez' son were back from St. Mike.

Chapter 31
Charles and Tamara

Out of the mudflats just below the point where the waters of the Klondike merge with those of the silt-laden Yukon a city laid out by Joe Ladue and Art Harper was growing like some strange organism with a definite energy and will of its own. Its *raison d'être* was gold.

Nearly twenty-four hours of sunlight at midsummer, high temperatures and abundant rainfall produced heavy vegetative growth during an intense though abbreviated season. Ditches became gardens of wildflowers and wild raspberries flowered and ripened quickly. Two varieties of cranberries thrived on the hills. Even domestic gardens flourished, with cabbages and root vegetables attaining phenomenal size.

Within a year the city would reach thirty thousand and more, with dance halls, saloons, hotels, a theater and various brothels and mercantiles. For her brief moment, Dawson would be the queen of the north.

There was no easy way to the gold fields, and yet the fortune seekers would continue to come, crossing over the Chilkoot Pass or nearby White Pass even during the frozen winter of '97–'98. Pack horses would founder in the drifts, stumble, break legs, fall of exhaustion. Three thousand died on the Skagway Trail and those who came after stumbled ahead over the frozen bodies of the dead.

By the summer of '97 the rush was already well under way, and craft after craft came shooting down through Whitehorse Rapids and Miles Canyon. Even a water spaniel managed to shoot the rapids successfully, and any number of kegs of whiskey on their way to the saloons of Dawson did likewise.

It was four hundred sixty miles from Whitehorse to Dawson. White canvas tents were pitched endlessly down the course of the Yukon. By midsummer Miles Canyon was almost a city in itself, though its population was transient. The miners were just passing through and in a hell of a hurry.

They beached boats and pitched tents. "How far is it to Dawson?"

"This is Dawson," an emergent city of Yankees in the Canadian Yukon, where bars and whorehouses were closed on Sundays in accord with Canadian blue laws enforced by the Royal Canadian Mounted Police.

Joe Ladue got rich with his sawmill and his sales of Dawson lots, but Art Harper had left—gone to Arizona, so the story went, to cure himself of tuberculosis.

August–September 1897

Tamara Rosavi, Frisco Rose, White Angel—she was gone to the boom town of Dawson to ply her trade. Charles Rostov Emerson was, he supposed, the most miserable man on earth. What was it worth, after all, for a man to be in the prime of life and already wealthy and yet to be lonely as hell? He lived with an interminable ache in his guts, a sense of heaviness day after day, desperate and hopeless yearning for a woman he knew was not to be his.

What was it he wanted?

I want her. I want her for my wife, no matter what Pa says, no matter what anyone says. What difference does it make if she's bedded down with a thousand men? That was a business matter. It wasn't that way with us, and maybe sex doesn't even have very much to do with it. She's gone and I'm as empty as a hole in the muck. I'm strong, but I'm not strong enough to deal with this. What the hell's love, anyway? A kind of lingering misery, a damned pain that won't go away . . .

"It wouldn't have worked. No way," Long John said. "Charles, my lad, you've got to have better judgment in these matters. Sure, I know she's pretty as any damned picture, but so what? It just ain't in 'er to love a man. I got nothin' against 'er, you understand, but she's all surface an' fluff. Some women just don't fall in love, not like the rest of us pore human critters. It's like they don't have the same needs, so to speak. An' that's why they're able to make their livin' the way they do."

Charles resented his father's words even though he knew that Long John was in all probability quite correct.

"To hell with that. Whatever she feels or doesn't feel, Pa, I know how I feel, and—"

"Charles, you'd break Ludmila's heart if you went after that one. An' it'd come to no good besides. Whatever happened with you two, take it for what it was. Your life's all out there ahead of you, son. Buck up, It's just a matter of time."

"How old were you when—"

"I fell ass over teakettle in love with your ma? About your age, truth to tell."

"And she was engaged to someone else at the time."

"There was two, three problems," Long John grinned, stroking his beard. "In Russia they kind of arrange things for the young ladies, an' it took me an' Ludmila a while to straighten matters out."

"You kidnapped her, in fact. Isn't that true?"

"Not exactly, but a gang of us did have to make tracks out of Sitka with the King of Alaska hot on our heels."

"What happened . . . to *him*?"

Long John glanced back toward the mansion and shrugged. "Pieter Dobshansky, that was his name. Had a leetle accident, you might say, up on the Chilkoot Pass. Anyhow, the problem got solved."

No amount of talk and no amount of other activity did any good. Charles took John Daniel and some of the other boys of the village, and Gracie as well, on a week-long hunting venture eastward, up into the Big Salmon Range, but not even this did any real good.

When they returned to Hootalinqua, now bristling with white canvas tents strung up by prospective miners on their way down to the Klondike, the sense of heaviness and futility descended on him even more intensely than before.

Nothing seemed to have any value. He spent a great deal of time brooding. He was unable to drive the image of the exquisite Tamara Rosavi from his mind. She inhabited his dreams and during his waking hours he was filled with leaden despair.

"Get back to work, any kind of work," Taos Danny told him. "Charles, it ain't fittin' for you to wander about like a chicken with its damned head cut off. Musi's got a bunch of repair work to do on the *Princess*. Why not give 'im a hand? *Trabajo*, my friend, *trabajo*. Work's the only thing what keeps coons like us from goin' stark ravin' crazy."

Charles considered Danny's advice and at length decided to return to the gold mine on Bonanza Creek. Skookum Jim and Tagish Charlie had already gone back downriver to rejoin the Carmacks. All were by this time no doubt happily engaged in burning out their placers to melt the permafrost and winching the sand and gravel to the surface to sluice it with water from the creek. His own claim was as rich as any of theirs, and though he did not feel an immediate need to produce additional gold, still it was something to do.

The fact that Tamara would be within a few miles of his claim, he concluded, had nothing to do with his decision to return to the gold fields.

Close by, but she might as well be a million miles away. She's not thinking about me. No, she's running a business, and the last thing she'd want is to fall in love. What, after all, could I do to lure her away from what she's doing? Nothing, nothing, nothing . . .

Suddenly he realized he was feeling better. Hope, a crazy, foolish hope had begun to flower in the back of his skull somewhere. With one mule to ride and two for pack animals he set out down the Yukon on the way back to Bonanza Creek.

He didn't mention Tamara to Skookum Jim or Tagish Charlie and he did his best not to think about her at all. Instead he labored on his claim, burning and digging and sluicing and accumulating a considerable pile of nuggets and fines. Sleep hardly seemed important at all, and when he was not at work in the hole, he began to construct a separate log cabin on his own claim. He drove himself like a man possessed, and within a month he had secured a second small fortune and had completed a sound, weather-tight cabin as well.

Once finished the cabin seemed decidedly empty. It was time for a little relaxation, he decided. With a full poke he talked Skookum Jim into accompanying him to Dawson.

"By God," Jim said, "you won't recognize the place, Charles. It's already bigger than Sitka. New buildings going up all over, and poor old Harper ain't even there to see it. He's on his way to San Francisco, that's what I heard. The lung disease is working on him. That's the truth. Sure, I'm ready. Let George and Charlie keep digging. I've got all the gold I need for now."

* * *

Charles Emerson was indeed dumbfounded at what had happened to the little settlement. He remembered tents and a few log buildings at the forks of the Yukon and the Klondike, and the beginnings of a city were now in the works. A number of streets had been laid out, dividing the area up into rectangles, and the place was virtually humming. Axes rang and hammers rapped like so many woodpeckers; foremen shouted and dray animals brayed. The smell of money underlaid it all.

Skookum Jim winked, shrugged, grinned, as pleased as a child with what was going on. "You got things to do." He winked. "Me too. McQuesten's back now, and he owes me a drink, by God. I'll be at Bill McPhee's saloon when you're ready to head back to the claims."

With these words he clapped his heels to the mule's sides, let out a yip-yip and sent his mount forward down the half-cleared roadway past a group of men working with a transit, a plumb bob and a measuring chain.

Charles urged his own mule ahead, recognized one of Ladue's men and halted.

"Mike Turner," he grinned, "what are you boys doing?"

"Top o' the mornin' to you, Charles me lad," Turner responded. "Why, we're layin' out a new San Francisco, that's what. Done named one street in honor o' your own ma, by heavens. Princess Street. You'll come to 'er about a mile up the line. Welcome to Fifth Avenue, lad."

"Fifth Avenue? Sounds almost civilized."

"It is, too. Hey, Bill, here's a gent you should meet—Charles Emerson, son o' Long John an' the princess."

The head surveyor walked over and Turner introduced the two men. Charles dismounted and shook hands.

"Bill Ogilvie. I'm layin' out a metropolis for Ladue and his partner. Just a matter of time until the world comes storming in here. You boys have hit about the biggest gold strike in the history of the world, I guess."

"Good to meet you," Charles said.

"Your ma, she's an honest-to-God princess? It's not just another north country yarn?"

Emerson nodded. "She's Russian. She and my pa came to the Yukon just about the time the Americans bought Alaska—in '67. There are a lot of princesses in Russia, after all—almost like it is with the Indians. My friend Carmack's wife is a princess too, and that's by adoption."

"Hammerwater Katie? Well, I heard that. Lying George will be chief of the Tagish one day if his father-in-law don't outlive him. Good to meet you, Charles. I'd half come to believe that all you Emersons were myths instead of real people, no matter what Ladue and McQuesten say. Is your dad really seven foot tall?"

"No, no he isn't. Just two or three inches taller than me."

"Well, he's a big one for sure then. Any chance Long John and the princess might show up here in Dawson? I'd sure be pleased to meet them."

"Aye," Mike Turner put in, "when's the big cahuna comin' down to visit us city folks?"

"Actually, they were talking about moving down to the gold fields for the winter. I'm expecting Pa any time now. Thought he'd be here last week, in fact."

"Jack McQuesten says he can shoot the eye out of a grizzly at a hundred yards—that true?"

Charles shrugged, realized that in contests between myth and truth, myth usually won out. "Yep. Haven't you noticed that every bear on the Yukon's got only one good eye? Long John's been working at it for years."

Turner laughed. "Knew it were true."

"I need directions, gents." Emerson swung back into the saddle. "I'm looking for Tamara Rosavi, Frisco Rose."

"We all are," Ogilvie smirked. Then, catching Charles' eye, he hastened on. "All right, then. Just ride on down Fifth Avenue here until you come to Queen Street, just on the other side of Princess. Turn left and go down a couple of blocks. You'll see a two-story place called the Dawson Rose, and that's it. Tell Jacqueline her favorite client will be in to see her tonight. She'll know who you're talking about."

"Narrow 'er down to twenty or so, anyhow," Mike Turner said, pounding Ogilvie on the back.

Charles nodded, tipped his fur cap to Turner and Ogilvie and clapped his knees to the sides of his mule.

The city of Dawson, he observed, was indeed like a strange sort of explosion in progress, with clusters of more or less disreputable-looking humanity moving along the wide, muddy streets. No women at all were in evidence on Queen Street. The men stood about, talking and drinking and cursing. Most appeared down and out, while a few wore jackets, vests and top hats. One, Charles noted, was selling some sort of patent medicine from the open end of a wagon, to the rear wheel of which a forlorn-looking monkey was attached by a cord.

At hand stood Sergeant Hayne of the Northwest Mounted Police, in full uniform, looking quite official and highly suspicious. Charles rode close by, primarily out of curiosity, called out to the Mountie and waved. Hayne glanced in his direction, recognized him, grinned and waved—then turned his attention once more to the snake-oil merchant's spiel.

Where had all these people come from? Mostly upriver via one paddle wheeler or another, Charles concluded, some of them with Musi and Okime. But what a sorry-looking lot they were—bums and hangers-on, profiteers and men without prospects. Such solid citizens of the north as existed, Charles reflected, were at work in the gold fields or supplying goods and services to support them.

Emerson tethered his mule to the hitching rail in front of Bill McPhee's Saloon and went inside in search of Skookum Jim. He found the big Indian sitting at a table with Swiftwater Bill Gates and Gussie LaMore. Gates had given Gussie her weight in gold in exchange for her favors on a more or less exclusive basis, with the promise she would marry him if he took her to San Francisco to live.

"Charles Rostov," Gates grinned, wringing Charles' hand and motioning for him to sit down. "You've met Gussie—sure you have. Just listen to this big coon behind the red beard. Blind drunk he is, but he can still preach a first-rate hellfire an' damnation, by God. Just listen to 'im."

"Crazy as a badger with a bad tooth," Skookum Jim said, grabbing the whiskey bottle from Gates. He took a long pull and shuddered.

Charles looked across the room. A large broad-shouldered individual in mud-spattered black robes and a red kerchief over his forehead paced back and forth and occasionally paused to thrust a big fist under the nose of one patron or another. The deep voice was quite audible even over the buzz of talk, and the subject indeed had to do with the conditions of men's souls and the likely fate of fire and brimstone for most of the degenerates present. About the man's waist was a wide ammunition belt; from one side hung a holster and pistol and from the other a Bowie knife whose length Charles estimated at twenty inches.

"Who the hell's the drunk priest, if that's what he is?" he asked.

"Goddamn Gossack shaman," Skookum Jim growled.

"No salvation from that one," Gussie LaMore sneered. "I knew him before Swiftwater Bill came to my rescue. The parts he keeps hidden aren't as big as the rest of him. Just a foolish old man—"

"Don't go tellin' Charles about your scarlet past,

damnit,'' Gates said, winking at Gussie. ''For sure, the nigger believes in the great God rotgut, just like a sensible man. Alexivich Karloff, that's his handle—Father Alexivich. But he ain't a priest no more, not since the old believers run 'im out of his church at Ninilchik.''

''Ran him out?'' Charles asked.

''Damn right. Seems like the not-so-good father managed to get two leetle fifteen-year-old gals in a family way at the same time. Now, one at a time them crazy Russians mighta stood for it, but two at once? That were pushin' things a mite too far. The big bastard come upriver about a month ago, and since then he's gotten thick with that lawyer that hangs around the Dawson Rose—the whorehouse that's run by that woman your ma helped out, from what I hear. That's the story, anyhow. So the lawyer's got 'im a cathouse on the one side and a whiskey priest on the other. A hell of a combination, I'm thinkin'.''

''I've come down from the diggin's with a poke full of gold,'' Charles said. ''My money's as good as anyone's, Tamara, and I'd be honored if you'd consent to have me as a paying customer. I want to spend this night with you more than anything on earth. The fact is I love you and I want to marry you; you know that. Say yes or I swear to God I'm gonna shoot myself in both legs, drink poison, put at least six bullets into my head and then wander off into the forest and die of loneliness.''

Tamara the Rose of Dawson rested her chin on her folded fist, stared into Charles' intensely earnest eyes, tried to resist smiling and failed. ''That really what you want? You think you want to buy me for the night, just like any other customer with a lot of money? I'm not going to marry you, Charles. You've got to get that through your head. I love you too, but in my own way. I'm a professional lady, and—''

''And I wish to be your customer. I'll play by the

rules, Tammy. I know what I'm doing and that's what I want."

Tamara sipped her rum and nodded. "We shouldn't spoil it, you know. I will always be grateful to you and your mother, Charles. And I will never forget our time by the river and all those mosquito bites. I—" The Rose of Dawson was furious with herself, for she could feel tears starting to her eyes. She blinked and drank down the rest of her rum.

"I'm not likely to forget either." Charles swallowed his own drink. "That's why I couldn't stay away. It's only twenty miles up to my claim, and I just couldn't get you out of my mind. Look, I was heartbroken as a damn fool kid when you left Hootalinqua without seeing me again, even though I knew you were going. Okay. Just for the hell of it, let's say you were trying to break things off clean. You didn't want to hurt my feelings. Let's even say you made love to me out of pity. You didn't feel anything at all. You were just being nice to Charles Rostov, okay? Shall we say that, Tamara?"

The Rose of Dawson wasn't really listening to Emerson. She was concentrating on the perfect dark brown of the two eyes that were staring into hers. "Oh, no, don't talk that way, Charles. Our day in the sunlight was . . . lovely. That is how I feel. Do you understand? But I don't see what we can do. Such is life."

"Let's say it anyway. It was just value for value, and now I wish to exchange a different sort of value for—"

"Charles Emerson, I don't wish to hear any more of this. Here, I'll pour you another drink. Be quiet now."

"All night," he said. "That's for a starter. I'm not going to let you sleep, either, Tammy. I'm going to make you—"

Tamara laughed, softly at first, and then hilariously. "Men are so vain about a very small thing. Goats have far more sense. I have watched them when I was a girl. The nanny just keeps on grazing and raises her tail, that's all. The billy stands up, sticks his nose into the air and pumps four or five times. Then he goes back to grazing also. People would be better off if they were like the goats."

"Nyet, Tamara, nyet. Let me tell you about the mountain rams. I watched them once from high up where they couldn't see or smell me. The woman, she waits and watches. The males, they kick at one another and then they back up and charge. They collide head on, over and over. Shake their heads, back up and then fling themselves at one another."

"And the ewe, she waits for the winner, is that it?"

"She waits for both of them. They both mate with her. But if the contest goes on too long, maybe she just wanders away and finds someone else."

"I don't believe this. Look, let's take the bottle of rum and go to my room. Rosita may come in here, or one of the customers. I enjoy . . . talking with you, but it is better for us to do it in real privacy."

"All right, but one more drink first. Yes, thank you. We are talking about the animal people, and we are trying to learn from them—we watch them and try to determine from that what we should do. Da? You drink too, Tammy. It's no fun being drunk alone. Have one more glass of rum and I will tell you about the wolves and the coyotes."

"Wolves," Tamara said, filling her glass. "In Russia in bad years the wolves come into the villages and kill anyone they catch outside."

"I have heard those stories," Charles said, "but I do not believe them. Maybe the Russian wolves are much different than the ones here along the Lot of Water. Once when I was hunting in the big mountains to the west, after I had been there for about a week three wolves came in to visit me. Two nights they did that, just sat there at the edge of the firelight, watching. So I talked to them, and they tilted their heads to one side and listened. The third night I tossed some meat to them—tossed it just a short way from where I was sitting. After a while they came in very slowly, and finally ate. I kept talking and then they sat closer, waiting for more food."

"What a story," Tamara said, breaking into delighted laughter. "I would almost think you were serious."

"I am," Charles replied, reaching once again for the bottle. "Those wolves, they slept there that night, and in the morning one of them was resting its head on the edge of my sleeping bag. A week later, when I was ready to leave, the whole pack—maybe twenty or more of them—came down out of the spruce forest and trotted along in front of me, single-file."

"I don't believe you."

"Well," Charles said, nodding, "it's the truth nonetheless. But what I wanted to tell you about wolves is this: they mate for life. Year after year I see the same pairs together. Different pups but the same two parents. If one is killed, then the other may take another mate or wander away from the pack and live alone. Once I met an old wolf, half his teeth gone, and a young badger; they had taken up together. The badger must have been doing the hunting for both of them, I don't know—"

"Well," Tamara said, "then that's the difference between wolves and humans."

"Yes?"

"Your wolves mate for life, or so you say. Humans don't. Oh, they get married, perhaps, but—"

"Some stay together as long as they live. That is what I would do. That's what you want, too. You just play at being a prostitute. It's a game. One day you will wake up, Tamara Rosavi."

She finished her drink, stood up unsteadily and whispered, "Take me to my bedroom. Give me all your gold, then. I will give it back later. Right now, Charles, before I change my mind."

Emerson laughed. "What makes you think I'm still interested?"

"Take me to bed, you son of a bitch. All this talk of yours has given me the vapors."

He rose from the table, half overturning it in the process, wobbled slightly and then lifted her like a small child. He staggered forward, his sense of balance peculiarly awry.

"Don't forget to open the door," Tamara said, biting his neck. "I think it's closed."

"Always had trouble with doors," he mumbled, pushing it ahead of him with his foot and then stumbling forward, Tamara still in his arms, onto her large bed.

Half an hour later Rosita looked into the room, found Tamara and her friend, both still fully clothed and tangled in one another's arms, sound asleep. She smiled, blew out the candles at either side of the room and closed the door.

In the morning Rosita woke her mistress. "*Mala suerta, señorita*. It is de Vris. He was here this morning and I have told him not to come back until noon. That one, he follows us everywhere we go."

Within moments Tamara was up and packing a few of her things.

"This girl's going to take a vacation," she said to Charles, who was drinking the coffee Rosita had brought him, trying to ignore the dull ache in his head, trying to wake up. "Charles, I want you to take me to your tent, wherever it is. I want you to give me refuge for a while. Will you do that for me?"

"No tent," he replied, "but I've got a nice new log cabin. By God I knew there was something missing. I need a woman, that's what."

"No time for banter. What Rosita siad is correct. Edouard de Vris followed me from San Francisco to Sitka—and now to Dawson. He's very rich, very powerful, and—"

"You were his mistress?" Charles asked.

"In a way, yes. He was, shall we say, very generous to me, but when I was able to leave, I did. I'm in absolutely no mood to deal with him right now."

"You want to go upcreek to my claim?"

"Yes, I'd like that very much—if you're willing."

Charles Rostov Emerson squinted at Tamara Rosavi and nodded. "There's nothing that would please me more, wife."

"You've got a head like granite, Charles, do you know that? All right, then. Take me to your log cabin and then you can show me your gold mine. Rosita, get me some of Sam's old clothes, will you? Tell Jacqueline I said to take charge of things until I get back, and you keep an eye on her. I'll get word to you in a couple of days."

"What shall we tell Señor de Vris when he returns at noon?"

"That I've gone up to—where? To Whitehorse, on urgent business. Say I left last night on horseback."

Charles Emerson, Skookum Jim and a companion rode slowly down Fifth Avenue to where Ogilvie, Turner and the others were happily engaged with transit, plumb bob and chain. A new intersection was being measured out and a small hand-scrawled sign had been stuck into the mud at the corner: *Turner Street*.

"Named one for yourself, I see," Emerson called to the surveying crew.

"Damned right," Mike Turner yelled back, squinting at Charles and Jim. The other, no more than a boy wearing too-large castoffs, had probably been taken on, Turner surmised, for room and board to haul buckets of gravel to the sluice boxes.

The three riders swam their mules across the Klondike River and proceeded upstream along Bonanza Creek, not hurrying, sticking to the parallel ruts that passed for a road.

When they reached the settlement at the confluence of the Eldorado and the Bonanza, Skookum Jim pointed ahead. A dozen men were hard at work leveling an area that looked to be about forty by seventy, while three others and a brace of mules were skidding in a log to the site.

"Guess she's going to do it, then," Charles said.

"Two stories high, just like the ones in Dawson," Skookum Jim nodded.

"More competition, then, way out here?" Tamara asked. "Well, there are so many coming in now that it doesn't make much difference. This way the miners have got a place to themselves."

"Belinda Mulroney," Charles said, "she's putting up a regular hotel. That's what it's supposed to be, a hotel. The newcomers are all staking claim up on the hill over there, and when the weather turns cold, they'll be more than happy to move inside. Meals and a place to sleep. It's one of the more honest ways of stealing gold, I'd say."

Tamara nodded and said nothing.

"I got question for you, Rose," Skookum Jim said. "Maybe you got an answer."

"I don't know, perhaps. What is it, Jim?"

"That crazy priest in Dawson—he's a friend of the Californio some of the boys say is your partner. Do you know anything about him?"

"Redbeard?" Charles grunted. "Made an impression on you, did he, Skooks?"

"Swiftwater Bill, he told me something. Just wondered if Tamara knew anything about him, that's all."

"Not much," Tamara replied, "only what everyone else knows, and I don't know that for certain. He was priest to the old believers in Ninilchik, but he left that behind him a few months ago. Jacqueline says she heard the villagers drove him away—for stealing, I think it was.

He claims to have studied religion in Moscow itself, but he was born here in Alaska. His father was a nobleman who was murdered by Indians when Alexivich was a young man. I'd suppose he's about sixty now, so that must have happened forty years ago, perhaps longer. Jacqueline could tell you a great deal more, I suppose, since he's been her client."

Charles and Skookum Jim exchanged glances. "The son of Alex Karloff." Charles nodded. "It's got to be, then. You had the puzzle all put together, Jim, didn't you?"

The big Indian nodded.

"The whiskey priest's father?" Tamara asked. "Who was he? Did you know him, Skookum Jim?"

"Knew about him, that's all. Charles, you think we should tell my father and sister? That was long ago, but—"

"Right," Charles answered. "If we can put it together, then most likely Karloff can too. Stories have a way of floating down the Yukon, and McQuesten knows the whole thing. Red Porcupine ought to be warned in any case."

"Warned about what?" Tamara demanded. "Is this some kind of family mystery? Well, I'm family too now, and I don't understand."

"You met my father, Red Porcupine, at Hootalinqua."

Tamara nodded and glanced at Charles, then back at Skookum Jim.

"Yes," Jim continued, "a long time ago my father killed the father of the crazy priest. That is what happened. My sister's mother was married to Karloff, but she is not his daughter. When the mother died, my father took her and she became sister to me an' Tagish Charlie."

"She's your half-sister, then—Red Porcupine was actually her father? Perhaps I shouldn't pry, but—"

"No," Jim said, "but the older Karloff wasn't her father either. That was Yuri Borodin, Red Porcupine's friend. I remember Borodin from when I was little. He played music and sang strange, sad songs. I was very young, but I still remember. This Borodin stole Kate's mother from her husband."

"The priest's father," Charles put in.

"Then what happened to Borodin?"

"He was dead without a mark when Red Porcupine found him. A poet's death. My father buried him and went to find Grushenka, my sister's mother. She was lost in the snow, almost dead. Red Porcupine took her to the priest at Nulato, far down the Lot of Water. That was when he killed Alex Karloff. When he came back later, Grushenka was dead and the priest gave my sister to him to raise."

Tamara shook her head, remembering the complexities of the stories and novels she had read as a girl. The intricacies of family relationships, she concluded, were no less involved here in the North American wilderness than they were among the Russian nobility. Indeed, nothing she had ever read of seemed quite so convoluted as the story she had just heard.

"We'll keep our ears to the ground," Charles said. "As long as Redbeard stays in Dawson there's no trouble. If he heads upriver, then it's a different matter. In the meanwhile we'd best talk the matter over with Carmack, Kate and Tagish Charlie. Hell, the old priest may not even know about any of this."

"Then why did he come to Dawson?" Jim asked.

Charles shrugged, leaned forward and pulled at one of his mule's ears. "Gold," he suggested. "Isn't that why the whole mob of outsiders came here? Thief, avenger or dirty old man, Karloff just naturally found his way to the one place where half the population is his own kind, and that's Dawson, Canada. Makes sense when you think about it."

Charles and Tamara took up residence in the new log cabin. Days and then weeks drifted by. She found an immediate interest in the mining process and worked both rocker and sluice while Charles was clearing the hole and setting up for the night's burn. The placer was rich and gold accumulated rapidly, even though the two of them often began their day's work late, since they talked and made love until considerably past midnight.

George and Kate, little concerned with news of the whiskey priest, made note of the late-flickering lantern. Shortly thereafter their own lantern could be detected casting a vague glow through the split-hide window of the Carmack cabin. Skookum Jim and Tagish Charlie shrugged, went to bed early and wished to hell their own wives were in camp.

Word spread up and down Bonanza Creek and spilled over into the drainage of Eldorado, by way of Grand Forks, that the notorious Mme. Rose was living with Charles Emerson. The miners didn't know what to make of this tidbit, but it provided a topic for many a long discussion. Some were of the opinion that if the rumor was indeed true, Charles Emerson was probably fighting a losing battle in his efforts to extract gold out of the frozen earth—a damn fool if ever there was one. Others, however, who had seen the elegant blonde young woman with the haunting light-blue eyes were of the definite opinion that Charles Emerson's luck went far beyond his having one of the richest placers in the basin.

"I Goddamned don't believe she's up there, no sir."

"Skookum Jim says so, an' he don't lie."

"Like hell he don't. Related to Siwash George, ain't he?"

"Tell you, I seen 'em together. She was wearin' men's clothes, but I'd know that face anywhere."

"You ever bed down with 'er?"

"Got to be royalty or damned near for Dawson Rose to unbutton your fly. For niggers like us she's just to look at, no matter how much dust we got."

"Heard she was up there running Charles' sluice for 'im."

"That don't sound right."

"Whoever he's got, it ain't Rose."

"Well, Swiftwater Bill's got Gussie keepin' house with 'im, an' he's the ugliest leetle shit on the Yukon."

"Gussie ain't Rose."

"Mebbe not, but if Gussie don't come in at least second, I sure as hell don't know who does. That woman's got the nicest set of titties I ever sucked on, I'll tell you."

"You claimin' you bedded down with Gussie?"

"Damn right. Swiftwater's bought an' paid for 'er, but she's still a workin' gal."

"Give 'er 'er own weight in gold, he did. A hundred an' thirty-four pounds an' four ounces. Hell of a price for a wife, by God."

"Particularly if she's still workin'."

"Jesus H. Kee-rist, Gussie LaMore don't weigh nothing like that much."

"Swiftwater didn't pay no mind even if she was wearin' a lead corset at the time."

"Her weight might surprise you. Those bazooms of hers got to weigh an appreciable amount."

"Well, I don't figger Dawson Rose is up there with Charles no matter what Skookum Jim says."

"You callin' him a liar?"

"Not to his face, that's for sure. That old coon might be fifty years old, but I still wouldn't bet against him even if he was havin' a wrestlin' match with a bear."

"Mebbe we ought to go up to Emerson's an' see what he's got."

"Ain't a bad idee. Ain't bad at all."

September brought Long John Emerson down from Hootalinqua, and the old mountain man set up on Carmack's number one claim. Musi and Okine were taking the *Princess* clear on down to St. Mike in the hope of being able to pick up a load of goods, paid for in advance. Supplies were running low at the Tagish village under the increasing numbers of would-be miners passing through. Taos Danny's Roadhouse & Trading Post had indeed been doing a brisk business, but Taos by now was out of practically everything and had to do some fancy trading of his own in the Nabesna and Tutchone vilages in a desperate attempt to keep his post stocked and open for business.

As Long John said, "Raven Man himself couldn'ta guessed there'd be this many damn fools comin' downriver. George, you wouldn't believe it. Tent villages all along the Yukon, leetle white flowers that have sprung up within the last month. Me an' Ludmila been talkin' about goin' outside to see what civilization's like for a spell, but from the looks of things, we ain't gonna need to."

Carmack pounded Emerson on the back and Kate gave him a long hug.

"He's married, Kate," George pointed out. "How many times do I have to remind you?"

Kate stood back, looked up at Long John and winked at him. "Well," she said, "I found him first. I set my claim long before Ludmila did. Ain't that so, John?"

"Been a long upriver pull since Red Porcupine yanked me out of the snow an' hauled me in to Tagish Lake. We go back a long way, Katie, an' that's the truth."

"He promised to marry me," Kate grinned.

"So you've told me once or twice," Carmack said, pounding Emerson on the back a second time. "Big John, you've just got no idea how much gold we've taken. We're rich, all of us—richer than any of us ever dreamed."

"You dreamed an' dreamed right," Long John said. "I'd given up, we'd all given up. But you believed in 'er."

"Your son has a friend now," Kate said, "the one

whose life Ludmila saved. She's a very nice person. George and I both like her, but—"

"I know," Long John replied, "an' there ain't one chance in a thousand that any good can come of it. Hovanski's kid brought the news upriver on his way over to Whitehorse. That's one reason I come down here two, three weeks ahead of time. As long as Musi an' Okime were chuggin' for St. Mike, I figgered I might as well ride along."

"One reason?" Carmack asked.

"Sure, that's one. Gettin' so damned crowded in Hootalinqua I figgered to bring Ludmila, John Daniel and Gracie down here for the winter. You do remember that daughter of yours, don't you? Truth is, the two of 'em are gettin' kind of thick. Might be best to house 'em in two lodges, so to speak."

"Maybe we ought to give in and let them get hitched up," Carmack suggested, "since that seems to be what they've got in mind. Old enough to bleed, they're old enough to breed. Hell, Gracie's a woman for all intents and purposes."

"Sixteen's a mite older for a gal than for a boy," Emerson replied. "Could be you're right, though."

"You two are disgusting," Kate said. "I don't know why I ever liked either one of you."

Emerson grinned and patted Kate on the head. "So Charles an' the professional lady are in the sack, eh? How long do you two figger it'll last? I mean, she's bound to get tired of spiled bacon, beans an' moose meat, ain't she?"

"It's a very strange lady," Carmack observed. "It's not as simple as you might think, John. I think they might make a go of it."

"She works the mine with him every day, just like a man," Kate agreed.

* * *

On the evening of the autumn equinox the boys at the forks gathered to set off a huge bonfire and to use up a keg of whiskey that Belinda Mulroney had sold them. When the sun, huge, orange and elliptical, finally dropped below the hills to the west of Grand Forks, they lit the fire, helped it along with a quantity of precious coal oil, shouted "Hurrah for the Yukon," and proceeded to get drunk.

Urged on by curiosity, several of the men had made trips to Charles' Emerson's claim, perhaps in the hope of actually seeing the notorious Dawson Rose, perhaps even imagining, under the influence of Dutch courage, that they might be able to avail themselves of her famed services. Whatever the case, rumors of elaborate orgies and the like at the Dawson Rose had preceded Tamara to Bonanza and Eldorado creeks.

Now, in drunken conclave, the miners decided to march on Charles Emerson's stronghold. Pitch torches blazing, singing half-remembered songs, shouting and whooping, they moved en masse up the drainage of Bonanza Creek, their hearts full of friendly malice.

It was well after dark when they reached the Emerson cabin. Stars were blazing across the sky. The season's first display of the northern lights was beginning to form, producing a series of red-violet tracings to the northeast. The temperature had dropped below freezing and the men's breath hung about their heads.

"We want the rose! We want the rose!" they began to shout in drunken unison.

"Dawson Rose, come out an' play!
Dawson Rose, come out an' play!
We got our tin—
We're by-God willin' to pay."

The chant was repeated several times, the intervals filled with whoops and hurrahs.

Some time passed and nothing happened. Some of the miners began to curse. The last of the liquor was drunk and tempers were beginning to run short.

"You goddamn whore," one man shouted, "get your white ass out here so's we can take a look at it."

This brought chuckles at first, then roaring laughter. More shouts went up and soon the men began to pour forth a veritable barrage of the vilest obscenities they could think of.

The door to the Emerson cabin opened and several figures were revealed in the glow of lamplight: five men and two women. Charles and Tamara, Long John Emerson, Skookum Jim, Tagish Charlie and George and Kate Carmack.

The miners were quiet for a moment, suddenly uncertain what to expect next.

They began to cheer, but the chorus was stilled by the blast of a shotgun not so far over their heads.

In the silence afterward a voice rang out. "This is Charles Rostov Emerson and you gents are trespassing on my claim. Get on home, you drunken bastards. Anyone else comes snooping around here, I'll shoot him and use him to burn out my gold."

Chapter 32
De Vris in Dawson

Once the rush was on, it became clear to the Canadian government that a monumental influx of Yanks, many of them poorly equipped, was certain to lead to widespread starvation and death by freezing when the lock of winter once more descended upon the Yukon. For this reason it was determined on good authority that no one with less than one thousand fifty pounds of supplies should be allowed to cross over into Canadian territory. The enforcement of the regulation was given to the Northwest Mounted Police, who established posts of inspection near the summits of Chilkoot Pass and White Pass. Those without the requisite outfits would be turned back.

An advertisement for the Seattle Clothing Company, T.M. Daulton, President, read:

> Seattle, Washington, is acknowledged to be the shortest, cheapest, and best route to the Alaska Gold Fields and the large majority will come and outfit here. It will be well to bear in mind that many articles are produced and manufactured locally and are sold more reasonably than in Eastern cities. Don't waste your money buying useless articles in the East and paying freight charges across the continent to find on arrival at Seattle that you might have saved twenty-

five to fifty percent, besides purchasing a better and more complete outfit here. We are receiving letters from all parts of the United States making inquiries about the costs of Provisions and Hardware, and have given below 'Supplies for One Man for One Year,' with prices prevailing at the present time. These prices, however, are subject to fluctuation. The cost of this outfit depends upon the wants and tastes of the purchaser. Our advice is: 'There is no economy in trying to save a few dollars on the purchase price of an outfit in the transportation of which is expended unceasing toil and hardships, and upon which your life depends.' Buy the best. It goes farther and is more satisfactory. Everything sold by us is put up by Experienced Packers in such a manner that it will reach its destination in perfect order.

Among the hundred eleven listed items were the following: Miners' Shoes, $2.75-$5.00 per pair; Sled, $5.00 and up; 300 lbs. Crown Flour. $7.50; 100 lbs. Granulated Sugar, $6.00; 25 lbs. Ground Coffee, $5.00; 6 packages two-inch Yeast Cakes, 20¢; 1 Gross Matches, 35¢. Unpriced items included fry pans, hatchets, hand saws, bits and braces, files, wicking, magnets, gold scales, and magnifying glasses.

October–December 1897

Long John Emerson shifted his lanky bones on the wooden bench, picked up a tin mug that Tamara Rosavi had just placed on the table in front of him and tried to sip from the edge of it. The coffee was scalding hot; he set the mug back down. His glance drifted to the wooden bedstead heaped with furs and blankets at the opposite end of the single room. By force of will he brought it back to the face of the exquisite creature who sat unmoving and unreadable across the table from him.

He cleared his throat and began speaking. "Truth to tell , ma'am, I feel more'n a little funny to be talkin' this way to a lady." He cleared his throat again and once more reached for the coffee. Holding it to his lips, he blew into it. "No, sir. I never expected in my life to be questionin' a female critter concernin' her intentions toward a son o' mine, but . . ."

Words seemed to fail him again. He looked so helpless that Tamara smiled a little. "Go ahead, Long John. Naturally, this does not come as a great surprise to me. Would it help if I assured you that my intentions are of the most honorable sort?"

"Mebbe I didn't quite put that right," Emerson muttered. "I never figgered you for anything but honorable, Miss Rose. An' Ludmila—well, you know how she feels about you. You're sort of a long-lost relative from the old country. No, ma'am, it ain't that. It ain't any, well, personal doubts at all. More about Charles himself, I guess."

Tamara rose with a gesture of impatience and stood beside the clay fireplace, her hands clasped behind her back. "I will say it for you, Mr. Emerson. Your son is naive about women. He's only twenty-nine years old, until recently a virgin and quite out of his element with a tough professional lady like me. You're afraid I'll take all his gold and leave him, or worse, marry into your family."

"Now come along," Long John said, also rising from the table. "This nigger never said any of that. First place, I got nothin' against professional ladies at all. To my mind, you're God's gifts to a sufferin' world. An' of course I know Charles ain't no virgin and also that he's a grown man. You twisted everything around, damnit."

"Then say it straight, Mr. Emerson," she ordered, looking directly into his eyes, her gaze like pale ice.

"Right," Long John agreed, returning her stare. "He's been hit hard. He's never been took that way before. I told him about Swiftwater Bill an' how Gussie likely kept on with 'er business even after he done give her all that gold an' built her a big house. Now I ain't sayin'," he added, putting up a hand to forestall the storm that he saw building in Tamara's face, "ain't sayin' at all you'd do anything of the sort, just that Bill Gates an' Charles is two different kinds. I reckon Bill figgered long as he got what he wanted from Gussie the rest didn't matter. But Charles, he's sort of romantic, you know. Ludmila raised him on a lot of books an' he's the kind to start brooding. Even if you're white as snow from now on, he's bound to get brooding on your past, an' you cain't deny you got one."

Tamara let her breath out slowly, at last nodded. "That's true enough, Long John. Would it surprise you if I said I love your son?"

"Nope. Nope, it wouldn't. I was pretty sure you did. An' if that's so, then I hope you'll consider what I'm asking."

"Which is that I leave and never see Charles again," Tamara finishd.

Emerson nodded. "It'll be hard on 'im, I know that, but in the long run—"

"It will be hard on both of us, sir," Tamara interrupted, her voice hard-edged with anger and with the effort of keeping back tears. "I have never been ashamed of my past, Mr. Emerson. I considered that I gave value for value, and I've earned everything I have. I want you to know that. But . . ."

Here her voice broke and she turned away from Long John. In a moment, however, she continued, her back very straight but her voice shaky with emotion as she spoke to the wall.

"But I think you're right about Charles. Yes, I'll do what you ask."

Long John put a bearlike hand on her shoulder in a clumsy gesture of sympathy, felt the stiffness of the muscles there. He reached into his pocket, withdrew the pouch that he carried and placed it by Tamara's clenched hand.

"This is just a little somethin' to, well, to make amends an' say no hard feelings," he faltered.

Tamara looked at the bag, felt its weight and stared up at Long John, streaks of red appearing in her cheeks.

"What's this?" she demanded. "Gold? You're buying me off?"

"No," he stammered, "that ain't what I. . . ."

She stood speechless for a moment and then spat an obscenity in Russian and hurled the pouch across the room.

"There's not enough gold in the Klondike to buy off Tamara Rosavi," she snapped. "I earn my gold, John Emerson. Take your money and tell your family that you've tricked Mme. Rose into leaving without it. Go!"

"Damnit, Tammy," Emerson began, distressed that she had taken the gesture so and angry at himself for not having foreseen her reaction, "I didn't—"

"Out," she shouted again, this time rummaging among the bedclothes until she came out with a small pistol, which she trained on Emerson.

"Don't figger you'll use that," Long John remarked, "but I reckon there ain't no talkin' to you. Oh hell, I am sorry." He gestured helplessly, nodded and turned to open the door.

As he strode away, he heard the door open once more—and a moment later a heavy object struck the ground behind him. He realized that Tamara had thrown the gold out, but he didn't turn to pick up the leather pouch. He continued back upstream to his own new cabin.

For a time Tamara's anger sustained her. As she packed the few belongings she'd brought with her from

Dawson, she tried very hard to convince herself that Charles was somehow partly to blame. He should have been there to defend her against his family rather than off on a hunting trip that Long John had cooked up to get rid of him. She tried to dismiss him as a mama's boy. What other kind needed protection from fast women at age twenty-nine? She tried very hard not to remember the warm lights in his brown eyes, the softness of his skin over hard muscles, the warmth of lying together and laughing, out of breath after making love.

"Well, it's for the best," she whispered to herself as she paused at the doorway and looked back at the interior of the little cabin. She did not believe her own words, but she said them hoping to convince herself. "I've always made my way alone. It's better not to get dependent on anybody. Love is a luxury for people who don't have to work for a living."

The single item that had cost her the most time in her preparations for leaving, her note to Charles, lay in the center of the table, three lines on a scrap of wrapping paper. Her other attempts were ashes in the fireplace, and what she had finally left was intentionally callous, designed to make him dismiss her, even perhaps hate her a little.

> Darling, it was a beautiful dream. A pity morning had to come.
>
> I will never forget our autumn.

She set out on foot, carrying her carpetbag and looking straight ahead as she walked through the settlement. Tagish Charlie was on the watch for her; he caught up as she passed his claim. He was riding one mule and leading another.

"Long John asked me to give you his mule," he said without preamble, "an' I thought I'd ride along with you.

Figgered it ain't good for a pretty woman to go all that way alone."

"Tell Long John Emerson to—keep—his damned mule," Tamara snapped. "As for the other, I'll be fine, Tagish Charlie. I've managed on my own all my life. No different now."

Charlie dismounted and walked beside her, leading both mules. "Okay, you don't ride the mule. I'll just walk along here with you and pester you until you do."

She didn't reply but continued striding along, her face set grimly.

"Look, Rosie—Tamara—I think Long John plain made a fool of himself on this one. Reckon he'll figger it out eventually. Reckon Charles will too."

"Please, Charlie, don't," Tamara cried suddenly. She stopped and turned on him a face of such despair that he was no longer able to think of anything to say. "Long John was right. I've made my life and there's no turning back. I'm a whore, Charlie, not a wife. I'm a damned good whore as a matter of fact. I'm not even ashamed of it. And right now I've got to get back to business. Long John just helped me see it."

"Tamara Rosavi, you're lying in your teeth and you know it."

"Look, Charlie," Tamara pleaded, "I'll ride your mule and you can keep Long John's if you don't want to ride on into Dawson to collect yours. But my friend, I've got to be alone. Please. Deal? I like you, but I can't stand this."

Tagish Charlie noted that Tamara's eyes were beginning to brim with tears. He hesitated, bowed to her look of desperation and silently strapped her bag onto the mule's back just behind the saddle. He helped her to mount and stood watching as she left, her back very straight.

* * *

Tamara chose not to ride into Dawson that first night, unready to enter her establishment in the full swing of evening. Instead she camped out high above the burgeoning town, partway up Midnight Dome. On its summit, Ladue and McQuesten insisted, the sun did not set for a week in late June. She slept under the stars, rolling herself tightly in her blankets. The temperature dropped well below freezing, and she rose stiff and chilled at first light. The day came up grey and gloomy, and as Tamara rode into the boom town, the sky began to spit down a few flakes of watery snow.

She took the mule to a livery stable and walked back down the wide, muddy central street of Dawson, past the silent board fronts of the many newly erected businesses to her own, the Dawson Rose. She went around to the side door and pounded until she heard Rosita coming to answer the summons, her feet thumping against the board floor as she muttered Spanish curses to herself.

A sound from the street, deserted at the moment, caused her to turn just in time to catch a glimpse of Tagish Charlie leading his mule past the alley. Both man and mule seemed to be on tiptoe.

"Charlie," she called out.

He stopped, looking vaguely guilty.

"You were close by all last night, weren't you? Spaseebo, thank you."

Charlie shrugged, looked sad and continued past, still maintaining the appearance of stealth despite the fact that he'd been discovered.

"Not open, not open yet. You go, *vaya*, come back later," Rosita called from within.

"*Hija de puta*, Rosita, let me in," Tamara called. The next instant the door swung open and Rosita drew her in, embracing her mistress against her broad breast.

"*Ay, querida*," she sobbed, "Miz Rose, I thought I

never see you again. But what happen? I thought you were in love."

"Back to the real world, Rosita." Tamara shrugged, swallowing against the lump in her throat. "You know how it is."

"Ah," Rosita sighed sympathetically. Then her voice dropped to a whisper and she said, "But you should get out of here right away. *Señor de Vris*, he is still here. He get pretty crazy when you run away, don't want to see him. He says he keel you if you don' come back real soon. Nobody knows what he's gonna do. You left Jacqueline in charge, but de Vris, he takes over anyway. Everybody's afraid of him."

"Afraid? Why would Sam be afraid of de Vris? Or Salmon-mouth Jack?"

"Not here anymore," Rosita replied. "Sam got disgusted, de Vris always telling him what to do, so he went to work for Swiftwater Bill."

"And Salmon-mouth?"

"He took Susie. They went off together, don't know where. Maybe out looking for *oro*."

"You're not afraid of him, are you, Rosita?" Tamara found that she wasn't very much interested in the problem of Edouard de Vris but was certain she would deal with it nonetheless.

"Me? No. He knows I slit his throat, zzzt," Rosita replied, drawing her finger across her neck.

"Well, I'm not either, but he is *bol*, a problem," Tamara said, her voice completely controlled as she looked directly at the man who had just appeared in the doorway leading from the kitchen out into the barroom. "Hello, Edouard. It's still early, but would you care for a drink?"

Charles Emerson, returning home from his hunting foray with Skookum Jim and a pair of pack mules laden with meat, was totally unprepared for what awaited him.

Sending Jim on with the mules, he entered the cabin alone. It was several minutes before he found the note, minutes in which he puzzled not over Tamara's absence but over the unnatural air of tidiness, the indefinable sense of emptiness. When he did find the square of wrapping paper with its few lines in Tamara's precise small penmanship, he read it through several times. He could not construe the message, could not get at its meaning. His mind was ready to accept anything but that Tamara had run out on him again.

When he could no longer escape that fact, he sat down abruptly on the wooden bench, feeling as if he had been punched hard in the pit of his stomach and couldn't quite catch his breath. He read the note over again and again. He rehearsed his last few days with Tamara, seeking some explanation, some hint of what was to come, but he could find nothing. A sense of bewilderment grew. How could his Tamara run out on him again?

Charles worked compulsively at the puzzle, finding some relief in the *why* to distract him from missing her and being so hurt.

It was several days before he learned of Long John's part in it. When he made the discovery, he very nearly came to blows with his father, who until now had always given him strength and even protection. However, they both knew he could win, so he sighed, biting back anger, and settled into cold politeness.

Charles thought several times of going down to Dawson, for he was fairly certain Tamara was there, but his pride would not let him go chasing after her again. He tormented himself with vision upon vision of her exquisite, laughing mouth, her beautiful, long pale body entangled with some stranger—the California lawyer de Vris, for instance. Tamara had told him about her relationship with the man and how he had followed her, first to Sitka and then to Dawson. Or the damnation-spouting priest the old believers had cast out, Alexivich Karloff.

It was actually worse to think of Tamara with men he knew—Anton Stander, perhaps, or old Jay Whipple, Frank Phiscator, Charles Constantine, the Canadian inspector of claims. Or Bob Henderson, from over on Eldorado Creek—no love lost there, and Henderson, Charles concluded, would be only too pleased to get Tamara for his own if he could.

For a moment he nearly decided to go up to Henderson's claim, to challenge the man and to kill him, but then reason returned. Charles hated Tamara and wanted her with an ache that was very nearly intolerable.

He threw himself into working his claim, spending twelve, fourteen, even sixteen hours a day digging and burning and digging some more, hauling up the bucketfuls of gravel by means of the hand winch, working the material with rocker and sluice. "Melts it out with 'is anger," Skookum Jim remarked. "Well, I'd be mad too."

Charles knew he was amassing a fortune, more than the sum of most men's dreams, but the knowledge meant nothing to him. All that mattered was the anodyne of hard physical labor.

Skookum Jim and Tagish Charlie frequently worked with him, but they found him a poor companion. He responded to conversation with a few grunted syllables or plain silence. He avoided his father entirely and wondered if Ludmila had not in large measure been responsible.

When Ludmila herself, John Daniel and Gracie appeared at the diggings, Charles kept his manner remote and chill. Ludmila began to stop at his cabin nearly every day to bring him something to eat. He greeted her, thanked her politely and continued working. As the weeks went by the cold set in and the days got shorter. Ludmila was increasingly worried about her son and spoke to Long John of the matter.

"It's woman fever," he said dismissively. "He's got to work it out himself. Ain't a blessed thing anyone can do for 'im. One of these days he'll wake up an' see he's been makin' a blue-assed fool of himself, an' then he'll find himself another 'un. Hell, I even had a touch of the fever once myself."

He grinned and undid the pins from Ludmila's long hair.

"Yes, and you solved it by kidnapping me away from my husband."

"Way I recollect the issue, you kidnapped yourself. Mebbe that's how he'll work it out, though."

"I don't think we did the right thing, Long John Emerson. I think now that perhaps I was wrong to warn you about her, knowing he'd be so close and remembering how devoted he was when she was ill. I like Tamara very much. She is a very good woman, whatever you thought. You have heard of her reputation, yes, and so have I. But you never had the chance to get to know her until after you came down here to Klondike River."

"Things'll happen how they happen, Ludmila. That leetle gal wouldn'ta left if she didn't want to. Might be it's time to bring the lad back to the world of the livin', though."

The next day Ludmila went to Charles' claim and refused to leave him alone until he had agreed to come to dinner the following evening. She insured his attendance by dispatching John Daniel and Grace to fetch him back in time for supper.

It was the dark time now, less than a week before Christmas, a fact of which Charles had been oblivious until he stepped into his parents' cabin. There he saw that Ludmila had decorated the window and the door with garlands of boughs and had set up a small spruce tree and trimmed it with ornaments of carved and painted wood, with paper flowers and strings of shell beads. The room was warm from a fire roaring in the clay chimney, despite the cold outside, and the air was fragrant with evergreen and cooking odors. Treats from the outside, purchased at the post in nearby Grand Forks, were heaped on the table. A dozen candles scented lavender and orange were burning from glass fixtures fastened to the chinked log walls. The place was transformed.

Gracie and John Daniel, Kate and George, Tagish Charlie and Skookum Jim were all present, all crowded into the small space of the Emerson cabin and all, it seemed to Charles, making a great effort to be cheerful.

Half of the damned clan, he thought, *damn near everybody in the world I care about except my Tammy. She's the one I need.*

Suddenly the decision was made, the solution so simple and so self-evident that he laughed aloud, astounding the assembled company. Impulsively he slapped Long John on the back, kissed Ludmila's forehead resoundingly.

"Ma, Pa," he said, thrusting his arms back into the heavy coat he had just removed, "thanks more than you can imagine. Wish I could stay for dinner after all this, but I have to be goin'. George, I'm gonna borrow your dogs if you don't need 'em for the next few days."

Carmack's eyes widened and he tugged at his mustache. Then he shrugged magnificently and nodded. "Figured you'd get there. Go ahead. My blessing."

Charles pushed away the barrage of questions that greeted his announcement, saying, "I've got urgent business to take care of. Should have done it two months ago, that's all. I only this minute remembered."

"But Charles," Ludmila argued, "you can't just go off into the night like this. Stay and have your dinner. Surely you can wait until morning, dear."

"Morning doesn't come for another two, three weeks this time of year," he said, grinning. "Nope, I told you, it's two months overdue now, and no darker than it'll be later. But if you could put up some victuals for me, I'd appreciate it. Be back as soon as I pack some gear, in about an hour. And Ma—" he paused, grinning at all of them and realizing they thought he had gone mad, "I love you. I love all of you, by God."

"Tolerate some company, son?" Long John asked, squinting one eye. "I got a couple of things I could take care of in Dawson, if that's where you be determined to go."

"I thank you for that, Long John, but no thanks."

The elder Emerson looked at his son steadily for a moment, nodded and put his arm around Ludmila's waist. "Come on then, princess wench," he said. "Let's at least get some grub packed up for the kid. He's got a courtin' gleam in his eye."

Within an hour Charles had the sled loaded, and with George and Throndiuk's assistance the dog team hitched, the animals snarling and bad-tempered for being roused out of their sleep and put to work at what they considered an unnatural hour. Carmack offered to accompany Charles, as did Skookum Jim and Tagish Charlie, but he refused them all.

He guided the sled out onto the frozen creek by the light of stars burning intensely through the air—that and a faint trailing aurora to the northeast. The glow reflected from the stark whiteness of a frozen world was plenty to travel by. The dogs had by now resigned themselves to their task and ran at a good pace, barking excitedly, their breath making puffs of mist about their heads.

The night was bitter cold, bone cold. Charles' breath had frozen on his beard and in the fur around his hood by the time he passed through the village of Grand Forks. He pulled his woolen scarf up over his nose and the cap beneath his parka hood down over his forehead. Then he decided he still felt as if the frozen night was taking the flesh off his bones.

Above him the aurora was Denato's glorious fireworks. It crackled and threw sheets of colored flame and an irrational impulse of joy made him shout out a long, wordless syllable like the shriek of a night bird.

Crazy as your basic shithouse rat, he thought. *She's just as likely to throw you out on your ear, you know. If she ain't come back in two months, it's because she doesn't want to.*

Thus he reasoned with his soul, but his soul wasn't listening. Gradually he became aware of the verse singing inside his head, tuneless tune that fit with the hiss and thud of the sled, the panting of the dogs.

> "Trip no further, pretty sweeting;
> Journeys end in lovers' meeting,
> Every wise man's son doth know."

Upon her return to Dawson Tamara Rosavi had not found Edouard de Vris precisely as she left him, nor was the Dawson Rose itself quite the same. With little authority beyond his own insidious self-certainty born of the simple power of wealth, he had converted the brothel into what amounted to his own club for wealthy investors.

These men had been lured north by the lawyer himself and by the scent of great sums to be made from the Klondike once the temporary hysteria of the rush passed and the true capitalists took over. To this end de Vris had been buying and swindling claims from drunken or dispirited prospectors and grubstaking others for future shares. The whole enormously complex scheme was dependent upon a fresh supply of bankrollers from the United States and even from Europe.

Using Tamara's establishment as his headquarters, de Vris already had controlling interest in more than half of the other whorehouses in Dawson, in the largest of the mercantiles and in the main docking area. He had also a silent partnership in Joe Ladue's land company. The seeds Jack McQuesten implanted in de Vris' imagination one rainy evening in San Francisco ten years earlier had now, after a decade of incubation, burst into full growth.

McQuesten himself, as he confided to Tamara, lived to regret that he ever ran into the successful San Francisco lawyer. At the same time, however, he reflected, "If it hadn't been your friend de Vris, it would have been some other, I guess. No real complaints, you understand. It ain't my gold he's stealin'—not yet."

On Tamara's return de Vris became extremely solicitous of her, assuring her that he had merely been looking out for her own best interests and cheerfully going over the ledgers with her. Then he led her to a table laden with champagne and Russian caviar and offered a toast to their renewed alliance. He even went so far as to propose marriage, which offer she smilingly declined.

De Vris nodded and admitted that their relationship was probably better without the encumbrance of vows. He then began to talk rapidly of his plans for the ultimate development of Dawson, the queen city of the North. But Tamara noted the hardness that came over his face, the scarcely perceptible narrowing of the eyes.

In most ways de Vris was much as he had always been—calculating and whimsical by turns, crafty and generous. But there were changes—yes, and perhaps even hidden desire to take revenge on her for having left him in favor of a man, so he had been told, who was hardly more than a wild Indian.

In her absence two things of note had transpired.

In the first place de Vris' appetite for opium had increased drastically to a dependency that consumed enormous quantities of money. Too, Tamara wondered if the lawyer's structure of manipulation and financial scheming might not be on the verge of collapsing with him. It was without question a matter of addiction.

Second, De Vris had a new partner. The precise nature of the partnership was not clear to Tamara, but the lawyer's primary companion was now the huge, shambling red-bearded whiskey priest, Alexivich Karloff. Morning and evening the dapper San Franciscan and the black-robed man of God, walked back and forth along Fourth Avenue or Queen Street, apparently discussing business dealings and other matters of common concern. It was a strange alliance, Tamara concluded, between the sophisticated atheist and the crazed prophet of hellfire and damnation, between the millionaire and the man who seemed oblivious to the lure of material goods.

Their single shared enthusiasm, or so it first appeared, lay in an appetite for the sexually perverse. Whatever vows to celibacy Father Karloff might once have taken, his present inclination was quite the opposite, for he was well known to the professional ladies of Dawson. It was clear that de Vris took great delight in acquainting the father with the most elaborate sexual techniques that his experience with the brothels of San Francisco might suggest. Alexivich Karloff was a willing student and had, so Jacqueline had informed her, a fertile imagination of his own.

Eventually de Vris confirmed the rumor that Tamara had heard: Father Alexivich Karloff had become a thirty-percent partner in all of de Vris' enterprises in Dawson.

"I wish to buy the Dawson Rose," de Vris announced. "I'll give you a fair price, Tammy, and you stay on as the proprietor of record. Don't shake your head, you little bitch. That's the way it's going to be."

"No, Edouard," she smiled, "that's not how it's going to be at all. We've been through this before."

"Do you suppose for one moment, ma petite, that I'm incapable of forcing my will upon you?"

Tamara sipped her wine. "If you don't get the opium problem under control, you soon won't be able to enforce your will upon anyone. Your fortune will be entirely in the hands of your friend Karloff. Are you two sleeping together now, or what?''

An expression of rage passed over de Vris' face, but then his aspect changed, softened. He emptied his wine glass, set it down on the table and appeared about to burst into tears. ''I *need* you, Tamara,'' he whined. ''Karloff is my friend, but I don't trust him, not the way I trust you. We've been through a lot together, haven't we? Can you help me, Tammy? It's true, the opium is taking me under. There are times when I don't even know my own mind. Father Alexivich, he laughs at me and describes the torments of the next world, the rotten old hypocrite. If there's a hell, he'll be burning in the hole right next to me. But he says that all one has to do is repent. What do you make of that? Is it possible?''

Tamara reached across the table and placed her hand over de Vris' clenched fist. ''Yes, I will help you, Edouard. I owe you that much, without question.''

So Tamara took it upon herself to bring de Vris' addiction within bounds. She shut down the Rose for a few days and locked Edouard into a room, where she administered decreasing dosages of the drug, ignoring his pleas and his occasional violent tantrums while she went about the business of reorganizing her enterprise, which had been allowed to run down during de Vris' disintegration.

Twice she was obliged to drive Karloff away at pistol point. The former priest cursed her roundly and declaimed against her as ''one whose sins be as scarlet, whose heart be black as the frozen darkness of winter.''

Another time he burst past her, Bowie knife in hand, and began to slash and hack at the furniture, demanding to be allowed to see de Vris. Tamara endeavored to calm the vandal while Rosita ran for the mounted police. By the time she returned with Sergeant Hayne, however, Karloff was in a jovial mood, sitting with Jacqueline, drinking and talking.

Tamara thanked the officer for coming so promptly and assured him that everything was quite under control. Hayne spoke briefly to Karloff, bowed formally to Tamara and strode back out of the Dawson Rose.

There were infinite details to be dealt with. Susie was gone now, Salmon-mouth Jack having made good his threat and dug a fortune out of the streambeds before coming back and claiming her as his bride. Rebecca had vanished as well, into the interior with a Nabesna hunter. To replace these two, Mme. Rose resorted to luring away the prettiest of the women she could find from competing brothels not controlled by de Vris. It proved no easy task, however, for in this city of tents and overcrowded hotel rooms populated almost entirely by men the favors of any woman, sexual and otherwise, were at a premium. In short, the professional ladies of Dawson were doing quite well where they were, and few saw reason to change locations.

Word had gotten around that the Dawson Rose was generally off-limits to all but de Vris, Karloff and their wheeler-dealer cronies. Along with the prominently displayed sign, *Closed Sundays*, that Sergeant Hayne had insisted be posted, Tamara put up another, larger display: *Come One, Come All.*

That night both Swede Anderson and Swiftwater Bill Gates set up court in the saloon area, buying rounds of drinks for the house.

Tamara devoted herself to her business tasks with almost demonic energy, setting herself goals each day that would absorb all her time if possible in the most mentally and physically demanding fashion. Whenever she found herself unoccupied, she would be overwhelmed with a sense of emptiness that was like a great black pit. She continued to miss Charles Emerson with terrible keenness, an intensely painful longing that had she allowed herself leisure time, would have sent her off immediately to Bonanza Creek, and Long John be damned. But she had decided that door was forever closed to her, a youthful folly that really didn't apply to her own life.

But one thing had changed irrevocably: sex.

She found it was no longer possible for her to perform the act mechanically, simply as a performance. After her time with Charles she felt gross repugnance toward allowing strangers to use her body, and she found that she could run the brothel quite efficiently without actually participating.

Edouard De Vris, once recovered, became a full partner in the Dawson Rose, buying in for forty-nine percent. He provided the funds necessary for extensive additions and shifted three of his own girls to the new quarters.

Since her return to Dawson Tamara had found sufficient reasons for not going to bed with Edouard, but now he became more demanding, and once in a foul mood declared that he intended to have her bound and raped by all his cronies.

"Very good," Tamara replied, "and later, when I find you sleeping, I will use a kitchen knife to turn you into a soprano—you and your besotted friend Father Karloff as well. The time is long past, Edouard, when you were able to force me to do anything against my wishes."

De Vris grinned, then burst out laughing. "There's never been one like you, Tammy. By the beard of Jesus, there certainly hasn't been. There's no other woman in the world I'd take your kind of abuse from."

Tamara smiled and shook her head. It was hopeless and she knew it.

"But what's a partner for?" de Vris insisted. "I need you. I've always needed you. No one else understands, for money or love."

Tamara had become quite skilled in distracting de Vris

to other subjects, acting as mistress of ceremonies to his orgies and once again serving as chief photographer. The few times she was not able to put him off, however, left her filled with a sense of betrayal of herself, a bleak feeling of hopelessness that she convinced herself was irrational.

Once after she thrashed de Vris soundly she brought him to lingering climax—almost, she feared, to the verge of a heart attack. He was sprawled across the bed and he mumbled something about having Karloff in on their next session.

"No, Edouard, nyet, nyet," she replied. "You may like Alexivich, but I find him disgusting. Under no conditions will I have anything to do with him. Jacqueline takes care of his needs. Let's leave it at that, shall we?"

"No conditions at all?" de Vris asked, a childlike smirk crossing his face.

"None, my dearest partner. If Jacqueline cannot fully satisfy the old reprobate, then you will have to attend to the matter yourself."

Quite rationally Tamara knew it was time for her to take her leave of Dawson. This time, however, she would not attempt to take her establishment with her. She was putting a good deal of money by, and when spring came, she would make a lightning departure in complete secrecy, perhaps to the East Coast of the United States or to Europe, more likely to South America or Australia, there to invest in more conventional enterprises and so escape her reputation if she could.

She was still young and beautiful, and wealthy besides. With these three assets put to work in the proper way, there yet remained the possibility of a good and long life in a world where she was not thought of as the whore of Babylon. Possibly she would run a clothing store, cater to the rich and respected.

Though love seemed out of the question, she was

confident of her ability to find a good and kind man for a husband, perhaps a college professor or a doctor. They would have children, raise their family, live comfortably and well. Rosita, of course, would go with her—but no one else.

At present, however, it was the dead of winter, so cold and dark that not even the spirit of Christmas seemed able to thrive. Dawson was locked in ice, the sun not even visible above the surrounding mountains at noon these past few days. The winter solstice approached, whatever significance that fact had in a world where noon was no more than a feeble glow beyond the southern ridges.

De Vris had decided to throw an elaborate entertainment, a saturnalia, for a small number of his closest associates—Johnson the banker, one of de Vris' employees; Chan the clothier, formerly the manager of de Vris' opium den in San Francisco; some New York money men; and of course the ever-present Red beard, Alexivich Karloff.

Tamara accepted the idea in good spirits and bent her energies and imagination to it, producing a Roman orgy. The Rose was closed to the general public on this evening. A long board set up in the main room was loaded with as many exotic dishes as it was possible to discover in Dawson in the dead of winter, as well as a great deal of liquor. Tamara herself prepared *pirozhki*, borscht and *obi non*—rolls stuffed with meat and cabbage, beet soup in the Russian manner and Uzbekh bread—at de Vris' request but presumably in deference to Father Alexivich. Tamara thought of the matter as one of keeping the peace, and with Rosita's help tended to the matter.

The guests were rigged out in togas; the girls saw to their costumes as they came in. The courtesans themselves were clothed in short gowns of diaphanous material fastened at one shoulder, leaving the other breast bare.

A dwarf sat at the piano and a thin, long-haired individual—male or female?—played Beethoven on the violin. Tamara had not seen the musicians previously but presumed them to be de Vris' imports.

The evening progressed as expected, the male guests increasingly intoxicated and heated as the girls sat on their laps and fed them or fondled them. Tamara, dressed as a goddess and wearing a long gown that covered her well, officiated but did not herself participate. At a signal from her two of the women sprang to the center of the long table and began to perform an erotic dance, ending by lying nude together and kissing, while the men at the table broke into hoots and cheers, reaching drunkenly for the performers.

"*Razvlyehkaityes*," Karloff bellowed. "Have fun, you daughters of sin, for Satan will burn out your bellies with his burning staff! All present here this night will burn in torment. And, that one," he proclaimed, pointing at Tamara, "she will nurse at Satan's staff."

Tamara studied the drunken Karloff, half supposing he might become openly violent. That problem could be dealt with when the necessity arose. For the moment she was worried about Edouard.

De Vris had hinted that he had a spectacular surprise planned, but she hadn't expected him to be quite so late. It now occurred to her that there had been something peculiar, even sinister, in the way he smiled when he refused to divulge his plan; his look was somewhere between a naughty child and a crocodile about to dine.

She decided to go looking for him, since her other guests were so thoroughly engrossed in their entertainment that she wouldn't be missed.

At that moment the door at the far end of the salon was flung open and a figure dressed entirely in black stood framed there, face hidden in an executioner's mask and even the hands covered in black gloves. "See who comes to join us," Alexivich Karloff roared. "Come in, Abdeil!"

"Brothers of the dark," the black-clad man called out, and by his voice that Tamara recognized Edouard.

Johnson, Chan, Karloff and the others around the table lapsed into expectant silence. All faces turned toward the ominous figure, slack and flushed. Tamara realized in a flash that they had been waiting for precisely this moment, that they had been privy to de Vris' secret plan. There was something feral, frightening in their hush, an electric spark that seemed to flow around the table. Tamara turned to flee but was caught by two of the toga-wearing guests before she could make the door.

These two dragged her back to the table, and other hands, Karloff's among them, joined to strip her naked and to pin her down spread-eagled on the clear space in the center of the board. As de Vris advanced and leaned above her, she noted three things: a heavy, sweetish odor of opium on his clothing and breath; his erect member, which emerged from an opening in his black tights and was the only flesh visible; and the glint of light that reflected from a knife he carried in his right hand.

"Edouard," she whispered, her voice tight with fear, "you're not going to kill me, are you?"

"Would I do that, Tammy?" he crooned. "Haven't you always been faithful to me, you bitch?"

He touched the tip of the blade to her throat, pressed just enough for her to feel a nip of pain. She moaned softly, tried without success to pull away from the hands that held her arms and legs.

"Come on, de Vris," muttered Alexivich Karloff, "I wish to see this performance. Fuck her, you overdramatic son of a bitch. I want my turn. I am hot!"

The others growled agreement, like a pack of hunting dogs who have sensed blood. . . .

With terrifying clarity Tamara envisioned a scene in which after she had been raped by each of them, Edouard

De Vris would ceremonially slit her throat. Perhaps the lot of them would drink her blood.

Don't be foolish. It is only a little dramatic performance. Edouard wants to frighten me and these others are enjoying the show.

But another voice spoke also, in cold certainty: *He could kill me. Not one of these men would ever say a word, and my girls would never be believed against the testimony of all these solid citizens, might even be too scared to talk.*

For the first time in her life she screamed aloud in pure terror but found her screams stifled by yet another pair of hands. Edouard was kneeling between her thighs, the knife still against her throat. Out of the corner of her eye, she saw that the other women had withdrawn to the edges of the room. They watched uneasily, some giggling nervously as if to convince themselves that this was all part of one of Tamara and Edouard's elaborate productions.

Chan was jumping up and down, one hand in his hair and the other grasping his still-flaccid penis.

"Vengeance is mine, saith the Lord," Karloff roared. "She must take all these salmon into her mouth!"

My God, what can I do?

"We'll both have her at once," de Vris cried. The idea had just occurred to him. "Rosavi, you suck the priest while I work on you from behind—or by God I'll use this knife on you. Turn over now, get on your hands and knees."

She started to obey as Edouard leaped to the table top. Tamara realized he had left the knife lying beside her. Karloff mounted the table as well, roaring with laughter, his penis in one hand and the other hand grasping Tamara by the hair.

She heard screaming, but whose voice? Rosita.

"*Bárbacos, bárbaros*, I will keel you if you do not

let my Tamara go!'' A shotgun blasted and splinters of wood fell from the ceiling above.

In the moment's confusion Tamara grabbed for the knife, but Father Alexivich attempted to pin her wrist. She screamed half in terror and half in rage, pulled her hand free of the priest's grip and had the knife in hand. She spun, slashing wildly, and Alexivich Karloff roared in pain and doubled over as the keen edge cut into his groin. Blood flowed between his fingers as he clutched his manhood, attempted to steady himself and slipped heavily from the tabletop to the floor, screaming curses in Russian and English.

''Tamara, you crazy bitch, what have you done?'' de Vris shouted.

The priest lay sprawled on the floor, his toga up over his head, a pool of bright blood forming rapidly and spreading over the polished boards of the floor.

''Murderess,'' Chan yelled. ''She has killed the priest, Mr. de Vris!''

''Stay away from Tamara or I keel you all,'' Rosita screamed, her voice breaking into sheer hysteria.

''Get the hell out of here, Rosita, or I'll turn the dogs on you. Your lady's bought it this time.''

Rosita stood her ground, the shotgun on Edouard de Vris.

Tamara grabbed for her clothing, pulled it about her as well as she could and stared down at the fallen whiskey priest. He wasn't dead—she could tell that much. His lips were still moving, he was still cursing under his breath, his face contorted with pain.

''Jacqueline,'' de Vris shouted, ''get over here and bind him up—he's hurt bad. Pull off your costume and use it for a bandage. Good God, there's blood all over everything.''

The citizens in their togas were vanishing, pushing

past Rosita as though she were not even there, struggling to find their own clothing.

"Goddamn all of you," de Vris shouted, "nobody leaves yet."

But a blast of frigid air from the winter darkness outside told him that someone had already bolted, not even stopping to change back into his own clothes.

At least, he reflected as he watched Jacqueline working to stanch the flow of blood from Karloff's crotch, Sergeant Hayne and his deputies were out of town, having been called down to Forty Mile on official business. Their absence would provide the time necessary to put a decent face on matters once again.

Tamara stood by dumbly, still in shock at what had happened, the blood-smeared knife in her hand. Then she allowed it to drop. It bounced on the floor, spun twice and lay motionless, glinting in the lamplight.

The dwarf and the violin player crept out from behind the piano, and de Vris, without even looking up, shouted at them to roust out a doctor, preferably a sober one.

Chapter 33
Yukon Justice

"I have been working like a slave since I came here, trying to get over the trail. I am not over it yet and furthermore do not think I will be in time to get to the Yukon this winter. Since I came we have lost our mule and one horse. I am undoubtedly a crazy fool for being here in this god forsaken country, but I have the consolation of seeing thousands of other men in all stages of life, rich and poor, wise and foolish, here in the same plight as I."

If a man had no money to purchase a horse, mule or ox, he opted for the Chilkoot Trail, shorter than the White Pass route but hell on wheels, to understate the matter somewhat. The last four miles to the summit exceed a thirty-percent grade. Indian packers and greenhorn miners alike fought their way up through ice and snow that winter of '97–'98. They climbed leaning forward, moving in lockstep. Malemutes and huskies climbed too, wearing saddlebags that weighed ten to fifteen pounds. If a dog began limping, the Indian packer sucked on its foot to free it of ice.

White Pass looked easier, even though the trail was longer. The way was easier—at first. But soon came the quagmires and canyons, roaring streams, tangles of boulders, cliff edges from which horses hurtled to death five hundred feet below. It was forty-five miles of hell and worse from Skagway to Lake Bennett.

In the Yukon they encountered a vast bleak land of endless forests, frozen streams and rivers, scant daylight and ultimately almost none at all. Temperatures fell to minus fifty and sixty and supplies were scarce as hens' teeth at all the way stations and in Dawson itself.

Hotel rooms in Dawson went for twelve dollars a night, while cots in tents were fifty cents or a dollar. A steak in Seattle was fifty cents, but in Dawson it was five dollars. A fifty-pound sack of flour now went for a hundred dollars and frozen moose meat was a dollar and a half a pound.

Then the essentials: Whiskey or rum was fifty dollars a bottle, cigarettes a dollar and a half a pack, cigars fifty cents each, and pipe tobacco ten dollars a pound. The costs were inflated in part because the Canadian government had imposed an import tax.

Men sickened with scurvy, but fresh vegetables were nearly impossible to come by. Milk was thirty dollars a gallon, eggs a dollar apiece, and a one-pound tin of oysters went for twenty-five dollars. Sugar sold for two dollars the pound.

Those who had gold made do; those who didn't went hungry.

December 1897

It was a small unheated upstairs room furnished with a bed, a washstand and a wooden table upon which a candle burned in a brass holder. Tamara alternately paced and lay on the bed, trying to shut her mind off and sleep, for she was physically exhausted.

At times she shivered uncontrollably, partly from cold, partly from exhaustion, partly from the sheer horror and unreality of the evening's events. She could not stop seeing over and over again de Vris in his ghastly executioner's costume, the blade at her throat. She relived her terror and her shame and then the big priest poised in front of her, his toga drawn back. Last of all was the man lying on the floor, blood beginning to pool about him.

She was sure hours had passed since Edouard thrust her into the room, closing the door behind them and saying, "Look, Tammy baby, it could be I can pull your pretty ass out of the fire. Depends on whether Karloff makes it or not. I can keep him from pressing charges, but if he croaks, I'm not sure what I can do."

He gripped her two arms tightly, pressing his fingers painfully into the muscle and putting his face against hers, speaking slowly through clenched teeth. "But one thing's damned certain. From now on we play my way, bitch, or your hide's nailed to the old barn door."

Then he grinned ferociously, squeezed her breast and left, locking the door behind him.

For a time she occupied herself by seeking escape routes, but she found none except for a single window, shuttered and providing nothing more promising than an unbroken drop to the frozen ground below. As she looked down, a small group of men rounded the corner, several of them bearing torches. They were all drifters and hangers-on, the semipermanent inhabitants of the various saloons. When the men saw her framed in the window, they pointed and let out a racous cheer.

"Show us your tits, Rosie," someone shouted.

"Dance purty on the end of that rope, now, gal."

"Hope they string you up naked!"

Tamara slammed shut the opening, but she continued to hear their muffled shouts and obscenities for some while, and an occasional missile rattled against the shutters or the side of the house.

Some time later she heard de Vris come back into the house, speaking a few words with another man, probably

Doublejohn or one of his sort who had been stationed to guard the door. Edouard had not spoken to her at all, and she knew that he was intentionally leaving her to ponder her fate in ignorance of the facts.

Did he die, that profane priest, that madman? Will Edouard allow them to try me as a murderess? It was self-defense, I was crazy with fear, but who will believe me? The Canadian officers are usually fair, but will the Dawson scum wait for them to return from Forty Mile?

The answer to the last question was obvious: *Not if they can help it.*

If Father Alexivich had died, there would be a mock trial officiated by de Vris and his supporters, and the outcome would be whatever the lawyer wished. She would be hanged if she did not cooperate fully, in effect becoming Edouard's slave, or perhaps she would be declared incompetent, her belongings and her person remanded to his custodial care. Perhaps no charges would be pressed at all so long as she acceded to de Vris' demands. He would save it up as a weapon against her. Yes, that was the likeliest outcome—or so she reasoned.

Or else they will hang me. But is he dead? All that blood— my God, I never intended to kill anyone.

She shuddered again and her mind circled back over the same agonizing path. The house was silent; it had been a long time since she heard any sound from outside. She went again to the window and opened the shutters. The alley was deserted, the rabble having long since grown bored with their entertainment and drifted back to their gin mills and poker games.

Tamara leaned out into the frozen night to contemplate the drop to the icy ground. *Fifteen feet, perhaps twenty. It probably wouldn't kill me, but broken bones, perhaps injury to the spine, paralysis . . .*

She could not force herself to crawl out through the opening and plunge to the rock-hard earth below. She closed the window, returned to the bed, thought of tying the coverings together to lower herself, thought of throwing the mattress out first to break her fall.

If I survive, where will I go? Charles—I couldn't do that to him, use him. No money, no friends I can get to without being caught. Nowhere, nowhere at all.

Tamara lay down on the blankets, closed her eyes, tried to force her exhausted mind to calm. Then she heard a prolonged pounding at the door and shouting. She sat up, her heart suddenly thundering.

Has the mob come for me, to take me out and hang me without a trial at all? She strained to hear the muffled but obviously angry raised voices.

Cursing at the repeated and persistent hammering, Edouard de Vris opened the door. His eyes were red and bleary and his breath reeked brandy. He had been plotting out how to turn circumstances to his advantage.

As the door swung wide a man several inches taller than himself, dark-haired and brown-eyed, sprang at the lawyer. The frost-covered giant shoved him back into the room and twisted his shirtfront so that the material dug painfully into his throat. "Where is she?" the stranger demanded. "Where the hell is Tamara, you diseased pig?"

Edouard de Vris twisted sideways, momentarily freed himself and drew his pistol from beneath his smoking jacket. "Keep your hands off me, friend," he grated, training the weapon on the other's chest. "Why don't you just calm down a little bit and tell me who you are before I ventilate your gut?"

"Name's Emerson, Charles Rostov Emerson. I've come for Tamara Rosavi. Heard you were keeping her here."

De Vris began to laugh. "So you're Charles Emerson. Yes, I've heard about you. Well, I'm afraid Tammy's got herself a little trouble with the law right now. Otherwise you'd be welcome to her, long as you like. Rate's a hundred a night, payable to me. A little extra if you want something more exotic than the usual, but certainly worth the price. Yes sir, Charley, I've seen old Tammy take it from three men at once, one in her—"

De Vris' taunting litany was cut short, for Charles, with a roar like an enraged bull, launched himself at the lawyer, knocking the gun arm down with one powerful blow that sent the revolver clattering across the floor. The next instant de Vris was lying on his back. Emerson, astride his chest, kept smashing his fist into his antagonist's face. De Vris attempted to fight back, but Charles' considerable advantage in size strength and rage as well as the lawyer's drunkenness made his efforts futile.

Charles continued to pound de Vris even after he could see that the lawyer was unconscious. Between what the half-hysterical Rosita had recounted when Charles arrived at the Dawson Rose and what the smirking de Vris had said just moments earlier, it was all Emerson could do to stop himself from bludgeoning the lawyer to death.

He sat over the man, breathing heavily, one fist still cocked for yet another blow. However, something wouldn't allow him to kill his defenseless rival. Charles rose wearily, picked up the revolver and searched through the unconscious man's pockets until he found a ring of keys.

Upstairs room, locked in. Rosita should know, and it would figure.

Tamara, her ear pressed against the door, heard the fight subside into silence, followed in a few moments by a voice calling her own name and the clatter of boots on wooden stairs. She could hardly allow herself to believe that the voice belonged to Charles Emerson, and she listened in silence until he had called several times before she responded with a joyous shout of her own.

In a moment a key turned in the lock and the door

swung open. Tamara fell against Charles. He wrapped his arms around her and buried his face in her pale hair.

She began to shake and then to laugh. Giggles welled up from some source over which she had no control. She clung tightly to Charles, trembling with her bizarre and ungovernable mirth.

He backed away a little and held her shoulders between his hands, staring intently into her face. "What the hell are you laughing at?" he demanded.

"Oh Charles," she gasped. Suddenly the bursts of laughter changed to sobs and the two mixed until she herself had no idea what she was doing.

She reached up, drew his head down, kissed him on the mouth, still laughing and sobbing. "Charles," she asked, "what took you so damned long?"

"A better question," he replied, squinting down at her, "is, why'd you run off that way? Goddamnit anyhow, Tammy. Listen, there's something you may not know about yet. Your friend downstairs was playing games with you, that's what I'm thinking—otherwise he wouldn't have had you all locked up. Stabbed that seducer of children, did you? Well, it looks like he's going to survive, unfortunately. Rosita found out. That lady's one loyal friend, Tamara. She acts like she's your own mother or something."

In his mad haste Charles had not unhitched the dogs from George Carmack's sled. When he returned to it with Tamara, he discovered that the dogs had not only broken into and devoured the store of dried salmon he had packed as dogfood, but also fought over the spoils and tangled their traces so thoroughly that it cost several precious minutes to sort things out. The dogs themselves were sleeping off their excesses in a large furry pile, and they snapped grouchily at being awakened again.

"Tammy," Charles asked as they worked with the

harness, "are you coming with me this time for good? Because if you leave me three times there's no telling what I'll do."

"I love you, Charles Emerson. All this time I felt I had lost a part of myself, as if half of me had been amputated. I would have come with you before, any time at all."

"Then why in hell did you leave? Didn't you know?" His voice was thick with suppressed anguish.

"I don't know. I thought you deserved a nice respectable girl. I thought you'd get over me. I don't know. Why didn't you come sooner?"

He stared at her, still holding a tangle of leather leads in his gloved hands, and suddenly he began to laugh away months of grief and the sheer joy of reunion and the sad irony of pride. He dropped the traces and wrapped his arms around her, ignoring the big white dog that growled threateningly at his movement. Man and woman clung together for a moment, luxuriating in the comfort of being together, of being whole again.

"I feel like crying," Tamara whispered.

"Me, too. Let's take a vow not to be stupid again."

"I promise never to be stupid again," Tamara solemnly agreed.

Two of the dogs began to discuss a point of difference and the couple had to separate them and sort out the traces once more before they could at last get under way.

It seemed a lifetime had passed since Charles set out from Bonanza Creek, but when they got out onto the ice of the Klondike, nothing had changed a great deal. It was still dark and clear; the stars blasted light from an icy sky. The Big Dipper had rotated perhaps a third of the way around the pole star, but that was all.

The sled dogs were tired. Even with Charles running behind while Tamara rode, they didn't make good time. This slowness displeased Charles. He had locked de Vris into the upstairs room when the lawyer was still only semiconscious after his beating, beginning to groan and spit blood from his battered mouth. While no one but Rosita had seen Charles since his arrival in Dawson, both Tamara and Charles knew it was only a matter of a few hours at best before the escape was discovered and a pursuit was mounted.

With luck they would make it back to Bonanza Creek, for there was no remedy but to join forces with one's allies. Charles knew enough about de Vris and his wealth to recognize a formidable enemy, for in their time together Tamara had shared much of her past with him, and it had long since been clear that Edouard de Vris was a man of far greater wealth than anyone else in the north country. That kind of money could buy whatever it wished, from armed assistance possibly even to some kind of hands off agreement with the Northwest Mounted Police itself—not with Hayne, perhaps, but who could speak for the provincial authorities? De Vris was a man to be reckoned with.

Charles snapped the whip over the dogs' heads, shouted at them, plodded along beside them as they panted and steamed in the frigid night.

No more than an hour out of Dawson the lead dog's trace snapped. Charles cursed the delay and mended the harness with a section of rawhide bootlace, but the repair didn't hold up for a mile. Seeing that no hasty repair was going to hold and that refashioning the line could take hours as well as materials he didn't have on hand, he was forced to cut the animal loose. This loss slowed the team to such an extent that Tamara insisted on walking behind the sled with Charles, at which point Charles freed the entire team.

"No point in hauling a sled along when we're both afoot," he reasoned. "George'll just have to come back for his rig. We can make better time without it."

The huskies and malemutes ran off upriver, heading for home and yipping happily.

"How far to Grand Forks?" Tamara asked as they walked on, huddled together against the cold.

"Two, three miles," Emerson answered. "I'll wake up Belinda Mulroney when we get there, see if she'll let us thaw out by the cookstove, maybe get us a pot of hot coffee."

In the dim whiteness of the starlit frozen landscape Charles and Tamara became aware of a sound growing out of silence, a tone at first like the ringing of a distant bell, this gradually resolving into the barking of a large number of dogs.

The two glanced at one another. Charles shot a glance back over his shoulder, saw movement, a spread-out line of their pursuers against the frozen waters of Bonanza Creek. He grabbed Tamara's hand and they ran to the far shore to hide among the trees there.

Too late. They will have seen us, two black forms cutting across the ice "Run for it, Tammy," he whispered. "Get up to the claim. Send Long John and Skookum, whoever you find. I'll keep 'em busy right here."

He reached inside his mackinaw and drew out a Smith & Wesson .44-caliber revolver.

The sleds had drawn even with them now, and they could easily hear the men's voices shouting to one another.

"Seen 'em cut over right about here."

"Spread out along the bank. They ain't going nowhere."

Charles gave Tamara a gentle shove. "Go!"

He knelt, leveled the Smith & Wesson and sighted on a spot in the midst of the searchers, who had gotten off their sleds and were lighting torches. He squeezed off the shot, and the .44 shattered the frozen air, echoing back from the far slope beyond the creek.

There was a moment's stunned silence and then a renewed babble of excited voices.

"Won't do you any good, Emerson. I've got a dozen men, all armed." It was de Vris' voice.

"Half a dozen. Hell, I can see all of you. You'll be the first, you pervert son of a bitch. Your boys know what you really are?"

Bad bluff, Charles thought. *He knows I can't tell from here. Wonder how many of the cheechako bastards have already come around behind me?*

He fired another shot, waited, heard a step on the frozen snow behind him. He whirled, pistol ready, but a double-action pistol was cocked on the other side of him.

"All right, gents," Charles said, putting his Smith & Wesson aside and raising both hands above his head, "I guess you've got me. Don't run trigger-happy just yet. I figure you'll end up hanging de Vris when you hear my story, anyhow."

"Got the hog at bay, Ed," one of Charles' captors shouted out, and in the next instant a match flared orange and ignited the pitch pine torch the man held.

The three who had surrounded Charles retrieved the .44 and bound his hands behind his back before they pushed him along out onto Bonanza Creek, where de Vris waited with the dogsleds. Several torches flared into life, and Charles was able to see the lawyer bundled up on one of the sleds, his face muffled to just below the eyes, both of which were puffy and colored red through purple to blue.

"My God, man," Charles laughed in a fit of perverse humor, "what did you do to your face? Ought to be more careful, Eddy, you really should."

One of the men standing with Charles, a big half-breed, drove a fist into the pit of Emerson's stomach. Charles leaned forward, sucked air.

"That's the way, Doublejohn," de Vris mumbled

through his scarf, "but don't rough our prisoner any more unless he makes it necessary. We don't want to kill him until he's had a proper trial."

"Trial?" Charles managed, still trying to catch his breath. "What the hell are you talking about, de Vris?"

"Attempted murder. Aiding the escape of a prisoner awaiting trial. Forced entry into my home," de Vris explained. "In the absence of properly constituted civil authority in our fair city we as citizens have the power to arrest and try the perpetrators of crimes."

"Sergeant Hayne agrees with you, does he? Under what law is it a crime for a woman to defend herself against rape and possible murder?"

"You'd better get your story straight, Emerson. Rosavi knifed Father Karloff at a quiet gathering of friends. I don't know what the nature of her quarrel was. I've suspected before that she may be subject to fits of irrational violence. In any case I'm sure it will all be made clear at the trial."

Charles struggled against his bindings, wishing desperately his hands were free. There was something about the lawyer's manner, he concluded, quite apart from anything the man had done, that aroused murderous rage. "Wish to Christ I'd killed you when I had the chance," Emerson muttered.

"More threats against my life? Perhaps you were in town longer than I thought. Perhaps it was you who incited Tamara Rosavi to make her crazed attack upon the person of Father Alexivich."

"Want to strip him bareass naked an' tie him to a tree?" Doublejohn asked. "What do you think, Mr. de Vris?"

"Certainly not, certainly not. We'll deal with this matter in accord with the laws of the United States. Boys, it's just a matter of time until Dawson's the capital of

Klondike Territory, with full statehood to follow in due course."

So that's what's on his mind. Governor de Vris. But first a trial with this shitheels lawyer and his friends, and after that they hang me, complete with legal niceties. That justifies the murder, and a little money will buy off the Canadian authorities when they happen in on things.

"Actually," de Vris continued, "Canadian law would do fine. But we have no judge, and the three mounted policemen were called down to Forty Mile just yesterday. Someone broke into McQuesten's warehouse—Indians, without question."

Charles Emerson groaned inwardly, shut his eyes briefly. So they would have a trial. *Keep running, Tammy. Get the hell out of here. It's our only hope.*

"You're judge and jury, then, is that it, de Vris? Well, let's get on with the hanging, then. What are you waiting for?"

"Patience, patience, my good fellow," de Vris chuckled. "Our party isn't quite complete. Ah, wait—I think I hear our friends now."

As the lawyer spoke, Charles heard male laughter, feet crunching the snow. Three figures emerged from beyond the trees and approached the circle of light cast by torches. Charles' heart sank as he realized the figure in the middle was Tamara, her face dead-white and her lips set as the others propelled her roughly forward.

The two fugitives were transported without further delay back to Dawson, where Charles was confined to the makeshift jail that the Mounties had erected at the end of the previous summer, while Tamara was returned to captivity in de Vris' house.

The stars had mostly disappeared and given way to the silvery light that preceded the brief period at midday when the sky would be faintly blue, although the sun would not be visible at all.

Tamara found herself more closely guarded this time, with Doublejohn stationed just outside her door on pain of death, de Vris declared, not to desert his post for the lures of the saloons, as he had done the last time. De Vris himself did not spend any time talking with her at all, but left the house almost immediately.

Before the short period of daylight had ended, however, he was back. "Time to go, sweet Tammy," he said cheerfully, sneering grotesquely from his disfigured face.

"Where are you taking me, Edouard? Is there a dog-fight in town?"

"We're going to see justice visited upon your boy-friend," he replied. "Court is in session. I want you to see this. You'll enjoy the spectacle, I believe. And I'll make certain you get the best seat at Emerson's hanging."

"If you go through with this mockery, Edouard, I'll see that you hang as well. If that doesn't work, I'll kill you myself. Charles' father is Long John Emerson—you've heard of him? Skookum Jim and his brother and George Carmack will all be after you, and so will I. You know I always do what I say I will. If you value your life, you'll put me on trial and turn Charles loose. Then I'll tell my story and let the city of Dawson itself decide."

"A war between Dawson and the men of the gold fields?" de Vris mused, closing his eyes and chuckling. "It might be interesting at that. I see that you haven't quite recovered from your mental infirmity, my dear. Doublejohn, will you assist me with the madam?"

The big half-breed responded to de Vris' call and came in through the open door grinning. He grabbed Tamara's arms, twisting first one and then the other pain-fully behind her back and securing them together with a short length of braided rawhide.

"I would think," de Vris added as Doublejohn shoved

her roughly ahead, "that you would speak more gently to me, considering that I've spent a good half my time today persuading Alexivich not to prefer charges against you for your senseless attack on him."

The "judge and jury," consisting primarily, Tamara observed, of men who had been present at the previous night's orgy, were waiting inside the Nugget, a popular saloon that de Vris owned. A fire roared in a big potbellied stove and a number of the town's less desirable element were gathered outside the roped-off area that had been set aside as a jury box.

A raucous cheer went up from the spectators when Tamara was brought in. Some local wit, most likely the one who had been outside her window the previous night, called out, "Hey, Rose, you gonna show us those titties this time?"

Charles had already been brought in and was standing near the bar, behind which Alexivich Karloff, as judge, sat on a high cushioned stool. However serious the wound may have been, Tamara reflected, Karloff hardly appeared much the worse for wear. His present figure stood in her mind in sharp contrast to the prone man in the blood-soaked toga who had writhed and cursed on the floor of the Dawson Rose less than twenty-four hours earlier.

In place as jury were half a dozen men, Johnson and Chan, Alfoxden, Doublejohn and two other of de Vris' hired men. They were present when she and Charles were captured on their way up Bonanza Creek; they frequently performed such tasks as physical intimidation, mayhem, even actual murder, as de Vris and his various associates required as a consequence of their dealings.

Tamara grew more and more hopeless as she surveyed the gathering. With the exception of Rosita and Jacqueline, both of whom stood near the door, she recognized no one who could be expected to be reasonably fair.

Where, she wondered, were McPhee, Gates, Turner, Ogilvie, Anderson, McQuesten? The only possible answer must be that they were intent upon their own business or hadn't even heard about Charles Emerson's plight.

De Vris opened the proceedings, taking the part of both prosecuting attorney and chief witness for the prosecution. He presented an eloquent if not strictly logical case, hinting at the vicious attack upon the "man of God" as if Charles had been responsible for that act. He tied it into the sanctity of the clergy and the sacred duties of the state, making reference to the founding fathers, George Washington at Valley Forge and President William McKinley as well as certain references to British common law. He concluded with a hint that a guilty verdict for Charles Emerson would be equivalent to striking a blow for the cherished freedoms such men as Washington and Lincoln had died for.

The spectators in the Nugget approved the speech overwhelmingly, responding with an outburst of applause and cheers that did not subside until Karloff pounded on the bar with a bottle, fixed the audience with his wild and furious stare and shouted for silence.

Charles looked about in the vain hope that he might find one friendly face in the crowd, but there was none. McQuesten or Gates at the very least ought to be present. Had they gone up to the claims to alert Long John and Carmack?

Two members of the jury were called upon as witnesses, Johnson and Chan, an irregularity that caused no one any more concern than the fact that the judge in the trial was Alexivich Karloff, an interested party in the affair. Since there had been no actual witnesses to the escape other than de Vris, these jury members testified to the general nature of the notorious Tamara Rosavi, subject of the jailbreak, and the vicious and uncalled-for attack upon Karloff. They also hinted strongly that they had seen

Emerson lurking about in the days preceding the stabbing and that he had certainly influenced the madam.

Tamara rose to her feet, shouting, "These are lies, nothing but lies, and you all know it. Why don't you just shoot us both? You know this is not a trial."

"I was there," Rosita called from the rear. "I will testify what thees pig of a *cura* was going to do to my Tamita."

The gathering hooted and shouted its disapproval, and Karloff eased himself down off the stool and limped toward Tamara. He raised the bottle he had been using as a gavel as if to strike her down. "Silence, both of you," he thundered. "One more word from this whore of Babylon and I will send you to the fires of Satan, and God will move my place up on the table of the Blessed for it. I am a man of the holy church!"

Rosita leaped forward, pushing her way through the assembled men, and was about to spring on the judge in defense of Tamara, but Doublejohn bolted from the jury box and stopped her, picking her up bodily and carrying her from the courtroom.

Karloff, meantime, facing Tamara's cold and unfrightened stare, seemed to calm somewhat and limped back to his stool behind the bar.

The travesty continued, growing ever more fanciful. Doublejohn, who had been the one to free de Vris from the room where Tamara and Charles had locked him, gave the only testimony that was even faintly related to the supposed charges against Charles.

Karloff felt called upon to deliver a long, ranting discourse upon the "scarlet bride of Satan" along with graphic details of her eventual tortures in hell. It was obvious that while de Vris may have persuaded his friend not to press charges against Tamara, the redbeard priest had not forgiven her. Most of the spectators, whose information was only through rumor, sided with the big priest and were not in the slightest concerned with what had actually transpired. Long familiar with the whiskey priest's hellfire and damnation diatribes and generally entertained by them, they began to grow restive, apparently wishing the more novel amusement of the trial and its inevitable conclusion, Charles Emerson's execution, to proceed.

De Vris, sensing the mood of the crowd, stepped forward and smoothly cut his friend's discourse short. "Thank you, Father Karloff. I'm sure that I speak for every man present when I say that we are always edified and improved by your magnificent sermons. That's particularly true on a solemn occasion such as this one."

He turned now to address both the jury and the spectators as he continued. "Gentlemen, regrettably I think we must all agree with Father Karloff. Certainly this community has suffered a moral decline, and in such a climate evil acts must inescapably increase. We have heard witness to just such an evil act on this day, how this young man, an outsider to our community, forced his way into my home, attacked and beat me without provocation and left me for dead—and certainly aided and probably induced a prisoner of this court to escape. There is strong evidence that Charles Emerson incited Tamara Rosavi, a woman known never to have been violent prior to her shocking attack upon Father Alexivich Karloff. Your Honor, with the court's permission I believe all the testimony is in. It is time to send the jury out to its deliberations."

"Well damn all of you," Charles bellowed. "The law says you've got to give me the chance to tell my story."

Karloff rapped the empty bottle against the bar, overruling Emerson, and pronounced the testimony complete.

Tamara rose again. "Wait," she called. "I wish to testify. I was there. I'm the one who's supposed to have been kidnapped. I'm a witness and I'm the one who should be on trial—I stabbed Alexivich Karloff, yes, but in self-defense."

A murmur from the crowd.

"Let the Rose say her piece, Judge."

"Let's hear what Sitka Rose has to say for herself. Mebbe then she'll show us 'er titties."

"By damn, I say Rose is better-lookin' than Maggie Laimee or Gussie LaMore either one!"

"Ain't big in the boobs, though, like Gussie an' her sister Grace."

"It is forbidden," Karloff roared. "Women are not permitted to testify in a court of law. De Vris himself says so."

"That's a lie," Tamara cried. "This is important. Everything de Vris has said is a lie. I was there—I tried to defend myself. Edouard de Vris held me captive against my will—no charges have been filed against me. Charles Emerson rescued me from—"

"You're not allowed to testify, Miss Rosavi," de Vris said. "You aren't even a citizen of the United States."

"And this isn't the United States," she shouted. "We're in Canada—Dawson's in Canada, everyone knows that. I demand that these proceedings be halted until Sergeant Hayne returns from Forty Mile!"

"By God, Mme. Rosavi," Karloff replied, "most of us here are citizens of the United States. I am Russian, like you, but I became a North American when the czar sold Alaska in 1867. Mr. de Vris and I and nearly everyone else present is a citizen of the United States, and we'll abide by our own laws."

"Damned right," someone shouted. "An' when we're done, we'll have de Vris an' his friend President McKinley annex the whole Yukon. The river belongs to us, not the Canadians."

Karloff took several large swallows from his glass of

painkiller and seemed to sink into a semistupor. He nodded, his eyes fixed in a fierce, glazed stare at Tamara.

"Wait just a damned minute," Charles shouted, looking around in disbelief. "You bastards really aren't going to give me a chance to testify? What the hell kind of trial is this?"

"He's right, Judge," one of the spectators called.

"Let 'im speak his piece," said another, and there was a general murmur of agreement.

Karloff roused from his torpor, winced, and stood up. "No," he roared. "No limb of Satan speaks in God's court."

"God's court?" Emerson asked. "Christ almighty, what the hell jurisdiction is this, anyway?"

"Blasphemy, blasphemy!" Karloff thundered. "I'll shoot you dead on the spot if you speak any more blasphemy."

Tamara shook her head in disbelief, but Charles broke into a harsh and despairing laughter.

"Gentlemen, gentlemen," de Vris said hastily, "as I indicated previously, I believe these proceedings are complete. The jury is instructed to go into the back room to deliberate. Bailiff," he added, addressing one of Doublejohn's compatriots, "restrain the prisoner, if you please."

The jury went out but returned within fifteen minutes with its verdict. "Guilty, to be hanged by the neck as soon as we get around to it." De Vris recommended that the execution take place immediately, but Karloff was inexplicably adamant that the hanging should not occur until the following day.

"He will be punished in the sight of God in the light of His day," Alexivich Karloff proclaimed. "So saith the Lord."

"What?" questioned a heckler. "Don't God see too good at night?"

Karloff's face seemed to swell at this new blasphemy. He drew his Bowie knife and slashed at the man who had spoken, grunting with pain as he wielded the blade. Edouard de Vris stepped forward and spoke quietly to Karloff, apparently saying the right thing, for the so-called judge subsided, returning his weapon to its sheath.

"Execution to take place at ten o'clock tomorrow morning, then, as soon as it gets sufficiently light," de Vris said. "Is that the court's judgment, Your Honor?"

Karloff nodded, bracing himself against the wall and closing his eyes.

"Court is dismissed, then," de Vris continued. "The prisoner is to be returned to the Dawson jail to await the performance of his sentence. Tamara Rosavi will remain in my custody until such time as she regains her senses—are those your wishes, Judge Karloff?"

The big priest nodded, waved his hand.

"No," Tamara screamed, "you can't do this! It's madness. Won't anyone here at least ride up to the Carmack claims to tell Long John Emerson what's happened?"

But de Vris and Johnson were already at her side. The lawyer slapped her once across the face, hard, and hissed, "Shut up, Tammy. You make a fool of yourself and I won't be able to keep them from hanging you right alongside your boyfriend."

They hurried her from the saloon back to de Vris' house, where she was once again locked into the little upstairs room.

"I know you hate me right now," the lawyer called through the closed door, "but later on we'll be friends again, Tammy. We really do need each other. We're exactly alike, you and I."

The insanity of the words stunned her. The entire preceding twenty-four hours seemed to revolve around a core of unreality, something so impervious to normal response that she could not imagine a reply to de Vris' assertion.

"I've got some business to take care of right now, but I'll be back after a while and we can talk. You know I love you, baby. That's what all this is for."

Tamara wanted to scream, but she forced herself to remain silent and soon she heard the front door close. She made an effort to gather her thoughts, to piece together some rational plan. She had slept less than three hours out of the past twenty-four and her mind was not working clearly.

They intend to hang him at ten o'clock, she reasoned. *That's what, twelve hours from now, fourteen. Maybe there's time to get up to the claim and bring help. Maybe—if the silly fools don't change their minds again.*

She sat heavily on the bed, her forehead resting against her palm. She was nearly overcome for a moment by the pure horror of the situation. "Oh God," she whispered. "No. No time for this. Can't do anything until I get out of here."

Resolutely she rose, tried the door, threw her weight against the handle as she jerked. It didn't budge.

"Go to sleep, Rose," Doublejohn growled from without.

It's the window, then, she thought.

She crossed the room, opened the shutters, leaned out. The drop looked no more inviting than it had hours earlier. Nothing stirred below in the darkness. There was absolutely nothing, no tree, no ledge, not a single protrusion to break her fall to the ground. Her stomach knotted as she imagined leaping, but she was resolved to do what seemed to be the only thing that promised some chance of saving Charles.

"Rosita," she thought, "and Jacqueline—Lucinda as well. My brave ones."

She remembered Rosita, face white with terror, standing her ground with the shotgun and dead determined to blast whoever would harm her friend. Then at the mockery of a trial that same loyal soul leaped forward once again to protect her mistress from the mad priest.

"If there's anything she can do, it will be done," Tamara reassured herself.

Perhaps at that moment the women were spreading their story among the old hands of Dawson. Perhaps word would get to Long John's friend Jack McQuesten or to Joe Ladue, millowner and founding father—but Ladue was now partners with de Vris and—

There was also Swede Anderson, Frank Phiscator, perhaps even Charles Constantine, the Canadian inspector of claims. Such men had been in the country for a long while, and they were a good-hearted lot on the whole. They had come as occasional clients to the Dawson Rose, and from Charles himself she had heard stories of their adventures and misadventures over the years. Some of them had literally watched Charles Emerson grow up, and McQuesten had been in the north country nearly as long as Long John Emerson himself. Perhaps such men, once they had been apprised of what had happened, would be able to organize a rescue party.

De Vris and Karloff, on the other hand, would at this moment be reinforcing the impression of guilt. They were almost certainly at the Nugget buying drinks for the crowd, celebrating the verdict over a dangerous criminal.

Tamara knew that she could not rely on the vagaries of public opinion, however, for there were far more newcomers in Dawson than old-timers. The new men, most without holdings, gravitated easily toward the wealthy and powerful Edouard de Vris.

Tamara drew a deep breath and began stripping the covering off the bed. Perhaps she could tie the blankets together. But most of the coverings were far too heavy to knot and she had no implement with which to cut the fabric. She decided that she simply hadn't the time to worry at unraveling the material, and so she set to work dragging the mattress onto the floor and across the room. She struggled to fold it and force it through the open window, but she had to work very quietly so as not to arouse the suspicions of Doublejohn outside her door.

She found that she was perspiring despite the bitter cold of the night, and she paused, half-leaning and half-sitting on the mattress as she caught her breath. It was beginning to look, she was forced to admit, as if there were no way she could break her fall in the slightest, for the mattress did not want to go through the window.

Jump and hope, she thought. *Perhaps there's no other solution. Well, Charles would do it for me.*

She stood and began to wrestle with the mattress again, making one final prodigious effort to get the thing squeezed out. She heard the faint rattle of a key being inserted into the lock on her door and reversed directions with the mattress, frantically dragging it back to the bed in a futile hope of getting it replaced before de Vris entered.

The key rattled, was withdrawn and another inserted.

Tamara lifted her head, puzzled over this circumstance. Edouard had chosen the wrong key? She listened as the procedure was repeated with a third key. A little flame seemed to be growing in her chest, a small flicker of hope.

"Rosita?" she asked softly—and then, when no answer came, "Rosita, is that you?"

"Sí, sí, now hush, Señorita."

After a few more attempts the door opened and the heavyset woman slipped through and closed the door behind her. Tamara thought she had never seen a more beautiful sight than the square grim-lipped face, and it was all she could do to keep from laughing aloud. Tamara hugged her old friend tightly, spun her around.

"*Silencio. Ay, lupita loca.* Listen quickly. I have

been busy, but I had to wait for Doublejohn to sneak away to the bar. Your Carlos is in the jail. It would take dynamite or else five teams of mules to get him out of there. Maybe if we shoot everybody, I don' know. Half the no-goods in town are guarding him. I think what's best is you get away, maybe get to his people. Señor de Vris, him or that *loco padre*, one of them keel you next time for sure."

Tamara sorted out the details and nodded. "Bless you, Rosita," she whispered. "Is there anyone we can send down to Fort Reliance? The mounted police are supposed to have gone to Forty Mile, but there must be someone at the post. And I need a dogsled. Can you get me one somewhere?"

Rosita looked as smug as was possible. "Of course, I see to all that already. Salmon-mouth Jack, he come in this morning. He has taken Jacqueline and Lucinda and they are going now for the *policía*. My good friend Dutch who runs the general post, he is waiting for you a little way up Fifth Avenue toward Klondike River. He has a dogsled. Hurry now. You always take so long. *Pero silencio*! Señor de Vris has put another watchdog downstairs. Doublejohn is probably back by now, so maybe the two of them are in the parlor getting drunk."

"*Bueno*," Tamara whispered. "Good-bye." She hugged Rosita, kissed her lightly and was gone.

The night was very dark and the only sounds Tamara could hear were the faint thunder of the sled and the harsh breath of the straining dogs. An occasional hissing of wind flurries blew dry snow into swirling devils, dim white forms on the edge of vision. A layer of cloud had drifted in to obliterate the stars and there was almost no light.

She stayed near the left bank of Bonanza Creek, sensing more than seeing the looming rise of land, and prayed that she would be able to find her way and not run up some tributary stream. She gave the dogs free rein, urged them onward into the darkness.

At one point she became disoriented in the swirling chaos of dark and spent many minutes worrying about whether they had turned around and were heading downstream once more. Then she saw an orange-red glow from fires in burn holes to either side of Bonanza. Her sense of direction restored, she called out to the dogs once again.

Rosita's friend Dutch had offered to go with her, but she persuaded both the merchant and Rosita to stay in Dawson, thinking it important that Charles have friends there in case the lynch mob grew impatient. She suggested to Dutch that he get hold of McQuesten at the ACCo store and alert Ladue, Gates and Constantine as well.

"Charles rescued me from de Vris and the whiskey priest, that is all. I was not a prisoner of any legal authority. I tried to defend myself; I still think they would have killed me. Rosita will tell you. Now I have to get Long John Emerson and his friends. Tell McQuesten I sent you. He'll listen, he'll believe you; Charles is his friend. And get Ladue and Constantine. He's the closest thing we've got to any real authority in Dawson. Please hurry, Dutch. God bless you and Rosita both."

She was making good time, of that she was sure. The dogs ran steadily and strongly. Dutch had one of the best teams in Dawson. He fed and cared for his animals so scrupulously that many of the miners thought him ridiculous; the general practice was to keep the teams half-starved and out in the cold to prevent them from "going soft." But somehow Dutch's pampered dogs managed to win most of the impromptu competitions that were occasionally gotten up, and more and more of the other team owners were considering his method with some respect.

Yes, the team was fast and well-trained and the sled in good condition. The animals were pleased to be on the move and they ran at quite a satisfactory clip. Tamara could not help being haunted by the recurring fear that they were making good time to some completely unknown and undesirable destination, however. She could not maintain any time sense of her own in the unending sameness of the frigid night. At times she thought they had been out for hours, and the next moment she re-examined her memory and decided that it had only been minutes since the last flicker of a kerosene lamp from the window of a cabin a few yards distant from the creek.

Fifteen miles to Grand Forks, five beyond that to the Emerson claim.

Again the smell of woodsmoke. She was certain for a moment that she had indeed gotten turned around and was approaching Dawson once more. But it proved to be merely a few cabins clustered at the mouth of a creek. She could discern more smoke illuminated from below, the miners' fires burning in the holes to thaw another few inches of muck to be dug out the next day.

Grand Forks, she thought, *is this it*?

Dogs in the settlement set up a clamor and her team tried to turn off to meet these challenges. She struggled with the animals, cracking the whip over their backs and shouting at them.

A voice called out, questioning. Tamara did not respond but urged the dogs ahead into darkness once more. Night closed around her again and she occupied herself with trying to recall exactly what the cluster of cabins near the mouth of Carmack's creek looked like. What landmarks, what trees or rocks or rises in the shore might give her a clue?

The silence of the night was shattered by a series of wild unearthly shrieks and low, moaning howls that brought her hair up on the back of her neck. Several of Dutch's dogs returned the calls and tried again to turn aside.

Wolves, Tamara thought, *wolves and coyotes as well*.

She repeated to herself as a litany the proposition that no one she knew of had actually been attacked by the predators. Charles claimed them to be merely curious, harmless unless attacked, possibly even friendly if given the chance.

Their calls came from both sides of Bonanza Creek, from upstream and downstream as well, eerie harmonies and countermelodies that sounded for all the world as if the wild dogs were producing a conscious musical composition. Something in the nonhuman music, something more than fear worked powerfully in a nonrational dark place in Tamara's mind and she could not keep tears from coming to her eyes.

After a time the sounds drifted off into the distance. Despite the terror they had roused in Tamara, she felt a sense of loss. The eternity of black silence returned and she fell back into the mechanical, time-distorting trance of travel.

Keep the bank to your left. Watch out for driftwood, downed snags embedded in the ice.

Chapter 34
Borodin's Music

America was on the move. Sixty thousand would head north to the Klondike and forty thousand would make it. Winter be damned, the Klondike-bound headed up from Dyea and Sitka, each with his thousand-plus pounds of gear and supplies, across the treacherous Chilkoot and the White Pass on their way to Whitehorse and Grand Forks and Dawson. The trail of '97 and '98 ran through the midst of sub-Arctic storms and brain-numbing cold. There was an avalanche on the Chilkoot and in a moment nearly seventy were dead. Frostbite and delirium took others, and the Lot of Water got its share as well.

No matter that all the most promising claims had already been staked; rumor had it that the seams of pure gold were virtually endless. This myth flamed so brightly in the imaginations of men that no amount of evidence was sufficient to dissuade them. Only death and high prices and barren placers would do that.

Up from St. Michael on the Lot of Water they came, fleets of stern wheelers burdened almost to the point of sinking. Three of the steamers ended up frozen into the Yukon ice some three hundred miles downstream from Dawson and remained there until the ice went out in May of '98.

In Dawson itself there was gold aplenty but precious

little to buy with it, for the Alaska Commercial Company and the other traders who had been quick to set up did not anticipate the size of the human tide that came both downriver and up. There was plenty of booze but nothing to eat except in the hands of hoarders. Wild game vanished and the forests were hewn down for lumber and firewood.

Summer brought salvation. Shipping moved up the river to ready customers, the citizens of a city in which every piece of finished lumber, every nail, every scrap of paper had to be brought in. Nevertheless, by the turn of the century Dawson would be the largest Canadian city west of Winnipeg.

Far to the south in Havana harbor the battleship *Maine* was sunk and Americans shouted, "Remember the *Maine*!" War with Spain broke out in the Caribbean and the Pacific; Teddy Roosevelt and his Rough Riders took San Juan Hill; and American victory was attained in December of '98. Cuba and the Philippines were taken with Guam and Puerto Rico. Hawaii was annexed.

And great, cloud-hung Denali was formally renamed in honor of the victorious president, William McKinley.

December 1897–June 1898

When the dogs began barking and pulling across the stream ice, Tamara thought for a moment she must be passing a settlement on the right bank. But the answering clamor came from directly ahead, on the ice itself, and she saw no trace of light and smelled no smoke.

In a moment a voice called out, "Who's there?" The tone was a familiar one of simple, self-assumed authority. Tamara puzzled with it while she attempted to straighten Dutch's dogs out and turn them back upstream.

"Identify yourself, dang it," the same voice shouted. "We're friendly enough except when we start killin'."

"Long John Emerson?" she called, hardly believing it possible. "Is that you, Long John?"

"The same, an' George Carmack an' the Porcupine brothers as well. An' you sound like Tamara Rosavi, if old Giyeg ain't et my senses. Where's Charles? Hold on an' we'll get us some light going here."

In a moment orange flickering flames blossomed, illuminating the tall, rawboned old man, broad-shouldered Skookum Jim, Tagish Charlie and the mustachioed George Carmack.

"Where's my boy?" Emerson repeated, seeing that Tamara was alone. "Carmack's dogs come back today an' we figgered Charles might need some help. Kate, she had a bad dream an' sent the whole pack of us out into the night."

For a moment Tamara found herself unable to speak at all. She fought back the urge to laugh and weep, her hands pressed hard against her mouth.

Carmack was cursing, shouting at the dogs as the two teams bristled and snarled at each other, both bent on fighting. Without being quite sure how it happened Tamara Rosavi found herself hugging the elder Emerson, clinging to her former adversary as if he were her own father and the world's last hope for salvation.

The sky that showed through the cell window gave no hint of light, but Charles Emerson was roused from an exhausted half-doze when rough hands pulled him to his feet and bound his arms behind him. De Vris, smiling pleasantly, stood next to Alexivich Karloff and pointed a pistol at his prisoner's head.

Doublejohn and a friend dragged Charles out of the cell and into the frozen street, where in the light of several sputtering flares a small knot of men waited to greet his appearance with mocking cheers.

"Goddamnit, de Vris, you cain't do this," a familiar

voice insisted. "There's me an' Swiftwater Bill here, an' there'll be others to testify that you boys have murdered Charles Emerson."

The voice belonged to Leroy Napoleon McQuesten, who had not learned until an hour earlier that Long John's boy was in town and about to be hanged. McQuesten found himself surrounded by the mob at the jail, the majority of whom were eager for a hanging and not overparticular as to its reasons. Although he had come armed, McQuesten found himself helpless in the midst of the bloodthirsty gathering.

"He had his trial, Jack," the lawyer returned. "Most of these men witnessed it and Alexivich Karloff was the judge. Not our fault the Mounties happen to be downriver, right, boys? Just keep out of it now. We've no quarrel with you, McQuesten. You've got a good job with the Alaska Commercial Company, and I certainly don't wish to have to make a report suggesting that you've operated in ways deleterious to the company's best interests."

"Been tried fair an' square," somebody shouted. "Let's hang the murderin' bastard now."

"You pigs," Rosita screamed, emerging from the twilight. "You try him like el coyote tries the rabbit."

"Ignorant Meskin whore," a voice countered, "oughta hang you an' all them other screwin' machines, too."

"The law of the United States and the law of God must be held inviolate," Karloff agreed, lighting a cigar.

"Heared you wasn't due to string 'im up till daylight," Bill Gates drawled. "Seems like you oughta keep your word on that part of it, anyhow. You was the judge, Karloff. I was told that's what you said."

"It is always light in the eyes of God," Karloff answered. "God sees all and judges fairly. When does it begin?"

"Such was the announcement," de Vris said smoothly. "Gentlemen, there's reason to believe that Emerson's criminal compatriots may be on their way here to disrupt our lawful proceedings. For that reason Judge Alexivich Karloff has seen fit to reschedule the execution."

"Correct, correct," the priest agreed.

"What happened, de Vris, your girlfriend get away from you?" another voice called out. A number of men present immediately recognized it as belonging to Joe Ladue. The Dawson honcho was standing a few yards distant, wearing a gun, but his arms were folded across his chest.

De Vris did not respond other than by a tightening of his jaw.

"Boys," Ladue said, "most of you know de Vris is my partner now that Art Harper's took his lungs down south. He's dealt fair with me in a business way, but that don't mean I've got to accept every scheme he's got goin'. De Vris, you an' the crazy preacher are violating Canadian and U.S. law every way from Sunday, an' a smart bastard like you knows it too. I suggest we all just cool down a bit an' wait for Hayne an' his boys to get back. There's nothing here as won't keep for a day or two."

De Vris glared at Ladue and shook his head.

"Charles Emerson," Karloff intoned, "have you made your peace with the almighty God? By my authority as judge I proclaim the hanging will take place immediately."

Charles stared at the torchlit faces crowding upon him. He shook his head and tested his bonds. He was having great difficulty in believing in any of this.

"Redbeard and the lawyer say I'm supposed to hang, boys, but what crime have I committed? Can you answer that? Sure, I whupped him a little, but I had to take his gun away first. Since when did fist fighting get to be a crime at all? De Vris, why don't you untie me and let the men see what kind of stuff you're made of? We'll have it out fair and square in front of witnesses. Boys, this thief was getting ready to murder Dawson Rose—him and the baby-raping priest and a couple of others who were on the jury. That's a fact—you heard what Tamara said at the trial. Me, I didn't even get to testify. The whole bunch of them was going to rape her and murder her, but she got hold of a knife and stuck the priest. Karloff, why don't you tell the men why you left Ninilchik? He got two little girls pregnant and the villagers drove him away, that's why he left."

Tammy got loose, somebody said. Stall for time, Charles Rostov. Minutes may count.

"De Vris," Ladue called out, "those are strong charges. What do you and Karloff have to say for yourselves?"

The mob was muttering to itself, shifting on its feet.

"Come on, you miserable cowards," Charles continued. "You going to give me a few last words, or don't you like the truth? What about a last meal? I've read that in the outside a condemned man always gets a last meal."

This request caused some dissent among the spectators. Although most were still firmly in favor of the execution, a number of the men now began to insist that the business ought to be handled according to tradition. "Man's inalienable right," several agreed.

De Vris was holding up his hand, trying to quiet the mob, when the full-throated roar of an ancient .55-caliber Hawken percussion rifle sounded and the ball hit a few feet above Karloff's head, creating a sizable hole in the jailhouse's wooden exterior. Most of the spectators instinctively crouched and some pulled battered fur caps down over their ears.

Long John Emerson, gaunt and sixty, almost legendary to everyone in the north country, was still a formidable figure of a man. He sauntered into the circle of torchlight, pushing home a second load into his old bear gun and replacing the wiping stick. Immediately behind and flanking him appeared Skookum Jim, Tagish Charlie and George Washington Carmack, all armed with pistols and rifles.

"Cut them down," Alexivich Karloff roared, but no one moved.

Leroy Napoleon McQuesten gave a long whoop. "Haw! Knew you'd pull it out of the fire, Long John. Didn't I tell you, Gates?"

"Damn right," Ladue said, moving forward, pistol in hand.

Swiftwater Bill Gates stepped away from the crowd and aligned himself with Ladue, McQuesten, Emerson and the Carmacks.

"Boys," McQuesten called out, "most of you know who I am an' you know I've been on the river a long while. Well, this here's Long John Emerson in the flesh, an' he's been here longer than any of us. It's his boy you're fixin' to stretch, or didn't you know that?"

"Arrest those men," de Vris shouted, his swollen face growing apoplectic. "Damnit, men, it's twenty to one at least, and there's a hundred dollars in it for each of you."

Karloff drew out both his pistol and his Bowie knife to brandish the weapons. "What do you call this? Is it justice? God Himself will help us to overpower these intruders!" He limped forward, his eyes blazing, and the crowd moved back away from him.

"Come no closer, Karloff," Skookum Jim warned. "You do not know me, but I know you. I am the son of the Tagish chief known as Red Porcupine."

Karloff stopped abruptly and fixed his eyes on Skookum Jim. "Then you are the son of a murderer. I will take your life in payment for an old debt."

With these words Karloff leaped forward, screaming wordlessly, and Skookum Jim met him head on. For a moment the two men struggled and then a pistol went off.

Karloff stepped back, the smoking weapon still in his hand and a stunned expression on his face.

In the uneven light of the torches it took a time for the redness to become fully visible. Blood was soaking into the priest's robes just above his ammunition belt. Karloff's mouth was wide open, but no words issued from it. Instead he collapsed into a heap at Skookum Jim's feet.

"He damn well shot hisself," someone cried.

Long John moved the barrel of his cap-and-ball Hawken from left to right and back again, fanning the crowd.

"Kinda like Russian roulette," he boomed. "Mebbe you boys got us outnumbered all right, but they's some more of you won't be eatin' breakfast this mornin', that's for certain."

Already a number of the spectators seemed to be losing interest in the proceedings and began to melt out into the darkness. Those who remained did not immediately express an opinion.

Tamara Rosavi appeared beside Charles Emerson, a pistol in one hand and a knife in the other. With the latter she began cutting through the cords binding her lover's wrists, even as she kept the weapon and one eye trained on Edouard de Vris.

"No, goddamnit," the lawyer screamed, scanning the disintegrating crowd. "They've killed Alexivich! Do something, you yellow . . . Doublejohn, stop them, for Christ's sake."

The big half-breed started forward, looked at the line of firepower arrayed against him, shrugged and muttered, "Not worth it, de Vris." He turned and walked away.

Edouard de Vris spun, his teeth flashing white in a snarl, and jerked off a shot at Charles and Tamara. The younger Emerson gasped and doubled over while Tamara cried out in horror.

Long John Emerson's .55-caliber Hawken roared blue-yellow flame and Edouard de Vris' head exploded in a red nightmare blur.

Something in the back of Tamara's mind, distant and unconnected with the present moment, noted an instant's twinge of pity for the fallen de Vris, but now he was nothing more than a distraction, a danger eliminated. Tamara dropped to her knees, laid her head against Charles Emerson's chest, pulled off one glove and thrust her hand inside the neck of his coat to feel for a pulse. She moved her fingers about, hardly able to breathe. Her own heart felt squeezed with terror. She felt something, a flutter, and moved her fingers down into the hollow of the throat. The pulse beat strongly.

"He's alive," she called turning her face up toward Long John. The giant was standing above her, watching tensely.

The old trapper's eyes dropped closed for a moment and then he pulled Tamara to her feet. "By God, girl, I guess you'll make a daughter-in-law after all. Charles never was stupid like his pa. Come on, Skooks, let's get the calf inside and take a look at 'im. Leroy, go scare us up a sawbones, will you? Must be a dozen of 'em in Dawson by now, big as it is."

McQuesten pounded Long John on the back, reached out and touched a wisp of Tamara's hair, motioned to Joe Ladue and Bill Gates. "We'll do better'n that, Slim Jeams. We'll see if we can round up a sober one."

Long John and Skookum Jim carried Charles back into the jail and laid him out on the cot. Carmack, Tagish Charlie and Rosita all stood by.

The bullet had entered just below the clavicle, high on the left side, and was lodged beneath the skin near the shoulderblade.

Within minutes Swiftwater Bill, McQuesten and Ladue were back with Dr. Tom Ryan in tow. Ryan studied the problem a moment, nodded and decided to operate while

Charles was still unconscious. He had only to make a small incision in the back and draw out the slug with pincers. Tamara and Rosita assisted, Tamara primarily by kneeling next to Charles' head and speaking soothing words to him when he began to mumble and groan before the operation was over.

"I love you, Charles Rostov Emerson. It's your duty to me to live." She had lapsed into her mother tongue.

Long John laughed uneasily and punched Carmack on the shoulder. "Damned if she don't croon Roossian just like Ludmila."

Carmack shook his head. "Shoulda just kept the damned gold to myself," he said. "Shoulda just told you, John, and nobody else. We'd still be rich and none of this woulda happened. Cheechakos all over the damned place, cities growing up right under our noses, the whole country's going to hell. I didn't use my head, by God."

Charles returned to consciousness while the sawbones was cleansing his wound with carbolic acid. He yelled out, swung and caught Doc Ryan with a hefty punch to the jaw, sending him backward onto the frozen dirt floor of the cell.

"Shit," Ryan growled, picking himself up, "you damned wild man, no wonder they meant to hang you."

Charles, still dazed, began to chuckle. He looked about, saw Tamara, his father, Carmack and the others. He grinned. "Haven't you heard the old saying? A man born to drown will never hang—something like that."

While the two women and sandy-haired Doc Ryan tended to Charles, Long John and a handful of his friends dragged the bodies of Edouard de Vris and Alexivich Karloff out onto the Yukon ice along with a quantity of firewood. With the aid of a considerable blaze and some hard work with picks and buckets the men managed to excavate a hole large enough to contain the remains of the priest and the lawyer. When de Vris and Karloff had been shoved into the cavity, Long John and his friends built more fires around the hole. The bodies, weighted with stones, were submerged in the ice. Then the fires were allowed to die down and the men kicked the coals about, scattering them and the unburned chunks of charred wood.

"Some kinds of fish," Ladue said, "they get froze solid an' stay that way all winter. Spring comes an' they just swim off. Don't think my former partner's gonna swim too good, though. Well, they went out together. Almost looks like they're huggin' each other, don't it?"

"These fish," Carmack said, "they're going to float all the way down to the delta when the ice breaks up."

"And prob'ly not going to smell so good when they get there, neither," Long John added.

"Don't smell too good right now," Tagish Charlie opined. "Some white men just naturally stink, and that's a fact."

By the time Sergeant Hayne of the Northwest Mounted Police appeared in the company of two fellow Mounties and Salmon-mouth Jack as well as Lucinda and Jacqueline of the Dawson Rose, it was several hours later. No trace of the morning's events remained unless one knew exactly where to look in the ice of the Yukon.

The mob had vanished and the erstwhile jury members and spectators also deemed it wise to become inconspicuous. But gossip spread through the various taverns like summer wildfire, and dozens of accounts emerged, complete with "authentic" details.

Long John Emerson invited the redcoats into the Dawson Rose for a drink. Stiff-backed Sergeant Hayne refused in behalf of his subordinates and himself even as his men gazed longingly after the two well-endowed women who had accompanied them up from Fort Reliance. Lucinda and Jacqueline had by now donned their working clothes in anticipation of the evening's business.

"Well now, Sarge," Long John drawled, "I don't know what I can tell you about all this. This child just come in from Bonanza Creek today, but by God the town seems quiet enough to me."

"It's likely somebody's been pullin' you boys' legs," McQuesten agreed. "Might be a good idee if you'd stay on an snoop around a mite, though. Never can tell what might float to the top."

"You bloody Yanks," Hayne growled, "I haven't the time to waste on games with bored miners."

"Well, I wouldn't go too hard on 'em, Sarge. Things do tend to get dull come winter," George Carmack counseled gravely. "You might want to haul those two women in, though, just as a sort of lesson."

"Lend some cheer to old Reliance," Long John agreed. "Nothin' like a pair of American fancy women to perk up a post in the howlin' wilderness."

Sergeant Hayne grimaced at the notion, glared at the old-timers as though he would very much have liked to pin something on them. Instead he turned to Swiftwater Bill.

"Come clean now," Hayne said. "Did you really give Gussie LaMore her weight in gold?"

"Damn right I did," Gates grinned. "You sure you don't want a drink?"

Hayne shook his head, motioned to his two men and got up. "The Canadian government doesn't want you damned Yanks taking the law into your own hands," he said. "You'd do us all a favor if you'd spread the word." With that he snapped a salute and turned away.

In March the Yukon River began to rise, shouldering up its winter sheath of ice, spilling over the surface and running silt-laden torrents above and below its solid skin. Then fractures appeared and the ice buckled and went all at once. It jammed just below Dawson and formed a rapidly rising lake behind it. The flood spilled the river's banks and inundated the town as high as Third Avenue. The city's population, swollen with the winter-long influx from the outside, drew back to higher ground, slept in saloons, stables, hardware stores and even in the small jailhouse.

Then with what sounded like thunder and earthquake all at once the water began to subside. The ice dam broke and a twenty-foot wall of silt and other debris went roaring toward the international boundary. Spring on the big river that only the old-timers still called Lot of Water or Kuikpak had arrived.

The days were rapidly growing longer as the season spun past the equinox. Returning formations of geese and ducks filled the skies. Wolves followed the migrating caribou, feasting on the mice and other small rodents that the ungulates stirred up and occasionally taking a calf that had strayed too far or a weak older animal. Grizzlies and black bears, revenously hungry, ate carrion, ripped apart rotten logs in search of big white wood grubs, sought fish in the smaller streams and devoured quantities of skunk cabbage.

The *Hootalinqua Princess* made her way down the long river, passing two larger, more elegant craft that had been lodged in river ice all winter and were now being repaired. She made stops at more than a dozen villages and towns before she found her way across the sound to St. Michael.

Here Musi and Okime bade temporary good-bye to the better part of their family, for the Emersons and the Carmacks were heading for the outside. They had booked passage for Seattle aboard the *Juneau Voyager*, whose endless round trips took her from St. Mike to San Francisco with a few stops along the way.

Aboard her were Charles and Tamara Emerson, Long

John and Ludmila Emerson, John Daniel Emerson, George, Klondike Kate and Countess Thunderstorm (aka Graphic Gracie) Carmack, Skookum Jim and Tagish Charlie. The brothers saw fit to leave their women and offspring in Hootalinqua village.

Taos Danny and Irena, with regrets, chose to remain in the village. Customers aplenty continued to pour down the river and the trading post was thriving. Even without the gold of the Klondike Taos Danny was well on his way to his own fortune.

"*Sayonara. Shinsetsuna ryoko,*" the Japanese couple called out as the *Juneau Voyager* pulled away from St. Mike.

But it was not a permanent parting, though Charles, Tamara, John Daniel and Gracie Carmack would remain for at least the following year at the Emerson ranch in Idaho. Charles and Tamara were to take up residence there and John and Gracie would be sent to public school. Long John and Ludmila, George and Kate Skookum Jim and Tagish Charlie, however, would be back on the Yukon before the end of summer to oversee the work at the claims on Bonanza Creek. These were operated in the interim by Tagish villagers under the supervision of old Jay Whipple.

Other denizens of the Klondike were aboard also, including Mike Turner and Bill Ogilvie, Swede Anderson, Hog-butcher Herriman, Swiftwater Bill Gates, Gussie LaMore and her sister Grace, also a working girl. Swiftwater Bill and the LaMore sisters were bound not for Seattle, however, but for San Francisco.

They brought their gold ashore at Seattle in duffle bags, boxes and suitcases. News of their arrival had preceded them, and Carmack, hailed as the discoverer of the riches of the Klondike, was beset by newspaper reporters and photographers.

When queried as to the extent of the gold deposits,

George pulled at his mustache, grinned and said, "Boys, it could be that this is all there is. Then again it could be that there's so much of the stuff we'll end up using it to pave the streets in Dawson. Get yourselves outfitted and head for the Chilkoot Trail, that's my advice."

Princess Ludmila, grande dame of the north country, was quite impressed with the bustling American city, complete with large buildings, churches, parks and colleges. The streets were crowded with horse-drawn vehicles of every sort and were illuminated after dark by gas or electric lights.

"It's very exciting," she said to Long John, "and when I was a girl, I dreamed of living in a place that had so many advantages—museums, operas, schools. Then you carried me off into the wilderness and I became a wild woman, a sow grizzly, content to live as you did."

"No reason we couldn't stay here if you like," Long John said.

She could see that his heart wasn't in it. "No, John, I want to go back to the Yukon. Perhaps later, when we get old, we can come back here—or perhaps to San Francisco. Tamara's told me so much about that city that it might be nice to spend some time there."

Long John laughed, hailed a carriage and guided his wife toward it. "Old?" he snorted. "This nigger's already as old as the hills. You're the only one who don't never seem to change none. Figger you'll plant me in another few years an' then go lookin' for some young buck."

"You have a strange imagination, Long John Emerson," she said as he helped her into the coach.

George Carmack, for no particular reason, began to roar with laughter. Katie glared at him and stepped up into the coach, and that was when Carmack pinched her on the behind.

* * *

They rented the fourth floor of the Butler Hotel, one of Seattle's finest. Carmack gave away nuggets for tips to the bellhops who undertook to carry the gold-laden luggage up the flights of stairs.

In their suite of rooms Tamara sent down for several bottles of French champagne and everyone drank to their success, young John and Gracie included. Then following Tamara's example they all hurled their empty glasses into the small marble fireplace.

The days that followed were full of excitement, and the clan, keeping together, toured the city and even took a stage up to a lodge on the lower slopes of Mt. Rainier.

"Don't know what we come here for," Long John chuckled. "They was plenty of rock an' ice where we come from."

Back at the Butler Hotel Skookum Jim and Tagish Charlie opened their windows wide and Jim began tossing fifty-cent pieces to the pedestrians below.

"Wouldn't buy much at Dawson prices," he said, "but down here it's a good hot meal in a fancy restaurant. Don't worry, I ain't going to bankrupt us. This dumb Indian's a rich man, by God. Look at them come running, would you?"

They went down to dinner on the ground floor level. Hammerwater Kate decided to go back to the rooms for an ostrich-plumed hat she had purchased earlier in the day. The maze of halls and stairways and corridors confused her, and she was gone for nearly half an hour.

"I think Kate's lost," Charles said. The waiter brought in roast duck and proceeded to set it aflame, to the great delight of John Daniel and Gracie. "Maybe you ought to go look for her, George."

Carmack rose, but Kate was on her way across the dining room, Bowie knife in hand.

"Katie, what on earth are you doing?" Ludmila asked.

"This place is worse than a spruce forest," Kate

replied, sitting down and placing the big knife on the table before her, "so I cut marks all down the halls and stairways. I won't get lost again now."

And Swiftwater Bill Gates? The little man who was known for his drunken rampages through Dawson showed up in Seattle a month later, just as Long John and his clan were making preparations to return to St. Mike.

"So what happened?" Carmack demanded. "Did you and Gussie get married or what? Where is she?"

"Hell, no, I didn't marry the whore," Gates replied, "beggin' your pardon, princess. Naw, I married her sister, Grace."

"But you gave her all that gold," Long John objected, squinting at his old friend.

"Did that. Man sees a nice pair of . . . well, you know what I mean, he just sort of loses all perspective on things. Anyhow, I'm gone bust an' now I got to get back to diggin' some more."

"Why didn't you marry Gussie?" Kate demanded.

"Well," Gates said, downing a shot of rye, "it turns out Miss Gussie was really Mrs. Gussie. Already married, by God, to a husband damn near the size of Long John here, so that were about the end of that.

"So I says, 'Grace, you ain't hitched already, are you?' "

" 'Nope,' she says.

"So I says, 'How about if I marry you, then?'

" 'Will you buy me a nice house over in the hills behind Oakland?' she asks.

" 'By God I will,' I says. So we done 'er."

"Well, where is Grace?" Long John asked, though he was almost certain he didn't want to hear the answer.

"In Oakland in that there big house I bought 'er. I spent two weeks trying to get 'er to bed and after that she done kicked me out. So it's back to the burn holes for this child, and pray the nuggets hold out."

It was the good time of year in Hootalinqua despite hundreds of miners passing through bound for the Hammerwater. All along the banks of the Lot of Water flowers bloomed in many-colored profusion, aspens shook their silver-green leaves in the sunshine, children laughed and the voice of living water was a joy to the ear.

The months from the breaking of Yukon ice until midsummer had been a dark time for Red Porcupine. He and Short Day, his beloved wife of more than fifty winters, had stood at the landing together and watched the *Hootalinqua Princess* churn down upon the back of the broad water carrying their sons and their daughter, yes, and their granddaughter and Long John Emerson and his family as well. Red Porcupine and Short Day stood together, smiling and waving good-bye, his arm tight around her waist, grown broad with the years. Neither of them spoke what was in their hearts—the fear that they would not see these loved ones again in this world.

They had each other, and they clung together that night as they had for many years past, taking comfort in each other's closeness.

The moon was full that night.

When it passed through its phases and came full once again, Red Porcupine woke to the knowledge that even Short Day had left him. She was lying quietly in their robes beside him as if asleep, but she did not rouse.

The old chief of the Tagish ordered that a great pyre be built for Short Day, and the mourning went on for yet one more cycle of the moon. It was a funeral of the highest dignity, on which Short Day could look back from the spirit world and be proud, although there were not nearly so many mourners as there would have been in the past. The village was thriving, but it was no longer a village of the Tagish and the Tutchones. More and more whites had chosen to stay, and most of Red Porcupine's people had either departed or become like the whites, following their ways and working for them.

His own two sons and Katie, his daughter, spoke English and not their own tongue. They sounded little different from Carmack or Emerson.

Before the official period of mourning was over Red Porcupine announced to such of his people as still followed him that he would be going away. He appointed Big Grayling, still strong and barrel-chested, to be chief in his place until George Carmack returned to take the position.

Next he went to Taos Danny Vasquez' trading post and asked the trader to write a letter for him, informing his family down south of Short Day's death.

He bathed, even though his mourning wasn't finished, put on his best clothes and set out from the village. It would be a long journey for him, more than four hundred miles as the whites counted distance, but he carried no food other than a little dried salmon.

The first part of the trip he made by water, taking his small hide boat out upon the breast of the river and riding the current down. At many places along the banks white settlements had grown up, including the large one at Dawson. But the settlements no longer troubled him, even though there were far more than he had imagined in the many years since he last came this way. The world was changing, that was all. He knew from the old stories that from time to time Raven Man decided to change everything, and this was one of the times.

He drifted with the current and sometimes he smoked tobacco in the strange whale-headed pipe Carmack gave him on the night of Kate's marriage. Several times he passed other vessels, rafts, barges, canoes, paddle wheelers, some going upstream toward the gold country, some coming down. To all of these he waved unsmiling greetings;

some returned his wave, astounded at the sight of the old chief in his ceremonial clothes, alone in his tiny craft on the great river.

At Beaver he saw the *Hootalinqua Princess* on its way back upriver; at the moment it was moored at the landing. Red Porcupine paddled toward midriver, caught the main current and went on by.

At the settlement of Nuklukayet at the mouth of the Tanana River, where the hunters of all the tribes came for trading, he beached his boat and continued on foot upstream along the big tributary river. Little had changed in this country, though in places a few white tents dotted the banks. There were a few villages of the Tanana people. Although some of these Indians came out to look at him as he passed, no one spoke. They understood his purpose.

The days were warm, the nights clear and lit with thousands of stars. He had left behind his people's fear of the dead, and it seemed to him that Short Day came at night to ease his loneliness.

The land began to rise around him, and from time to time when he cut across a ridge he could see the white peak of Denali floating in the blue air above purple foothills—Denali and the lesser giants that rose close by the great one.

He came into the drainage of the Kantishna, where many summers before he had gone with his friend Yuri Borodin, the laughing one who was half Russian and half Tagish, the one who sang and played an instrument that made music like water falling over stones. Red Porcupine could no longer remember the name of the three-cornered wooden box with strings, although he had known it in that long-ago time. He did remember the name of the beautiful girl with hair the color of the setting sun, for she was the blood-mother of his daughter, whom he and Short Day had taken as their own.

Grushenka, yes; he could remember her face so clearly

that it seemed she might step out into the path at any moment, hand in hand with Borodin, and laughing. Red Porcupine had not returned to this country in all the years since that winter when he came through the snow to discover Yuri Borodin sitting beneath the frozen tree, his musical instrument in his hands as though he had sat down to play for a moment and simply forgotten to get up.

"Toklat River," he said. "That was where I found him."

Perhaps he is still there. . . .

The voice, he realized, was inside his own head, but it sounded so real that Red Porcupine turned to look behind him. There was nothing there, except that at the edge of his vision there was a hint of movement.

Red Porcupine tried to count the years since that winter and found that he could not be certain. In between had come a lifetime, many lifetimes. He and Short Day raised their three children: Long John Emerson and Ludmila came, and after them other whites; and now there was hardly any place left for the Tagish. The Emersons had been his family also, and their children as well. He knew that their lines would merge, for young John Daniel and his granddaughter had been as if made for each other since the time they were tiny, and this was a good thing, this merging of one good thing with the other.

He climbed steadily now, and another night passed. He felt the chill of the ground and the air only slightly, for such discomforts were not important. Only reaching his destination was important.

He wrestled again the next day with the matter of time. It was a very long time since he passed this way, and yet nothing had changed. The land was eternal, and it seemed that he had returned after a very short time, after perhaps a brief night's dreaming.

Somewhere during the course of the day he became

aware of a presence walking with him. Frequently he turned, hoping to catch a glimpse of his companion, but always it would be nothing more than a flicker at the edge of vision, a suggestion of movement in the branches of brush, something like a giggle he thought he heard but could not be sure about.

Another night passed and the next day he climbed above a lake that he remembered as if it had indeed been only a short night's dreaming since he saw it last. The Tanana village at the lower end of the shining blue water was deserted; only a few depressions in the ground showed where it once stood. But on the bench of ground above the lake on the far side he thought he could discern the outline of a cabin still standing.

It was midafternoon when he reached the lodge. A thrush sang in the warm silence and springwater still trickled over stones, just as he remembered. Part of the cabin's roof had fallen in, but the walls remained.

Red Porcupine was tired. It had been a very long journey, and he was not sure now why he had come. If it was Yuri Borodin he sought, he should have gone directly to the Toklat River, but something had brought him to the headwaters of the Kantishna instead. He sat down on the grassy earth and leaned against the logs of the wall. Away to the south, its peak gleaming gold in the slanting rays of sunlight, Denali soared unchanged, impossibly distant, a glimpse of the other world.

He let his eyes close for a moment and was awakened by laughter and music like the water of the spring singing over its rocks. Red Porcupine opened his eyes.

Yuri Borodin sat across from him, his balalaika—yes, that was the name—in his lap, his fingers moving over the strings. Grushenka sat beside him, both of them singing something very beautiful. They smiled at him in greeting.

He heard the laughter again, the joyous giggle that

had been troubling him like a spirit all day. He turned his head, for the sound was much closer now.

It was Short Day as she had been many years earlier, her eyes wide and sparkling, her figure lithe. "Welcome, husband," she said, her eyes bright with love. "I am glad you are awake now."

"Yes, old-timer," Yuri agreed, still strumming his instrument, "I thought you would sleep forever. It's good to have you with us."

"Sing! Help us sing, Red Porcupine," added Grushenka of the hair like sunlight. "We need you to sing with us to make it right."

Red Porcupine clasped Short Day's hand and laughed. "What is the song?" he asked.

"Just sing, don't ask foolish questions," Short Day whispered, elbowing him gently in the side.

Red Porcupine opened his mouth and sang to the music of the balalaika, the falling-water music, the music of wind dancing among aspen leaves, of birds falling from the air and catching themselves, the music of salmon gleaming beneath the surfaces of rivers, the music of spirits coming into a beautiful dream for a time and then passing out, the music of a mountain peak rising like the syllable of creation at the center of the world.

The music rose into the sky and vanished and Red Porcupine rode the ripples of song with Yuri Borodin and Short Day and Grushenka. The ripples spread wider and wider and they rode air and soared and drifted beyond Denali, beyond the white mountain of beginnings and into the laughter of Raven Man, his eyes gleaming stars in the darkening sky.

ABOUT THE AUTHOR

Judith Shears was born and raised in Calaveras County, California, and educated at California State University, Sacramento, receiving her M.A. in creative writing in 1979. Poet and critic as well as novelist, the author now lives at her hideaway in Woodpecker Ravine, not far from Grass Valley, in the California Mother Lode Country. She's married to novelist Bill Hotchkiss and has a teenaged daughter, Anne, as well as a pet wild turkey named Walrus.